CoDex

1962

CoDex

1962

Sjón

Translated from the Icelandic
by Victoria Cribb

MCD / Farrar, Straus and Giroux

New York

MCD
Farrar, Straus and Giroux
175 Varick Street, New York 10014

Part I, *Thine Eyes Did See My Substance—a love story* was originally published in Icelandic in 1994 by Mál og menning, Reykjavík, as *Augu þín sáu mig—ástarsaga*
Part II, *Iceland's Thousand Years—a crime story* was originally published in Icelandic in 2001 by Mál og menning, Reykjavík, as *Með titrandi tár—glæpasaga*
Part III, *I'm a Sleeping Door—a science-fiction story* (*Ég er sofandi hurð—vísindaskáldsaga*) was originally published along with Parts I and II in Icelandic in 2016 by JPV Publishing, Reykjavík, as *CoDex 1962*

The quotation on page 360 is from *Gangrimlahjólið* by Loftur Guðmundsson, published in 1958 by Almenna bókafélagið, Reykjavík. The interview with María Guðmundsdóttir on pages 455–57 is from *Morgunblaðið*, September 15, 1962.

Library of Congress Cataloging-in-Publication Data
Names: Sjón, 1962– author. | Cribb, Victoria, translator. | Sjón, 1962– Augu þín sáu mig. English. | Sjón, 1962– Með titrandi tár. English. | Sjón, 1962– Ég er sofandi hurð. English.
Title: Codex 1962 / Sjón ; translated from the Icelandic by Victoria Cribb.
Other titles: Codex 1962. English
Description: First American edition. | New York : Farrar, Straus and Giroux, 2018. | "Originally published in Icelandic in 2016 by JPV Publishing; Iceland. English translation originally published in 2018 by Sceptre, Great Britain" — Verso title page.
Identifiers: LCCN 2018020046 | ISBN 9780374125639 (hardcover)
Subjects: | GSAFD: Epic fiction.
Classification: LCC PT7511.S62 C6313 2018 | DDC 839/.6934—dc23
LC record available at https://lccn.loc.gov/2018020046

Our books may be purchased in bulk for promotional, educational, or business use. Please contact your local bookseller or the Macmillan Corporate and Premium Sales Department at 1-800-221-7945, extension 5442, or by e-mail at MacmillanSpecialMarkets@macmillan.com.

www.mcdbooks.com • www.fsgbooks.com
Follow us on Twitter, Facebook, and Instagram at @mcdbooks

1 3 5 7 9 10 8 6 4 2

This book has been translated with financial support from

 ICELANDIC LITERATURE CENTER

To Ása, Júnía and Flóki,
to my mother and father,
to my friends, both living and dead.

CONTENTS

PART I

THINE EYES DID SEE MY SUBSTANCE

a love story

I

1

'If we were to enter by night the main square of a small town, let's call it Kükenstadt, in Lower Saxony (judging by the architecture and the signs above the shops lining the square), we would find the atmosphere typical of such towns after midnight. Everything so wondrously quiet that it puts one in mind of the dormitory at a summer camp for obedient children; every house in its place with the night tucked up under its eaves; the whispering about the cares and events of the day fallen silent. A small boy with an umbrella has incorporated the town into his realm.

The boy may have continued his marauding westwards, but he has not left the little town of Kükenstadt entirely at the mercy of its dreams: in the middle of the square a statue keeps watch over the citizens.

It is the sculpture of a chick, caught mid-sprint, its neck thrust out and head raised to the sky, beak gaping wide and stubby wings cocked. The blue moon is mirrored in the black marble like a night-light left burning for a child who is afraid of the dark.

It is from this chick that the town draws its name, and despite its diminutive size – only about seven times larger than a living chick, and that's not saying much – it ensures the inhabitants of Kükenstadt more peaceful rest than most big city saints can grant their flocks, for in the hearts of the sleepers the memory lives on of how the chick saved their forebears from being slain by a ferocious berserker who once rampaged across the Continent, annihilating everything in his path.

But were it not for the fact that my life-story begins in this very town which owes its existence to an inquisitive chick; yes, if it did not begin here, in a three-storey building on the square, we would tiptoe out of the dormitory town of Kükenstadt, closing the door softly behind us.

* * *

There's a sound of moaning coming from the building, as those who have an ear for houses will notice, but these are not the sighs of the suffering or the sick, oh no, these are the agonised moans of ecstasy, the crescendo of sexual climax; the groan that results from being bitten on the neck and gripped tight around the buttocks.'

'So it's a whorehouse, then?'

'A creeper sprawls across the front of the house, parting round the windows and the sign over the entrance: GASTHOF VRIESLANDER. The plant is in such a tangle under the eaves that it looks as if it's about to lift the roof off.'

'Lift it off! I want to see inside, see who's moaning . . .'

'This is no longer a house of pleasure but an ordinary guesthouse, run by an honest couple who upped sticks and abandoned their farm to make way for an autobahn. They didn't get much for it, but God and good luck were on their side and they bought this den of iniquity for a song when the Party outlawed immorality from the land.'

'Lift it off!'

'Close your eyes, then. Can you picture the square? The chick and the shops? Gasthof Vrieslander, the tangled creeper and the roof? Good. No, don't open your eyes. I'm going to put my hand inside your forehead – yes, go ahead and wrinkle it – and now you can watch it entering over the square, pale grey like a monster's claw in the ghostly glow from the street lights and the moon over the church.'

'God, how weird your hand looks – so huge. And what long nails you've got, I hadn't noticed that before—'

'Shh, concentrate! I press my thumb against the eaves of the roof at the front, grip the join with my fingers and gently prise the whole thing off, taking care not to break the chimney.'

'Yes, we wouldn't want to wake anyone.'

'Then swing it over the square with a smooth flick of my wrist and set it down, and now the chick has acquired a roof over its head. More importantly, it can't see what we're up to. Listen to it cheeping with curiosity: "Can I see? Can I see?"'

'Oh, it's so adorable.'

'Don't feel sorry for it. It'll soon give up protesting and stick its beak under its wing.'

'Goodnight, little chick.'

'It'll fall asleep while we carry on exploring the house. Can you see me poking my long fingernails into the joint between the façade and the gables?'

'Yes.'

'And pulling the façade forwards?'

'The joints are cracking like sugar glue.'

'Now I'm laying it down on the square.'

'It's just like a doll's house.'

'Indeed. Here on the ground floor is the reception with an office leading off it; directly opposite the desk you can see the door to the dining room, and through that door there, the one with the oval window, is the kitchen. As you see, there's nothing indecent going on here: the guests are respectably asleep in their rooms on the three floors, while the staff lie work-worn in their beds under the rafters.'

'So what are those noises coming from the office, then? From what I can hear it sounds like panting and gasping.'

'You're quite right, let's take a peep inside and see who's panting . . .'

'In a deep leather chair at the desk a red-haired youth sits hunched over the yellowing photographs of buxom girls, his hand working away in his lap . . .'

'Who's the pervert?'

'The guesthouse servant boy, an orphan the couple brought with them from the countryside, who they use to do the chores no one else wants to.'

'What's his connection to your story?'

'He's only really a minor character, poor thing, but all will be revealed later: I'm not telling the story here and now, merely setting the scene. Well, do you notice anything else unusual when you see the house opened up like this?'

'Like what?'

'Well, take a look. How many rooms are there on each floor, for example? I'm not saying any more . . .'

'Hang on . . .'

'If I lift off the upper storeys so that you can look down on the first floor from above as if it was a maze, what happens?'

'That's what you mean, ah, now I see . . .'

'The rooms on the first floor of the Gasthof Vrieslander have secret doors concealed in the wallpaper. They open into narrow, winding passageways that lead to the priest's hole, a compartment behind the panelling of room twenty-three.

This once provided a refuge for the spiritual and secular leaders of the town, and any others who were forbidden from being seen in the company of ladies of pleasure, for the madam's house contained many rooms to cater for the diverse needs of her children.

But what the mayor and priest didn't know was that for a handsome sum the ordinary guests of the brothel could watch them through a peephole in the wall of room twenty-three; so the proportions of the pillars of society were on everybody's lips, so to speak.'

'But who's that? Oh, she slipped round the corner. It was a woman, wasn't it?'

'You've got a good pair of ears. That's an old man who lives at the guesthouse, because houses that play a major role in stories generally have a pensioner or two thrown in.'

'He looked awfully effeminate in that nightie, with his arms held out in front of him like a hare . . .'

'You hit the nail on the head there. His name's Tomas Hasearsch, or "hare's arse", and he's lived at the guesthouse ever since he was a boy.'

'Then he must have a tale or two to tell from the days when clients could expect to find more than just a hot-water bottle waiting for them in their rooms.'

'Wait, I'll get him. Come on, old chap, stand here at the edge of the floor.'

'He's asleep.'

'Yes, he sleepwalks, wandering the passages like a ghost in an English spine-chiller. He sometimes talks in his sleep too, and he can be pretty crude at times, I can tell you.'

'God, it must give the guests the creeps to be woken by the sound of indecent whisperings through the walls.'

'Shh! He's moving his lips, lifting his geriatric blue hand and addressing the sleeping town—'

'Can I see? Can I see?'

'Quiet, chicken! This is unsuitable for young birds.'

'Yes, shame on you for thirsting after smut!'

'The old man goes on: There you are, poppet, ah, bring the towel here, pass Bellalolalululili something to dry herself with. So Lululilibellalola's little man was spying, was he? And did he see something nice? No, goodness me, child, that's nothing compared to his cannon; no, I'm not telling anyone his name: he comes here in the mornings when most of the others have left, my heart's angel, wearing a black mask, and I'm the only person that knows who he is – well, and maybe one other. Oof, now Lolabellalililulu's tired, be a good boy, rub some ointment on her bruises and tell her some funny gossip from town . . . What's the postmaster been up to?'

'Stop that right now – he's grabbing his crotch!'

'The old man continues: If boysy's good to Lililolalulubella she'll play with the little chap, she'll give her little boy something nice around his winkle, oh yes, she will . . .'

'Don't get carried away with this filth.'

'All right, all right. The old man falls silent – there, I'm pushing him back into the passage, and now I'm up to my elbow in the picture you've conjured up of Kükenstadt town square.'

'Is there anything else I ought to see? I'm feeling a bit dizzy . . .'

'Ready, now I'll snap the upper storeys back on, then the front, and the roof on top. And now I'll whip my arm out of your head . . .'

'All I can see are yellow spots, shooting in front of my eyes like comets, but when I close my eyes the square appears just as you originally described it, only now I can see inside the guesthouse, I'm familiar with every nook and cranny.'

'But don't you notice a change from earlier? We're drawing closer to the story and its first signs should be visible . . .'

'Yes, wait a minute, that's strange, now there's a light shining in one of the attic windows . . .'

'Marie-Sophie X is asleep.'

'Who's she?'

'She's the woman I come closest to calling my mother.'

'A young girl sat reading a book in bed, the eiderdown in a ruck at her feet and her soles resting on the monogram embroidered on the cover in cross-stitch. She had piled up the pillows behind her back and tucked a cushion on to her lap, on which she was resting the book. A candle stub flickered in a holder on the chest of drawers by the bed, casting a syrupy yellow light over the contents of the room. There wasn't much: a chair, a wardrobe, a chamber-pot, an oval mirror and a gaudy picture of a saint hovering in a forest clearing with a little hut in his hands. A maid's black uniform hung from a hanger on the wardrobe door, books lay heaped on the chair. There were two doors to the room, one leading to the staff lavatory, the other to the landing.

The girl drew an invisible thread from word to word with a bitten-down nail, sensing the writing between the lines with her fingertips. Every now and then she would close her clear blue eyes and ponder what she had been reading, and her left hand would lift of its own accord to fiddle with the dark plait that lay over the lace front of her nightgown. Every time she turned a page she frowned, and when the story was full of action she rubbed her big toes together and drew up her feet.

She paused increasingly often to reflect on the book. The clock on the floor below chimed three and a moment later the silver bell in the town-hall tower struck four.

— This book's a bloody thief of time. Oh well, I'll read one more page, then I'm going to sleep.

* * *

— And the comets?

— They're angel dandruff, which burns up in the outermost layers of the atmosphere and the ash falls to earth where it turns into tiny guardian spirits for the smallest animals, plants and minerals, just as the volcanic ash from Mount Hekla has its origin in the embers that swirl from the devil's beard when he's careless around the fires of hell, but they, on the other hand, turn into demons that fight the good spirits for power over all living things. So the battle between good and evil is waged even in your socks – they look to me as if they're made of cotton.

— What nonsense is the man telling you, little Siegfried?

— He was telling me about the stars.

— Is that so? We must be getting home now.

— What about elephants? Are there devils in elephants too?

— Come on, I said!

— Goodness me, yes, there must be quite a battle being waged in them.

— And in my braces?

— Ugh, yes!

— COME ON!

The slave was left standing alone by the hut as the man took the boy by the hand and led him over to the gate where the guards saluted and let them through. He watched father and son climb into a gleaming Mercedes-Benz and drive away.

* * *

— Marie-Sophie?

    — Yes?

    — Can I talk to you?

    — Talk to me.

    — You're alone.

    — All alone.

    — Darkness hangs over the land.

    — I can see it through the skylight; there are no stars.

    — I looked out over the earth: it was asleep.

    — Everyone except me.

    — You too.

    — But I'm reading a book.

    — You're asleep.

    — Am I asleep? Oh my God, is the candle still alight?

    — It is burning, as you too will burn.

    — Now I'm in for it. This is an old house; it could burn to the ground in a flash!

    — I'll watch it for you.

    — Thanks.

    — It's hard to find anyone to talk to these days. No one dreams any more; the cities are blacked out and the only sign of life among humans is the breath that rises from their houses on a cold winter's night. But then I noticed you. You were dreaming; that's how I found you.

    — Me dreaming? I wasn't dreaming; you were drawn to the light. Oh Lord, I've forgotten to close the shutter! I must wake up. Wake me up, whoever you are.

    — Call me Freude.

    — That's no answer. Wake me up.

    — I'm the Angel of the West Window, the skylight above you, and I've blacked it out – you needn't worry.

    — Are you here in my room?

    — Yes, I'm always in your window, at your window.

    — This is a fine mess you've got me into! I'm not allowed to entertain male guests at night. You'd better get lost double-quick or we'll both end up in hot water. She's tough on morality, the Inhaberin – the proprietor's wife.

— Well, I'm not exactly male.

— I don't care; your voice is deep enough. Get out!

* * *

The slave returned to the work hut, to his comrades in slavery, to the supervisors and the ceramic falcons that stood on the shelves, their fierce eyes glaring out over their creators: a shaven-headed congregation of men who kneaded them and formed them from black clay.

It was hot in the hut: cruel birds like these had to be fired in vast kilns in which the white flames licked the spread wings and splayed claws.

He silently resumed his work, dabbing yellow paint on to the eyes before the falcons went back into the fire.

* * *

— I'm not going anywhere, I can't!

— Then shut up and let a tired chambermaid get some sleep!

— I'm bored . . .

— I'm not a diversion for bored angels.

— What were you dreaming?

— What kind of question is that? Didn't you just say you'd been drawn to my dream?

— Yes, but you must describe it to me.

— I want to know who you are; I'm not accustomed to describing my nonsensical dreams to strangers.

— But I'm not a stranger, I'm always with you.

— Well, I like that! You may hang around my window, thinking you know me, but I don't know the first thing about you. For all I know, you may be a scoundrel, planning to get me in the family way.

— Now, now . . .

— Don't now, now me, my good man. It wouldn't be the first time in the history of the world that one of your lot has had his wicked way with a woman.

— Eh!

The girl tosses and turns in her sleep and the book slips from her hand, but the angel catches it before it falls to the floor. He opens it at random and skims the text.

— Marie-Sophie!
— What?
— I see here on the left-hand page that the slave has finished digging his way under the perimeter fence of the camp. Let me read a bit for you – then perhaps you'll remember the dream . . .
— Oh, for goodness' sake read, then at least you won't keep prattling!

* * *

When he sticks his head up out of the hole a crow flaps by over the pale field, croaking: *Krieg! Krieg!* He vanishes back into the ground for a moment, then a suitcase and a pink hatbox with a black lid appear on the edge of the hole.

* * *

— That's nothing like the story I was reading . . .

* * *

He crawls out of the hole and takes a deep breath. It's unbelievable how fresh and invigorating the night air smells out here in the field; unthinkable that this is the same air that lies like a stinking fog over the village of death behind him.

* * *

— That's nothing like my book . . .
— But this is what you were dreaming.
— You must be joking. I was reading a love story.
— When you fell asleep the story continued in your dream, taking

a new direction. I've read the book from cover to cover, but this is a new edition. Listen:

* * *

But he can't dwell on his thoughts about the sky: he's on the run. Carefully picking up the hatbox, he wedges it firmly under his left arm, seizes the handle of the suitcase and sets off in the direction of the forest, leaving . . .

* * *

— Which is what you should do.

    — He's on his way here.

    — So what? As far as I'm concerned, the people I dream about are welcome to visit me. Go and find your own book to fall asleep over . . .

    — Goodnight, Marie-Sophie.

    — Goodnight.'

II

'Gabriel bestrode the Continent, his celestial soles planted on the Greenland ice-cap in the north and the Persian plateau in the south. The clouds lapped at his ankles, billowing the snowy skirt of the robe that hid his bright limbs and all his blessed angel-flesh. Chains of pure silver spanned his chest, azure epaulettes graced his shoulders and his glorious head was wreathed in twilight so the flood of bright locks would not turn night into day. His expression was pure as the driven snow; a crescent moon glowed in his eyes, a fire that erupted in an annihilating blaze at the slightest discord in his heart; an ice-cold smile played about his lips.'

'Now that's what I call a proper angel.'

'Gabriel stroked downy-soft fingers over his instrument, a magnificent trumpet inlaid with opals, which hung about his neck on a roseate thong plaited out of poppies from the fields of Elysium. He spread his heavenly wings, which were so vast that their tips touched the outer walls of the world in the east and west, and the feathers swirled over the earth, falling like a blizzard on fields and cities. He shook back his sleeves, grasped the trumpet, braced his shoulders until the epaulettes touched his ears, flexed his knees and thrust out his holy hips. Hosanna! He raised the instrument.'

'Hosanna!'
  'Shut up!'
  'No.'

'Gabriel laid the trumpet to his lips, puffed out his cheeks, emptied his mind and prepared to blow. He concentrated on listening for the tune, hosanna, waiting for the right moment to let it sound out over the world that lay at his feet.'

'And?'

'Gabriel had long awaited this moment, but now that it was nigh he had difficulty pinning down his feelings; he wavered between anticipation and fear, euphoria and despair. On the one hand he felt like a well-trained player who has been forced to sit on the substitution bench for game after game, though everyone says he's the most talented member of the team, and now that he has finally been sent on to the pitch it was to save the team from a hopeless situation. HOSANNA – he would do his best. On the other hand he was afraid of the emptiness that would follow in the wake of the clarion call; naturally there would be turmoil and confusion after he sounded the trumpet and he would take part in the cataclysmic events that ensued, leading a fair host of warlike angels into battle against the powers of darkness, but when it was all over he would have nothing to look forward to and nothing to fear. The Lord giveth and the Lord taketh away. The angel didn't know whether he felt happy or sad.

He was surprised at himself. He had always imagined that when the time came he would seize the trumpet in both hands and sound the blast without hesitation; that it would thunder in his mind like the very voice of the Creator, finding its way to his lips without hindrance; that all he would have to do was take up position and amen: doomsday in heaven and on earth.

Gabriel knitted his fair brows in an effort to banish these thoughts. He lowered the trumpet for a moment and ran the tip of his sweet tongue over his lips, closing his limpid eyes and swaying from his hips. He imagined the tune trapped in his nether regions, in his withered rectum, and that he could free it by rhythmic movements of his pelvis so that it would rise like a lifebelt from a sunken ship, ascending his spine to his wondrous brain where it would bob up on the surface of his consciousness. The angel's head nodded, his neck veins swelled, his fingers clenched the instrument, his stomach muscles cramped, his knees shook a little, his feet trod sand and snow. The tune eddied in his brain fluid like blood in water: Leluiala, iallulae, aiallule, ullaliae, eluiaall, lleluaia, auaellli. The angel sensed it was coming, thank God. He drew a mighty breath through his sublime nostrils.

Stretching his eyes so wide that they shot out sparks into the abyss, forming seven new solar systems in the process, he glared at the doomed earth below. Aallelui! Sinful mankind lay abed, snoring, breaking wind, mumbling and gulping saliva, ugh, or grappling with another of its kind, drunk with lust, exchanging bodily fluids.'

'That's disgusting!'
'The occupations of the wide-awake were no more savoury.'
'Go on.'

'Gabriel shuddered; it was clearly high time judgement was called down upon this rabble. He saw platoons of plague scouts storming over the Continent, sweeping from country to country, torching towns and cities; armed with hard steel they answered to tyrants who sat twisted with bloodlust in their underground bunkers, desecrating the map of Europe; with panzers, helmets, shields and guns they trampled growing fields, ripped up forests by the roots, pissed in rapids and rivers, massacred mothers and children, murdered and maimed; to strike and stab was their pride and joy: they paid no heed to judgement day.

The angel trembled with righteous anger. Hosanna, glory be to God in the highest, woe to them and woe to them; soon they would suffer the ultimate fate and their cold corpses be robbed of their robes of state.

Stripped of power they'd be nothing but worms' bait.

He heard air-raid sirens wailing in the cities – those human fiends made a worse racket than the devil himself – but now they would get a taste of some real doomsday music. ALLELUIA! ALLELUIA! ALLELUIA! The tune surged against the angel's inner ear, sounding absurdly like the death cries that emanated from below, strong and full of promise about the great battle in which the angels of heaven and devils of hell would strive for men's souls in a magnificent show-down. Hah, mankind's sordid struggles would end the instant the notes poured forth from his fair trumpet: Creation would be over-turned, the firmament torn, the oceans set on edge, the rocks split and the guilty cast down while the virtuous were raised up to the highest heights on high. Yes, such is the song of the end of days!'

'Bah!'

'Gabriel tried to curb his fury, he must get a grip on himself: the trumpet was a sensitive instrument and the note would go awry if he blew too hard. He relaxed his shoulders, breathed out slowly and counted the tempo in his head: One-two-three *A*, one-two-three *A*, one-two-three *A*, one-two-three *A*, one-two-three *A*, one-two-three *A*, one-two-three *A*. Gabriel was about to inflate his magnificent lungs afresh when he caught sight of searchlights cleaving the night above the capi-tal of the Kingdom of the Angles – a blasphemous name; oh, good heav-ens, they were groping like crude fingers up under the costly robe.

The angel was chaste, yes: no one was going to get an eyeful of his Jerusalem. He yanked his robe tight about his holy body and the heavenly garments swung modestly against the shining limbs, concealing the sweet treasure between his legs, which was a good day's work by God and ineffable, *Kyrie eleison*. But Gabriel could not prevent the twisting movement from running the length of his body. His glorious head was flung back, one of his brightly glowing locks fell out from under the dusky headdress and obscured his view of the earth, and the tune went awry, slipping out of his consciousness and sliding into the amygdaloid nucleus of his brain like a snake into its hole.'

'No!'
'Oh yes! It was the work of Lucifer Satan – he who passes through the world with delusions and dirty tricks, sowing the seeds of heresy in human hearts.'
'Woe to him!'

'Gabriel smelled the scent of lady's mantle (*Alchemilla vulgaris*) and brushed the hair from his eyes: he was standing on a verdant plain under a crystal sky; tens of thousands of suns cast their rays on fields and meadows; doves (probably *Gallicolumba luzonica*, which is marked out for the Saviour by its blood-red breast feathers) cooed in olive groves (*Olea europaea*), and she-tigers (*Panthera tigris*) gave suck to kids (*Capra hircus*) on the banks of a tinkling brook. Away on the horizon cherubs hovered over marble cliffs.

The angel was in Seventh Heaven, his home, as far from mankind's vale of tears as could be imagined. He heaved a sigh of relief: doomsday appeared to be over. All was quiet, the Almighty had conquered – for ever: AMEN!'

'Amen.'

'Gabriel observed from the shadows of the olive trees that it was approaching suppertime in heaven (everything casts a shadow there even though the suns are always at their noonday zenith – I mention this merely for information) and suddenly he felt an overwhelming sense of fatigue throughout his colossal frame.

He was truly exhausted after his descent to earth, aie; now he had no greater desire than to return to his blessed lodgings in the house of the Father on the main square of Paradise City. He longed for a perfumed bath; to lie in the foaming holy water of the silver tub and let the tension seep out of his body. In the evening he would go out on the square and dance on the head of a pin with the guardian angels.

The angel spread his weary wings, adjusted the goodly trumpet, raised himself into the air and headed for his quarters.'

'Praise be to God.'

'Yes, let us praise His holy name, but don't forget that Satan has taken charge of the Lord's show.'

'Oh dear!'

'And although the story will now turn to other matters for a while, he has not had his final word.'

'Gabriel?'

'He'll come into the story again – later.'

'Kiss me.'

'How much will it cost?'

'You can have one free for the she-tigers: I identified with them; they were so utterly adorable.'

'Thanks.'

'Not at all, the pleasure was mine.'

3

'The cook was hard at work kneading a voluminous mass of dough on the kitchen table when Marie-Sophie came down in the morning. The servant lad sat at the end of the table, forming gingerbread men from the lump of cake-dough he'd been allotted, shaping small human figures with his large hands, digging a nail in the soft dough to divide legs and arms from body, pricking eyes and mouths with a roasting skewer.

— Thank goodness you're here!

The cook turned her plump face to the girl without missing a beat in her kneading: the dough danced on the table, took to the air and smacked down, turned, stretched and contracted, like a squirming brat refusing to have its nappy changed. The cook was wholly in its power, her massive body quivered and quaked, right from the small feet, which performed quick dance steps under the table, to her double chin, which bulged and compressed, all in obedience to the origin of the movement – the dough.

— Well, I don't know how much of a blessing it is, I'm not working.

Answered the girl, pretending not to notice the boy who was bending over his creations with a wolfish grin on his face.

— I haven't had a Sunday off in ages.

— Sweet Jesus, I wasn't going to ask you to help me, no, dear child, nothing could be further from . . . No, no, no . . .

The cook lowered her voice and motioned Marie-Sophie closer with a toss of her head, which is how she directed everything in the kitchen when she had her hands full with the cooking; with lightning-quick motions of the head she drew invisible lines in the air, connecting hand to pepper-pot, grip to ladle, fingers to saucepan lid.

— Why am I put upon like this?

The cook darted suspicious eyes at the boy, all the while nodding to Marie-Sophie until the girl was up close to her quivering flesh.

What is it with fat people, anyway? thought the girl, now partnering the cook in her dance. I always feel closer to them than I want to be. Is it because the distance between men's hearts must always be the same, regardless of a person's girth?

— What have I ever done to those people?

The cook raised the dough aloft and kneaded it at head height as if by this means she could absorb the impact of the dreadful news she was hugging to herself but now wished to share with the girl.

— Why do they have to stick him in the kitchen when you lot have the day off?

Marie-Sophie glanced over her shoulder at the pimply, red-haired youth, chief protagonist of the first major event of the day at Gasthof Vrieslander; the gingerbread figures dwindled in his hands and his face was so flushed that you'd have thought he was sharing the oven with his progeny.

— I do declare I'm afraid of him!

The girl found it hard to believe that the cook, who was still brandishing the ever-moving globe of dough aloft, would not have the measure of this scrawny boy – the dough must weigh nearly twelve kilos.

— Isn't that going a bit far?

The cook squinted at Marie-Sophie and whispered:

— We're not talking about physical violence, dearie, he's not man enough for that, oh no, what do you think he's gone and done?

Marie-Sophie couldn't imagine what the boy had done that could take this worldly cook by surprise: the woman had experienced a thing or two in her time, after all, having worked with her backside and bosom under men's noses ever since she could remember. The girl had heard all the stories after the rum baba distillations in the evenings: "Because you have to make rum baba in the evenings, child, as it needs to stand overnight."

But today, apparently, the cook was shaken:

— He's using psychological violence against me, the filthy little beast!

She slammed the dough down on the table so hard that the kitchen reverberated. The boy jumped and for a moment the grin fell from his face, but when the banging and rattling in the cupboards had subsided it lay again between his sticking-out ears like the gaping flies on a pair of trousers. He was agonised: he was the type who smiles when he gets into trouble – which led to frequent misunderstandings. This time it was the cook who misunderstood him: And he just sits there laughing at me!

The boy tried to hunch lower over his gingerbread in the hope that his face wouldn't show – as if that would change anything. The cook had kneaded his disgrace into the cake-dough. The guesthouse regulars would eat it up with their morning coffee and later in the day they would pass it out the other end. And with that his unfortunate prank and the shame of being scolded like a randy dog in front of Marie-Sophie would have become part of the world's ecosystem.'

'So what on earth had he done?'

'The cook began to knead life back into the dough, which had lain limp between her hands since being slammed on the table.
 — *Mein Gott*, I can hardly bring myself to talk about it . . .
 — Yes, you can, I'll see that he gets his comeuppance.
Marie-Sophie pretended to glare at the boy. He was obviously relieved, though he was trying not to let it show. The poor wretch had been drooping in reception all night – honestly, it was rotten of them to order him, still heavy-lidded from the night shift, to assist the hung-over cook with the baking. Was it any wonder if the lad resorted to a little mischief to keep himself awake over the gingerbread?
 — Just look!
The cook jerked her shoulder at a baking tray which was on a chair by the door to the backyard; it had been placed as close to the edge of the chair as possible without actually falling on the floor. Under a page from the *Kükenstadt-Anzeiger*, the town newspaper, a cake-shaped lump could be seen – this gingerbread was clearly a reject.
 — What do you think it is?

Before Marie-Sophie could answer the cook began to edge them both in pursuit of the dough, which was creeping off in the direction of the rejected baking tray.

— *Mein Gott*, you'll never guess!

The cook made the sign of the cross in the air with the tip of her nose as she transferred the dough from the table to the wall by the back door and proceeded to knead it there.

Marie-Sophie was no longer indifferent to this kitchen drama in which she had unwittingly become a participant. She felt queasy from having the quivering formlessness before her eyes, the heat from the oven was suffocating, and she was seized with the fear that she might never break free from her intricate dance with the cook. It was her day off, it was Sunday, she had slipped downstairs to grab a bite to eat. Her fifteen-minute date with a simple breakfast was developing into an interminable tragedy in which answers were sought to major questions about honour, morality and evil in the human soul. And, as befitted a great showman, the cook spun out her testimony to the very brink of anticipation:

— There it is!

The boy flinched. The cook spat out the words. Her proximity to the object of disgrace, the forbidden confectionery, made her blood boil to such a pitch that it seemed she might pass right through the wall into the yard and Lord knows where, with the cake-dough held aloft like a banner of censure.

Marie-Sophie no longer saw any chance of escaping with her sanity intact from this kitchen of the absurd; the cook would never bring herself to expose the evidence in the case of "Propriety versus Clumsy Hans"; the gingerbread men would end up so small in the boy's hands that he would split the atom, and she herself would never make it to her date with that glass of milk, slice of bread and pear, even though her business was first and foremost with them on this Sunday morning – she would starve to death in a kitchen.

The girl now reacted quickly: she tore herself away from the cook and made as if to whip the newspaper off the baking tray when the boy leapt to his feet:

— I didn't mean anything by it . . .

Marie-Sophie nailed him with her eyes:

— Yes, you should be ashamed of yourself. Apologise and then beat it to bed . . .

The boy scratched his fiery red thatch, untied his apron and moved hesitantly to the door.

— I'm sorry, Fräulein, Frau . . .

He yawned unconvincingly, shrugged his shoulders, examined his toes, turned up his nose, did his best to look chastened and directed his words at the girl and the cook in turn.

— Don't know what got into me, no sleep, yes, just . . .

Marie-Sophie signalled to him to scram but now it was as if he were rooted to the spot: of course, he was waiting for her to uncover the tray, but she wasn't going to give him that satisfaction. She turned to the cook, who had stopped kneading and was now herself again: an overweight woman with a headache. Their eyes met and Marie-Sophie said what she had been meaning not to say ever since she set foot in the kitchen:

— I'll finish the baking with you, shall I?

The cook shook her head.

— No, dearie, I couldn't let you do that; you haven't had a Sunday off in ever such a long time, my goodness me, no.

She handed the dough to the girl and trotted over to the pan cupboard from which she extracted a bottle of cooking rum and a cup without a handle. The boy was still standing by the door, staring rigidly at the cook. The grin spread over his face as she filled the cup.

Marie-Sophie laid the dough on the table: what an idiot the boy was, why didn't he get lost?

She looked askance at him but her only answer was the grin now splitting his face in two, accompanied by a twitching of his shoulder towards the larder door.

The cook raised the cup and hissed at the boy as she sipped the rum:

— See what you've done to me!

And then Marie-Sophie understood what was rooting the boy to the spot; she heard what he had heard: from inside the larder came a muttering. She hushed the cook and the good woman crossed herself.

Marie-Sophie crept to the larder door and put her ear to it: there was no mistaking the sound: someone was moving around among the jars of pickled gherkins, the *wursts* and wine – a thief? A pregnant woman with an insatiable lust for pickled gherkins? A sausage snatcher, or a dipso who had lingered too long in Paradise and been unable to make his escape when the cook turned up to work that morning? She tiptoed to the table and picked up a rolling pin.

— Sweet Jesus!

The cook was near to tears over what the Lord had given her to bear that morning. Marie-Sophie put a finger to her lips, handed the boy a meat tenderiser and directed him to the kitchen door: he was to watch the exit, she would open the larder and brain the thief, and if he tried to escape through the yard door the cook would be in his path and that was one female there was no getting round.

Marie-Sophie counted up to three in her head, took a tighter grip on the rolling pin, flung open the door and burst out laughing: a gaunt figure in a tattered rag of a coat, with a poor apology for shoes on his feet, was sprawled the length of the larder floor. Of course it wasn't the man's vagabond appearance that made the girl laugh but the fact that in his fall he had pulled down a string of sausages, which now encircled his head like a crown, while on his left breast a gherkin perched in place of a medal.

He was holding a hatbox. He was my father.'

4

'Head hanging, Marie-Sophie shuffled her feet on the plump angel that was woven into the carpet of the guesthouse office.

— When something like this happens, no one can have a day off, not you, not me, you must understand that?

The owner was sitting behind her in a red leather-upholstered chair, mopping the sweat from his brow with a white handkerchief.

— I'm far from happy about this, but we owe these people money. They brought the man here last night and we were forced to take him in.

Marie-Sophie bit her lip: the owner and the Inhaberin, his wife, had stormed into the kitchen just as she was about to wet herself with laughter over the scarecrow in the larder. And now she felt as if she had actually done so.

— I know no more about him than you do and we don't want to know anything, remember that.

Naturally they had gone crazy when they saw the chaos in the larder, at least that's what Marie-Sophie had thought. The owner had dealt the boy's cheek three cuffs from his store of blows, then shooed him out into the backyard, while the Inhaberin steered the weeping cook out into the passage and poured the rest of the cooking rum down her throat, and Marie-Sophie was ordered to tidy up the kitchen and then report to the office where "they would have a word with her".

After this they had stripped the thief of his regalia – the sausage crown and gherkin of honour – and between them lugged him upstairs to one of the rooms.

Marie-Sophie had done as she was told and now the owner was, as it were, "having a word".

— If anything should happen – I don't know what – we're completely blameless, or you are anyway, I'll see to that.

The girl said nothing.

— We take care of our people, you know that. And that's why we want you to look after him.

The owner glanced around nervously.

— Can I offer you a barley sugar?

Marie-Sophie sighed heavily: what was she doing here? What was the man asking of her? To look after this sausage emperor or gherkin general or whoever it was that they'd found in the kitchen? She knew nothing about nursing: he could hardly be very important if they wanted her to do it. And what was this about "if anything should happen"?

— Or maybe you don't have a sweet tooth? Good for you.

The owner had risen to his feet and was pacing up and down the office, stopping short every time somebody walked past reception. He rattled on about sugar consumption and tooth-care and praised the girl to the skies for her abstinence in the sweet department.

Marie-Sophie didn't know what to do. Every time she meant to put her foot down and tell him that unfortunately she couldn't take this on, it was her day off, and anyway she was bound to kill the man instead of curing him, her attention was distracted by some aspect of the room's furnishings: the curtains of wine-red velvet, the gilded desk or the risqué painting over the bookcase. These reminders of the building's former role somehow hampered her in finding words for her thoughts.

She no longer knew how to say the vital "no".

A movement at the office door sent the owner flying into his chair; he wiped his handkerchief quickly over his bald pate and almost shouted:

— Then I think we – I've covered the main points of the matter.

The Inhaberin swept into the room, slamming the door behind her.

— Well, I never! I didn't know we were going to broadcast it all over town that we're hiding a fugitive.

The owner waved the flag of truce in his wife's face.

— You were ever such a long time, dearest . . .

The Inhaberin stuck her nose in the air.

— Huh, as if you had the faintest idea how long it takes to undress a full-grown man.

Her husband converted defence into attack.

— On the Western Front we had to—

She turned to the girl.

— Well, dear, he needs a bath . . .

The thief, who Marie-Sophie now gathered was not a thief at all but a desperate fugitive, was awaiting his nurse in room twenty-three on the first floor of the guesthouse.

He was sitting stark naked in a hip bath beneath the window. The curtains were drawn and in the gloom the girl made out the most pathetic figure she had ever laid eyes on: his head lolled on his breast, his arms hung lifeless to the floor and his legs knocked together at knees as swollen as bruised pomegranates.

— So, what do you think of the creature?

The Inhaberin pushed Marie-Sophie before her into the room and shut the door behind them.

— It wasn't easy to get him out of those rags, I can tell you: his drawers and socks were grafted on to him like a second skin.

Marie-Sophie tried not to look at the pathetic creature in the tub: red flecks covered his back and arms, his belly was distended like that of a baby. He was shivering. The girl put her hands over her mouth: what on earth was the woman thinking of? Letting him sit bare-arsed like that in the empty bath? She grabbed the cover off the bed and wrapped it around his nakedness – that way less of him was visible too.

— He's all yours, then. The boy'll bring the water. He'll put it by the door and knock – he has no business coming in here.

The Inhaberin clapped her hands together and turned on her heel.

Marie-Sophie nodded and wrapped the bedcover more tightly round the poor invalid: God, he was so thin that the shoulder-blades and vertebrae jutted out of his back like wings, like the teeth of a saw. She looked at the Inhaberin, shaking her head helplessly: what were they thinking of to place this corpse in her care?

The Inhaberin pretended not to understand the girl's expression.

— When you're finished, move him in there . . .

She pointed to a light spot, no bigger than the pupil of an eye, on the wallpaper above the bed.

— In the priest's hole?

— I've put clean sheets on the bed and everything should be there. But if you need anything, ring the bell.

Opening the door, the Inhaberin peered out into the passage, then pulled it to again when she heard someone on the stairs.

From the passage came a monotonous stream of senile complaint: Herr Tomas Hasearsch bade the Almighty Lord to take him away from this miserable place where God-fearing souls were cheated of their gingerbread men on their day of rest. They listened to him struggling with the lock of his room; after an eternity a door was heard opening and closing.

But now it seemed the Inhaberin was no longer in a hurry to leave.

— I bet the old sod's laying an ambush for me. He can sense what's going on; after all, he grew up in this house. Do you think he shut the door properly behind him?

The invalid sneezed.

Marie-Sophie hugged him tighter and looked daggers at the Inhaberin: if the woman was trying by her indifference to demonstrate that she knew nothing about caring for invalids, the message had been received loud and clear.

The Inhaberin screwed up her eyes. She surveyed the pair under the window for a long moment, then snorted:

— You're young; you think you know it all, but I'd keep an eye on him if I were you. He's not as pathetic as he looks: I thought I'd never wrestle that scruffy box out of his grasp.

She gestured with her left foot to the hatbox, which lay on the floor along with the rest of the invalid's worldly goods: the ragged clothes and a suitcase that plainly didn't have room for much.

With that the Inhaberin swept out, slamming the door behind her.

The girl Marie-Sophie stayed behind: in room twenty-three. On the first floor of the Vrieslander guesthouse. In the small town of Kükenstadt. At the mouth of the Elbe. In Lower Saxony. Alone with a half-naked man. An hour ago she had been ready to brain him with a rolling pin; now she was expected to nurse him. War raged in the world.

Marie-Sophie rolled up her shirtsleeves, dipped her elbow in the water and poured it into the tub.

— Right, dear, on with the washing.

The invalid flinched: *the boy had brought the water in two buckets and was dying to get into the room*: a tremendous stench rose from the tub as the soap began to work on the dirt that covered the man's skin like a parasitic fungus: *she'd told the boy that the Inhaberin had forbidden it; this was no amusement show*: the red flecks seemed sore, she stroked them gently with her fingertips: *then the idiot boy had said he wanted to see them*: she carefully soaped the swollen armpits: *See what?*

— There, do you think you can stand up?

Marie-Sophie clasped the invalid under the arms and raised him to his feet to make it easier for her to wash his chest and stomach: *The kittens, of course!*

— See, you can do it.

The invalid stood upright in the tub, his arms dangling limply at his sides: *she hadn't known whether to laugh or cry*: there were small scars on his chest as if someone had stubbed out a burning finger there: *did the boy really think she was drowning kittens in the best room of the guesthouse?*

— I suppose we'll have to clean you there too!

Marie-Sophie quickly dabbed soap on the man's privates: *Yes, if they were to be dispatched to heaven the boy thought it only natural that it should be done in decent surroundings*: she looked away and blushed: *In soapy water?*

— My God! Where have you been?

She snatched back her hands: *Yes, the boy imagined it would be quicker that way*: the invalid's back was so burned with faeces and urine that festering wounds emerged from under the filth: *the Inhaberin had told the boy and he wanted to see how it was done*: she bit her lip and continued to run the bar of soap down the man's thighs:

*Did she put the kittens in a sack or did she hold them under water with
her bare hands?*

— There, nearly done.

The invalid whimpered when the girl touched a badly healed sore
on one shin: *she had told the boy he was an idiot*: the man's insteps
were bruised and chilblained with cold: *the boy had lost his temper
at that*: she reached out, grabbed the bucket of water, stood on tiptoe
and rinsed the soap off him: *then she had added that he was a darling
idiot*: the invalid gasped as the lukewarm water sluiced over his body:
this had mollified the boy: she helped him out of the tub and dried
him: *and the boy had said, with an enigmatic look on his face, that she
could expect a little something from him later*: the invalid buckled at
the knees, she wrapped the bedcover around him again and led him
into the priest's hole: *she had thanked the boy and gone back into the
room with the buckets of water as she had to wash the invalid.*

Despite its small size, the priest's hole was the most luxurious room
in the guesthouse. On the wall facing the bed there was a cunningly
contrived *trompe l'oeil* window with a regal frame and curtains of the
richest velvet. An Armenian rug, an Indonesian frankincense burner,
carved bedroom furniture from China, hand-painted porcelain decorated with Japanese geishas, a dancing Shiva from India and a laughing
brass Buddha from Siam were such a fair testament to turn-of-the-
century taste that Marie-Sophie thought she had developed tunnel
vision when she helped the invalid into the opulence: this *embarras
de richesse* was to be their setting for the next few days.

She laid the invalid in the emperor-size bed, put a nappy on him,
drew the bloomer-pink eiderdown over him and arranged the embroidered silk pillows under his head.

Lying there in that enormous bed the invalid, who had looked frail
enough before, now reminded Marie-Sophie of a piece of flotsam on
a storm-tossed sea.

He was ridiculous.

She burst into tears.'

5

'Marie-Sophie sat on a chair by the stranger's bed: she had rearranged his luggage countless times by the wardrobe: nothing could be touched until he regained consciousness and told her what was to be hung on hangers, what should be arranged on the chest of drawers or desk and where he wanted his shaving things; in his case or by the wash basin? Some gentlemen were so particular about their things; the cook had told her that shortly after the guesthouse opened an Icelander had stayed there, who never unpacked his trunk. One morning when she brought in his breakfast and straightened the bedclothes, she had spied him rummaging around in his trunk like a pig in a rubbish heap, muttering to himself something that sounded like "findin', findin'". Strange man, she'd thought; is he forever reminding himself of everything he does? She pictured him going for a walk in a forest, arms outstretched, grinding out words at every step like a mill: "Out for a walk, out for a walk!"

The girl laughed out loud at this thought and the comatose sleeper turned over in bed. She clamped her hands over her mouth and felt the blood rushing to her cheeks.

Here I sit laughing like a goose. What will the poor man think if he's woken by the sound of giggling and the first thing he sees is me, scarlet in the face and shaking with suppressed laughter?

She swallowed her laughter and adopted a serious expression, but then she remembered the cook's story of the muttering Icelander – "Out for a walk, out for a walk!" – and couldn't contain her mirth. The cook had eavesdropped at the Icelander's door to hear whether he said: "Eat, eat!" when he enjoyed his breakfast, but no, he recited a peculiar grace that seemed to have no end because in between chewing his sausage and swilling his beer he had continually apostrophised the Lord: "*Gott,*

Gott!" At that the cook had run squealing downstairs to the others and could hardly stammer out the words to tell them about the phenomenon in room twenty-three. The following day all the guesthouse staff, including old Tomas, eavesdropped on the Icelander and had a good laugh at the man's piety.

Ach, those foreigners can be a caution! I can just picture his face when he opened the door and found the passage full of people either howling or crying with laughter. "*Guten Tak,*" he said, after studying this parcel of fools for a long moment. "*Guten Tak!*" And at that even the Inhaberin couldn't hold back a smile.

Tee, hee, "findin', findin', *Gott, Gott*", – if only all the guests were like that Icelander.'

'Ha, ha, ha!'
   'Later this man became a famous author.'
   'No, stop it at once, you're killing me!'
   'Eat, eat!'
   'Ha, ha, ha!'

'Marie-Sophie shook with silent fits of laughter, she ached all over, there was a shrill whistling in her ears, but gradually the spasms became fewer and further between and she felt the memory being shaken out of her like a fever. She dried the tears from her eyes: she was standing by the fake window.

Have I lost my marbles or something? I've staggered over here in a fit of cramps without even noticing, bent double and crying at the reflection of my own face. What on earth's the matter with me? I've always been a dreadful giggler – and they trust someone like me with an invalid!

The girl exclaimed aloud at her reflection in the glass, gave a quick sniff and spun round. The invalid had lifted his shaven head from the pillow. She gasped; he examined her out of black eyes. They were brilliant with fever and seemed huge in his hollow face, enquiring: why were you laughing? She retreated from his regard and groped in the neck of her dress for an excuse.

— Once we had – here at the guesthouse, which is where you are by the way, at Gasthof Vrieslander, that's to say – we had a guest, I know I mustn't laugh at guests, the Inhaberin forbids it, but anyway he was from Iceland and there was a misunderstanding, like all jokes, you know, they laughed and laughed – Oh Lord, how are you supposed to understand when I don't understand what I'm on about myself? – but they almost died of laughter out there in the passage, because, so, because he said "eat, eat", that's why I was laughing.

But she couldn't come up with an answer.

Marie-Sophie closed her eyes in the hope that the invalid would copy her, just as long ago she used to lull her brother to sleep, but when she opened them again he had screwed up his own and enlarged the question: Am I in hell? She pressed herself against the window until the frame creaked and stared dumbly back: yes, he was in hell and she was the fool who was supposed to look after him. Was there something he'd like? Was he thirsty? Would he like a drink of vinegar? Hungry? She could ring down for some pepper mash, a stinging-nettle salad or pickled gravel. Was he hot, perhaps? She would place glowing coals at his feet. Cold? No problem, there was plenty of ice in the kitchen.

God, what on earth have I got myself mixed up in? What did they want to bring the man here for? This is no job for an out-and-out birdbrain like me!

The girl watched anxiously as the invalid ran his eyes over her body from top to toe: she was a puppet on a string; he was a puppeteer, taking her apart limb by limb in search of a flaw in the handiwork, a crack in the varnish. Were her legs well enough turned? Did he need to whittle a smidgen more from her waist? Could her elbows be better planed? And what about her cheeks, perhaps the red was a touch too hectic?

She felt inadequate.

What's going through his mind? He's behaving as if he owned me. He was better when he was dozing.

Marie-Sophie's body parts hovered in mid-air above the bedstead, rotating before the invalid's eyes, while her head loitered alone and uneasy by the window. It seemed to her that he paid particular attention to her hands: why was that?

She noticed that her right hand was clenched in a fist while the left was floating right under his nose, so she hurriedly clenched that as well to hide her nails, which were bitten to the quick. He gave a low whimper; the lines of pain around his mouth deepened and his eyes grew still larger. She started.

Oh, he's frightened!

Hastily she opened her fists, clasped her fingers over the eiderdown and tried to smile reassuringly: it's all right, it's only me, Marie-Sophie, silly Marie-Sophie, it's all right! But before she could say a word the invalid had closed his eyes again, let his head sink back on the pillow, turned to face the wall and sighed.

— Ugly, I know.

— No, it's not that.

Marie-Sophie came to herself again where she stood by the bed, helplessly wringing her hands: now she'd hurt his feelings. What could she do? What should she say?

— You're not ugly!

She shouted at the poor man. He gasped, screwed his eyes even tighter shut and didn't answer: his shaven head twitched on the pillow, the eiderdown trembled and after a few panting breaths the invalid sank into a silent stupor.

* * *

THE CHILD AND THE DWARF

Once upon a time a child was travelling on a tram with its mother when a dwarf got on board and took a seat near them, attracting the child's fascinated interest. It pointed at the dwarf and said, loud enough for him and the other passengers in the carriage to hear: Mummy, look how small that man is! Why's that man so small? Mummy, that man's smaller than me! He is a man, isn't he, Mummy, isn't he? Mummy, he's so small, and so on. The dwarf looked around tolerantly because children will be children, and the passengers looked tolerantly back for the same reason. And since mothers will be mothers, the mother bent over her child and whispered in its ear: Shh! You mustn't say that, we don't say things like that, perhaps he doesn't like being that small, no, just as you would feel if you had a big pimple on your nose, I'm sure he doesn't want people talking about it, so let's be nice to him and stop talking about how small he is.

The child shut up at these words, the dwarf stretched in his seat, straightening his coat on his shoulders, and the passengers nodded to the mother in recognition of her timely and successful intervention.

When the child and its mother had finished their journey, the child had yanked the bell-pull and the driver had opened the doors with a loud hiss, the child stopped by the dwarf on its way out and said in a loud voice: I think you're big!'

* * *

'Hee, hee!'

'The silence thundered in the girl's ears: a nice situation she was in! She drifted around the room, stopping by the bed every now and then and slapping her thigh in disgust.

That's torn it, now you've gone and insulted a helpless man! What next?

Marie-Sophie was relieved that the invalid was asleep, or dozing, or at any rate that he was lying with his eyes closed: after her uncouth behaviour she felt she didn't have any right to look into those big black eyes of his; that they were all he had left, the only part of him that was still alive, and a stupid girl like her should have the wit to leave them alone.

She pretended to make herself busy, drawing back the curtains and shaking them, then closing them again and shaking them some more. She arranged his belongings yet again, propping up the suitcase with the hatbox in front of it, then laying the case on its side with the box on top of it – from his luggage she couldn't really see that there was anything that remarkable about the man. What kind of VIP was it whose only luggage was a grubby case and a hatbox? Admittedly it was odd that a man should be lugging around a box that was clearly designed for a woman's hat – but hadn't she herself arrived in

Kükenstadt with all her worldly goods in her father's hunting bag? And she hadn't thought there was anything odd about that. Anyway, what had given her the idea that the invalid was remarkable? Oh, it was the way he had looked at her and taken her apart. Her soul blushed at the mere thought of it. And it was something the Inhaberin had said to her; yes, it was that he was important – she hadn't said remarkable – and that they would come and have a word with her. The men who had brought him? But the Inhaberin had refused to say any more. Apparently it would be better for her not to know too much; her role was to keep him alive during the days he stayed with them. Days? The matter was settled!

Marie-Sophie smoothed the towel and examined herself in the mirror, tilting her head on one side and putting a hand to her cheek, smiling.

— Yes, Karl dear. You won't get to see this maiden today – she's looking after an important invalid . . .'

'What nonsense is this about your father being important? Was he any more remarkable than other fathers?'

'Shh, all will be revealed—'

'I hope so, or I'll begin to suspect you of exaggerating.'

'All in good time, I mustn't lose the thread, don't interrupt . . .'

'I'll interrupt when I want explanations or have a comment to make. I'm your best critic, as you're well aware.'

'Marie-Sophie was about to sit down by the invalid's bed when she heard someone entering room twenty-three.

She crept to the door and listened to find out who it was: the owner, and he wasn't alone. She opened the door a crack and peered out.

— There you are!

The owner looked apologetically at the two men who were standing on either side of him, while they looked enquiringly at the girl.

— I can never remember where the entrance is to this – this den of iniquity . . .

Marie-Sophie had seen the two men before; they generally came in the evenings and drank coffee in the dining room. The owner used to join them and they would talk in low voices, sometimes till dawn or until he got drunk and the Inhaberin bore him off to bed.

— Would you mind having a word with these gentlemen, Maja dear?

Marie-Sophie raised her brows. Well, I never: Maja dear! The owner wasn't in the habit of calling her Maja, no one called her Maja, nor did she want them to. But it was clear he was all of a jitter so she'd better do as he asked.

The owner introduced the girl to the two men and explained that they wanted to ask her some questions about the visitor. She needn't be afraid; they had brought the man here. One of them asked her whether the man had said or done anything she thought they ought to know about.

Marie-Sophie thought hard but couldn't remember a thing. It seemed to her only natural that the man should mutter in his sleep, and it was none of their business that he had dismantled her.

No, nothing had happened that was worth repeating.

Then they said they had heard voices when they came into the room, how did she account for that?

The girl blushed to her toes: oh no, did they have to ask her about that? Now she would have to tell them that she had been talking to herself, how embarrassing. The two men pressed her for an answer and she confessed to chattering to herself, adding that she didn't have much else to do, left alone with a mute like that. Might she perhaps be allowed to pop up to her room for a book? She was afraid that otherwise the loneliness would drive her round the bend.

No, out of the question; the two men said that waking or sleeping she must keep an eye on the man. Reading books would only distract her attention from the finer points of his behaviour.

Sleeping? The gentlemen weren't asking much. Marie-Sophie had the impression that they hadn't a clue what they were asking her to do, or what they expected the invalid to get up to. Anyway, as if someone in as much pain as he was would have any tricks up his sleeve.

She asked if there was anything in particular they wanted her to watch out for? What if he used sign language? Should she perhaps peer under the bedclothes every now and then and try to read his hands? And what was to be done when she had to spend a penny – she was only human, after all – what if something interesting happened then?

Marie-Sophie pictured the invalid running round the priest's hole with his finger in the air, following the skirting board, moving up the walls and ceiling, and muttering to himself reams of incomprehensible mumbo-jumbo.

The two men listened patiently to the girl's ramblings, and in response to her last point asked the owner to see to it that she was given a chamber-pot for her use.

With that they took their leave of her, and the owner threw up his hands and followed them out like an obedient dog.

Marie-Sophie slammed the door of the secret compartment and plumped down at the dressing table: this got better and better! As if it wasn't bad enough that she had to change the nappy of this stranger who lay there in bed as lively as a washed-up jellyfish, now she had to do her business in front of him as well!

The girl glanced round for some place where she could use the potty in private: leaning against the wall was a handsomely carved wooden screen.

She stood up, unfolded the screen and propped it against the bedstead with the decorated side facing the wall; it depicted Japanese women bathing in a pool, spied upon by greybeards.

— Better not give him any ideas, seeing as they believe him capable of anything . . .

If Marie-Sophie stood on tiptoe she could see the invalid over the top; squatting, she could see him through the joins, so there was no longer any danger of his leaping out of bed, talking some outlandish gobbledegook and behaving in an otherwise sensational manner without her witnessing the whole thing.'

6

'When seized with impatience, women – fictional constructs of the female variety, that is – often stalk over to the nearest window and stare out. Usually it's the kitchen window, demonstrating that they are oppressed housewives, or alternatively the drawing-room window, indicating that the woman is a prisoner in a smart mansion in the best part of town.

As the woman examines the familiar view – dreary grey apartment blocks in the former case, the bright lights of the city in the latter – the thoughts that pass through her head are initially incoherent, aimless and connected primarily to what keeps them immured within the four walls of home. But as the interior monologue progresses, her thoughts become clearer. The woman manages to put two and two together, for instance placing an equals sign between what she wears and her husband's penis, which she is required to admire at night with adjectives from his own mouth.'

'Rubbish!'

'In the end, the awareness of her miserable lot condenses in her consciousness, like the menstrual blood in her lap, until it bursts out in a primal scream: I want to be free! I want to know my body and own it myself. I want to live for myself and nobody else. I want the freedom to . . .

Yes, a series of visions follows in the wake of her declaration of independence, based on the noun "will", the verb "to want". The woman pictures herself in situations that are in reality symbols of her desire for freedom and consequently as varied as the women themselves. The woman's level of education and self-realisation are also bound to influence this dream vision, this Holy Grail that she will dedicate her life to seeking from now on.

FREEDOM!

Isn't it interesting how oppressed minorities invariably conclude their intellectual analysis of their situation with this same cry: freedom?'

'No! Get on with the story.'

'May I remind you that you are not sufficiently well versed in the history of narrative to start getting uppity. The fact that I'm introducing you to the basics of feminist thinking on narrative at this point is not irrelevant; I'm doing it so you'll understand the singularity of my mother Marie-Sophie's position in literature. She lived before the age of feminism and this will influence her behaviour in the story that is to follow.'

'If you ever get round to it.'

'I've sometimes wondered whether the naivety of those who go forth into the world to regain their freedom – note that I say regain, thus assuming that mankind is born free – is a consequence of that primal scream passing through their minds, hearts and right down to their colons, purging them of all impurities, all corruption. And whether the strength of these sword-girt fools lies not least in the fact that they will chop down their oppressor before he can choke to death on his last gale of laughter. Because what could be funnier than a fool fighting for her life?'

'An intelligent person letting a fool bore her to death!'

'Anyway, it was only after my attention was drawn to the detail about women and windows that I caught myself walking over to the nearest window when I was feeling churned up inside, and all I could think of was the analogy in those feminist books – because I, of course, am neither a fictional construct nor a woman . . .'

'Or so you think!'

* * *

'Marie-Sophie stood by the fake window in the priest's hole, prattling away to the invalid. He was asleep but she had decided to act as if he were awake. She didn't know whether he was aware of her presence: if he sensed her there it would surely be more entertaining for him

THINE EYES DID SEE MY SUBSTANCE 49

if she showed some sign of life, behaved less like a female mourner at his deathbed and more like a dizzy girl who plucked amusing facts from existence – perhaps then he would want to live?

She pretended to look out of the window: the canvas, which was strung across as a fake backdrop to the glass, depicted a faded Paris street scene. The painter had managed to cram in everything that a straitened cleric in a small north German town would imagine as *la vie Parisienne*. There was the Seine, the coquettish demoiselles, the lanterns in the trees, libertines with unshaven chins, doves canoodling under the tables of pavement cafés, dandies with moustache and vanity cane, illuminated signs inviting people to come and peep under the skirts of the neighbour's daughter, the Eiffel Tower looming tall and erect in the distance. But Marie-Sophie had no interest in this impoverished dream: she looked through the painting, across the room on the other side of the wall and out through a gap between the curtains . . .

— What can you see?

Marie-Sophie spun round. No, the invalid hadn't spoken; she had been thinking aloud. But what could she see? She might as well tell him; although he was asleep she could speak for them both. What else did she have to do? So she leaned against the window and pretended to look out:

— You're in the town of Kükenstadt, which is situated on the banks of a large river and has a wharf for the barges that transport cargo down to the big port. Not many travellers pass through the town, most continue straight down the autobahn to the city, yet in spite of this you can always meet a handful of strangers in the square. As a rule these are tourists, that breed that wanders the world with the sole purpose of comparing it to life at home.

If they come here at all it's to see the altarpiece in the modest church by the square. This piece, which is the size of a man's hand, shows the Passion of Christ, and in addition to being one of the smallest of its kind in the world, according to the three lines devoted to the town in the tourists' travel-bibles, the painter's perspective is considered somewhat out of the ordinary as well, for the cross is viewed from the back and the only glimpse of Christ himself is of elbows and knees. The fact that the artist, whose identity no two people can agree on, didn't widen the cross by the trifling amount necessary to hide the Saviour completely – thereby sparing himself the persistent slander that he couldn't paint people – is precisely what makes our altarpiece such an ideal subject for controversy.

After the tourists have stood a good while before the altar, bickering over the merits of this palm-size icon, in muted tones of course, they emerge into the open air and shake off the solemnity that reigns even in the little church here in Kükenstadt, by poking gentle fun at that matchless work of art, the chick, which greets them in the square: naturally it is not the custom where they live to waste expensive stone on sculpting such humble little creatures.

More often than not, the tourists find the chick so hilarious that all the joking gives them a thirst and they appear, breathless with laughter, in the dining room downstairs. There they drain their beer, wink at one another and shake their heads in delighted wonder at having finally found people even odder in their habits than those who await them at home. But will you hark at me, prattling on about visitors? You're one yourself and it would make more sense for me to tell you about all the other stuff. Would you like that?

Deciding that the invalid wanted to hear more, Marie-Sophie went on:

— It's Sunday and the sun is shining, small clouds are floating on the horizon, the breeze is stirring the flag over the town hall: a yellow pennant bearing a red two-headed bird, a chick that has been lent an imperial cast, while in its claws – they are called claws, aren't they, on chicks? – it holds an onion flower and a spray of hops. Those versed in heraldry know how to interpret this.

Anyway, men and women are promenading around the square with children in prams or milling around their legs, then there are those who are on the lookout for someone to take future Sunday promenades with, and finally those who have promenaded through so many Sundays that now they are content to sit about on benches all day.

As you can hear, this is a terribly ordinary square in a little town near the North Sea, a pocket version of the squares you find further south on the Continent – not that I'm suggesting it's a direct copy of those . . .

— No, only an idiot would go to the trouble of planning a town square . . .

Marie-Sophie imagined the invalid's voice as deep and strong, rather than wounded and weak like its owner.

— . . . they come into being of their own accord. Roads meet, houses come face to face with other houses, and one day when people step out of their front doors they find themselves standing in a square . . .

— Yes, and you must have seen for yourself that our square is just as you described; something that came into being without anyone's attention or interference. Oh, what am I saying? What can you have seen? You only got here last night, under cover of darkness.

Now it's day and the sunlight flashes off the golden boot over the cobbler's, the golden pretzel over the baker's and the gilded cutlet over the butcher's. I've always found this last one rather ridiculous, but the butcher clearly got swept along with the rest when those pots of gold paint turned up at the grocer's . . .

— So people gild their existence here?

— Yes, it became an obsession; the grocer's, for example, is more like a temple than a corner shop. The owner got saddled with the leftover paint and used it up by decorating the shop inside and out, and I gather that his home is equally dazzling. By the way, the story is that the owner was sent off on the train with all the rest, and the man who took over the shop and flat was the son of the town's Party chairman – but not many people shop there any more, though almost everything under the sun can be found in the countless boxes and shelves that line the walls. For one thing, the old owner knew exactly where to lay his hand on everything – every snip, every nub was in its place in an equivalent box or jar in his head – and, for another, no request ever caught him out. "Butterfly wings . . ." He would mutter the brand-name several times under his breath before abruptly falling silent, and then it was as if you could hear a compart-ment opening under his skull-cap; and in the twinkling of an eye he would have swarmed like a monkey up the ladder that slid along a rail round the shop and somewhere up by the ceiling he would open a tiny cupboard, then hurtle back down to the floor, where he would lay the object on the counter and begin slowly and meticulously to wrap it up. Ordinarily you never saw him move faster than a snail on its way across an infinite lawn, but it was as if the flurry and pounce in search of the required item were motivated by a terrible fear that he would fail to find the blackbird's eyes, child's rattle from Prague, or whatever it was the customer wanted, before the cupboard door slammed shut again – for the last time – in some recess of his mind and with that all these priceless objects would be lost in oblivion.

— Which is where he took them when he was put on the train . . .

— Ye-es . . .

Marie-Sophie sighed and fiddled with her nose as if waiting for the invalid to continue. They both remained silent for a while, then he mumbled and she jumped, remembering that she was his voice too.

— So today there's no one left in Kükenstadt selling spare parts for Creation?

— No, the son of the Party chairman can't for the life of him remember where a single item is kept in the shop; he's insensitive to the smaller things in life – he worked in tank manufacturing before . . .

The figure in the bed groaned. The girl bit her lip: goodness, how boring she could be. Before she knew it she had begun harping on about the miserable side of life. She had meant to amuse the invalid with funny stories about Kükenstadt, but now here she was, standing over him, complaining that life in the town had taken a turn for the worse since war broke out.

She sat on the side of the bed, smoothing the eiderdown over her afflicted roommate: her patient, yes, she permitted herself to call him that, though she had no claim on him and would much rather be somewhere else: at the café between the barber's and the bakery – Café Berserk – which, in spite of its splendid name, was more commonly known as "the Barbary". Her boyfriend, Karl Maus, was probably sitting there at this very moment, looking sulky after the servant boy had brought him the message that she, his girlfriend, would not be able to meet him today. And of course it wouldn't help that he'd had to pay the cost of a beer for the bad news: "People should understand that there's a price list," as the boy used to say. Which meant he had been rewarded twice for his pains, because she herself had paid him with a kiss on the cheek. That boy would make something of himself one day, though he was still a bit gormless, so spotty, scruffy and randy, but with the exception of himself God alone knew how rich he was in the equivalent of glasses of beer. On high days and holidays he ran errands for every Tom, Dick and Harry in town; no matter what the job, the price was fixed: everyone paid the same – except her.

Karl had once lost his temper when he saw her kiss the boy for ironing the kitchen linen. It was Christmas and she had wanted to get off early so she could go out on the town with her Karl: they were going to buy each other presents.

"How can you kiss that little twerp?" he'd asked as they sat on a bench in the zoo – so called by the town council because a handful of farm animals from the neighbouring countryside languished there in pens, allowing small children to feed them stinging nettles and gravel. She had answered Karl that no doubt she would one day employ caresses to cajole him into doing the household chores, if this war ever ended and if they, well, if they . . .

— Then I kissed his scarlet face in front of the children skating on the duck pond, and since then he hasn't said another word about my dealings with the boy.

Marie-Sophie gazed bleakly at a shaft of sunlight that was piercing the peephole in the priest's hole and flickering on the invalid's eyes. He grimaced and tried in vain to shift away from the light. She stood up, went over to the hole and peered out through it while loosening the white ribbon that confined her hair in a ponytail: the brightness stung her gloom-accustomed eye, the pupil contracted in her blue iris and a tear sprang out of the corner. She dried her cheek with the ribbon, then plugged the hole with it and turned away.

— But the war goes on. Karl and I still sit in the park on my days off, though one night long ago all the animals were stolen, and eaten, of course; now there are no beasts left except the crows quarrelling in the trees, and us, and it doesn't occur to anyone to call it a zoo. . .'

'Now she's going on about sad things again . . .'
    'It's the times.'
    'Hold me.'
    'All right . . .'

'The world went black before Marie-Sophie's eyes: her account of the zoo's fate had made her so unhappy that a lump the size of a twelve-week-old foetus formed in her throat and seemed about to choke her. The pain spread through every nerve, her senses grew raw; the dim lamp on the chest of drawers cast an unbearable glare about the little compartment; the smell of carbolic soap from the invalid hit her like a gust of wind.'

'All because of a few animals?'
    'No, the animals' disappearance from the park had made my mother realise that she'd been ignoring the war raging in the outside world; by concentrating on her daily chores and following the same routine on her days off she had managed to keep the world as it was. And because everyone she knew did the same, it wasn't until she described the atmosphere in the town to my father that she realised the war was more than merely news of heroic victories in the lands of inferior races who had been impertinent to her countrymen; it had also had a deleterious effect on life in Kükenstadt.'
    'You mean that people don't understand their destinies until they can talk about them or picture them?'
    'Yes, even Adam and Eve were content for the first few years after they were expelled from Paradise – they didn't realise what their punishment was for the theft of the apple. It took young Cain to open their eyes to the fact that the human race had been deprived of its immortality.
    And this uncomfortable fact gave rise to a new word: death.'

'Marie-Sophie was roused from her gloom by a tap on the door.
    Outside stood the cook wearing a secretive expression and holding a tray of steaming food.

— Well then, here I am . . .

She winked at Marie-Sophie and pushed the tray at her, but when the girl went to relieve her of it, the cook tightened her hold and jutted her chin.

— Aren't you going to invite me in?

Marie-Sophie squeezed quickly out of the room and shut the door behind her. The cook recoiled, goggling.

— Well, I never!

She thrust out her bosom and snorted.

— I was ordered by the proprietors of this guesthouse to take a meal to our new guest and now you're denying me entry. When I'm ordered to deliver something, in this instance hot food, soup, bread and boiled cabbage with slices of sausage, it is my custom to place the tray on the table and ask the person concerned, in the civil tone that is second nature to me after my long experience of serving and catering, whether he or she requires anything else, after which I leave, and that and no more was my intention on the present occasion.

She let go of the tray with one hand, rolled her eyes heavenwards, slapped her brow and cried:

— What have I done to deserve this?

Marie-Sophie sprang into action, grabbing the tray before the food slid off: she had to butter the cook up or the woman would go straight down to see the owner and pour out her life-story to him, though he was sick and tired of this tale, which invariably began with the words: "I hadn't turned three when I baked my first loaf, up till then I had only been entrusted with the kneading . . ." And ended on these: ". . . and when I was sacked from Bayreuth for sleeping with the Icelandic tenor Gardar Hólm – did I say sleep? No, they said that (Siegfried himself had got involved by then), which was a pack of lies – I swore I'd never let anyone walk all over me again, no, and certainly not a mere slip of a girl who wasn't even born when I was working for the Wagner family and the finest voices of the century used to sing the praises of my cooking. No, I shouldn't have to put up with this, not at the Gasthof Vrieslander, which is the lowest-class establishment I've ever worked for, and you know it!" After the cook's grand finale the owner usually lost his temper and vented his fury on some poor scapegoat with a tirade of abuse.

Marie-Sophie was afraid he would order her to go and shovel coke and entrust the cook, or goodness knows who else, with the task of nursing the invalid, which was unthinkable.

— Oh, it's all so strange . . .

The girl set down the tray, then put an arm round the cook's shoulders and made her sit down on the bed in room twenty-three.

— It's strange for all of us; I don't know what to make of it myself. Sitting there all day long, keeping watch over something that's nothing and yet so dreadfully mysterious . . .

The cook gave her an understanding look and patted her thigh.

— We were just discussing in the kitchen whether you were up to the job, and opinions were divided. Of course, we're not sure what it is that you've been entrusted with, but the waiter thinks it's hardly decent to make you do it – you're so young and so, you know, alone with a strange man, eh?

The cook shot a glance at Marie-Sophie's ample bosom.

— Is there anything in what he says? I mean, that room you're in, you know what I . . .

Marie-Sophie flushed dark red: how dare the cook imagine that she was servicing the invalid. Not only had the woman seen him with her own eyes in the kitchen that morning, and you would have to be physically and mentally deranged to mistake the puny wreck that had toppled headlong out of the larder door for some lust-crazed Don Juan – but she should know that Marie-Sophie was a respectable girl.

— You're blushing! You're not answering. It's all right, you can rest assured that we're not going to rush out and spread it around town. They made us promise not to mention it to a soul that he's here, and we're on no account to let the other guests sense that there's a commotion in the house. Well, I did tell old Tomas, but he's one of us after all, and no one listens to his nonsense . . .

Marie-Sophie didn't reply. What were the owner and Inhaberin thinking of? The cook and the geriatric next door had the biggest mouths in Kükenstadt; no human frailty lay outside their scope and they were as happy to spread scandal about the magistrate's financial embarrassment as the vicar's wife's constipation. Tomas looked on gossip as his duty because he was writing a history of Kükenstadt, while the cook was on a vain crusade to uphold moral standards in the town.

But now it was guaranteed that everyone, whether they cared to or not, would hear about the lewd goings-on in the priest's hole at Gasthof Vrieslander.

— Anyway, I haven't got time for this . . .

The cook pretended to be on the point of leaving but didn't budge an inch, in the hope that the awkward silence would reward her with news. After they had sat without speaking for a while, the cook got up from the bed.

— The boy'll come and fetch the tray later – I've got to pop into town – don't hesitate to report the man if he tries it on . . .

She patted Marie-Sophie on the cheek.

— You let me know if there's a problem. We're right behind you. You do think it'll be all right, don't you?

Then off she went without waiting for a reply.'

7

'Marie-Sophie was feeling dull in the head from the monotony of the day and from being entrusted with something – she didn't know exactly what, but it was clearly of great importance and only she could do it, namely to sit shut up in a darkened room on a sunny Sunday with a sleeping stranger.

She picked at her food and sipped the blackberry juice; she was famished but didn't like to shovel her meal down in front of the skeleton in the bed. The invalid wouldn't touch his food; he hadn't even reacted when she brought in the steaming tray and tried unsuccessfully to wake him by waving the appetising sausage under his nose.

— What kind of man who's desperately in need of a square meal would turn his nose up at a fat pork sausage?

The girl stole a quick glance at the invalid; from under the eiderdown came a series of loud rumblings. She shook her head in bewilderment.

— And then his guts yowl like thirteen thousand wild cats in a trap.

What could she do to restore his appetite? Perhaps he'd prefer to eat alone. That was common among eccentrics, and as far as she could tell he was not quite like other people. Perhaps that was why she was looking after him; perhaps that was what made him special. Yes, she was nursing him for the two men who apparently thought the world of eccentrics and laid a heavy burden upon themselves, or rather upon others, so that a rare shoot should be allowed to thrive instead of withering and dying at the hands of wicked men. And the reason she had to observe and memorise whatever he might say was naturally because rare shoots grow up to bear wondrous blooms and strange fruit.

It was lucky for the owner, the two men, the invalid and Marie-Sophie that she had a green thumb like her grandmother and so knew a thing or two about gardening.

— I don't suppose there's much difference between you and a Jerusalem artichoke when it comes to perking things up.

Marie-Sophie hurriedly propped the invalid up in bed and piled the cushions behind his back. She laid the meal tray on his lap and placed the knife and fork in his limp hands.

— The trick is simply to water the plant, then leave it alone, because no flower will deign to grow while it's being gawped at. So I'm going to sit on the chair over here by the door, turn my back to you and see whether you'll eat then.

She drew the chair from the desk and sat down.

— And in the meantime I'll tell you a story about an eccentric old woman, not just because I think you'll enjoying hearing about people like yourself, but because I haven't heard it for ages and I think it's such a good one.

The story tells of an old crone who lived in the forest where my great-grandfather was a warden; like you she preferred not to eat in front of others.

What do you think?

The invalid's guts rumbled in reply.

* * *

THE OLD WOMAN AND THE KAISER

Once there was an old woman who lived alone in a cottage in the middle of a forest. She was a recluse and had no dealings with the inhabitants of the surrounding villages and farms except on Saturdays when she went to the market with mushrooms, roots, salves and other concoctions which she brewed from the herbs in the forest.

What made the old woman different from the other misfits in the region (there were plenty of them but they were generally allowed to live unmolested with their quirks), was that nobody could persuade her to sit down and eat with the other stallholders at the end of the working day, yet on the other hand she was not shy about answering the call of nature in full view of her colleagues, preferably when they were eating.

The reason for the old woman's behaviour, and why no one interfered with her habits, was not that she was particularly coy, had taboos about table manners or was a witch, as the children believed, but simply that she was rumoured to have broken bread with the Kaiser himself.

It's only natural that after one has broken bread with a Kaiser one is above common social niceties.

They had met in the forest when the old woman was a young girl and the Kaiser a mere prince. The future Kaiser was out hunting thrushes with his retinue when he spotted a fox slinking through the undergrowth and saw at once that this was no ordinary beast. No, it was none other than the golden vixen that had haunted the forest for as long as the oldest folk could remember. She was every hunter's dream quarry but as she was exceptionally sly and cunning she had always evaded their bullets and arrows. No one was a true hunter among hunters unless he had a tale to tell of his dealings with this fabled beast; how he had caught her by the golden brush but she had slipped from his grasp like a snake. To prove their story they would raise two fingers and show those present the glistening dust that clung to their tips, while those who were in the tedious habit of adapting proverbs would say: "Better a fox in hand than three in the bush".

So the golden vixen represented a pipedream for many.

The young prince was filled with a fierce desire to capture the beast. He called to his men but they were so busy shooting thrushes that they neither heard nor heeded when he drove his spurs into his Arab stallion and headed off alone on the foxhunt.

The pursuit passed through the length and breadth of the forest. The golden vixen scurried along the forest floor, through bushes, under tree roots and over streams. The prince pursued his quarry with zeal, revelling in the agility of his oriental steed. He longed to catch the vixen alive so he could present her to his father as a gift, thereby softening his mood, as he and his father had fallen out over the prince's relations with women, or rather his lack of appetite for

Adam's rib, a lack that had become so notorious around the world that the other emperors made merciless fun of his father at emperors' conventions.

Little by little the vixen drew the prince and stallion deeper into the forest, further than they had ever been before, and the prince had to spur his mount on when the nettles became so thick that the horse had difficulty finding its footing. But at last the vixen grew weary of the chase and the prince managed to corner her in a narrow clearing in the heart of the wood.

The prince reined in his horse, making it sidestep to block the entrance to the glade and close in on the golden vixen. He approached her warily. She crouched down on the forest floor, suspiciously eyeing the man who had come closer to her than any other. Hatred smouldered in the predatory grey eyes; they trapped the prince's thoughts, and for a moment he sensed he was standing in the presence of an enigma that was infinitely greater than a mere sly fox whose cunning had made her a legend among inept country bumpkins.

Thunder growled in the distance and the stallion grew restive beneath its rider. The prince gripped the reins, curbing his steed, and when his gaze returned to the vixen she seemed to fade before his eyes, the golden pelt lost its lustre and she sank slowly into the ground. He rubbed his eyes and shook his head in disbelief. There was no longer any vixen in the depths of the glade; in her place were two snow-white pearls.

The prince ground his teeth with vexation, but thought to himself that it would be better to return to the Autumn Palace with two pearls than empty-handed. He dismounted, tethered his horse to a low branch and entered the depths of the glade. But he had no sooner bent down to pick up the pearls than lightning flashed over the forest, gleaming on the vixen's terrible needle-sharp teeth right by his fingers. He snatched back his hand and, black now as pitch, the vixen reared up on her hind legs, snarling: 'You'll have cause to remember, unhappy man, that a dumb beast has got the better of you.'

And with that the vixen darted past the prince, between the horse's legs and out of the glade.

The horse went mad with fear. The prince ran over and tried in vain to control the rearing beast but the stallion tore itself free and struck its master to the ground.

When the prince regained consciousness he was no longer in the clearing but lying in a humble but neatly made bed. A savoury aroma of soup filled his senses; from the next-door room came the sound of a woman singing. The prince cast off the skilfully embroidered quilt that his benefactor had spread over him, rose to his feet with a groan and limped over to the window. His whole body ached from the fall and he felt as if a glowing lump of coal were stuck to his brow. The sight that met his eyes in the rain-lashed glass was a sorry picture of a face, all battered, bruised and crowned with a garish snuff rag, which was binding a handful of thick leaves to the lump of coal on his scalp.

'I look like a caricature of Dante,' the prince grumbled to himself; he was known for his enthusiasm for literature and the fine arts: 'And I haven't got a stitch on.'

He glanced around in search of his clothes but they were nowhere to be seen so he decided to lie down again, and just as he was clambering into bed, pink princely rump in the air, a young girl entered the room. She didn't laugh, she was beautiful, she was his saviour, she was carrying a tray of steaming soup and a loaf of bread.

While the prince tucked into the soup, the girl told him how she had been gathering nuts when the thunderstorm broke. As she was running home she had narrowly escaped being trampled by a horse doing St Vitus's dance along the path. Shortly afterwards she had stumbled across a man, lying battered and concussed on the bank of a quagmire that had swallowed up many a good lad. This had been none other than the prince himself. Of course, she couldn't leave him lying there in that terrible storm so she had lugged him home with her. Which is why he was now sitting here, eating her soup. How was it, by the way?

Well, the prince couldn't deny that the soup was delicious.

The storm lashed the forest for seven days and seven nights.

What passed between the prince and the girl during this time nobody knows, but on the morning of the eighth day he took his leave, restored and wearing patched breeches, and in parting he gave her a ring; it was an exquisite object of pure white gold, engraved with a double-headed eagle picked out in rubies.

When three months had passed since the future Kaiser's visit, the girl stopped attending the Saturday market and wasn't seen again until six months later. People suspected that she had been with child and had given birth to a little boy whom she had hidden in a cave in the forest.

Although men went on expeditions in search of the boy, he was never found, and this was taken as a sign of how well his mother knew the forest. She who was constantly wandering through its darkest thickets in search of herbs and berries for her potions and elixirs would have no problem hiding an infant in the murky depths of the wood.

The story goes that the girl had hidden her son by the future Kaiser in order to wait for a time when the nation faced great peril and disaster and its people would be ready to accept him as their spiritual and secular guide who would lead them into a new age. But until the boy steps forth in the fullness of time, protected by his origin, his virtues and the treasure his father laid by for him, which is hidden in the cave, he will not age a single day beyond twenty-one.

Of the girl, his mother, on the other hand, the story goes that she grew old like other people and became an eccentric crone, living alone in a hovel in the middle of the forest and conforming to the rules of neither God nor men when she sold her produce at the market.

In the end she dropped dead in her porridge without leaving behind any clue as to where men could find the cave, the boy or the fabulous treasure. When a search was made of her dwelling nothing was found but what you might expect from the hovel of any old wise woman.

The prince became Kaiser and was nicknamed 'the Virgin King' by wits, because he was never linked to any woman but the girl who had rescued him from becoming one with the soil on that long-ago autumn day. He became an enthusiast for skilled embroidery and swan breeding, he frittered away the riches of his realm on artists and risky speculations, and he drowned young and disastrously childless, as official historians claim. But a sign of the truth of this little tale is that when a post-mortem was carried out on the prince's body it transpired that his private member was made of gold.

It should be added that for a long time after these events children playing on the edge of the forest would hear the boy creeping about in the undergrowth like a fox, while young girls who ventured in among the trees would feel a young man's eyes upon them. And many a girl dreamed of meeting the Kaiser's secret son on some lonely path, falling in love and living happily ever after.

But now so long an age has passed that the forest has lost its aura of fairytale, the golden vixen has not been seen since the death of the old woman, the children no longer fear the hidden boy and the young girls head for towns and cities in search of husbands.

That's what I did and found my Karl.

The mouse is run, my tale is done.

* * *

— Thank you for the meal.

Marie-Sophie was so shocked when the invalid addressed her that she almost fell off her chair, but when she turned round with: "You're welcome!" on her lips, he played the same game as before and shut his eyes. He had finished everything but the sausage.

— You're welcome, anyway.

In Marie-Sophie's humble opinion, it was wrong of the two men to ask her to watch the invalid like a cat waiting by a mouse-hole. There were no finer points of the invalid's behaviour to observe; he didn't behave in any way at all, he was too weak for that. If anything, he perked up when she forgot about him or pretended to ignore him.

The girl felt she was beginning to get the hang of her nebulous duty.

The door of room twenty-three opened.

Marie-Sophie jumped: she was getting fed up with these constant comings and goings. What was the point of taking a wreck into the guesthouse, then denying him the peace and quiet in which to become human again?

— It's as busy as a lavatory at a children's birthday party.

She got up and flounced over to meet the visitor, ripping open the door of the priest's hole.

— What now?

— Heh, heh, she's right, the girl's all edgy . . .

The waiter muttered into his bowtie as usual, pretending not to notice Marie-Sophie's anger:

— I've just come to fetch the tray if I may, heh, heh. We felt it wasn't right to send the boy, a callow youth . . .

He squinted past Marie-Sophie. She scowled at him and went to get the tray.

The waiter continued his conversation with his confidant, the bowtie.

— So this is Paradise, heh, heh. I've been wanting to get an eyeful of that for a long time. You used to hear enough about it here in the old days . . .

— You can tell the proprietor that the sick man has eaten and said thank you for the meal.

Marie-Sophie shoved the tray at the waiter.

— The sick man? You call him sick. Is he ill then? Is it catching?

— No, I call him sick because it's such a funny word, it rhymes with chick!

Marie-Sophie slammed the door in the waiter's face.'

8

'— You're doing a good job, no doubt about it . . .

The owner had come at suppertime and praised Marie-Sophie's performance.

— I hear he's spoken to you, said thank you and I don't know what else? They'll be happy, I should think they'll be bloody pleased when they hear about that. Yes, there's no doubt you're the right man, I mean, right girl for the job. And it's clear that you must stay, yes, I think we'll have to . . .

He grew awkward and started rubbing the hip flask in his back pocket.

— Ahem, do you think you could, well, er, stick around? Better let the wife . . . She knows how to . . . I won't be a moment . . .

Marie-Sophie heard him pause on his way downstairs to reception to take a fortifying nip from the flask, before going to find the Inhaberin, who was on duty in the dining room which converted into a tavern in the evening. "They only come here to drink, they don't eat a sodding thing, why do they think someone sits for an hour every day writing out decorative menus for them? I ask you." The Inhaberin never received an answer to this question. Marie-Sophie couldn't bring herself to tell her what everyone else knew: that the cook was useless, the waiter rude, the china chipped and the choice of dishes, so beautifully written out on the menu, hadn't changed since the paint dried on the sign outside the inn.

The noise from the dining room magnified as the owner entered, dipped when the door shut behind him, then rose again as he came out accompanied by his wife.

Marie-Sophie listened to the Inhaberin huffing her way up the stairs, her husband rambling on, clearly in great agitation, but when they entered the room they fell momentarily silent.

— So . . .

Whispered the owner to his wife. She whispered back:

— So what?

— So here we are.

— I'm aware of that . . .

— I mean, er, good grief, is that the time? It's probably best if I leave this to you . . .

— You're not going anywhere!

The Inhaberin gripped her husband by the upper arm and hissed:

— It was your talents at the card table that got us into this mess, so you'll jolly well accompany me every step of the way while I extricate you from it!

Marie-Sophie peeped out of the priest's hole.

The Inhaberin let go of her husband and turned smiling to the girl.

— Ah, there you are, we were just saying how diligent you've been . . .

The owner gave a quick sniff and looked daggers at his wife:

— Yes, we've decided to give you a bit of a pay rise for all this, yes, indeed.

The Inhaberin jabbed him with her elbow and shook her head slowly and menacingly. He beamed at Marie-Sophie.

Marie-Sophie beamed back: it was a great blessing for the staff of the Gasthof Vrieslander that the owner's method of getting back at his wife was to be kind to them.

— And you're to take the next few Sundays off . . .

The owner dodged his wife like a rabbit, she spun in a circle when her blow went wide, he fled squeaking into the passage, she shook her fist after him, he stuck his head back through the door and made a face at her, she tore off her shoes and hurled them after him, he parried the missiles with his arms and clicked his tongue, she groaned, he laughed and left.

Marie-Sophie pushed the door of the priest's hole to and waited patiently while the Inhaberin discussed with God and the devil the minuteness and flaccidity of her husband's penis. When the woman had finished conversing with the two supreme powers she cleared her throat and spoke gently to the girl behind the door:

— Are you there, dear?

— Er, yes . . .

— You know me, don't you?

— Er, yes . . .

— You know I'm not the sort of person who corrupts young girls?

— Er, yes . . .

— Neither I nor my husband tolerate any immorality here at the guesthouse, am I right?

— Er, yes . . .

— Though many people in our position do: they turn a blind eye, have a weakness for an easy profit, simply raise the price of the accommodation, do you understand what I'm getting at?

— Er . . .

— No, we set great store by employing decent, hardworking and God-fearing staff, and we set the same standards for ourselves, don't we?

— Yes . . .

— And that's why we employ you and not someone else, isn't it?

— Er, yes . . .

— I don't quite know how to put it but I think you catch my drift . . .

— Er . . .'

'Is the woman deranged? Is she never going to get to the point? Isn't it obvious that she's trying to ask the poor girl to sleep in the priest's hole with the wretched man? Sorry, your mother with your father.'

'EXACTLY!'

'Marie-Sophie yessed and noed her way through the Inhaberin's cate-chism. At long last, the woman got round to stating the request that was so difficult to put into words and required a preamble so convo-luted that it came close to the book of dialectic that was opened when God halted the construction of the Tower of Babel. After the Inhaberin had asked the girl whether she would mind, whether she would consider, whether it would be all right to approach her about, whether it would be against her better judgement to spend the night with the foreigner in the priest's hole, Marie-Sophie asked her to wait a moment and went into the invalid's room.

She looked at him enquiringly. He had pulled the eiderdown over his face.

— Should I stay with you tonight?

Through the eiderdown she thought she saw a wicked twitch lift the corner of his mouth, and as far as she could tell he nodded his head.

— I see, my good man, so you're like that, are you!

Marie-Sophie called out to the Inhaberin that of course she would sit with him, but she wanted her mattress, her bedclothes and the book she was reading. If they expected her to sleep then they could hardly complain if she looked at a book.

— Because reading books is a kind of dream sleep, you see.

The Inhaberin said she would fulfil all Marie-Sophie's wishes; she was an angel and deserved only the best. With that the woman left, whooping hurrah, while the girl stayed behind, which was all she could do.'

'Amen to that.'

'Marie-Sophie held her breath: yes, there it was again; scratch-scritch-scritch from the wall. Then nothing for a while.

Scratch-scritch-scritch. Silence. Silence. Scratch-scritch-scritch.

She had noticed the noise after the Inhaberin left; first there was a light tap, then at regular intervals a scratch-scritch-scritch, which seemed to follow her movements around the priest's hole.

Scratch-scritch-scritch by the head of the bed; if she moved to the foot, scratch-scritch-scritch there.

Marie-Sophie put her ear to the wall and listened for a solution to the puzzle. She pressed her ear to the flocked wallpaper and waited for the peculiar sound. But nothing happened, no scratch-scritch-scritch could be heard unless she was moving around the room, and she tested this by pacing back and forth in the confined space, which seemed to have acquired paranormal properties. Immediately the scratch-scritch-scritch moved along the wall with great alacrity.

At a loss for an answer, she was glancing around when her eye fell on a glass tumbler on the desk; she took it and carried it noiselessly to the source of the mystery. At first she could hear nothing but the hum inside her own head, but when her hearing sharpened she realised that she was listening to someone who was listening to her through a glass on the other side of the wall.

The girl flushed with rage: predictably, that disgusting Tomas was eavesdropping, hoping to hear an echo of the sin they all seemed to believe was being committed between her and the invalid. Hah, she would damn well let him know that she knew what he was up to in his underpants in there.

Marie-Sophie moved away from the wall: scratch-scritch-scritch. She listened intently to where the old man's glass stopped, then paused a moment before crashing her glass viciously against his. A shrill scream carried through the wall and the girl gave a cold laugh: the old sod deserved it; perhaps now he'd stop pinching her when she made his bed.

Old Tomas had pretty much behaved himself for a while after Karl had torn a strip off him for groping her, affecting a shivering and shaking every time Karl's name was mentioned. But then this went the way of all flesh, like everything else at the guesthouse. Tomas seized every opportunity to shriek at Karl: "I could show this young whipper-snapper a thing or two, and neither of them pretty, if I was his age, if I had the stomach to knock down a coward who can't be bothered to fight for his country but hangs around at home, making fun of old soldiers." And Karl retaliated by asking time and again who the old bag was who loitered all day in reception, whether she had been sitting there long or might even be dead and so whether it wasn't about time she was boiled down to make soup for the Scots.

Karl was right that old Tomas had become terribly effeminate with his high-pitched voice, and so shrunken that the waistcoat that reached down to his thighs today would be as long as a ball-gown on him by the time death invited him to dance. But when Karl went too far and smeared lipstick on the ancient face, crammed a woman's bonnet on his head, thrust a bouquet of flowers into the blue-veined hands and dragged him trembling out into the square to auction to the lowest bidder, Marie-Sophie decided the joke had gone far enough and intervened in the game.

Karl had been livid with her for defending old Tomas: hadn't she lent him the lipstick? Hadn't she laughed with the rest? Perhaps she wanted the old pervert to go on harassing her? Marie-Sophie retorted by saying that in her opinion Karl was spending more time these days getting on his high horse with an impotent old trout than ingratiating himself with her. Karl hit high C: Impotent? How did she know that? Was there something between them? Marie-Sophie cut short the conversation.

She hoped the owner and Inhaberin would make sure Karl didn't get wind of her night with the invalid; if he could be suspicious of the servant boy and the old man, he was quite capable of exploding with jealousy over a bed-bound invalid.

The girl sighed: it was a fearful poison that seethed in the glands that dangled between men's legs.

Marie-Sophie was squatting on the chamber-pot behind the screen when the Inhaberin marched into the secret compartment with the girl's eiderdown in her arms, followed by the servant boy with the mattress on his back, the cook with a tray of cake and milk, the waiter with matches and a bundle of candles, and the owner bringing up the rear with a small Bible-like volume in his hands.

The girl stemmed the flow, wiped herself, leapt to her feet, pulling up her knickers, covered the chamber-pot and greeted the retinue that was turning around itself in the confined space. They whispered to one another, walked on tiptoe, moving as slowly as they possibly could, and their consideration for the occupants of the secret compartment was so excessive that what ought by rights to have taken a minute took nearly three-quarters of an hour: would Marie-Sophie like the mattress by the bed or in the middle of the room? A bit nearer, perhaps? Further away? And the book? On the chair by the bed? On the desk? The cupboard? Mmm? And the cake and milk? The eiderdown? Mmm? The candles?

By the time they had nothing left to do but tuck the girl up in the book, spread the milk and cake over her, put the mattress on the desk so she could read it while she ate the matches and sipped the candle wax, they had had their fill of gawping at the invalid who slept like an angel through all the commotion.

The Inhaberin snapped her fingers, the retinue formed a single column behind her, then they sang softly but terribly gaily the lullaby of Tanni the Cur as they left the room in single file:

> Two little birds, woof-woof-woof,
> nimble with their fingers, woof-woof-woof,
> sweetly sing, woof-woof-woof.
>
> Tanni watches,
> Good boy Tanni watches.
>
> Two little fishes, woof-woof-woof,
> good with their hands, woof-woof-woof,
> sweetly swim, woof-woof-woof.
>
> Tanni watches,
> Good boy Tanni watches.

The servant boy's red head was the tuft on the end of the singing tail; he turned back in the doorway, thrusting a hand inside his shirt:

— This is for you, the only one that escaped from the kitchen this morning . . .

He handed Marie-Sophie a folded napkin and disappeared into the passage after the others.

Marie-Sophie sat on the edge of the invalid's bed, fingering the boy's gift; so this was the object of disgrace itself: a chubby gingerbread boy with an erection.

The girl laughed to herself: it was a good thing that somebody at the guesthouse was entertainingly nuts.

The invalid turned over in bed; Marie-Sophie didn't look up

from the crude gingerbread boy; her breathing deepened. The invalid sighed; the girl ran a finger down the sugar-glazed body; her eyelids grew heavier. The invalid coughed; she looked deep into the black raisin-eyes; her head sank on to her chest.

The gingerbread boy coughed.'

IV

9

'The night after my father's arrival in Kükenstadt, the townspeople's subconscious lives broke free of their bonds. Everyone dreamed and the angel Freude was hard pressed as he dashed from mind to mind, conscientiously recording what went on there.'

'What did the people dream?'

'There's no time here to detail every single dream and nightmare, but since you're keen to get to know the character of the town I'll tell you a few that seem to me to reflect the story and its times.'

'Please do.'

* * *

(FROM THE ANGEL FREUDE'S BOOK OF DREAMS)

'I enter an attic and think it's my room. Against the wall on the right there's a desk, with shelves above it containing books, pebbles and a rusty crown.

A pale child, I can't see whether it's a boy or a girl, is sitting on the bed by the window, holding a cardboard box. I go over to the child.

There's a small pike in the box: it's alive but strapped tight with splints and bandages, and there's a plaster stuck over its eyes.

I remember that I've come to take the plaster off the fish.

I know this will blind it.'

Gertrude A—, housewife, 47 years old

'I'm on the deck of a cruise-ship. There are several other people there and they're all a little underdressed, given that the sky is overcast.

A girl who can't be more than seven years old is going from passenger to passenger, offering them a basket of sugar-glazed pig's trotters. My fellow travellers decline these delicacies with indulgent smiles and this infuriates me; the trotters are so liberally glazed that the sugar is nearly an inch thick.

I beckon the girl over and grab a handful of trotters.

The instant I sink my teeth into the first trotter and the sugar coating cracks with a satisfying crunch, the crowd begins to levitate from the deck.

The people gather over the ship and the more trotters I gnaw the coating off, the higher they rise into the sky.

I feel it serves them right for being so rude to the little girl and I wolf down the trotters until the crowd has vanished into the sky.

The captain comes down from the bridge, thanks me with a firm handshake and says: "Those clouds are like scorpions."

The captain is Axel the butcher.'

Conrad B—, optician, 68 years old

'A black-haired girl in a pink dress beckons me to join her in a wood-land clearing.

I don't recognise her at first but then realise that it's Elisa, a girl who was in my class at school.

In the middle of the clearing there's a pram that is iced over with frost, though the sun's beating down.'

Ferdinand C—, watchmaker, 35 years old

'I'm standing outside a hotel, waiting to pick up a woman.

When I enter the lobby a nurse comes towards me and I realise that it's a hospital.

She asks me what I want.

I say I've come to pick up the pictures.

We walk along wallpapered corridors and she orders me to wait in a large ward. I look around and the beds appear to be luxury four-posters.

When the woman comes back she is naked.

I'm filled with lust and put my arms round her, running my hand over her crotch.

When I stick my fingers inside her, her belly suddenly expands, then contracts again.

I'm holding a roll of film.'

Wilhelm D—, railway guard, 23 years old

'I'm standing by the cooker, waiting for the water to boil for tea.

When it begins to simmer I arrange a saucer, teaspoon and cup on a tray.

I snatch back my hand: a spider has spun a web over the sugar bowl.

I try to fish it out alive with the spoon but discover that it's dead. It falls into the bowl.

I stir the sugar carefully in search of the spider's corpse; the legs break off its body and scatter through the sugar.

I go to the window and scrape the sugar out. Other things come to light: the flesh and skin of a trout. I chuck them out of the window too.

I've been doing this for quite some time when it occurs to me that it might not be such a good idea as there could be someone below; children playing, for example. I lean out and find myself looking down on two shiny top-hats.

There are two men under the hats. They are being hoisted up the wall of the house in a basket.

I'm just withdrawing inside the window when they become aware of me and look up.

They're women.'

Helmuth E—, pastor, 51 years old

'I'm holding Klara's little boy by the hand. We're on our way to church but it's taking us a long time; the ribbons on his shoes keep coming undone.

I tie them up again.

They must be properly done up when the pastor christens him.'

Käthe F—, midwife, 80 years old

'Georg holds out a red balloon to me. I refuse to take it.'

Axel G—, butcher, 56 years old

'I'm at Café Berserk. Facing me across the table is a man absorbed in the weekend edition of the *Kükenstadt-Anzeiger*.

I read the front-page news: "Last blind man executed in Milchbürg!"

The paper is upside down.

I find it side-splittingly funny but I can't laugh.

I feel as if I've got a great lump of clay in my mouth that I can neither swallow nor spit out.'

Elisa H—, secretary, 29 years old

'I'm quarrelling with my mother. She's lying under a quilt on the living-room floor.

— Get up! We're going skiing with Tristram and Isolde.

— Skiing? But you can't even swim . . .

I start to cry.'

Gisele I—, cook and housekeeper, 62 years old

'Everyone in the house has come into my sitting room and the street outside is filling with people. There's something wrong with my wireless.

Günther, the horse dealer, is sitting in the window, relaying what comes out of the set to the crowd below; it's like a mixture of laughter and singing.

I can tell people are not sure what to make of it.'

Carl 'Blitz' J—, pensioner, 73 years old

'A drunk comes into my shop and asks me to mend a split seam in the armpit of his jacket.

I tell him to leave but he won't listen and asks me to sew on a button that's hanging by a thread from his flies.

I say I'll get the police to take him away if he doesn't leave the shop at once. Then he asks for a glass of water.

I'm about to dash past him to fetch help when I notice the teasing glint in his eye. I hesitate a moment, then say: "Of course, sir, in Kükenstadt we don't begrudge a thirsty man water."

But when I go round the back there's no more running water and the cups have all disappeared. I call out to the man, pretending I have to wash up a glass and asking him to be patient.

Then I sneak out of the back door and knock at the barber's but he tells me sadly that the water has run out and all his cans of shaving foam are broken.

It's the same story wherever I go: the baker is in despair; he has neither water nor measuring jug. There's a state of emergency at the café where unscrupulous customers have drunk all the water and stolen all the glasses and cups.

I go from house to house and street to street, out of the town, across fields and meadows, until I come to a thick forest – there I give up.

I'm standing by a low hovel that hadn't been there before.

I think to myself that if the wealthier citizens of the country have neither drink nor anything to drink out of, it's pointless seeking help from the inhabitants of a poor dwelling like this.

Then an old man with a grey beard appears in the doorway of the hovel, pushes a rusty ladle at me and asks: "What will you give for this poor ladle?"

I answer: "My soul."

He passes me the ladle and asks: "Oak or vine?"

I assume he means the handle of the ladle and answer: "Oak."

The old man smiles at me and reaches up into an oak tree that stands behind the hovel, overhanging its roof. He tears a leaf from a twig, lays it in his palm and closes his fingers over it.

A crystal-clear juice trickles from his fist and fills the ladle to the brim.

I mean to thank the old man but find I'm now back where my journey began. I hear the drunk coughing out front in the shop.

I walk slowly into the shop, taking care not to spill any of the oak-juice, hold out the ladle to the drunk and apologise for having nothing else to offer him. And he says: "My thirst offers thanks, my good woman, for the elixir of life that it seems to see here in this noble chalice."

I pass the drunk the ladle; he takes it in both hands, drains it in one gulp and sighs gustily.

After that he says thoughtfully: "Oak or vine?"

I gasp; for there stands not just the hermit who gave me the ladle but none other than the Führer himself in one of the many disguises he adopts as he travels about the land, keeping an eye on his subjects.

But I know I haven't sold him my soul; it was already his.'

Ilse K—, draper, 52 years old

'Fräulein R— has asked me to see her after school. I'm waiting for her in the corridor outside the classroom.

She calls out to me from inside the room.

Fräulein R— is standing by the blackboard with the class register in her hand, watching a white cat that is lying on an open atlas on the desk, giving birth to black kittens on the Atlantic Ocean.

The kittens slide out of the cat as if they were on a conveyor belt, and answer Fräulein R— with a feeble squeaking when she reads out the names of my classmates.

I wait in terror for my turn to come.'

Heinrich L—, 13 years old

'We're playing Cowboys and Indians; me, my brother Tomas and our friend Hermann from next door. Tomas is the Indian and he's hiding.

We find him in the boiler room and tie him up.

Tomas is quick to free himself but instead of continuing the game and choosing one of us to be a cowboy with him, he opens the boiler, takes off his clothes and throws them into the furnace.'

Klaus M—, music teacher, 39 years old

'I run along the ridge of a roof, slide down the tiles and come to a halt on the edge. I'm not alone.

A few yards away something is bumping about on the eaves.

At first it looks like some kind of armour-clad animal, a mole or a large hedgehog, but when I get closer it turns out to be one of Rossum's universal robots; it's the size of a newborn baby and it's climbing up the roof.

I decide to follow the robot to find out if it can talk.

But when it clambers over the ridge and rolls down the other side with a loud clatter, I hear women's voices.

I hide behind one of the chimneys and peer round it:

Standing on the edge of the roof below are the mother and daughter from next door.

They're laughing at the robot, which is lying on its back in the gutter, helpless as an insect. I want to call out to them but I can't remember their names – and I feel that without those there's nothing I can do.

I watch the mother and daughter until they've laughed their fill, then the daughter spins the robot round with the toe of her shoe while the mother lifts her dress to mid-thigh. The robot starts to climb up her leg.'

Erich N—, chimney sweep, 31 years old

'An old woman sets a ram, a cock and a horse on me. I run as fast as my legs will carry me.'

Henkel O—, historian, 97 years old

'I'm sitting in the back seat of a car travelling at high speed. A man in black is sitting in front with Zarah Leander. She appears to have a red velvet ribbon round her neck. The man turns to the woman and it becomes unbearably hot in the car when he says: "Now I'm going to brake!" Her head loosens from her body and falls into my lap.'

Hannah P—, schoolgirl, 16 years old

'My grandma has a pet tigress.

Grandma's been raising the tigress in her kitchen for six years but now it's time to take her outside. Close up she seems nice and friendly to children, but from a distance you can see a gleam of claws and teeth.

It's my job to take her out for a walk.'

Günther Q—, printer, 59 years old

'A dress-coat hangs in my wardrobe, dripping.'

Frieda R—, teacher, 39 years old

'It's a spring morning and I'm on my way to work. I'm only a few yards from the town hall when evening falls. I stop and wonder whether I should turn back. Then I hear a stuttering engine noise. It's coming from Pastor Helmuth's garden.

Before I know it I'm on the other side of the garden wall.

Someone has arranged apples in a wiggly line across the lawn. I follow them. The engine noise gets louder and I find myself behind the house.

There's no one there. The noise is coming from above.

There are two women standing on the edge of the roof, looking down at me. One of them is wearing a black gown with her hair in a bun, the other has her hair loose and is wearing a sky-blue dress.

The one in the dress is standing behind the one with the bun, with her arms round her and her hands clasped over her lap.

The engine noise is coming from under the woman's gown and I realise that the stuttering engine is the reason why evening has fallen.'

Manfred S—, council employee, 43 years old

'I watch Daddy tickling Mummy. She's laughing so hard that I run into the kitchen.

There's a man sitting there with a helmet on. He's staring down at an empty soup bowl.

I go up to him and ask:

— Doesn't your mummy give you anything to eat?

He asks back:

— Will you be my mummy?

And I answer:

— Until tomorrow.

Then the man picks up some scissors and begins to cut my nails over the bowl. When the bottom is covered with clippings he says:

— Now you must cry, Mummy, or I won't get any soup.'

Imogen T—, 7 years old

'I go to the door. The State Prosecutor is standing outside with two police officers; he shows me a search warrant.

I let them into my caravan.

The police officers go straight to a book lying on a chair by the bed, pick a page at random, tear it out of the book and hand it to the Prosecutor.

He folds the page like a napkin, holds it up in the air and nods gravely to the policemen; the crease resembles the profile of the American Jew Ehrich Weiss who taught me the "seven-knot trick".

I bend my tongue to the root but the skeleton key is not there.'

Dr U—, illusionist, (?) years old

'I'm standing on a jutting crag with my daughter Hilde. Seven aero-planes come in from the sea and fly over us with a loud droning. I don't recognise the make or the markings that flash on their wings, so I'm hesitant to wave at them.

The planes bank and wheel in over the shore, then come in to land on the grassy sward that runs up to the crag where we're standing.

I walk towards the planes – Hilde shows no interest in them but carries on playing – and I'm nearly there when the pilots jump out and take off their helmets: they're black goats.

I run towards Hilde but the pilots get there before me.

They corner the child on the crag and begin to scold her for various things I know she hasn't done.'

Margareta V—, seamstress, 28 years old

'I'm standing at the altar with my wife; we're getting married for the second time.

Someone slaps me on the shoulder.

The best man, Air Marshall Goering, smiles at me. I look round and see an empty pew where I thought my son Sigi was sitting.'

Sigismund W—, bank clerk, 63 years old

'My sister-in-law comes visiting with a bolt of cloth, saying she's been asked to deliver it to me. I'm to use the material for curtains.

I ask her who the benefactor is. She leaves without answering.

I unwind the cloth: printed on the pink linen are pictures of my husband and me in the most extraordinary sexual positions.

I'm not shocked.

I examine the cloth thoughtfully; the further it unwinds, the fainter Boas's image becomes and the clearer mine is.

In the last pictures I'm alone, making love to myself.'

Gretl X—, female worker, 22 years old

'I'm flying in a biplane. There are two women in the passenger seats behind me.

They call me Macheath.

I'm immortal.'

Rudolf Z—, servant boy, 17 years old

10

'Gabriel soared over the sapphire-green meadows of the Realm of Heaven, listening devoutly to the eagle-whoosh of his famous wings. His journey home had gone well despite the divine weariness that had spread through every quill and plume of his angelic frame, and when the spires of Paradise City rose scintillating on the horizon, their glorious radiance moved his tongue in a psalm:

> O Jerusalem divine,
> How my spirit for thee doth pine,
> For the light that doth shine
> From thy raiment divine.
> Where thy children line
> Baskets with berries fine.
> Gladdened with wine,
> Forgotten is all repine,
> They glow like a bramble . . . spine.

Gabriel knew of no more glorious sight than Paradise City when he returned worn out from a long journey such as that which now lay behind him.

But in truth the archangel was not, as he thought, in flight, nor had he accomplished his day's mission: "To sound the trumpet for battle in heaven and on earth, to fight in said battle, and to conquer." No, in reality he was hanging like a firefly trapped in a web of deceit spun by eight-footed Satan.

It was night, Gabriel straddled Europe, his supple body frozen in an absurd attitude; his right foot resting on the Greenland ice-cap and his left on the Persian plateau, clutching the robe to his lap, the trumpet jutting obscenely from his hand, his silver-bright head flung back into the depths of space and his mouth primly pursed like a spinster's.

The only sign of life was his eyes, which quivered beneath their lids, astray in a dream.

On the crystal-clear backdrop of heaven beyond the spires Gabriel saw the Lord's hosts flocking to the city: Seraphim clove the air with Metatron at their head, singing "Kadosh! Kadosh! Kadosh!"; Ophanim swooped in formation from the clouds on their way home from the life-spark mines, and blazing Cherubim on guard duty circled the seven city gates.

Gabriel beat his wings harder, unaware that the tiredness coursing through his body was spun from an evil thread; it was human – tantamount to corporeal – and had its origin in memories from the ancient of days on earth, when he had caught God's sons, the giant Grigori or Watchers, fornicating with the daughters of Eve.

The archangel had informed the Almighty of the crime and carried out the ensuing purges with such zeal that the Father Himself had seen fit to intervene and reprimand him before the eyes of all: "Dear child, we do not force anyone to confess to sins he has not committed."

But as the Almighty knew what motivated Gabriel in the purges – compensation for the fantasies that had seized his mind when he witnessed the sacrilegious union between the incandescent substance of the Watchers and the doomed flesh of woman – the archangel was allowed to set up as many show trials in Paradise as he wished.

And it fell out as the Father had intended: by the time the raids against the Grigori had ended and the ringleader Röhmiel had been cast into the darkness of hell, Gabriel had managed to suppress within himself any desire to watch the obscenity that must characterise any sexual congress between immortals and mortals.

Right up until the moment when the fiend Satan – in a base attempt to postpone Doomsday – trapped Gabriel in his net.

* * *

Archangels such as Michael and Uriel have many tasks to wear them out, and it is thus inevitable that they should from time to time grow weary. (In his important work *De Civitate Dei* or 'The City of God', St Augustine of Hippo, for example, puts forward the following explanation for the existence of the same species of animal in lands separated by sea, that in the days of the Creation the angels flew around the globe with the beasts, setting them down according to the orders of the Creator. And one need hardly add that this was no easy task. – Ed. H.G.) In general, the fatigue of angels is most unlike the weariness that we mortals know, as it does not threaten their lives in the same way as toiling from morning to night can cripple the human labourer and shorten his lifespan . . . These divine beings are immortal, they have a refuge at the high seat of God and from Him they derive their spiritual and physical nourishment. (Here the author is speaking figuratively; he is not claiming that angels are made of flesh and blood. On the contrary, it was the author's contention that the heavenly 'flesh' in fact consisted of rays of light emanating from the divine love. – Ed. H.G.) . . . On the other hand, God's angels experience sin in a similar way to how we experience the diminution of our strength: sin dulls the glittering tissue that constitutes the angels' bodies, and instead of reflecting the incandescence of Jehovah, they absorb it. They become filled with pride – and fall.[1]

* * *

The frisson of lust, which Gabriel in his innocence mistook for weariness, now assaulted him like a nightmare. Even the flood of light from the golden roofs of Paradise City could not restore his strength; his legs grew heavy as lead, his wings would not obey his commands. Losing the power of flight, he plummeted to earth with a deafening shriek.

Gabriel came to his senses in a woody grove: a blue sky with a single sun shone through the canopy of trees – the ten thousand suns

---

[1] 'On the distinctive natures of angels' by Helmuth Adler (*Radiant Life – Icelandic Unisomnist Newsletter*, no. 3, 1979).

and crystal vault had vanished – but the rays of the single sun were so strong that they made his eyes water.

When the angel had wiped the tears from his eyes and blinked until he grew accustomed to the glare, he almost let out a shriek of terror: he was lying with his head in the lap of a young maiden who was passing the time by plaiting a garland of rose petals (*Rosa rubrifolia*) and rosemary sprigs (*Rosmarinus officinalis*).

Gabriel choked back his scream and clamped his eyes shut in despair. He felt so faint that he wouldn't be able to lift so much as a finger in self-defence if the maiden were to make advances to him, let alone flap his wings and fly away before someone caught him *in flagrante delicto*, as it was called in the books of the Last Judgement. He couldn't follow this thought through to the end – to be caught in these demeaning circumstances, no, it would be too cheap an entertainment for that hellish pimp Pharzuph and his queens of shadow.

He decided to feign sleep; the instant he recovered his strength he would shoot up the blue arc of heaven like an arrow from a bow.

Gabriel was startled out of his lamentations; something wet had brushed against his foot. What was happening? Had she started to grope him?

He opened one eye a slit: a unicorn calf (*Monoceros imaginarius*) was snuffling interestedly at his soles, seemingly about to lick them. O Lord! How was he supposed to feign sleep under this sort of torture?

But just as the unicorn was about to apply its tongue to the defenceless angel, the maiden looked up from her pastime and shooed him affectionately away. The calf bleated crossly but obeyed the gesture and trotted off.

This good deed altered the angel's view of the maiden.

He saw through half-closed eyes that she was not only good-hearted but wondrously fair, and he drank up her beauty like the very elixir of life: clear blue eyes, a tip-tilted nose, rosy cheeks and a well-shaped mouth graced her snow-white visage like a constellation. Her fair hair fell loose over shoulders that had never known the burden of sin, her delicate hands deftly plaited the flowery garland, her small virginal breasts rose and fell under the fine weave of her dress.

Well, the archangel could hardly feel threatened by such a beautiful, unspoilt maiden – the latter quality attested to by her power over the unicorn calf, which now stood in the middle of the grove, chewing the buds off a Venus flytrap (*Dionaea muscipula*) which grew beside the trunk of a pomegranate tree (*Punica granatum*).

Gabriel had never before been in such close proximity to the weaker sex – not even when he announced to the Blessed Virgin Mary that she was to give birth to the Saviour. The great tidings had been delivered without physical contact: the future Mother of God had been standing at the kitchen table, kneading dough, while the angel had knelt in the larder doorway, and the glorious words had hovered in the air between them, blazing with fire. Though the angel had lost count of the paintings that supported his impression of the event, he was now so intoxicated by the maiden's beauty and the warmth from her lap that for all he could remember he might have pressed his lips against Mary's right ear and kissed her.

Gabriel puckered up: then what objection could there be to his offering this young maiden something similar? What was acceptable to the Holy Virgin ought surely to be welcome to this little sister of hers who was cradling his head in her lap. He opened his eyes wide and grabbed at the maiden.

But she was not as preoccupied with her flower arranging as Gabriel had supposed.

Nimbly eluding his hands she sprang to her feet and laughed at him as he rolled over, heavy as a sack of coal.

Gabriel sat up in the grass, trying to get his bearings.

The unicorn was lying beside the Venus flytrap, making idiotic ruminating noises, but the earth seemed to have swallowed up the beautiful young maid: what foolishness had led her to flee from him as if from an old satyr? It didn't take a theologian to see that he was an archangel. Who else would have sixteen wings and a halo?

The unicorn shot him a dirty look.

The angel clambered to his feet, wiping the sweat from his brow with the hem of his robe. He had to find the girl: she mustn't think he wished her any harm. No, it would be most unfortunate if she were to spread that about.

Forming a trumpet with his hands, he walked around the grove, shouting in every direction: "I am an angel! I am an angel!"

But his calls received no response apart from the ruminating noises emitted by the unicorn calf, which grew louder every time he uttered the word "am".

Gabriel soon tired of his conversation with the calf's digestive system, but decided to repeat one more time for form's sake that he was an angel, now adding that he was the special friend of virgins. And would you know it, at that the maiden jumped giggling out of the bushes.

She ran to him, placed the garland on his head, skipped away from him and halted just within reach, but the moment he stretched out a hand to her she frisked away with a squeal.

The angel clapped a hand to his brow: the symbolist who had put together the unicorn and given him to maidens was a genius indeed: the state of virginity was obviously nothing but absurdity piled upon absurdity. If he wanted to offer the maiden a thing or two, he would have to follow the example of the fabulous beast with the head of an antelope, the body of a horse, the beard of a goat, the legs of an elephant, the tail of a pig and the horn protruding from the middle of its forehead, two ells long and twisted.

Emitting a loud neigh, Gabriel lumbered off in pursuit of the maiden.

The chase led them the length and breadth of the grove. It was rather mismatched on account of the large age gap between the players: the angel was coeval with the world, the maiden in her thirteenth year. She was as fleet as a hind and instantly retreated whenever he was lucky enough to catch hold of her dress or ankle. But the feel of the young flesh was so inflaming that the angel was unable to stop and pursued the maiden until finally he tripped over a knotted root and was unable to rise again, however much she teased him.

Gabriel lay back, his chest heaving with exhaustion. He admitted defeat: clearly the maiden didn't want an annunciation and he would have to respect the fact. But perhaps she would like to play with him later?

The angel glanced over at the maiden and saw the unicorn come trotting up behind her with its spear in the air. He was about to yell at her to look out when the animal feinted at her and she fell screeching into Gabriel's arms.

The maiden seemed to like it there.

She immediately started making her own annunciation to the angel.

These maidens certainly were odd creatures.'

'Has he fallen then?'

'Dew glitters on the onion fields around Kükenstadt . . .'

'Meaning what?'

'Let's go there.'

VI

11

'Marie-Sophie thought she had only nodded off for a moment when she came to under the eiderdown on the mattress on the floor beside the invalid's bed: from the square outside came the rattle of cart-wheels and the lethargic hoof-beats of the dray horse.

The girl started up with a jerk: she must throw on her clothes and get the dining room ready before the regulars turned up for their morning coffee. No, what was she thinking? She had to stay here in the priest's hole with the invalid until he left – if he left.

I'll die of old age in here . . .

She reached out for her clothes which lay neatly folded on the chair by the desk and blushed: what was this? She didn't remember having folded them. Could the invalid, a strange man, have undressed her and put her to bed? And her book was open as if she had been reading it – or he had been reading to her as if she were a child. Had the night turned the world upside down, converting patient into nurse and nurse into patient? It wasn't as if she didn't know what to think, but it was most embarrassing.

I won't put up with this for a minute longer . . .

Marie-Sophie peered over the side of the invalid's bed: he was asleep, his suffering face revealing nothing about the events of the night.

The girl wrapped the eiderdown around her, sprang to her feet, snatched her clothes from the chair, darted behind the screen and dressed herself: a pungent smell rose from the chamber-pot which she hadn't had time to empty last night.

I'm going mad . . .

She took the potty out of the priest's hole, holding it at arm's length, and laid it by the door of room twenty-three. The raw Monday light penetrated between the curtains, flashing on the motes that hung in the air waiting for someone to come and inhale them.

Marie-Sophie drew back the curtains, opened the window and breathed in the new day: on the far side of the square, between the draper's and the butcher's, a young man was leaning against a lamp-post. He was struggling to light a cigarette that seemed to have a life of its own between his lips, flicking nimbly away from the flaring match he raised to it.

The girl smiled at the man's clumsiness.

Look at him, always the same old butterfingers . . .

It was Karl.

Marie-Sophie stuck her arm out of the window and waved to him. Karl tackled the self-willed cigarette one final time but it got the better of him. He looked over at the guesthouse. She saw him notice her and beckoned him to come across the square so they could talk. He shrugged, pushed the hat back on his head, snatched the cigarette from his lips and dropped it on the street, grinding it underfoot, then turned on his heel and walked away without returning the greeting of the girl in the window.

What have they done to me?

She hissed with rage: damn the day off she had missed yesterday and damn the fact that she had to change the nappies of a fully grown man who was none of her concern; there was no way she was going to let the owner and the Inhaberin deprive her of her boyfriend.

Marie-Sophie had had enough of being a good girl.

Hearing the front door of the guesthouse open, she climbed on to the window sill and peered out through the leaded panes: the owner was standing on the pavement below, having a drink. The servant boy came out of the house carrying a small table.

— No one'll want to sit out here today, it's going to rain cats and dogs – anyone can see that.

The boy put down the table and stared up at the sky.

— I don't give a damn about your weather forecasts; the wife tells us to run a pavement café and that's what we'll do – for all I care the fools who sit out here, going along with her pretentious nonsense, can be struck by lightning. And here's one for you.

The owner gave the boy a box on the ear.

— Now get back inside and fetch the chairs, you bloody weather-cock!

Marie-Sophie clenched her fists with rage: she'd had it up to here with the blows the owner dealt out to the boy every morning in an attempt to work off his hangover.

I'll see to it that the boy's weather forecast comes true – and it won't be him that gets a wetting but that swine of an owner, thought the girl.

She jumped down from the window sill, fetched the piss-pot and positioned herself so she could follow what was happening on the pavement and empty the pot without being observed.

She waited.

The servant boy arranged the chairs around the table while the owner fussed, finding fault with how far the chairs were placed from the table and which way they faced; his hangover made him ultra-sensitive to distances and ratios.'

'Tell me about it! I once woke up at a composer's house – I wouldn't be surprised if that was on a Monday morning too. And when I went into the living room the musician was sitting stark naked at the grand piano, knocking together a sonata.'

'You know artists? I don't know any.'

'That's a shame. They're generally quite amusing; pickled in drink and self-pity, of course.'

'My father used to associate with them, but he never brought them back to our house . . . '

'Anyway, where was I? Oh yes, the composer sat there wearing nothing but his prick, his big head hanging over the keyboard. The sun shone on his curly hair and his left hand scuttled like a spider across the keys, spinning wonderful phrases, while the nicotine-yellow fingers of his right hand held a fountain pen, with which they trapped the sounds in a web of paper where the black notes glittered on the lines like flies . . .'

'Now who's telling stories within the story?'

'Me.'

'And who can't stand digressions?'

'Me.'

'So what do you say?'

'Sorry?'

'I should think so.'

'Marie-Sophie held the cup of wrath in a firm hand, making sure nothing slopped over the brim: the servant boy and the owner were so preoccupied with solving problems of relative space and distance on the pavement below that they didn't notice the chamber-pot hovering over their heads like a gilded rain-cloud.

— Wouldn't it be better like this?

The servant boy grabbed a chair and pushed it defiantly under the table with a loud screech. The owner ground his teeth.

— Or like that perhaps?

The boy scraped the chair back.

— Eh? Bit closer?

The chair legs grated on the paving stones. The owner raised his hand to strike.

Marie-Sophie released a torrent of golden liquid from the chamber-pot.

The owner gasped as the cold urine struck his head, poured down his neck and ran between his shirt and his skin.

The servant boy looked up with a smile.

The girl winked at him, drew herself and the cup of wrath back inside and descended in one bound from the sill and into the priest's hole.

She closed the door carefully as she listened to the owner swearing; his curses made such a fitting dawn chorus that morning that she hummed along.

The invalid looked enquiringly at Marie-Sophie. She hushed the man she was supposed to be encouraging to talk, a fact that amused her. Then she yanked the bell-pull that hung by the doorpost and heard a faint ringing in the kitchen:

— I hope they'll send the boy up with our breakfast.

The invalid nodded gravely: he had to keep on the right side of this girl who had begun the day by running around with her chamber-pot. This suggested that she was at home in this house that had all the appearances of a set for a great whore-atorio; from where he lay he couldn't avoid noticing the bite marks in the black silk pillows, the nail stuck in the wallpaper above the bed and the red crêpe shading the light-bulb to soften the imperfections of the flesh.

He stole a glance around him: there ought to be a reminder of the Father and Son somewhere around here.

— Good morning.

Marie-Sophie stood over the invalid: he seemed to be awake, and although he didn't look as if he could hear her any more than he had yesterday – his eyes were spinning like tops in his head – she was so pleased with herself after her morning's work that she just had to say good morning to somebody.

Yes, there it was! The invalid fixed his gaze on a finger-length brass crucifix over the door.

Marie-Sophie studied the invalid: was this stare his way of saying good morning? Wouldn't it be typical if he decided to recover just when she had got herself all psyched up to tear a strip off the owner?

The invalid's face twisted in a wry smile: nothing boosted the carnal vigour of Christians like the knowledge that the heavenly Father and Son were watching over their every move.

What was so funny? Marie-Sophie followed the man's gaze: Oh my God, was the potty on the table? And completely empty too!

The invalid watched her spring into action, whip the chamber-pot off the table and vanish behind the screen: the crucifix convinced him that he had been brought to a brothel. And so the girl, this early bird who dashed around with her chamber-pot, must be the siren-whore whose role was to madden him into confessing.

The man listened to the girl swearing to herself: yes, here people must start the day by hoping that "the boy" would bring them breakfast. He could imagine what type "the boy" was: a pale-eyed muscle mountain in his forties whose name began with a letter towards the end of the alphabet and who was filled with resentment against the world because on his first day at school he had been read out last of all the class.

He used his remaining strength to peel off his smile and sink into oblivion.

From behind the screen came a sigh of pleasure as a stream of liquid sang in the chamber-pot.

Marie-Sophie had just managed to finish before the door of room twenty-three opened.

Well now, it's the owner himself or the Inhaberin. It'll do them good to learn to bring people their breakfast. Who knows? By the end of the day they might find themselves without help. Who knows where I will be by then?

The girl covered the chamber-pot and went out to meet the newcomer.

The Inhaberin had slept badly and wore a scowl.

— We need to talk.

Marie-Sophie smiled as if butter wouldn't melt in her mouth: the Inhaberin measured every minute she slept in carats. She had been a member of the Unisomnist Association before the war and, although the movement had been banned, Unisomnists still gathered every night on the lowest level of the astral plane to synchronise themselves.

"Her nerve endings have been ruined by spoiling," as the cook said, referring to what the Inhaberin had told her in confidence: that her family thought she had lowered herself by marrying the plumber who today was the owner of Gasthof Vrieslander. "As if he 'owned' anything!" Old Tomas claimed that the Inhaberin was addicted to sleep because she was having an affair with an Indian warlord on some higher plane and the reason the "owner" allowed this to go on was that he only existed between his wife's inverted commas.

But today the Inhaberin was to be pitied: no one deserved to be rudely awoken by a urine-soaked husband.

Marie-Sophie took the tray from the woman's hands.

— How kind of you to bring up his food yourself.

The Inhaberin looked down her nose.

— You're very generous today, Marie-Sophie, but don't try to throw dust in my eyes. I should think the drenching you gave my husband was enough for us to be going on with.

The girl looked uncertainly at the Inhaberin: she had been hoping for the servant boy to share a laugh with, or the owner so that she could add insult to injury by demanding compensation – holidays, etc. – for the incident with Karl. But she didn't dare take any liberties with this woman, who would kill for forty winks.

The woman looked Marie-Sophie coldly in the eye.

— My husband's beside himself, I could hardly understand a word he said, but from what I could gather I thought the town must have been hit by an air raid at the very least and that I alone could have prevented it.

The Inhaberin pursed her lips and continued:

— Do you think it's remotely amusing for a spiritually minded person to be woken by a carry-on like that, by the yelling and blustering of a husband drenched in piss?

Marie-Sophie gulped: it was her fault that the Inhaberin had been toppled from her astral plane, from the embrace of the Indian prince into a dingy grey morning in Kükenstadt. She deserved what was coming to her for being the cause of such a poor exchange.

— Answer me! Do you think it normal for someone to wake his wife by hurling himself on her bed, wet as a dog after a dip in the river, and screaming for vengeance?

The Inhaberin extracted the girl's fingernails with her eyes.

— Well, say it!

Marie-Sophie's grip tightened on the breakfast tray.

— Say what?

— That this is no way for a fully grown man to behave!

The girl had to choke back her laughter: the Inhaberin hadn't come here to berate her after all; she hadn't the slightest interest in her husband's sufferings. What she wanted was sympathy. And Marie-Sophie was grateful for this chance to add fuel to the bad feeling between this couple who were responsible for turning her boyfriend against her.

— Well?

The Inhaberin stamped her foot and hissed:

— Or perhaps you side with him in this act of domestic violence?

— Are you mad? Why do you think I gave him a royal drenching this morning? Because he uses violence against me too.

The woman gasped.

— The bastard!

She was about to rush out of the room when Marie-Sophie flung down the tray, took a firm grip on her arm and held her back: the Inhaberin was angrier with her husband than the girl had guessed; she was out for blood. And although fortunately the woman was sane enough to realise that she was bound to meet with more understanding from the authorities if she killed her husband because he had raped a member of staff than because he had woken her from her dreams, nevertheless the guesthouse couldn't afford a murder investigation, not while the invalid's life depended on them.

— It's not what you think.

— Oh?

The Inhaberin couldn't hide her disappointment.

— So he didn't rape you, then?

Marie-Sophie snorted.

— No, I wouldn't let anyone rape me, least of all – forgive me for saying so – your husband.

The invalid listened patiently to the girl. She sat beside him on the bed, feeding him watery gruel and the tale of her triumphs.

He had feigned unconsciousness when she entered the room with the tray: he meant to hover on the brink of starvation until they gave up on him and shot him, but the girl clearly had orders to get some food down his neck, whether he was conscious or not.

The girl obediently raised him up, put the bib on him and commenced shovelling. The invalid chewed feebly, dribbling enough of the gruel out of his mouth for her to believe he was dead to the world: he wondered whether the absurd story she was telling him was part of her orders; did it contain hidden elements designed to elicit unwary comments from him? Something as innocent as: "Really? She gave you time off to visit your boyfriend, did she?"

During the interrogations they had twisted his most banal statements into proof of an international conspiracy against the Führer's rightful view of existence. But as the girl continued her story, he began to doubt that it was learned by rote and merely an act; it was too convoluted and ridiculous for that.

Marie-Sophie finished feeding the invalid. She rang the bell and took out the tray: the Inhaberin had been upset enough to believe every word she said: her husband was trying to come between Marie-Sophie and Karl. If it wasn't violence to prevent a girl her age from meeting her intended, then what was it? God knows what the man was up to! And although the woman was generally dead against Karl and his visits to the guesthouse, she had given the girl permission to pop out at coffee time; of course the Inhaberin couldn't watch the invalid herself as she was going egg-collecting in the countryside with her husband, but the cook would sit with the man for the hour that Marie-Sophie was away.

When the servant boy came to fetch the tray and they had laughed themselves silly, Marie-Sophie scribbled a message on a napkin, folded it neatly, drew her butterfly on the front and asked the boy to run along with it to Karl. Payment was cheap and easily achieved: one kiss on the cheek.

Marie-Sophie whistled "His name is Valdimar, he's simply wunderbar!" as she returned to her charge in the priest's hole: now all she had to do was kill time. The two men were due at noon for a report on the invalid's condition. The Inhaberin was going to see to it that they would agree to his being left in the care of the cook.'

'Marie-Sophie went to the skylight and opened it, took off her maid's uniform and laid it on the bed, fetched a mother-of-pearl box, which she kept hidden beneath her underwear on the bottom shelf in the cupboard, and bathed her face in the steaming water in the basin. Taking a sliver of perfumed soap from the box, she rolled it carefully between her hands.

The two men had given their permission, though she had nearly blown it when they looked in on her and the invalid in the priest's hole. They had asked her – yes, because now it was she who knew him best – whether she thought it was safe to let the cook look after him.

After spending the night with the invalid she had somehow taken it for granted that he would stay with them at the guesthouse for ever and ever, that he was like a new Tomas who anyone could look after, and she had answered the two men against her better judgement that the cook was no novice when it came to nursing, no, someone who had nursed on the battlefields in the last war ought to be up to coping with this pathetic creature. However, the truth was that the cook had the greatest contempt for nursing and said you could tell what kind of "profession" it was from the career of Florence Nightingale, yes, apparently she'd been a fast piece and there was no need to ask the colour of her lamp.

The two men conferred, with grave faces.

Marie-Sophie grew uneasy and began to repeat the words "last war" as if to convince them that the cook was all right and that she herself knew what she was talking about: "In the last war, yes, wasn't it supposed to be the last war?"

At that they shot her a look and asked in unison: "Why are you talking about war?"

She was taken aback by the sharpness of their tone: the question blew up like a storm in her ears; the vowels merged and consonants scattered in a discordant choir that roared in her head. But as her inner ear grew accustomed to the roaring she discerned within it the voices of the men who had been dearest to her in her childhood.

She heard the distressed cry of the headmaster when her classmates surprised him by hiding in a ditch and jumping out at him; she heard the suppressed moans of pain from her Uncle Ernst, who couldn't swallow without wincing; she heard the sobbing of her father who wept alone in the kitchen when he thought she and Boas were asleep.

And she heard other things.

The male-voice choir in her head sang the homecoming song:

Like a shot bird
your hand flees
my hand.

Like an eclipsed moon
my eyes darken
your eyes.

Like the shadow of a flame
your child plays
my child.

And those who had fought so that the battle lines would never be drawn up around those hands, those who had shielded the brightness of those eyes by facing up to what no man should have to see, those who had no life to look forward to but the lives of their children.

Yes, who was she, a little girl like her, to rub their noses in the fact that they hadn't brought an end to all wars by surviving one bloody world war?

She said she didn't mean anything by it, it was just something people said.

They shook their heads indignantly and left her alone with the invalid.

Marie-Sophie pulled on a pair of deceptively warm stockings and poured a rose-print dress over her head: the world could do with cheering up today, overcast as it was and ready to burst into tears. She fetched her lipstick from its hiding place in the cupboard, dipped her little finger in the tube and applied the colour to her lips with her fingertip: not too much for the moral majority in the middle of the day – not too little for Karl.

When they were alone again in the little compartment, she had recalled for the invalid the feminine war wisdom that she hadn't dared to mention to the two men: somewhere she had read that all beings were sexless in sleep; he was out for the count and so ought not to be offended by what she had to say.

* * *

A TRAVELLER'S TALE

In the years after the First World War a tramp travelled across Europe, visiting women who had lost their husbands and lovers on the Eastern and Western fronts: Flanders, Tannenberg, Gallipoli, the Dardanelles, the Somme, Verdun, the Marne, Vittorio Veneto. They knew the roll-call of names and the despair it evoked.

The tramp went from country to country, city to city and house to house. There were more than enough war widows and he visited them all.

On pitch-dark nights when the widows lay unable to sleep, sighing with longing for gentle fingers to stroke their cheeks and hard muscles to flex against their thighs, the tramp would appear without warning in their rooms, like the moon from behind a bank of cloud. They welcomed him with open arms.

There was always something about him that reminded them of the departed, that one little thing that had made him unique, made him theirs. Some recognised the unruly lock of hair that fell over his left eye, others the crooked thumb on his right hand, and others the birthmark by his Adam's apple where they had kissed him in a final farewell.

The tramp would undress in silence and allow the widows to survey him before he joined them under the covers, cold from his night's wandering.

And they would guide him through every movement that had characterised their lovemaking with their husbands, their lovers.

In the morning he would be gone.'

'I've heard this story before, I know who the tramp was.'

'So who was he?'

'Franco Pietroso was a nondescript functionary who worked in the Italian war ministry, sending out death announcements to the fallen's next of kin. Except that instead of doing what duty commanded, he stuffed the announcements under a chair, got in touch with the widows and pretended to be from their husbands' regiments, claiming that he was on leave to attend his mother's funeral.

When Franco Pietroso had won the women's trust with this deception, he regaled them with tales of the debauchery at the front, saying that there were plenty of Red Cross girls to entrap the soldiers in their toils, and you could count on the fingers of one hand those who resisted the temptation.

The poor widows, who had not the slightest idea what life was like in the trenches, any more than Franco Pietroso had, and assumed that their husbands were alive and well and cheating on them, sought "comfort" from their confidant.

In the end Franco Pietroso was exposed; a soldier who was supposed to be dead caught him with his "widow". And the story goes that when he was hanged, the gatekeeper of hell, unable to find the crime of "cuckolding dead men" in his books, turned him away.

He won't gain admittance there until a war widow declares her love for him, despite knowing what kind of man he is.'

'That sounds plausible – and I must admit that the man's name fits with what I know about him – but I'm afraid the truth is not so pretty.'

'If the widows had known the tramp's origins one can be sure they would not have welcomed him with open arms, no, they would have buried their faces in their pillows and shuddered in speechless horror when the ghastly presence lay down under the covers beside them.

He's cold from his night's walk; my burning flesh will warm him.

So they had thought, but they hadn't noticed that the tramp's body temperature remained the same even in the heat of the action. He was not cold from his long walk.

He did not exist.

Yes, the reason why winter frost and women's embraces had no power to touch the tramp was quite simply that his name was not recorded in the book of the living; the ruling powers had not intended him a place in Creation.

It was the widows' frustration that had created him from the mortal remains of the men they had loved and lost.

The body parts had torn themselves off the rotting corpses on the battlefields and been borne across Europe by wind and water. In a gneiss cavern deep in the bowels of the Alps, beneath the Jungfrau, to be precise, there gathered kneecaps from Flanders, fingernails and guts from Tannenberg, tonsils, spleen and ligaments from Gallipoli, hipbones, eye sockets, testicles and gums from the Dardanelles, lungs, soles, vocal cords and pituitary gland from the Somme, tongue root, shoulder-blades and colon from Verdun, lymphatic system and cheek muscles from the Marne, and a pair of kidneys from Vittorio Veneto. Combining with a host of other body parts they assembled themselves into a man with everything that a man should possess.

That man was the tramp.'

* * *

'And you think that's more credible than the story of Franco Pietroso?'

'I don't think anything; that's how the story goes.'

'The invalid dozed during Marie-Sophie's tale and she didn't seem to care whether he showed any reaction to the content.

When he stirred he thought the girl was interrogating him about his movements during the period from 14 August 1914 to 11 November 1918, and he shrugged. Even if he told her what he remembered, she wouldn't get any feathers in her cap for that: every fart and belch could already be found recorded in the archives of the Third Reich – everything that is, apart from the time between his being led out of the camp by the hand of fate and their finding him again and depositing him here with this talkative girl.

There was a knock on the door and the girl admitted an older woman into the priest's hole and told her there was no need to do anything for the man in the bed, it would be best to leave him be; she'd be back in an hour anyway.

He murmured some gibberish and pretended to sleep.

Marie-Sophie tidied away the lipstick and soap, combed her hair and pinned it back with a silver clip, pulled on her cardigan, locked the room and went down to reception.

The owner was standing behind the desk. He scowled when he saw the girl.

— An hour! Not a minute more . . .

The old man sat at his ease by the front door, parroting the owner's words.

— An hour! Not a minute . . .

She blew them both a kiss and sped out of the guesthouse.

Marie-Sophie headed across the square. She paused by the draper's, examining her reflection in the window and rearranging a lock of hair that refused to stay in its place by her left temple. Inside, Fräulein Knopfloch was bending over a whopping great mass of black velvet, measuring tape in hand.

Marie-Sophie nodded to her. She was sometimes allowed to buy leftover pieces of expensive fabric for a bargain price; often they were enough for a shawl or a dress.

The woman was too engrossed in marking off the roll of cloth to return the girl's greeting, but an enormous man wearing such a tight suit he must have borrowed it from his youthful self, who was standing at the counter with a huge bunch of silk ribbons in his big hands, smiled all the more sweetly at her. She bridled: why was this recent widower pulling faces at her? Had he been blinded by grief? Why on earth would a blooming girl like her take a second glance at a buffoon like him? Did she look like some loose-living tart?

Marie-Sophie darted a glance at the window pane to reassure herself that she looked no more tarty than usual – which is to say, in every way respectable – only to catch the eye of the man who had now come over to the window. There was no mistaking it, the old sod was flirting with her. He ran a coal-grimed hand over the bunch of silk ribbons and formed silent words with his thick lips: "O, come my dear, let us be joined/ Together in my black lair!"

The girl shivered; her heart missed a beat at this snatch of the old song. She backed away from the shop and bumped into a boy who was lost in contemplation of his watch.

What am I thinking of? Time's passing and Karl's waiting!

Marie-Sophie stuck out her tongue at the suitor on the shop floor. Fräulein Knopfloch looked askance at her and she shrugged at the spinster.

The man could tell her whatever lies he wanted. As soon as they took the invalid away she would be a free woman again and could ask forgiveness for her sins all over town.

The girl quickened her stride.

Her heels clicked on the paving stones, her footsteps counting off the seconds; every step was half a second, click-clack, click-clack, that made a hundred and twenty a minute, click-clack, click-clack, three thousand six hundred a half-hour, click-clack, click-clack, click!

Clack! I've got fifty-four minutes left.

She swung out of the square and into Blumengasse where no flowers grew. The street was nothing but a rubbish tip; dustbins stood along the soot-stained walls and it was obvious why the householders couldn't be bothered to put on their lids: anyone who chose to hang about in this tip was bound to fit in with the scenery.

I only hope God doesn't know about this. He gave men the power of speech so they could name everything under the sun, but I bet He'd think the naming of this dreary spot had gone a little awry. What would he say, for example, if he sent an angel here to raise up the sinners and the feathered one came back with the following description: "I landed on the square, walked round the corner by Fräulein Knopfloch's and found the sinner in a filthy tip called Flower Street."

How are men to reply when He asks them about this slip-up?

"There used to be flowery meadows here in the olden days!"

I don't suppose the Lord would believe that for a minute; He must know that Kükenstadt is a town built on a mud flat – they joke about it enough in the surrounding countryside.

He might think of striking us all dumb for such a blunder.

Marie-Sophie paused a moment under the sign at the end of the street.

But I'm wearing a flowery dress and I'm walking along you, so today you can be called Rose Bloom Street and we'll just have to hope that the Creator changes His mind about striking us dumb – I'm going to need my tongue to soften up Karl.

Herr Abend-Anzug, Karl's neighbour, was standing on the doorstep, apparently unsure whether he was coming or going.

He was awkwardly attired, out of keeping with the hour – in starched evening dress and patent-leather dancing shoes – and had plainly been loitering there for some time, because when he caught sight of Marie-Sophie he called:

— Good evening!

The girl bid the man good afternoon and made to slip past him but he sprang backwards and took up position in the doorway.

— I've heard you're a good girl, and I believe it.

He waited expectantly for an answer.

Marie-Sophie adopted the neutral expression that had proved useful in her dealings with amorous guests at Gasthof Vrieslander: she had neither the interest nor the time to listen to speeches about her character.

Herr Abend-Anzug tweaked the topic of conversation.

— Yes, I'm sure you are.

She twitched up the corners of her mouth and this reaction satisfied the man. He laughed:

— Mama's no fool.

It transpired that Herr Abend-Anzug had not blocked the girl's way in order for her to solve his existential problems on the doorstep.

— But the same can't be said about the swine I imagine you've come to visit. We don't ask much of the residents of the attic, but things can go too far; you couldn't hear yourself speak for the racket he made when he came home this morning.

Marie-Sophie paled.

— When he wasn't bawling out the "Internationale" he was crashing the furniture around, or goodness knows what. Some people wouldn't have hesitated to call the police.

Herr Abend-Anzug looked the girl solemnly in the eye.

Marie-Sophie didn't know what to think: Karl furniture-moving, singing the "Internationale"? He despised the Communists, they had treated him badly. He had read her a call to arms he'd written for the Chimney Sweeps' Union, at the urging of radicals who had then failed to publish it. He must have got roaring drunk – to be caught engaging in Communist activities could mean big trouble.

— Yes, my mother and I were just talking about how sad it is to see you in the clutches of such a brute. My mother said these very words: "What's she hanging around with that Karl for, a good girl like her?" And she added: "It should be child's play for her to get a decent boyfriend, a pretty girl like that . . ."

— I'm grateful to you and your mother for your kind words about me, but it sounds from what you say as if Karl must be ill – I'd better go and nurse him so you and your mother can indulge in your little dreams in peace.

Marie-Sophie bowed politely to Herr Abend-Anzug but this had the opposite effect than intended on the dandified man, who now became a little too gallant, given that she was just a humble chambermaid.

— Perhaps the young lady would care to partake of an early dinner with me, or whatever you call a splendid afternoon repast. I've been called up – don't you know? – to fight the Slavs, and I'm taking the train this evening; that's why it's dinnertime for me now.

Herr Abend-Anzug went down on one knee.

Marie-Sophie squeaked "Good grief!": the man clearly had little faith that the war was being won if he meant to propose to her right here on the doorstep.

— They all want to make widows of us.

Herr Abend-Anzug looked awkwardly at the muttering girl as he rolled up his trouser leg, stuck his fingers down his sock, drew out a bundle of notes in a worn elastic band and dusted some cake crumbs off it.

— It would delight my mother more than words can say if I were to be seen dining out at a smart restaurant with a young lady such as yourself.

Marie-Sophie smiled sweetly at him and shook her head in reply.

— Thanks for the chat, Herr Abend-Anzug. And for your mother's sake, please come home alive from the front.

At her last words the man stood up, stepped aside and fumbled at his brow for the brim of his non-existent hat.

Marie-Sophie knocked tentatively on Karl's door but received no reply. She knocked harder and listened for any movement in the room: what the hell was Karl playing at? She had managed to escape from work and he couldn't even be bothered to drag himself out of bed. It was a bit much for a fully grown man to be so hurt about missing a single Sunday at the so-called zoo.

She slapped the flat of her hand on the door and turned abruptly away.

— Go ahead and sulk, then!

A door opened on the floor below and a white-haired old lady, the size of a seven-year-old child, appeared on the landing.

— It would take the trumpets of Jericho to rouse Herr Maus, my girl!

She hobbled halfway up the stairs and held out a hand to Marie-Sophie.

— I've been up and down these stairs like a yo-yo ever since noon trying to wake him, though I'd rather not; he's so nice when he's asleep.

Between the gnarled arthritic fingers was a little folded napkin with a glimpse of a pencilled butterfly: Marie-Sophie's message to Karl.

— A young lad came by. He was supposed to give this letter to Herr Maus but said he was afraid of him, so I offered to deliver it. You must take it, dear; I don't like having another person's post in my possession, I'm always tempted to read it – and you're here now anyway.

The girl went down to the yo-yo and took the letter.

— Do give the lad my regards; he was ever such a charmer, unblocked my kitchen sink for me, told tales about your boyfriend and accepted no more than the price of a pint of ale for the whole thing.

The old lady simpered and crept off downstairs.

Marie-Sophie considered the message: perhaps she should make another assault on Karl's door and just say hello – that way he'd be in a better mood next time they met.

Before she could make up her mind there came a whisper:

— Has she gone back inside?

Karl darted red-veined eyes out on to the landing.

The girl nodded at her lover: his pale face was deeply creased from the pillow. There were wretches and then there were real wretches.

He opened the door a crack and beckoned her to come up to his landing. Marie-Sophie shook her head: she didn't like the way Karl looked: he was half dressed or undressed, the blond hair plastered to his forehead, a bloodstained hanky bound around his right ankle.

— I've been standing out here for quarter of an hour already – I'll be late.

Karl clutched his head and moaned:

— That degenerate at Gasthof Vrieslander's not the only one who needs nursing.

— What did you say?

— You've got plenty of time for the man you're hiding at the guesthouse.

The girl glanced round nervously.

— What do you know about that?

— You were with him last night. Is there anything else I should know?

— How do you know I didn't just read my book and go to bed as usual? I've nothing to hide.

— I didn't see a light in your window.

— Were you spying on me; were you in the square to spy on me?

— I was keeping an eye on you; you're the woman I love.

— For all I know you might have been with some other girl and shown yourself in the square this morning so I wouldn't suspect.

— Bah!

— So how come you got piss-drunk, then?

— Drunk? I caught a chill.

— I bet!

— Bah!

— If you two mean to go on quarrelling like this you can do it in your room!

An obese man stormed out of the flat opposite and brandished a pen under Karl's nose.

— The stairwell is a communal area and its primary purpose is for entering and leaving the building.

— Call this a building?

Karl shrieked, clutching his head in agony.

The man hastily withdrew the pen and made an expert aerial sketch of Karl's features.

— Good, good!

The illustrator rushed back into his room and slammed the door.

— You can find me in the zoo on Sunday if you can be bothered.

Marie-Sophie set off down the stairs.

— Jew!

The girl froze in her tracks as the word reached her ears.

— He's a Jew.

She looked up. Karl had disappeared from the landing but his door stood ajar.'

13

'Close your eyes, point to the east, point to the west, point to the one you think is the worst.'

'Maus, Karl Maus, Marie-Sophie's boyfriend.'

'You're shaking . . .'

* * *

'*Das Kabinett Des Herrn Maus*

(The girl looks hesitantly at the half-open door, shivers, then plucks up the courage to approach.)

MARIE-SOPHIE: Karl?

(The landing rears up behind the girl, tipping her in through the door.)

MARIE-SOPHIE: Talk to me . . .

(The room lies in darkness apart from the steel-grey daylight seeping in through the grimy little window above the unmade bed. The girl recoils from the shadow of a wardrobe on the wall facing her; the shadow falls slanting from the wardrobe, through the light, across the window and along the ceiling, to loom over the girl like a clenched fist.)

MARIE-SOPHIE: Karl? Are you there?'

'Get out of there, girl!'

'(The door slams shut. The girl whirls round. Herr Maus is standing by the door. He spreads himself out until his body fills the wall and his head is framed by the doorposts and ceiling. She's afraid but smiles at him.)

MARIE-SOPHIE: God, I didn't know where you'd got to . . .

(Herr Maus laughs hoarsely, the darkness playing ugly tricks with his face: his lips appear blue-black, his nose like the barrel of a gun, his eyes sunken. The girl fumbles nervously for the silver cross that she wears round her neck. Herr Maus spits from between tobacco-stained teeth.)

KARL: Have you any idea what you've got yourself mixed up in?

MARIE-SOPHIE: Mixed up in? I'm nursing a sick man; you should see him, then maybe you'd understand that there's nothing fishy going on.

(Herr Maus lowers his voice until it's no more than a whisper but the words pierce the girl's ears.)

KARL: You naïve little fool! Why do you think they make you stay with the hook-nose? So they themselves will get off scot-free if anything happens.

(Herr Maus tries to laugh but chokes. He hawks into his palm, shoves his hand quickly into his pocket and deposits the disgusting gobbet of phlegm there.)

KARL: And you can bet your life they'll find out that it's no ordinary vermin problem you've got at Gasthof Vrieslander.

(The girl glances round for an escape route. Herr Maus emits something between a spasm of laughter and a cough. The girl backs away from the man's bodily noises, moving further into the room, towards the window – the shadow following her.)

MARIE-SOPHIE: Excuse me, but how do you know we've got a guest if no one knows about him? You haven't visited me for a week. What if I say you've made the whole thing up – that it's nothing but delirious raving?

(Herr Maus takes a step towards the girl. The floorboards creak, the walls of the room close in, the window narrows.)

KARL: You say I haven't been at the guesthouse for a week?

MARIE-SOPHIE: Yes.

KARL: What do you mean?

MARIE-SOPHIE: I mean no . . .

(Herr Maus thrusts forward his unshaven chops, whining.)

KARL: I mean no . . .

(The girl walks boldly towards Herr Maus.)

MARIE-SOPHIE: I haven't got time for this, Karl; you know perfectly well what I mean.

KARL: Herr Maus, you mean. I keep Karl's body in the wardrobe over there – do you want to see it?

(Herr Maus seizes the girl brutally by the shoulders, drags her hard against him and rolls his bloodshot eyes – the shadow above them takes on a human shape.)

KARL: But of course you haven't time to say hello to your deceased boyfriend, you've got to hurry back to work to screw that Jew!'

'The disgusting bastard!'

'(The girl tries to tear herself free but Herr Maus tightens his grip, his knuckles whitening, shoulder-blades cracking.)

MARIE-SOPHIE: How could you think such a thing? The man's desperately ill . . .

KARL: Ha! That was then. He can hardly be ill if you can fuck like rabbits in that priest's hole.

(Herr Maus grinds his teeth with fury, shaking the girl violently to emphasise his words.)

KARL: Perhaps you don't make much noise; no, you know how to do it quietly – Karl told me that. Didn't you, Karl?

(Herr Maus yells over the girl's shoulder. From inside the wardrobe there's a bumping, the sound of coughing and a weary voice.)

VOICE IN THE WARDROBE: Yes.

KARL: You see, Karl was at the guesthouse yesterday.

MARIE-SOPHIE: Rubbish!

KARL: (Smugly.) Tell her!

VOICE IN THE WARDROBE: I was in old Tomas's room; you almost deafened me when you banged on the wall . . .

(The girl gasps.)

KARL: See! Karl and I tell each other everything. He's told me all about you and how good it is to fuck you. Sometimes you cry afterwards – Karl likes that.

MARIE-SOPHIE: Karl dearest, let me go.

(The girl begins to cry.)

KARL: See, what did I say? Do you believe me now? Mmm? Do you believe me when I tell you I know what you're doing with the degenerate they're hiding at the guesthouse?

MARIE-SOPHIE: Yes.

KARL: I can't hear you.

MARIE-SOPHIE: Yes!

KARL: What?

(The girl looks up at Herr Maus with tear-stained eyes.)

MARIE-SOPHIE: YES!

(Herr Maus stares at the girl with an unhinged look in his eye. An uncontrollable spasm distorts his face and the girl's terror changes to amazement when the upper part of his head begins to elongate. It stretches from the eyebrows and ears, like a thick sinew, and twists in an arc round the room until the crown of his head touches a teaspoon that is lying among the handwritten drafts of a heroic poem on the rickety table by the wall facing the window.)

* * *

Little Karl is amusing himself by turning over palm-sized granite paving stones in front of a well-to-do house. He grubs around in the dirt under them, finding pebbles or stumps of root that he rolls between his fingers before tossing them on to the neat lawn.

The small boy turns over one stone after another, finding a pebble, a root stump.

He comes to a stone that won't budge. After making several vain attempts to shift it with his bare hands he runs into the house.

Little Karl sneaks into the whitewashed kitchen, goes straight to a cupboard containing gleaming silverware and takes out a teaspoon, slips it into his pocket and slinks out.

He pushes the spoon into the soil beside the stone, levers it up, turns it over, then puts his hands to his mouth.

In the dirt lies a sparrow, teeming with maggots.

— MUMMY!

* * *

(Herr Maus's head shrinks back to its former shape with a snap, he flings the girl away and she lands on the bed under the little window.)

KARL: You fucking whore!

(Herr Maus storms round the room in a frenzy that seems likely to tear him apart limb from limb. The girl casts despairing glances at the window and door – which narrow before her eyes to crusted sphincters.)

MARIE-SOPHIE: (Cries out.) Karl!

(Herr Maus gets a grip on his thoughts, stops by the girl on the bed and bends over her.)

MARIE-SOPHIE: (Whispers.) Let me out . . .

KARL: (Kindly.) I'm sure Karl would let you out, my dear, if he wasn't locked in the wardrobe.

(From inside the wardrobe comes a pitiful mumbling: "It's true, Marie-Sophie, I'd let you go.")

KARL: But I'm not Karl, I'm Herr Maus and Herr Maus demands that people show him respect. Herr Maus likes people to say: "Your Excellency!" when they're pestering him for favours – then he's generally quite amenable.

MARIE-SOPHIE: Your Excellency, please can I go? I've been here far too long, the Inhaberin will kill me, the owner will lynch me, the cook will murder me, and the two men will wring my neck if I'm late back to the guesthouse. I've got to get back . . .

KARL: Of course, dear Fräulein, of course. Nothing would seem more absurd to us than to keep your ladyship here against your will!

(Herr Maus holds out his hand to the girl and she takes it hesitantly. He raises her to her feet and leads her to the door.)

KARL: Herr Maus has manners, Herr Maus is a gentleman in his dealings with virtuous young girls but hard and ruthless in his dealings with the wicked. There's no question that you belong to the former category, is there?

(Herr Maus twists the girl's arm behind her back until they're standing close together; the pretence of gentleness vanishes from his face. He begins to cackle.)

KARL: Is there? (Fighting back laughter.) You're unquestionably pure in body and soul? Isn't that so?

MARIE-SOPHIE: (Hesitantly.) Your Excellency knows that perfectly well.

KARL: So perhaps we might ask the Fräulein one final question? (The laughter rattles in his throat.)

MARIE-SOPHIE: Stop it!

(Herr Maus grips the back of the girl's neck, forces her head forwards, presses his mouth against her right ear and howls with laughter.)

KARL: Ha, ha, ha! How did you do it? You and the Jew? Ha, ha, ha!

(Herr Maus forces the girl to her knees.)

KARL: Bloody hell, girl! Ha, ha, ha! Can't you answer a simple question?

(The girl can't speak for the pain.)

KARL: Tell me how you did it or I'll show you! Ha, ha, ha! That's a good one. Ha, ha, ha! As if I knew anything about how those circumcised hogs mount their sows.'

'Why on earth doesn't she just tell the swine some lie and get shot of him?'

'(Herr Maus releases the girl's arm but tightens his hold on her neck. He is no longer laughing.)

KARL: (Wearily.) Then you leave me no alternative but to show you what I mean . . .

(Herr Maus drags the girl on her knees further into the room, forces her head down to the floor, squats behind her, lifts up her dress, jerks her knickers down to her knees and holds her in an iron grip while he gropes one-handed on the rickety table.)

MARIE-SOPHIE: (In a muffled voice.) Karl, I'll scream, I can't breathe.

KARL: Our name is Herr Maus; scream all you like – it's a great pleasure for us to scream with a contemptible little sow like you!

(The girl cries out. Herr Maus bellows. The shadow rages round the room like fire in a storm, the wardrobe shivers and shakes.)

VOICE IN THE WARDROBE: For God's sake, leave her alone!

KARL: Shut your mouth! We made a deal and it stands!

(Herr Maus gives a low whistle, he's found what he was looking for – it glitters in his hand as he bends forwards and brandishes it in front of the girl's eyes.)

KARL: It's shaped something like this, isn't it?

(The girl's dilated pupils reflect a corkscrew jutting from Herr Maus's powerful fist.)

MARIE-SOPHIE: NO!'

'No! To hell with you and your sickening story! I'm off!'

'Don't go, please? Don't leave me alone with Karl Maus and my mother. Please. Stay with me until the horror is over; I can't bear it alone.'

'Promise me you'll get it over with as quickly as possible and you won't wallow in the gory details, and I'll stay. Do you promise?'

'Yes. My God, I'm not doing this for fun. I have to describe everything as it happened or the story won't be true and the follow-up will be absurd.'

'Give me the truth, then. I'm listening.'

'(Herr Maus looks from the girl to the corkscrew with an expression of astonishment.)

KARL: What are you saying? I was always given to understand that pig's pricks were twisted like their tails. Perhaps you couldn't feel it properly when the hook-nose stuck it up you; perhaps this will help refresh your memory.

(Herr Maus raises the corkscrew aloft behind the girl – she faints and slumps to the floor. Herr Maus loosens his grip on the girl's neck, examines her deathly pale face and listens for her breathing. After a long interval the girl regains consciousness.)

MARIE-SOPHIE: (In a cold, neutral voice.) Yes, it was twisted like a corkscrew, a pig's tail, a narwhal's tusk.

(Herr Maus flings the corkscrew away with an expression of disgust. The girl is momentarily relieved. Herr Maus looks at her and is moved to tears.)

KARL: My child! Your mother's lap – your most holy shrine – has been defiled and you can't even see it. As it is written in verse twenty-three: "Beware of those who, abetted by the urging of the flesh, promise you a share in the Father, for they are liars and fornicators, spawn of the serpent Leviathan, who begot them upon himself in the outermost darkness. With the snares of lust they will strike the eyes from your souls: you shall not see, nor shall you be seen".

(Crazed with fear, the girl struggles to rise to her feet but Herr Maus presses a fist between her shoulder blades and leans all his weight on it.)

KARL: But despair not, for there is a chance of salvation for those who have been defiled.

(Herr Maus unbuttons his flies with his free hand.)

KARL: If a just man steps forth and touches the soul-blinded in the same manner as the tempter, but with the word of God on his lips, he will be able to direct the Father's eye towards the defiled one; and His divine gaze will raise up the sinner.

(Herr Maus sighs and pulls out his penis.)

KARL: And here comes the one who is prepared to sacrifice himself for you, my child.

(Herr Maus stiffens the penis in his hand.)

KARL: He is dumb, this poor wretch, so I'll have to twitter his prayers for him. (Panting.) Our Father, which art in heaven . . .

(Herr Maus pushes his penis against the girl's dry crotch.)

KARL: . . . hallowed be thy name . . .

(He hesitates, lowers his head and addresses his penis solicitously.)

KARL: No, damn it if I'll soil you in that pig's outpourings.

(Herr Maus moves his penis up an inch and jabs it into the girl.)

(The girl screams.)'

14

Up from the road starts Coal-black John
Calls to young Lily so fair:
O, come my dear, let us be joined
Together in my black lair!

My maidenhead you never will get.
Tra-la lalla-la.
A mantle will cover it when I am dead.
Tra-la lalla-la.

But the churl he had two heavy hands,
He caught Lily fast, said he:
Coal-black gets what Coal-black wants,
My wench. Not a word said she.

My maidenhead you never will get.
Tra-la lalla-la.
Darkness will swallow it when I am dead.
Tra-la lalla-la.

She's turned into a nimble hind
Fled to the woods away,
He's taken the shape of a cruel hound
And snatched her as his prey.

My maidenhead you never will get.
Tra-la lalla-la.

The soil will sully it when I am dead.
Tra-la lalla-la.

In coal-grey boots to his forest tower
Strides John at a furious pace,
Blackened with blood, with a lily flower
Fading in his embrace.

My maidenhead you never will get.
Tra-la lalla-la.
'Twill glut the worms when I am dead.
Tra-la lalla-la.

'Tra-la lalla-la, tra-la lalla-la. Marie-Sophie pulled down her dress and held the skirt tight against her lap.

She wanted to get out, out, out, she's turned into a nimble hind. Karl had got to his feet but though she was looking right at him, meeting his eye as he stood with a glazed expression struggling to pull his damned trousers up his hairless legs, she didn't see him, tra-la lalla-la; where he should have been there was nothing but a dark stain, and when he cleared his throat with a low rattle she didn't wait for more but tore open the door and fled out on to the landing. The man must be crazy if he thought she was going to listen to his bloody whining after he had raped her.

Marie-Sophie raced down the stairs, trying to tidy her hair, button her cardigan, keep her footing and wipe the sweat from her neck as she went; there was muttering behind every door: We told you so, yes, you should have listened to us. When she reached the front door she turned round and yelled back: Why didn't you do something? The chorus of mutterers retreated from the doors and scattered to their former occupations: one listened to a speech on the wireless, another checked on the dough on the kitchen worktop, the third continued his shaving; so it goes. In a corner by the staircase four children were engrossed in playing with a mouse in a chocolate box, turning it over and over so wall became floor, became ceiling, became wall, and listening absorbed to the rodent's pathetic squeaking as it scrabbled around in the darkness. At Marie-Sophie's yell, the children glanced up quickly from their game and looked her carefully up and down. Tears welled in Marie-Sophie's eyes and she groped behind her for the door-handle; she wasn't going to cry in front of these children. The eldest, a fair-haired girl with a hare-lip and dark brows, left the group and came over with her hand outstretched: Why are you crying? Marie-Sophie: I'm not crying. A lisping boy at mouse-play: Yes, you *are* crying! Marie-Sophie: (in a choked voice) I'm not! Lisping boy: You *are*, my sister says so! Marie-Sophie began to weep. The girl hushed the boy, stood on tiptoe and patted her cheek: You've only yourself to blame for going up to his room. Her tone was cold; Marie-Sophie recognised in it the voice of the old lady who lived on the floor below Karl. She gripped the girl's arm hard, twisted it and whispered so the other children wouldn't hear: Your time will come, little girl! She raised her free hand to strike: And give your granny this from me! The girl parried the blow before it struck her pale cheek: (low) It's already come. Marie-Sophie lowered her hand: I'm sorry? But the girl tore herself away and darted back to her playmates. The children stuck out their tongues and pulled faces: Coal-black gets what Coal-black wants, tra-la lalla-la, Coal-black gets what Coal-black wants, tra-la lalla-la. The mouse in the chocolate box squeaked.

Marie-Sophie stumbled over the threshold, out into the street where the daylight hurt her eyes: was it still light? Surely night had fallen while she was with Karl. Could daylight really endure what he had done to her? A deed so wicked that the sun ought to have fled over the horizon. Marie-Sophie longed for night.

Dear God, grant me night, if it's in Your power to call down darkness over this hole of a town, grant me a black sky to hide me on the way home; on a grey day like this there are no shadows for a dishonoured girl to hide herself in. Grant me pitch-darkness so I can get back to the guesthouse unseen. Please say for Marie-Sophie: Let there be night! Amen.

She bit her lip and waited for an answer.

From the second floor of the house came a whimpering – Karl was hanging out of the window like an obsolete flag: Marie-Sophie, come back, I still love you.

The sun came out from behind a cloud; the clip in the girl's hair sparkled, her yellow cardigan glowed, the roses on her dress bloomed, her shoe-buckles gleamed. Marie-Sophie radiated light like a jewel on a rubbish tip and she paled with fury: Karl had defiled her, nature had betrayed her, and now the Lord had scorned her simple prayer.

— The devil take you, if he hasn't already got you!

— But Marie-Sophie, I love you!'

'That was then!'

'Her heart clenched like a fist, she started running along the street: she was late, the cook would kill her: What are you thinking of, girl! Then she would say . . . no, she couldn't tell anyone what Karl had done . . . yes, the cook would understand her, she had seen it all, that woman. She would undoubtedly hug her and stroke her hair: My dear child, there, there! And shoo away the waiter and the boy. Then she'd lead her by the hand up to their rooms and draw a hot bath for her: There now, scrub that filth off you; look, I'll put some of my bath-salts in and afterwards your body will be as pure as your heart, dearie! Meanwhile the men would hover down in reception; speechless over what had happened, they would plot with furtive eyes and gestures of the hands to teach Karl a lesson he wouldn't forget in a hurry. Yes, that's how it would be when she found her way back into the embrace of her workmates, her friends, at Gasthof Vrieslander.

It took all the girl's efforts to make herself invisible. It was as if the townspeople had been released from a spell, cast off their customary cold indifference and been filled with a hysterical love for their fellow men. They stood alert on every pavement, acted like fellow citizens, paraded themselves and noticed others, raised their hats, nodded their heads, shook hands, and candidly discussed the chicken in one another's pots. Some were plucked: No, really? Do you roast it, then, and get a good crispy skin? Others were skinned: Yes, that's how I like it! That's the usual way. Or seared: Really? Do you joint it and boil it in a broth with vegetables and black pudding? When they had finished these ingenuous exchanges, people parted with a handshake: Do give my regards to your husband and remind him about this evening's meeting. Or: I do hope your wife's earache gets better. And in passing: Any news of your son? No? Yes, those boys are lazy about writing home. Goodbye, madam! – Goodbye, sir!

Marie-Sophie hugged the walls and skulked in alleyways whenever she thought she spotted a guesthouse regular among the passers-by, reasoning that if she neither looked at nor listened to the people she met, they wouldn't be able to see or hear her.

Go away, I want to go home, to bed, I want to sleep, you don't exist, I don't want to be here, go away, I want to sleep, I don't exist, tra-la lalla-la, fading in his embrace, tra-la lalla-la.

She half ran, paused, broke into a run again, waited, went on, stopped, and dashed along, like an avant-garde dancer in a newsreel she had seen with Karl in the early days of their courtship: the poor man had flung himself from pillar to post, crouched down and jerked to and fro to the accompaniment of clashing cymbals, dustbin lids, pots and pans, or whatever it was that the musicians banged to make such a cacophony. The man was dressed in light-coloured overalls with a pointed hat on his head, while on his feet he wore big shoes that hindered his movements. At the end of the news item he was asked what the performance was supposed to represent and he had replied, still sweaty and grimacing from his efforts: This is Germany today. The audience had collapsed with laughter; God, she and Karl had thought they'd never be able to stop laughing. The poof's reply – for what else could he be with his face all made up like that? – had become a saying with her and Karl; every time they saw something absurd they had only to catch each other's eye and repeat the first three words: This is Germany! to collapse into helpless giggles. Oh, oh, oh, I'll die laughing: if only all newsreels were this good, ha, we wouldn't need any Hollywoodstadt.

I'm Germany today, tra-la lalla-la, at a furious pace, tra-la lalla-la.

Marie-Sophie didn't slow her frantic pace until she reached Flower Street, where, on rounding the corner, she discovered that the street had narrowed at the other end until only a stick-figure could have squeezed through and instead of the guesthouse appearing on the far side of the square, all that could be glimpsed was a sliver of its corner. Flower Street had been transformed from earlier that day: doors had opened in the grey walls, above which red lamps illuminated the sides of the houses, and the purple roofs leaned in to meet in the middle, shutting off the street over the girl's head.

I'll make it through, I'm like a cat, I was like a kitten when I was a little girl, in and out of all the windows, under the sofas and fences; the cook says I'm nothing but skin and bone: You've no flesh on you at all, my girl, what are men supposed to grab hold of if there's nothing on your bones? But I don't care, I'm glad: being a waif will come in useful now. The pain's the same whether the body's large or small, but that bastard Karl would have hurt me even more if there had been more of me. I'll get through.

She wrapped her cardigan tighter around her and set off: figures, the like of which she had never dreamed of, stepped out on to the pavement and screwed up their eyes as the fresh air touched their pinched faces, like cats when someone blows in their eyes. God, they were as grotesque on the outside as she felt on the inside. A man with a gigantic head stretched his calloused paws out of a doorway, hooked his deformed fingernails into a crack in the pavement and dragged himself puffing and blowing over the threshold.'

'Is there no end to this freak show? What happened when she got home, hmm? How was your poor father?'

'Try to control yourself; she's in a mental state that's hard to describe. I'm doing my best!'

'Tch!'

'Marie-Sophie was about to make a detour round the huge-headed cripple when he gave an almighty shriek and hurtled out on to the pavement where he landed right by her feet and started rubbing his behind. From inside the house came a whisper.

— This is my doorway, you freak!

Big-head shook his fist in the direction of the whisper and rumbled some ugly curse about what gave her, a woman who didn't even own her own crack, the right to shoot her mouth off?

A head and foot appeared in the doorway.

— Don't you try and talk dirty to me, old man; you know who this girl's protector is?

Marie-Sophie was taken aback: were they whispering about her? The whispering couldn't refer to the face and foot in the doorway, they didn't belong to a girl as she understood the word: the gaunt face was covered in pale powder and garish rouge, the varicose foot stretched a silver shoe with a rapier heel. No, a girl was a young woman, someone aged no more than twenty like herself.

— My good madam! Could you spare a trifle for an old soldier?

The girl yelped when the cripple pinched her knee.

— Excuse me, I didn't mean to frighten you, but with the way I look I've come to expect people to back off. I lost my legs in the last war and now I can't take part in this one. Does madam have a small coin she could spare?

Marie-Sophie stared at the begging head: how could she have failed to notice this creature before? Kükenstadt was so small that a man who looked as if he had been drawn by a five-year-old ought surely to be the town freak.

— Change?

The cripple suddenly struck his brow.

— I mean, madam knows how this sort of business goes, doesn't she? I hold out my hand – looking mighty hungry – and beg for alms from your purse. You put a little something in my hand, averting your face – I understand and don't take it personally – and continue on your way. You feel better – you've been called madam and given God's blessing – and I've now got enough for meat stew or a pilsner, depending on how generous madam has been. Shall we try again?

The girl didn't answer. Around the beggar's neck was a sweat-stained priest's ruff: now she was sure she had seen the man somewhere before.

He flushed.

— Ah, you're wondering why this unfortunate war hero should be so attired. There's no time for my life-story, hmm hmm, but I suppose I was an army chaplain, God's servant on the Western Front; because even there men had need of their crucified Jesus when the going got tough. Yes, many're the last rites I've administered to the blown-up bodies of God's children with this hand that now patiently awaits your alms.

The beggar spread out his fingers and before Marie-Sophie knew it she had slipped him a coin.

A hoarse voice swept down the narrow street like a cloud of dust on an autumn morning:

— A war hero with healing hands?

A shorn-headed woman in a scarlet dress stood on the pavement diagonally opposite them, sucking on a cigarillo through a foot-long holder.

— There can be no doubting the priestling's love of the truth . . .

The cripple flinched and hung his head. Crop-hair jerked her head and breathed out the words in a stream of blue tobacco smoke.

— You should tell your benefactress about the acts of charity you carried out with your feet; it would be a laugh to see her reward you for those good deeds.

The legless man clenched his fist around the coin and darted pleading eyes at Marie-Sophie. She looked in bewilderment from the man to the head in the doorway, receiving a stare as sharp as the stiletto that had driven the man howling from the house.

— Don't waste your pity on a child-killer.

The girl was shocked. The accused hid his face and whined:

— Don't listen to them.

But Marie-Sophie knew better: she had devoured an article about the child-killer Moritz Weiss in the weekly magazine *UHU*. The magazine was a treasure trove of information, publishing lace patterns alongside blueprints for tanks, and she was allowed to read it at the house of the kind woman next door, in return for helping with the housework.

At first she hadn't been allowed to read the unsuitable pages, the articles about corruption, degeneracy, crimes that were common in the old republic. The kind woman kept a close eye on her reading and said firmly: "Turn over!" every time Marie-Sophie came to them. Either the woman knew all the issues off by heart or else she sensed whenever the next spread contained a picture of a murderer, pervert or corrupt politician. It didn't matter whether she was somewhere else in the house at the time or standing out on the steps chatting to the postman; at the very second, the very instant the girl touched the corner of the page her voice would ring out: "Turn over, two pages, thank you!"

But when Marie-Sophie began to leaf through the paper backwards, upside down and at every other imaginable angle to fool the woman, and everything the woman said was punctuated with the exclamation: "Turn over!", she gave up on the girl and after some debate they agreed that she was old enough to learn about the shady side of life.

Which was precisely where Moritz "Bloodfoot" Weiss belonged.

* * *

"Bloodfoot" Found!
— Berliners celebrate after years in the shadow of child-killings.

Moritz Weiss was a trainee priest and child-killer, and no different from others of that ilk: those who knew him were unanimous in declaring that he had a heart of gold. He was abstemious in his intake of alcohol and tobacco, a volunteer at the church soup kitchen and a true friend to the older members of the parish. He worked hard at his theological studies – and if he had understood Nietzsche it's not inconceivable that he would have made it to bishop.

No one could have dreamed that Moritz Weiss, that dear chap with the big head, was the scourge of Berlin's little children, none other than "Bloodfoot" himself.'

'Are you sure you want to hear the story of Bloodfoot?'

'What do you think I am?'

'Then I'll leave it out.'

'Of course I want to hear it, isn't everyone obsessed with murderers nowadays?'

'Have you ever shaken hands with a murderer?'

'No, but I've shaken hands with an author.'

'Apparently that doesn't have the same cachet.'

'Really?'

'So I'm told.'

'Make me better acquainted with Bloodfoot then, and be quick about it!'

'Bloodfoot went about his child murders in the following way: he would sneak into the sacristy of the university chapel in broad daylight, "borrow" a priest's habit and hasten to the scene of the killing, one of Berlin's numerous public parks.

There he would hide in the bushes and spy out his small victims.

If an unfortunate nanny took her eyes off the little charge that she had promised to guard with her life, the monster Moritz Weiss would creep over the lawn to where the innocent victim sat wondering at creation and deliver a kick to its soft skull. Afterwards the murderer would dive into the dense undergrowth and wait for the nanny to return and find the infant, the crushed apple of some unknown parents' eye, whose name he would learn from the evening papers.

The nannies' shrieks of horror sounded like holy music to Bloodfoot's ears; just so must Mary have cried out when her Son committed his spirit to the Father on the cross. The comparison was not wholly absurd: the only sound the infants emitted when the heavy foot smashed into the back of their skull was a mournful sigh.

After the murders, Moritz Weiss savoured the echo of the grown-ups' wails, which gave him peace of mind and enabled him to carry out his daily tasks in the service of the church of the suffering mother of Christ. But, as is the nature of echoes, the propitiatory sounds would gradually die away. And the trainee priest would be driven to don his bloodfoot once more.

Weeks became months became years; the number of victims rose to twelve.

The authorities were helpless in the face of this wave of killings: conventional policing methods, increased surveillance wherever the murderer was thought likely to strike, and countless arrests as a result of information from mediums and detective novelists, who saw in the tragedy a golden opportunity to promote themselves and their work, had not furthered the investigation one iota.

The child-killer, who had been christened Bloodfoot, remained at large in Berlin and no one could do a thing about it.

Then one day a street urchin, on the prowl for purses in the park, saw a scrap of paper fall from the trouser leg of a clergyman who was passing through his hunting ground, a path that wound along beside the park wall. Since the boy was a pickpocket – i.e. he relieved his fellow citizens of the loose change that weighed them down on their walks – he had no interest in things people shed of their own accord.

He picked up the scrap from the path, and although it was nothing but a yellowing newspaper cutting, he set off in pursuit of the cassock-clad figure, waving the paper and shouting: "Mister! Mister! You dropped something!" But when the gentleman failed to acknowledge the boy's call and instead half ran across the playground, the boy was hurt and couldn't be bothered to chase him any further.

— That's what comes of being a pickpocket. No one trusts us; we're even feared by those who should have a better understanding of human failings than most. But I suppose it's like that in all walks of life: the pros and cons cancel each other out.

Muttering something along these lines to himself, the street urchin smoothed out the cutting. He had resolved to throw it away, since he'd had bad experiences of being caught in possession of printed matter that didn't concern him, but first he meant to read it.

He was brought up short: the cutting was a seven-month-old police notice warning people to keep a close eye on their children as a full moon was due and psychiatrists believed this increased the likelihood that Bloodfoot would go out on the prowl.

The street urchin spat on the notice, crumpled it up and stuck it in his pocket. He knew the park like the back of his hand and knew that the clergyman couldn't have gone far; if the man turned out to be the wolf in priest's clothing that he suspected then the boy was in luck: Bloodfoot happened to be wanted by more than just the department of criminal investigation.

When the detectives' exhaustive search for Bloodfoot began to have an adverse impact on Berlin's more normal criminal activities, Black Max, king of the underworld, had taken matters into his own hands and sent out word among his associates that whoever delivered the child-killer into his hands would not go unrewarded – and since Black Max was in a position to pity that poor Jew boy Nelson Rockefeller, it's clear that this offer was not to be sniffed at.

The boy combed the park as deftly as he did the back pockets of the bourgeoisie, and it wasn't long before he spotted the priest. And the priest was not behaving in a manner befitting a clergyman; he was crouching behind a hedge, spying on the children.

Everything happened very fast.

The street urchin whistled to the other pickpockets in the park, the pickpockets whispered the news in the ears of the burglars, the burglars talked to the whores, the whores nudged the pimps, the pimps got in touch with the book-keepers, the book-keepers passed on the message to the managing director of the casinos, the managing director of the casinos rang the director of the national bank, and the director broke off his meeting with the finance minister to go and see the man who, according to the Communists, held Germany in the palm of his hand.

Black Max was reclining on a massage table at his headquarters beneath the Reichstag building, listening to one of his catamites reading the latest issue of the adventures of Sexton Blake while the other six smoothed his flesh with Assyrian oils.

The king of crime was dreaming about what would happen if the detective came to Berlin and they clashed. He himself would fight like a son of a bitch, Blake nobly, and both with great resourcefulness.

— Why isn't life like the storybooks?

He murmured in mellow tones under the boys' agile hands and a vivid image of the English detective's physique.

— The German police are useless, it doesn't seem to matter how much money I ply the milksops with; they couldn't find a naughty child if they were pregnant with it.

It's not fair that men like Sexton Blake should be fictional, not fair to the public or to me. People would feel better if they knew a man like that existed in real life, and I would have a worthy adversary to spar with.

Black Max slipped into his favourite daydream:

It was a dark and stormy night, with thunder and lightning. Black Max and Blake stood face to face on the edge of the Reichstag roof, revolvers in hand. They pulled their triggers simultaneously, but neither gun fired a shot. Both laughed sardonically, flung down their weapons and began to wrestle. Sexton Blake used the oriental method of fighting known as jiu-jitsu while Black Max fought like a termagant, biting and scratching for all he was worth.

The battle could only have one outcome.

Blake drove Black Max to the very edge of the roof with well-aimed kicks and hand-chops, and as Black Max teetered on the brink Blake said: "You shall commit no more evil deeds; tomorrow mankind will waken to a new dawn, to a new world in which white slavery will be as unthinkable as the idea that a scoundrel like you should ever have walked this earth!"

To which Black Max instantly retorted: "Aren't you stuck in a role, my dear Sexton? Aren't you confusing me with the crime-queen Stella? I've never invested in women – boys are more my thing!" Then, with the last of his strength, he seized Blake and dragged him with him in his fall.

On the way down they exchanged a lascivious kiss.'

'Have you forgotten about Marie-Sophie in all this nonsense? Wasn't she rushing home to Gasthof Vrieslander?'

'You wanted to hear the story of Bloodfoot, so shut up and listen!'

'I thought there would be more to it than this.'

'Marie-Sophie shook her head; the street had been closing in while she recalled the story of Bloodfoot: what on earth was she thinking? She didn't want to get stuck in this part of the magazine, she wanted to turn the page, turn the page, turn the page; but however hard she concentrated, the kind woman's voice would not reach out to her across time. She had to get out of the street and the story of Bloodfoot before the story finished and she became trapped there; the gap between the gables was now so narrow that Big-head and the crop-haired prostitute – she couldn't be anything else, the girl saw that now – were standing side by side in front of Marie-Sophie.

— I've got to go!

Marie-Sophie's voice was choked with tears.

— I don't belong here.

They stared through the girl.

— I'm not one of you.

A hand was laid on her shoulder.

— We know that.

The deep voice raised the hairs on the back of Marie-Sophie's neck.

The speaker stepped forward.

He was a dwarfish man of middle age, dressed in a white suit and lilac shirt, with a hand-painted silk tie round his neck and crocodile-skin moccasins on his feet; in his arms he held a poodle and he was dusting imaginary dandruff from the animal's curly, pink-dyed pelt.

The girl let out a gasp: it was none other than Black Max himself.

— Do you think you might allow us to finish our story?

He tapped his nose with a ring-bedecked little finger.

— Then you can do as you like . . .

The crime lord screwed up his eyes.'

'See! Everyone has the right to have their story told to the end.'

'Black Max's eyes widened when the director of the central bank brought him the news that the child-killer had been found. He sprang to his feet on the massage table and stood there with legs apart, penis erect and fist clenched in the air, shouting in his nakedness:

— I was once a child and it was fun; I was cuddled and coddled, I was bathed and had my botty powdered, I was petted and praised, I was given a flag to wave on high days and holidays and I was spanked until I developed a taste for it.

Children and child-lovers of this world! I owe you a debt!

The king of the underworld did not make idle promises.

The street urchin had started up a conversation with the "priest" and delayed him by asking him to teach him the children's hymn "O Jesus best of brothers". And although the lines of the verse wrenched at Moritz Weiss's heart, he was so afraid of giving away the reason for his presence in the park that he didn't dare do anything but give the rascal a Sunday-school lesson then and there.

So you could say that the child-killer Moritz "Bloodfoot" Weiss was almost relieved when Black Max's henchmen came up behind him and clamped a chloroform-soaked cloth over his nose and mouth as he was quavering the second verse of the hymn in duet with the boy for the ninety-third time.

They carried him discreetly from the park, put him in a fetid storeroom in the city sewer system and trussed him up like a pig.

There he was left to stew while Black Max thought up his sentence.

* * *

Black Max squinted up at Marie-Sophie between her breasts; the gables of the houses thrust them ever closer together until the poodle was squirming against her belly; they had come to the closure of the story, the closure of the street . . .

— And what do you think I did?

Black Max smiled.

— It's none of her business.

The girl flinched as Bloodfoot's tepid breath filtered through her dress and cooled on her thigh. The head in the doorway hissed:

— Let Maximilian Schwartz be the judge of that!

Crop-hair smacked the cripple on the skull.

— The papers left out one detail, did you know that?

Marie-Sophie didn't want to know and shook her head.

But Black Max pretended not to understand and continued:

— First he was stripped – I wanted a photo of the scum in his birthday suit – and what do you think came to light? He had collected the newspaper cuttings and cobbled them together into underclothes – the brute positively rustled as he murdered the tiny tots.

Well, I thought that since he was so attached to these news announcements he could hardly be satisfied just by wearing them next to his skin, so what do you think I did?

Black Max gave Marie-Sophie's bosom a triumphant look. She closed her eyes and tried to think about something nice instead. He laughed:

— I had the whole lot stuffed up his arse!

The prostitutes tittered. The poodle barked. Moritz Weiss howled.

— After that he was dressed in his sheep's clothing again and the boys took him to the park where they cut off his legs and hung them in a tree over his head. The police found him later that night after an anonymous tip-off.

— Dead, don't forget!

Bloodfoot's face was right by the girl's thigh and he spat the words out of the corner of his mouth.

— You killed me, you bastards!

Black Max forced his foot between the girl and the murderer and stamped on the swollen stump where Bloodfoot's left leg had been. The cripple whimpered:

— I had a right to a fair trial.

— Like the children?

Came a whisper from the doorway.

— Like the children?

Echoed Crop-hair.

The atmosphere in the street grew fraught, and Marie-Sophie would have witnessed a second execution of Moritz Weiss – whores are resourceful, they would have found some way to perform in the cramped conditions – if Maximilian Schwartz, better known as Black Max, hadn't given them a sign to shut up.

A film of sad world-weariness formed over the yellow eyes of Berlin's crime lord; he stroked the poodle thoughtfully before looking up, taking a light hold of the knot of his tie and saying softly:

— Didn't we all have a right to a fair trial?

Without waiting for an answer Black Max jutted his jaw and loosened his tie and the button of his collar so the slit in his throat gaped at the girl.

His voice descended to a mocking rattle.

— I demand a trial for myself and my dog.

Black Max held up the dog; across its middle lay a deep tyre mark.

— I want a trial!

The wig slipped off the head in the doorway; the skull was smashed, showing a glimpse of brains.

— So do I!

Crop-hair pulled up her dress; her belly was covered with stab wounds.

— Can I join in?

The street urchin leaned out of a window above them, noseless and waving his genitals.

— And me? I was raped.

Whispered Marie-Sophie, who had begun to assume that she would spend the rest of eternity with these people. Moritz Weiss gave an ear-splitting screech:

— Raped? You were lucky, look at me!

Crop-hair slapped his face and stroked the girl's cheek with the same sweep of her hand.

— No, love! You don't belong here – Maximilian said you could go.

Black Max nodded; the story was over.

The street closed up.

For a moment Marie-Sophie felt like a dried lily, pressed in a book.

Marie-Sophie was alone; Black Max and Moritz Weiss had vanished along with the whores and the street urchin. She drew a deep breath.

The street was a magnificent boulevard leading to a spacious square.

On the other side of the square stood a grand hotel:

Gasthof Vrieslander.'

15

'Marie-Sophie set off across the square towards Gasthof Vrieslander, hoping she wouldn't meet anybody, that no one would see her arrive, that everyone in the guesthouse would be too busy shirking their duties in the owner and Inhaberin's absence. She wanted to slip up to her room unseen and lock herself in, then wash and have a good cry in the powerful shower – so no one would hear a thing.

She prayed that the owner and Inhaberin were still on their egg-jaunt; the woman was quite capable of behaving like a reformed prostitute and he was about as convincing in his morality as a lecherous priest.

Marie-Sophie hurried past the statue of the chick, darting it a murderous look.

— I'll throttle you if you squeak: "Can I see?"

But it wouldn't have mattered if the chick cheeped or squeaked; all eyes rested on her, she was on everyone's lips: "There goes that Maya-Sof! Look how the shame clings to her like a drunken shadow . . . So it's true what they say about girls who allow themselves to be raped . . ."

The imagined gossip weighed the girl down and she dragged her feet the last steps to Gasthof Vrieslander, bowed beneath her shame. The guesthouse door stood open, the gloomy reception area awaited within and beyond it the stairs – the top steps vanishing into darkness.

Marie-Sophie caught her breath, bending over, resting her hands on her thighs and gathering strength for the final sprint up to the attic. An out-of-towner sat at one of the tables, eating smoked *wurst* from the point of his knife. He looked shiftily at the girl and began to pack up his picnic.

She almost smiled: the Inhaberin and the owner were not back. The woman usually ordered her husband to order the servant boy to order anyone who didn't buy their refreshments from the guesthouse to clear off the pavement. The Inhaberin was convinced they were uncouth farmers to a man and that it was down to her to teach them city manners – they couldn't tell the difference between quality pavement-café furniture and fence-posts: "How would they like it if we marched our guests into the countryside and sat them down on the fences around their miserable hovels?" But Marie-Sophie had more important things on her mind than some unknown peasant's picnic: in a poky garret on the second floor of a house on Spülwasserstrasse was a man who loved her; she needed to wash off that love.

The girl picked up her skirt and dashed into the guesthouse, looking neither right nor left, passing straight through reception and up the stairs where she ran slap into old Tomas. She turned her face to the wall and side-stepped so the old man could pass: she had nothing to say to this ally of Karl's. He seized her by the shoulders and cried as quietly as he could: "God, is shocked, God, is shocked!"

Marie-Sophie tore herself free: she couldn't care less about the state of the old man's deity. It served the old fool right for choosing a god in his own image.

She sprang up the stairs but things got no better on the landing: the waiter and the servant boy were standing by the door of room twenty-three, shaking with suppressed emotion; the former was in a good way to gnawing off his own knuckles, the latter was bouncing up and down like a piston.

Something dreadful had happened in the priest's hole.

— Poor invalid!

Before the tears could fill the girl's eyes the old man burst on to the landing, crying in the same low voice: "She's back! She's here!" And crashed into the girl who was thrown into the arms of the servant boy who was flung backwards on to the waiter who grabbed the doorhandle to brace himself against the blow.

The door flew open and they tumbled into the room in a heap: the

THINE EYES DID SEE MY SUBSTANCE 149

cook was sitting on the bed, where one of the two men was standing over her, watching her cry.'

'What an ugly shambles!'

'Yes, my mother wasn't given much peace to recover after what that scum Karl Maus did to her.'

'But surely this farce is a bit over the top?'

'To tell the truth, I would have preferred it if the story had featured a more solemn, momentous homecoming, but this is how it was; she was fated to think more about the invalid than about herself on the day of all days when she alone deserved people's undivided sympathy.'

'I feel for her.'

'Marie-Sophie clawed her way out of the heap: from the priest's hole came a stream of invective which was answered by the gnashing of teeth.

The invalid wasn't dead, then.

The girl leapt to her feet, tidied her clothes with quick movements of her hands, wiped the mask of humiliation from her face and stormed to the door of the secret compartment.

The cook turned purple with rage when she caught sight of her:

— There she is! Oh, *mein Gott*, talk to her, not me, she's confused him, she's corrupted him . . .

The man blocked Marie-Sophie's path, silenced the cook and gestured to the three men on the floor to get up at once and take her outside. He waited in silence while the servant boy and waiter helped the cook from the room, and once the door had closed behind old Tomas who brought up the rear, trying to cheer the woman up with a piece of scandal that was transparently invented on the spur of the moment, the man stepped aside and let the girl into the priest's hole. The invalid seemed to have slid out of bed; he was writhing on the Armenian rug while the second of the two men tried in vain to grab hold of him. He wriggled from the man's grasp, naked and quick as a hare that has come to its senses after being flayed.

Marie-Sophie bent down to the man and whispered in his ear:

— Allow me: he's always so docile when I'm with him . . .

The man straightened up and thanked her with mock courtesy for bothering to drop by.

Pretending not to hear, the girl touched the invalid's shoulder and he calmed down; she laid a gentle hand on his arm and he stood up; she gave him a light push and he sank down on the bed; she held a cupped palm under his neck and he lay down; she spread the eider-down and cover over him and he closed his eyes.

She sat down on the bed beside the invalid, turned to the two men and saw that their anger had evaporated.

— What happened?

They glanced at one another, then told her that shortly after she had left the guesthouse the man – who we'll call "L—" – well, he'd woken up and started behaving in a threatening manner; he was raving, or so the woman who was sitting with him thought, but she soon began to suspect that he was playing with her because every time she approached him he pretended to be asleep, but the moment she took her eyes off him he stared at her and pointed to his nether regions – crudely, she thought. Well, she gave him an earful, she said; told him he'd better behave if he didn't want the rug pulled out from under his feet; she'd met men a darned sight stranger than him in her time. Does the woman have a theatrical background, by any chance?

Er, yes, you could call it that. Marie-Sophie testified to the cook's culinary work in the service of opera.

The two men continued: it had finally dawned on the woman that L— needed to relieve himself and was asking her to help him, but she told the man that he had a nerve: all she had been asked to do was sit with him for a little while; she had no intention of watching him do his business, he could perfectly well hold it in until that silly girl came back – yes, that's what she called you – only then he managed to reach down to the chamber-pot under the bed . . .'

'Look, dear, haven't we had enough scatology in this story already?'

'No, no, this is only the beginning . . .'

'Marie-Sophie shuddered; she could hardly imagine that the invalid would do something as crude as the two men's account seemed to imply. Anyway, L— had no sooner got his hands on the chamber-pot than he began to play on it and the woman thought her last hour had come; the man ran his fingers around the rim and tapped it on the side making alternate humming and clinking sounds, resulting in such a blasphony that the woman blushed to the roots of her hair, and when he raised his voice in a hypnotic drone she was powerless with shame; she'd never heard such a croaking before.

The two men paused in their tale and asked Marie-Sophie whether L— had ever sung to her. And if so, what?

The girl shook her head: what was going on? What did it matter if this man sang and played on his potty? Who was he, anyway?

They ignored her questions: the man had contrived with his playing to hypnotise the woman into a strange state in which the room had spun before her eyes for a good while and once that nonsense was over she says she imagined she was in a nursery; she was walking down the room with a milk jug in hand, but every cradle held a chamber-pot and in every chamber-pot was a turd, and every turd was bawling like a baby . . .'

'You're not right in the head.'

'Come on, it's all symbolic . . .'

'I don't think I care for symbolism of that sort.'

'The cook's adventures were making Marie-Sophie feel ill: what did the two men mean by this detailed recounting of her nonsense? The woman had clearly committed some dreadful misdemeanour and was trying to cover up for it with this ridiculous pack of lies. Once Marie-Sophie would have found it funny, but after what had happened to her that day she had no stomach for listening to other people's cock-ups. She wanted to be alone with the invalid.

The girl sighed.

— The cook's obviously had a peculiar experience, but I wouldn't call it exactly life-threatening—

She got no further. The two men interrupted her simultaneously: the woman had been so disgusted at this sight that the trance had worn off, and when she had recovered her senses and screamed at him to behave or she'd pull the rug out from under his feet, he had rolled out of bed and on to the floor in a trice, and there he was lying, clinging to the rug for dear life when we arrived to warn you that he's not safe here any longer.

The world went black before Marie-Sophie's eyes: what were the men saying? Were they punishing her for going out? Were they going to take the invalid away from her? Then who could she tell the thing that she couldn't tell anyone?

The two men prepared to leave: "We'll come for him after closing time; he must be ready to leave by then."

— Why?

She hid her face in her hands, peeping out at them through her fingers.

The men stared at her, saying they didn't understand her; she'd seemed happy enough to get away from him at lunchtime. Was there something she wasn't telling them about her relationship with L—?

Marie-Sophie sniffed and answered in a shaky voice:

— No, it's just that I'm worried he won't be able to cope with travelling, not in the state he's in. Can't he stay with me, with us here at the guesthouse, a tiny bit longer? I won't leave him again.

The two men conferred in whispers before telling the girl that it appeared someone had informed on him. She asked who in the world would be interested in hunting down a scarecrow like him? They answered that although the man in the bed gave the impression of being a half-mad skeleton who'd wrapped himself in skin for the sake of appearances, there were people in certain circles who believed he held the outcome of the war in his hands; they themselves hadn't a clue what it was that L— knew or was capable of, and though they were keen to find out, it was none of their business – their role was simply to ensure that he got out of the country alive, and that's what they meant to do.

Marie-Sophie smiled coldly: they talked to her as if she were an idiot; fine, she was perfectly capable of acting dumber than she really was.

— So you're saying he's supposed to change the course of world history with his potty-rattling?

But the two men saw nothing wrong with what the girl said. They

THINE EYES DID SEE MY SUBSTANCE 153

nodded gravely: perhaps this peculiar music was the key to world peace – anything was worth a try.

— I'll have to remember to pack his instrument when he leaves, then . . .

They agreed and left.

17.13. The invalid reaches out a hand and lays it on the back of the girl who is sitting beside him on the bed: he had listened to her conversation with the two men; she was on his side – that was good. The girl was funny; she'd given him the idea of fooling around with the chamber-pot when that woman was driving him crazy with her questions about their supposed love affair. Now the girl turned to him, but it was as if she didn't see him.

Who did she see?

Marie-Sophie scrutinises the invalid's face: was he looking at her? Where was the hand on her back heading? Perhaps he wasn't as helpless as she had believed?

Karl's image flickered over his face.

The girl tears his hand from her waist and spits out:

— You too!

The invalid wrinkles his brow: him too? Why was she yelling at him? What had happened to the amusing girl of that morning?

Marie-Sophie leaps up from the bed and moves as far into the corner by the door as she can get, pressing her face between the walls until the tip of her nose touches the innermost angle where they meet: God, what would she give for the walls to split ninety degrees, then she would be standing on a corner and could walk away, to somewhere far away.

But there, in the shadowy world of the corner, lurks Karl along with Herr Maus. Throwing out their arms, they mutter: "It's no ordinary vermin problem you've got at Gasthof Vrieslander."

The hallucination smacks Marie-Sophie's cheek with the back of its hand and she recoils into the priest's hole.

A strange sensation of weeping fills the invalid's breast. Fumbling for the girl, he catches hold of her skirt: sympathy, it was a long time since he had wept for anyone but himself, yet now he wanted to cry for this girl and for all those who, like him, had been robbed of sympathy by their enslavement.

— Leave me alone!

Marie-Sophie snatches her dress from his hand: where could she go? Nowhere! Where were the people who loved her? Nowhere!

The invalid watches the girl snuff out the light and sit down at the dressing table.

She looks at herself in the mirror.

— That's what you are: darkness in the darkness.

18.06. The invalid props himself up in bed, coughs and calls to the girl: "Come here . . ."

She doesn't react.

He sighs heavily; the girl's refusing herself sympathy, refusing to let him show her any sympathy . . .

18.57. Marie-Sophie listens to the invalid tossing and turning: when she first switched off the light, he had fumbled for her in the darkness; now he was asleep. She retches and weeps in turn.

19.43. The invalid opens his eyes a crack: the girl is still sitting at the mirror. The temperature's rising in the priest's hole and he realises that the moment is drawing near when he will be allowed to weep with her . . .

21.38. Marie-Sophie jumps to her feet. The heat in the compartment has become unbearable. She strips off her cardigan.

— Have they gone mad in the kitchen? God, they're burning the entire coal ration, they're going to kill me! Burn me like a whore . . .

The invalid watches the girl fling open the door and swing it back and forth to cool herself, but it's as if she's blowing on embers; the temperature in the compartment rises and she breathes in gasps.

— Christ, it's like a furnace; I'm sweating worse than a glass-blower . . .

She disappears from the compartment. He hears a heavy blow and swearing, then she comes storming back in, growling like a caged lion.

— Would you believe it, the bloody proprietor's only gone and nailed the window shut! I'm dying! This is killing me!

Marie-Sophie undoes the top button of her dress and wipes the sweat from her throat: the wallpaper creaks, the varnish on the furniture bubbles.

She gives the invalid a quick glance.

— You must be suffocating under those covers . . .

— I am.

The invalid answers the girl at normal pitch, but she doesn't have time to wonder at this – she's burning up – and she whips the boiling cover and eiderdown off him.

— There, that should make a difference . . .

But Marie-Sophie says no more, her impatience drains away when her gaze falls on the man: the invalid is as grotesque as a Romanesque statue of Christ, minus a cross and wearing a nappy instead of a loincloth.

She goes to the door, takes hold of the glowing handle and shuts it: "I was raped . . ."

A tear springs from the corner of her eye and she raises a finger to her eyelid.

Her fingernail gives off a spark.

The compartment burns up.'

16

My substance was not hid from thee,
when I was made in secret,
and curiously wrought in the lowest parts of the earth.

Thine eyes did see my substance,
yet being unperfect . . .

Psalms, 139:15–16

'Marie-Sophie rises from the ash heap by the door: the temperature in the priest's hole has dropped but the smoke from her body still hangs in the air after the burning.

She opens the false window and the veil of smoke is sucked out into the cool Parisian night of the painting: on the further bank of the Seine a young man is leaning against a lamppost, struggling to light a cigarette.

It's Karl.

She scratches his face off, scraping away the paint with the nail of her index finger until there's nothing left but brown canvas.

The clock in reception struck eleven, the sound of merrymaking rose from the dining room: the owner had returned and was jovially drinking toasts with his companions, who thanked him for the drink in a manly chorus.

Marie-Sophie roamed around the priest's hole, wringing her hands.
— What am I to do?

The invalid lay naked under a layer of ash, snoring. She sat down beside him and brushed the ash from his face and hands.

— I'm clean, it felt good to burn with you, but they're going to take you away from me, take you away, just when I want you with me for ever, even if you do snore like a pig – even though I once promised myself I'd never live with a man who snored.

She dusted the invalid's lips and he woke up. Her mouth turned down.

— Don't go? Where can you go? Do you have to go?

The invalid quietly hushed the girl but she couldn't control herself.

— If you are going, tell me everything: what are you running away from, will you come back? Tell me everything, I must know everything!

He sat up in bed, slung his thin bird's legs to the floor and she helped him on to his feet. He addressed her in a suffering voice.

— Where's my suitcase? There's a robe in my case, can I have it? I had a box too . . .

The girl opened the suitcase and found what he wanted, a midnight-blue robe dotted with silver stars, and he put it on carefully, sliding his arms slowly into the sleeves like a man who has recovered his dignity but isn't sure if he cares for it any longer.

— I'll show you all there is to see. The box, didn't you have it somewhere?

— It's here.

Marie-Sophie laid the box on the bed. It was a battered oval, an ornate pink hatbox, the lid marked: Dodgson & Tenniel – Hatters of England. He contemplated it fondly for a moment.

— Could you put it on the table over there?

The invalid gave a low sigh and pointed behind him to the dressing table. The girl moved the box to the table.

— Here?

— And would you please hang a cloth of some sort over the mirror? Thank you.

Marie-Sophie didn't really know how to behave: what had come over her invalid? He was an invalid no longer, no, he had the air of a surgeon in an operating theatre or a master of the dark arts in his laboratory, directing his acolytes around him. Yet it was only a few hours since they had burned together, melted into one being, in the scorching room. She huffed.

— Well, if that's the way he wants it, if he's going to pretend nothing's happened between us, then he's welcome; I'll expect no good from men from now on.

She covered the mirror with a towel, watching the invalid, or whatever he was, from out of the corner of her eye as he undid the white band that held the lid on the box. Muttering to himself in a language she didn't understand, he lifted off the lid. He cheered up the moment he saw the contents of the box, then bent and lifted out what appeared to Marie-Sophie to be a petticoat of salmon-pink silk. He called to her softly.

— Come here!

She came closer; he laid the silk cloth on the table beside the box and drew out another like it. The girl didn't like the look of this: was it underwear? Was he an unscrupulous black-marketeer? That would be a fine thing, to have nursed someone of that sort! She stood on tiptoe to get a better view over the man's shoulder. He unwrapped one silk cloth after another until a red lump the size of her forearm was revealed. She looked from the invalid – the man, the guest, or whatever she should call him now that he had changed – to that thing in the box and back again. His eyes shone with joy and after a brief silence he whispered over his shoulder in a choked voice.

— How do you like it?

Marie-Sophie was speechless: How do you like it? Like what? That red block of wood? That meat loaf? What did the man mean? After all they had shared he showed her a blood-red lump and wanted to know what she thought of the object. Either the man was making fun of her or he was insane. Oh well, whichever it was, she'd better answer him as he was no longer her invalid but a guest, and it went with the job that you had to treat guests as paying customers, as the Inhaberin called them, even when they were barking mad.

— How do you like it?

— Er, I don't know.

She tried to look stupid. He stepped aside, put a hand on her shoulder and gave her an affectionate push towards the table.

— Touch it.

He took her hand to guide it towards the lump but she wrenched it back.

— What's the matter? You gave me back what they'd taken away from me: love. In return I want to share with you the only thing I own . . . You needn't be afraid . . .

— Oh, it's just that I prefer to make my own decisions, not just about how I dress, what I think and eat, but everything else as well, including how I stick out my finger to poke something.

— Not poke, touch gently.

Marie-Sophie lightly tapped the tip of her right forefinger on the lump, which was cold and moist to the touch.

— It's some kind of clay, isn't it?

The guest, the man, the invalid nodded.

— What are you doing with a lump of clay in a hatbox, behaving as if it's your heart and soul? People might say that you, well, once I reckon it would have been considered a bit odd to show your sweetheart – if I may be so bold – a lump of clay in confidence like this.

— Just wait.

He twisted a signet ring from his little finger, gripped it by the band and pressed the seal into the clay. The girl looked at him enquiringly.

— Touch it now.

Marie-Sophie hesitated: he'd said he loved her, hadn't he? Wouldn't it be best to do as he asked, did it matter that he was mad after all? It would be a pity if they parted on bad terms; it had felt so good to sit with him and talk a lot of nonsense while he dozed, blushing when he woke up and looked at her, and it had felt good to burn with him. She couldn't prevent him from leaving or them from taking him – well, what was she supposed to do? Pounce on them like a lynx and gobble them up, fasten her fangs into them and tear them limb from limb? Others would probably come in their place and she wouldn't have room in her stomach to devour all those she killed. She wanted to fight for him but in the circumstances she would have to make do with playing this absurd game with him. That way he would be happy and she perplexed when they parted, which aren't such bad emotions at such a time.

— Touch it now.

She stroked the tip of her finger lightly over the surface of the lump: God! It twitched like a maggot and vibrated slightly. What on earth was it? A sea cucumber? The girl had never seen a sea cucumber but had a clear picture of one in her head; a sea cucumber looked pretty much like this, yes, as thick as an arm, tapering at the end where the mouth was. The creatures did have mouths, didn't they? Marie-Sophie looked up from the prodigy.

— Does it bite?

The man shook his head and rubbed the imprint of the seal off the lump of clay, which squirmed under his touch, then lay as motionless as a block of wood. The girl looked enquiringly at the man she loved: what alchemy was this? What magic?

He drew the chair from the desk and offered her a seat with a swivel of his right hand. She sat down and waited for him to explain. Taking a deep breath he put his hands together as if in prayer, closed his eyes a moment, lowered his head and raised his hands to his face so the fingertips rested under his nose. The atmosphere in the room grew charged: darkness gathered around the thinking man and the darkness was so deep that the girl had the feeling that the wall had disappeared and she could see into another room behind it. A glow illuminated a golden wall, glimmering from seven candles in a man-high candelabra. The candles smoked, the smoke flickering from the flames in ever-changing symbols or letters in a language she could make no sense of. A second later this eternity was over and he straightened up, his face wide-awake.

— I'm called – I am – Loewe! I'm delighted to make your acquaintance.

He bowed and smiled at the girl, who gulped.

— And this thing that I have shown you, resting on its silken bed in that hatbox, is my child – my son, if we wish to be precise – and he will be your child too, if you are willing to help me, to give birth to him with me.

Marie-Sophie gaped in bewilderment at the man, at this crazy invalid who she couldn't help loving: what did he mean by his child? Their child? This repulsive lump that squirmed like a giant, chopped-up maggot when she touched it. How romantic! She shifted on the bed, hoping that her movement could be interpreted as: "Well, I suppose I should be getting along!" or "You don't say! You're called Loewe? And you have the material for a clay boy in the box on the table? And I can give birth to him with you? Well, it's a nice offer, but perhaps you could explain a little more clearly? I'm just a simple country girl but, ignorant as I am, I've always thought that little children, chicks, the birds and the bees, were made in quite a different way from this." Marie-Sophie raised her eyebrows and shrugged. He smiled back encouragingly.

— Er, I think it's probably best if I leave you to it. You're so much better and I expect you've had enough of me hanging over you chattering this past couple of days . . .

She leapt to her feet and went to the door with the intention of leaving, then turned to her poor, deranged man and held out her hand to him.

— It was nice to meet you, Herr Loewe – sir, I mean.

Loewe took the girl's hand, studied her, then shot a quick glance at the hatbox.

— Believe me.

Marie-Sophie knew he wouldn't let go of her hand and that she was ready to give it to him. They held hands. He led her into the room, she led him into the room.

— I've devoted my life to creating this lump using dust from under the Altneu Synagogue in Prague, dew from the roses that bloom in the Castle gardens, rain from the cobbles in the ghetto, and more, much more.

— What? You must tell me everything.

Marie-Sophie and Loewe paced around the room, as far as its small size permitted, back and forth with the light swing of a Sunday promenade, as he described to her how he had collected his bodily fluids: phlegm, blood, sweat, nasal mucus, bone marrow, excrement, urine, saliva and sperm, kneading them slowly but surely into the clay over the years, along with nail parings from his fingers and toes, hair and flakes of skin. The girl shuddered during the recital, but nothing could surprise her any more; from now on nothing bad could happen. She swung their hands to and fro, and she could happily have hummed along to his speech if she hadn't found the whole thing sufficiently absurd and amusing as it was.

He finished his account and they took up position before the table, gazing with starry eyes at the lump of clay in the hatbox, red-cheeked like parents admiring their firstborn in its cradle. She clasped his hand tighter: Our child!

The girl felt new emotions stirring deep within her soul: twisting, no more than a movement, a rhythmic dum-de-dum, dum-de-dum. They were followed by other movements, haphazard, yet apparently born from the same rhythm: Dah-da, dahh-da-da. Now Marie-Sophie felt the urge to touch the lump again, the stirrings in her mind were attuned to its movements; quick twitches and then a vibration: Dum-de-dum, dah-da, dum-de-dum, dahh-da-da. She concentrated on the dark colour of the lump, listening for the sensation, then became aware of Loewe's breathing at her side. He was breathing steadily and deliberately through his nose, she could hear the whine of the breath as it forced its way down his nasal passages and out through his nostrils, making them flare and the lobes of his nose tremble.

I hope he hasn't caught a cold; it could kill him, the state he's in.

Marie-Sophie was about to turn to him and remind him to take care of himself, not to let himself catch a chill, when: Dum-de-dum, dahh-da-da, dum-de-dum, dah-da, dum-de-dum, dahh-da-da. She became the feeling and he became the breath passing slowly and steadily in and out of his body. Marie-Sophie realised her eyes were closed.

His eyes are closed too, yet I can see the lump – my child – quite clearly.

They turned to face one another and their gazes met through their eyelids.'

'God, that's so beautiful!'

'Yes, Marie-Sophie and Loewe met in each other's eyes, they crossed over into the dim antechamber of the soul where lovers dwell when they close their eyes together, where thought flutters on rose-pink curtains and we look in even as we look out.

The girl stepped into the living darkness to join the man and he walked into the darkness to join her.

She opened her eyes and looked herself in the eye, but it was not her face that was reflected in her pupils, it was he who stood within the arched windows, looking out at himself through her eyes. Dum-de-dum, dah-da, dum-de-dum, dahh-da-da. The girl heard the feeling throb in her body which now housed Loewe, and she felt how the breathing in her new body resonated with the dum-de-dum, how they pulsed together in harmony, each lifting the other: Dum-de-dum, tiss and whee in the nose. He pointed at the lump and now she saw a child begin to take shape in the formless mass. He stroked the clay carefully with her hands; she stretched out his hands and stroked the backs of her own hands, following them on their journey over the unformed matter: a cupped palm formed cranium and nape, dah, tee, then the throat, up a little, and there was a chin; the side of a hand marked out a mouth; thumb pinched against forefinger, a nose; little finger pressed the clay down into eye sockets and mounded up a forehead. Holding the neck carefully he shaped the shoulders in the twinkling of an eye: Dum-de-dum and whee, tiss and da-da. She followed the movement with his hands, letting his eyes stray over her body, watching it work, watching how her shoulders undulated when he ploughed the clay up with a sure touch and freed the child's short arms, taking what came off and kneading it into tiny patches that he placed on its breasts to make nipples. With the tips of her forefingers he sketched a ribcage and drew lines in it with the tips of her other fingers, whiss, dum-da. He paused and counted the ribs: one, two, three . . .

— Twelve.

Marie-Sophie was startled by her masculine voice and emitted a low chuckle. Loewe looked up from his work and laid finger to lips as if to hush her but blew her a kiss instead, then carried on. He slid her hands under the lump, moulding the two lowest ribs, cupped her palms over the stomach and ran them down the abdomen and out to the hips where he pushed her thumbnails deep into the clay and separated the legs: Dum-de-dum, dah-tee, whiss-de-dum, dahh. He kneaded legs and feet, then rolled the excess material thoughtfully between her fingers. He looked at the girl in his body, drew the towel over the mirror a little to one side, and looked at himself in her body. She caressed his cheek.

— I know what you're thinking, but I want it to be a boy. I long for a little boy who will be different from the rest, a peace-loving boy who will grow up to be a good man.

Loewe shaped a little willy and balls which he placed between the clay-child's legs.

— There's no question of his sex.

Marie-Sophie gave a low chuckle, and he pinched a tiny scrap off its foreskin and used it to fill in the crotch, before sticking the top joint of her little finger into the clay below, and there was its rectum. The girl saw the blood rush to his cheeks and thought she could feel herself blushing.

So that's what I look like when I blush, she thought, dum-de-whiss, tee and dah. I'm actually quite pretty when I blush. Oh, how little we know about ourselves, how little we see of ourselves, yet everyone else knows all about us.

He looked at her. She wanted to kiss him. She kissed him on the neck, where she liked to be kissed, rather harder than intended. He tilted her head in the hope of another kiss and puckered up her mouth. She smiled.

— Let's get on.

Loewe sighed shyly and continued with his creation. The girl stepped back from the table and took a good look at the lump, which increasingly resembled a real baby: and just like a real baby, all its proportions were so improbable that it was hard to imagine the ridiculous body ever growing, elongating and taking on the appearance of an adult male.

* * *

METAMORPHOSIS

One morning when Jósef L. woke up at home in bed after troubled dreams, he found himself transformed into a giant baby. He lay on his weak back, which was soft as a feather cushion, and had he been able to raise his head at all he would have seen his belly, distended and pink with a protruding, unhealed navel; the bedclothes hardly covered this bulging mound and seemed ready to slide on to the floor at any moment.

His limbs were pathetically spindly compared to the rest of him, and waved awkwardly without his being able to control them at all.'

* * *

'Not more stories!'

'But this is a literary allusion.'

'So what?'

'It adds depth to the story of Marie-Sophie and my father, the invalid, making it resonate with world literature.'

'I don't care. Tell me about the child, tell me about you.'

'You mean that?'

'Yes, dum-de-dum, or I'm off.'

'Well, then, whiss!'

'Dah-da.'

'Tee!'

'Loewe gently picked up the child-lump and laid it on its stomach: he passed nimble fingers over its back, moulding shoulder-blades and spine, hips and buttocks, crooks of knees and ankles. Dah-da-tee. Dum-de-dum-whiss.

My child! thought Marie-Sophie when he turned the lump over again. Now, who do you take after, my boy?

Loewe was busy moulding fingers and toes, drawing lines on palms and soles, excavating temples and nape of neck, and forming ears which he placed rather high on the head. Marie-Sophie put a hand on her beloved's shoulder.

— We must give him a face. Do you know, he reminds me a bit of my brother, and perhaps of myself, with those little ears like shells, sticking out a bit, yes, like a calf.

She watched him give the clay a face: the boy's features were pure, he had high eyebrows and cheekbones while the cheeks themselves were chubby and the mouth sensitive with a pronounced Cupid's bow. Loewe opened the mouth and stuck her finger inside, pressing the clay into palate, gums and tongue, and turning when he had finished to the girl in his body.

— Could you open your mouth for me, please?

Marie-Sophie did as Loewe asked, gaping at him awkwardly while he stroked the fingers of both her hands over his tongue.

— Thank you.

He smoothed the clay under the boy's eyes and tweaked him here and there. The girl closed his mouth: in the hatbox on the table before them lay a sleeping infant who was wonderfully like them both, and suddenly she was seized with an incomprehensible restlessness: whatever were they thinking of to let the poor little mite lie there naked and helpless in a dirty cardboard box? It was plain that they knew as little about children as they did about anything else – what a couple of misfits! Wasn't it obvious that people like her and the invalid were not to be trusted with small children?

She wanted to pick the child up at once and press him to her bosom. She wanted to cuddle this dark son of hers against her, rock him gently and sing quietly and reassuringly some of that loving nonsense that the warmth of a defenceless baby calls forth on our lips. Marie-Sophie fumbled instinctively over her flat chest, and suddenly missed being in her own body, but she didn't want to disturb Loewe who was absorbed in putting the finishing touches on their child; she shifted his feet uneasily behind him: what should she say? Give me back my breasts? No. So she whispered:

— Isn't he cold? Shouldn't we cover him?

Loewe finished polishing the clay and now began crimping it at knee and elbow; he didn't look up from his work but answered her question as if he were talking to himself, breaking off every time he wrinkled the child.

— He can't feel anything. Not yet. Later. Be ready with something then. A blanket.

Marie-Sophie stroked a finger across his brow, the brow of the man in her body.

— His forehead, could you draw a line like this across his forehead?

He examined his own face.

— Does it make sense for him to look like me?

— Yes, it's a nice line and doesn't seem to have been caused by worry or anger; it's just there. And it's so mysterious when babies are marked out in some way, when there's something in their appearance or air that we usually think of as a sign of having lived a long time. It gives you the feeling that they've come from far away, bearing a message perhaps. I think it's healthy for people to have children like that around them.

Loewe nodded and applied the nail of her forefinger to the boy's forehead.'

'Yes, it's true, can I touch it?'
    'Later. Time's pressing on, they haven't got all night . . .'

'Marie-Sophie admired how the man ran her agile fingers over the child's body: the creation was nearly finished and she could hardly wait for his eyelids to quiver and existence to be mirrored in his eyes for the first time.

Yes, good point! They hadn't yet given him his sight.

Loewe stood silently by the table, critically surveying his handiwork; she tugged at his, her arm, and pointed to her, his eyes. He stuck his thumbs into the clay-boy's face and enlarged the eyeholes.

— They're in my trouser pocket.

The girl fetched his trousers from the cupboard and slipped a hand in the left pocket, but there was nothing there; it had a hole in it.

— I'll mend this for you.

— No, please don't, I use that pocket for things that can be lost or even should be lost. People love finding things when they're out for a walk, and that's my way of taking part in the informal pavement trade. I use the other pocket for things I've found and want to keep.

He laughed apologetically on hearing his girlish voice.

Marie-Sophie put his hand in the right pocket and, sure enough, there was a leather pouch among the coins and scraps of paper, and through the leather she felt two round objects: the eyes that were destined for their boy's head.

Loewe took the pouch from her and extracted the brown eyes and two frames of a film strip – one showing Adolf Hitler making a speech, the other showing the same man at dinner, wiping a gravy stain from his tie – and he laid the pieces of film, one in each eye socket, placed the eyeballs on top of them, then closed them with clay scrapings from under her nails.

The work was done. Marie-Sophie and Loewe looked into one another's eyes, swapped bodies again and examined the fruit of their hands: on a dressing table in a vulgar priest's hole off room twenty-three on the first floor of the Vrieslander guesthouse in the small town of Kükenstadt on the banks of the Elbe lay a fully formed child. The work seemed very good to them. Now nothing remained but to kindle life in the small clay body.

My father held the ring and asked my mother to do so as well, and together they pressed the seal into the tender flesh, midway between breastbone and genitals.

I woke to life and her eyes saw my substance.

The town-hall clock struck twelve.

The twelfth chime echoed over the town like a premature farewell.

There was a knock at the door.'

VII

17

'Gabriel saw nothing wrong with the maiden's passionate annunciation; the hands that he had admired at their garland weaving were certainly deft, the well-shaped mouth seared his face and throat, and the small breasts now rose and fell against his robe. No, on the contrary, the maiden's caresses convinced the angel that he must have known her in the days of old, that they were meeting after a long and painful separation; he mimicked her every movement and touch.

There came a point when the maiden touched the angel's skirt.

He seized her hand: wasn't that going a bit far?

The unicorn calf's idiotic snorting under the pomegranate tree was getting on Gabriel's nerves: the calf had been making strange noises ever since they started kissing, thereby preventing the angel from losing himself completely in the fire. Wouldn't it serve the beast right if he went all the way with the maiden and enjoyed her in a manner that the monstrous creature would never be able to experience?

The angel released the maiden's hand and half closed his eyes. She stroked slowly up his legs, the folds of his robe bunching between her wrist and forearm. He held his breath; the interplay of soft palm and fresh air felt blissful on his thighs.

Gabriel was on the point of swooning in ecstasy when the maiden whipped back her hand and let out a shriek. He looked down his body but couldn't spy anything that could give her cause for alarm: had she overreached herself at last?

But the maiden was not the only one to be alarmed, the unicorn calf literally jumped out of its skin: the antelope jaw distorted in a terrible scream, the horse body shuddered and shook in a fit of convulsions, the elephantine legs lengthened and shrank by turns and from under the pig's tail came an insane hubbub and stench, yes, as if a whole legion of foul-breathed demons were blasting on trombones.

The angel blenched: he had been led into a trap!

His lust evaporated, he launched himself into the air in a trice and paused at a safe distance from the grove: the calf was metamorphosing into a demon. Around its horn appeared a pewter crown, upside down, the points piercing the flesh of its brow, and to the clown's immeasurable joy black blood began to trickle down its face. It shook its head, rolled its yellow eyes and licked its face with a forked tongue three feet long.

It was none other than the cacodemon Amduscias, hell's court composer, he who tortures the damned with his unbearable clashing and banging.'

'But who was the maiden? Who was the honey-trap?'

'Gabriel wailed with terror when he discovered who it was that stood by the monster with the unicorn's head: Lilith!

Black hair cloaked the curvaceous body of the first woman, she who had joined Satan's band, the tresses parting over her breasts and loins; between her wet labia glistened predatory teeth.

He clamped his hands over his eyes but the witch's image slipped through the backs of his hands and etched itself on his mind's eye.

— Look at me, look at you . . .

Lilith smiled at the angel. He clapped his hands over his ears but the witch's voice filtered through his fingers:

— Gabriel and Lilith, Lilith and Gabriel . . .

The angel put his hand over his mouth: she was trying to brainwash him into heresy; by answering he would give her an opening to attack. The golden rule in dealing with the devil's emissaries was not to let them lure one into chat as they were either fluent-tongued rhetoricians or speech-impaired morons who could in either case ensnare the strictest of believers.

Amduscias pushed himself forward and the latter mood was on him. The demon struck a pose, flung out his arms and bleated:

— Gusgi laig Gagriel, Duski laig rubby-pubby, Busbi laig maig babieth . . .

Then he rolled his glaring eyes, crouched down, puffed out his cheeks and began to strain with abominable gasps and groans.

Gabriel spread his wings and rose higher into the sky: what was the meaning of these farcical antics? What were they trying to tell him?

Out of the demon there now poured a stream of horns, bassoons, alpenhorns, trumpets, clarinets, pan pipes, oboes, saxophones, tubas and cornets. And finally flutes, forcing themselves lengthways out of the devil's backside.

The newborn wind instruments wriggled in the grass like snakes, farting feebly at the angel who recoiled in disgust.

Lilith shouted over the wailing of the instruments.

— If you fear me, you fear yourself . . .

He shook his head in bewilderment and prepared to fly away.

But the expression in Lilith's eyes made Gabriel hesitate: he was an archangel – the blood-red hearts of men, the sun-white hearts of angels and the pitch-black hearts of the damned were open books to him. What he read in the she-devil's heart was compassion, commiseration, complicity, comprehension, communion . . .

She pointed to her crotch and whispered: Sister . . .

At last Gabriel understood what Lilith was trying to tell him: the horrible thing between her legs was the mirror image of the enigma he hid between his own.

The Archangel Gabriel's nightmarish screams echoed through the solar system and beyond; they bounced from star to star, reverberated between the galaxies, until she was woken from her restless slumber by his – her – own screams.

The angel was confused by the remnants of his dream and unsure of what sex she was or what had happened, but he did remember that by an ugly trick the serpent Satan had performed his will through her: the old corruptor of souls had by a neurological ruse led the doomsday melody astray in the angel's chaste brain and sneaked it into the amygdaloid nucleus, seat of olfactory and sexual sensation. Gabriel knew that although it might sound like an innocent prank by Beelzebub to confuse her senses in this way, the consequences had been catastrophic: she had dreamed that she was female.

Gabriel brushed the glowing lock of hair from his eyes; beneath her twinkled the cities of the Continent that was now to meet its doom. He raised the sacred trumpet to blow, but her lips wizened like burning parchment against the mouthpiece, her fingers writhed on the polished metal like maggots, and instead of the angel's lungs filling with the Holy Spirit she retched. GABRIELLE was disgusted at the thought of obeying the divine command to sound the blast for the battle between light and darkness – SHE had lost all inclination to play the instrument, this engine of doomsday that had accompanied HER for as long as SHE could remember, ever since SHE was a golden-haired boy-child rehearsing in the Almighty's throne room – SHE no longer knew who SHE should side with in the dreadful conflict that would follow the blast.

Gabrielle felt tears of rage forcing their way into her eyes, and this was a new sensation.

She had been betrayed, not by Lucifer and his fiends, no, Lilith and Amduscias of the delusion were merely instruments in the hands of the truth that had craved revelation at this fateful moment: Gabrielle had a definite sex, she was an angel in the feminine; a nonentity who had neither name nor status in heaven and could be found nowhere except in books by old ladies learned in angel lore.

But who had blinded Gabrielle? Who had deluded her as to her own nature?

Gabrielle struggled against tears and blasphemy.

She tore off the trumpet and flung it at the sun, which now rode high over Bikini Atoll, and there the instrument melted, yes, it went up in smoke along with her youth and everything she had stood for in the minds of devils, gods and men.

Gabrielle spread her wings and kicked off from Planet Earth. She found to her joy that she had not lost the gift of flight. She soared lightly over the earth: her departure would not make a decisive difference to the course of universal history. The human race was possessed of such a strong urge to self-destruct that sooner or later they would invent something that would surpass her wind instrument. The Prince of Darkness would continue to rove around the abyss in search of night quarters for his homeless shadow army; she didn't know any jokes black enough to console that joker. And as for the powers that be . . .

— That's us!

A woman's voice illuminated the eternal darkness; the glow reso-nated a moment on the moons and nebulae – everything became nothing and nothing became everything.

Gabrielle stood meekly in the palm of Sophia's hand, celestial soles planted on her index finger to the north and her wrist to the south. Gentleness lapped her ankles and fluttered the snowy skirt of the robe that hid her bright legs and all her blessed flesh.

And she is no longer part of our story.

But Gabrielle was wrong to believe that life on earth would continue after her disappearance; her disposal of the trumpet in the aforemen-tioned manner had greater and more momentous consequences than simply her own emancipation.

Before the beginning of time, the Creator of heaven had engraved every movement and groan, every gesture and victory cry of Arma-geddon, on the instrument; and since his handiwork was now shat-tered into its atoms in the sun's ocean of fire, there was no question of that course of events ever being played out to the end.

The power struggle between light and darkness was over.

The angels and fiends, who had clashed over Creation in everything from the smallest blade of grass and most minuscule mayfly to the highest mountain ranges and deepest canyons, put aside their quarrels and headed for home. They floated up from the battlefields like a ribbon of mist, up to heaven or down to hell, leaving nothing behind but everything.

At 12.27 in Kükenstadt, time stood still.

The earth is no longer the divine or diabolical place we know from old books: without hate or love, cradle or grave, it is a matter neither for stories nor poems.

Sic transit gloria mundi . . .'

'Is it all over then?'

VIII

18

'Time was murdered three years ago.

Heaven and hell are closed, the trumpet will not be blown, angels will not descend to earth, no devils will rise up from the abyss, the dead lie quiet in their graves. Nothing lives, nothing dies.

* * *

An ambulance, which has been painted black and converted into a hearse, waits in a paved square in front of a three-storey building. A withered creeper covers the front of the building from pavement to eaves, parting around the sooty windows and the faded sign over the half-open front door: GASTHOF VRIESLANDER.

On the other side of the whitewashed door waits Loewe, my wretched father, wrapped in a woollen blanket, clutching a scruffy hatbox in his claw-like hands. He stands between two men wearing wide-brimmed hats, long leather coats and gleaming boots; one holds the door-handle, the other a battered suitcase.

The curtains do not move. The dough does not rise on the kitchen table. The mouse in the boiler room will not finish giving birth to her young. The pendulum of the clock is fixed in mid-upswing.

It is a moment of parting.

In the reception area behind them stands a group of people with words of farewell on their lips: a grey-haired old man clenches his fists, a sullen waiter examines his palms, a tearful cook throws up her hands, a randy serving boy clasps his knuckles to his chest, a drunken proprietor rests a hand on the hip flask in his back pocket, a stern Inhaberin lays her fingers to her lips.

But the farewell will not reach the invalid's ears.

Their tongues have withered in their mouths, their eyes have shrivelled in their sockets and their desiccated faces are twisted in a ghastly smile.'

'Is nothing happening? Make something happen!'

'Do you see that there's a button missing from the left sleeve of the invalid's jacket? The thread's hanging loose down his arm. Pull it and what happens?'

'He's blinking and peering round but he can't force out a word.'

'What do you think he wants to say?'

'Let's go?'

'Loewe swallows the dust in his throat, licks the scum from his mouth and whispers: "Let's go".

The words tear apart the silence like the command of a demonic god.

The fetters of death fall from the two men and with mechanical movements they continue from where they left off three years earlier. But they are so weak that the one holding the door-handle hasn't the strength to open the door any further. He looks helplessly at his colleague, the suitcase falls from the latter's hand with a thud that shakes the guesthouse, and by leaning against the door together they manage to edge it fully open. They tramp with heavy feet out into the night with my father between them, still clutching the hatbox, drag him to the hearse, lean him up against the side like a plank while one of them goes back for the suitcase and the other struggles with the rear door of the vehicle, and when the former has lugged the suitcase out into the square and the latter has managed to open the back, they pummel the invalid and his luggage inside, laying him flat on the coffin-rest, then shuffle along the vehicle and struggle together to get in on the driver's side; the door swings open with an ear-piercing screech, one of them loses his footing, sinks zombie-like to the ground and stiffens, while the other treads on his shoulder and slumps into the vehicle where he seizes the ignition key with both hands and manages after several attempts to start the engine, then, gripping the steering wheel, he heaves himself up in the seat, puts the hearse in gear, stamps on the accelerator and drives off.

The hearse crawls a complete circuit of the darkened square, the engine noise booming off the houses and shaking the gold-painted signs over the shops; from the coffin-rest Loewe sees the globe swinging over the grocer's shop, the pretzel over the bakery, the cup and saucer over Café Berserk, the razor over the barber's and the spool of thread over the draper's.

The invalid doesn't see how the booming of the engine hurls open the doors of the church and reverberates in the nave until the lime crumbles from the walls and the palm-size altarpiece falls to the floor. On its back appears the front of the painting of the Saviour from Nazareth; the wound in his side, the nails and the crown of thorns would have put an end to all controversy over the artist's ability or lack of it.

Nor does he see how the memorial to the inquisitive chick receives the engine noise in blind silence: blue moonlight will never again be reflected in the black stone eyes, its story will never again be recalled for amused tourists – in the beer cellars of Kükenstadt there is no one to lend it his voice and cry: "Can I see?"

The hearse swerves round the corner of the town hall.

The only thing Loewe can hear over the engine noise is the driver grinding his teeth when his fingers lock on the steering wheel and he expends the last of his strength on turning it. Once round the corner death overtakes the driver; he sinks down into the passenger seat, the steering wheel slips from his grasp and straightens up, and the hearse rolls down the street towards the river.

The square vanishes from my father's sight, but for one moment, when the hearse drives over a bump in the road, the roof of the guesthouse appears.

A candle glimmers in a window.

In the attic room sits Marie-Sophie, the dear child, on the edge of her bed, her face buried in an open book. The candle stub in the holder on the chest casts a glow on the contents of the room: the chair, chamber-pot and wardrobe. The saint has vanished from the gaudy picture over the bed, the hut that rested in his hands lies shattered in the forest clearing, its inhabitants scattered like matchwood among the ruins.

But the syrupy-yellow light of the candle does not fall on the girl's face or the pages of the story, it stops at the plait on her neck, leaving her in the shadow of her own head, bowed in sorrow.

The angel Freude no longer taps at Marie-Sophie's west window – he collects no more dreams in his book – and even if he did return there would be nothing there for him: she is not dreaming, she is not awake.

As the window disappears beneath the hill the hearse's engine falls silent and the girl's name rises from the invalid's lips like steam from newly ploughed earth after a sunny day, and he strokes his twisted bird's claw of a hand over the lid of the hatbox: "Marie-Sophie . . ."

The hearse crawls noiselessly down the street over the last stretch to the riverbank, and Loewe sees the only people who had been out and about on that long-ago night: four men who are standing in front of the police station; on the steps three military policemen are roaring with laughter over a bit of sausage which one is balancing on another's nose, while a young man, who looks as if he has lost his inner poet, stands with one foot in the gutter. He stares up the street, smiling on the side of his face that is turned towards the uniforms. The invalid wrinkles his brow anxiously as the hearse brushes against the upper arm of this unfortunate man who seems worn down by the wait. He is unaware that this is the citizen of Kükenstadt he knows best apart from my mother: Karl Maus. And Karl Maus will never know that what he has been waiting for all this time has been and gone, leaving behind only a black stripe like a mourning band on his sleeve. He continues to wait.

The hearse runs through a road block, slows down and stops on the riverbank; a barge is floating low in the water against the dock; the helmsman, who had been sitting on the rail smoking his pipe when the blast came, lies sprawled on the bank, thoughtfully contemplating the cold ashes.

Loewe stretches out on the coffin-rest and kicks the rear door until it flies open, then crawls out of the hearse with the hatbox clasped under his left arm, dragging the suitcase behind him with his right. He looks round in search of life; there's no one here to help a poor wretch who doesn't know where he's going.

But out on the river floats a silvery feather from the Elbe's guardian angel, and a single pitch-black bristle from the beard of the Elbe's demon lies like a thwart amidships.

It's as big as a Viking longship and the quill of the feather reaches to the shore like a gangplank. My father struggles over to it with his luggage. He perches on the beard bristle, puts down the suitcase on the vane at his feet and hugs the hatbox to him. A good while passes like this with nothing happening: the Elbe no longer flows to the sea, its rushing voice is silenced.

The only movement in the eternal night is the invalid's ribcage, which trembles with his weeping, and the only sound is the sob that bursts from his throat and is carried over the doomed Continent, over woods and fields, over towns and cities, over lakes and plains, over hills and mountain peaks.

Europe becomes Eurweep.

At the Ural Mountains in the east and Gibraltar in the south the gust of weeping turns back on itself in search of its origin and blows my father off the beard bristle. He rises to his feet, spreads his arms, captures the sob, and lets it carry him out to sea on the feather.

> Puff-puff-puff, Puff-puff
> Puff-puff-puff, Puff-away,
> Puff-puff-away, Way-away,
> Puff-way-away, Way-away,
> Way-way-away, Way-away . . .

Loewe's silvery vessel rocks on the North Sea. Off the coast of Denmark – level with the small towns of Natmad and Bamsedreng – lies a ship at anchor, its navigation lamps illuminating the night, lights burning in every porthole, coloured bulbs glowing up the mast and stays, its name painted in white letters on the black hull: *GODAFOSS*.

The invalid sits huddled on the beard bristle in a world of his own; it is not until the feather has floated to the ship's side and the swell has begun to drive it away again that he wakes up to the fact that the ship's engines are revving, the ship's whistle is being blown. He leaps off the bristle, seizes it with both hands and paddles for dear life to the side of the ship, where he grabs his chance to bang on the hull with his oar. After he has been tapping on the hull for some time, succeeding only in scratching at the letter "A" in the ship's name, the silhouette of a man appears at the rail, and a moment later a rope ladder is thrown over the side and a sailor swarms down it. He pays no attention to the feather and beard bristle, having apparently seen stranger craft, but addresses my father in a bizarrely singsong language, conveying to him with the help of hand signals that he wishes to throw him over his shoulder and carry him aboard, but they'll have to leave the suitcase and hatbox behind. When my father cries: "No!" and bursts into tears, the stranger gives this puny wretch a thoughtful once-over, then tosses him and his luggage over his shoulder without a word and climbs aboard, where they are met by his double. The second man whips the invalid over the rail and sets him down at his side, simultaneously greeting him and laughing at him.

The invalid looks small on the deck, the throbbing of the engine shakes him from head to foot, the wheelhouse towers over him, the flood of lights hurts his eyes and at the top of the mast he sees a flag bearing the accursed symbol flapping on its pole.

The sailors put their arms around my father's shoulders and yell, one in each ear:

— *Kalt?*

The invalid grasps what they mean, but before he can answer they lead him between them inside the ship and it's warm there.

From below decks rises the cheerful sound of dance music and a babble of drunken voices.

My father looks enquiringly at the sailors but they shrug their shoulders and push him before them down a narrow passage, round a corner and down some stairs, down more stairs, down more stairs.

The noise of partying grows louder the deeper they descend into the bowels of the ship, until it is a fantastic hubbub, and when they reach the saloon the invalid gets a brief glimpse through a sand-blasted glass door of a man in a monkey-suit leapfrogging over a two-metre-tall Negro wearing a bowler hat. He is relieved when they continue down the passage; however ridiculous a figure he may cut, he's simply not dressed for a party like that.

Two men stand in the cabin doorway.

Inside the cabin a ragged-looking man kneels before an open suit-case.

Taking a few small things out of the case, he proceeds to show them a knotted root that resembles a man with crossed legs, a copper etching of a white adder and a troll without legs, and a jar containing a golden herb.

They shake their heads.

He holds up his palms and raises his brows, and there is a flash from the ring he's wearing on the little finger of his left hand. They point to the ring and nod.

He gives them the ring.

They break it in two.

He lies down on the bunk, clutching the hatbox to his chest. They leave.

He waits for the whistle to blow for departure.

The whistle blows for departure.'

'The ship cleft the world-night and headed north. I was in the hatbox.'

'And now you're here.'

PART II

ICELAND'S THOUSAND YEARS

a crime story

I

(In the Beginning)

1

'Once upon a time there was a berserker who had such a wicked temper that he couldn't bear the presence of any living thing. At first he made do with attacking the life around him – this was in the south of Asia – but after he had killed everything within reach he packed up his few personal belongings, which consisted of a pair of tongs the size of a fully grown oak tree and a henhouse on wheels, harnessed himself to the henhouse, grasped the tongs in both hands and set off on his great journey of destruction.

Now some may find it perplexing that the brute should have spared the chickens he kept in the battered hutch. But this was because he lost his appetite in his murderous frenzies and couldn't bring himself to eat his kill. Instead he dragged the corpses into piles, strewn here and there over the bloody field. This was a most wasteful way of working and by the time he had finished he was too exhausted to start slaughtering chickens with all the effort that entails. And so the years passed without the berserker ever finding time to tear apart his hens. Gradually he learned the knack of eating their eggs, gaining great satisfaction from gobbling down whole generations of unborn poultry. His method of eating eggs was as unnatural as the thoughts that accompanied it. As soon as the poor feathered creatures began their broody clucking he would seize them one after another and suck the eggs out of their rumps.

Ah yes, his nature was godless and cruel.

Anyway, the story of the berserker's travels tells that he stormed across the Continent, henhouse in tow and tongs aloft, beating and crushing everything in his path. He leapt over the Bosphorus and strode up through Europe. There he encountered a river, the Elbe, and decided to follow it to the sea. Fair and abundant was the life on its banks. But the heaps of the slain piled up in his wake, the river water became tainted with blood, and from its mouth a crimson slick spread all the way to the ends of the earth where the island of Thule, or at least the West Fjords peninsula, was then in the process of forming.

One morning the berserker woke up and began to suck at his hens. Now it so happened that when he raised the final hen's rump to his lips it was not an egg that he sucked up into his ugly chops but a chick that was very much alive. This miracle had come about because the berserker's method of egg-collecting had stretched the creatures' backsides so wide that the chick had hatched inside its mother.

If the berserker had paid more heed during his killing spree the day before, he would have noticed the chick living contentedly in its mother's backside and poking its yellow head out of her behind to feed. But he didn't and so the inevitable happened: the chick was hoovered up into the berserker's jaws. And if the berserker hadn't hesitated a moment at the ticklish feeling that a feathered chick is apt to create on the tongue, the chick would have ended up in his stomach and given up the ghost among all the egg yolks, shells and whites.

The berserker's jaw dropped; he rolled his thick tongue around his chops in search of the alien object, he cleared his throat, he spat, he gave a sudden snort, he coughed, he put his fingers down his throat, he stuck out his tongue, he panted like a dog, he screeched, he opened his jaws wide and examined his reflection in the shiny surface of the tongs. All in vain, for you see the chick had ducked into a deep cavity in the berserker's wisdom tooth where it remained cowering during the fearful upheavals. The berserker would no doubt have stayed there for ever and a day, belching and grimacing, if just then some butter-flies hadn't wafted over to him on the morning breeze. They captured his attention with their bewildered fluttering over the hop fields and called him back to his daily chores.

The berserker was filled with enthusiasm for his work. He ripped and tore on every side in pitched battle with the butterflies which, in addition to being tediously careless of their fate, kept seeking out the orifices in the berserker's body for all the world as if there were something good to be found there. By the time evening fell, the sun began to bleed over the wasteland and the berserker rested his weary

bones after the day's toil, decisive victory in his battle with the butter-
flies and the piling up of the slain in the aftermath, he had forgotten
all about the interloper who had made itself at home in his mouth.

The chick meanwhile was snug in its crazed host's wisdom tooth.
Like other young creatures it was naively accepting of the trials that
life has to offer, whether these consisted of the exile of its people,
regular growth spurts, or simply being swept willy-nilly from its
mother's warm posterior into a berserker's fetid gob. Indeed, the
transformation in the chick's circumstances preoccupied it less than
the fact that it was mastering the art of cheeping.

The only thing the chick missed from its former abode was the
possibility of peeping out at the world from time to time. Now it only
got a glimpse of the big wide world when the berserker launched
screaming into battle with his adversary, life, while the chick sat in
his hollow wisdom tooth like a poor student in the upper circle at
the final rehearsal of *Götterdämmerung*. But as it did not dare on its
little life to stick its head out between the berserker's teeth, what it
saw was not worth the telling: the odd panic-stricken human being,
a fleeing family of hares, a shivering juniper bush.

The chick was not merely inquisitive, it was young and inquisitive,
and so this paltry ration came nowhere near to satisfying it. When
the berserker ground his teeth over the construction of the piles or
slept with jaws clenched, which he did for fear of being invaded by
creepy-crawlies, the chick would cheep with all its might and main:

— Can I see, can I see?

Until the berserker stirred and gaped in astonishment.

— Can I see, can I see?

The berserker couldn't gather his wits. He not only lacked the
brains to get to the bottom of the voice that was interfering with his
killing – he could barely finish wringing some creature's neck before the refrain would start up:

— Can I see, can I see?

No, it also contradicted his sense of identity to be driven on by
something other than himself. He was seized by bewilderment and
found himself utterly at a loss when his enemies lay, lifeless corpses,
at his feet, yet the cheeping continued to reverberate in his head:

— Can I see, can I see?

And so one day the thought lanced into his thick skull and put down roots there: that this must be his "inner voice".

He put on a self-important face and announced loud and clear:

— I have heard my inner voice. And my inner voice is curious. It wants to see, it wants to examine. I want to see. I want to examine. To know more and more things. I'm curious about everything that lives or dies – though perhaps more about what dies – and above all it is curiosity that drives me on my otherwise inexplicable travels.

Before the chick entered the scene, the clock that ticked in the berserker's heart had not been some creature that said "eter-nity". No, it was a formidable mechanism that thundered:

> That-whidge-duvn't-deftroy-me-makef-me-ftronger!
> That-whidge-duvn't-deftroy-me-makef-me-ftronger!
> That-whidge-duvn't-deftroy-me-makef-me-ftronger!
> That-whidge-duvn't-deftroy-me-makef-me-ftronger!
> That-whidge-duvn't-deftroy-me-makef-me-ftronger!

Anyway, where was I? Oh yes, at this point in the story the berserker was near the mouth of the River Elbe. His journey had taken longer than he'd have liked because nowadays he was no longer remotely satisfied with merely piling up his victims in artistic heaps; on the contrary he felt absolutely compelled to dissect and study them in minute detail before embarking on any pile-building.

But nothing seemed to satisfy the inquisitive chick that the berserker was allowing to run the show. The berserker was by now utterly worn out with splitting bones, tearing apart tree trunks and crushing stones.

— Can I see, can I see?

Shrilled the chick, and the berserker toiled away. One imagines that these labours would have been the death of the berserker had it not been for an event that saved him from such a plebeian fate.

The berserker had cast himself down in exhaustion to sleep and he must have been a ridiculous sight lying there on his back with his mouth open wide – it was the only way he could get any peace from his persistent inner voice, which could be heard chirping reedily:

— Can I see, can I see?

But it grew quieter as sleep overcame the chick. Next morning the berserker and chick awoke in an onion field – the onion crop was coming on nicely in Lower Saxony at the time – which was at the foot of a hill that separated it from a nameless cluster of huts around a patch of dirt.

Anyway, the berserker and chick had awoken, the former to further feats in his battle against life, the latter to new discoveries about this same life. The berserker leapt to his feet with sleep in his eyes and a strong reek of onion in his nose. The dew shone on the stiff onion stalks as far as his bleary eyes could see. The fresh earth and those green shoots poking up from it irritated every nerve in his body before running up to his brain and ringing all the alarm bells there. In a flash he pictured the vegetation sprouting from the soil and growing into a ludicrous tangle that would wind itself around his feet and trip him up. The aftermath would be an easy matter for his enemy: there he would lie, helpless, until the onion plants smothered him and the earth piled up over his body.

He would die.

The berserker went crazy. The doomsday clock boomed in his heart: "That-whidge-duvn't-deftroy-me-makef-me-ftronger! That-whidge-duvn't-deftroy-me-makef-me-ftronger! That-whidge-duvn't-deftroy-me-makef-me-ftronger!"

The chick braced itself in the wisdom tooth; the killer's hour had come, and the berserker tore round the onion field like a tornado. He kicked up onions, ploughing them from the earth with hands and feet, sending showers of soil soaring into the sky like Gothic spires. In no time at all the berserker had managed to defeat the enemy, and once he had quite literally turned the field upside down he embarked on expunging all life from the onions that lay around him, like a sniper whose cover has been blown.

Under normal circumstances, that is to say if the berserker had been himself, he would have made light work of the onion butchery. But as he was busy crushing one bulb after another in his fist the chick could no longer restrain itself, and the berserker heard his piping inner voice urging him to investigate the onion:

— Can I see, can I see?

The berserker opened his jaws to hear better, the onion appeared before the chick's eyes and it immediately wanted to see what was inside – it had never seen an onion before – so it cheeped with genuine, youthful curiosity:

— Can I see, can I see!

The chick watched enthralled as the berserker's stubby fingers peeled layer after layer from the onion, and it was beside itself with excitement as every new layer appeared:

— Can I see, can I see!

The berserker was becoming anxious; he sweated and had difficulty getting the onion off the onion. His inner voice, that inquisitive inner man he had discovered within himself, had begun to grate on his nerves: what the hell was there to see in a blasted onion?

— Can I see, can I see!

The chick went into overdrive, flapping its wing stubs, popping its eyes, craning its yellow neck and squawking:

— Can I see, can I see!

When the berserker managed with trembling fingers to peel away the final layer – and it transpired that there was nothing there, yet the voice continued to yell for more – he lost his wits. He wept, he laughed, he spun in circles, he stamped his feet, he wailed, he quietly sniffed, he seized his head, he flung himself flat on the ground, he beat the earth, he swore, he counted his fingers, he whined, he tore off his clothes, he recalled his childhood, he barked, he whistled a tune, he grabbed his penis and swung it in circles. He stiffened, he sighed.

The berserker stood rigid in the ploughed-up mire that until a short time ago had been a field; a naked, lost troll. The mink-like nature had been extinguished in his breast, the mechanism had worn out, and no "That-whidge-duvn't-deftroy-me-makef-me-ftronger!" sounded there any more. The peace of madness had descended upon him. He hung his ugly head, a mild expression on his face, and rubbed together the thumb and forefinger of his right hand as if fondling the nothing that the onion had contained, muttering, "Eter-nity, eter-nity."

Then he raised his eyes, as surprised and dopey-looking as anyone would be if they had nothing left in life but these three questions –

"Who am I?", "Where do I come from?" and "Where am I going?" – aware that the answers lay in the history of his life up to that fateful moment which, in addition to teaching him to ask these questions, had robbed him of his memory.

The chick, which had been quiet during the mayhem, huddling down in the root of the wisdom tooth, now saw its chance and broke the silence with a short, hesitant cheep.

— Can I see, can I see?

Which probably meant something like: "Is everything all right, foster-father? The world has returned to normal, hasn't it?" Because few things trouble the young more than disorder; that is to say, it doesn't matter how absurd or unfair the world is, so long as things proceed as normal. But it couldn't find words for this in any other way than to cheep:

— Can I see?

The berserker went berserk. He took to his heels in mad flight from his inner self, launching himself off the hill and hurtling in a great arc over the cluster of huts, all the way north to the Arctic Circle where he landed in such a violent belly-flop that every single bone in his body was smashed to smithereens. There he lay rotting for nearly forty years, to the great benefit of all animal life. His spine still juts up from the sea and is known today as Trolls' Cape.

Meanwhile what of the chick? When the berserker soared in a great leap over the rooftops, his face a death mask, every muscle strained in a greedy cry of: "Death, come to me now!", the chick flew out of his gaping jaws and landed in the middle of the village. And naturally it survived the fall.

The villagers knew that if the chick hadn't driven the berserker mad their days would have been numbered, and they were not content merely to name the place "Kükenstadt" after their saviour, no, they even raised a memorial to it on the patch of dirt that later became the town square. And there the statue of a chick stood, as one can see from old photographs, until the town was razed to the ground towards the end of the Second World War.'

II

(17 June 1944)

2

'By 1944 the art of making ocean voyages was taken for granted by mankind to the extent that few things seemed more natural than putting to sea, even when the destination lay beyond the horizon.

There were many reasons for this.

People were no longer afraid of sailing over the edge of the world. The earth was no longer as flat as it looked. Scientists had long ago proved that it would be more accurate to describe it as a ball floating in space and revolving on its own axis at the same time as it revolves around the sun. The moon and planets do the same. They revolve simultaneously around themselves and around the sun.

To begin with, adults were rendered as dizzy as children by the notion that the world was like one gigantic ballgame; it went against every instinct. Their eyes could no longer be trusted, plains had turned into slopes, and if anyone happened to say that he had stayed in one place or another he was laughed at. Not to imply that the public had this knowledge on the brain. No, when it came to daily life this world view amounted to little more than mental gymnastics for experts to amuse themselves with in specially built institutions. Ordinary people didn't have the time; they were too busy with other things, such as eating soup made of carrots, onion and cabbage parcels.

Or sailing ships.

By 1944 it was, of course, many centuries since none but super-heroes had been expected to sail over the horizon. Seafarers knew as well as anyone else that the earth was round and did not let the fact disturb them. If they had to sail uphill, so be it.

Nor would it occur to them for a moment that all land had sunk when there was nothing visible on either side except the coal-grey sea. Even if they had received no news from home for forty days and forty nights. No, at this point in the history of the world's voyages brave captains steered their ships by compasses that turned magnetic needles to point to the North Pole, whichever way the vessels were lying in the water. Sails were no longer used except in pleasure boats or antique craft.

Instead of sails there were engines the size of cathedrals and the average ship was so swift that it could easily overtake any sea monster that chanced to cross its path. Indeed, these ships were made of such high-quality steel, tempered and burnished and coated with super-strength paint, that there was no longer any need to keep a lookout posted to watch for that eight-tentacled menace of the seas, the giant squid. All that remained was for the ships to lift off from the surface of the sea and head for the moon.

But in spite of technology and the wonders of shipbuilding, it so happens that the sea-road that was easily navigated yesterday may have turned into a thirty-fathom-high cliff today. And such is the case when this story opens.

The sea is wild.

The passenger ship *Godafoss* is pitching midway between the deep troughs of the seabed and the outer limits of the universe. The body of the ship is nothing but a shining slug, contracting when a wave swoops over it like a midnight-blue bird of prey. In other words, this is an unremarkable ship by world standards, but to the tiny nation that launched it on the terrible waters of the ocean it is a titanic vessel.

And we are bound to agree with the childish notion that a coat of paint and a noble-sounding name are enough to convert a trawler into a metropolis on an even keel – for there seems to be something in the delusion.

The ship is unsinkable.

Now it appears on the crest of a wave. It is thrown forwards and for an instant appears to be on its way over the edge, with nothing remaining but to plummet into the jaws of the ocean that await green and greedily howling below. But just as we think it's about to happen – and the story will swiftly be over – the wave breaks under the ship and instead of being projected over the edge, it hangs in midair, where a moment before there had been water.

In a cabin in second class lay a man who had the advantage of most on board in that he was seasick and therefore didn't care whether the ship was hanging in midair, on its speedy way to foundering with all aboard, or merely continuing its hopping and skipping. The malady had him in its grip – and he had the malady.

Rolling to the wall and rolling away again, rolling to and rolling fro, rolling and rolling, back and forth like chaff and corn, like corn and chaff. He drove his head into the pillow: if only he could keep his head still for one moment the lump would leave his throat. And if the lump left his throat, he would be able to catch his breath. And if he could catch his breath his stomach muscles would relax. And if his stomach muscles relaxed, his colon wouldn't contract. And if his colon didn't contract, perhaps he would be able to keep his head still for a moment.

So it is to be at sea.

It was not only the blessing of seasickness that diminished his interest in his circumstances: like other landlubbers he thought himself nowhere until he had land in sight. And since only intellectuals or madmen can have an opinion of limbo – and he is neither – he was more homeless now than he had been in the hour that he had abandoned his God in the death camp.

That is where he was coming from; where he was going he didn't know. He was leaving, that itinerary was good enough for him. Rolling to, rolling fro, rolling and rolling. He keeps a tight hold on the hatbox that he is clutching to his chest. It's a matter of life or death and even the nausea isn't enough to weaken his grip. This box contains everything he owns: an infant made of clay, or the likeness of a child, as it might seem to others. But it is not his alone. That is why it is a matter of life and death that nothing should happen to the child.

But who is this seasick wretch?

As a matter of fact it's my father, the Jew Leo Loewe, who has arrived here after walking across Europe with a stopover in the small town of Kükenstadt, where he met my mother. And now he's crossing the sea with me myself, newly created.

My name is Jósef Loewe, I am made of clay. The motion of the ship has no effect on me. I sleep in the darkened box.

And my sleep is the sleep of the dead.

* * *

TUBAL'S ARK

He had slept with an angel. That was the last thing Tubal could remember when he awoke. They had begun their affair when he was in his 140th year; the angel was considerably older.

It happened like this:

Tubal's parents thought him introverted and peculiar and didn't dare leave him alone at home when they needed to go out. And since they found him so odd, and he was their only son, they felt it would not do to have any fewer than all seven of his sisters looking after him when they themselves were away. It was not only because he was odd that they took such good care of him, no, he was a late-born son and there was little likelihood of their conceiving another; Naphtachite was 816 years old and his wife nearly 700 when the Lord blessed them with little Tubal. It happened like this: the angel of the Lord said to Naphtachite's wife: "The Lord sayeth: See, thou art with child. A son I give to thee. Thou shalt name him Tubal."

One day, when Tubal's parents went out, leaving their only son in the care of his seven sisters, the girls became fed up with childminding. This was in the days when the sons of God walked the earth, taking women as they pleased. The sisters had hitherto missed out on the fun because they were always minding Tubal. The youngest was 179, the eldest 246, and they were all women. It wasn't fair. They sat together in the kitchen, discussing the problem. Tubal was alone in the living room. He was playing with a doll. The boy wasn't much trouble and his sisters were discussing this very fact:

"He just lazes about or sits in a corner doing nothing," said the first.

"They should be glad he's not like the other boys, shooting arrows in each other's faces," said the second.

"He mostly plays with our old toys; he's hardly going to come to any harm doing that," said the third.

No sooner had these words been spoken than a shrill scream came from the living room. The sisters looked round as one. Tubal was scolding the doll for dirtying herself.

"Let's just take him with us," said one.

"They'll kill us," said another.

"It's better than hanging around here," said yet another.

Tubal came to the kitchen door. He was a pretty boy.

"No one need find out," said the seventh.

The sisters got themselves ready – and Tubal too – for a date with the sons of God. Once he was wearing a dress, with his hair hidden under a veil, it was hard to tell that Tubal wasn't the eighth daughter of Naphtachite and his wife. This was in the days when God's angels walked the earth.

The angel boys were quartered in an army camp outside the city walls. Great were the marvels it contained and there was a strict guard on the gate. The sisters had to pout to gain admittance. They hid Tubal among themselves and he got past the guard unobserved. In the middle of the camp was a square to which the sisters now headed to show themselves off.

The sons of God came one by one to examine them. They were connoisseurs of the daughters of Adam's line and were surprised not to have seen these girls before. Each sister was more beautiful than the last and the sons of God led them to their tents forthwith. They even competed over the eldest who had been afraid of being left on the shelf.

Tubal alone remained.

And the angel Elias.

Their courtship was slow. The angel took this shy young girl under his wing and used to lead her outside the camp and wait there with her until her sisters had finished amusing themselves with the sons of God. It was all very debauched and the angel drew his feathers over the scene so the young girl wouldn't be corrupted. Then one day the angel Elias said to Tubal, whom he took for the eighth sister: "Now you are 160 years old."

But when Tubal corrected him and revealed that he was a boy, they made love. For the only son of Naphtachite and his wife loved the angel.

He was a son of God.

Tubal looked around. He was covered in feathers and lying in a huge nest. The nest was in a hole that had been hacked out of a tree using some enormous, convex tool. High on the wall facing Tubal hung his dress, a beautiful shimmering brocade that one of the sisters had given him in parting when she went to heaven with God's son Josh, to whom she had borne a son, who was a giant.

Behind the dress was an oblong opening, just wide enough for a slim man to slip through. Tubal and Elias had entered through this crack, for the angel could stretch and contort his body in every way imaginable. This was one of the things that made the angels superb lovers and sought-after husbands, that and their good manners, and the promise of a new and better life – if the relationship worked out.

Tubal clambered to his feet, breaking out in gooseflesh when the feathers tumbled off him. Where was the angel? It wasn't like Elias to leave him to wake up alone after a lovemaking session. They usually sat a good while in the nest, talking about everything under the sun. The angel was well versed in the books of gods and men, and would either impart his wisdom verbally or give Tubal a scroll to consume so the events would pass before his eyes like shadows on a screen.

Tubal's favourite was the Creation story, especially the part where Adam named the beasts. Or when the Lord searched for a soulmate for Adam, and tried him out with everything from a butterfly to a giraffe before he hit upon the idea of Woman. Yes, he knew whole scrolls by heart, did the angel Elias, and on top of that he knew all about the authors. Tubal enjoyed these tales no less. The things those authors got up to! The things Elias and Tubal got up to!

The floor rocked beneath his feet and he inched his way along the side of the nest to the dress. When he snatched it to him, rain lashed his face. It cascaded in through the hole and Tubal thought to himself that he didn't want to stay here a moment longer. Reaching for the crack he hauled himself up. There he hesitated for a second, before remembering that he was alone. The angel wasn't there to grasp his hips and lift him up to the crack. This had always marked the end of their sessions together.

Tubal was halfway out when he discovered that something fairly significant had been happening to the world while he was asleep. For one thing, the tree was tilting strangely and swaying to and fro. Not as if before a wind; no, when he brushed the rain from his eyes there was nothing as far as the eye could see but rough waves. And the rain was no ordinary rain. The heavens were emptying themselves over the earth. Lightning of supernatural scale exploded from coal-black continents of cloud and thunder crashed with such force over the tree that Tubal, son of Naphtachite, little brother of the seven sisters and lover of the angel Elias, was flung backwards into the nest hole.

He hid his face in his hands and wept. When he had wept for a good while, he hung up the fine dress across the opening so the rain wouldn't fall on him. After this he carried on weeping. And that was all he did.

The days passed and Tubal wept in unison with the skies. He didn't have the wit to feed himself but, as he was in the quarters of a holy being whom he loved and who loved him, small creatures emerged from the bark of the tree and crawled into his mouth and down to his stomach. This was his nourishment; they sacrificed themselves that he might live.

What happened next is that the rain began to let up and Tubal's weeping lessened accordingly. He rose to his feet hiccupping and peered out of the tree. Yes, it was nothing but a heavy shower. So he cried a little more. The rain stopped. And Tubal stopped crying.

The world was awash with water. Everything that had once had the breath of life in its nostrils, everything that had lived on dry land had been obliterated from the face of the earth. Tubal realised that everyone he knew was dead. He began to whimper.

But his whimpering turned into song. For he now saw that the waters were going down. Winds blew over the earth and before long mountain peaks rose from the surface of the sea like islands.

The tree drifted before the wind and Tubal sat in the crack, singing like the adolescent he was. One day he saw a raven. It was fun when it perched on the tree beside Tubal and they exchanged croaks. Life was delightful. Or would have been if it weren't for his stomach pains. They grew worse as the boy's journey continued and his belly began to swell. He blamed the unusual diet – those little creatures that sacrificed themselves so that he might live – but his belly continued to swell.

The raven went on its way. The next visitor was a dove, which Tubal caught and ate. By then the surface of the earth had dried out and Tubal was now so large that he slept outside, which is how he caught the dove, for it arrived like a thief in the night. Rolling to, rolling fro. The tree drifted along the coasts of many lands. Tubal was on an ocean, heading north.

One morning Tubal was woken by a thud. He sat up and looked to see what was happening. He had been carried to a rugged island, indented with bays, and the tree was crunching against a colossal headland. When he saw the situation his mouth was filled with sweet song:

> Ah ee-aiya, ah-aiya
> Aiya-a ee, aiya-a ee.
> Ah ee-aiya, ah-aiya
> Aiya-a ee, aiya-a ee.
>
> Ah ee-aiya, ah-aiya
> Aiya-a ee, aiya-a ee.
> Ah ee-aiya, ah-aiya
> Aiya-a ee, aiya-a ee.

Which means: "God is Lord!"

When he came ashore he saw that what had been holding the tree upright in the water was the angel Elias. The angel was dead but his body lay entwined in the roots of the tree like ballast, like a child in the arms of its father.

Tubal buried his friend and wept. Then he went into labour and gave birth to the children Eilífur (that is, "Eternity") and his sister Eilíf.

They were trolls.'

* * *

'Have you started?'

'I was just setting the scene.'

'So I haven't missed anything?'

'The story begins at sea. I was meditating on voyages past and present. I'll come back to them later, so you should be able to pick up the thread.'

She takes off her green leather coat and hangs it over the back of a chair in the living room where they are standing. A beautiful woman, giving off the scent of rain. He indicates a bowl containing the remains of some soup made of carrots, onion and cabbage parcels:

'Would you like a coffee?'

'I wouldn't say no to something stronger . . .'

She runs a hand through her rain-wet hair.

'Have a look and see if I've got anything . . .'

She takes the soup bowl and goes out into the kitchen which adjoins the living room. She opens the cupboard under the sink and tips the leftovers into the bin. Behind it are the corpses of wine bottles and a small bottle of brandy. She looks inside and reckons there's enough for a French coffee.

'You can't imagine what sort of day I've had.'

The woman appears in the kitchen doorway and leans against the frame. She scratches her shin with her toes while waiting for a response. He doesn't respond but watches as she stirs brown sugar into the coffee. She sighs:

'I know, I need to shave my legs.'

'I'd be grateful if you got on with it.'

She sips from the cup and enters the living room where she makes herself comfortable in an armchair facing the sofa. He roots around among some papers on the table in front of him. The woman lights a cigarette.

'I'm ready . . .'

3

'My father stuck his head out from under the quilt, craned his neck and thanked Poseidon for his hospitality with a stream of green bile. If he had forced himself up and gone out into the passage he would have seen that he was in a microcosm of a city with everything that one would expect to find there: the cabins were houses facing on to narrow streets, the smoking room was a café, the saloon a restaurant, the engine room a factory, the bridge a town hall, the deck a square, the hull the city walls, and so on for as long as one can be bothered to stretch out the metaphor. It was a reality he was familiar with.

Anyway, he never discovered the fact. After he had done obeisance to the god of the sea he noticed out of the corner of his eye that there was a man standing in the recess behind the door. He couldn't remember anyone coming in so didn't know how long the visitor had been there.

They studied one another.

The visitor was a broad-shouldered black man, dressed in a suit that reached to just below mid-calf and barely covered his elbows. His shirt was open at the neck and the blue lamp over the door gleamed on his black chest. He wore sandals on his feet.

My father was a mess.

There was a knock at the cabin door. The visitor pressed himself further into the recess and gave my father a sign to keep quiet. When there was a second knock and no one answered from inside the cabin, the door was flung open. There stood two hulking great brutes in sailors' uniforms. They peered into the darkness, seeing nothing but my father who raised his head from where it was hanging over the side of the bed and looked back glassily. These were the men who had hauled him aboard. They had taken a gold ring from him, broken it in half and split it between them. What did they want now? He vomited.

The *Godafoss* chose that moment to go into freefall.

The giants were hurled out into the passage. The door slammed behind them. My father laid his head back on the pillow. The visitor gave a sigh of relief. He went over to my father and knelt down. Both sighed. The visitor addressed my father in English:

— Those guys are crazy, man; I don't know what I did to them. They were licking stamps and postmarking envelopes in the captain's cabin. They went mad when I wished them a happy Independence Day. I was on my way to the dance. I'm lucky to be alive, man.

My father took a deep breath and whispered in German:

— Please forgive me, I am not myself.

The visitor nodded understandingly and my father took this as a sign that he should introduce himself. He began:

— Born . . .

The visitor followed suit:

— Oh, you mean that. I was born in the shanty town of Dream On, today just a nameless suburb of Atlanta. That's in the United States. My father was Jimmy Brown, preacher at the Church of the Black Pentecostalists. He was famous for handling poisonous snakes for the glory of the Lord, but they were mostly toothless little critters. I myself was christened Anthony Brown and I was eleven years old when I set out on a trip to the store that would take me halfway round the world but never back home again.

My daddy had asked me to run out for some bottles of milk, milk being the main diet of the snakes that he kept in a steel drum in the shoe closet to the left of the bathroom door, our house being so cramped. The milk made them docile and easier to handle. I didn't drink milk any longer myself: I'd seen its effects on critters that were lower but also more dangerous than me. Well, I was walking along our street, heading for the neighbourhood store that was on the corner a few blocks down. You could buy most things there that a black family needed, like corn and kidney beans.

I was about to step into the store when some kids drove past in a black Plymouth, though they themselves were white. It was a rare sight in this part of town that was known as Nigertown – I thought it was called after the creek they used to call the Niger that ran down the middle of the main street, Brook Road, which by some strange quirk hadn't been concreted over. Or at least that was the explanation my daddy gave me when I asked about the name.

Anyway, I had eyes for nothing but the fancy car; I was car crazy like all boys, and didn't stop to wonder why these white schoolboys were driving through the neighbourhood. I went into the store and bought what I had been told to: seven pints of milk, and three times three inches of pork rinds that were my wages for the errand. I've always had a thing for pork rinds – sure hope you can get them in Iceland. Only, by the time I came out again the kids had driven right round the block, swearing at the old ladies and whistling at the young ones, spitting at the old-timers and throwing nuts at the children. I'd like to make it clear that I didn't hear about this till later so it had nothing to do with what happened.

As I stood on the sidewalk, chewing the pork rinds, blissfully unaware of anything else, the punks climbed out of their car and surrounded me. They seemed in high spirits. And so was I.

I held out the goody bag.

— Howdy, pork rinds?

Well, they jumped me. And I did what I usually did when people jumped me. I threw them off. I didn't want to hurt them, you know, it was just my upbringing. This went on until it was time for me to hurry home with the milk. My daddy didn't take kindly to idling; he was a strict man, there was no idling anywhere near him. And they were getting mad too, those kids. I held up the shopping bag and said:

— Well, boys, the snakes'll be getting hungry.

They didn't like that one bit. Maybe they thought I was belittling them by holding up the bag, which of course I hadn't put down. They grabbed whatever came to hand – a length of piping or a bottle, I don't remember which, man. Anyway, I was forced to put down the bag. That was all it took.

Only, when I'd turned the boys upside down and didn't really know what to do next, I saw an elderly man standing on the sidewalk, who was dressed so fancy that I was sure I'd be punished big-time.

That was my benefactor.

Anthony Brown fell silent and waited for my father to react to the story. But he had fallen asleep since he didn't understand a word of English. Anthony Brown sighed, took the hatbox from his arms, placed it on the top bunk and jerked him to his feet.

— This won't do, man, this won't do at all.

My father stirred at the manhandling, but before he could offer any resistance Anthony had tossed him over his shoulder. And out of the cabin he went, into the corridor, down the corridor, up another, up and down, round and about, until they came to the ship's saloon. A dance was in full swing; the saloon was decorated with balloons and such a complicated tangle of red, blue and white paperchains that it resembled the intestines of a blue whale. On the wall above the captain's high table hung a picture of a man with bushy, grey whiskers. And above that was a banner bearing the handwritten slogan: 17 JUNE 1944.

A band was playing on the stage by the dance floor and a man in a monkey suit was wandering among the merrymakers asking: "Was I all right?" "Great show!" answered the guests and carried on drinking. And singing. There was singing at every table, though not always the same song.

Anthony went straight to the captain's table where he laid down his burden. My father slumped into a velvet-upholstered chair beside a sleek, plump person, the tenor Óli Klíngenberg. Óli was on his way home.

He leaned forwards and addressed Leo:

— Good evening, eh . . .

This refined "eh" with which he capped his sentence was an affectation that Óli Klíngenberg had picked up in Vienna where there are numerous open-air cafés in the streets and squares. The waiters can't hear what the customers are ordering. And the customers can't hear the waiters saying, "What?" So both say: "Eh?"

The singer held out his hand with the back uppermost.

— You are new here on board, sir, eh?

Anthony nudged his shoulder at my father who sank forwards in his chair until his face touched the wrist of the tenor Klíngenberg who snatched back his hand, thus saving the helpless man from making a disgrace of himself. Leo's lips briefly brushed his knuckles, before Anthony dragged him upright again.

— As if one were the Pope! Shrilled the tenor, drawing back his hand, relieved by this insubstantial kiss. He looked at his dining companion, Georg Thorfinnsen, former captain of the *Miskatonic*. He too was on his way home.

— Evening, young man.

Georg nodded to my father and my father asked if he had seen his hatbox. Ignoring this, the captain pointed out that he would have to put on a lifejacket like everyone else if he meant to join in the fun. The master of ceremonies announced that now the Icelandic National Anthem would be sung, led by the opera singer.

— Well, please excuse me, eh?

The saloon fell silent as Óli Klíngenberg rose to his feet and all eyes followed him as he walked to the stage and took up position in the middle. Bowing neatly he gave the pianist a sign to begin.

> O, God of our land-eh! O, land of our God-ih!
> We worship thy holy, holy name-eh!
> Thy crown is woven from the suns of heaven-ah
> By thy legions, the ages of time-eh,
> For thee a single day is as a thousand years-ih
> And a thousand years are as but a day-ah,
> An everlasting flower with a quivering tear-eh
> That prays to its God and then fades-ih.
>
> Iceland's thousand years, Iceland's thousand years-ah
> An everlasting flower with a quivering tear-eh
> That prays to its God and then fades-ih.

My father had lost consciousness long before the partygoers chimed in with the tenor. Not tomorrow, nor the day after, but the day after that their homeland would receive them. Some would be welcomed, others would go straight to jail, but they were all on their way home. Until then their life would be "life on board". Their whole life would be an echo of "life on board".

But who am I to chatter on about this? I who have never even been conscious on a ship that sails between lands bearing a cross-section of humanity on board. I don't know – yet I catch myself repeating these clichéd three words as if they meant something to me: "Life on board".

I say them out loud, letting them resound in my mind until they stir up a poignant sense of regret that is obviously borrowed from stories told by those who can truly recall a time when people clubbed together to pretend that there was nothing more natural than the dinner service having a life of its own and being constantly on the move, while respectable matrons staggered around like winos. That there were two species in the world: the pale-green *Homo terrestris* and the salt-encrusted *Homo marinus*.

But it is not true that there were only two species.

* * *

My mind conjures up a ship's dog called Sirius. At mealtimes you had to keep an eye open so he wouldn't slip into the saloon to scrounge for food, taking advantage of the bounty provided by the passengers' lack of appetite. I remember him scampering around on deck, barking at the gulls that followed the floating village on its voyage over the deep. I can picture him snuffing around on the bridge, and I can see him tied up in the mess boy's cabin in heavy weather. Sirius, if I had sailed the seas with you I would have hugged your sea-wet body. We would have raced around the ship until someone got fed up and temporarily separated us. And when we met again I would have smuggled you a titbit.

Sirius, loyal and true, a friend in need. I, a seven-year-old boy, you the ship's dog, my friend. We two friends; material for a *Boy's Own* story.

The sun is setting beneath a southern sky. The native drums herald the coming of night and the girls' frenzied dancing in the glow of a huge bonfire. My father, the captain, gets a certain look in his eye when the chief's daughter smiles at him. I have come to recognise that look, and you recognise it too, Sirius. We both know that if he follows it up he will be merry when the ship sails in the morning. Then he'll be very kind, will my father, and when he is kind, he lets me steer. He lifts me on to a box at the wheel and I steer dead ahead, away from the island where the natives wave us off: "Aloha!"

A musical deckhand from the north of Iceland sits in the stern, thanking them on our behalf by playing an Icelandic seaman's waltz on a ukulele he had traded a pocket knife for. A new day has dawned in the life of the little sailor and his dog. Beyond the far horizon exciting adventures await them:

Light in the Depths. Jósef discovers documents indicating that the Nazis are preparing an attack on his father's convoy. Will Jósef and his dog manage to find the U-boat lair and prevent the Nazi attack? Who is the one-eyed man who steals from house to house under cover of night? A nail-bitingly exciting tale for boys of all ages.

The Cold Room. Jósef and Sirius get wind of a plot by a former officer of the Third Reich to bring Europe to its knees again. Did the Allies ever find the Nazis' infamous "Machine of World Destruction"? What is the Cold Room, where is it and what secret does it hold? A terrifically exciting book by the author of *Light in the Depths*.

Gleam in the North. When Captain Leo accepts an assignment to transport a cargo of gold through the ice floes of the Arctic, neither he nor Jósef nor Sirius have a clue what lies in store. Strange flashes in the sky prove to be more than just the Northern Lights. Are aliens from outer space following the ice-breaker? And, if so, do they come in peace? A new title for fans of the Jósef and Sirius books.

Revenge of the One-eyed Man. Jósef is more than a little shocked when he returns to his home town to discover that his old arch-enemy, "the One-eyed Man", has become a respectable citizen. Is he all that he seems? And who is behind the series of crimes terrorising the townspeople? The Jósef and Sirius books have long possessed the hearts and minds of boys of all ages.

The Tasmanian Werewolf. What is Jósef to believe when a peaceful group of Aborigines from Tasmania ask for his help in defeating a werewolf? Is it a case of primitive superstition? Or does the nearby atomic power station have a dark secret to hide? The fifth book about the companions Jósef and Sirius will surprise even their most devoted fans.

I miss you Sirius, my imaginary canine friend, and have never missed you more than now when I must leave you and continue my father's story. But my tale will probably suffer the same fate as the *Boy's Own* stories. When the war was no longer on everybody's lips and the interests of the average Western boy had turned to other kinds of dangers and villains, the authors were forced to bow to the times and the inclinations of their readers.

* * *

The ship sails on its way. High above it there is a cloud of small birds. They drift north-west before the wind, in the same direction as the ship.

They are black and twitter:

"Chirr, chirr!"

Isn't it time we caught sight of land?'

(18 June 1944)

4

'The smell of porridge spreads through the house, wafting as usual to the nose of the boy who is sleeping in the closet in the attic. Instantly wide awake, he lifts the quilt, climbs out of bed and checks whether there is anything on the sheet or his pyjama bottoms. No, there's nothing there and he's pleased with himself. He does a little skip to the chair and begins to dress in the clothes that await him folded on the seat. His sister laid them out ready yesterday. A smile flickers over his sensitive mouth when he sees that she has gone to the trouble of ironing his bowtie. He knots it round his neck, pulls down his shirt-sleeves, lifts the trapdoor and lowers himself through the hole.

The door to his sister's room is open but she's not there. His father's door is ajar. There's no one there either and the bed is unmade. The boy carries on downstairs, following the promise of good porridge. No one can cook oatmeal like his sister. To his mind she has a stature and importance that are out of all proportion to the three years that separate them in age. She has run the household ever since their mother vanished: their parents were on a boat trip to the island of Drangey, organised by the Icelandic Swimming Association, when suddenly, in the blink of an eye, she was no longer on deck with the other passengers.

Their father, unable to cope following the tragedy, buried himself in solitary contemplation of the manuscripts that he read to pieces on specially made light tables at the University of Iceland.

The girl took care of father and son.

So the boy is startled when he sees that it is his father the palae-ographer who is stirring the saucepan, not his sister. Usually the brother and sister have the morning hour to themselves while the old man eats his rations up at the graveyard before going to work – even on holidays. But no, today it is the old-timer, all two metres of him, who stands over the porridge pan with the wooden spoon like a darning needle between his huge fingers, just sort of poking at it.

— Good morning.

Says the boy, sitting down at the kitchen table.

— Speak for yourself . . .

The old man runs his free hand through the white hair that cascades handsomely over his shoulders, then turns quick as a flash from the hob and dishes up into a bowl for his son. His movements are so sure that if the man weren't a swimming champion many times over the boy would have thought he had spent all morning practising serving porridge. He picks up his spoon without saying a word. His father bangs the saucepan down on the hotplate, reaching for the cream pot in the fridge and splashing it on to the heaped porridge in a single movement.

— Get that down you.

And with that a strange day begins in the boy's life. Outside the citizens are about to start celebrating the fact that yesterday they became an independent nation with a pure-blooded Icelandic President. Admittedly he's no "President Jón", like the old indepen-dence hero, Jón Sigurdsson, who adorns the first stamp series to be issued by the free country in defiance of its old imperial Danish overlord. No, he is someone they know even less about than the deposed king, whom most citizens eligible to vote at least got a chance to set eyes on when he visited the country in 1936, and who is remem-bered for his excellent table manners. (He had a firm, confident handshake too.) But since when has the nation ever really known their standard-bearer?

The new President is merely a sort of civil servant; he's even got black shadows under his eyes. But no one complains – he makes people feel as if they have nothing to fear from the foul pit, full of spectres, that is the present day. The boy knows this because his father told him so.

— Where can your sister have got to, hmm?

The old man has turned off the heat under the saucepan and is holding a half-gallon jug. The boy darts a quick glance over his shoulder and catches his father emptying two bottles of aquavit into the jug.

— Of course she assumes we won't be going anywhere in the meantime . . .

The boy doesn't know how to answer this but the old man spares him the trouble.

— No, old chap, she's like your mama. She's realised that not just anyone is invited to this fancy independence party of theirs. We're better off staying away . . .

He drops heavily on to a stool facing the boy and half empties the jug in a single swig.

— No, it's not enough to have posed for that little scribbler Tryggvi, wearing a damned potato sack, eh?

He strokes the beard that flows palely down over his chest like the fleece of a prize-winning ram.

— You'd have thought a fellow had grown a beard and put flesh on his bones purely in order to pose for the coat of arms of a nation that can't even tell the difference between a dragon and a serpent.

He wipes his mouth on the back of his hand and grimaces like a man with three rows of teeth:

— No, the mountain giant will "just, you know", as the hoi polloi from Skuggahverfi would say, hmm, he'll "just, you know" have to stay at home. Then why, I ask, why the devil did they have to change the coat of arms anyway? The old one is much more like the pathetic rabble I see every day: the bull looks like a badly shorn ewe, the eagle like a plucked cockerel, the dragon like a dog with asthma, and the giant like a mincing actor who's forgotten his lines.

The old man slams his fist on the table, making everything jump. The boy can't swallow his porridge: this is no longer his story; in that he's a fourteen-year-old Reykjavík boy who goes into town on the second day of the new republic and meets up with several of his classmates. They huddle together and share a cigarette down by the wall of the East End School before heading into the centre to watch the preparations for the festivities. Then they run up to Camp Ingolfs to cadge spirits from the GI who asks for nothing but a kiss from each of them in return for the bottle. Yes, the day passes in high jinks of this kind. They grab a bite to eat in the sales tent or at a pub, since they're all on their summer vacation or doing holiday jobs. Then at the dance in the evening they plan to ogle the girls, and are pretty hopeful that the girls will ogle them in return.

But no, that's not how the boy's day is going to pan out. Instead, the main protagonist of the day will be his eighty-two-year-old father and he himself will only be a minor character in that drama – or perhaps merely a spectator. The old man reaches a furtive hand down to the floor and snatches up a massive oaken staff.

— At least I got to keep the bloody stick . . .

He brandishes it over his head, smashing the light-fitting above the table.

Fragments of glass rain down on father and son.

* * *

THE OLD MAN AND THE MARE

This is how your grandfather died.

Ignoring the protests of foolish farmhands, he ordered them to shoe a crazy mare that everyone else agreed was fit for dog-meat but that he insisted was a child's ride and had named Cinderella to underline his point.

After they had chased the mare up hill and down dale, calling and stretching out their arms as if they had finally worked out how to capture nature itself, they managed to corner the beast in the shoeing pen by the farm. But no one dared go near her. It fell to your grandfather, the old-timer – he was born in mid-September 1778 – to shoe her.

Well, after wishing the lily-livered cowards to hell and beyond, your grandfather crept up on the mare with a "Steingrímur's iron" in his hand. This was a home-made horseshoe named after himself, and with hissing and threats he managed to hook it round the animal's near hind leg. He drew the hoof to him, fitted the shoe and positioned the first nail – but as he raised the hammer for the blow the mare decided that it was not her time that had come but his:

she flung off the shoe and gave him a good kick in the head, sending him flying backwards in a great arc to land at the foot of the farm wall.

Man of steel as your grandfather was, he rose to his feet unaided, glared fiercely at the group standing round him in a semicircle and staring at him aghast, and snarled:

— What are you gawping at, you bunch of gutless milksops?

Before anyone could tell him that the mare had left a nail in the middle of his forehead, he fell down unconscious. The first thing the homeopath Haraldur Skuggason did when he came to visit him was to ask for a pair of pliers.

For several days men took it in turns to try to prise the nail out of his forehead. Of course it was bloody useless: the mare had been sired by a *nykur*, a water monster from Lake Kappastadir, and your grandfather came from Trolls' Cape. Then, on the third day, he sat up and bellowed so deafeningly that people looked up from their haymaking in the meadows.

> The warrior wakens
> his whistle dry
> a desperate desire
> to drain an ocean

A young girl was ordered to water him. This proved such a daunting task that she ended up having to pour sour whey down his neck morning, noon and night. The horseshoe nail made your grandfather so thirsty that he drank unceasingly, but only if your grandmother brought him the drink.

One night, deciding she'd had enough of carting whey to your granddad, she seized the pliers that lay on the chest by his bed. Straddling the old man, she gripped the nail with the pliers and after an interval of rocking the blood gushed into the air like a geyser, right in your grandmother's face. You can guess what happened next!

It was not the only thing to gush out of the old man.

Yes, that's how your father was conceived.

That is why you are here.

* * *

The day passes something like this.

The old man wanders round the house, managing to keel over in a stupor in every room in turn, before rising almost immediately from the dead only to pass out again in the next room. And he begins every resurrection by telling his son the story of his conception. In between times he bellows to himself that it is no coincidence that it should fall to him, and no other living Icelander, to be chosen as a model for the giant in the new republic's revised coat of arms. The boy follows him to make sure he doesn't hurt himself. As if he could prevent the troll from destroying himself or anything else that gets in his way. He tells his friends the old man is ill.

Usually it is his sister who watches over the colossus on his pere-grinations round the house. On these occasions the boy shuts himself in the attic, puts on his balaclava to muffle the sound of what's going on downstairs and tends to his stamp collection. The old man thinks it a foolish pastime.

Now they've reached the bathroom. The old man sits on the side of the bath, shaking his fist at the window. The hubbub of the cele-brations carries in through the vent in the top right-hand corner. He leaps to his feet, cups his hands into a foghorn and yells at the smartly dressed people on their way down to the square:

— Long live the rabble-public!

The boy draws the curtain across the window. He knows that this display of bad temper is not because the old man was neither offered a seat of honour and a woollen blanket at the ceremony at Thingvellir nor invited to take part in recreating the coat of arms as a "tableau vivant" on Lækjartorg Square. No, he is aggrieved because his son will not follow in his wake as a swimmer, and, what's more, he suspects that his daughter is carrying on with a soldier. The boy knows that this is quite true.

He also knows that he stopped wetting his bed the day he cut off the tip of the middle finger on his right hand, the very day he – Ásgeir, the son of Helgi, the son of Steingrímur – was due to begin training with the Poseidon Swimming Club.'

IV

(11 March 1958)

5

'The first creature to wake up that morning is a black nanny-goat which is lying outside by the wall of a shed in the back garden of a dignified wooden house on a street leading up from the centre of a small town in the corner of an inlet on an island located in the north of the mid-Atlantic.

She scrambles to her feet, darting yellow eyes around to check on the world. Everything is in its place and tinted with red. The rainwater glows in a brimming bucket by the corner of the shed. The goat heads over to it.

When she has drunk her fill an early spring fly settles on her. She shakes it off and waddles over to the house at number 10a Ingólfsstræti.

She's hungry.

* * *

Leo Loewe is at the National Gallery of Iceland, attending the opening of a photographic exhibition entitled "Faces of Iceland". The Minister for Culture is giving a speech on how landscape and weather shape the soul of the nation – and how the soul engraves itself on the visage of its people. He speaks extempore, the words flowering on his tongue like buttercups on a mountain-top. He himself is not tall, for men of vision seldom rise as high as their thoughts. Therein lies the beauty of his opening speech.

— This interplay between land and people, this story of man and nature, these glad tidings are captured by the photographer at a single instant in time. The eye of the camera opens by the miracle of technology and sees the truth: that man and country are one. Iceland speaks to us in faces that have been turned towards snow-white mountain peaks, red-glowing lava and berry-blue moorlands. For generation after generation the nation has celebrated its landscape and this celebration is reflected in its cloudless expression.

Here the minister pauses in his speech and the exhibition guests thank him with some shy clapping. Turning to the photographer, a tall man with hawk-like eyes, the minister places a hand on his arm. The photographer does not stir but inclines his head, thereby signalling to the minister that he is ready to hear more. The minister removes his hand from the artist, leaving it dangling motionless in the air between them.

— So it is not only today's children of Iceland who look out at us from these pictures; no, when our eyes meet theirs we come face to face with Iceland's thousand years. And we must ask ourselves whether they like what they see . . .

(Dramatic pause.)

— Yes, we must ask ourselves whether we have "followed the path of righteousness, with good as our goal", as the poet said. Mr President, ladies and gentlemen, I hereby declare the exhibition "Faces of Iceland" open.

This time the applause is vigorous and the photographer bows to the President, the Minister for Culture and the guests, most of whom have their picture included in the exhibition. People disperse around the gallery in search of themselves, Leo Loewe among them. The walls of the gallery are hung with the portraits of almost every living Icelander, arranged according to county and settlement, except for Reykjavík where they are in alphabetical order by street name.

In the gallery housing the citizens of Reykjavík, Leo comes across the anthropologist who accompanied the photographer on his three-year circuit of the country. He is standing in the midst of a group of tweed-clad gentlemen sporting bowties, university types. The anthropologist himself towers over them, silver-haired, with a coarse-ground pepper-and-salt beard. There is a frisson of anticipation among the men and some have started to smoke. The anthropologist is telling them something amusing. He speaks like a man of the people, with a hard northern accent, forcing out the words between clenched teeth as if he had a half-eaten trout's head in his mouth.

— There's something I must show you . . .

The anthropologist beckons them to follow him and leads them straight across the gallery to where the letters I–H are hand-painted in black on the wall above the pictures. Leo, tailing along behind, sees the anthropologist searching with his finger for a particular face on the wall, while the group around him waits expectantly.

— Ing-ing-ing-ing . . .

The finger hovers over the pictures.

— Ingólfsstræti!

The finger stops but Leo can't see exactly where because the academics all lean forwards as one – and fall silent. Leo inches his way closer; he lives on Ingólfsstræti. The anthropologist awaits his colleagues' reaction, anticipating tears of mirth; he himself is at bursting point. But instead of a gale of laughter swaying them like buckwheat, the tweed figures slowly straighten up and look at one another awkwardly – no one looks at the anthropologist. Once they have adjusted their bowties they all discover simultaneously that the girl with the drinks tray has come to their rescue.

The anthropologist is left standing there with superfluous laughter in his throat. Perhaps Leo can laugh with him? Yes, though anthropology often makes a mockery of people with its eccentric sense of humour, there is no need to punish the anthropologist personally for this. Leo approaches the wall. Ah, yes, there are his neighbours. The anthropologist bleats something.

— Best approach him warily. Let's see: 2 Ingólfsstræti, 3 Ingólfsstræti, 4 Ingólfsstræti (no one lives there, that's the Old Cinema), 5 Ingólfsstræti, 6 Ingólfsstræti (where's Hjörleifur?), 7 Ingólfsstræti . . .

Leo is just getting to his house when the anthropologist emits a dreadful howl of laughter:

— Behehe, behehe . . .

He gulps, rolling back his tongue as Leo looks at him encouragingly. Leo searches for his picture on the wall. The anthropologist is whining with laughter. Then Leo spots himself; his name is typewritten in clear letters on the strip of paper beneath the black frame:

Leo Loewe, overseer.

But the picture is not of him at all but of a big toe. It fills the entire frame with its dark, deformed nail and a coarse tuft of hair on the joint.

— Behehe, behehe, behehe . . .

The anthropologist bleats, pointing at Leo. Other exhibition guests come flocking over, with the President and Minister for Culture in the vanguard. The photographer presses his lips to Leo's ear and breathes:

— You are what you see . . .

— Behehe . . .

* * *

— Behehe, behehe, behehe . . .

The goat is trapped by the horns in Leo's bedroom window. Having chewed down the *Coleus* plant that stands on the sill, she now wants to get back out into the morning but this is proving hard.

— Behehe . . .

Leo shakes off both anthropologist and sleep. He sits up. The goat's head is hidden by the curtains but the animal's struggles seem full of despair; she kicks the window pane with her forelegs and snorts angrily. The flowerpot is tossed out from under the curtains and lands on Leo's bed, showering the newly woken man with dirt and broken pottery.

— I'd better sort this out before she pulls the window out of its frame. She's annoyed enough people already . . .

He leaps out of bed and yanks back the curtains. Startled at the sight of the man, the goat goes berserk and splinters start flying from the woodwork. Leo reaches out a hand to lift the catch but the goat snaps at him. He whips back his hand and she recommences kicking the wood. He puts out his hand, she snaps. Etc.

Footsteps are heard upstairs. Mr Thorsteinson, Leo's landlord, a member of the Reykjavík House-owners' Association, is up and about. He doesn't like the goat. Were it not for the fact that she is an ally in his battle against Mrs Thorsteinson's scheme of turning the patch of yard behind the house into a garden, she would long ago have been sent back to the rubbish tip.

Leo knows this but the goat does not. She keeps up the same behaviour, finally succeeding in biting him. He squeaks soundlessly and thrusts his hand into his armpit, then dives into the kitchen and fetches a pot of parsley to offer his tormenter. It works. The goat tucks in and Leo manages to lift the window latch with his free hand. He eases the goat's head out of the window, followed by the parsley pot.

The goat is violet in the morning sun and the udder that bulges out from between her hind legs shines a rosy pink.

So it is to be a goat.'

'What kind of a way is that to describe a goat?'

The woman leans back on the sofa, smoothing the dress over her stomach – a twinkle in her eye. But the storyteller doesn't react to the joke. His eyes grow wet.

'I owe more to that goat than almost anyone else.'

'Really . . .'

'My father found her when she was hardly more than a kid. He was walking along the Gold Coast on the west side of town with Pétur Salómonsson Hoffmann, the uncrowned king of Reykjavík's rubbish dumps, when they heard a pathetic bleating coming from a cardboard box marked with the logo of a local coffee merchant, but we'll leave his name out of it. Pétur wouldn't go near the box, saying he didn't touch Masonic stuff like that, it resulted in nothing but trouble – that's assuming it wasn't a merman. But my father feared neither Freemasons nor sea monsters. He opened the box and looked straight into the yellow eyes of a kid that had been left there to die. It craned its neck towards him and bleated appealingly.

He freed the baby goat from its prison, took it in his arms and told his companion that this was a pure diamond. Pétur snorted: "Goats are unnatural creatures, they don't understand Icelandic."

"I'm keeping her anyway." Leo clutched the creature tighter, prepared for a long argument about goats. It wouldn't be the first time he had disputed about such things with Icelanders. But nothing came of the argument. Pétur had spotted a gold ring inlaid with precious stones.

He rubbed the dirt off the ring, handed it to Leo and asked if this was what he was looking for. No, it wasn't the right ring. Leo's ring was still in the hands of robbers, split in two. Pétur said he would continue to keep an eye out for it – though he didn't understand what was so special about it; gold was gold.

Anyway, the kid, which was as black as coal, was christened Ambrosia. Goat's milk is the food of heroes.'

'I won't argue with you about that.'

'Leo bandages his wound and sighs when he looks in the mirror and catches sight of the suit hanging on the lavatory door. Today he had meant to be so very smart, never smarter than today of all days. But now his bandaged hand would protrude from his elegant sleeve like a picture puzzle for everyone he encountered. They would all want to know how he had hurt himself. And how was he to answer? That he had been bitten by a goat? That would only lead to further questions, which might in turn lead to others, and he had no desire to answer those.

Leo takes his suit down from the peg on the lavatory door and flicks off some imaginary dust. No dust has ever fallen on it. Every Saturday morning without fail for the past seven years he has taken it out and brushed it. The temptation to put it on was great, especially at first. But he refrained, since nothing must be allowed to spoil the hour when it finally came. The suit is tailor-made, of black wool with three buttons, but when he pulls on the trousers he discovers that he has lost weight since he bought it.

Today is the formal occasion for which the suit was made.

Leo puts the kettle on. He takes a bottle of milk from the fridge and a scrap of sponge from the side of the sink, intending to pick up both at once but hampered by the bandage. He pours the milk into a soup bowl and puts in the sponge, then takes it into the pantry that opens off the kitchen.

Leo fumbles his way forwards in the gloom with his bitten hand. Besides what you would expect to find in a pantry there is a set of copper vessels. The largest stands on a simple electric hotplate. It is boiling and drops are dripping from the pipe that connects one vessel to another until it turns into a spout that tapers down to nothing. Leo checks the spout: a minuscule droplet glitters there, while in the crystal-glass beaker below there is a golden flake the size of a child's fingernail. Making gold is a time-consuming business.

He lays down the bowl and after groping along the top shelf on the outer wall he takes down some jam jars and lines them up on the shelf below. My crib is revealed, a rather ancient and somewhat dented hatbox. Standing on tiptoe he slips his good hand underneath it, gets a purchase on the box and checks whether he has enough strength to lift it down without tipping it. He manages.

He carries the box carefully to a wooden table by the door, removes the lid and arranges it so that the contents are illuminated by the strip of light that falls into the pantry between door and frame:

— So, little Jossi, how are we today?

Leo brushes his fingertips over my forehead, very gently so as not to disarrange it. Reaching for the bowl of milk, he squeezes most of the moisture from the sponge and begins to bathe me. With light strokes he wipes the grey child's body, and the clay from which I am made absorbs the milk. The bluish-white goat's milk seeps into me like the maternal care I never knew.

He turns me over and plies the milky sponge under my back and bottom. Then he squeezes the rest over my chest, rubbing it into my breast on the left-hand side so the heart gets its share. He has done this every morning and evening for the fourteen years that have passed since he was carried off the ship in Reykjavík. But from today Leo can set about trying to retrieve the gold he needs to quicken life in the little figure in the hatbox. That, in addition to the small amount of gold he has managed to make for himself, should be enough for a new seal.

— There, there, old chap, Daddy will be home by suppertime and then we'll be Icelanders, you and I.

He turns round in the pantry doorway.

— Icelanders, Jossi, imagine!'

6

'It was on a Tuesday that my father had gone, a few weeks earlier, to the Ministry of Justice with the form he had filled in so many years before. The official who received him was a dignified middle-aged man, small-boned, with bushy eyebrows and a steel-grey five o'clock shadow. He rested his elbows on the desk with the form between them like a bowl of porridge. He was waiting for a call, that much was plain, for whenever there was a pause in his conversation with Leo his eyes would dart to the telephone.

— So, you are applying for citizenship?

My father said he was.

— And how have you enjoyed your stay so far?

He eyed the phone. My father nodded.

— Very much.

— And that is why you are now applying for citizenship?

— Yes.

— Leo Loewe; you're German?

The official rested a finger on my father's name.

— No.

— Just as well . . .

He ran his finger down the form with one eye on the phone. It remained silent.

— Right, there are some questions I need to ask you.

— Please, go ahead.

The official cleared his throat, then said with heavy emphasis:

— Do you speak Icelandic?

Leo paled: this question implied so much more than merely whether he knew the language. The official was in effect asking Leo if he was worthy of citizenship.

The country was full of people who had lived there longer than him but had not yet become Icelanders. There were Danes, Germans, Norwegians, Frenchmen and Englishmen who had never got to grips with Icelandic. Their speech was broken, ungrammatical. They were a laughing-stock. The Danes were considered especially ridiculous.

* * *

Two years after he had arrived in the country Leo had worked with a Dane on the construction of a funfair. The man had completed an advanced education in the management of fairground rides and held a Master's degree in Tivoli Studies from the Royal College of Engineering in Copenhagen, but now he had to make do with labouring with Leo and a bunch of Reykjavík bums who had been press-ganged into the job from the city's late-night watering holes. The low-lifes were respectful to the Dane, keen as they were to finish the job as quickly as possible so they could get back to the fun at the illicit drinking dens, but the foreman lost no opportunity to humiliate him. When the Dane said good morning:

— Goo' morn!

The foreman wouldn't answer. If the Dane happened to repeat his wishes for a good morning to his co-workers the foreman would turn to the low-lifes who were loitering bug-eyed from lack of sleep around the coffee shack and bellow at them:

— For God's sake, say "goo' morn" to the bacon-eater so he'll shut up!

After that the Dane wouldn't open his mouth for anything less than a matter of life or death. But it soon came to that.

— I don' tink dis is strong *nok* . . .

They were busy erecting the Ferris wheel and the Dane was worried that the struts supporting it were not strong enough. The foreman, on the other hand, was adamant that they were and bawled back:

— This *nok* was welded by Icelanders in the factory down by the bay here and if it's not good *nok* for you, you can bugger off back to Denmark and shove your Danish *nok* where the sun don't shine!

The Dane became obsessed with those struts. For the rest of the

week he went around alone, muttering to himself that this business
with the struts wasn't good *nok*, while the foreman winked at the men
and roared until the funfair echoed:

— He's *nokk*ing again!

Shortly afterwards the Dane was caught red-handed, alone in the
middle of the night, trying to tighten the bolts that pinned the struts
to the ground. He was fired on the spot and told he should be grateful
he wasn't being charged with sabotage. The following day Leo and
the other labourers' first task was to loosen the bolts again. After the
funfair opened the Dane became its most loyal customer. He would
be standing by the box office with his tuppence ready when the ticket
girls arrived at work, and he wouldn't go home until the last batch
descended shrieking from the gondolas. But the Icelandic struts held
firm *nok*. It was painful to watch this intelligent Danish engineer lose
his job, his family and finally his wits.

In the end the customers and staff of the funfair found his presence
so oppressive that the Danish ambassador was forced to intervene.
The fairground specialist was arrested after a protracted pursuit around
the funfair and it took a dozen policemen to coerce him on board a
ship to Copenhagen. He went off in a straitjacket and the country
was considered well shot of him.

When Leo learned of the fate of his former co-worker he decided
to master Icelandic as well as is humanly possible for a foreigner.
But the first thing his tutor in the Icelandic language impressed
upon him was that he would never achieve a perfect grasp of the
tongue.

— Never!

Dr Loftur Fróðason, librarian, reiterated his words by raising a
finger and flexing the muscle of his forearm at the elbow, causing his
finger to quiver like a barometer needle indicating low pressure. The
lessons took place in the National Library that housed the Icelanders'
literary heritage – which was all a closed book to Leo and, according
to his teacher, would remain so for ever and a day.

Leo's fellow pupil was Mikhail Pushkin, a Russian Embassy
employee who had been unable to finish reading the Icelandic–Russian
dictionary before being summoned to serve in Iceland. Apart from a

fair knowledge of Icelandic vocabulary from A to K, all he could say when he arrived in the country was:

— A man of Muscovy am I.

And although this caused amusement wherever he went and people were forever buying him drinks on the strength of his attainment, it was in no way sufficient for the job he was supposed to be doing. Comrade Pushkin was a master chef at the Russian Embassy; that is to say, a KGB spy.

— Icelandic is like a mountain spring, a great and mighty river, so clear that one can see to the bottom wherever one looks. At times it has flowed with the light current of narrative, at others cascaded in the roaring rapids and whirlpools of poetry. During the spring thaw streams have run into it from far and wide, bearing with them dirt and clay, but they have never succeeded in muddying the deepest wells. They have formed no more than streaks of sediment along the banks, and gradually the grime has sunk to the bottom and vanished out to sea.

Loftur slammed the book shut and glared at his students. Had Leo Loewe or Mikhail Pushkin grown up by such a river, sipping from it with tender, childish lips? No, and so they would begin every lesson by drinking a glass of pure Icelandic water.

— The main characteristics of the Icelandic language are as follows: it is pure, bright, beautiful, soft, strong, splendid, ingenious, rich, and so, it follows, especially well suited to literature. That is the opinion of respected linguists from all over the world. If you wish to argue with them, be my guest!

No, neither Leo nor Mikhail trusted themselves to enter into a debate with foreign professors. Loftur laughed.

— I thought not. Now listen to this!

He took a violin down from the wall and began to play. The tune was poignant and vigorous by turns. The notes poured from the instrument until Leo was no longer in the poky little basement under the Icelandic National Library, no, all those literary riches lifted from his shoulders and he was sailing slowly up the Vltava. He is seven years old; Prague lies behind, a picnic ahead. He leans over the rail; the river water boils against the hull. Towers and town squares. Now he is playing with his sisters in a woodland clearing; a magpie flies overhead with a piece of glass in its beak. Now he is running down to the river; his father is sitting on the bank. An old black hat is silhouetted against the dazzling water. Now he takes a bite of rye bread with sweet pickled herring; the fish oil trickles over his tongue and the onion crunches between his teeth. Now he dives into the water; a barge sails past with engine throbbing. A tram. Now he wakes up in his mother's arms; the journey home always makes him sleepy.

— That is the song of Iceland!

Loftur put down the violin and Leo returned to his adoptive land. The basement had grown darker. He looked at Mikhail and saw from the sensitive expression on the Russian's face that he too had returned from far away. The Icelandic teacher seized a rattle from the desk.

— And this is what it sounds like in other languages . . .

He shook the rattle. It was an ugly racket that left both Leo and Mikhail unmoved.

At the end of the first lesson Loftur handed his students an Icelandic primer for complete beginners and told them they could teach themselves that stuff. He would help them with their comprehension and their feel for the language's infinite possibilities.

— Infinite!

This is how the Icelandic classes were organised. They consisted mainly of practical exercises in acquiring mastery of the language of the medieval Golden Age. Only once did Leo see the doctor at a loss. He was demonstrating the language's rich vocabulary to his disciples by competing with them as to whether Icelandic or their own languages had more words for various concepts. And all evening long he had trumped them.

Then the moment came when he challenged them to name all the words they knew for the thing that grew out of the rear ends of the beasts of the earth, and began immediately to list the contributions of Icelandic to this area:

— *Rófa* on dogs or cats, *hali* on cows, *skott* on mice, *stertur* on horses, *spordur* on fish, *dindill* on sheep, *stél* on birds—

— Excuz mi . . .

Here Mikhail interrupted the doctor, something that had never happened before, since he was an exceptionally courteous man.

— *Stýri* on cats, *vél* on birds . . . Yes, Mr Pushkin?

— Gan yu dell mi vhat zis is galled?

He stood up and began to fiddle with his waistband.

— What what is called?

The doctor didn't know whether to look at the Russian's face or at his fumbling fingers.

— Zere is no vord in Russian.

Leo averted his eyes; the man was pulling down his trousers. The doctor flapped – or waved, or shook, or wagged, or brandished – his hands at him. At his hips and behind him.

— Now, now, man, control yourself! You must have a word for that in Russian – more than one, no doubt.

— No, no, Doctor, listen to Pushkin, I am delling druth . . .

The suffering in the Russian's voice was so undeniable that the doctor and my father looked round as one; his eyes were filled with a childlike plea for mercy.

— Well, let us see . . .

Loftur put on his glasses.

— But you mustn't think that this is going to become a habit.

— No, no, only zis vonce.

The Russian pulled down his trousers, but instead of taking out his John Thomas he turned his backside to them. And everything was not as it should have been. Leo leaned forward: there was a bulge in the underpants where they should have been empty. Pushkin looked over his shoulder, briefly whipped down his pale blue pants and said pleadingly:

— Vhat is zis galled?

The chef-spy's audience gasped: he had a tail. It was the size of a finger, hairless, with joints visible beneath the bluish skin.

— Nobody knows vhat zis is galled in Russian . . .

Mr Mikhail Pushkin looked hopefully at the doctor. But it did little good. The tutor was stumped: although words existed in Icelandic for every thought on earth, and he knew them all, his pupil's overgrown coccyx had been left out of that tremendous lexical creation. After some thought:

— Well, the bone is called the tailbone. So I suppose it's a tail?
Pushkin burst into tears.

— No, no, Dr Fródason, Pushkin iz not pig or dog.

Dr Loftur comforted him by saying that in the next lesson they would have a go at inventing neologisms. Perhaps they could come up with something if they combined their efforts.'

'A Russian with a tail? I thought the Red Ogre was dead . . .'

'No, it's true. I feel kindly towards Pushkin; he and my father became good friends.'

'And he had a tail?'

'Actually the phrase they invented for it was a "rear-projection".'

'So in other words he had a rear-projection?'

'Yes, he showed it to me when he came to Iceland several years ago. He was in Gorbachev's entourage at the summit meeting with Reagan. He could even wag it – not much, just a little. It's called atavism or reversion to an ancestral state.'

'Really, aren't you the know-all?'

'Leo and Pushkin graduated after a three-year course of instruction. In parting, Dr Loftur Fródason gave them each a newly issued set of stamps featuring pictures of Iceland's principal manuscripts. A group of scholars had chosen them, making their decision after a prolonged dispute. Dr Loftur was a member of the committee.

— It is our hope that these stamps will help us in our struggle to compel the Danes to return the manuscripts to us.

This was Leo Loewe's first experience of the Icelanders' special relationship with stamps.

* * *

— Yes, I speak Icelandic.

Leo spoke loud and clear so the official wouldn't fail to recognise that here was a model candidate for Icelandic citizenship.

— That's good to hear.

The official stuck a finger under his left eyebrow and lifted the tuft of hair from his eye. Then the phone rang and it didn't take him long to snatch up the receiver.

— Yes, wasn't it?

He listened a good while, then put his hand over the receiver.

— What do werewolves eat?

Leo didn't realise the official expected him to answer.

— What do they eat?

The official whispered. Leo whispered back:

— People? Aren't they man-eaters?

The official shook his head, astonished at the foreigner's ignorance, then continued his telephone conversation.

Leo kept silent.'

7

'Leo walks down Ingólfsstræti. It's five weeks after his interview and four hours and seventeen minutes until his case will be put before parliament. And what is a waiting man to do? Where is the best place to do something like that? Leo goes to a café.

He takes a seat at the long table in Café Prikid. It's fairly empty since it's a weekday today and still early. "A coffee, please, and the morning paper." He drinks it black and opens the paper at random. Oh, why did he have to do that? On the left-hand page he sees that they're burying Ásgeir Helgason today.

There are three obituaries: a long one by Ásgeir's brother-in-law, a short one signed by Hrafn W. Karlsson on behalf of the Icelandic Philatelic Society, and the third a farewell from his colleagues at the Reykjavík Swimming Pool. They are all tinged with awkwardness. Murders are so rare here that obituaries for murder victims are outside people's experience. It's clear from the notices that Ásgeir had accomplished nothing beyond collecting stamps and fussing around naked men, activities that are described in exaggerated and elevated style. Is it perhaps because the murderer has not yet been caught and the authors of the obituaries hope he will feel remorse when he reads about the victim's virtues? As if he hadn't known him. Here everyone knows everyone else.

Even Leo knew the murdered man. Ásgeir Helgason was one of the unluckiest individuals he had ever met. During the time Leo had been going to the swimming pool the man had continually lost fingers and toes, even earlobes.

After reading the obituaries Leo feels he knows Ásgeir's father, Helgi, rather better than the man himself. The father appears to have been a champion swimmer and an expert on Icelandic manuscripts.

— Apparently it was a grisly sight . . .

Leo looks up from the paper. A red-haired man with a Jack-of-Spades beard in the same shade has taken a seat beside him. He leans towards Leo.

— His tongue had been cut out.

— What?

— I heard it from a woman I know who's married to a policeman. He was first on the scene.

Leo is in no mood for such talk; today is a day of celebration. The redhead's voice grows reedier.

— He knew something, it was a warning to others.

Leo closes the paper, picks up his purse and begins to count out the coins for his coffee. He puts the money on the table and stands up. The other continues:

— His stamp collection has vanished.

— Why are you telling me this?

— What? I'm just making conversation.

— Well, good day . . .

Leo hurries out of the café.

* * *

The official had concluded his conversation about the diet of were-wolves by hissing at the person on the other end of the line:

— Go to hell! They've got their heads up their arses and from what I can hear so have you!

He continued the interview as if nothing had happened.

— You have a clean record, I see, and here is a statement from the Czechoslovakian Embassy that you did nothing unlawful while you were domiciled there. What, I thought you were German?

The official glared at Leo.

— I'm from Prague.

— I hope you're not a Communist?

— No, I'm apolitical. I'm an alchemist.

— Oh, is that to the left or right, politically speaking?

— You could categorise it as an occult science.

— I know that, I was just testing you. An alchemist, that means someone who makes gold, doesn't it?

— Yes, but it's primarily a system of spiritual exercises.

The official assumed a blank expression.

— Where do you stand on the Chrysostom theory of Iceland's settlement? Was there a sect of "*Krýsar*" or Irish mystics here when the Norsemen arrived? Are we all "golden mouths", hmm? Did Egyptian shades hold court in Krýsuvík a thousand years ago?

— I find it highly unlikely . . .

The official livened up.

— Pah, it's all a load of codswallop anyway. What about the Heruli? That's not such a mad idea, is it?

— Er, I don't know that one . . .

— Good for you, it's a disgrace to the Icelandic nation to claim that they're descended from a race who worshipped pigs. Don't bother mugging up on all that stuff.

A long pause.

— Right, here's the reference from Reykjavík's Chief of Police. You appear to have a spotless character.

The official put down the papers.

— But if there's anything we ought to know, if there's anything you want to tell me, it would be better if you did so now. Better for all concerned . . .

* * *

When Leo had first arrived in the country he had picked up an application form for prospective citizens. But as it ran out before he got round to filling it in, he had given up on the idea. It was only when the stamp dealer Hrafn W. Karlsson explained to him why it was impossible for him to stay any longer in the country without becoming a full citizen that he realised the sooner he got on with applying, the better.

— Say you're arrested with some of these stamps – that you had a fire at your house, for example, and the firemen found them – you would be deported from the country, you know, without so much as a by-your-leave. But Icelandic citizens aren't treated like that. *They*'re simply sentenced to a spell in jail at Litla-Hraun and can go home again once the case has been forgotten about.

— They are above board, aren't they?

Leo ran his hand over the files that lay on the counter of the Reykjavík Stamp Shop: red thirty-five-aurar stamps featuring an erupting Hekla and a black "five-aurar" overprint. The printing was clumsy, the overprint tilted at every angle: upside down, over to one side, in some places double. It was late in the evening because Hrafn wouldn't do business with him until after closing time.

Leo didn't care; he knew it was because he was a Jew, while Hrafn was a former member of the Association of Icelandic Nationalists. All their dealings were marked by Hrafn's embarrassment at associating with Leo. If they met in the street he could never be sure from one day to the next whether Hrafn would greet him. Sometimes he looked at Leo as if he had never seen him before, though if he was in the mood he would acknowledge him like anyone else. Understandably Leo did not like associating with Hrafn, but he had no choice.

Hrafn tapped a thick finger on the envelope.

— So, you don't actually know what you're selling me?

— Are they stolen goods?

— You're asking the wrong person. You won't tell me where you get the stamps from . . .

— I was asked not to.

— And you won't say who buys them from you either?

— I wouldn't dream of it.

— Good.

Leo had no idea what he was mixed up in. All he knew was that in Iceland stamps are somehow more than just sticky labels indicating postage paid. Indeed, there are whole families in the city who make their entire livelihood from dealing in these goods, as they have done for three generations. The stamps he sells Hrafn come from a different source, however. He received them from a man whom he suspects of working at the Gutenberg State Printing Press.

Their encounter took place at night. Leo couldn't sleep as was often the case when they were busy at the town's fish-meal plant and a miasma of guano lay over the city. Locals call this stench "the smell of money" and sleep like millionaires, while men like Leo suffer from insomnia. Even though the reek of rendering flesh and fat was stronger outside in the open air than in his little basement flat, he preferred to be somewhere he could go for a run to shake off the horror stories that the smell evoked.

* * *

FROM THE STORY OF THE ZEBRA PEOPLE

Turning a man into a zebra is not as far-fetched a process as it may at first sound. All the Germans needed for the task was an old or new prison, a dedicated workforce and a group of people who had been selected for the transformation. There were old prisons available in every occupied territory but in some places they embarked on new constructions and whole prison villages were erected. If the prisons were in use, some of the existing prisoners were pardoned, their sentence was reduced, they were given the choice of working on the conversion of the place as community service, and so on.

The choice, where possible, of the oldest and most inhumane prisons illustrates the ingenuity of those responsible for operation *Zebrastreifen*. Those of us who found ourselves in the black hole on the outskirts of P— had been transported there for a variety of crimes. I met men of every nationality, race, creed, political belief and sexual orientation. They ran the gamut from adolescents to geriatrics. What we all had in common was that by the end of our stay we had been transformed into zebras.

The method the Germans used for this task is a testament to their sharp sense of pragmatism. The cells were packed; instead of putting two men in a two-man cell they would put in five, and this alone was enough to transform our physical attributes. The transformation could occur rapidly or over a long period. I suppose I was there for some seven months, which was the time it generally took to bring out the main characteristics of the animals: a stripy body, swollen belly, matchstick legs with knobbly knees, sticking-out ears on a bony head and alienated eyes.

During the very first weeks of the transformation I felt a growing stiffness in my body, my back grew bent from the simple fact that in a crowd one makes oneself small. Since nothing was done by the prison management to improve conditions in the cells, although they now held three people more than they were designed to, apart from our being given a thin blanket to cover ourselves or fold under our backsides on the stone floor, we had to take it in turns to sleep on the bunks, walk the three paces that separated them and stretch our bodies by hanging from the sill of the tiny, deep-set window that provided our world light during our stay there.

At first relations in the cell were good; we agreed that we would not let them break us down. My cellmates, of whom there were to be quite a number during my months in P—, had in some cases been imprisoned before and knew something of the art of preserving one's sanity in circumstances like these. The first commandment was never to talk of our families or other loved ones outside the walls. The second was not to discuss our reason for being there. The third was to share all food parcels, tobacco and other items we might be sent.

To cut a long story short, all these commandments were broken. The third least often, however, because all our communication with the outside world was swiftly cut off. And soon the atmosphere in the cell grew thick with worries about sweethearts, wives and children, or else flared up in quarrels about politics, religion and sport, or, as time went on, types of beer and the appearance of matchboxes.

What illustrates our ignorance better than anything else is that we devoted our greatest efforts to clinging on to the tatters of our souls, to our mental health, instead of to caring for our physical bodies. We didn't know that these were what the Germans were principally interested in; they couldn't care less whether the soul in the zebra's body was whole or splintered.

About three months after my arrival in P— I saw my first zebra. We had been let out of our cells for the weekly fifteen-minute circuit of the prison yard. The yard was segregated so we couldn't communicate with prisoners from other blocks, and there we were made to circle at regular intervals and speeds. If prisoners were caught quickening their pace in order to stretch themselves they were instantly punished with a truncheon blow to the thigh.

It was an unbearable exercise which succeeded neither in strengthening the body nor clearing the head. It seemed principally designed to remind us that we were not only prisoners of the Germans but also of our own bodies. I was obsessed by the longing to run around like a madman, crowing and gambolling, back and forth, from wall to wall. During these weekly sessions we didn't care whether the sky was blue or black, it lay over us like a millstone carrying us round and round like worthless chaff. It was probably this caricature of physical exercise that led to our being so careless of our bodies when we returned to the cells.

Anyway, it was during this circling that we saw the first man in our prison who had metamorphosed into a zebra. (I write "our". You don't have to stay long in hell before you begin to regard it as home.) What happened was that several of the guards suddenly came running out of the prison, firing their rifles in the air. We immediately flung ourselves on the ground, clasping our hands behind our necks as we had been taught the first time we were led out into the yard. The guards often amused themselves by checking our reactions and obedience in this way. They would make us lie prone on our stomachs until some newcomer couldn't resist the temptation of raising his head to see what was going on. The man would be punished with a beating while the rest of us were made to repeat the exercise until the fifteen minutes were up.

This time, however, there was evidently something serious afoot. We hadn't been lying with our faces in the dirt for long when another group of prison guards came out leading an unrecognisable creature between them. It was the size of a man but looked so grotesque that I couldn't believe my eyes. Yes, I saw it out of the corner of my eye, for we had become adept at surveying our surroundings from this position. One turned one's eyes as far as they would go in their sockets, and by avoiding focusing on anything in particular one could take in a surprisingly large area.

Following on the heels of the prison guards leading the creature were black-uniformed SS officers and two men in civilian clothes who obviously belonged to the Gestapo. They trooped past us with the moaning creature and vanished through a massive door in the wall of the yard furthest from me.

It wasn't until we had been given the signal to rise to our feet and ordered to return to our cells that I realised what it was I had seen. At first I had thought it was a close-shorn sheep that the prison guards were amusing themselves by dragging around the prison on its hind legs before slaughtering it. Many of my fellow prisoners had interpreted the sight in similar terms, for we had all experienced the guards' sense of humour in one way or another.

But the presence of the ravens and vultures excluded the possibility that this was any sort of joke; the guards were always on edge when these crack troops of the Third Reich visited the prison to interrogate those imprisoned for their political views or acts of resistance. No, once we cellmates had compared notes and every possibility had been considered, it became clear to us that what we had seen was, yes, incredible though it may seem, a zebra.

A long silence followed this discovery; we sat quietly, lost in our own thoughts. The creature appeared vividly before our minds' eye: the protruding mouth, black hooves like clenched fists, stiff limbs indicating that it was unnatural for it to walk upright, and the dark stripes on its flesh, yes, what were they?

For my part, it was the swollen abdomen and sleepless eyes that I noticed we shared with the animal.

We stole glances at one another and at parts of our own bodies. You see, we were beginning to realise what the Germans were plotting. We were all in one way or another marked by their plan to turn us into zebras; we all showed signs that the transformation had begun.

* * *

So, in other words, Leo was returning home after going for a run to shake off the memory of some such tale of prison-camp life, and had just rounded the corner of Ingólfsstræti when he walked straight into a short man in blue overalls. As they collided, the man in blue handed him a brown envelope, then continued on his way without paying the slightest heed to his shouts and calls. Leo understood why when he saw the policemen who now came racing in pursuit of the man.

What did he do with the envelope? Nothing. He put it on the

kitchen counter and it was still there when he came home from work the next day. What's more, he had received an addition to his collection of unasked-for packages.

In the sink lay an unstamped envelope that had been slipped through the kitchen window:

> Mate,
> you've got something of mine.
> Keep it safe. More later.
> V—

A week later another letter lay in the sink:

> Mate,
> take it to Hrafn the Nazi.
> Sell it for a good price. 10% commission.
> V—

Leo hadn't a clue who had or hadn't been a Nazi in Iceland. To tell the truth, he hadn't realised there were any Nazis here, only nationalists belonging to every party and a few boys who played at dressing up. He had learned this from the shower attendant at the swimming pool. But now he had to look up a man described as a Nazi, just like that, as if it were a job title. And as if that weren't bad enough, he was supposed to do some sort of business with him, though what he didn't know.

The envelope from the mysterious V— lay on the kitchen counter. Though it didn't look in any way remarkable, he handled it warily. Weighing it in his hand he discovered that it was about as heavy as your average accounts book. He put the envelope down on the kitchen table, took a seat and carefully lifted the flap. Tilting his head, he peered inside; it contained some papers, he thought. Secret documents, perhaps?

— Do you know someone called Hrafn the, er, nationalist?

Leo addressed the shower attendant in a low voice. He was standing by the lockers, drying himself. The shower attendant wiped the white tiles with a large mop and muttered into his chest:

— There are lots of Hrafns.

Leo slipped the elastic band from his wrist – it had the key to his locker attached – and in so doing revealed the tattoo of his prisoner number from the death camp. The attendant stole a look at it as he flicked the mop under a radiator:

— And there are lots of nationalists.

— Well, I just thought I'd ask.

Leo opened his locker and began to get dressed. The shower attendant disappeared round the corner of the row of lockers. Leo was fully dressed and on his way to reception when the attendant intercepted him.

— When I was a boy I used to collect stamps. They say it's healthy for little children to handle delicate things. You learned to snip them off the envelopes and soak them, unless of course the envelope itself was likely to become a treasure of postal history, in which case you put it in a folder. Then you put the stamps on a piece of paper and pressed them dry. Then you could begin the classification by type and date – and by watermark when you were older and trusted with chemicals. Yes, you could amuse yourself with this for days on end, right through the night . . .

The shower attendant fell silent and allowed a swimmer to pass. When the swimmer was out of sight he continued:

— You sought out rare stamps, running errands to the shops for the old ladies in the neighbourhood in return for being allowed to poke about among their papers. That's how I found, for instance, an envelope with a combination of coarsely perforated two-shilling stamps and finely perforated four-shilling franks, posted in Djúpivogur but postmarked Hamburg!

He lowered his voice:

— The old woman hadn't a clue what she was giving me in return for fetching her a bottle of milk and some rye bread. Hah, she died last Christmas; don't you think her heirs would go nuts if they found out about this? There would be hell to pay.

The shower attendant laughed quietly into the back of his hand.

— Bloody hell, I'm going to have a comfortable retirement.

Leo held out his hand, intending to congratulate him on his booty, but instead of accepting his handshake, the attendant gripped him by the collar, pulled him into a cubicle and hissed:

— You're not to tell a living soul about this! I'll kill you . . .

Leo swore blind that he would never mention the fact that the shower attendant at the swimming pool had as a child acquired by dubious means an envelope with coarsely perforated two-shilling stamps and finely perforated four-shilling franks, posted in Djúpivogur but postmarked Hamburg. The attendant released his grip on Leo and patted the front of his shirt.

— You've never considered going in for stamp collecting yourself?

— No.

Leo said, bored, glancing over the attendant's shoulder. He had to escape from this ludicrous situation.

— Why not?

Leo held out his twisted hands.

— I don't find it so easy . . .

The attendant held out his own: he was missing two fingers on his left hand and the tip of the middle finger on his right.

— One manages.

He scratched his head with the end of the mop handle.

— All the same, you should drop by the Reykjavík Stamp Shop.

He winked.

— They've got very good tweezers; you only need two fingers to use them. Still, no need to mention that I sent you there.

Leo thanked him for the information and promised to examine the instruments at the Reykjavík Stamp Shop. And, no, they would never find out who had directed him to do business there. The attendant stepped aside and let him out of the cubicle.

The incident with the shower attendant had rattled Leo so badly that when he got home he had to go and lie down. Whatever had compelled the man to lecture him on the joys of stamp collecting? Hitherto they had barely passed the time of day, apart from that one time when the shower attendant had informed him that the Nazis had played truant from modern Icelandic history. The subject had arisen from the attendant's interest in the fact that Leo was circumcised.

Leo eventually came to the conclusion that the shower attendant's lecture about stamp collecting must have been in reply to his question about Hrafn the, er, nationalist. That's how Icelanders generally evaded all topics of conversation, using instead a philosophical mode of discourse. They were incapable of discussing things directly. If they contributed anything at all to the conversation it was in the form of a short anecdote or examples from natural history.

If the question was whether human beings were by their nature good, the first contribution might begin as follows: "What won't the Arctic tern do . . . ?" The second contribution might be: "When I was a girl . . ." And the third: "In the Tún neighbourhood they used to say . . ."

Yes, the shower attendant had been hinting to him that the answer was to be found at the Reykjavík Stamp Shop.

The Reykjavík Stamp Shop stands on the corner of a street on a hill overlooking the town centre. The shop is on the ground floor but the actual stamp business takes place in the two back rooms. A brass bell jangles whenever someone enters, as it did when Leo turned up with the envelope from the mysterious V—. An adolescent with a giraffe-like neck was bending over the glass plate on the counter, examining stamps from different parts of the globe and finding them ridiculous. He sniggered, muttering to himself that the Portuguese should forget about issuing stamps altogether:

— Huh, look at that!

Leo walked over to the counter and took up position there. After a long moment a chair was heard scraping the floor in a back room and shortly afterwards a man appeared in the doorway, sitting on a chair that he had propelled all the way there with himself on board. He was pear-shaped, as often happens when sportsmen put on weight, wearing a white shirt with rolled-up sleeves and khaki trousers hoisted up to his nipples. He craned his neck towards the customer, examining him through a magnifying glass that was gripped in his right eye socket.

— Yes?

— Good afternoon, my name is Leo Loewe. Is Mr Karlsson in?

— Yes?

— Could I speak to him?

— Yes?

After a momentary silence the youngster said in adenoidal tones:

— Iss 'im, innit. Doncha know Hrafn?

Leo reddened.

— Excuse me, I haven't been here before.

He placed the envelope on the counter.

— Um, I was asked to find out whether you would be interested in this?

Hrafn pulled himself to the counter.

— Loewe, you say . . .

Leo pushed at the envelope. Hrafn screwed the loupe deeper into his eye and curled his lip as he picked up the envelope and opened it.

— I'm not really buying much these days . . .

The magnifying glass fell on to the glass counter top.

What's more, Hrafn W. Karlsson gaped so wide that there was a gleam of teeth. Leo gasped. In the stamp dealer's left wisdom tooth there was a flash of gold, ill-gotten gold. It was Leo's gold. He was determined to recover it by any means necessary, and to do so he would have to keep an eye on Hrafn.

So it was that Leo allowed himself to become a courier of anomalous, and therefore valuable, stamps. He lived in expectation of V— sneaking an envelope through his kitchen window. Hrafn the Nazi paid for the contents and Leo put the proceeds into a secret bank account at a branch in the East Fjords.

This did not change until the Postmaster General discontinued the bad habit of constantly overprinting stamps, since by then the powerful stamp-dealing clans had turned to other, even shadier pursuits.

After this turn of events, Leo no longer had the opportunity to keep an eye on the gold in the mouth of the Nazi at the Reykjavík Stamp Shop. And it was then that he remembered Hrafn W. Karlsson's comment that if he meant to get involved in any criminal activities in Iceland, it would be an advantage for him to be an Icelandic citizen.'

8

'Leo bowed his head:

— I've done a bit of stamp dealing.

— Who hasn't . . . ?

The official smiled. Then his smile dropped away, he frowned and said sternly:

— Fourteen years? You've been here fourteen years, yet only now are you applying for citizenship. Is there some reason why you haven't been in more of a hurry?

The official was interrupted by the telephone; he snatched up the receiver and turned away. Without meaning to, Leo heard him repeating Lucian of Samosata's description of the inhabitants of the island of Glassia for the person at the other end:

— They're made of water; w-a-t-e-r! It's eternal winter there, or they would melt and turn to vapour; v-a-p-o-u-r! That's what happens when an inhabitant of Glassia dies; the sea mist that hides the island is made up of the dead. It's obvious . . .

My father met the eyes of the President who hung in a gilt frame on the wall behind the official.

'Leo is sitting on a bench in Austurvöllur Square, watching the starlings pecking up the breadcrumbs he has scattered on the grass. They're such funny little creatures, so lively and chatty with their "chirr, chirr" – followed by some complete gibberish that no one can understand. Not even Leo, who has been in the country as long as them, for one could say he had travelled here alongside these spotted birds with their copper-black, metallic-blue plumage. They are foreigners, and nobody is fooled when they manage to mimic

as pure Icelandic an avian as the redwing. Mr Thorsteinson, the
landlord at 10a Ingólfsstræti, wages a heroic war against them.

— They squeeze into every crack like rats. They're inside the walls
all over the house, twittering away on every crossbeam: hear that?
And they're crawling with fleas. My wife wakes up every morning
bitten all over. The cat won't even look at them. How do you deal
with birds like them down in Europe?

The cathedral bell strikes three. And exactly seven minutes later
there is a change of tune. A death knell. The church doors open and
the funeral procession slowly emerges. The coffin is followed by a
man of a very great age, supported by a young woman. From the
man's massive shoulders and chest Leo guesses that this is the swimming champion Helgi Steingrímsson with his daughter. His son-in-law
follows hard on their heels, carrying a bunch of flowers.

Hrafn W. Karlsson is standing by the corner of the Parliament
House, his hair wet-combed, dressed in a black suit: he's lost a bit of
weight. Why wasn't he at the funeral? Leo rises to his feet and bows
his head out of respect for the dead. The coffin is eased into the
hearse, the back is closed and the engine starts up.

Leo looks up and sees Hrafn W. Karlsson appear in the cathedral
doorway, wet-combed and dressed in a black suit: he's put on a bit of
weight.

The Hrafn in the church doorway greets his double on the corner
with a brotherly grin.

— Are you all right?

The official studies Leo. His watery-blue eyes remain fixed on
him.

— Oh yes, I'm just trying to find the words to explain why it's so
long since I arrived – and why I'm only bringing the form to you
now . . .

— Have you seen a doctor?

Leo glances down at his body: does he look ill? As usual in the
case of fully dressed men all that can be seen of him are his hands
and head. They should be all right, or at least they were the last time
he looked in the mirror.

— You speak Icelandic?

The official drums his index finger on the table. The conversation is getting out of hand. Leo feels the cold sweat breaking out on his forehead.

— Yes, as I told you, I speak—

— Do you have a health certificate?

— A health certificate, oh yes, of course, I thought, er, er . . .

Leo laughs apologetically and hands the official the envelope that his doctor, Axel Freydal Magnússon, had given him the last time he had a check-up. The official opens it and glances briefly at the contents, then ticks the appropriate box on the form. After that he stands up, peers out into the corridor, closes the door, then comes and perches on the edge of the desk.

— You see, it's like this, I'm putting together a theory about the origin of the Icelanders. Do you mind if I run it by you? My wife's sister's husband doesn't understand it; he's a fool. It was him I was talking to. He has just as good access to a telephone as I do. Do you have a phone?

— Yes.

— Do you use it much?

— As often as I need to.

— Good, we're vying with the Canadians as to which country has the greater telephone usage. They're ahead at the moment. We're number two in the world. Anyway, where was I? Oh yes, you see, when the original settlers came to Iceland they didn't just find a scattering of Catholic hermits with nothing better to do than march up and down the beaches swinging their censers and singing hallelujah against sea monsters. No, the land was settled, all along the coastline and far inland. It was the home of creatures that cared nothing for God, Óðinn or any other heavenly father . . .

Leo is flummoxed. The official studies his expression, then says:

— You haven't read up on Icelandic history?

— I've attended lessons with Dr Fróðason.

— Tch, what does he know?

Realising that the question is rhetorical, Leo remains silent. The official reaches for a fist-sized stone that is lying on a pile of files on the far corner of the desk. He weighs it in his hand, then passes it across the desk to Leo.

— For example, what do you make of that?

The official lowers one eyebrow and raises the other. Leo examines the rock. It is dark brown and rough on the surface but smooth in the cut. And in the cut there is a fossilised fly, a bee.

— It's a fossil.

— Yes, and where do you think it comes from?

Leo shakes his head.

— Mmm? Guess.

— I don't know . . .

— Guess.

— Er, France . . . ?

The official bursts out laughing.

— France? No, my dear fellow, this comes from Mount Esja.

He flings out an arm, pointing to the mountain, framed in the office window, that is a landmark to every Reykjavík-dweller.

— And what does that prove?

— That there were bees here?

— Exactly! And what does that prove?

Leo says nothing since the official is wholly caught up in the irresistible momentum of his argument.

— It proves that there was an abundance of honey here. And what does that prove? Mmm?

The official rocks back and forth on the edge of the desk.

— It proves that the ancient Greeks were right! This was the home of Scritifines, pantheists and mead-drinkers. Iceland is ancient Thule where the most savage barbarians, or should I say wild animals, used to dwell, long before the coming of the Irish monks or Norsemen.

They were mainly Scritifines, though personally I am of the opinion that the Greeks didn't realise that they were all one and the same race, and the pantheists and mead-brewers were simply different social groups among them. The Scritifines were crazy barbarians who ate nothing but each other or unlucky travellers. It is not hard to picture the nurseries with baby Scritifines hanging from every bough in leather pouches, yelping sweetly and growling contentedly as they suck the marrow from the finger bones or ribs of foreign seafarers.

You look shocked – no one has told you. That's hardly surprising since it's been hushed up. The history books have been censored and if foreign travel writers so much as breathe a word about this there is a huge furor and someone is paid to respond to them with yet another tome about how we're the descendants of Norwegian chieftains.

A staple ingredient of travel tales from Iceland used to be reports of how the people here thought nothing of giving away their children to anyone who wanted them but on the contrary demanded a high price for their dogs. The dogs were unfailingly described as earless and tailless, badly trained and vicious. There are no accounts of the children except that they generally came from litters of thirteen to seventeen siblings. Well, the Icelanders objected to these reports and gradually they were forgotten.

But I ask you: why in the world should English, German, Dutch or French explorers be interested in buying our tailless dogs? And why were children always mentioned in accounts of this trade in dogs? Have you considered that? No, the real reason has been so thoroughly hushed up that no one refers to it any longer. You have lived here for, what, thirteen years and never heard a word about it. Well, of course it had nothing to do with trading dogs or giving away children.

He pauses to emphasise what is to follow.

— Those doglike creatures were werewolves.

— I see . . .

— What Blefken, Peerse, Krantz and other worthy men were telling the world was quite simply that this was a good place to buy werewolves. These were experienced merchants, talking to their peers in code. All the nonsense they dressed their stories up in was primarily to frighten others off coming here; they didn't want just anybody getting access to their supplies. And there is no reason to be offended by the fact. That's just business . . .

There is a knock at the office door. The official starts up and off the desk.

— Yes?

The door opens and a dark-haired man with a square face and pointed ears sticks in his head. He nods when he notices Leo, then addresses the official:

— Perhaps you'd have a word with me when you're finished here?

The official says he'll be with him in a quarter of an hour. The other is satisfied and withdraws. The moment the door has closed:

— Do you know who that was?

— Wasn't it the Minister . . . ?

— Did you notice his appearance?

— He looks like the father of his country.

— Yes, yes, but don't you think he looks a little like an older version of the boy in *I Was a Teenage Werewolf*? Could be his father?

— Er, perhaps his haircut . . .

— Exactly! Well, let me tell you what werewolves eat: night-darkness and snow. Where in the world is there a land better suited to such creatures than here? Indeed, how else can one explain all the accounts of black men, that is, black-haired giants with bushy eyebrows, in our literary heritage? A Briton called Sabine Baring-Gould came here to travel round the country in the summer of 1861 and published his account in 1863. A fine book but not one word about werewolves.

Well and good; two years later he publishes a book about werewolves. Coincidence? Hardly. And where did he get most of his information about werewolves? From Icelandic sources. Was he mad? Hardly. He wrote thirty novels, well over a hundred scholarly works and a history of the saints in sixteen volumes, as well as writing the hymn "Onward Christian Soldiers". A highly educated man . . .

The official looks at the clock and begins to gabble:

— Yes, and Bram Stoker says straight out in *Dracula*, or perhaps it's the Count who says it, that he himself is descended from Icelandic werewolves. Do you really think it's a coincidence that the Icelanders have the longest heads on earth? In other words, there were still werewolves living here when the Norsemen stepped ashore. And inevitably there was a degree of interbreeding. I mean to say, the characteristics are still coming out. Can you do this?

The official leaned forwards and lowered one eyebrow to his cheek while lifting the other to the roots of his hair. Leo tried to emulate him but failed.

— You see, I'm the one descended from the saga hero Egill Skallagrímsson, not you. There is werewolf blood in all that line. His grandfather was Kveldúlfur, "Evening Wolf", who used to go crazy at the full moon. Now people are claiming that he was mentally ill, a manic depressive. No, my friend, he was a hairy-pelted werewolf . . .

My father had never heard such a feeble excuse for wild eyebrows and rapid beard growth. The official seized the pen from his breast pocket, reached out and scribbled something on a piece of paper behind him, muttering:

— Skallagrímur Kveldúlfsson. Trance, transform, transformation, transmutation . . .'

He stood up and went back behind the desk.

— Anyway, my friend, I just wanted to try my theory out on you. It's still taking shape. I'm supposed to be giving a lecture at the Lodge and I had the idea of presenting it there. It's good to hear other people's opinions of one's ideas while one's still in the process of forming them.

The official smoothed out the form; he'd sobered up from his theorising.

— Anyway, where were we? Oh yes, there was the business of your name; you must take an Icelandic name.

Leo was well prepared for this part of the application.

— I'd thought of the name Starri.

— Starri – a "starling"? Yes, not bad. May I ask why?

Leo merely told him he liked it.

— And whose son are you?

— My father was called Abraham.

The official scribbled the name Starri Abrahamsson on a memo and considered it, raising his brows.

— It'll do. Then that seems to be it. The matter will be dealt with at the spring session of parliament; it'll be a piece of cake, a mere formality . . .'

'But your patronymic isn't Starrason . . .'

'Quite right, I'll come to that later.'

9

'The time has come. The honourable Prime, Agriculture and Justice Minister gets up to speak in the capacity of the last-named office. Leo straightens in his seat. He has been sitting in the public gallery of the Althingi, Iceland's parliament, for an hour and a half, waiting for this very moment.

In the meantime he has listened to a debate on the extension of the territorial waters to twelve miles, which reached its climax with the proposal of a parliamentary resolution that if the English kicked up a fuss the Icelanders would claim full sovereignty over the Scottish isles that had been settled by the Norsemen before they found sanctuary here in Iceland. The speaker concluded by saying that he had already drawn up similar proposals for the annexation of Greenland, Newfoundland, the west coast of Norway, New York and the whole of Ireland. The debate on this issue was postponed.

Now it is the Minister for Justice's turn to take the floor.

— Honourable Mr Speaker, I would now like to propose a parliamentary bill on the granting of citizenship . . .

At these words there is a good deal of noise in the chamber and Leo leans over the gallery rail to see what's happening. The MPs are leaving the room since it's well past coffee time. A handful remain, however, and Leo gets the impression that they are waiting in suspense for the Minister for Justice to continue. When he does so by reading out the names of the fortunate, Leo has difficulty breathing. His heart pounds in his chest, hammering faster the further down the list, and closer to his name, the minister gets. He holds his breath.

— Leo Loewe, hereafter known as Skallagrímur Kveldúlfsson.

Leo exhales so violently that the MPs raise their heads in search of the bellows. He pulls himself together, coughs apologetically and retreats behind a pillar. There has been a dreadful mistake: he doesn't want to be known as Skallagrímur Kveldúlfsson. When the minister has concluded his recital of the bill on new Icelandic citizens, Leo peers round from behind the pillar. Frantically scanning the chamber, he catches sight of the official who dealt with his application. He is standing in a room adjoining the chamber, with his bushy eyebrows, and a pile of documents in his arms.

What is Leo to do? He tries to catch the official's eye by raising a hand, but it is no use. He doesn't want to draw any more attention to himself than he already has. If the MPs become aware of him the Speaker could regard it as a disruption of the session and have him thrown out. Then they would find out who he was. And then his dream of becoming an Icelander would be over. And then there would be no hope of his being able to do what is required to quicken life in his little boy. He sinks down on the bench, doomed to bear the name of Skallagrímur Kveldúlfsson – if his application is even accepted.

The session proceeds with a debate on the bill. At first the members don't seem to have any objections. One MP asks about a Hungarian woman whom he knows to have applied. Why is she not on the list? The Speaker directs him to propose an amendment to the bill if he is so keen for the woman to become an Icelandic citizen. And with that the debate seems to be over.

But just as the Speaker is about to put the bill to the vote, a man rises from his seat, a man so huge that Leo wonders if he is ever going to stop. For a moment he forgets his misfortune and gawps at the human colossus who lumbers over to the podium and rests three fingers on the side of the lectern that had previously been occupied by the entire hand of the Minister for Justice. Leo, who has never seen such a freak before without having to pay for the privilege, can't take his eyes off him.

The Speaker announces:

— The honourable third supplementary member . . .

The big man growls low and briefly inclines his head.

— By your leave, Mr Speaker?

The Speaker nods and gives the member the floor. The giant draws breath, a procedure that takes some time, though he does leave some oxygen behind for the others present. He invariably delivers his parliamentary speeches in verse and is famous for it. Now he begins and the House of the Icelandic Althingi resounds:

PARLIAMENTARY VERSE

Did a fellow hear aright,
can I have lost my mind?
The chamber rings with a dire slight,
a famous name maligned.

Father of Egill the bushy browed,
beloved of the Icelandic nation;
no foreigner should be allowed
to harm his reputation.

Kveldúlfsson in his grave would turn
at parliament's suggestion,
so I say either let us adjourn
or declare it out of the question.

Your bubble reputation will burst;
the report of the ages: How shoddy!
But let it be known that Skúli cursed:
Over my dead body!

At these words there is a loud murmuring among the few MPs present in the chamber. Leo's noisy exhalation had caused them to overlook the inappropriateness of the name, but now that they have been reminded of it in such a forceful manner they must respond vigorously. Their blood calls them to their duty, the pursuit of justice; the rhythm of the quatrains has recalled them to themselves; the song of Iceland has brought a hectic flush to their cheeks. Although he didn't fully understand the verses, Leo has grasped enough to see that he is in trouble. And the man's thunderous declamation seems to have carried to the cafeteria, for the chamber fills up in the twinkling of an eye, as does the list of speakers. Hrafn W. Karlsson's twin brother passes around the chamber, topping up the members' water glasses, for it seems they all intend to speak, to make their voices heard.

The minister is not amused by this incident, and if we didn't know that the werewolf theory was codswallop, it would be precisely at a moment like this that he would be inclined to shape-shift. Instead, he summons the official, and the bushy-browed man slinks into the chamber. He squeezes apologetically behind the cabinet benches and begins to go through the paperwork with the minister.

Leo presses himself harder against the pillar; the way things are going it would be best to lie low. Honourable members from every constituency and party feel duty bound to have their say. One speaks entirely in questions:

— Have we "followed the path of righteousness, with good as our goal"? Is it surprising that we should ask ourselves this question? What is all our rich heritage of sagas worth if riff-raff can come here from all over the world and appropriate the names of our forebears? Are they intending to begin a new age of settlement here? Are our founding fathers, the blood-brothers Hjörleifur and Ingólfur, fated to meet again in the telephone directory, instead of in the Fields of the Immortals? Are we not to answer these questions with a resounding "no"?

The next three speakers largely concur with the previous speaker, while wasting a great deal of hot air on arguing whether Ingólfur had gone to Valhalla or to Hel, the Underworld. A supplementary member from a country constituency brings the house down by commenting that judging by the state of the capital today its founder ought to be in hell. But that's just his little joke and the gravity of the matter reasserts itself. Even the Communists, who admittedly have assumed a different name by this point in time, are scandalised. This fellow sports gold-rimmed spectacles.

— I must say that the government seems to me to be in pretty bad shape if it passes such things without criticism. I support the government, I can't do otherwise; I do. But I will not put my name to this. I wish to draw the attention of the honourable members to a recent article on personal names . . .

He waves an issue of the socialist literary journal above his head.

— It emerges that the public is getting carried away in utter absurdity when it comes to naming their children: Dion, Lucky, Boy, Tyrone, Roy . . .

He leafs through.

— Gibbon, which is *nota bene* the name of a species of monkey; Oliver; the middle name Wayne, and so forth. And who is to blame? Have the Icelanders' IQs plummeted? No, this land is inhabited by well-educated, intelligent people, as parliament is bound to agree. But no one can withstand overwhelming odds. A tidal wave of vulgar American culture is pouring over the land, the legitimate offspring of the occupying force at that atom station, Keflavík Air Base. Only yesterday I heard teenagers referring to their parents as "guys" and "chicks" . . .

The member gets sidetracked into banging on about the NATO base issue and is booed down. The next recommends that people should be kind to their children and give them nice names which they won't be teased about. For instance it's a fine custom to christen children after deceased relatives, especially if the name comes to them in a dream. The member himself is named after his great-grandmother, bearing the middle name Annas.

While all this is going on, Leo sweats in his refuge behind the pillar. It was never his intention to trigger conflict amid the nation that has fostered him for the fourteen years that have passed since he was carried ashore here, a wretched foreigner. His greatest desire is to become one of them, not to sow dissension.

The parliamentary session dissolves into chaos, there are shouts from the chamber and the members ignore the jangling of the bell and the Speaker's calls for order.

— What's the man called?

— Leo, Leo Loewe . . .

— Can't he just keep that name?

— It's not Icelandic!

— Excuse me but it so happens that there is a small boy living in this town called Leo Love and I am not aware that he has been sent to jail for the fact.

— Whose son is he?

— His parents are Icelanders.

— That's a whole different kettle of fish!

— What does Leo mean? Doesn't it mean "lion"?

— Loewe, that means "lion" too.

— So the man's called Lion Lionsson?

Laughter.

— Has the honourable Prime and Justice Minister lost his tongue?

No, the Minister for Justice is conferring with the official who has been scurrying in and out of the chamber during the debate. At this point the minister signals to the Speaker that he wishes to speak. Then he takes the floor and asks for quiet.

— Honourable Mr Speaker, I have now examined the facts of this case with officials from the Ministry of Justice . . .

Leo peers round the pillar.

— It seems that the name Skallagrímur Kveldúlfsson was written in the relevant box on the form by mistake. I have been assured that the applicant had no part in the affair, indeed he is quite blameless, as confirmed by the character reference from the Chief of Police that accompanies his application.

Leo emits a private sigh of relief: it's going to be all right. The minister continues:

— But as we have been unable to contact the man in question, in spite of repeated attempts – he is neither at work nor at home – we don't know which Icelandic name he was intending to adopt. This leaves us with two options: either to leave him out of this bill and reconsider his application next year . . .

The Minister for Justice pauses and looks out over the chamber. If he looked up at the gallery he would see my father, a picture of misery: there are limits to how long he can keep the clay child moist. The goat's milk helps, but the clay will soon begin to crack. And what will Leo do then? He shudders with horror at the thought of having to form the boy again, thus obliterating his mother's touch.

The minister:

— Or else to come up with a name for him here and now. He can always change it later in accordance with the legislation on personal names. I repeat that this is a mistake, the government had absolutely no intention of smuggling a Skallagrímur Kveldúlfsson into the national register. And I strictly advise the opposition against trying to capitalise on this case for other purposes. Those of us fortunate enough to be born and bred Icelandic should understand the desperation that must beat in the breast of the person who waits poised on the threshold of receiving their Icelandic citizenship. For humanitarian reasons I therefore propose that the latter alternative should be chosen.

The members answer:

— Hear, hear . . .

And start scribbling down various names. But the minister raises his hand and concludes his speech:

— So as not to waste any more time on this affair than we already have, the government proposes the following: as has been mentioned, a direct translation of the name Leo Loewe could well be "Lion Lionsson". Naturally, that will not do, but with a minor adjustment we arrive at the eminently suitable and good Icelandic name of "Jón Jónsson".

And so the bill is put to the vote.

And passed.

— Hear, hear!'

10

'Jón Jónsson stands on the quayside, fishing. He is an Icelandic citizen and according to the law on citizens' rights he is now free to fish all he likes in the nation's precious territorial waters. So he intends to celebrate by catching something for his pot.

— Are they biting?

The voice is deep and singsong. My father looks round and sees a powerfully built black man standing there. He's wearing a light camel coat and gold-rimmed glasses, and holding a small case. Judging from its shape it contains a trumpet. An American jazz musician, Leo guesses, though it strikes him as odd that the man should speak Icelandic.

— I've only just got here.

— Hey, how ya doin'?

The black man approaches him with outstretched hand.

— Don't you remember me? No, of course you don't remember me.

Leo takes the man's hand, examining him politely: no, he can't place him. He ought to remember if he'd seen him before, let alone been introduced to him, as he's black.

— How do you do?

Leo nods, waiting to hear more.

— I was with you on the *Godafoss*. You were as sick as a dog, man, right from . . .

The black man laughs.

— You made me look bad by snoring through the national anthem!

— Really, I did? I'm sorry.

— Listen, I've clean forgotten your name.

— My name's, er, my name's Jón Jónsson.

— You don't say? I could have sworn you were a foreigner.

A foreigner. What's the man talking about? If anyone's a foreigner it's him; black as the ace of spades. But as Leo is now an Icelander he must react as one.

— Really? Thank you.

— Not at all. Anthony Theophrastus Athanius Brown.

— What?

— Just call me Tony, everybody does.

— Of course, yes, I'll try to remember.

And then he gets a bite. My father reels in the line and the fish. It's a sea scorpion. He frees it from the hook and is about to throw it back when Anthony grabs his wrist.

— Wait! I know how to cook that.

And Leo recognised him by his grip.

— How did you come by such a terrible name?

Anthony Theophrastus Athanius Brown is sitting at the kitchen table in Ingólfsstræti, chopping carrots and onion. After Leo told him he had been granted his citizenship earlier that day, he wouldn't hear of anything but their celebrating the fact together, as old shipmates. And since Leo said he was on his way home, they did their celebrating there.

— It was something of a misunderstanding.

Answers my father, and tells Anthony the whole sorry tale. Anthony finds it so side-splittingly funny that he cries with laughter – managing to offend Leo three times during his fit of mirth. But from time to time Leo too is carried away and joins in the laughter. Anthony walks over to the cooker, still chuckling.

— Why the hell did you take up citizenship, my friend? I've been here as long as you and I wouldn't dream of it.

Leo is startled. The man must be lying. Although they travelled to the country together and he speaks good Icelandic, there is no way he can live in Iceland. Why should he be granted a residence permit any more than any other member of his race? Black people are as rare in these parts as thunderstorms, no, grapevines, no . . .

Anyway, it doesn't make sense.

— You've been in Iceland all this time, since 1944?

Anthony scrapes the vegetables from the chopping board into a flameproof dish where the sea scorpion is lying together with de-seeded tomatoes, celeriac and parsley.

— Did I say that? It must have been a slip of the tongue. Hell, you've got some mighty fine vegetables here, man. Where do you get them from?

— There are some kids who go round the neighbourhood from house to house. I think they sell them for their father.

Leo has no intention of letting the man off so lightly. For all he knows, Anthony may be here about the boy, about the gold-making. This is actually the first time Leo has ever admitted a stranger to his flat, but what if that pest extermination man who came round to the house to poison the starlings saw something, yes, although Leo didn't let him out of his sight for the entire half-hour it took? No, he can't take any chances.

— I'm sorry but this visit is over.

— Say what?

— I can't stand it when guests lie to me.

— I'm sorry, man, there's no need to take it like that.

— I heard you say quite clearly that you've been here for fourteen years. Thank you for the visit.

Leo folds his arms and nods firmly. Anthony throws up his hands.

— All right, but you mustn't tell a soul. It's actually a state secret.

Leo promises. Anthony takes a deep breath and says through clenched teeth:

— I am here on behalf of the University of Iceland's Faculty of Theology.

They sit over their coffee in the dining room while the theologian tells his story. After touching on the main points of what he had told my father before, he takes up the thread where he left off in the cabin nearly fourteen years ago. Anthony Brown was, as it happens, an expert in comparative religion, and scholars of this discipline require outstanding memories as their field rivals entomology for its sheer number of characters and protagonists.

— Yeah, man. As I was telling you, I was lying there in the street on top of those troublemakers. The fancily dressed gentleman stood over us, inspecting us as if we were something weird and wonderful from the bottom of the sea. I sneaked a look at him, expecting to get a whack over the head. But instead of thrashing me, as I richly deserved, he held out a silver cane and prodded my enemies in the backside. They yelped at the prodding and I saw that he was laughing inside at how uncomfortable they were about feeling the cane so near their assholes, since we could all see that he was aiming right at them and just playing at not hitting them. Well, I didn't have the heart to pin them down any longer, and the white trash made off while I got to my feet and dusted off the rust-red dirt of Nigertown. The snappily dressed gentleman handed me his card and told me to come and visit him.

The next day my daddy the prelate took me down to Atlanta's police headquarters. He was as sure as I was that the card would be my ticket to several years in a chain-gang and all that time I would be made to crush rock for "President" Woodrow Wilson. But after we'd cooled our heels at the station for a whole six hours, we were informed that I had done nothing wrong, though a big, strong Negro like me should behave himself all the same. I promised, and my father gave me a clip on the jaw in front of them to show that I meant it.

We went straight down to the post office where we learned that all it said on the card was that a man by the name of "Lord Butter-Crumbe" lived at the "Beau-Soleil" estate. When we heard this I decided that whatever my daddy said, I would learn to read. I was nearly twelve years old and suspected that life had more to offer than Bible stories, snake farming and hard knocks.

Since Nigertown had started out life as a cluster of slave shacks belonging to Beau-Soleil, and since my people knew almost nothing but horror stories about that estate, it was with a slight tremble to our knees that several days later my daddy and I lifted the lion's paw that served as a door-knocker. It fell with a dull thud.

He was a pederast, my daddy and I spotted that the moment we stepped into the entrance hall, or anteroom, that was decorated with paintings and statues of naked men. But I was big and strong; I would be more than capable of handling a fruit like Lord Butter-Crumbe. That's what my daddy insinuated after he had shaken hands with the lord on the agreement that he was to become my guardian, starting the very next day.

What did he want with the youngest son of Jimmy Brown?

Well, the man had three interests. He had an anthropological interest in wrestling, an erotic interest in naked men, and a theological interest in "Negroes", as he called me and my people. He would take care of my upkeep and education until I graduated from college if in return I would deign to wrestle for him, seeing as how I was a naked man and black by nature. It was 1917 and falling into his hands saved my life. That same year my six elder brothers threw away their lives for nothing in the trenches in Europe.

Well, in accordance with the old man's theories, alongside wrestling tricks I studied theology, or rather I studied Roman and Greek mythology. I wove the knowledge into the wrestling holds and tricks, and so I was able to recite, for example, all the known stories of Helios while I dealt with my opponents. So there was really no question of majoring in anything other than theology when I was sent at last to the University of Berkeley where they were experimenting with educating people like me. Anyway, I acquitted myself pretty well; I wrestled and studied, that's all I knew. After graduating I began my travels; I've done research and collected data in every corner of the world, never staying anywhere long as a rule. This is the longest I've lived anyplace since I left Nigertown at eleven years old.

Towards the end of the war I received a letter from the Faculty of Theology here in Iceland. They'd heard a humongous – that is the right word, isn't it? – amount of praise for me and wanted me to come over and put together a syllabus for a course on comparative religion. It was a combination of pleasure and work for me as I had always been on the point of heading here to study the Norse myths. That's how come I was on board the *Godafoss* when we first met.

You were carried off the ship on a stretcher and I was arrested. Naturally I went ashore, as you do, but there was nobody there to meet me, though I suspected that the three men standing by a nearby car were looking out for me, but before I could catch their attention the police came along and took me off to jail. It was all sorted out when I showed them the letter from the Faculty. Someone had forgotten to tell the men I was black. Otherwise life hasn't been too bad. I live pretty much like a shadow; I've never been inside the university, but they visit me and pick my brains when they need to.

But the country cottage at Thingvellir is nice and I'm well paid – in true Icelandic fashion I've got more than one job. I guess what I miss most is the wrestling. They aren't too keen on letting a black man grapple with them here, as I've discovered on more than one occasion. But once I wrestled with Helgi Hjörvar. He was a tough customer. We have a mutual acquaintance out west.

Yeah, man, that's how things are with me.

Leo bends over the clay boy, bathing him with milk. Anthony left some time ago. They plan to meet again. He wants to have this big, strong man on his side when he deals with Hrafn W. Karlsson and his twin brother, the parliamentary attendant.

In the back garden of a tall timber house at number 10a Ingólfsstræti a little goat dozes. She is enfolded in the fairest thing the world has to offer: a spring evening in Reykjavík.'

V

(A Spring Evening in Reykjavík)

11

'The man who fills the watering can from the tap by the cemetery gate on the corner of Ljósvallagata and Hólatorg has no intention of tending to the graves of the dead. He comes from the countryside and wasn't acquainted with any of those who lie in the Reykjavík graveyard. Not that it would make any difference to his business here if he did; he would simply avoid the graves of his relatives as he did when he lived in the West Fjords and made use of the churchyard there. It is only at night that he can perform the work that brings him here, as it did there, from spring to autumn. His motives are not honourable, as he would be the first to admit.

But needs must and life is expensive.

We follow him down the slope and along a path to the oldest part of the cemetery. There the grave markers are made of iron that was originally painted black, and more often than not there are knee-high railings around the plot. The moon dips in and out of the clouds and the chill spring wind whistles in the trees above his head. But he's indifferent to the eerie conditions. He's completely fearless, endowed as he is with second sight, and he's on good terms with most of the departed.

He stops by the grave of Ólafur Jónasson, student (b. 1831 – d. 1868), puts down the watering can and sets to work. He unbuttons his coat and we see that the garment is lined all over with pockets. The light catches a garden trowel that juts like a red claw from his breast pocket; his other pockets are stuffed with similar tools, as well as seeds and seed potatoes.

While the man from the West Fjords gardens in the cemetery – he knows the place like the back of his hand, going from one grave to the next, sowing here, turning the soil there, watering – the dead are busy with their own affairs.

For so it is in the Old Graveyard on Hólavallagata, I can't answer for other places, that by night it transforms into a pleasure garden for the dead. They stroll here and there in their shrouds or sit on benches discussing issues of eternal interest, while others idly toss gravel against the cemetery wall. Materialists, who hadn't for a moment anticipated a life after death, hold themselves aloof from the rest, attending cell meetings and arguing about whether there's a life after this one that they're living against their will and in defiance of science. Only the odd person can be heard complaining about getting neither to heaven nor hell, which has been the state of affairs for God's creation ever since 1941 when the trumpeter Gabriel sealed both the Pearly Gates and the portcullis of hell by incinerating his instrument in the bonfire of the sun.

It is the recently deceased who gather in the air above the cemetery where there is a good view over the city to east and west, north and south. They're naturally livelier than the old-timers on the benches below. They romp around, turning somersaults and generally enjoying life after death. Among their number is Ásgeir Helgason, the shower attendant, whose funeral took place barely seven hours ago.

Then he lacked a tongue, four fingers, three toes and both earlobes, to mention the most important bits. Now everything's back in place and he can start over. From sheer exuberance he swims the length and breadth of the graveyard: oh, if his father could only see him now. He powers through the air with elegant strokes. The fear of water that plagued him in life, and led to his father's forever finding fault with him, is history. Breaststroke, backstroke, crawl, butterfly, treading water, he can do them all.

On one length Ásgeir spots the West Fjords man bending over a grave and planting potatoes. He dives.

— Boo!

But the graveyard farmer doesn't turn a hair at the haunting by the late shower attendant. He looks calmly over his shoulder and studies Ásgeir's spiritual body before retorting suddenly:

— Boo!

Ásgeir starts so badly that he tumbles backwards through a handsome poplar tree. The other grins, turns back to the grave and says mockingly to the loam:

— New here, are you?

Fascinated by the man, Ásgeir floats over to him.

— Is it that obvious?

— Well, we have an understanding that you lot leave me in peace in return for my keeping quiet about what goes on here. People getting together and that sort of thing . . .

He lowers his voice.

— And not just men and women, if you know what I mean.

Ásgeir is all ears and the West Fjords man continues:

— No, here you see hard-bitten old trawlermen fondling vicars, nurses getting off with ordinary housewives, and I don't know what else. I expect they think it's all right to give in to it now they're dead. But it would be a pity if their families got wind of it, if you know what I mean?

— I'm sorry, I didn't know – about the understanding.

— That's all right.

The man stands up, sprinkles water over the grave and moves on to the next. The shower attendant follows him: this man is well informed about the affairs of the dead and it would be better to learn etiquette from him than to make a fool of himself in front of the other ghosts. The afterlife is quite different from how Ásgeir had imagined it; he had almost hoped that he would end up in some kind of hell.'

'Whoa, there! He wanted to go to hell?'

'Ásgeir had strange needs . . .'

'The shower attendant positions himself behind the man and tries to think of something to ask him. But it's difficult to know what to say when you're a greenhorn in a new place where all the laws of nature are obsolete.

— Do you make something from this?

— Well, if you know what you're doing it works out fine.

— Is it mostly potatoes?

— I've got all the root crops: turnips, swedes, carrots, radishes, then cauliflower, scurvy grass, white cabbage, parsley and chives. They're over there. I've been experimenting with tomatoes, basil and other herbs in the mausoleum too: there's a huge demand for fresh herbs at the restaurants. I can't complain. And these here are strawberries.

He rakes up the soil around the three-leaved plants on the grave plot of Jóhann Skúlason, joiner (b. 1867 – d. 1943).

— These aren't for sale, they're for my kids. I've got everything, really, except rhubarb. People don't want rhubarb on their graves here in the capital. At home in Ísafjördur it wasn't a problem. Perhaps you wouldn't mind?

— I've nothing against rhubarb as such.

Ásgeir wants to keep the man sweet so he can pick his brains. The gardener's face lights up.

— Where are you?

— Where am I?

— Where's your grave?

— It's down by Sudurgata.

— Down by where?

— Er, Sudurgata . . .

— You really are a greenhorn, aren't you? This graveyard has named streets and numbers, French-fashion. Some nob introduced the practice several years ago.

The West Fjords man beckons Ásgeir closer.

— The snobbery here's something awful. If you're down there that's supposed to be a terribly posh area. I won't be able to get away with planting rhubarb there. There would be an outcry. By the way, you're Ásgeir, aren't you?

— Yes, how did you know that?

— I do read the papers.

— Oh, you mean that.

The West Fjords man takes off his gardening glove and scratches his red Jack-of-Spades beard.

— Is it right, what I heard, erm . . . ?

He puts his glove back on.

— Ah, it's none of my business. I shouldn't be sticking my nose in . . .

— Go ahead and ask.

— No, I don't like to.

— Go on, it's all right, honestly.

The West Fjords man gives a low whistle, then says quickly:

— Is it true your stamp collection's gone missing?

* * *

The Grettisgata Ghost was thirteen years old when he was found more dead than alive under a stack of loading pallets in the yard of the Freezing Plant. At first the accident was a mystery. People found it extraordinary that the weakling boy had managed to mutilate himself so badly: his guts were hanging out, his face was a bloody pulp and his trousers were round his ankles. After a detailed inquiry, however, the police came to the conclusion that he had rocked himself to death. For the Grettisgata Ghost was none other than "Kiddi Rock", Kristján Hermannsson, a rock'n'roll-mad GI bastard from Lokastígur.

Folk memory has it that Kiddi saw every single showing of *Rock around the Clock* during the months it ran at Stjörnubíó cinema. He talked in quotes, could hardly walk for the twitching of his hips, hey-heying, and clicking of his fingers, and for the first time in his life he appreciated the fact that his ancestry included a story of forbidden love between a Mohican girl and a nineteen-year-old cowherd from Stavanger in Norway.

The posing, the raven-black hair and congenital boxer's nose turned him into Kiddi Rock in the eyes of the girls, whereas the boys carried on calling him "Krissi Chick" – as they used to before his life was revolutionised by rock'n'roll. But the insult "Chick" backfired on his tormentors because kids from other neighbourhoods assumed it referred to Kiddi's success with the girls, and when he was seen with the prettiest chick in Nordurmýri and also with Donni Halldór's sister in the same week, the boys couldn't take it any more.

Kristján Hermannsson took a long time to die. He may have been a second-generation townie boy and so lacked the toughness of his forebears from Trolls' Cape (his grandfather had been the biggest child born in Iceland in 1874, his mother the largest born in Reykjavík in 1928, though in her family's eyes she was a puny little thing), but he had an inbred tenacity like others of that stock.

* * *

Height/weight of newborn infants on Trolls' Cape, 1900–1908

Name	Height	Weight
Arnaldur	96 cm	14.1 kg
Áshildur	98 cm	14.7 kg
Birna	97 cm	13.4 kg
Björn Ólafur	93 cm	12.8 kg
Brynja	100 cm	15.2 kg
Einarína	100.5 cm	11.5 kg
Eiríkur	92 cm	13.3 kg
Finnur	97 cm	12.5 kg
Grímur	95 cm	13.0 kg
Gudrún	97.5 cm	12.2 kg
Helgi	89 cm	11.3 kg
Hildur María	92 cm	14.0 kg
Jón	100 cm	15.7 kg
Jón	103 cm	12.3 kg
Kristján	106 cm	13.0 kg
Kristrún	100.5 cm	15.2 kg
Leifur	95 cm	13.8 kg
Margrét	96.5 cm	13.4 kg
Ragnar	104.5 cm	14.0 kg
Rannveig	99.5 cm	12.9 kg
Sigurlinni	101.5 cm	15.5 kg
Thór	96 cm	15.0 kg
Thóra	89 cm	13.5 kg
Average:	97.3 cm	13.6 kg

* * *

Anyway, it was a long battle and Kiddi Rock did not regain consciousness until the very end of his time on earth. The day he died there was a young medical student on shift. She didn't believe for one moment that his injuries were self-inflicted. He might well have been an incorrigible dance-maniac, and some of his injuries may well have been caused by his losing his footing during a rock'n'roll move on top of the stack of pallets, but she was quite sure he hadn't sodomised himself.

She noticed that the boy was finally managing to give up the ghost. Sitting down by his bed, she held his hand to help him on his way. In the midst of his gasps he opened his eyes and looked at her. She leaned forwards and asked:

— Is there anything you'd like to tell us, Kristján dear?

And Kiddi Rock answered:

— See you lader alligador . . .

He kept his word, which was how the Grettisgata Ghost came into being. He keeps to the lower end of the street from which he takes his name and can usually be seen in the underpass leading from Grettisgata down to Laugavegur and the Stjörnubíó cinema. His head jerks, his eyes glow, and he says: "Hey-hey-hey!" Or else takes his place in the queue for the cinema, then vanishes when he gets to the ticket window. In all other respects he's harmless.

And yet, over the years he has come down hard on several of his old schoolmates and their sons, presumably in revenge for the fact that they once called him Krissi Chick.'

'Ásgeir Helgason is uneasy after his conversation with the graveyard farmer: people seem more interested in tracking down his stamps than his murderer. What kind of society was this turning into?

— Hi, Uncle!

The Grettisgata Ghost waves at the shower attendant, then continues to shuffle his feet by the cemetery gate on the corner of Ljósvallagata and Hringbraut. Ásgeir floats over to him.

— What are you doing here?

— Well, I don't know where else I'm supposed to be.

It hadn't occurred to Ásgeir that his nephew Kristján would be waiting for him in the graveyard. They hadn't had much to do with each other while they were alive. Helgi Steingrímsson had refused to see or speak to his daughter ever again after she fell in love with a GI and fell pregnant with Kiddi as a result. Ásgeir felt he should say something to the boy.

— Your mum's well, Kiddi dear. She's in Philadelphia.

— Good for her, she always wanted to go to Philly.

— No, I mean she's in the Philadelphia Congregation. She's living with a decent man. He speaks in tongues. And wears zip-up shoes.

The Grettisgata Ghost grins.

— Zip-up? Like that, is it?

Ásgeir is at a loss for an answer. What on earth had he meant by that? It had just slipped out. He hadn't a clue what "Preacher" Thorlákur wore on his feet. His nephew regarded him through narrowed eyes.

— Do you have some unfinished business on the other side? Is there something on your mind? Or someone, perhaps?

Kiddi spits over the cemetery wall and the spittle lands on the shoulder of a man who is passing. He stops and looks up at the sky in search of the guilty party, but as there are no birds to be seen he makes do with cursing all birds before continuing on his way. Ásgeir's eyes grow blank: there's something about those shoes he needs to look into. He pictures large feet and smells snuff, no, stewed coffee. He snatches at Kiddi.

— Is there any way of getting out of here?

Kiddi rolls his eyes, clicks his fingers and flips up the collar of his jacket: yes, the teen rocker Kristján Hermannsson has found a way of shrugging off the astral bonds, the spiritual thread that ties the dead to the cemetery. The method is simple: at a certain point in the evening a curtain is sometimes drawn back from a kitchen window in the apartment block opposite the Grund retirement home, to reveal the face of a man with an unruly mop of hair.

— The guy's so terrified of the dark that he sucks you to him.

Kiddi laughs.

— The poor sod can't get enough of it. I sometimes drop in on him on my way into town. Knock inside the kitchen cupboards, rattle the china, flap the dishcloths and that sort of thing. He sits on the kitchen bench, rigid with fear, waiting for the haunting to stop. He gets a kick out of it. Last time I was there I saw him reach for a notepad and write on it "Mar-lon" as I left. I guess I'd been thinking of Brando or something. Anyway, he should put in an appearance any minute.

They wait.

— Hey, Uncle, what gives with Granddad?

— Your grandfather?

The curtain twitches.

Ásgeir floats over the city. It's all so delightful. He sees his house. He sees the lake. He sees the Music Pavilion. He sees the park. He sees the Free Church. He sees the Reykjavík Stamp Shop.

Ásgeir parts from his nephew above the Music Pavilion Park. The Grettisgata Ghost is on his way east to Snorrabraut to greet cinema-goers from the nine o'clock showing of *King Creole*. Keeping to a height of around twenty-three metres above ground level, Ásgeir whooshes north along Lækjargata, then takes the tight turn up into Thingholt. Slowing down, he perches on the roof of the house that stands on the steep slope above the Stamp Shop. From there he can see through the window of Hrafn W. Karlsson's office. He slips through the evening-cold window pane. In the right-hand corner of the room, viewed from the door, is a cupboard on feet six centimetres high. Underneath it, the calf-leather spine of Ásgeir's own stamp album can be glimpsed, and you'd have thought that this was what had drawn the deceased stamp collector. But no, he doesn't bother himself with that, moving instead, like a living person, to Hrafn's desk.

A newspaper lies open on top, spread over various philatelic catalogues, and there one can read that this very evening Óli Klíngenberg is holding a concert at the Idnó Theatre.

A note has been scribbled next to this notice: "Fetch tkt. bef. qtr to 7."

Óli Klíngenberg is standing at the front of the stage, resting his ring-bedecked, milk-white, small but pudgy right hand on the grand piano which is carefully positioned so the pianist, some Norwegian, is only just visible.

Óli emits a low cough.

He hasn't sung much in public since returning to the country towards the end of the war. No, most of his time has been spent attending to spiritualist matters, for when he had been in the country for some three years and no one had so much as hinted that perhaps he ought to hold a concert, he remembered that when he was small he had been what they call "receptive". When they lived on the farm at Smjör-Hali he had associated with four elf boys, and later, at their house on Lindargata here in town, with a blue-haired Indian called Sansia who inhabited a leg of their living-room sofa. It wasn't much compared to some, but enough for him to quickly gain a reputation in the city's spiritualist circles. And it was to prove plenty more than enough when a medium called Mrs Benediktsson persuaded him to fill in for her one evening with the Unisomnists.

— Dear boy, they're not really interested in ordinary people, more in famous types: the author of the Tarzan books has been coming through recently. And it's only one séance . . .

Said the lady and off she went to say goodbye to her lover who was leaving for America to study physics on a hurdling grant. (But she didn't prove too farsighted there since they were both later found in the back seat of Hannes Benediktsson's Lincoln at the bottom of the east harbour.) Since then Óli Klíngenberg has been one of the busiest mediums in town.

Now he is holding a concert at Idnó. It's in aid of repairs to the Unisomnist meeting house. He is quietly clearing his throat when Ásgeir slips under the door of the hall. He squeezes between the audience's legs, craning his neck to right and left in search of Hrafn W. Karlsson's feet. And finally, finally, he locates them. Yes, there they are. The villain is sitting in the front row with his wife, wearing zip-up shoes. Yes, he's wearing lined, zip-up shoes!

Óli is just finishing clearing his throat and is about to raise his voice in song when he happens to glance into the auditorium and sees the shower attendant's shaggy head peering out from between the stamp dealer's legs.

The tenor gulps, then belches out like a hardened trawlerman:

— My nem's Ágei Elgason.

The audience roars with laughter. But is abruptly silenced.

— Rabn W. muhdered me! Jus' look undeh the cubbahd!'

VI

(26 August 1962)

'— Scientists have referred to us as "The Light in the North". And that's what we are, no more no less. By reading the Scriptures with slide-rule in hand and a rudimentary knowledge of mathematics, anyone who cares to can prove that all paths of light lead to Iceland, whether they are calculated abstractly from the roots of the Cheops pyramid or traced by finger on a map, in the footsteps of the men of Atlantis. This news is spreading fast among civilised nations. If you happen to meet an Englishman, for example, he will almost certainly be informed of Rutherford's theories, and an old German is likely to know this intuitively, whereas a man born in Benin knows nothing of Iceland. But where is Benin anyway? Who made this coffee?

This coffee is piss-poor. But it hasn't been easy for us. Like the story of the Jews, who are the only nation apart from the Icelanders to have received direct orders from God to light the way for the world, the history of Iceland has been a series of disasters, exiles and humiliations. Our exile, however, was such that no one was sent away, we have always lived here, thank God, but we were made exiles in our own country. We may be the only real Jews left on earth. What happened, for example, to the race of Benjamin?

The people of Isaac, ice-axe, ice-acre, Iceland. Pass me the sugar!

Will you pass me the sugar, please? On paper we may have been Danish subjects but in our hearts we were the children of the land of ice and fire. The Danes have never understood the first thing about us. They call the founding of the Republic a victory for whingers. They say we whinged our way to independence. But I ask you, if it's true, what's wrong with that? Are they complaining that we didn't fight them? No, we are a peaceable nation, men of letters and cunning as foxes. Look how we're dealing with them over the Manuscript

Question. Why do you think the Danish nation is coming over to our side, contrary to the will of the Danish government? Is it because we're driving them mad with our whingeing? Do you mean to finish the Christmas cake, boy? It's supposed to stretch to tomorrow's coffee break too.

No, nowadays we let them beat us at sport. After the war we gave them a pasting in every arena you could think of, but then it emerged that the Icelandic nation was going ahead with its demands for the return of the manuscripts. What was to be done? The Danes weren't happy; we were not only independent but forever wiping the floor with them at athletics or football, so there was no way they were going to return the manuscripts. Well, the sports movement came to the rescue. They understand that this is a temporary measure. Our high achievers agreed to undertake the task. In return they have received a huge increase in funding for sport. And now we just keep on losing. The Danish government can't make head or tail of it. I heard this from a board member of the Drengur Youth Association. That's in Kjós district. They held the meetings there. Other nations should follow our example.

Anyway, boys, "*Arbeit macht frei*"!

The speaker claps his hands and people rise from the tables in the cafeteria of the Midgardur Ceramics Factory. Leo finishes his coffee and goes into the workshop. He has worked here for the past seven years, overseeing the tableware department. The company's production is split in two: tableware and ornaments. The ornament department is supervised by the man who held the floor during the coffee break: Thorbjörn Arnarson, ex-wrestler, horse breeder, mountaineer, versifier and chess player. He's a decade short of his century but still runs up mountains, rides horses and women, composes verses and plays chess, although he no longer wrestles except for fun at the Wrestling Association's annual shindig. People never tire of the hilarious sight of him flooring the country's crown princes of wrestling and pinching them in the balls. He sometimes pinches the apprentices at Midgardur in the balls too. If he's in a good mood he'll creep up behind them as they are bending over their clay, grab them by the crotch and ask:

— What do you say to that?

Not releasing his grip until they answer. It's just a bit of fun that lightens the atmosphere in the workplace.

Leo likes Thorbjörn; he's an artist who has developed a unique style from a blend of Art Deco, National Realism and his own idiosyncratic ideas about the appearance of the Norse gods and ancient heroes. Statues of these characters form the core of his artistic output and are exceptionally popular with the Icelanders. It's said that every home, business and institution in the land boasts a statue by Thorbjörn from Midgardur.

Njáll, the hero of the eponymous *Njáls saga*, graces the desks of the intelligentsia; Thór brandishes his hammer Mjölnir in the offices of go-getting directors; students who excel in Icelandic are rewarded with the saga hero and poet Egill Skallagrímsson; the goddess Idunn with her golden apples adorns living rooms; Freyja and Gunnar of Hlídarendi are popular confirmation gifts; in the countryside Njáll's wife Bergthóra stands side by side with the outlaw Grettir; horsemen own Hrafnkell Frey's Priest; gifted children are given the dwarfs Mímir or Fjölnir; no fisherman's home would be complete without the sea-god Ægir; Baldur "the White" is a favourite with religious types, and so on. But most remarkable of all is Ódinn who straddles his eight-legged steed Sleipnir with the ravens Huginn and Muninn on his shoulders. He belongs to a privileged few.

Perhaps the reason for this popularity is that despite their small size – they are no bigger than is customary for such mantelpiece knick-knacks – the statues are so cleverly proportioned that when the Icelanders call them to mind they loom as large as the Hraundrangar sea stacks.

Which are no mean size.'

'They're collector's items these days. Loki was on sale at the flea-market in Kolaport the other day and they were asking an arm and a leg.'

'There's one thing you should watch out for if you're planning to buy something by Thorbjörn – there are forgeries in circulation.'

'And how can I watch out for them?'

'You must check whether they're stamped on the base with a serpent coiling round an M and biting its own tail.'

'Of course you'd know all about that . . .'

'The only ones that didn't sell were Hallgerdur Long-breeches and Freyr. She was basically unpopular while his statue was considered obscene. If you come across one of them you've got it made.'

'Really, I've never seen them.'

'I've got several examples of both; my father smuggled them out. I keep them in a bank deposit box.'

'They must be worth a fortune?'

'They're not for sale.'

'It's a shame people threw so many of them away.'

'Yes, and now the national has become international and the international national. Or so I'm always reading in *Morgunbladid*.'

'The ceramics factory was located on a back lot towards the bottom of Laugavegur. There was a cowshed there until 1951 when Thorbjörn purchased the plot and moved Midgardur to the city. Leo was part of the working party who tore down the cowshed and mucked it out, which is what he was doing when Thorbjörn turned up to see how things were progressing. He was accompanied by his brother and right-hand man, Gudjón.

By one of those coincidences that are always so satisfying in stories, it so happened that Gudjón had been doing work experience at the ceramics workshop run by the SS in conjunction with the prison camp at Dachau, which was one of the strange byways Leo had passed through on his journey from Prague to Reykjavík.

Gudjón immediately recognised his old workmate, although he was standing there in the dung channel with a flat cap on his head and a shovel full of cow shit. He struck up a conversation with Leo and after they had exchanged greetings Gudjón began to interrogate him for news of this and that character who had worked with them on the ceramics in the old days, for all the world as if they had gone to the same primary school. Leo was sorry to have to tell him that he thought these characters were almost certainly all dead.

This left Gudjón silent.

But as he was a cheery cove by nature like his brother, he shook off the bad news and introduced Leo to Thorbjörn with the words that if anyone in Iceland knew how to glaze a dinner service it was this here foreigner.

— Is that a fact?

Asked Thorbjörn.

— Er, well, you know . . .

Answered Leo, who had already picked up the local lingo.

— Of course it's a fact!

Said Gudjón, looking his brother in the eye.

— The eagle service!

Thorbjörn raised his brows.

— The eagle service . . .

Leo muttered into his chest:

— The eagle service . . .

And with that he was hired.

It is unusual for a foreigner to attain a good position at an Icelandic company, but Leo's outstanding knowledge of ceramics in general, and glazing tableware in particular, resulted, before six months were up, in his taking over the position of overseer from Gudjón who turned to management instead.

One of Leo's tasks at Midgardur was supervising the production of souvenir plates of various kinds. He went over to his work table and examined the prototype of a plate that they planned to produce alongside the issue of a five-and-a-half-krónur stamp to commemorate the centennial of the National Museum. The stamp showed part of the medieval door-carving from Valthjófstadur, in which a knight is trampling a dragon to pieces and rescuing a lion from its claws.

A piercing shriek was heard from the ornament department, followed by a deep male voice rumbling:

— What do you say to that?

It was Sunday, but as the ancients didn't observe rest days, neither did Thorbjörn. Leo concentrated on the stamp plate. He needed to propose a good background colour for the plate itself, a colour that would enhance the stamp. White would have been best from the point of view of cost but it wouldn't work because the stamp would merge into the background, surely?

He called out to Kjartan, a talented draughtsman whose job it was to realise Thorbjörn's sketches of the dragon interlace that decorated most Midgardur products.

— Do you think you could draw me a version of this, tracing a gilt border round the stamp? It occurred to me that then it would stand out against the background even if it's white.

— Classy . . .

Kjartan took the plate over to the drawing board. Leo went out to the cloakroom where the staff telephone was located. He put a ten-aurar coin in the slot and dialled a number. It rang for a long time and he was about to hang up when it was answered by a man who seemed to be having considerable difficulty in getting the receiver to his face.

— Hello . . .

— M-Mr Loewe, Loewe?

— Yes . . .

— This is Pushkin, yes, yes, yes . . .

— Hello, you're back from Krýsuvík then . . .

— Did you ring me?

— Yes.

— How do you know I was in Krýsuvík?

— You told me.

— What, that was just a joke.

— I need to see you.

— Oof, I'm a bit tied up right now . . .

— When would be convenient?

— Ooh, yes, yes, nearly finished, nearly finished . . .

— I'll be finished by five.

— Pushkin wasn't talking to Leo, Pushkin is with an informer.

— Were you able to check for me?

— Hee, hee, yes, yes . . .

— I'll be home by about half past five.

— Bye, comrade, ha, ha . . .

— Bye . . .

— Ha, ha . . .

Leo hung up: Pushkin was clearly in bed with some female. It was extraordinary what a hit he was with the ladies in spite of his tail. Or was it because of his tail?

Leo sat on a stool in the garden, milking the goat. He pulled the teats with a steady motion, causing the hot milk to squirt into the bucket with a rhythmic hissing. There was no other sound in the world. Pausing in his work he zipped up his jacket. The wind was picking up and the odd raindrop traced its outline on the paving stones that ran along the side of the house. Pull, hiss, pull . . .

— Mr Loewe?

He looked up and saw a short but lithe figure in a white tuxedo, with a black bowtie and sunglasses as dark as his sleekly combed hair, peering round the corner. It was Pushkin.

— You're very smart!

— Oh, there was cocktail party at the embassy.

Pushkin lit himself a Chesterfield cigarette and blew out the smoke with a thoughtful expression.

— Herring, herring, herring . . .

Leo saw a shadow appear at a window on the second floor:

— Listen, why don't you go inside, this'll take a while. Anthony's here, and there's hot coffee in the pot.

— *Spasiba.*

Pushkin disappeared round the corner.

The goat bleated angrily; Leo had inadvertently pinched her teat when the Russian threw him that chummy "*spasiba*".

He had certainly smartened up his appearance and manner since Leo saw him last, but then he'd had a good model, none other than Alexander Alexeyev, who had learned how to dress when he was posted to Paris after the Second World War and managed more often than not to be a step ahead of the existentialist Sartre when it came to guessing the length of that season's coats. Also, that autumn all the weeklies were bursting with sensational news about the film *Dr No* which told of the adventures of 007 – the true heir to John Dee, magician and spy to Her Majesty Elizabeth I, and a real man of style.

This brightened the existence of men like Pushkin. There was little glamour attached to being a Soviet spy in Iceland: nothing ever damn well happened there. The Left had little to say as they were never given access to information that mattered. They were mainly pre-occupied with reporting one another for various accounting swindles to do with the importation of propelling pencils, razorblades, tyre irons, and other small items they were licensed to buy in from Bulgaria.

Pushkin's principal source of information at the US military base down on the Reykjanes Peninsula was a mentally handicapped man who did various odd jobs for the steward in the enlisted men's mess hall. There he picked up little crumbs that to Pushkin seemed better than nothing, such as flyers about entertainments at the base: dances, bingo, barbecues and so on. In return Pushkin rewarded him with various kinds of badges and flags, since the idiot didn't drink.

By this means Pushkin had managed to scrape together enough information about the movements of the military force at Keflavík Air Base for his superiors in Moscow to promote him.

* * *

OPERATION BELLA

Women in the West do not enjoy the same degree of respect as they do in the lands that are governed by a Communist vision of the two biological genders of *Homo sapiens*. As you are no doubt aware from your sojourn in countries oppressed by global capitalism, Western women are utilised principally for bearing children and spoiling men. You would never see a Dutch woman using a welding torch at a shipbuilding yard, or a French girl laying paving stones, nor would Spanish señoritas be caught dead carrying coal, oh no. And the respect these women enjoy is correspondingly small or non-existent. Yes, even if a woman in Brussels is beaten to a pulp by her husband she can't get rid of him. Things do not work as well there as in the egalitarian Soviet Union where we can get married and divorced in five minutes flat if we so desire. Nor are these women able to exercise the human right of choosing their own bed-mate according to their whim. No, they are subordinate to their capitalist husbands. In your work you will exploit this knowledge, together with your understanding of

Communist teachings and the natural attractions that an upbringing in the spirit of Communist ideals has conferred on you; this will be your contribution to the Permanent Revolution.

* * *

Pushkin moved out of the embassy kitchen on Gardastræti and into a two-room bachelor pad in the Hlídar district. His new mission was to charm lonely Reykjavík ladies with the same skill that he had formerly brought to cooking "badger filet on a bed of red cabbage" for the ambassador.

That is how he became the Romeo of the switchboard girls from the various businesses and institutions. He was an expert in weighing them up and reeling them in. Many of them had recently arrived in town, they were without exception badly paid and lived in basement flats or lodged with strangers; that is to say, they were easy prey for a handsome Russian who was also so charmingly clumsy and had such a funny way of speaking. There was no shortage of these women.

How did he get them to work for him?

Well, irrespective of their political sympathies, they turned coat in support of world peace when he laid on the table such evidence as photos of nuclear bunkers belonging to Icelandic authority figures, proof that they were primarily concerned with saving their own skins; the general public could roast and burn in the nuclear bonfire for all they cared. The pictures showed innocently unsuspecting errand boys from the Reykjavík Area Cooperative passing whole pallets of dried fish, water, smoked lamb, peas, collections of the Icelandic Sagas, black pudding, liver sausage, lamb suet, the yearbooks of the Iceland Touring Club bound in leather and gilt, singed sheep's heads and legs, sour whey, curds, mare's cheese, angelica, stockfish, bilberries and copies of *Icelandic Humour* down through a hatch in the lawn behind the government minister's handsome residence. Yes, his back view was instantly recognisable as he stood there in his shirtsleeves, directing a boy towards a stack of barrels marked "seal fins" – as one could see with the aid of Pushkin's magnifying glass.

To prevent the women from realising they were being brainwashed, he used to slip them various small presents. (In addition to treating them to the odd night at Hôtel Valhalla.) He slept with them – it wasn't as if they had trouble attracting men, no, but he was highly trained in the art of lovemaking. His training had involved a spell in the KGB "Swallows' Nest" where he was manipulated into various positions that were to prove a novelty in the land of ice and fire.

That was the clincher.'

14

'The representatives of the two superpowers sat in the kitchen at Ingólfsstræti, sizing one another up. It was the first time they had met. They had introduced themselves. Midway between them on the ice-blue kitchen table was a plate of pancakes, and both had mugs of coffee in their hands. Neither the Soviet spy with the tail nor the American theologian with the bull neck touched the pancakes; neither had ever set eyes on such a species of man before.

Pushkin broke the ice.

— I have rear-projection . . .

Anthony agreed whole-heartedly.

— Me too.

And put three sugar cubes in his coffee.

— Really?

— Yeah, it's totally *verboten*.

— Oh, no one has told Pushkin this . . .

— I'm sorry, man, I don't know how it is in the Soviet Union but back home in Louisiana . . .

Anthony waved his hand with a light "ooh-la-la".

— Not to mention if you're a "Negro" born and bred, then it sure ain't no "please Mama" . . .

Pushkin adjusted the knot of his tie, glancing out of the window as if seeking an escape route should the kitchen suddenly fill with one-hundred per cent Icelandic police officers on the lookout for men with illegal tails, brushes, sterns or scuts. Drizzle spattered the window panes; it grew dark.

— What do they do to you?

— Well, what do they do to any criminal?

— Criminal?

— Yes, can you call it anything other than a crime? The punishment could be anything from hard labour to the electric chair . . .

Pushkin broke out in a sweat.

— But no one can help it . . .

— That's debatable . . .

Answered the theologian.

Pushkin shuddered and raised his mug to his lips; everything they said about these capitalists was true. At that moment Leo came indoors with the milk pail. Anthony laid his black fists on the table, spread out his fingers and examined his nails. Pushkin blew on his coffee and stared at the far rim of his cup. Leo fetched a funnel from the kitchen cupboard and began to decant the milk into bottles. No one said a word until Anthony leaned back in his chair, making it creak.

— Sorry, man, we were just discussing the fact, me and Comrade, er . . .

— Comrade Pushkin.

Supplied Pushkin.

— Yes, me and Pushkin have real objections . . .

Pushkin sighed and nodded in agreement.

— Aie . . .

Leo paled: he had been so happy as he milked Ambrosia for what he had believed was the last time before his son was born. Afterwards he had brushed her and promised that when her role as the boy's wet-nurse was over he would send her to a good home in the country.

Anthony continued:

— It sounded like a good idea yesterday, just grab the guys and you hold them down while I pull out their teeth. Done and dusted, man.

— What?

Exclaimed Pushkin.

— Yeah, and we don't even know whether the other guy has one in his tooth or not . . .

— Whose teeth are we going to pull out?

Asked Pushkin.

Leo was thoughtful: Anthony Theophrastus Athanius Brown was right. Of course it was madness. They could be charged with assault, kidnap, or whatever you call extracting people's teeth against their will. He couldn't expect these men to put their reputations on the line for him; after all, he hardly even knew them well enough to call them his friends. If the plan – what bloody plan? – went wrong they would all end up in jail. Then Anthony and Pushkin would be deported while he himself spent several months kicking his heels inside and in the meantime his son would turn to dust; the boy would come to nothing.

Leo distantly heard Pushkin saying:

— No, no, that's not right . . .

The adventure was turning into a nightmare before it had even begun: Anthony Brown had managed to hide among the Icelanders for seventeen years, so why should he sacrifice himself for the private miracle in Leo's hatbox? The same thing had happened to him as happened to most foreigners who wound up on this godforsaken rock. They couldn't bring themselves to leave, whether under duress or of their own free will.

In other words, Anthony was enjoying his stay.

Although he had suffered a major bout of homesickness after Kennedy Junior came to power, he had undergone an abrupt recovery exactly ten days ago when Miss Monroe checked out of the American dream (it was none other than the myth of the dark prince and the goddess of light that he had been intending to research when he returned to his homeland). Mythological logic indicated that now the young lady was out of the picture, it wouldn't be long before Kennedy himself fell. So Anthony had no reason to go home; after all, man, his family were long since buried under the green sod, six feet under, not an inch less.

The reason why more pressure could not be brought to bear on Pushkin, on the other hand, was that the intelligence department of the Soviet Embassy couldn't afford any more scandals. As if there hadn't been more than enough in recent months, what with all kinds of scoops by the *Vísir* newspaper – and that damned stupid blunder at Lake Kleifarvatn. And, to top it all, the two men would never know why on earth they had become embroiled in this lunacy.

If Pushkin and Anthony had to explain why they had got involved in nocturnal burgling raids on the mouths of Icelandic citizens, the only explanation they would have for their conduct was that they had been helping a man mine for gold there. It wouldn't look good, no, it would look terrible. And while Leo kicked his heels in jail, the boy would turn to nameless dust; little Jósef would turn to dust; he would disintegrate into dust.

In the autumn of 1989 an unnamed biology student rents a basement flat in a house on Ingólfsstræti. While his mother is cleaning the flat before he moves in, she finds an old hatbox in the pantry that her son, the biology student, intends to use as a study. She puts the box out on the pavement along with all the other junk the flat contained; it's extraordinary how much rubbish some people accumulate. A gang of kids appears and once they have gone, so has the hatbox. The children open the box in a backyard by some dustbins. It contains nothing but grey dust. They pour it out. The gust of wind that wanders round the corner at coffee-time whips it out of the yard and carries it into the street where it blows away, away into the blue yonder.

No, my father couldn't ask his comrades to do this. He turned white, groped for the edge of the table and collapsed on the floor.

When Leo came to his senses he was lying on the living-room sofa with a cold compress on his forehead. Pushkin sat in a chair reading a Hebrew dictionary. Anthony was standing by the radio, bending his head to the speaker from which a drawling voice was praising Dizzy Gillespie and co's version of the song "My Heart Belongs to Daddy". Leo sat up; it was dark outside. How long had he been lying there?

— Time?

The dictionary flew out of Pushkin's hands and landed on the window sill. Anthony looked up from the wireless.

— It's late, man, pretty late . . .

Leo lay back with a pained sigh. Pushkin poured water into the glass on the coffee table at Leo's side and waited impatiently for him to take a drink. When Leo had done so, he began:

— I have rear-projection, not real objection; I will do whatever I can to help you get what you want. Comrade Brown no longer has real objection. He is just tired; he's been wrestling with men from YMCA all day.

Anthony raised an apologetic hand.

— Every Sunday.

Pushkin straightened his bowtie and brushed a finger over his eyebrow. He opened a gold-plated cigarette case with a deft movement of the hand, took out a cigarette and tapped the filter on the lid.

— Mr Loewe, our friend of the oppressed black race is right; it would be better if you told us straight out why you're in such a hurry to get hold of these men's molars.

— You see, we're not Icelandic citizens like you, man; the authorities will take a different view of things if we get on the wrong side of them.

Anthony sucked his teeth.

— So we need a real good reason . . .

Leo bowed his head and turned on his heel. They followed him into the kitchen where he opened the pantry door and motioned to them to step inside. They obeyed. He went in after them and shut the door. A red light-bulb sprang into life. The three men became massive shadows in the resulting dim illumination.

My father squeezed his way to the back of the pantry and took the hatbox down from the shelf. Anthony and Pushkin leaned forwards as one when he placed it on the table, lifted the lid and unwrapped the pink silk from what it contained.

The soft red glow fell on the well-formed image of a child that lay there as if in a womb. It was a little boy, a sleeping boy, who seemed to come to life in the irregular interplay of the light and the shadows thrown by the onlookers. (His expression shifted and it looked for all the world as if he were smiling.) Then my clay breast slowly rose – and fell even more slowly. It was I who breathed.

Two gasps.

One of the men saw in me a magnificent fulfilment of the relationship between man and God; the other the achievement of a man who has broken free of all ties with the divine.

Pushkin now recounted for Anthony and Leo all that was known about the twin brothers Hrafn W. and Már C. Karlsson. Most of his

information derived from the archives of the Soviet Embassy, the rest
he had discovered by drinking whisky with his Icelandic informers.
They wouldn't touch vodka so he traded with his opposite number
at the British Embassy, whose informers turned up their noses at
everything but vodka.

— This is why Pushkin is sometimes a little tiddly – Ishelanders
drink so much whisky; Pushkin drank only vodka at home in Russia.
But here Pushkin must not say no – no, it's part of the job.

Anyway, Pushkin had received the information about the Karlsson
brothers from "MILO" who worked on the switchboard at Iceland
Prime Contractors, sat on the committee of the Conservative Women's
Association "Incentive", and had been in the same class as the twins
at the West End School.

— She's good woman, could be Russian . . .

Pushkin proceeded to read aloud from a small notebook:

— Hrafn and Már are the sons of Karl Hadarson, a mechanic, and
his wife. Karl died several years ago and his wife is a patient at the
Kleppur Mental Hospital. The brothers graduated from the Reykjavík
College and were nationally renowned champion sportsmen in their
youth. During the winter of 1943 to '44 they attended a course in
youth association studies in Germany and were on their way home
when your paths crossed aboard the *Godafoss*. They were not part of
the regular crew but worked their passage as deckhands. For some
reason their names cannot be found anywhere in the Steam Ship
Company crew lists, of which we have copies at the embassy.

At the end of the war they retired from sport and Hrafn W. opened
the Reykjavík Stamp Shop with the profits from the commemorative
stamps the brothers had postmarked at sea on 17 June 1944. (The only
set known to exist.) Már C., on the other hand, took to drink. After
being caught with his trousers down at the City Hotel Christmas Tree
Celebration he managed to clean up his act. He worked as a police
officer before becoming a parliamentary attendant. Hrafn W. is
married to the daughter of a car salesman here in town and they have
three children. Már C. has been associated with various disreputable
women but currently lives alone. Hrafn has done well out of the stamp
business and built himself a house in an upmarket neighbourhood

whereas Már rents a two-room apartment in the Melar district. And, as we know, Hrafn W. is currently serving a prison sentence for the murder of Ásgeir Helgason.

In his brother's absence Már C. has been running the Stamp Shop and I gather that eyebrows have been raised about the apparent intimacy between him and his sister-in-law.

Pushkin put down his notebook.

— What do you want to do?

He looked at the clock.

— By all accounts Már should be at an AA meeting and Hrafn at a meeting of the Freemasons' Lodge. He's given a police escort to and from prison like a head of state.

Leo scratched his head.

— You're the expert when it comes to this sort of operation.

Anthony folded his arms.

— I suggest we start by snatching Már. We don't know where he's hiding the gold so we'll need time to put pressure on him. I get the feeling too that he'll be a tougher nut to crack than Hrafn.

Leo and Pushkin agreed.

— Good.

Anthony clenched his fists and flexed his biceps.

— I'll get myself ready. Please excuse me.

He went out into the hall, fetched his trumpet case from the coat rack and vanished into the lavatory with it.

Pushkin and Leo pored over floor-plans of the Freemasons' Temple: the dark blue lines delineated room after room, dark corners and maze-like passageways. In the honeyed glow of the lamp over the coffee table the document resembled a map of one of the fabled labyrinths in the Ancient World.

— It's just a regular Lodge meeting so he should be somewhere around here.

Pushkin planted a finger on a square in the centre of the building. Leo gasped.

— Are we going to break in?

— No, are you crazy? They've booby-trapped the entire building with firebombs. Oh, yes, if anyone inappropriate, that's to say the section of humanity that does not belong to the Freemasons' order, should blunder into any of these heptagonal, round or beehive-shaped chambers where the sacred rituals take place, the whole caboodle will go up in flames. Boom! The temple will burn to the ground, taking its secrets and the trespasser with it. It's no coincidence that this is the only large property in town that the fire brigade has never been allowed to inspect, let alone hold plans of, as is usually the case with big buildings. In fact there's an arrangement that if the Freemasons' Temple does catch fire from "natural" causes, the fire brigade is merely to ensure that the fire doesn't spread.

— Are you serious?

— Yes, they can hose down the neighbouring houses and the outside of the building but they mustn't set foot inside. It's an unwritten rule. You've come up against stamp collectors and I'll admit that that's no joke. In a small society like Reykjavík that sort of business would drive anyone round the bend, but what not many people know is that the Freemasons' Lodge in Iceland is one of the most pernicious in the world. Why should that be? Well, it was founded by the Philatelic Society. When stamp collecting became a popular pastime the hard-core of old-school collectors realised that there was nothing—

— Gentlemen!

They looked up from the blueprints: Anthony stood in the living-room doorway, his head blocking the light from the hall, creating a magnificent silhouette of a man. When he stepped into the light they saw what he had been up to in the lavatory. He had donned a skin-tight black bodysuit, decorated with white brushstrokes depicting a skeleton, his head hidden by a hood with slits for eyes and mouth, which formed the skull. Altogether he was: "El Negroman!"

This is how he had been dressed when he wrestled in Mexico City where he had spent three years studying comparative religion as a postgraduate.

— They enjoy wrestling, and I made my living from it . . .

He ran a hand over his abdomen.

— I met some fine people there, like Paz. I wouldn't be surprised if he won the Nobel Prize one day, though he's not much of a wrestler.'

15

'The black car crawled along a dark street where vandals had smashed the bulbs of the street lights by throwing stones, and stopped diagonally opposite a peach-coloured wooden house with a black roof and black window frames. It's our three friends, Leo, Anthony and Pushkin in the car. They have, in other words, embarked on their risky venture and their first stop is the AA meeting house. No one knows what goes on there unless they've experienced it for themselves. And once someone has set foot in an AA meeting it's as if he's been grabbed by the throat should an outsider ask for information about the workings of the organisation. (*What follows is therefore based on conjecture and guesswork alone since I myself have never attended a meeting of this organisation. But if you, dear reader, continue with this tale, in spite of my confession that what follows is nothing but make-believe, there's one thing I can promise you in recompense: it's an incredibly exciting story that will hold you gripped to the very end.*)

Lights blazed from every room in the house but only in the downstairs rooms could movements be seen. The windows had steamed up and all that was visible of the people attending the meeting was their heads, all facing in the same direction, towards a wall where the organisation's banner hung next to the national flag. There, a dejected-looking figure could be glimpsed.

The three friends made themselves comfortable in the car. Pushkin smoked a cigarette, Anthony sat in the back seat, going over wrestling moves in his mind and muttering their names:

— Cross-buttock aloft, half-nelson, body-scissors . . .

The engine purred quietly below the sound of the gospel emanating from the radio. Leo was the only one who was obviously tense. Sweat beaded his upper lip and he was gnawing at the nail of the index finger on his right hand. He tried to focus on the catarrhal tones of the man who was expounding on the fourteenth chapter of Paul's first epistle to the Corinthians:

— Is it so that speaking in tongues is pleasing to God? Yes, did the apostles not speak in tongues? Does not Paul say that he is superior to others in the art of allowing the Holy Spirit to flow unhindered through his body in the language that he verily speaks? The only thing he warns his brothers and sisters in Corinth against is that too many should speak in tongues simultaneously, or that those who speak should not understand themselves. Speaking in tongues is a gift of grace granted to those who are pure in spirit, pure in body . . .

— Shabba-dee-da-da-da-dee-da-a, baba-ba-bee-bibbibbidddeedooa, dooah . . .

Anthony raised himself up in the back and drummed on the seat in front of him:

— Babba-dabba-deea, baba-deea . . .

— Let's see what's happening . . .

Pushkin switched off the headlights, opened the glove compartment and turned on the radio receiver concealed inside, which was evidently custom-made for cars of this type. He turned a large dial until a man's voice could be distinguished through the hissing and crackling:

— I started drinking with my father. I was only twelve. It changed my life bzzzzzzzz . . .

Pushkin adjusted the tuning.

— Bzzzzzzzzzz my father stopped beating me and we both took to thrashing my mother. She was Swedish. I was brought up on a diet of jam, redcurrant jam; she called it fruit soup . . .

The speaker broke down, but after a lengthy silence he continued through his sobs:

— That's no food for an Icelandic boy.

His audience responded with a combination of snorts and throat-rattling. Pushkin opened a compartment under the handbrake and took out a small medical bag. He opened it, revealing a collection of ampoules, pill bottles, tubes, syringes and the like.

— This is not going to be much fun. Amphetamines, anyone?

My father raised his eyebrows just as the next man cleared his throat.

— My name is Már C. Karlsson and I'm an alcoholic. I had my first drink in the Scouts. We were both in the Scouts, my brother Hrafn and I, in the Niebelungen Troop. This was on a hike up Mount Mosfell. One of the older boys had brought along a flask of brandy. Once we had planted the troop banner, someone pulled out the cork. I can still hear the pop in my mind. In my memory the mountains seem to echo with it. Whenever I drive past it's as if someone's standing on the mountain, popping their finger in their cheek: Plop!!! It still echoes there.

And then: Dig-k, dig-k, dig-k.

Or: Glug, glug, glug.

Or more like: Ghunk-ghunk . . .

That first sip. There was something magical about tasting the liquid on one's tongue, flooding one's mouth, cascading over one's tonsils. I remember passing the flask to Hrafn but he looked at me as if I'd lost my marbles. I thought he was stupid not to want to follow me Lethe-wards, for with the very first sip I heard it calling: "Friend, friend! I'll look after you, my embrace is great, my waters are wide, wide as the abyss, I am as empty as the abyss of thirst." After that first sip my throat was never dry again.

Oh, how I envied my brother Hrafn for refusing that bitter chalice! Today I realise that I was driven by an inferiority complex. I was never as good-looking as Hrafn, never as clever or respected, but of course I shouldn't have let that get me down; I mean, he could never match up to me at hammer-throwing.

Well, things didn't get any better at the sports college in Nuremberg, no, that's when they really got out of hand. I could still more or less run, jump, throw and shot-put but that didn't last long. I have so much to thank my brother Hrafn for; he stood in for me more often than not, setting various records in my name. This is a secret but I know you'll keep it, just like everything else that comes out at these meetings.

Yes, although he's in prison today, for something he didn't do, he's still a pillar of strength for me in my battle against Bacchus, or "the Führer" as we brothers like to call him.

The audience tittered.

Pushkin was humming something that sounded like a hymn but couldn't be: the man was a godless Communist, as Leo had gathered from his reaction to the miracle in the pantry. Yet when the Russian finished his humming and wiped a tear from his eye, my father was unsure. And he was not alone. Anthony Theophrastus Athanius Brown laid a great black paw on the singer's shoulder.

— Say, is that Orthodox?

At this Pushkin flared up in his seat: the man who had sung himself to tears only a few seconds before had reverted to being a ruthless Soviet agent.

— No, that was the "Cosmonaut's Lullaby". Popovich and Nikolayev sang it to each other when they met on their space missions right here above Iceland. But what do you care? You're only interested in the unbelievable up there in heaven, in gods and angels and all that crap, but there's more out there that's beautiful than the invisible, let me tell you. And that's the human creature itself – the whole, undivided human body with its nerve-controlled consciousness – which is beautiful in all its labours from cradle to grave. But it requires a poetic frame of mind to place man in circumstances in which he is able to shine like a newly manufactured tractor in the morning sun. And that's where the Soviet Union wins out. You Americans tell stories of paperboys, shoe-shine boys, errand-boys and bellboys who become millionaires, but they tell us absolutely nothing new about the human condition. For what's new about people being driven by greed? No, stories like that are old hat. They're journalism. It takes a Communist approach, an epic consciousness, to create adventures like the one that took place over our heads the other day.

Do you think anyone at the arch-capitalist American space agency would ever come up with a proletarian lullaby in space? No, old Nazis like Wernher von Braun and others of his ilk rule the roost there, and I can't imagine them seeing the beauty in a duet between a shepherd boy and a lumberjack. They don't have the words to describe how the two of them float over the continents of the world as light as, light as . . .

Pushkin was now completely under the influence of the amphet-amines.

— As . . .

He frowned at his distorted reflection in the windscreen, and it provided the answer.

— As lambs, yes!

The next speaker was a man with a deep, booming voice and a polished narrative that indicated he had rehearsed his story a thousand times before.

— My name's Arinbjörn Egilsson and I'm an alcoholic. It happened like this: one morning thirteen years ago, that's five years after we became a free nation among the nations of this world, I happened to walk past a playground for small children on Freyjugata, on my way to work, and saw that something special was afoot. I slowed down to see what was happening, since the progress of youth is one of my main preoccupations, whether it's onward or upward. For tomorrow belongs to them; we are nothing but the godfathers of the Icelandic Republic, at most half-brothers of the true Icelanders who were born after 17 June 1944. We were born under the Danish Crown that fitted us badly at best. But are they not crowned by the Northern Lights that dance airily and independently over this northerly island nation? The wonders of heaven are not our coronets, no: our part is merely to admire, polish and preserve them.

As I was saying, the children were making an unusual amount of noise. Their clear voices echoed in the morning air, they tussled energetically in the October breeze, there was an atmosphere of antici-pation. "What's going on here, young man?" I asked a fair-headed urchin who in the heat of the game had been driven howling to the concrete wall that fences off the playground – a highly necessary precaution since the streets are full of fast-moving motor cars which present a major hazard for the youngsters, let us not forget. "Thliding," anthwered the little boy.

Here one of the audience interrupted Arinbjörn:

— Excuse me, didn't you mean to say "answered"?

— Didn't I mean to say what?

A third voice:

— Yes, you said "anthwered".

Arinbjörn was wrong-footed. He caught his breath, muttering:

— What did you say? Anthwered?

— First you said "thliding", then "anthwered" . . .

— Oh dear me, well, thank you for correcting me. I really wouldn't want to inflict that sort of thing on you. Yes, thank you very much, I only meant to sort of, sort of spice up the story by saying "thliding", like the little lad did – after all he was only a child – instead of "sliding", but I should have refrained, oh dear me, yes, I shouldn't have done it; speech impediments are so infectious. Er, perhaps it would be best if I stopped at this juncture?

Silence.

— I leave it up to your judgement.

Silence.

— Well, then . . .

Arinbjörn cleared his throat and hissed his *s*'s for the remainder of his speech.

— "Ssliding," answered the little lad, pointing across the playground to what at first appeared to me to be a monstrosity of shining metal – not a heap, no, please don't misunderstand me, it had a very definite shape which wasn't revealed until five handsome, musclebound young giants from the city engineer's office set it up.

— And what have we here, my little friend?

I asked the urchin but he had stopped crying and run off to the shiny steel miracle, since the piping of the children was now so insistent that it could best be described by the word "buzzing", yes, goodness me if they weren't buzzing, or "burbling" perhaps, or was it more like "humming"?

Well, I beckoned one of the childminders to come over and speak to me. She obliged. "It's a slide," she answered when I interrogated her about the construction in the middle of the playground, which stood gleaming in the winter sun that peeped over the rooftops as if to bid good morning to the first generation of the republic. "A slide," I said. And there was I thinking "slide" was a verb.

— And what do you want with something like that here at the playground?

I asked.

— It's for the children, she replied.

Me: Which children might those be?

Her: Why, the ones you can see here.

And what did I see? Well, I saw something that led me down the thorny path of alcoholism. Our little children had formed a seemingly endless queue behind the construction, which I later referred to as a "slippery slope" in my articles in the *People's Will*.

— Hah!

Snorted Comrade Pushkin:

— Is the old sod trying to imply that he was driven to drink by that? He's always had a weak head for booze and drunk too much of it; he headbutted Stalin's favourite cousin on a friendly visit to Leningrad in 1948.

Amphetamines, anyone?'

16

'After Arinbjörn Egilsson had spoken for close to an hour on the slide affair and its impact on his drinking, people began to trickle out of the meeting. Pushkin switched off the radio and the twin-hunters took up position to ambush their first victim. It was not long before Már C. emerged on the doorstep. A woman was standing there in a cleaner's overall with a beehive hair-do and her left eye blackened, sucking on a cigarette. Már zipped up his jacket, knotted the double-checked KR football-club scarf round his neck and said goodnight.

They shadowed him down the road and managed to corner him by the back entrance to the Stamp Shop where he had naturally intended to prepare for the next day's wheeling and dealing by weighing up useless junk by the pound for unsuspecting youngsters and ignorant foreigners. It was not to be. Pushkin pounced on him like a polecat, stabbing him in the shoulder with a syringe full of a tranquillising drug.

Now Anthony Brown was standing by the boot of the Volga, his chest heaving with effort, while the prisoner was inside and remarkably subdued considering what had gone before: Már C. Karlsson lay curled up like a wolf cub, his breath whistling through a broken nose. A Russian man's sock bulged out his cheeks, and his hands and feet were bound with shoelaces.

Inside the car Pushkin was sitting behind the wheel. He lit a cigarette and wiped the sweat off his forehead with the back of his hand.

— Damnation, there's no way I can drive like this.

He slipped off his laceless patent-leather shoes and placed his bare soles on the accelerator and brake.

— Hell, it's cold.

Muttering to himself:

— I must write a report on this, get a bloody form for it. Make them put carpeting on the pedals so your feet don't freeze to death when you've just been involved in hand-to-hand combat. Hah, who knows, I might be rewarded for carrying it off like that. What do you think?

Anthony got into the car and heaved an arthritic sigh. Pushkin looked in the rear-view mirror and caught the black theologian's eye.

— Have you ever heard, seen or read about a man pole-axing his adversary with his shoes, tying him up with his laces and gagging him with his socks?

Anthony was out of humour and didn't answer.

— Hah! It'll be named after me, you can bet your life on it! Comrades, what you learned today was the unique "Pushkin Method" for overpowering lunatics.

Anthony refused to enter into the Russian's fantasy. Pushkin nodded his head encouragingly.

— Damn it, he was quiet when you packed him into the boot . . .

— That's the "Brown Method".

Replied the theologian dryly.

— What does that involve?

— I told him I was a homo.

Leo ripped open the front door and climbed into the passenger seat. He was holding a locket the size of a two-krónur piece. It was the sun cross that had been hanging round Már C. Karlsson's neck and had flown off in the frenzy that had seized the man when he sensed the drug overwhelming him. He had torn off his KR scarf and the shiny object had spun out into the night. Leo had found it in the gutter.

The gold glowed in the illumination from the street lights, and the glow was like the very spark of life.

Hrafn W. Karlsson appears in the doorway of the inner sanctum, leading an ass. The brothers of the Lodge stand in two rows, forming a corridor, with the Grand Master standing at one end, wearing a robe that is on the large side. They are smartly dressed, with the intention of looking like a single consciousness in one and the same suit, with one and the same bowtie round their necks and the same unbuttoned trouser flies. They raise their swords.

— Baphomet!!!

The ass flinches slightly at the shout but the kind man who fetched him from the menagerie in the basement, which he shares with a billy-goat, thirteen ibises, a deranged alligator and an eternal lamb that can carry a banner, strokes his flank with a firm hand – and he relaxes. He little suspects who they are, standing there in their best clothes, with trousers flying low and sabres in hand. Asses aren't much given to reflecting on human status or power and are so perverse in their habits that they submit most readily when someone is cruel to them, beating or starving them, for example. The Freemason could learn a lot from the ass. And it's worth pausing here to consider that when the glorious race of horses came close to extinction, to vanishing entirely from the face of the earth, the ridiculous ass made a reasonable job of sticking it out. Who bore the Saviour on its back into Jerusalem? Yes, he chose a mount from the donkey family, a fact with implications that the Freemasons alone appreciate.

It is for this reason that a permanent secretary of a government ministry, a civilian bank manager, a director of a coffee-roasting company, a city mayor, a director of a water company, an ordinary director, a half-German master gardener, a man incapable of anything, a master baker, a butcher's merchant, a director of the Central Bank, a wholesaler, a government minister and a cathedral priest are all toasting a silly ass in a bizarre chamber on the temple hill on Skúlagata in Reykjavík on the evening of 26 August *anno domini* 1962. The ass Baphomet couldn't care less about any of this. He can smell roses. It's suppertime. The brothers of the Lodge sheathe their swords and turn on their heel. They stand back to back, each taking a single red rose from his left-hand breast pocket.

Hrafn W. Karlsson leads the ass anticlockwise round the chamber. He pauses in front of each man in turn, the ass is given a rose, and the brother takes his penis out of his trousers and strokes its tip against the beast's grey flank while it munches on the rose petals. This is an ancient ritual and absolutely no thoughts of a sexual nature pass through the minds of the ministerial permanent secretary, coffee-roasting company director, city mayor, director of the water company, master gardener, the man incapable of anything, the baker, butcher's merchant, director of the Central Bank, wholesaler, government minister or cathedral priest when the sensitive skin on the tip of their penises touches the ass's hide. The priest brings up the rear in this gathering of the great and good, whereupon Hrafn W. Karlsson exclaims:

— Hoysan, hoysan!

And leads the ass out of the Masonic chamber.

Only one thing remains: to collect up the droppings, for of course the beast has let out a few during such un-asinine proceedings. This is Hrafn's role on his return, for such is his Masonic punishment for having taken a man's life; he's been reduced to ass-keeping.'

* * *

'This is unbelievable!'

'You find it odd that I should describe a Masonic meeting taking place on the twenty-sixth of August rather than on the big day itself, three days later, which is both Christmas and Easter to the Freemasons?'

'Oh, and you think that's what struck me most about this implausible farrago of lies?'

'Yes, because it was so out of the ordinary. But the thing is that one of the King of Sweden's chamberlains was in the country – you see, he was the Grand Master of the Swedish Masonic Lodge, of which the Lodge in this country is nothing but a minor offshoot.'

'I find the business with the animals a lot stranger than the fact that they held their service on an ordinary Sunday.'

'Consider this: is it any coincidence that the Icelandic Freemasons' Lodge was formally founded shortly after Circus Zoo visited the country? Up until then they had made do with the skulls of these species. Afterwards the skulls were sent north to Akureyri.'

'You don't say . . .'

* * *

'Outside the building life follows its normal course. The townspeople are going to bed. Lights are turned out in Skuggahverfi. Tomorrow is Monday, the start of a new working week in the life of the bustling

Icelander who breaks his back with toil in the service of his country, for the republic is still in its infancy and everyone wants it to grow up to a healthy maturity. A lonely Flamenco dancer bewails her fate on the steps of the National Theatre. But the trio in the car parked in an unlit alley across the road spare no thoughts for the health of the republic. Nor does the man who lies bound and gagged in the boot.

No, while the Freemasons tuck into a meal after honouring their ass, Loewe, Brown and Pushkin wait for the chance to realise the second part of their plan to retrieve the gold that my father needs in order to kindle life in his only son. Meanwhile, the bound man in the boot is plotting how to escape and thwart their plans.

By the time the peace of midnight has descended on the town, the Freemasons are sated. A movement at the back door turns out to be caused by the waiter Sigurdur. He props one buttock on a dustbin and lights a half-smoked Cuban cigar that he has filched from the Masons' table. After that he retrieves a brandy glass from his jacket pocket and takes a sip.

Anthony Brown pulls his hood over his face and eases himself noiselessly out of the Volga.

Then Pushkin says:

— Last night I dreamed about the night porter from the City Hotel.

Leo has nothing to say to this unexpected announcement.

— I thought I was on the top floor of a building that was actually a bleached skull. A thick mane of grass grew from the scalp, covering the whole thing like green rushes. At the same time it was like a huge, spreading quilt. I began to roll around in the quilt, like you do when you're a kid, and it was fun because it was big and thick and smelled of wild flowers. When I had rolled around in it for some time and reached the place where the headboard should have been, that is, towards the back of the crown where the skull slopes down to form the nape of the neck, I became aware of a man under the long grass. He sat up and began to romp around with me.

When I woke up I realised it was the night porter from the City Hotel. I don't know the man from Adam; I've only glimpsed him coming off duty. Isn't there something alchemical about this?

He looks at Leo.

— A skull, a man from Skálatún?

Leo ponders this.

— Skeleton?

Pushkin shakes his head. Leo frowns.

— Head, caput, capital . . . City Hotel . . . Capital city!

Pushkin nods.

— Not bad, I myself prefer "state of mind".

Leo bursts out laughing.

— My God, we're turning into proper Icelanders!

The waiter Sigurdur jumps when Hrafn emerges from the back door. He hides the brandy glass and cigar behind his back and asks in a gasp as he swallows his smoke:

— Not driving?

— No, I'll walk . . .

— Oh! Back in town, are you?

Hrafn sends the waiter a poisonous look. Is the bloody man making fun of him? He knows perfectly well that he's still in the clink. The waiter was shelling the lobster in the kitchen at eight o'clock when Hrafn arrived with his police escort. Nobody would fail to hear about it when he was released. Look at the bastard, cheeks swollen with suppressed laughter.

— The boys are playing a hand of whist down at the station. I want to give them a chance to finish.

Sigurdur the waiter, red and blue:

— That's kind of you.

— By the way, for the record, I'm innocent . . .

He waves a hand at the waiter and continues on his way. The waiter coughs up his lungs. Pushkin puts the Volga in neutral and it rolls noiselessly down the hill. It crunches on the odd piece of gravel but that's not enough to catch Hrafn's attention as he strides down Skúlagata towards the police station where the evening shift are wiping the floor with the night shift at whist. When autumn comes and the primary school teachers who work for the police during the summer holidays have to go back to wrestling with the tribe of youth (that gum-chewing, aitch-dropping, tic-ridden, grammar-violating nation within a nation), it is customary for them to lose to their uneducated colleagues at cards.

The Volga rolls like a softly padding predator in pursuit of the stamp killer, Hrafn W. Karlsson. Leo holds his breath. As Hrafn passes the Slaughterhouse, Anthony Brown will whip him into an alleyway and overpower him. Then Leo and Pushkin will leap out of the car. Pushkin will give the man an injection of sedative and once he is unconscious Leo will find his wisdom tooth and tear it out. After that they will anaesthetise the man and lay him beside his brother. Then they'll split up. Leo will ring the police and say something along the lines that Ásgeir the shower attendant has been avenged. The police won't make a fuss, since how are they supposed to explain to the public that a convicted murderer has been taking a stroll along the seashore when he should by rights be sitting chain-smoking on a mattress in jail, reflecting on the error of his ways and preparing himself for a new life?

Hrafn is light on his feet for a man weighing some 130 kilos. The stone-cutting at the house of correction is keeping him fit and Leo's eyes open wide when their quarry vaults agilely over the fence at the crossroads with Frakkastígur. He's not far now from his appointment with the Mexican champion wrestler, Negroman.'

17

'Anthony Brown blocked Hrafn W. Karlsson's path and flung his arms round him in a bear hug. He crushed the breath out of the stamp dealer so he couldn't utter a word. Pushkin slammed on the brakes and leapt out of the car with his medical bag. Leo caught up with him just as he plunged the morphine needle deep into Hrafn's back-side. The stamp dealer slumped down, mumbling some nonsense about snow-buntings. They dragged the man further down the alley to a pen where a few scrawny lambs watched the struggle without interest. Pushkin went over to the corner of the building to keep a lookout.

Leo straddled Hrafn W.'s chest and wrenched his jaw open. He peered inside for the gold tooth but in the darkness of the alley there was no gleam of precious metal that would bring life to the little clay body. He fumbled with his pliers until he found the wisdom tooth in the upper left-hand jaw, then applied them to the tooth and tugged vigorously. The man's head came too, but the tooth wouldn't budge, and after my father had swung it back and forth for a while Anthony grabbed his arm and whispered that perhaps it would be better if *he* pulled out the man's tooth. My father gave way to the scholar of comparative religion, a little disappointed to have no part in the action. Anthony said:

— Hold his head.

My father did so, pleased to have something to do. Anthony jerked the pliers with all his might. Leo saw the stamp dealer's dilated pupils contract momentarily as his wisdom tooth came out with a crack.

— Here, take the gold!

Anthony passed my father the pliers. He freed the tooth, held it between his fingers with a professional air, then went round the back of the building to examine it better – there was an outside light on over the staff entrance. Anthony heaved Hrafn W. to his feet. He was smiling foolishly, a trickle of blood running from the corner of his mouth down his chin. The black man beckoned to Pushkin to bring the car down the alley; there was no need to risk letting the cargo escape into the street. It looked to him as if Hrafn needed another dose of the drug, since he was reviving and reaching the stage where he wanted to sing for the world.

— O, the bonny bluebell . . . !

Anthony clamped a hand over his mouth.

Leo's blood ran cold when he raised the tooth to the light and saw that the metal was nothing but bog-standard Icelandic orthodontist's gold. Had they pulled out the wrong tooth? The lambs in the pen seemed infected by his fear; they fled and huddled together by the wall furthest from the alley.

— Aren't you coming, man?

Anthony stuck his head round the corner and whispered as loudly as he dared:

— We've gotta get out of here.

Leo saw the steam rising from his mouth and realised that the temperature had dropped below freezing while they were occupied with Hrafn. Shivering, he turned up his collar. They would have to have another poke around in the man's mouth. He ran into the alley. Pushkin had reversed the Volga down it and was now standing by the boot, ready to open it and dope the prisoner Már who was going demented inside.

— I don't know if I dare risk it.

He drummed his fingers on the black paintwork. There was frost on the rear windscreen.

— Can you give me a hand, Mr Brown?

— Not unless you give this one another dose . . .

Pushkin looked at Hrafn in astonishment.

— Hell, these guys have hard heads . . .

He fetched the medical bag from the front seat, filled the syringe with another dose and prepared it.

— Damn, it's chilly here, are we by the freezer unit?

Hrafn W. tried to say something through Anthony's thick hand. He was clearly coming to his senses and the black man tightened his hold on him. The sheep were now bleating fearfully in the pen. Leo stepped forward and showed them the tooth.

— We'll have to take another look, this is the wrong one.

Pushkin jabbed the needle into Hrafn's upper arm. As he did so, Anthony relaxed his grip for a split second, which enabled the prisoner to jerk his head aside, and now he evidently had more on his mind than bonny bluebells.

— Fuck you! You don't know what the hell you've got in the back of the car . . .

Hrafn's voice was hoarse. Leo looked into his eyes. They were yellow. Hrafn inflated his lungs like a swimmer:

— HRA . . .

The scream was inhuman and faded into a canine howl as the drug overcame him once more. A bitch gave an answering howl from the Skuggahverfi neighbourhood. It had an ugly sound. Anthony flung Hrafn away from him and he crashed into the slaughterhouse wall, then slid down on to the road.

— It's no good, we've gotta get out of here.

Leo poked a finger in the man's mouth but there was nothing there. Pushkin dragged him to his feet, pushed him towards the car, then loosened the belt of Hrafn's trousers and pulled them down.

— That'll raise some questions!

He said after they had spun down Skúlagata and were bowling south along the road heading for the hill of Öskjuhlíd.

— Iceland's one of the few countries where you can still spread rumours about men being sexually attracted to sheep. Why, I don't know, I probably haven't been here long enough, but it's come in very handy.

— What do we do now?

— We dump him up by the hot-water tanks.

Anthony placed his forearms on the seat backs in front of him and rested his chin on the ledge between Leo and Pushkin.

— This has been quite enough excitement for an academic like me, man; no one wants to lose his job and all, right?

Nobody spoke.

After their defeat in the battle with the stamp dealer, Leo had reconciled himself to having to use the tiny amount of gold he had already made, along with what could be melted down from the sun cross. Without the missing gold the boy would be a little out of kilter with his fellow citizens: deaf, lacking arms, diabetic, mentally handicapped or predisposed to cancer. But he was prepared for that: it wouldn't be the first time something similar had happened in the creation of a homunculus.

Up ahead, the hot-water tanks towered on the hilltop like the walls of a medieval castle, forming a black silhouette against the grey sky. The slopes were a tangle of dark foliage, covered with the man-high scrub that seems like a fairytale forest to the citizens of Reykjavík. The trio took the airport road along the western slope and from there drove up the gravel track to the foot of the tanks.

— Right, here we go . . .

They climbed out of the car and walked round behind it. The prisoner had not made a sound since they raced out of the alley by the slaughterhouse.

— Is he, do you think he might be . . . ?

Sighed Leo.

— I very much doubt it.

Answered Pushkin, putting a hand on his shoulder.

— This car is designed especially for this kind of transport. But we'd better proceed with caution, all the same. Either the drug has put him to sleep or he was knocked out when the car bumped out into the road, or . . .

Pushkin raised a finger; he was in his element.

— Or he's lying there, having squeezed out the sock and freed himself from his bonds, waiting to take us by surprise. After all, this is the one-time Nordic hammer-throwing champion.

He lowered his voice:

— But we might have just the thing to deal with that.

Opening the medical bag of tricks, which seemed to contain yet another chemical weapon, he took out a rubber tube and a gas canister with a tap. He squeezed the tube into the spout and pushed the other end under the lid of the boot. Then he popped an amphetamine pill and turned on the tap. After a lengthy pause:

— If Mr Karlsson is not in the Land of Nod by now, I must be dreaming that I'm standing in the middle of the night on Öskjuhlíd hill pumping Lysergene gas into the alcoholic twin brother of a convicted murderer, who is, *nota bene*, in the boot of my car. With me is a giant black man dressed in a Mexican wrestling costume that's rather on the tight side and the Czechoslovakian Jew, Jón Jónsson, I'm sorry, I mean the Icelander, Leo Loewe, a sorcerer who has in his possession the clay image of a small boy. Later in my dream this little figurine will come to life and perform a variety of miracles. But that is material for another dream.

As he spoke these words the terrifying sequence of events began. The whole thing was like one of those appallingly violent comics that are banned in Iceland. The dream-character forced his way out of the car boot with the door on his shoulders, quite unlike the man they had originally bundled in there: his jacket and shirt had burst off his body but by great good fortune his hands and feet were still bound – and he still had the sock gag in his mouth.

That didn't last long.

The man turned blue in the face, his eyes popped out on stalks, and his throat rattled with deep sucking sounds as he swallowed the pair of socks. (Leo retched as the bundle of synthetic fibres bulged in the man's throat before sinking like the moon down his oesophagus, lifting his ribcage on the way.) The stay in the car boot had done him no good at all.

Már C. flung back his head and howled like a beast. Every single bird on Öskjuhlíd hill flew off whatever perch it had found, whether twig, tussock or rock. And then ghastly things began to happen to the face of the former parliament attendant: the bones of his skull behaved as if they were made of liquid plastic: his forehead sloped back, the root of his nose and lower jaw thrust outwards as if punched from inside by a clenched fist. His eyes changed colour, from sky blue to yellow, his pupils became black slits. And the fangs burst out of his gums, flashing like scimitars.

— What the hell is going on with these brothers?

Pushkin glanced round for an escape route. Anthony ducked his head between his shoulders, the instinctive wrestler's reaction, and retreated a few paces as part of the same tactic. The man continued his metamorphosis, tearing off his fetters; hair sprang out all over his body at the exertion, and, in the blinking of an eye, muscles had begun to ripple where before there had been flab. He opened his jaws wide and licked them with his long wolfish tongue. And then Leo saw what he so desperately needed: there was the gold in the wisdom tooth of Már, who was of course none other than the stamp dealer Hrafn W. Karlsson. Why hadn't he realised it before? Of course the villain had made his pathetic wretch of a brother take the rap for him. It all made sense.

Hrafn turned his head towards my father, saliva foaming at the corners of his mouth, his eyes blazing like funeral pyres in a hurricane. He extended his claws, a murderous weapon flashing on every finger, and braced himself to pounce on Leo. But he hesitated. My father drew out a pistol, an ancient weapon that he proceeded to load so nimbly that Pushkin and Brown could hardly believe their eyes.

The werewolf howled with fury when Leo tore a silver cufflink from his shirt (for this is how mystics are generally attired) and rammed it down the barrel of the firearm. The savage beast gathered itself in a leap and vanished into the night. My father threw the keys to his friends.

— Meet me at Ingólfsstræti!

Anthony Brown caught them in the air and my father ran off after the monster. Thunder rumbled over Faxafloi Bay . . .'

VII

(Anniversaries)

18

'Darkness; birth of Confucius.

In 413 BC Nicias' fleet disperses during a lunar eclipse. The Spartans see nothing terrifying in the workings of the heavens and proceed to massacre the Athenians.

Then 1,958 years later Alessandro Farnese, Duke of Parma, is born. When he is seventeen, the composer Hans Leo Hassler is born. Seven years pass before Pope Pius bestows the title of Grand Duke of Tuscany on none other than Cosimo I de' Medici. In 1576 the great plague lays low the painter Titian and in 1583 the composer Simon Besler is born. He is exactly two years old when the Duke of Parma captures Antwerp and eighteen when Olivier van Noort completes the first Dutch circumnavigation of the New World.

Then in 1610 the Polish King Wladyslaw is elected Tsar of Russia, in 1619 Frederick, the Elector Palatine, assumes the crown of Bohemia, and in 1626 the Battle of Lutter am Barenberge breaks out. It ends with the Catholic League trouncing King Christian IV of Denmark. In 1628 the Sultan of Java attacks Batavia, two years before the birth of the flower painter Maria van Oosterwyck, and a whole thirteen years before the composer Johann Samuel Welter first sees the light of day. In 1667 the existence of hurricanes is first recorded in print. This happens in Jamestown, Virginia. So much for the seventeenth century.

The fires of the Mývatn eruption surround the church at Reykjahlíd and the lava flows into the lake, where it can still be seen today. The lava still feels warm when Johann Georg Hamann is born in 1730; his hobby is playing the lute. Then we have to wait until 1770 for the birth in Germany of Georg Wilhelm Friedrich Hegel, none other than the inventor of dialectic. And he is no more than a six-year-old boy when the English defeat the American rebels in the Battle of Long Island. Then in 1783 the first hydrogen balloon in the history of mankind is launched into the air and reaches an altitude of 2,952 feet. It is unmanned, and only six years later the French National Assembly issues its Declaration of the Rights of Man and of the Citizen. In 1798 the Castlebar Races take place in Ireland, in which the French army routs the English.

Anyway, in 1813 Napoleon defeats the Austrians at Dresden, and in 1816 Lord Exmouth bombards the nest of corsairs at Algiers, while the music critic, composer and music teacher Hermann Kipper is born exactly ten years after that piece of ethnic cleansing. In 1828, meanwhile, Uruguay achieves independence following peace talks between Brazil and Argentina. And four years later Black Hawk, chief of the Sauk Indians, surrenders to the white man. In 1837 yet another composer is born, Heinrich Urban, who is already an accomplished musician (after all, he is twelve) when the Mexican nation gives birth to the poet Manuel Acuña who is to be famous for his nocturne. The Italian mathematician Giuseppe Peano of Cuneo, on the other hand, enters the world a year before Edwin Drake becomes the first man to successfully drill for oil. That is in 1859 and will bring various changes in its wake, both economic and social, in the six years that pass before the birth of Emmuska "Scarlet Pimpernel" Orczy.

She is two years old when a volcanic eruption breaks out in the Vatnajökull ice-cap in Iceland. That same day Umberto Giordano is added to the tale of the living and of composers. Then the writer Theodore Dreiser is born in 1871. Then the chemist Carl Bosch is born in 1874. Then the automobile manufacturer Charles Stewart Rolls is born in 1877. Then the composer Joseph John Richards is born in 1878. Then it is a sad day in 1879 when Rowland Hill, the man who invented the postage stamp, dies in his eighty-fourth year. His contribution to civilisation cannot be overestimated. In 1882 Jaroslav Křička, composer, and Hubert Marischka, director of the 1941 Viennese comedy *Invitation to the Dance*, are born. They are only twelve months old when the island of Krakatoa erupts with a force of 1,300 megatons. The tremor is felt over much of the world, including Iceland.

The astronomer A. Borrelly spots asteroid number 240 and calls it

Vanadis. That is in 1884. The year of 1886 is well endowed with composers, for that is when Rebecca Clarke and Eric Coates are born, the latter also known for his skill on the viola. A year later we turn to Stadarhraun in Mýrasýsla county, Iceland, where the boy Jónas Gudlaugsson is born. Now time passes and Man Ray is born in 1890 in Philadelphia, and on his second birthday no one can talk of anything but the fire at the city's Metropolitan Opera House. In 1896 the English defeat the inhabitants of Zanzibar in the "Thirty-eight-minute War" which lasts from 9.02 to 9.40 a.m.

In 1897 A. Charlois observes asteroid number 427 and names it Galene. In 1899 Cecil Scott Forester is born; he will write the Horatio Hornblower series. In 1900 the Battle of Bergendal takes place in which General Buller of the British Empire team wipes the floor with the army of the Boers and their leader Botha. Then I think we've reached the age of inventions.

In the first year of the new century, the present century, the Ritz brother Al enters the world. The following year the composer Herbert Menges is born, while in 1903 Xavier Villaurrutia, a Mexican poet who wrote about the nightlife of angels, is born. The next piece of news is that in 1908, at Stonewall in Texas, the Johnsons have a boy whom they christen Lyndon B. Two years earlier Max Wolf observed asteroid number 605 and called it Juvisia. In 1909 the saxophonist Lester "Prez" Young and the cycling champion Sylvère Maes are born. Then in Macedonia the child Anjezë Gonxhe Bojaxhiu enters the world; later the street children of Calcutta will name her both Mother and Teresa.

In 1912 Edgar Rice Burroughs publishes the novel *Tarzan of the Apes*. And exactly a year later the philosopher Donald Mackenzie MacKinnon is born. The same day a historic aeronautic event takes place in Kiev when Lieutenant Pyotr Nesterov, of the Imperial Russian Air Service, takes to the air and completes a backward loop in his monoplane. On the second day of the war in 1914 the Germans bomb Usdau in the Battle of Tannenberg, while out on the cold North Sea the trawler *Skúli fógeti* hits a mine and sinks. On the same day asteroid number 794 appears in the telescope of Mr Palisa. He names it Irenaea. Two years pass and then Romania declares war on the Austro-Hungarian Empire.

In 1922 the aloof Finnish runner Paavo Nurmi sets a world record in the 3,000 metres of 8:28.6. Three years pass before the birth of the drummer and band leader, Tony Crombie, who is to drive Reykjavík wild in the spring of 1957. The year of 1928 is eventful: sixteen people die in the second worst accident in the history of the New York subway; sixty-two nations sign the Kellogg–Briand Pact, thereby outlawing war from the world, and Mangosuthu Gatsha Buthelezi, the Zulu leader, enters the world. A year later the discus-thrower Elizabeta Bagrintseva is born in the USSR and the writer Ira Levin in the USA.

The International Peace Convention is inaugurated in Amsterdam in 1932, on the same day as the births take place of the cosmonaut Mikhail Nikolayevich Burdayev and the composer François Glorieux; a strike by 200,000 English textile factory workers also begins. In 1935 P. Shajn hits the jackpot by discovering two asteroids on the same day, number 1369 Ostanina and number 1387 Kama. Then Alice Coltrane and Tommy Sands are born in 1938, when George E.T. Eyston sets a new world land-speed record of 345.49 mph. That year there is a banquet in Paris at which an unfortunate incident occurs when the Chilean artist Oscar Dominguez throws a glass at the Romanian Victor Brauner who loses an eye. Erich Warsitz becomes the first man to fly a jetplane, a Heinkel He 178. The same day, in 1939, his countrymen in the government of Hitler's Germany demand the right to rule the Polish Corridor and Danzig. Thus begins the Second World War. The following year there is another historic moment for aviation when the Caproni-Campini CC-2 jet makes a successful maiden flight in Milan. In the United States the jazz guitarist Warren Harding "Sonny" Sharrock is born, while G. Strommer is fortunate enough to locate asteroid number 1537, which he names Transylvania.

In 1941 the cosmonaut Yuri Vasilyevich Malyshev, who will fly both Soyuz T-2 and T-11, is born, while down south in Persia the Shah abdicates in favour of his son Reza Pahlavi. The actress Tuesday Weld is born in 1943 and the following year the composer Barry Cunningham is born. That day 200 Halifax planes attack oil refineries in Hamburg. In 1945 American forces land in Japan following the capitulation of Emperor Hirohito, "son of the Sun". A year later in Iceland the first car makes it over the Siglufjördur pass after the road has been ploughed and graded for eleven years in a row.

In 1951 the exhibition galleries of the Icelandic National Gallery are formally opened in the National Museum building. In 1952 Emil Zátopek wins the twelfth Olympic marathon in a time of 2:23:03.2. In 1955 the *Guinness Book of Records* is published for the first time. In 1957 the Americans conduct an experimental explosion of an atom bomb in the Nevada Desert.

In 1958 they explode one in the South Atlantic while the Soviet Union launches Sputnik III with two dogs on board. In 1960 Anita Lonsbrough sets a swimming world record in the 200 metres breaststroke of 2:49.5.

In 1961 "Tiger Trainer" Miss Mabel Stark appears on the American TV show *What's my Line?*.'

* * *

'So what?'

'None of these came close to the miracle that took place in the kitchen of the basement flat at 10a Ingólfsstræti in 1962, on 27 August, at five minutes past eleven:

When I was born.

Later that same day the Soviets exploded a 4,000 megaton atom bomb on Novaya Zemlya, while the Americans launched Mariner II which went all the way to Venus.

I call those pretty good omens.'

19

'It was nearly eleven in the morning by the time Leo had melted the gold from Hrafn W.'s tooth and the solar cross. He poured it into the mould and waited for it to cool.

The battle with the philatelic werewolf had ended on top of the water tanks. The cold autumn wind ruffled the monster's fur as he loomed against the moon, which was shining fitfully through the clouds. My father stayed at a safe distance. Hrafn stood on the brink, rocking menacingly so the moonlight shone on and off in my father's eyes. Hrafn was obviously planning to push my father over the edge, letting gravity and the rocks crush every bone in his body. He sprang.

Leo Loewe crouched with lightning speed. The werewolf flew over him, landing on his back with a heavy thud. The brute howled with pain and lay motionless for some time, naturally hoping that his enemy would make the mistake of checking to see whether he was completely done for, at which point he would devour him. When it became clear that this wasn't going to happen, he rolled over on his stomach and wearily climbed to his feet.

My father stood with legs braced, holding the pistol straight out in front of him in classic shooting pose, ready to fire at the werewolf which was approaching him with slow steps.

— Damn . . .

Growled Hrafn W. Karlsson indistinctly, his coarse wolf's tongue better shaped for lapping up blood than forming words. He threw in the towel.

— I'm far too old for all this . . .

My father retreated a step and pulled back the trigger so the monster would see that he was serious about using the weapon. The other barked:

— Take the bloody thing, then . . .

The stamp dealer reached with the long bestial nails of his thumb and forefinger into his mouth and plucked out his wisdom tooth as if there were nothing to it. He flung it at my father who caught it in the air.

His fist closed over the tooth. The moon disappeared behind a cloud.

When it shone out again Hrafn W. Karlsson had vanished.

Leo broke the mould off the signet ring. He polished it and drew it on to the middle finger of his right hand. His work would soon be complete. He went out into the living room and woke Anthony and Pushkin who were sleeping there in chairs. They hurriedly rose to their feet and followed him into the kitchen where they took up position on either side of the table while Leo went into the pantry and fetched the hatbox.

He laid it on the table, took off the lid and unfolded one cloth after the other, all of the finest silk, which flowed over the sides like living tissue. He carefully lifted the clay child from the box and laid it on the table. Then he drew the ring from his finger, pronounced a few well-chosen words and pressed the seal into the clay.'

* * *

'To be born is like climbing out of a forest pool into burning sunlight; one moment you're boiling, the next you get goose flesh.'

* * *

'Leo wrapped me, the shivering baby, in the eiderdown he had bought long ago, and stooped over me, crooning. In the eighteen years that had passed since his arrival in Iceland he had amassed all the things necessary for looking after a child. Anthony and Pushkin gaped as romper-suits in every colour of the rainbow emerged from drawers and cupboards, along with nappies and flannels, underwear, rattles and pinwheels, bottles and dummies, jumpers and hats, socks and mittens, teddy bears and dolls that would have sufficed for a whole children's crusade.

I was no longer dormant clay but a purple boy who wriggled and grizzled as my father put on my nappy and dressed me in a soft cotton top and sky-blue romper-suit decorated with lilies.

Anthony nipped out into the passage and returned with a small book that he laid at my feet.

— It's the custom to give the baby a present, isn't it?

It was the book *Icelanders on Other Planets* by Gudmundur Davídsson.

Pushkin reached into his pocket and drew out a skeleton key.

— Might come in handy . . .

And laid it in my hand.

Then there was the present that arrived in the post.

The goat bleated in the garden, a pair of uniformed legs came and went past the kitchen window, and a moment later something fell through the letterbox: a letter that had taken more than four years to travel the five minutes from Kvosin to Ingólfsstræti.

Reykjavík, 5 March 1958

Dear Swimming-pool customer Loewe,

I want to start by apologising that you have to read this letter. I am no good with a pen and the occasion is awkward, I realise that. I don't know you, although we've sometimes had a nice chat together when you've come to the Pool where I work. Not many people bothered – to talk to me, I mean. You won't have noticed, being a foreigner and all, that I have a speech defect. Well, perhaps not a defect, but my grammar's no good, I don't talk proper Icelandic. I'm quite unlucky in this, seeing as how I'm Helgi Steingrímsson's son.

I've decided to take my own life. So I'd like to ask you to take care of this envelope with coarsely perforated two-shilling stamps and finely perforated four-shilling franks, posted in Djúpivogur and postmarked in Hamburg. I once let slip that I owned it and so I thought it would be best for you to have it. But it's not for you.

If you should ever have a son you are to use this to allow him to do what he wants. If, for example, he is afraid of water, you're not to make him take up swimming against his will.

Thank you from me,
Ásgeir Helgason

P.S. I know my death will attract attention, but I had to get H.W.K. into trouble somehow. It was me who put my stamp collection under his cupboard. Don't tell anyone. He once swindled me out of a five-aurar stamp with a reversed "three" overprint. Afterwards he sold it at auction in Copenhagen.

I was nine years old. I was a child.
Á.H.

On the evening of my first day, after my father had bathed me, powdered me, put on my nappy, dressed me in my night clothes, laid me in the cradle and tucked me in, he told me a bedtime story. A tear quivered on his eyelashes.

* * *

CREATION STORY

Once upon a time the universal father and son were travelling through the cosmos; they were heading for home and still had a long way to go. The father was carrying his sleeping son in his arms. After six days of walking he was so weary that he paused by a galaxy. He laid the sleeping boy on a nebula while he himself stretched out in the void and fell asleep. Shortly afterwards the little universal boy was woken by a meteorite brushing past his nose. He almost sneezed aloud but that would have made an almighty din and since he was a good boy he held his nose and sneezed politely so as not to wake his father.

The boy played with some comets, trying to catch them and hold them fast by their tails. He enjoyed feeling the warm tails brushing his palms as they slipped through his clenched fingers. The game carried him away from his sleeping father. The boy saw a cold sun that he wanted to examine more closely, but before he knew it he had come face to face with a big black hole.

The sun sank into the black hole and he reached out for it – too far. The black hole gripped the little hand and pulled the boy slowly and inexorably towards it.

— Oh!

The universal boy began to cry. He shouted and called but his weeping was sucked into the blackness and his other arm vanished inside it too. He was drawn closer to the black hole, closer and closer, until his head vanished, then his shoulders, then his body, closer and closer, then his legs; everything vanished into the black hole except the big toe on his left foot. When the universal boy had vanished this deep into the black hole the tip of his nose became cold and for a moment he stopped crying.

— Atchoo!

He sneezed, making the universe echo.

The universal father started awake. He raced over and saw the tip of the universal boy's toe sticking out into space, and taking hold of it he snatched the boy out of the black hole. The father embraced his boy, comforted his son and told him he must never do that again.

— I'll never leave you, Daddy.

The universal boy stopped crying.

His father dried the tears from his eyes and kissed his little hands. Then he saw that under the nail of the ring finger on his right hand, which had sunk deepest into the black hole, was a rim of grime. The universal father took out his big knife. The mighty blade flashed in the void and the edges sparkled.

The son held out his hand, his finger, his nail, and his father cleaned underneath it. He scraped a bit of black clay from under the nail, black clay from the bottom of the black hole. The universal father wiped the point of the knife on his son's fingertip, leaving the bit of clay there. Then he sheathed the knife and showed the boy how to make a ball from the scrap by rolling it between his fingers, which he did. The universal father and son now headed for home.

They walked hand in hand through infinity. The father either hummed a tune or sang verses, while the son played with the little ball of clay. When they were nearly home they passed a small galaxy. In the galaxy was a solar system. In the middle of the solar system was a star and around the star revolved a planet. It was a blue earth that revolved on its own axis while around it revolved a grey moon. Everything was revolving around everything else.

The universal boy found the earth beautiful and shrank his hand so that he could touch it. His hand passed the grey moon, through the atmosphere, round below the South Pole, and he let the earth sit on his palm, allowing it to spin there. The father watched his son raise the earth to his face, which was bathed in blue light.

The son studied the white clouds and black hurricanes, the golden lightning and silvery Northern Lights. The lights were playing in the sky above an island near the North Pole. The boy looked at his father and back at the island, back at his father and back at the island. Then he shrank his other hand and pressed the black clay into the corner of a bay on the island. Before he withdrew his hand he pressed his index finger firmly into the clay.

And the universal boy's fingerprint laid down the guidelines for streets and gardens, parks and squares.

Today it is known as Reykjavík.'

* * *

'Goodnight.'
'Chirr, chirr . . .'

PART III

I'M A SLEEPING DOOR

a science-fiction story

I

~~Rutting Season~~ Rite of Spring

(1 April 1961)

1

'Although I'm going to say that it all began in Reykjavík on the first day of April 1961, it could just as well have been two or even three weeks earlier – though hardly any more than that. And, with the same proviso, it must have ended on the same date the following year, or possibly one to two months, at most ten weeks, later, though I find that highly unlikely as I've not uncovered any evidence of a birth that premature. It would have created such a sensation that it's bound to have left traces in the press or other contemporary sources.

In the account that follows I shall therefore stick to the aforementioned date: 1 April 1961. The event could just as well have taken place somewhere else, in the countryside or a fishing village, for instance, but I choose to place it in Reykjavík, in the centre of town, in the street where I grew up. I do so partly because this was when the population of Reykjavík first outnumbered that of the rest of the country, and partly because I want to place myself squarely in the bigger picture. I first saw the light of day in Iceland's capital, I've lived there all my life and I fully expect to die there.

Above all, though, it is for form's sake that I want to establish a time and place, not only so you'll be clear about when and where the action is set, but to give this opening chapter a weight and stature commensurate with what is to follow – in other words, to leave you in no doubt that my story is in dialogue with other major types of narrative, with that long, resounding roll-call that encompasses everything from visionary poems in medieval manuscripts to futuristic films, from topsy-turvy verses to the four gospels, from folk tales of drug-induced ghosts to gossip columns in the papers, from travel accounts written by intelligent women to comic strips about mutant children, from pop lyrics to publications on psychology, from pornography to chess commentary – so that in its clarity and profundity my introduction will be on a par with the best scholarly accounts by those gifted anthropologists who can, by means of a complex yet clear line of reasoning, instantly convey their readers back across time to the image of a hand left by one of our foremothers on a cave wall in Altamira, when discussing the old children's game of placing a hand on a cool window pane, breathing on it, then taking it away, so that there appears for a brief moment the hot image of a small hand, a hand as different from my cold, hard ones as hot breath is from frost-chilled glass.'

'I'm holding your hand, Jósef, resting my palm on the back, touching the soft skin. There's warmth under there. You're still alive.'

'The sheep-worrier. Did I show you what happened to him?'

'That comes later. Tell me about 1 April 1961 . . .'

'This is how I picture it happening:

In the very instant that the mighty clapper of the clock in the Thorsteinsons' dining room, on the first floor of the house at 10a Ingólfsstræti, had finished striking twelve midnight, on the eve of Saturday, 1 April 1961, a car drove quietly up to the house on the garden side and parked in the lee of the wall, leaving its engine idling though its headlights were off. From where he lay under his eiderdown in the basement – hands folded on his breast, waiting for the horn and ivory gates between the worlds of waking and sleep to open and let him in – my father Leo Loewe heard, over the purring of the diesel engine, Mrs Thorsteinson's quick footsteps descending the stairs leading from the kitchen to the back door. It could only have been her: the couple were childless, the maid had gone home for the day once she'd cleared up after supper and Mr Thorsteinson was at choir practice. The Song Thrushes, the male-voice choir to which he belonged, were busy rehearsing for their upcoming tour of the Holy Land, where they were scheduled to perform at the Church of the Nativity in Bethlehem, on the shores of the Sea of Galilee, on the Temple Mount in Jerusalem and in the Garden of Gethsemane, in addition to paying a visit to the capital Tel Aviv to be photographed beside the olive tree that was planted beside the Knesset building in honour of a former choir member, the baritone Thor Thors, who, as ambassador, had led Iceland's delegation at the United Nations in support of the establishment of the State of Israel. Rehearsals for a tour of this magnitude tended to drag on for hours so Mr Thorsteinson was unlikely to be home before morning.

Mrs Thorsteinson slowed her pace when she reached the bottom step, as if belatedly remembering my father sleeping in the room below the stairs, or – in view of what lay ahead of her that night – perhaps she was assailed by doubts about her plan. Whichever it was, her hesitation didn't last long. Stealthily she opened the back door, and my father heard the clicking of her heels on the pavement outside, followed by a car door opening and closing, then saw the glow as the headlights were switched on, and heard the diesel purr deepen into a growl as the vehicle moved away.

At which point the gates of sleep finally opened to admit him . . .

* * *

THE SECRET OF THE BLACK TRIANGLE I & II

(Taxi 69)
A cloudy, dark blue April night enfolds the black Mercedes-Benz taxi parked at the rear of the service yard behind the fish-meal processing plant. It's shortly after midnight and the only light competing with the dense gloom is the pale yellow glow of the dials on the dashboard, which is enough to enable the young driver, Örn Ragnarsson, to see everything he desires in the rear-view mirror when the woman in the back seat strips off her fur: her tailored suit of bottle-green wool accentuates every line, every curve of her body.

"She can't be wearing much underneath," is the first thought to form in his mind. "Maybe nothing at all." His gaze lingers on her hips, on the hollow between her firm thighs, where the dip in the short skirt hints at what awaits him under the taut fabric.

Still without taking his eyes off the woman, the taxi driver leans forwards and switches off the two-way radio. Before he can say a word, she has unbuttoned her jacket to reveal a thin, silky blouse through which he glimpses a low-cut black bra. She lets him look at her for a moment, then unzips her skirt, pulls it down to her knees, props her legs up against the seat in front of her and wriggles out of it. She hands him the skirt and he lays it on the passenger seat beside him. Then, lifting up her buttocks, she reaches under her see-through petticoat and starts easing her panties down the same way. Five seconds later a pair of lacy black silk knickers has joined the skirt on the seat beside him.

The temperature in the car is stifling. The engine's running, there's a steady blast of hot air from the heater, the meter's ticking. On the American base radio station they're playing the theme from the film *Exodus*. Through the flimsy petticoat he sees the shadow of the black triangle between her legs, framed by tan nylon stockings and the dark red straps of her suspender belt. He loosens his tie and undoes the top button of his shirt.

Smiling faintly, the woman pulls open her blouse, thrusting up her breasts until the rosy-pink nipples are peeping over the black cups of her bra. A delicious, warm scent rises from her ripe body. He takes a deep breath, hastily scanning the darkened yard as he does so, though there's no risk of their being disturbed at this hour of the night. He steals a glance at the clock on the dashboard. Twenty-three minutes past twelve – it won't be long before the cab company notices he's missing. If this is to go anywhere, he needs to do something about it right now.

He twists round to look at the woman in the back seat.

The tip of a pink tongue peeps out from between her full, red-painted lips and she moistens them by moving her tongue slowly from side to side. When she parts her thighs, her petticoat is stretched tight and rides up to her hips, revealing a dark bush of hair between her suspenders. She gives a low moan.

Without more ado, he drags off his jacket, clambers between the front seats and squeezes into the back beside the woman who reaches out and pulls him down on top of her, thrusting her body against his as if she had no greater desire than to give herself to him. Their lips meet in a long, passionate, tremulous kiss. There's a roaring in his ears. The woman's ardour is so violent that it frightens him. With wild abandon, she teases his mouth, cheeks and throat with her lips, rubs his stiffening penis through his trousers with red-varnished nails, fingertips and palm. A frisson of fear runs through him as he feels her unbuttoning his shirt to expose his chest, freeing his belt, undoing his flies.

When they finally break off their long kiss he manages to turn his head towards the dashboard, peering out of the corner of his eye at the illuminated dial of the clock: it's twelve thirty.

— Listen. Listen?

Whispers the driver breathlessly as she kisses him greedily again.

— I've got . . . I've got to be back at the cab company in fifteen minutes.

She clamps a hand over his mouth and leans back on the seat, kicking off her black high heels, propping her right leg on the back of the passenger seat, bracing the left against the door, clasping his buttocks and pulling him harder against her until he feels her wet labia closing round his cock.

Never before has a woman been so eager for him. But when she thrusts her hips forwards and sucks his penis into her hot loins, he's incapable of satisfying either of them. There's a minute of frenzied lust. Then sparks fly before his eyes as the sperm spurts out in quick jerks into her vagina. It's over.

While the taxi driver adjusts his clothing, the woman lies unmoving, her eyes closed. But he has no doubt about the meaning of the expression that crosses her face: overwhelming disappointment. The darkness outside suddenly intensifies as the heavens open and raindrops start drumming on the roof of the car.

He squeezes forwards between the seats, climbs behind the wheel, pulls on his jacket and checks himself in the mirror, wetting a finger with his tongue to tidy his hair, cursing under his breath all the while: he was quick, damn it; far too quick.

The woman doesn't say a word or even look at him as he passes back her knickers and skirt. She begins to get dressed. He turns up the radio, and the combination of booming rain and the Marcels' doo-wop version of "Blue Moon" somehow makes the woman's air of silent accusation more bearable. He pretends to stare pensively out into the night while actually watching her reflection in the curved windscreen. She slips into her knickers, eases on her skirt the same way it had come off, zips it up at the hip, smooths down her blouse, pulls on her shoes and buttons up her fur coat.

She flicks her head and the stiffly lacquered chestnut hair falls back into shape. The taxi driver retrieves a packet of cigarettes from behind the sun visor, shakes one loose and is about to extract it with his lips when he hesitates and glances over his shoulder at the woman. Her face has hardened. He notices the red crocodile-skin wallet in her hand.

— Stop the meter, driver. I'm getting out here.

(Lady on the Prowl)
She had materialised out of the April night, as unlooked for as the rain-shower that had driven her to seek shelter. Fáfnir Hermannsson was startled by a knock on the back door, but before he could get up from the typesetting machine where he was surreptitiously setting a pamphlet on the nuclear threat for his aunt in the Women's Peace Movement, she had let herself into the print shop and appeared in the compositors' room where he was working.

"Reykjavík Aphrodite". The words sprang into the typesetter's mind as he rose from his chair to greet the woman. She was drenched. The rain trickled from her dark hair, causing her make-up to leak down her cheeks in multiple streaks of black and blue, from her eyes to her red lips. Water dripped from her thick fur coat on to the floor, collecting in a pool at her feet.

"A Red Indian princess, covered in war paint, with a beaver skin draped over her shoulders." Taking a handkerchief from his trouser pocket, he wiped the ink off his hands.

"A pedigree bitch after a swim." He stood in front of her, unable to guess her age or background: a society lady in distress; the well-kept mistress of a managing director or politician; a daughter from a good home, sneaking out on the town in her mother's fur; an officer's bit on the side; an actress? Soaked to the skin like that, all women looked the same.

— What do you want?
The question came out more coldly than intended and he imme-

diately regretted it. But when the woman opened her mouth to answer, her teeth were chattering so badly that she couldn't utter a word. She tried again but her shivering got the better of her. Stepping forward, he put an arm round her shoulders and guided her into the coffee room.

This was a long, narrow space opening off the corridor between the compositors' room and the print room. It contained a plain kitchen unit, a cupboard and a table with seating for seven. At the far end, an old cast-iron stove was blazing merrily. Having steered her towards it, he helped her out of her coat. She turned to the stove and held out her hands, alternately rubbing them and spreading out her fingers. He pulled aside the plate on top of the stove to allow the heat to rise straight up and she bowed her head, the raindrops falling from her hair on to the black metal where they evaporated with a quick hiss. Even with the flames playing over her wet face, her teeth were still chattering.

He went over to the cupboard and took out a thick towel.

— You could do with warming up. Can I offer you a coffee?

She stared for a moment at the towel he was holding out to her, before taking it. Then, after nodding in reply to his offer, she began unbuttoning the jacket of her green suit, while the typesetter went over to the kitchen counter and started making the coffee.

Now he is standing at the counter with his back to the woman, while the boiling water drips through the filter. He can hear her drying herself with the towel but resists the temptation to steal a glance. Pouring the coffee into a cup, he calls out:

— Milk and sugar?

When he receives no answer, he turns round. The towel has been spread on the floor beside the glowing stove and the woman is standing on it, stark naked. A halo of red light flickers around her, licking over every curve of her body. The cup trembles in his hand.

— What – what the hell are you doing?

Even as he stammers out the words, he feels the pull of the woman's body. Although dazzled by the fiery halo, he can see with increasing clarity her naked beauty, the alluring lines of her figure, the darkness of her pubic hair against the milk-white skin at the top of her thighs.

He feels as though a hot wave is crashing over him, as though he has been swathed in a blinding flash of light. Now she's swaying her hips provocatively, her hands straying to the object of desire: the black triangle.

Bewitched by the woman's irresistible charms, the typesetter is drawn ever closer. Her arms twine themselves around him. With nimble fingers she slides the braces from his shoulders and pulls his trousers down to mid-thigh. Then hauls him down on to the towel where she gets him on his back and straddles him. For an instant he sees the flames glittering on her wet labia as she opens herself and slides on to his cock with such force that he plumbs her depths.

An electric current seems to course through the typesetter's body. He tries to tip the woman off but she grips his cock inside her, riding him harder, her hands on his chest pushing him down on the floor as the sperm spurts into her receptive womb. His rapturous moan mingles with the sound she emits:

A frustrated groan.'

'What are you doing?'
   'Taking off my jumper. This is making me hot.'
   'Sorry, that wasn't the intention.'
   'I'm not complaining. Tell me more.'

2

'At the time these events took place in the early hours of 1 April 1961, it was received wisdom among the psychiatric profession in Iceland, as in the world at large, that women's sexual needs received only a limited outlet through intercourse; in fact, their sexuality was largely sublimated into household chores and caring for others. So it was a common problem that when their children grew up and their husbands became increasingly preoccupied with their jobs, women were denied a natural outlet for their desires. Behaviour, which in young women resembled the nesting instinct of a female bird and went hand in hand with a healthy desire to reproduce and make a good home for their offspring, was, when displayed by older women, regarded as a dangerous sign of sexual dissatisfaction. The symptoms of restlessness generally appeared shortly after the children had left home, at which point these women would embark on a campaign of home improvements, rearranging the furniture, buying new wall- and floor-coverings, collecting expensive ornaments and redesigning all the rooms. Unsurprisingly, this put a great strain on their husbands and the situation could not always be rectified by redirecting the wife's energies into good works, taking her away on foreign holidays or getting the family doctor to prescribe her tranquillisers or strong sleeping pills.

Mrs Thorsteinson was no exception. She was thirty-two years old and still hadn't got pregnant. At first she believed the fault lay with her, that there was something wrong with her physically – an old injury resulting from an incident in her youth – or that some aspect of her daily routine, diet or habits was preventing her from conceiving. But when she finally plucked up the courage to complain to her closest friends, she realised from their reactions that the problem lay with her husband and his unusual behaviour in the marriage bed. Yet she had only told them half the story.

Her first reaction was, predictably, to redecorate the house. In no time at all the Thorsteinsons' dignified living quarters had been transformed. Where before there had been turn-of-the-century respectability – all thick velvet and gleaming hardwood – now there was a violent clash of colours everywhere you looked: in the carpets, rugs, tablecloths, runners and curtains, in the paintings that consisted of nothing but squares, circles and triangles of varying sizes, in the curved kitchen cabinets, in the Danish furniture designed more with microscopic amoebas than comfort in mind, all of which were as much of an enigma to Mr Thorsteinson as his wife's body. In other words, every detail of the childless couple's sea-blue, grass-green, rose-red and sunshine-yellow home testified to the conflict that was raging in Mrs Thorsteinson's soul and endocrine glands.

Mr Thorsteinson thanked heaven that his parents were no longer alive to witness his wife's destructive urges. They'd had their doubts about her from the beginning. It was all very well, but who was this shop assistant their son had met over the tobacco counter in the Reykjavík and Area Coop? And, more to the point, what was he doing patronising a shop run by a cooperative that undermined the influence of Reykjavík's business elite, the class to which he belonged? Going to meet the girl, obviously. It was easier to lower yourself than to aim high. Would she ever belong in their world? No. Would it end in disaster? Yes.

They had turned out to be right about that as well. Mr Thorsteinson, having no choice but to weather the disaster, concentrated on building up the engineering firm that he ran with his maternal uncle Andrés – who was managing director in charge of him, one trainee and the girl who answered the phone – and on taking under his wing the "fledgelings", as he called the young bachelors who joined the Song Thrushes, offering them extra rehearsals after the official choir practice was over.

Which is where he was tonight – one hand pressed firmly against the abdomen of a young tenor, the other on his back, telling him to pant, to breathe until his abdomen expanded into the palm of his hand – at the moment when Mrs Thorsteinson realised that the redecoration of their flat was complete.

* * *

THE MYSTERY OF THE BLACK TRIANGLE, III & IV

(Friday evening to Saturday morning)
It's past two in the morning. There's not a cloud in the sky but the city's still wet from the earlier downpour. The streets glisten; corrugated iron and windows gleam. The illuminated signs in the city centre seem brighter. Down by the harbour the moon draws a mysterious forest of shadow and light from the masts of the trawlers and fishing boats. Beyond them, the coastguard vessel *Freyr* is moored close to the harbour mouth where the crew can put out to sea without delay when duty calls them to defend the fishing grounds, those Solomon's mines of the deep, alive with herring, the silver of the sea, and cod, that yellow currency that buys Icelandic trawler owners admittance to the waiting rooms of the world's banks.

Iceland's gunboat is larger than any of the fishing vessels moored further inside and painted entirely grey, apart from the coat of arms on the wheelhouse. There the blue, white and red colours of the flag adorn a shield mounted on a black slab of lava, while flanking the shield are the four guardian spirits of the land – the eagle, dragon, giant and bull – each picked out in a different colour. Standing in *Freyr's* bows under a green canvas, its long barrel stretching the material taut, is a gun, a rare weapon in this weaponless nation.

The second mate, Carl Steinsson, is on watch.

At the present moment, he's sitting down below in the cabin, immersed in *The Hamster Wheel*, a weird novel by his neighbour, Loftur Gudmundsson. At hourly intervals he takes a break from the peculiar antics of the fictional Gydling clan and the monotonous perpetual labour of the office staff, who are forever wielding the same rubber stamps and wrapping up the same parcels – which is exactly how he pictures life on shore. Laying down the book, he goes up on deck, scans the docks and checks that no one has been tampering with the gangplank. At weekends you always get a few drunks wandering into the harbour area. More often than not they try to come aboard; usually it's just drunken antics but occasionally they're after the first-aid box. He has just returned from one of these patrols, settled on the bench and re-opened his book, when he is confronted with the sentence:

"Then he sees the mouse-haired girl dance past in the fragrant artificial dusk; a shadow on the chest of another shadow, a skeleton in another skeleton's arms . . ."

There's a sudden noise from above.

Slamming the book shut, he grabs his torch.

A moment later he's back on deck, scanning the docks. He directs his torch at the gangplank; all is as it should be. He walks clockwise round the ship, first aft, then forwards along the rail on the seaward side, heading for the bows. There's a human figure standing in the shadow of the gun.

Carl shouts:

— Who goes there?

He tries to trap the figure in the torch-beam but it retreats, ducking out of sight behind the barrel of the gun. He grips the torch tighter, knuckles whitening, bracing himself to use it as a weapon. When he is only a few feet from the intruder's hiding place, he barks out the command that is usually enough to persuade uninvited guests to surrender without a fight:

— Give yourself up. I'm armed . . .

For a minute nothing happens. Then, to his astonishment, the mate feels his breathing growing shallower, quicker – and, even more bizarrely, discovers that he's got a hard-on. Transferring his torch to his left hand, he puts his right into his trouser pocket and adjusts himself to make it less obvious.

A woman in a fur coat steps forward into the light. Before he can react, she's come right up to him. She reaches out her left hand, not in the least coy about letting the mate see the gleaming symbol of marriage on her ring finger, and strokes firmly down the powerful shaft of his confined penis, creating an even larger bulge in his trousers. The mate groans as the woman drops to her knees in front of him and unbuttons his flies. She moves her head towards his swollen manhood, and in the light of the torch he sees her drawing back the foreskin prior to rubbing him with her fingers. Then her head is touching him, and she's moistening her lips with her tongue before applying them to the tip of his erect organ. She takes a quick breath, grips his penis between her lips and lowers her head until more than half of him has disappeared into her mouth. Her fingers slide simultaneously under his scrotum, gently clasping and caressing his testicles.

And so the woman teases the mate with fingers, lips and wet tongue, until his penis begins to twitch in her mouth, at which point she pinches the root so hard that the head swells against her palate. Without releasing her grip, she rises to her feet and whips open her fur, having already hitched up her green skirt and pulled her silk knickers to one side. Then, turning away, she stands, legs apart, thrusting her soft buttocks towards him, and the mate glimpses the edge of the black triangle between her legs.

— Now shoot . . .

The instant his penis has entered her she releases her grip and the hot sperm gushes out in powerful spurts. Then she rams herself backwards with such force that the man is slammed against the gun. The torch drops from his hand and rolls flickering in a half circle on the deck before going out.

The woman sighs bitterly. The second mate, Carl Steinsson, loses sight of her. By the time he has retrieved and switched on the torch, he's alone again on the coastguard ship *Freyr*, as if she'd never been there.

(Smutty Interlude)

The door of the prison has barely closed behind the newly released inmate when a woman rounds the corner from the right. Walking straight up to him, she links her arm through his and leads him away.

Jón "Bull" Thorgeirsson isn't used to being pushed around – he's the strongest man in town and makes a living from standing silently by while men cleverer than him collect their debts – and after a three-week stint inside he would have been glad of a chance to breathe in the fresh April night air undisturbed. But instead of shaking off the fur-coated woman who has so boldly helped herself to his arm, he allows her to pull him into a dark alley round the back of Hallveigarstígur. He does so because of her quick whisper in his ear as she grabbed his arm:

— Let me feel how frustrated you are after three long weeks without a fuck.

He doesn't have time to wonder who the woman is or how she knows about his sentence, and right now he couldn't give a damn because she's shoved a hand inside the waistband of his trousers and is grabbing his balls. The shaft of his rock-hard member presses hot against her forearm. With her other hand she hitches up her green skirt, then guides his right hand to cup the black triangle between her legs. To his delight he discovers she's not wearing any knickers. He runs his fingers down over her curly-haired mound of Venus, jabbing one between her soaking-wet labia. She's ready. By the time he's undone his flies and feels the cool night air on his hard cock, he's ready too.

Propping the woman against the wall, he seizes her behind the knees and lifts her off her feet, simultaneously ramming his organ deep inside her, right up to the balls. Then, holding her tight as she crosses her legs behind him and drives her sharp heels into his back, the ex-con takes her body with urgent lust.

A window opens upstairs and the silhouette of a balding head pokes out.

— Clear off or I'll call the police!

Without missing a stroke, the ex-con flings back his head and bellows at the man in the open window:

— Shut your gob, you little prick . . .

He has no sooner spoken than the tingling prelude to orgasm spreads through his loins. Lights explode before his eyes. He grits his teeth, feeling the sperm pumping out of his penis into the woman's vagina as if he's filling her up.

Deflated, he slackens his grip on the woman. Lifts her off his penis, lowering her until her feet touch the ground. She wriggles out of his grasp. He leans against the wall, staring down at the gravel, watching out of the corner of his eye as she smooths down the green skirt and wraps herself in the fur.

As she turns to walk away he hears a cold laugh at his ear.

— You haven't changed, still can't last a bloody minute . . .

It's the laugh of a girl he once, thirteen years ago, took by force in Siglufjördur. The following morning some kids had found her lying on the seashore below the machine shop. She had been taken to hospital in Akureyri and never returned to the village. And he had made himself scarce too, heading south to Reykjavík.

— Dísa? Dísa "herring" . . . ?

He looks up, her name on his lips. But instead of receiving her answer, he sees standing in a half circle around him the balding man from the window, now accompanied by a police officer and the prison guard who less than half an hour ago had processed his release from jail.

It's a short walk from the dark alley behind Hallveigarstígur down to the house at 10a Ingólfsstræti.

Mrs Thorsteinson – who we now suspect of having been Dísa "herring", the fish-factory girl from Siglufjördur, before she moved south to the city where she did a number of odd jobs (filleting salt-fish, scrubbing floors, washing and mending, cleaning rooms and serving tables at the City Hotel) before becoming a sales assistant in the tobacco department of the Reykjavík and Area Coop where she met her future husband – returns home from her nocturnal adventure, creeps in by the back door, and this time, remembering my father asleep in the basement beneath her feet, slips off her shoes, and, without disturbing him, tiptoes upstairs in her nylon stockings to the kitchen door, which she opens and closes behind her with the same stealth as before.

Now that she is home she goes straight to her bedroom, strips off her clothes, tosses the damp fur into the corner, throws down her muddy high heels, drops the jacket and skirt of her suit on the floor at her feet, and proceeds to chuck bra, stockings, suspender belt and silk knickers on to the bed or the chair by the dressing table. Stark naked, she examines her body in the oval mirror. Turns her mouth down, tries to squeeze a few tears from the green eyes, to sniff or summon up a lump in her throat, tries to feel guilty or ashamed of her behaviour. But her only emotion is glee, a ticklish joy that she still possesses the power to pull men, to arouse their lust, feel their hot, hard penises in her hand, mouth and cunt, and their sperm spurting inside her.

Not one of her four "flings" had satisfied her – true, she has yet to experience that pleasure with anyone but herself – but there will be time enough for that later; tonight she has achieved what she set out to do. There's no turning back. From now on she is going to make full use of the newfound freedom that the events of the night have kindled in her breast. Without putting on a stitch of clothing, Mrs Thorsteinson leaves the bedroom.

She pads around the flat, watching her naked body moving from room to room, admiring her reflection in hall mirror, bathroom cabinet, the glazed doors of the kitchen units, the window panes of the darkened dining room, the photo frame on the sideboard in the drawing room containing her in-laws' wedding picture – the only trace that remains of them in the reception rooms – until she is standing in the doorway of her husband's bedroom.

The hall light casts her shadow into the room, stretching it across the floor and up the length of Mr Thorsteinson's bed until its head is resting on the pillow. That's the closest she intends to get to his bed from now on. Although you can hardly move in there for all the furniture and other bits and bobs that used to belong to the old couple, she can't immediately see anything to reflect herself in. Gripping the handle, she takes a step backwards and is about to close the door when she notices a small ray of light flickering on the black triangle between her legs. It's the hall light bouncing off some round object that is peeping out of one of the countless drawers in the bureau – the nerve centre of her father-in-law's one-time fishing empire – which is now wedged between wardrobe and grandfather clock:

The old man's monocle.

A laugh escapes her when she works out the source of the beam. However tiny, her naked reflection is there in the eye-piece.

And the very second it dawns on her that, however unexpectedly and indirectly, the sanctimonious ship-owner Thorsteinson has achieved what he failed to do in life – to see her naked – I imagine it happening: yes, I dare say that in the very instant that Dísa's body shook with cold laughter, deep in her womb, awash with male outpourings, the silent event took place: an egg from her left ovary was fertilised. And with that the first child of 1962 began its development.'

* * *

'This conception was all the more remarkable since, owing to the unpredictable nature of the female body, a rare event occurred in Dísa "herring" Thorsteinson's womb: sperm from each of the four men with whom she'd had intercourse that night succeeded in entering her egg, but instead of splitting into four and embarking on the development of quadruplets, the egg closed around the genes from the testicles of the taxi driver Örn Ragnarsson, the apprentice typesetter Fáfnir Hermannsson, the ex-con Jón "Bull" Thorgeirsson and Carl Steinsson, second mate of the coastguard ship *Freyr*, to create a female embryo of unique complexity.'

'Was there a notice about it in the papers? FIRST CHILD OF 1962! Accompanied by a photo?'

'Mr Thorsteinson didn't want that.'

'Did he know how the child had been conceived?'

'He must have known he wasn't the father. But that wasn't the reason: in the middle of the girl's forehead was a round birthmark that made her look like the child of a savage, marked out for the gods with a purple sun of eagle blood and soot. But the Thorsteinson family were Christians.'

* * *

'The starting gun had been raised, the shot fired.'

3

'This ushered in the time of mass copulation, the conception of the 4,711 children – 2,410 boys and 2,301 girls – who were born alive in 1962: night and day, morning and evening, on weekdays and holidays, in lunch hours and coffee breaks, smoking breaks and school breaks, during mountain hikes and country dances; in the upper echelons of society as in the lower, and not least in between; outside in the open air – where the mountain's high and the valley's deep, on tender nights beside the silvery sea, when the stars begin to fall, in that good old mountain dew, when skies are grey, where skies are blue, in that twilight time, with the Northern Lights a runnin' wild, when snow falls all around, by the old dirt road, where the Hagi bus stops and goes – and inside, in garages and apartment blocks, office buildings and shops, factories and sheds, ski huts and carpenters' workshops, art galleries and warehouses, country cabins and boarding schools, fish factories and petrol stations, fishermen's huts and cinemas, net sheds and dairies, clothes shops and school buildings, knitting factories and mail-boats; reclining on teachers' desks and in grassy dells, on the floors of cloakrooms, bathrooms and pantries, on sandy beaches, living-room sofas and rag rugs, in bathtubs, hot tubs and swimming pools, under shop counters, billiard tables and birch shrubs; sitting in armchairs and dentists' chairs, on stony beaches, church pews, garden furniture and apple crates; standing against car doors, front doors and washing machines, bookcases, kitchen shelves and churchyard walls, there met in long, wet kisses the lips of electricians and schoolmistresses, air hostesses and cobblers, journalists and doctors' receptionists, actresses and milk-lorry drivers, vicars and schoolgirls, fish-factory women and paediatricians; there clothes were stripped off by fortune tellers, deckhands, bakery girls, barbers, seamstresses, joiners, midwives, bank clerks, hairdressers, warehouse managers, waitresses, foremen, cook-housekeepers and draughtsmen; while, with hesitant fumbling fingers, farmers, engineers, plumbers, bus drivers and watchmakers groped for the hooks on the bras of switchboard operators, hired hands, housewives and nannies prior to fondling their warm, soft, oval breasts; the members of 4,661 men stiffened and the vulvas of 4,661 women (there were fifty pairs of twins) grew wet; husbands lay with wives, lovers with mistresses, husbands with mistresses, lovers with wives – and also wives with mistresses, lovers with husbands, mistresses with mistresses, lovers with lovers, though these unions produced no offspring other than enduring memories of the coupling; rapists assaulted their victims; fingers, lips and tongues stroked erogenous zones; penises were rubbed, licked and sucked; buttocks were gripped; backs were clawed; wet pussies enclosed hard cocks; hymens tore; ejaculations were premature; orgasms were achieved, and women took on board the nineteen litres of sperm that were required to produce the 4,711 children to which they were to give birth in 1962.'

The Dance

The curtain is raised. Fluorescent bulbs bloom into life in a series of clicks and flashes, and in their illumination there appear in the middle of the stage twelve cots and twenty-one oxygen tents lined up in two rows. The cots, plain, everyday affairs, are on wheels. The oxygen tents stand on white-painted steel legs. Eight of the cots are covered with light blue, loose-knit woollen blankets, four with pink. This is the chorus:

Girl: 12 January 1962 – † 13 January 1962
Girl: 13 January 1962 – † 13 January 1962
Girl: 21 January 1962 – † 21 January 1962
Boy: 24 February 1962 – † 27 February 1962
Boy: 1 March 1962 – † 14 April 1962
Girl: 13 May 1962 – † 14 May 1962
Girl: 13 May 1962 – † 17 May 1962
Girl: 5 May 1962 – † 21 May 1962
Boy: 7 May 1962 – † 25 May 1962
Girl: 19 May 1962 – † 26 May 1962
Girl: 27 May 1962 – † 27 May 1962
Girl: 28 May 1962 – † 29 May 1962
Boy: 22 June 1962 – † 23 June 1962
Boy: 27 June 1962 – † 30 June 1962
Boy: 10 February 1962 – † 11 July 1962
Girl: 30 April 1962 – † 11 July 1962
Boy: 10 February 1962 – † 16 July 1962
Boy: 16 July 1962 – † 16 July 1962
Boy: 9 July 1962 – † 18 July 1962
Girl: 19 July 1962 – † 19 July 1962

Boy: 31 July 1962 – † 31 July 1962
Girl: 1 August 1962 – † 1 August 1962
Boy: 29 March 1962 – † 3 August 1962
Boy: 9 July 1962 – † 4 August 1962
Girl: 13 February 1962 – † 7 August 1962
Boy: 1 July 1962 – † 18 August 1962
Boy: 17 August 1962 – † 20 August 1962
Girl: 3 September 1962 – † 3 September 1962
Boy: 1 October 1962 – † 6 October 1962
Boy: 18 November 1962 – † 18 November 1962
Boy: 27 November 1962 – † 27 November 1962
Boy: 18 December 1962 – † 18 December 1962
Girl: 16 December 1962 – † 23 December 1962

At first silence reigns. The odd high-pitched, fretful cry, brief sigh or feeble whimper emanates randomly from a cot here, a cot there. There's a low humming from the oxygen tents.

Then the boy who lived for two days in May raises his voice. His weeping is bitter, his voice hollow. He is the precentor. The first to join in with him is the oldest member of the chorus, a girl who lived to the age of twenty-three weeks. Then, one after the other, the rest of the children chime in. The wailing spreads from cot to cot and echoes in the oxygen tents. The small bodies shake, their lower lips tremble, their curled fists beat the air (so tiny, so tiny), their frail blue legs twitch in aimless kicks. With mumbling and sighing, grizzling and hiccupping sobs, they perform the first movement of the choral work:

— We were stillborn, premature, the umbilical cord wrapped round our necks, our endocrine systems defunct, our intestines blocked, our brains damaged, our lungs collapsed.

We departed as quickly as we arrived.

Dear brothers and sisters, born in 1962, we await you here.

4

'GOD'S BLOOD

The instant the word sprang to His lips, God acquired sight. He saw that He was omnipresent. He saw Himself from every angle, from above and below, from all sides at once. And as God had no awareness of up or down, here or there – everything was simultaneously the beginning and the end – His consciousness was whole and undivided, while being present in every nook and cranny of the world that was coming into being. (*Stone axe–microchip.*) He was both one and many. His mouths opened.

10^{-47} seconds after the light had begun to flow it reached God's eyes wherever He was present. The glare was so dazzling that He instinctively raised a hand to shield them. (*Mosaic–Marburg virus–parrot feathers.*) But just as an infinite number of hands were passing an infinite number of mouths on their way to shield the countless eyes, the light fell on the back of God's hand, and to His astonished delight it passed right through, streaming red from His palm.

The blood-coloured radiance was easy on the eye. God moved His hand back to His mouth and held it there. As the vapour of His breath blended with the colour, phenomena began to appear through a pink haze. (*Nervous system of an earthworm–galaxy cluster MS 0735.*)

Out in the cold black void, the light projected images made of the incomprehensible substance from which the Creator had created Himself.

And God is still holding His mighty hand before His mouth.

* * *

The accompaniment to the protracted groans of lust and childbirth that echoed in Iceland from 1 April 1961 to the close of 1962 was no different from the everyday symphony that generally heralds the arrival of a whole year's cohort of children: the booming of car and tractor engines intermingled with the humming and whining of domestic appliances and plant machinery on the one hand, and the shouts and calls, clapping and stamping of humans on the other; the belching and farting of kids in school playgrounds, swimming pools and back gardens found an echo in the cursing and swearing, throat-clearing and coughing, laughter and gasping of spectators at sports meetings, theatres and sheep round-ups; jazz, classical and pop music emanating from dance halls, music schools and gramophones mingled with the clatter of crockery, the burble of the radio news and conversations in workplaces, cafés and homes about affairs major and minor, domestic and foreign – all of which is well documented in autobiographical novels in which every sentence and paragraph glistens with the poignant tears of happy nostalgia shed by their authors: *200 porpoises run aground on Bardaströnd; Yuri Gagarin is the first man in space; Askja erupts; the Berlin Wall is built; the Duke of St Kilda sings for Reykjavík's tax director; Marilyn Monroe is found dead in bed; neo-Nazis hold a march in Fossvogur Cemetery; Watson, Crick and Wilkins win the Nobel Prize in Physiology or Medicine; lightning strikes the cowshed at Nedri-Hóll in the Stadarsveit district killing five cows; the Soviets build missile launch pads in Cuba; the* Morgunbladid *newspaper's April Fool's joke is the discovery of the saga hero Egill Skallagrímsson's hidden silver; Ringo Starr quits as drummer of Rory Storm and the Hurricanes; Adolf Eichmann is hanged in Israel; Hótel Saga is built in Reykjavík's Melar district; Yuri Gagarin visits Iceland, only coming up to the shoulder of the newly crowned Miss Iceland when photographed with her at the airport; the Telstar communications satellite is launched and television images are broadcast between continents for the first time; the first issue of the* Spiderman *comic is published by Marvel, and so on and so forth* – in all respects but one: in the twenty months during which that year's quota of children was conceived and born, the vault of heaven rumbled with the most powerful nuclear explosions ever seen or heard on earth.

Night after night, man-made Northern Lights shimmered in the skies over Siberia, over atolls in the Pacific, while by day corpse lights flared against the clouds, lights so powerful that they appeared as bright as the sun from 1,500 kilometres away. Every third day, for 690 days in a row, nuclear devices were detonated above ground, 139 by the Soviets, 86 by the Americans, 225 in all – with a combined explosive charge of 245,000 kilotons or 7,000 times the power of Little Boy and Fat Boy, the bombs dropped on Hiroshima and Nagasaki, including, as they did, both Tsar Bomba and Starfish Prime, one of which caused the biggest explosion of all time on earth, the other in the skies.

Yes, never before or since have the mighty war drums of the superpowers been beaten more frenetically or with graver intent. By the end of 1962, the radiation in Iceland's atmosphere had reached unprecedented levels.

What happened was inevitable:

Children of the 1962 generation mutated . . .'

II

From tape a)

(17 June 2009)

5

The midnight sun gleams on the still waters of Lake Thingvellir, doubling the island of Sandey in the middle and tinting with purple the high rock wall of the Almannagjá Ravine.

The geneticist raises his glass to eye level, squinting through it above the fiery-brown, fifty-year-old Japanese single malt – a gift from the CEO of the drugs giant Hoffmann-La Roche's Northern European group while they were still on speaking terms. Luckily he'd stashed it away in the boathouse and forgotten all about it during the seven fat years, only to find it again this evening among the containers of turpentine and brush cleaner, and the empty wine bottles. Who would give him a gift like that today? He frames the view with his glass, lining up the surface of the whisky with that of the lake before raising it to his lips, taking a mouthful and swallowing it slowly, mentally calculating the cost as he returns the glass to the table beside the bottle. The name of the whisky is sandblasted on the side in Japanese and English, together with the year 2005 and the minimum price of ¥1,000,000.

— Seven millilitres, ten thousand yen . . .

The sound of his voice, emerging unnaturally loudly in the evening stillness, startles the geneticist; he hadn't meant to speak out loud. He is alone on the deck down by the boathouse – away over in the cottage among the birch trees, he can hear the guests enjoying themselves: friends of his fourth wife Dóra, mingling with a bunch of celebrities from the media, entertainment and art worlds, people who accepted an invitation to the annual 17 June party only because his name was on the card; people she describes as friends of theirs whenever their names crop up in conversation with members of her old sewing circle, though the same names fill her with nothing but contempt when she comes across them in reports of premieres, openings and concerts or on the covers of the gossip rags – so he finishes his thought, saying:

— Ten thousand yen, fifteen thousand krónur . . .

Waves lap at the rusted tracks that run from the boathouse down to the water. The carriage still sitting on them has fallen apart beneath the rotting planks of the *Birna*, his father's old rowing boat. He used to go out fishing for trout in her with his father and three brothers, first as a tow-headed five-year-old and, for the last time, at twenty-four, when he and his father rowed out on to the lake together and, despite having recently graduated from medical school, he hadn't a clue what to do when the oars slipped from his father's hands and his body sagged gently forwards off the thwart into his son's arms, a sudden death – but even in the manner of his passing the old man had almost certainly trumped anything his son would ever achieve, since there was something historic about dying in full view of the ancient Icelandic assembly site, the Law Rock, the ruins of Snorri Sturluson's booth; it hinted at the fulfilment of a life's vocation, and indeed this became a leitmotif in the obituaries for the author, radio broadcaster and Socialist Party MP who had, in all he did, placed the independence of his country and people before himself – whereas these days the crumbling boat merely served as a re-minder of all the hours the geneticist had promised to spend with his younger son restoring it, making it watertight, painting and re-launching it, but which he had in fact spent dashing around the world, peddling the 'Northern Lights' that shimmered in the Icelanders' genes.

— Ten thousand krónur . . .

He takes a sip, a little smaller than the first. Then adds at a pitch designed to carry to an absent audience:

— This is where I became the man I am . . .

The geneticist falls silent and glances at the tape recorder on the table beside the whisky. It's an old Norelco 95 dictaphone that he bought on Saturday, 25 September 1976, the day before he started work in the Neurology Department at the University of Chicago Medical Center. The machine, cutting-edge technology in its day, had been a pricey purchase for a medical student on a tight budget, but Anna, his first wife, had urged him to buy it, aware that he wouldn't rest until he had got one, if a 'portatape' was what it took to make him feel on an equal footing with the senior consultant in his department: he couldn't care less about the more junior doctors, let alone his fellow students, always comparing himself to the man at the top, a position he intended to occupy himself one day. That Saturday they had taken the train down to Logan Square and bought the dictaphone from Abt's Electronics, and Anna hadn't so much as batted an eyelid when he went for the most expensive model. He often missed the ease with which she had been able to read him, the simple ploys she had used to prepare him for new situations and prevent him from falling out with people who couldn't tell the difference between scientific fervour and ordinary arrogance. In a perfect world she would have accepted his invitation to become his secretary after their divorce.

He presses record, pulls the machine closer and makes sure the microphone is pointing his way. The cassette buzzes in chorus with the last evening flies. A golden plover pipes in the distance. The neologism 'portatape' was his own invention.

'That's the crackling noise you heard – the machine being dragged across the table top.'

The geneticist clears his throat and starts again:

— This is where I became the man I am. A little to the east of Sandey . . .

He gestures towards the island.

— By mid-July a big shoal of trout tends to form there – Arctic char weighing one, one and a half, up to two kilos – and my father's family used to fish for them with nets every summer for as long as they lived on the tenant farm at Bláskógar. After they gave up farming and the last generation had moved to the city, my father was the only one of his brothers and sisters to keep up the custom of 'bringing in the char', as he called those fishing trips – because it wasn't a formal business, not like the kind of angling practised today by milk-fed middle managers who turn queasy at the thought of eating the fish the guide has lured on to their hooks – and my brothers and I joined him on the trips once we were considered grown-up enough.

Taking another sip of his drink, he murmurs:

— Twelve thousand krónur . . .

Then continues in a carrying voice:

— As I was saying, I came into being on my first ever trip to bring in the char. Once we had reached the fishing ground to the east of the island I was given the job of sitting in the bows and guiding the whole enterprise. I felt it a great honour that Dad should entrust me, the youngest member of the crew, with such a responsible job, which consisted of my pointing down at the water and yelling incessantly: 'Fish, fish!', while he and my elder brothers dragged in the net. How successful the catch was I couldn't say, though as far as I remember it was good, in excess of what we needed. But when my brothers tipped the char out of the net and they formed a frantically wriggling mass in the bottom of the boat, I snatched away my feet with a screech of terror. It was the first time I'd ever seen a fish fighting for its life; up to then I had always waited with my mother in the cove below the boathouse to welcome Dad and my brothers ashore with their catch already dead. My brothers laughed at my shrieks, taking out their pocket knives and bloodying the trout with practised movements, stabbing the well-sharpened blades through the top of the gills and cutting down to the throat, since the fish weren't to be knocked on the head; their skulls had to be kept intact to ensure the proper taste when the Bláskógar siblings gathered for the annual 'head-feast' at Dad's house, the day after we got back to town. I looked at Dad as he sat in the stern, quietly rolling up the net, with the inevitable *Udarnik*, or Bulgarian worker's cigarette, in the corner of his mouth. His silence and the bittersweet blue smoke blowing over to me on the breeze had a calming effect, so I stopped my howling, although by now the fish were not merely writhing but writhing in their own blood. As we rowed back to shore, the twitching of the tails at my feet grew gradually more sporadic and I summoned up the courage to inspect our catch, this pile of dying fish with their trembling gills and sudden death spasms, which all looked exactly alike. And I remember thinking in time to the rhythmic gurgling of the oars that this explained why . . .

He stops talking and we hear him drag the whisky bottle closer, unscrew the top, lift it off the table and pour some into his glass, then screw the top back on, replace the bottle on the table, push it away and pick up the glass.'

'Ah! I know that sound: that creaking and singing is a flock of swans flying past.'

The geneticist watches the swans' singing progress over the lake, holding the whisky in his mouth until the flock has vanished behind Raudukusunes Point and his tongue has begun to sting. Only then does he swallow.

— Eleven thousand krónur.

He sips his drink again, muttering:

— Thirteen thousand.

Then, putting down the glass, he leans back in his chair and stretches with a cracking of collar-bones and shoulder-blades: where had he got to in his account of the fishing trip?

— The char . . .

Before the geneticist can pick up the thread, he breaks off, jerks upright, flexes his shoulders, runs his fingers quickly through his white crew-cut, strokes the grizzled hair on his cheeks, looks around in bemusement, claps his hands and clasps his fingers, and only then does he work out the cause of his restlessness: his palms and fingers are missing the worn leather of the American football that he usually fiddles with whenever he needs to free up his mind for deep concentration – squeezing it, spinning it on one finger and tossing it from hand to hand – which keeps his old sack of bones occupied in the world of terrestrial mechanics, allowing his inner man to kick off from the dirt patch of habit and soar heavenwards into a world where imagination is the only law of nature that matters.

The geneticist glances at his hands. With their position, the distance between them, the curve of his fingers, he has unconsciously sketched the outline of the ball.

What was he about to say?

He chucks the imaginary ball at the rotting boat.

What was the moral of the story?

The ball strikes noiselessly against the hull, bouncing off the flaking paint where wind and weather have obliterated all but the last three letters of the name: *R-N-A*.

How did he become the person he is on that fishing trip fifty-five years ago?

He catches the ball on the rebound.

And a play on a book title pops into his mind:

The Fish is Always Alone.

Yet he still can't find the words to express the thought he remembers dawning on him, as a child in charge of the catch, when he saw the bloody heap on the bottom of the boat, a heap in which, except in size and colour, every fish was identical to the next – like his three brothers who strangers were always telling him were spitting images of the same man, their father, whereas he himself took after his mother: how there at last he had found the explanation for his father's habit of always referring to 'the fish', 'the trout', 'the char' in the singular, when it was obvious that he was referring to a whole shoal of the creatures: yes, for the same reason that he always avoided the plural when referring to the human race, the future socialist MP talked about the fish of Lake Thingvellir in the singular. Just as humankind was 'Man', so the fish were one entity, one species: 'the Trout', as in 'the Trout does this' or 'the Trout does that'. But the comparison couldn't be pushed any further because unlike 'the Trout', which has perfected the ability to live as both one and many, 'Man' is badly afflicted with a sense of individualism that distinguishes him from all other creatures on earth: an unhealthy resistance to the instinct of putting the interests of the collective before his own, of sharing what he acquires with others, of taking no more than he needs, of adapting to society as best he can. In this way the gift of 'Knowledge' had corrupted 'Man' – since all gifts are accompanied by their antithesis and the antithesis of 'Knowledge' is 'Capitalism'. The geneticist knocks back sixteen thousand krónur worth of whisky and snorts:

— Damn it, as if I'd have been capable of thinking like that at five years old.

First there's silence, composed of birdsong, lapping water and whispering leaves, then a single remark:

— Damn it, as if I'd have been capable of thinking like that at five years old.

Then there's a summer's night and a man being silent again. He kneads the air between his hands. If he'd learned any important lesson on that long-ago summer's day, it was neither that the trout was a true socialist nor that it was a homogeneous ingredient in fish-head soup. The nearest the future geneticist came to grasping a 'big truth' on that fishing trip was when his father shifted from the stern to the centre thwart and took up the oars, turning the boat in the water until the sun was behind him, then setting a course for the cove by the boat-house, where his youngest son is now sitting, nearly six decades later, remembering with a shiver the sudden chill he experienced when his father's shadow fell on the stiffening bodies of the char and on himself, huddling in the bows. He understood then that as long as one individual was big enough to overshadow them, it didn't really matter if 'Man' and 'Trout' were plural or singular, individualists or community-minded.

But he couldn't offer up this lesson as his answer to the question posed by the magazine about how he – as one of five famous individuals – 'had come into being'.

Besides, the answer lay elsewhere.

At the end of June 1962, the summer he turned thirteen, he had been on his way home from a trip to town with his fellow workers at the Reykjavík Freezing Plant – they'd been to the nine o'clock showing at Stjörnubíó of *The Woman Eater*, a film about a mad scientist called Dr Moran who, with the help of the drummer Tanga, son of the king of the rainforest, feeds young women to a flesh-eating Amazonian tree and uses the resin to develop a serum to bring the dead back to life – when he came across his parents sitting in 'the Green Goat', their Russian GAZ-69 jeep, which was parked in front of the house. This was their usual refuge when they wanted peace and quiet to 'talk things over', as they called it, since neither of them would ever admit that they had rows. The brothers were old enough by now to notice how shaken up their parents seemed after these 'discussions in the car', and how, increasingly often, one of them would remain sitting in the front seat long after their conversation was over.

There was a knot in his stomach as he ducked out of sight behind the garage of the house opposite. From his hiding place he saw, through the jeep's dirty rear windscreen, the silhouette of his mother holding an open newspaper in her clenched fists and thrusting it in her husband's face. His father's silhouette firmly removed the paper from her hands and put its arms around her. After a while she freed herself from his embrace and wiped her face. The driver's door opened and his father got out, then he opened the passenger's door for his wife and helped her up the steps to the house. Once the front door had closed behind them, the future geneticist hesitated a moment before running over to the Goat and quietly climbing in.

On the floor lay a crumpled spread from *Morgunbladid*, the mouthpiece of his father's political opponents – a lying rag that was never allowed over their threshold – and his first reaction was the childish idea that his mother must have provoked the quarrel by bringing the paper home from the bookshop. He smoothed out the spread. Across it was printed in large letters:

Sleeping pill thalidomide
— thousands of children left with birth defects

The article was accompanied by a photograph of two newborn babies, a boy and a girl. They were lying on their backs on a white sheet, their bodies slightly out of alignment with their heads, as is common when infants are posed for photographs, but instead of arms and legs, or hands and feet, they had tiny stumps, each bearing a fin that looked more like feathers or a fringe than fingers or toes. One of the children had its eyes screwed shut in a grimace, the other wore a puzzled look.

Two weeks later, his mother went to Denmark for an operation on her leg.

The geneticist raises his glass and peers through the whisky at the lake and the island of Sandey, so radiantly black against the midnight sun.

— Thirteen thousand . . .

Childhood

(27 August 1962–3 September 1972)

6

— Thirteen . . .

The geneticist's voice echoes tinnily from the small speaker of the dictaphone until a neatly manicured feminine hand picks the machine up off the coffee table in Jósef Loewe's sitting room and stops the recording with a long, blue-varnished nail, causing the tape to stutter, the voice to hiccup on the last word:

— . . . thoug-shunD.

In the ensuing silence the woman sits holding the dictaphone while she studies the man dozing on the sofa opposite her: Jósef Loewe is lying at an awkward angle, a pile of large, embroidered cushions supporting his spine, the high sofa-back curving around him like the outstretched, dirt-brown, velvety wings of a swan mother rearing up in defence of her young. But it would be hard to imagine anyone less like a cygnet than this man.

He is middle-aged, borderline soft in the body, dressed conserva-tively in a red-checked flannel shirt, a large, moss-green V-necked jumper, loose, pale khaki trousers, brown socks and grey felt slippers. His face is smooth and beardless, his cropped hair greying and thin-ning on top, his round head presently drooping between collar-bone and shoulder, his pale hands resting in his lap – not relaxed but stiff as if they belonged to a ventriloquist's dummy – and at first sight he's just a man dozing a little crookedly on his sofa at home. But the eye needn't rest long on Jósef Loewe before it perceives what his posture, clothes and hair are concealing: on the crown of his head, his forehead and jaw, the skin is stretched tight over strange bony excrescences. And the same bony growths, only larger, are visible on what can be seen of his arms, ribcage and legs.

This is not the first time he has nodded off during the silence-punctuated soliloquy from Thingvellir. The woman has played the tape to him more than once. She feels Jósef has a right to hear the recording of the man who has booked this interview with him.

The sounds of the summer night are soporific.

* * *

THE NET

When Hrólfur Zóphanías Magnússon was a boy living out in the suburb of Laugarnes, it was common knowledge that there was a whorehouse in Fischersund. None of his friends actually knew what a whore was, or what they got up to in their houses, but the word, with its hint of a wicked woman (that much they suspected), was wreathed in such mystery that there was an absolute taboo on entering the short lane that connected the centre of town to the west end; no one dared set foot there.

The braver boys in his group went on an expedition to the town centre to see for themselves but all the women they spotted in the vicinity of Fischersund – and spied on from a safe distance in the hope of getting closer to the truth about the nature of a whore – turned out to be so like the boys' own mothers, sisters, aunts and even grandmothers that they concluded whores must either be different in the head from ordinary women or else be hiding some physical deformity under their clothes: a possibility they didn't dare think about, especially after the doctor's son came up with the theory that they were hermaphrodites.

In those days the Goldfish Bowl was the only shop in Reykjavík where you could buy tropical fish. Hrólfur was ten going on eleven and fish-mad according to his family: in his room he had three large tanks (holding 30, 60 and 120 cubic litres) as well as any number of jam jars and bowls serving as hatcheries and nurseries, accommodated wherever they would fit on bookshelves, floor or window sill. So when the Goldfish Bowl relocated from Laugavegur to Fischersund, this presented him with something of a headache.

Hrólfur was on notice with the fish: if he didn't shoulder the entire responsibility for their upkeep and cost – which he did by delivering the socialist paper the *People's Will* and by hawking *Vikan* in the street – they would be flushed down the loo. By faking illness he had twice prevailed on his father to drop into the shop on his way home from work and buy food and weed for the gouramis to spawn in. And another time he had talked his eldest brother's girlfriend into buying a filter for the guppy tank by claiming that he'd been picked on by some rough kids who hung around at the bottom of the street, in the car park by Steindór's Taxis. He felt he must be a bad boy to send her to a terrible place like Fischersund but justified it by telling himself that if she got trapped there and turned into a whore, he would go down and rescue her – though not until they were both grown up and his brother had forgotten all about her.

When the girlfriend discovered that there weren't any bullies loitering in the car park and told him that from now on he could look after his own 'disgustingly smelly fish', the moment arrived when he had to go to the Goldfish Bowl himself: his swordtails had developed fin rot and he needed the owner's advice on the right medicine – and anyway he couldn't have trusted an amateur with a veterinary matter of this gravity.

He got off the bus at Lækjartorg Square and set off along Austurstræti in the direction of Fischersund. But there was suddenly so much to see along that 250-metre stretch: East German liquorice at the Coop, new piggy-banks at the Agricultural Bank, hand-knitted mittens and scarves at Thorvaldsensbasar. Having frittered away half the morning like this, lingering so long in the shops that the staff had begun to eye him with suspicion, Hrólfur Zóphanías finally reached the cab company at the bottom of Fischersund. He found a place round by the dustbins that allowed him to see five metres or so up the lane and waited for his chance.

When it looked to him as if the lane was likely to remain whore-free for the next few minutes, he sprinted across the road, making a beeline for the door of the Goldfish Bowl, which luckily turned out to be located right at the bottom, almost on the corner of Adalstræti.

It was a huge relief when the door swung shut behind him.

Inside, the atmosphere turned out to be the same as it had been in the old basement on Laugavegur: the all-pervasive stench of the owner's sweat, the ceaseless humming and gurgling of pumps blowing air bubbles into the tanks and stirring the green tendrils of weed, the fish looking from a distance like multicoloured moving points of light, like shining fairies flying through an enchanted forest. But it would be wrong to claim that nothing had changed. Since his last visit, the owner's daughter had undergone some indefinable or at any rate mysterious transformation. He could see it in the way she moved as she netted the midnight-red fighting fish that lurked alone in its tank, a fish he had long coveted but hadn't yet saved up the money to buy.

Dipping the net into the water behind the fish, she chased it around the tank with nimble movements of her wrist – movements repeated a moment later in her hips – until eventually the fish grew tired. Then she lifted it deftly out of the water, popped it in a plastic bag, twisted the opening and tied it in a knot.

The incident came back to Hrólfur Zóphanías Magnússon, geneticist and chief executive of CoDex, as he sat one night in a velvet-padded cell, on exactly the same spot as he had stood forty years before, struck dumb by the change in the owner's daughter. After the Goldfish Bowl moved out, the premises on Fischersund had housed a funeral parlour for many years – instead of fish tanks the walls were lined with empty coffins – and after that a dry cleaner's had moved in, replacing the coffins with washing machines.

These days the site was occupied by the strip club Bar Lewinsky and Hrólfur Zóphanías was waiting in one of its private rooms for Aleta, the Ukrainian girl he had been chatting up in the bar earlier, to draw back the curtain. He had guessed at once from her figure that she was a transwoman who, although well on the way, had not yet completed her transition. How far she had got he would hopefully find out in a minute.

The curtain was drawn back.

Aleta undulated towards the man in the armchair. She swivelled her right hand at the wrist – like the owner's daughter long ago, he thought, like the owner's daughter – and caught him in her net.

* * *

After she danced for him the geneticist had taken her phone number, though Aleta hadn't attached any importance to this. But several weeks later she had received a phone call from the biotech company CoDex, offering her a job as a researcher. And now here she is, sitting in Jósef Loewe's basement flat, waiting for him to wake up.

* * *

The recording of the geneticist had been in the dictaphone given to her by his assistant, along with a box containing twenty unused 180-minute cassettes, some folders, a Polaroid camera and other material relating to the study. Before conducting the first interview, she had removed the cassette from the machine without listening to it and put it in an envelope with the questionnaires, intending to return it when she went to headquarters to hand in the results of the first three sessions.

It wasn't until October 2010, as she sat in the visitors' lounge at a state institution waiting for her interviewee to get ready – inevitably, given the nature of the study, many of the participants were in hospitals or institutions – that it occurred to her to check what was on the battered old 180-M Philips mini cassette, which looked as if it had been in the machine for years. The worn label had been written on, rubbed out and crossed out so often that it was covered in scribbles, but under it all you could still make out what she guessed to be 'Dr Magnusson'. She put the tape in the dictaphone and heard the rustle of the wind in leaves, the twittering of redwings, the lapping of waves and finally the brisk cough that removed all doubt as to who was about to speak.

The geneticist's voice was familiar to every child in the country; even the least talented could make a decent stab at mimicking it. For years he had been a regular on radio and TV news and chat shows in his role as chief executive of the genomics biotechnology company CoDex (which had from day one been reporting news of incredible scientific advances) due to controversy over the company's access to the Icelanders' medical records, from which it was creating a database of the nation's genetic information, the so-called 'Book of Icelanders' (an idea sold to parliament and public on the pretext of its benefits to mankind – the Icelanders' pure genomes were to be used for discoveries that would liberate the inhabitants of Planet Earth from every imaginable disease, from cancer to the common cold – though it appealed primarily to people's sense of nationalism and greed, and, as it later turned out, the project was bankrolled by overseas drugs giants); due to its successes on the financial markets at home and abroad; due to CoDex's subsequent bankruptcy and the fact that so many people, carried away by the talk of genetic purity and massive profits, had bought shares in the miracle; due to his resurrection and refinancing of the company; and due to his idiosyncratic views on Iceland's history and culture, and especially its literature, since he made a big deal of his youthful dream of becoming an author and claimed that all his tinkering with his 'juvenile scribblings' had, when the time came, given him the edge over his foreign competitors who were unacquainted with the Icelandic cottage industry of 'rolling out a plot'. But since the instantly recognisable voice – with its hard cadences and strident pitch, which always made the speaker sound as if he were standing out of doors, talking into the wind whichever way he turned – was bound to attract attention, Aleta immediately stopped the tape and took it out of the machine. She didn't know what she was to say if someone asked why she was listening to the geneticist droning on about prices and millilitres.

As she was slipping the tape into her bag, a nurse appeared at the door and helped in that day's interviewee, a woman in her forties, wearing a long, azure dressing gown, her pure white, neatly combed hair parted in the middle and falling over her shoulders and arms and forwards on to the cotton gloves she wore on her hands, though it couldn't conceal the symptoms of the genetic disorder that had caused the skin of her face and limbs to break out and harden into tightly packed hexagonal eruptions reminiscent of drying scales, forming a kind of 'fish skin' that was finest on her fingertips and the end of her nose but became progressively coarser the larger the skin's surface area, the scales growing as big as a hand and ranging from red to green, passing through yellow and blue wherever broken veins and swelling were thrown into the mix.

She rose to her feet and held out her hand to the woman in the dressing gown.

— Hello, I'm Aleta Szelińska . . .

The woman didn't answer or take her proffered hand.

For a long moment the woman studied Aleta studying her, giving her a chance to look away or steal another glance at her scaly cheeks, then announced hoarsely:

— You're all right. You're not one of us but we're on the same team . . .

7

For two years Aleta conscientiously followed her instructions:

i) She maintained confidentiality about all aspects of the project, the client and the participants.
ii) She took a Polaroid photograph of each participant at the beginning of the interview.
iii) She went through the entire questionnaire with the participant.
iv) She entered the main information in the appropriate places on the form during the interview.
v) She labelled the tapes, questionnaires and envelopes according to an agreed numerical code.
vi) She put away the material in folders, which she secured and sealed with red wax.
vii) She handed in her work on the second and fourth Thursday of every month.
viii) She was not permitted to form a relationship with any of the participants.

Until, that is, she met Jósef Loewe, a man of nearly fifty, who was suffering from an exceptionally rare condition known as 'Stone Man Syndrome' or, in medical terminology, as *Fibrodysplasia ossificans progressiva*. This disorder causes the body to react abnormally when the muscles or other soft tissues are damaged by forming new bone tissue over the site. The sufferer ends up imprisoned in a 'double' skeleton, as stiff as a dummy in a shop window. The first sign of the disorder is a deformation of the big toes.

* * *

QUESTIONNAIRE FOR PROJECT HZM/0-23 (<u>PRIVATE</u>)

Tape no.: _____ Date of interview: __ / __ / ____
Time: __ / __ / __ Place: _____

a) Name:
_____

b) Date of birth:
_____

c) Place of birth:
_____

d) Parents (origin/education/occupation):
_____
_____
_____

e) Childhood residence:
_____
_____
_____

f) Education:
_____
_____

g) Childhood hobbies:
_____

h) Marital history:
_____
_____

i) Children:
_____
_____

j) Adult residence:
_____
_____

k) Political views (may be omitted):
_____

l) Religion (may be omitted):
_____

m) Adult hobbies:
_____
_____

n) Memorable incident:
_____

o) Memorable dream:
_____
_____

_____
Name of interviewer
(in block capitals)

_____
(Sign.)

* * *

Aleta was so exhausted after her interview with the white-haired mermaid – which was the name the participant used for herself, quite without irony, beginning most of her answers: 'we mermaids', cf. 'we mermaids inflame men with lust, it's true what the fairytales say' – that when she got home she crashed out on her bed, fully clothed, and lay there staring at the ceiling as its colour deepened into blue with the fading daylight; as afternoon gave way to evening.

The mermaid had spoken so quietly that it had been an effort to hear what she said, and to ensure the dictaphone would pick up her voice Aleta had been forced to sit as close to her as the arms of their chairs would permit, holding the machine a finger's length away from the woman's withered, unmoving, red-painted lips. When, to make matters worse, the woman had answered her questions at far greater length than Aleta had anticipated (her orders were to keep each interview under 120 minutes so it would fit on a two-hour tape), her sojourn in the visitors' lounge had developed into a form of mental and physical torture. The interview lasted for just under five hours. For the last seventy minutes Aleta's right hand, locked on the dictaphone, had been completely drained of blood. Her breathing had synchronised to the second with the mermaid's. Their breasts rose and fell with the same gentle rhythm. Their shoulders touched and Aleta had grown so queasy from the warm scent of vanilla rising from the woman's dressing-gown-clad body that all her attempts to convert the relentless whisper into mental images of the backdrop to the tales of childhood and school days in the Westman Islands, in the village half buried under a black layer of volcanic ash, were disrupted by flashbacks to the white mounds by the old salt factory in Drohobych, the town where she herself was born.

Inside her an alien voice kept repeating the same formula at brief intervals: 'She's white-haired, you're black-haired. You're black-haired, she's white-haired . . .'

The bedroom ceiling above her was now indigo, verging on black. Aleta reached out a hand, fumbling for the cord of the table lamp without taking her eyes off the ceiling, found it and, groping her way to the switch, turned it on; indigo gave way to yellow.

Although up to now no session had gone over three hours, and five hours was sheer insanity, it wasn't the gruelling length of the interview with the mermaid, the concentration (or lack of it) or the pain in her right hand and arm that had proved the greatest drain on Aleta's strength.

After all, this wasn't the first time she had 'cheated' on the timing. When other interviews had required more than one cassette she had thought 'it can't be helped', since the recordings would be the sole surviving witness to these lives, the only chance the participants would have to tell their story in their own words, their own voices – and, since the geneticist's assistant hadn't yet complained about her wasting tapes, Aleta had gone on letting the interviews overrun. As for the concentration the whispering demanded of her, the deformed jaws and damaged vocal cords of many of Aleta's previous subjects had made them far harder to understand than the softly spoken mermaid; and as for real pain, that was something Aleta had got to know on her journey from the Ukraine to Iceland.

No, in the end it was the woman's repeated mantra about not being 'one of us but still on the same team' that proved the final straw; the strain of having to be on one's guard for five whole hours to make sure the recording didn't contain the slightest suggestion of doubt that she was who or what she purported to be.

Aleta had thought those days were over: the mermaid had sharp eyes.

She sat up and started to undress, wriggling out of her coat, kicking her leather boots across the floor, pulling off her jumper and skirt, removing bra, nylon stockings and knickers and flinging them in the direction of the laundry basket. Then, grabbing the bag from the bed, she went into the bathroom.

Yes, during the interview the mermaid had repeatedly addressed Aleta directly, drawing her into the story, turning her into a participant in her experiences. After describing the memorable incident when, at seven years old, she had discovered that she wasn't destined for the same kind of life as other people – during a meeting of the Bethel Pentecostalist congregation it had finally dawned on her who the pastor was talking about when he said that, although not all children in the islands were created in God's image, the congregation had a duty to remember them in their prayers, something she'd heard the bald preacher saying every Sunday for as long as she could remember, with the result that she had been conscientiously praying for herself every evening: the little child she had pitied for not being created in the divine image had turned out to be her – the mermaid had shot a glance at Aleta and whispered:

— You'd know all about that.

Of course, Aleta could have agreed, admitting that she knew from personal experience what it was like to be struck by the realisation that mankind was divided into two kinds of children, the clean and the unclean (and which kind she belonged to), that such a moment had been branded on her consciousness too, but she didn't permit herself so much as a nod: she had no intention of encouraging any further impertinence from the old lady; in point of fact, Aleta knew the woman wasn't that old – she was born on 25 September 1962, which made her two years short of fifty – but the scales on her face, the colour of her hair and the arthritis that twisted her shoulders all made her seem much older than she really was, so one inadvertently thought of her as 'the old lady'.

Aleta put her bag down on the stool by the bath, pulled out a packet of cigarettes and a lighter, lit one, turned on the mixer tap, and sat smoking on the loo while waiting for the tub to fill.

Towards the end of the interview the mermaid had lowered her voice yet further, squeezing Aleta's knee with a gloved hand.

— I haven't told you anything you don't already know.

Releasing her grip on Aleta's knee, she had raised a hand and pointed at her own breast, whispering:

— I'm soft where it matters.

At this Aleta had smiled sympathetically. She had opened her mouth to say: 'Of course it's who you are inside that matters, goodness can appear in all manner of guises.' But before she could speak, the mermaid had whipped open her robe, revealing to Aleta the softness she was talking about.

From the neck down, over her breasts with their blue-black nipples and her flat stomach, the rough scales gave way to pale, silvery skin, with the softness and sheen of precious silk or the belly of a plaice, right down to her crotch with its dark red tuft of hair, like a tangle of wet seaweed. A strong smell of brine rose from the white skin, mingling with the scent of vanilla.

The mermaid whispered:

— This soft embrace was enjoyed by dozens of grateful sailors from the ships that docked in the islands, from when I was thirteen until two years later, when what I got up to 'alone' in the bait shed every night was discovered by my mother and the pastor of Bethel, who caught me *in flagrante* with three deckhands from the *Birtingur*, a capelin boat from Ísafjördur. After that I was expelled from the Pentecostalist congregation. Though, needless to say, no one thought to ask what my mother and the pastor were doing there in the middle of the night. From then on my school friends were forbidden to speak to me and my teachers stopped caring whether I turned up or not, though both were merely a formality by that stage. Shortly afterwards I was kicked out of my home and after fending for myself from Easter to the beginning of summer – the local tramp used to let me stay with him, and once or twice the manager of Hótel Heimaklettur let me lie on a mattress in the boiler room in return for being allowed to lie on top of me first – I was picked up by social services and sent to a children's home on the mainland. I ran away whenever I could, seizing every chance I got to have sex with men. After one of these escapes they told me I was being sent for a preventative appendectomy at the City Hospital, but when I woke up after the operation I discovered that they'd removed my womb at the same time. Later, I took myself abroad and slept with a succession of men in Copenhagen's Christiania district, in Amsterdam, Tangier and Marseilles, until nine years ago my arthritis got the better of me and I couldn't walk any more, so I decided to come home.

Aleta cursed the intrusive memory of the mermaid's story, too many details of which coincided with her own. Stubbing out the cigarette in the sink, she dropped it between her legs into the toilet bowl, then stood up and flushed. The woman's voice faded.

— Shouldn't a person die where they came into being? Like the sea trout . . .

Which was when Aleta remembered the geneticist's recording. She pulled over her bag, took out the tape and put it in the dictaphone, pressing the play button and fast-forwarding to the comment:

— This is where I became the man I am . . .

She turned off the tap, lowered herself into the bath and leaned her head back, resting her neck on the rim and feeling the tiredness flowing out of her body as she listened to the geneticist attempting to understand himself.

This intimate glimpse into his thoughts gave her a feeling of security. It put them on a level. As far as he was concerned, Aleta didn't exist. He might see her name on one of the questionnaires, but she thought it unlikely he would ever listen to the recordings himself. The interviews would be digitally transcribed by a CoDex minion; he would never even hear her voice.

But from that day on the geneticist would no longer be the distant authority figure who communicated with Aleta through his assistant.

Now she knew more about him than he did about her.

She would never return the tape.

* * *

Jósef Loewe stirs on the dirt-brown sofa.

Aleta bends over him and blows cigarette smoke in his face.

He starts awake and tries to avoid the smoke.

Aleta laughs:

'You're such a bore!'

8

'Which brings the story back to me.'

Jósef steeples his fingers.

'There aren't many of us on this earth who can describe what it felt like to enter the world. Most people find it hard enough to remember what they did yesterday, let alone a week, three months or thirteen years ago. But from the moment I awoke to life on the kitchen table in the basement of 10a Ingólfsstræti to the present day, I can remember everything that's ever happened to me, every waking moment, every thought, every dream. Whenever I choose to summon them from my memory, past events appear vivid in my mind's eye, whether they took place on the afternoon of 27 August 1962 or the morning of 27 August 2012. Thoughts and actions return as brief glimpses – like the luminescent form of a giant squid rising from the depths to light up the night-black sea – so fleeting that it requires special training to see and hear them, innate cunning and strength of mind to catch and hold them still in one's consciousness, patience and mental agility to untangle them.

If a handful of wool is carded until every thread lies alongside the next it will eventually cover a whole room – and so it is with memories. Gone about the right way, it will take as long to revive the past as it took to experience it in the first place.

This is my gift: to remember everything, to experience it all twice over – and to tell the tale.

* * *

From the very first moment my senses were fully formed: my eyes could see, my ears could hear, smells wafted past my nostrils, flavours enveloped my tongue, my skin perceived the touch of air and matter.

I drank it all in. And through the medium of words I can convey you to any time or place that is stored in my acid-bright memory.

I am a time machine.

* * *

The day after I drew my first breath, I woke to find Leo Loewe, my father and creator, inspecting his handiwork. To prevent me catching cold he had half-wrapped me in an eiderdown and sat cradling me in his arms, examining my small body from head to toe, stroking me all over in search of flaws or inconsistencies. He took my head gently in his hands to reassure himself that there was a skull beneath my scalp; he squeezed my arms to feel the bones under the soft flesh; putting his head on one side, he raised me to his ear and listened to my heart-beat; he palpated my abdomen to check that the organs were in place, then moved his fingers round to my back and felt for my kidneys; he tugged gently but firmly on my legs to make sure the tendons and joints would hold. When he turned me on my right side to run his fingertips down my spinal column and count the ribs, my head was thrust against his chest and I heard for the first time the beating of a human heart:

My father's heart. It was beating fast.

Leo Loewe was in a state of high emotion, filled with elation at having successfully kindled life in the clay boy who, at great personal sacrifice, he had brought unscathed to a refuge far from the wicked-ness of the world, crossing the enemy-occupied Continent, the U-boat-infested seas; fearful all the while that I might not be perfectly whole, that something might have gone wrong during the nearly two decades that had passed between the moulding of the child from a lump of clay and the moment when the spark of life was ignited in the inert substance, transforming it into flesh and bone, guts and fluids, nerves and veins. Clay can dry out and crack, and although he had been at pains to keep the surface moist and soft, there was a risk that something might have gone wrong inside; after all, the clay had been kneaded with a variety of bodily secretions that are sensitive to storage, heat and damp.

Like other new parents, my father was moved above all by having taken part in the miracle of life, that perpetual process by which newly embodied consciousnesses are summoned into being in the cosmos; all different, all unique in their desire for the same thing as all those who have gone before: "to live life to the full".

After counting my bones, not once but three times, my father laid me on my back and wrapped me in the quilt. I remember the goose-flesh prickling my limbs as the cold cotton touched my skin, and I remember too how quickly my body formed an alliance with the eiderdown and filled with a spreading warmth.

> *Ay-li-lu-li-lu* . . .

Leo held me in his arms, crooning in his mother tongue:

> *Unter Yideles vigele,*
> *Shteyt a klor-vays tsigele* . . .

I tried to keep my eyes open. It was interesting, this crack in my father's face that opened and closed, stretched and compressed with his grimaces, producing the lullaby about the white kid that traded in raisins and almonds:

> *Dos tsigele iz geforn handlen –*
> *Dos vet zayn dayn baruf* . . .

The cadence of the lullaby and the warmth of his breath caused my eyelids to droop.

> *Rozhinkes mit mandlen*
> *Shlof-zhe, Yidele, shlof* . . .

He smiled at me and crooned the last line again, inserting my name instead:

Shlof-zhe, Yosef, shlof,
Shlof-zhe, Yosef, shlof . . .

In his arms slept a boy-child of flesh and blood, of that there could be no doubt.

For the first few months I received all my nourishment from the milk of the black nanny-goat that Leo kept in the garden behind the house on Ingólfsstræti. I grew so hungry for it that when I heard the clatter of the lid on the pan in which my bottle was sterilised, I began to quiver like the wing of a fly, my whole body shaking with anticipation, and, had I known how, I would have bawled with impatience.

From time to time, Mrs Thorsteinson from upstairs – who, before she had her daughter, used to complain about the goat and tried repeatedly to persuade her husband to get rid of it on the grounds that it was an embarrassment to have an evil-tempered, evil-smelling beast where by rights there should have been roses and redcurrant bushes, and it wouldn't hurt if they could get shot of the foreigner at the same time – would send her maid down to our basement to solicit a bottle of goat's milk for Halldóra Oktavía, which was the name the couple had given to the baby Mrs Thorsteinson conceived with her four lovers on that historic night.

My father always welcomed the maid, however busy we were, telling her to take her mistress the milk with his warmest wishes for the mother and daughter's good health, adding that he was sure Mrs Thorsteinson would do the same for his son. But despite the sincerity of his polite sentiment, Mrs Thorsteinson never offered to share any of her bounty with me when her breasts were full – and my father would never have dreamed of demanding such a thing, though the goat's supply had begun to dry up by the spring of 1963.

No, my hands never clutched at a mother's breast, my lips never closed over a nipple, warm mother's milk never bathed my tongue or flowed down my throat.

Leo wondered at times if the reason I was so quiet – yes, I was a contented child, and never wailed or raised my voice; my whimpering and cooing were so muted that he was never sure if I'd actually made

I'M A SLEEPING DOOR 403

a sound or if it had simply formed in his head as he watched me wriggling in my cradle – was that my body was unacquainted with the sustenance that is human milk; that a clay boy could never become human unless he fed off another person, imbibed the cannibalistic drink of life.

When he realised that all he had to offer that was in any way equivalent to Mrs Thorsteinson's white breast milk was his own red heart's blood, he banished these thoughts once and for all: the idea of rearing me on blood was such a travesty, would be such a gamble if put into practice. Leo was creating a saviour to deliver an important message to a new age, not an insatiably bloodthirsty monster like those who had pushed the world over a precipice while the precipice had looked the other way.

I can still feel his little finger tickling my mouth as he felt my palate and tongue to check that everything was all right: the frenulum not too taut or slack, the palate not too thick or cleft, the root of the tongue neither shrivelled nor over-grown. At other times he would rest my head in his hand, stroking my throat with the tips of thumb and forefinger, or lay his palm on my chest to measure the strength of my breathing – but all was as it should be. After this examination he would sigh heavily. All he could do was wait and hope that the day would come when I found my voice. If I really turned out to be dumb he would have to teach me other methods of communication – art, dance, literature, music – employing every means possible to ensure that when the time came I could reach a mass audience and carry them with me.'

'Which you will. There's still time left.'

'Thanks, Aleta, you're sweet. Let's have some brandy.'

'Only once did Mrs Thorsteinson deign to come downstairs in person to request milk for her daughter. One Sunday morning at the beginning of March there was a peremptory knocking on our door. I was lying in my cot, which Leo had rolled into the cramped living room so he could keep an eye on me from where he was sitting at the dining-room table. He was drinking tea and nibbling ginger biscuits while poring over a book of sheet music that he had acquired from an antiquarian bookshop on the first floor of a house on Laugavegur, playing in his head the silent sonata *In futurum* by the Prague-born Erwin Schulhoff. We both started up, I from a doze, he from the composition's furious silences. Before he could get up to answer the door, the visitor had let herself in. Footsteps approached along the hall. A moment later Mrs Thorsteinson paused in the living-room doorway.

Her red hair was in curlers under a dark green scarf, below which she wore a dressing gown of shiny black silk with a repeated pattern of Japanese pagodas and puffy clouds woven in even blacker thread, and burgundy-coloured mules with nut-brown pom-poms and varnished wooden heels. The fifteen-month-old Halldóra Oktavía was perched on her mother's arm like a princess on her throne, dressed in a velvet pinafore with a lace collar and sucking on a dummy with loud smacking sounds.

Mother and daughter filled the doorway as if intending to block our exit. Leo looked at the woman enquiringly. She didn't react.

Seconds passed.

Then it dawned on my father what a ridiculous position he was in, caught halfway between sitting and standing, like a chimpanzee doing a bowel movement in its trousers.

Cheeks reddening, he straightened up, put down the sheet music and cleared his throat.

— Good morning.

Mrs Thorsteinson walked into the living room, running her eyes over my father's spartan furnishings with a studied indifference that could be interpreted as either respect for his privacy or suspicion about what sort of "junk" he had "brought into her house". The sheet music didn't escape her notice. She said sharply:

— I hope you're not in a choir, Mr Loewe.

Although I was lying there with the eiderdown pulled up to my chin, limiting my view of the room, I could sense how nervous my father was in Mrs Thorsteinson's presence.

He was tongue-tied, tripped over his words, made grammatical errors, pronounced the Icelandic *s* like the Czech *č*, forgot how to say the most commonplace words and ordered them haphazardly into sentences – thereby confirming all the woman's prejudices about the defective foreigner in the basement.

— Not that it's any of my business.

Mrs Thorsteinson peered into my cot.

— Dook, Dóra, dee de dickle boy.

She leaned forwards so the little girl could see me too.

— Id dere a dickle boy in our house? A dickle boy fow wus?

Halldóra Oktavía subjected me to a searching stare. Her dummy emitted a loud pop. Her mother lowered her towards me. I gazed back, fascinated, noticing that one of her eyes was blue, the other brown.

Halldóra Oktavía paused momentarily in her sucking, her lower jaw grew slack and the dummy slid forwards between her parted lips, releasing a rope of drool from behind the disc, which oozed down her chin, collected there in a large drop, then fell on to my forehead.

The drip of saliva ran into my left eye and I recoiled like a beetle lying on its back. I shook with fright. I emitted a tremulous squeak. I kicked my legs in the air, shedding the quilt and sending the knitted bootees flying off my feet.

Mrs Thorsteinson reached out to cover me, then paused and withdrew her hand, glancing over her shoulder at Leo who was hovering uneasily behind her, and addressed him in the same language as she had used with Halldóra Oktavía:

— He've got fuddy big does . . .

She turned back to the cot, pointing at my tiny feet.

— Hasn't he?

My father stepped up to Mrs Thorsteinson's side.

Yes, indeed, my big toes were not as they should have been. The top joints were crooked, slanting towards the other toes, as if they had been crushed against their neighbours. Leo gasped. How could he have failed to notice? Had his boy's clay feet been squashed against the sides of the hatbox, resulting in a malformation of his toes? Could it have happened the morning he took me out to bring me to life? But he didn't have time to give it any further thought just then.

Halldóra Oktavía jerked her head and sucked on her dummy with a loud smack.

The Icelandic public were to become familiar with this abrupt jerk of the head when Halldóra Oktavía became temporary governor of the Central Bank during the financial crisis of 2008 to 2009.'

The Dance

The stage is darkened. We hear stagehands pushing cots and oxygen tents to the front. They are clad in black from head to toe, but as our eyes adjust to the lack of light, they begin to resemble embodied shadows, alternately pushing, dragging or carrying between them puzzling dark shapes, which they arrange here and there on the stage behind the cots and the oxygen tents. After this, they withdraw into the wings.

Fluorescent bulbs click into life, illuminating those present:

Girl: 12 January 1962 – † 13 January 1962, Girl: 13 January 1962 – † 13 January 1962, Girl: 21 January 1962 – † 21 January 1962, Boy: 24 February 1962 – † 27 February 1962, Boy: 1 March 1962 – † 14 April 1962, Girl: 13 May 1962 – † 14 May 1962, Girl: 13 May 1962 – † 17 May 1962, Girl: 5 May 1962 – † 21 May 1962, Boy: 7 May 1962 – † 25 May 1962, Girl: 19 May 1962 – † 26 May 1962, Girl: 27 May 1962 – † 27 May 1962, Girl: 28 May 1962 – † 29 May 1962, Boy: 22 June 1962 – † 23 June 1962, Boy: 27 June 1962 – † 30 June 1962, Boy: 10 February 1962 – † 11 July 1962, Girl: 30 April 1962 – † 11 July 1962, Boy: 10 February 1962 – † 16 July 1962, Boy: 16 July 1962 – † 16 July 1962, Boy: 9 July 1962 – † 18 July 1962, Girl: 19 July 1962 – † 19 July 1962, Boy: 31 July 1962 – † 31 July 1962, Girl: 1 August 1962 – † 1 August 1962, Boy: 29 March 1962 – † 3 August 1962, Boy: 9 July 1962 – † 4 August 1962, Girl: 13 February 1962 – † 7 August 1962, Boy: 1 July 1962 – † 18 August 1962, Boy: 17 August 1962 – † 20 August 1962, Girl: 3 September 1962 – † 3 September 1962, Boy: 1 October 1962 – † 6 October 1962, Boy: 18 November 1962 – † 18 November 1962, Boy: 27 November 1962 – † 27 November 1962, Boy: 18 December 1962 – † 18 December 1962, Girl: 16 December 1962 – † 23 December 1962 . . .

Behind them, incandescent bulbs begin to glow in a series of chandeliers hanging low over the stage. They come in all different shapes and sizes, some made of black or white plastic, others of pale or dark grey glass, and shed a white light on the objects the stagehands have arranged there:

A raised platform, on which stand six cots, four highchairs, three prams and a play-mat decorated with pictures of moons and moths.

As we become aware of movements in the cots and prams, the stagehands carry in toddlers and seat them in the highchairs, then lay four more on the play-mat. The children have bruised heads, blue lips, bloodshot eyes, and burn marks on their arms and bodies, from water, fire and electricity.

Boy: 19 November 1962 – † ? 1963
Girl: 27 July 1962 – † 9 February 1963
Girl: 8 August 1962 – † 14 February 1963
Girl: 30 March 1962 – † 16 February 1963
Girl: 21 October 1962 – † 3 March 1963
Boy: 1 August 1962 – † 1 April 1963
Boy: 7 June 1962 – † 4 April 1963
Girl: 27 February 1962 – † 10 April 1963
Boy: 9 February 1962 – † 15 April 1963
Boy: 11 November 1962 – † 1 May 1963
Girl: 3 December 1962 – † 14 May 1963
Boy: 30 June 1962 – † 16 May 1963
Boy: 19 July 1962 – † 8 August 1963
Boy: 11 December 1962 – † 3 October 1963
Boy: 5 February 1962 – † 26 October 1963
Girl: 29 May 1962 – † 26 October 1963
Boy: 6 May 1962 – † 14 November 1963

Behind the prams and cots, the highchairs and mat, three boys and a girl enter and come toddling into the pools of light. One of the boys is dripping seawater, another is muddy, the third is as ashen-faced as the girl he is leading by the hand.

Boy: 14 January 1962 – † 16 July 1964
Boy: 10 February 1962 – † 4 September 1964
Boy: 30 July 1962 – † 30 September 1964
Girl: 1 July 1962 – † 18 October 1964

They are joined by five more children. One boy comes cycling in on a red tricycle, another is straddling a home-made car, propelling himself along with his feet; one girl is pushing a frilly doll's pushchair, another is clutching scissors and a pair of hot curling tongs; the fifth child is pulling along a sailing boat, made from an STP oil can. They are pale and bruised, crushed and broken.

Boy: 10 May 1962 – † 5 January 1965
Girl: 6 August 1962 – † 18 February 1965
Girl: 4 October 1962 – † 9 October 1965
Boy: 24 June 1962 – † 14 November 1965
Boy: 9 February 1962 – † 23 December 1965

Footsteps herald the arrival of two more girls and one boy. They trot on stage and take up position on the platform with the younger children – blood crusted in their hair and salt in their mouths.

Girl: 9 August 1962 – † 13 January 1966
Boy: 29 October 1962 – † 10 July 1966
Girl: 10 November 1962 – † 20 December 1966

The chorus deepens, the newly arrived voices increasing the range, supplementing the sighs and whimpers with babbling and primitive words: 'daddee' and 'nana', 'mama' and 'oh-oh' – and the beginnings of intelligible sentences: ''top it' and 'Me no go bye-byes' and 'Teddy cuggle'.

The first obituary written for a child born in this year includes the following description:

> She was a bright little soul, full of beans and as busy as a bee. Wonderfully imaginative too and unusually interested in all she heard or saw. People couldn't get over how grown up she sounded in some of the things she said.

This little darling, who died in her fourth year, now leads the chorus in the second movement:

— We fell out of our mothers', fathers' or siblings' arms; we rolled off tables, out of beds, down the stairs; we walked off cliffs, in front of milk lorries and vans; we swallowed a coin, a prune stone, a glass bead, the button of a smoking jacket, which got trapped in our windpipes; we ate scouring powder, we drank caustic soda, we poured boiling water and coffee over ourselves; we ran with scissors or with a teaspoon in our mouths; we got meningitis, whooping cough and pneumonia; we suffocated in cots, beds and prams; we got shut in doors; we were washed out to sea.

Dear brothers and sisters, born in 1962, we await you here.

9

Jósef Loewe puts his head on one side, slumping deeper into the sofa and pressing back into the thick cushion that supports his neck, as if he can't talk about himself without a certain distance between himself and his audience, Aleta, the young woman with the questionnaire and the tape recorder; as if the gap between them grants him the narrative detachment he needs for his story to be believable; as if only by seeing the woman from a distance, from head to toe, can he respond to her reactions to his account of the main events in his own and his parents' lives – instantly adapting the plot and focus to prevent her attention from wandering or himself from losing faith in what he has to say. Or perhaps Jósef has unwittingly resorted to one of the oldest tricks of the trade, whereby storytellers are not content merely to have power over their audience's minds but must also take control of their bodies at the very beginning of their tale by lowering their voices and leaning back, thus compelling their listeners to lean forwards – after all, they've come to hear what the storyteller has to say. By means of this synchro-nised shift they establish who is the guide and who the travellers on the coming journey, for at the outset they all cherish the same hope:

That their roles will remain unchanged to the end of the story, that the speaker will hold the listeners' attention, that no one and nothing will be lost along the way, least of all the story itself, which can at times seem loose underfoot, precipitous, slippery, boggy and over-grown, or cleft by sudden bottomless chasms into which everything falls: plants and animals, men and monsters, gods and death itself, together with all the ballads and fairytales that come into being at the meeting of these types, in town and country, in the sky and at the bottom of the sea, by night and by day, in the spirit and in the flesh – though, if all else fails, the guide has up his sleeve a thread that will help him navigate his way out of the fieriest pit, causing a path to open through mountains and wilderness.

Yes, it is the storyteller's tiny initial withdrawal that lures the audience over the invisible border into the storyworld – thereby confirming that all true literature speaks to the body as well as the mind – and, sure enough, Aleta now leans towards Jósef by exactly the inch or two that he has leaned back into the cushion.

$$* * *$$

'I was the silent child. I was the child who stood by while the other children played. The child who waited quietly while the others fought over who was to be first in line for the seesaw, first at the back of the bus on the school trip, first at the table for the chocolate cake. I was the child who didn't speak unless spoken to, by adults or other children, either to the teacher at the nursery when my legs were soaked up to mid-thigh, or to the boy sitting next to me at the cinema when he emptied a full bottle of Coke into my lap, to the postman when a letter fell out of his sack on the pavement, or to the child who stood under the eaves when a pile of snow was about to fall off the roof. I was the child who replied to every question with a nod or a shake of the head, or a mumbled "I don't know" when answering was unavoidable. I was the quiet child who pottered about alone in the far corner of the playground, who sat at the back desk by the wall in the row nearest the classroom door. I was the child who never volunteered for the role of the prince in the *Sleeping Beauty* musical, who never shot his hand up when the blackboard was to be decorated for Christmas. I was the child who neither laughed aloud nor cried in the presence of strangers. I was the dull child, ignored by adults when they spoke to his father in the street, never talked about behind his back by the other children. I was the child whose name no one can remember when they're looking at old class photos.

A person is a composite of the times they live through – a combination of the events they have witnessed or taken part in, whether willingly or not; a collection of dreams and thoughts, whether their own or strangers'; a concoction of deeds done by themselves and others, whether friends or enemies; a compilation of stories remembered or forgotten, from distant parts or the next room – and every time an event or idea touches them, affects their existence, rocks their little world and the wider one too, a stone is added to the structure that they are destined to become. Whether this is to be a town square or a path beside a pond, a bridge or a beer factory, a Portakabin or a watchtower, a palace or a university, a prison camp or an airport, not until after they are dead and buried will their true dimensions – their role in society – be revealed; they will only be complete when there is nothing left of them but ruins; a fading gleam in people's memories; the occasional photograph in the albums of family or friends; the odd tangible creation; belongings now dispersed; everyday clothes and one smarter outfit; name and social security number scattered through the public records; death notice and obituary yellowing in a newspaper, none of which can ever be reconstructed . . .'

He's expansive now; no evidence here of the silent boy or the weary invalid.

'That's depressing talk.'

'Though I spared you the conclusion: . . . *any more than their physical remains, disintegrating in the grave.*'

'Thanks for that.'

'This is the preamble my father used to trot out by way of a refusal whenever I asked him to tell me his story. He would claim he was nothing but the sum of everything he'd experienced during his lifetime. And who would be interested in that? People have trouble enough coping with their own lives. Only after he was gone would I see what his purpose had been.'

Jósef smiles wryly.

'Luckily he left behind a load of cardboard boxes full of papers that I've been able to draw on. After he died, I was lumbered with the task of reconstructing his story . . .'

Aleta ignores the note of self-pity.

He goes on:

'If you want to succeed, you have to read the Man in the context of the World.'

Jósef picks up a folder from the coffee table and, opening it, starts leafing backwards and forwards through the plastic sleeves until he finds what he's looking for. He pulls out two yellowing newspaper cuttings, closes the folder and places it flat on his knees, laying the cuttings on top.

'For example, what do you suppose these two news items have in common?'

Aleta joins him on the sofa. The cuttings come from the inside pages. She skims the headlines:

Sheep-worrier at Large in Borgarfjördur

Body Discovered on Ring Road

The first is labelled in red biro *HWK 29/08 '62*, and the second *HWK 07/09 '62*.

He waits, as if expecting Aleta to answer his rhetorical question.

She waits for him to go on.

'Well, they record the demise of Hrafn the stamp collector, the first reporting how he went around biting the throats of sheep while in his werewolf state; the second how his body was found lying naked by the side of the road near the Agricultural College at Hvanneyri. My theory is that he was on his way to seek help from the local vet when his frenzy began to wear off.

And that's not all . . .'

Jósef reaches for a small photo frame that stands on a crocheted mat on the sideboard by the sofa and hands it to Aleta. He gives her a sign to wait while he locates a handwritten sheet in the bundle of papers on the table. Then, taking the glasses that hang from a chain around his neck, he props them on his nose and begins to read.

PORTRAIT OF MY MOTHER

Throughout my childhood and teens the first thing that met my eyes when I awoke was a photograph of my mother.

This black and white portrait, the size of a playing card, used to be propped against the base of the lamp on the table between our beds, in a bronze-coloured copper frame, designed to look more expensive than it was – with two dark grooves along the sides and decorative swirls at the corners that tickled my fingertips when I stroked them.

In the photo under the shiny, convex glass, my mother has her right profile to the camera and is looking slightly down and to one side, so both her eyes can be seen, the soft daylight picking out her features. Her expression is serious, yet gentle. She is pensive. Her dark hair is combed into a fringe that falls over her forehead from under a black cloche hat that covers her head to the nape of her neck. She's wearing a white jacket with the collar turned up against her long throat, a deep seam running from the neckline down her slim shoulder to the edge of the picture.

The background is divided into two slanting halves:

The upper half shows a light-coloured wall with a horizontal flaw at the top. For a long time I thought it was a crack in the plaster, though later I decided it must be a decorative moulding, but at the very beginning – before my vision was sufficiently developed to interpret perspective – I was under the impression that my mother was balancing a plank of wood on her head, since the line ran straight across the picture, touching the top of her hat.

The lower half is black – apart from three white spots floating at breast height on the dark plane in front of my mother, forming the three corners of an equilateral triangle. They are fuzzy, like stars in a night sky seen through the worn lenses of an old pair of hunting binoculars, or city lights receding in the rear-view mirror of a fast-moving car. This is the most mysterious element of the picture, yet it also serves to accentuate the beauty of the woman, the purity of form repeating itself in variations; the dark triangle between the points of light confirming the classical proportions of her face.

At times I would trace the light in the picture, following it from the glimmer on her dark fringe, down the smooth forehead to the tip of her nose, and from there to her cheek, upper lip, the corner of her mouth, her shining lower lip, then down to her white throat, and up again under her eyes. There was so much warmth in those bright planes that I had no need to imagine the feel of her cheek against mine, my face grew hot simply from looking at them. And the flush in my cheeks was accompanied by a silent yell of joy that went racing through my mind and body, causing a sudden tingling in the roof of my mouth. I felt my mother's gravity must be put on, as though any minute she would burst out laughing at the photographer's ridiculous instruction not to smile while he was taking her picture. She, Marie-Sophie, who was always so cheerful; the chambermaid who only ever saw the good, the beautiful in everything, even in the darkest times.

Not to smile – how on earth was she to manage that? He might as well forbid a lily to bloom.

At other times I would allow my gaze to be guided by the dark planes, starting at the nape of her neck where the shadow was blackest and moving up to where an unruly lock of hair led me to a partly shadowed ear, then over that and on to her temple, her cheek, down her cheekbone to her nose, out along one nostril and from there up the bone of her nose into the corner of her eye.

Then I would be gripped by the feeling that my mother was genuinely sad, that in the instant the camera shutter opened and closed she had been struck by the thought that this picture would be the sole confirmation of her existence, that she had ever been born and known what it was to feel. And I would touch the frame, stroking it and thinking:

But you didn't know then that you'd meet my father the invalid; that you'd nurse him back to life; that together you were destined to create me.

Fortunately, it was much rarer for my eyes to stray down that melancholy path of shadows. When they did, I would find my way back to the long lashes, under which a distant light glittered on the black pools of the eyes. At this, my mood would brighten.

The last thing I did in the evenings, before laying my head on the pillow and pulling the eiderdown up over the tops of my ears, was to place the frame so that the picture would be directly in my eye-line when I awoke.

As soon as I was able, I would rise on my elbow, still groggy with sleep, and switch on the lamp. Then I would sit gazing at her, leaning my head against the cool wall, until my father came back into our bedroom having got breakfast ready, and helped me into my clothes or, once I was old enough, chivvied me to get up and dressed myself.

There were times when the picture shifted and was no longer aligned exactly with the crack in the varnish on the bedside table, and once – or twice perhaps – it was facing away from me when I awoke, as if she had decided to turn round during the night to see how my father was doing.

Then I would find myself looking at the back: the brown speckled card that supported the picture in the frame, held in place by four copper clips, and the extendable foot attached with a shiny ribbon, while in the bottom right-hand corner there was a small, oval sticker with the silhouette of a swan and the name of the manufacturer:

Andersens Ramfabrik – Odense.'

Jósef sighs and lowers the sheet of paper to his lap, where it slips from his hand.

He has nodded off again.

The Dance

Black-clad stagehands go about their work, pretending they're invisible, but in the darkness the eye can make out four shadows walking on to the stage carrying a long platform which they place behind the one that's already present. There's a clicking of fluorescent bulbs, the various chandeliers flicker into life.

Girl: 12 January 1962 – † 13 January 1962, Girl: 13 January 1962 – † 13 January 1962, Girl: 21 January 1962 – † 21 January 1962, Boy: 24 February 1962 – † 27 February 1962, Boy: 1 March 1962 – † 14 April 1962, Girl: 13 May 1962 – † 14 May 1962, Girl: 13 May 1962 – † 17 May 1962, Girl: 5 May 1962 – † 21 May 1962, Boy: 7 May 1962 – † 25 May 1962, Girl: 19 May 1962 – † 26 May 1962, Girl: 27 May 1962 – † 27 May 1962, Girl: 28 May 1962 – † 29 May 1962, Boy: 22 June 1962 – † 23 June 1962, Boy: 27 June 1962 – † 30 June 1962, Boy: 10 February 1962 – † 11 July 1962, Girl: 30 April 1962 – † 11 July 1962, Boy: 10 February 1962 – † 16 July 1962, Boy: 16 July 1962 – † 16 July 1962, Boy: 9 July 1962 – † 18 July 1962, Girl: 19 July 1962 – † 19 July 1962, Boy: 31 July 1962 – † 31 July 1962, Girl: 1 August 1962 – † 1 August 1962, Boy: 29 March 1962 – † 3 August 1962, Boy: 9 July 1962 – † 4 August 1962, Girl: 13 February 1962 – † 7 August 1962, Boy: 1 July 1962 – † 18 August 1962, Boy: 17 August 1962 – † 20 August 1962, Girl: 3 September 1962 – † 3 September 1962, Boy: 1 October 1962 – † 6 October 1962, Boy: 18 November 1962 – † 18 November 1962, Boy: 27 November 1962 – † 27 November 1962, Boy: 18 December 1962 – † 18 December 1962, Girl: 16 December 1962 – † 23 December 1962, Boy: 19 November – † ? 1963, Girl: 27 July 1962 – † 9 February 1963, Girl: 8 August 1962 – † 14 February 1963, Girl: 30 March 1962 – † 16 February 1963, Girl: 21 October 1962 – † 3 March 1963, Boy: 1 August 1962 – † 1 April

1963, Boy: 7 June 1962 – † 4 April 1963, Girl: 27 February 1962 – † 10 April 1963, Boy: 9 February 1962 – † 15 April 1963, Boy: 11 November 1962 – † 1 May 1963, Girl: 3 December 1962 – † 14 May 1963, Girl: 30 June 1962 – † 16 May 1963, Boy: 19 July 1962 – † 8 August 1963, Boy: 11 December 1962 – † 3 October 1963, Boy: 5 February 1962 – † 26 October 1963, Girl: 29 May 1962 – † 26 October 1963, Boy: 6 May 1962 – † 14 November 1963, Boy: 14 January 1962 – † 16 July 1964, Boy: 10 February 1962 – † 4 September 1964, Boy: 30 July 1962 – † 30 September 1964, Girl: 1 July 1962 – † 18 October 1964, Boy: 10 May 1962 – † 5 January 1965, Girl: 6 August 1962 – † 18 February 1965, Girl: 4 October 1962 – † 9 October 1965, Boy: 24 June 1962 – † 14 November 1965, Boy: 9 February 1962 – † 23 December 1965, Girl: 9 August 1962 – † 13 January 1966, Boy: 29 October 1962 – † 10 July 1966, Girl: 10 November 1962 – † 20 December 1966 . . .

The assembled children are as quiet as can be expected. A three-year-old boy sits on the floor with legs crossed, cheeks resting in his hands, dozing. Small scuffles can be heard among the girls. The youngest children grizzle and sigh without restraint.

A murmur passes through the group.

Light bulbs descend from the darkness above them, one at a time, until they are all hanging at the same height over the platform. Then they come on, red, green, yellow and blue.

The children do not speak. Those capable of standing straighten up and tidy their clothes. But none of them move from their place.

Twelve boys and two girls now enter. The girls and one of the boys are being pushed in wheelchairs by the three eldest boys. The stage-hands help to lift them up on to the platform and they each hobble to their places where they take up position and gaze out over the auditorium.

Boy: 8 February 1962 – † 10 January 1968
Girl: 12 January 1962 – † 18 February 1968
Boy: 7 September 1962 – † 30 September 1968

Boy: 24 August 1962 – † 8 April 1969

Boy: 22 November 1962 – † *12 May 1969*
Boy: 23 December 1962 – † *26 December 1969*

Boy: 24 March 1962 – † *1 October 1970*
Boy: 22 February 1962 – † *17 November 1970*

Girl: 7 August 1962 – † *29 January 1971*
Boy: 14 March 1962 – † *10 March 1971*
Boy: 16 April 1962 – † *4 April 1971*
Boy: 19 June 1962 – † *10 October 1971*
Boy: 15 December 1962 – † *26 December 1971*

Boy: 17 June 1962 – † *12 March 1972*

Four of the new arrivals show on their bodies the signs of having been hit by a car, two of having drowned, four of having died in their sickbeds, one of having burned to death in a house-fire, and three hang back so the cause of death is unclear.

The oldest boy steps forward. He speaks clearly, if a little slowly and slightly too loudly, as he is making an effort to articulate:

— The reaper cuts his swathe. He points to the promising corn. He points to the flushing rosebuds.

The other thirteen children hold up their arms and start waving them as if swaying before a warm breeze. The girls put their wrists together, forming flowers with their hands; the boys spread out their fingers to form ears of corn.

The oldest boy:

— He says: 'You, you, you, you – and you.'

The children point out into the auditorium, repeating the oldest boy's last words:

— You, you, you, you – and you!

The oldest boy starts swinging his arms, imitating a man cutting with a scythe.

— He swings the scythe until it sings.

The thirteen children copy the oldest boy's movements, repeating his words:

— The scythe sings!

Some of the younger children start swinging their arms and swaying from their hips, as if acting out a story through dance. They point to one another, murmuring:

— You, you, you, you . . .

The oldest boy:

— The man sings with his scythe, sings the reaper's song that only they know and no one else will ever hear . . .

The thirteen children and the oldest boy now chime in with the younger ones:

— You, you, you, you and you!

The thirteen children and the oldest boy keep repeating the word 'you', lowering their voices until it is no more than a whisper and finally fades out.

— We ran in front of cars, we were found in pits full of water, we were burned inside huts, we were found at the bottom of swimming pools, we were incurable. We disappeared from our homes; no longer flung our arms round our parents' necks; our tears and laughter were silenced, our chairs empty at mealtimes, our beds empty at night. We disappeared from the gaggle of our brothers, sisters and cousins; we were no longer there in the playgrounds with our friends; in the classrooms with the other children.

They fall abruptly silent.

The silence is broken by the oldest boy who takes a deep breath, inflating his little chest, then rises up on tiptoe, holding his head high, and declaims in a glad voice:

— Then, at the end of time, a young man with flowing hair and beard, clad in a shining robe, will appear at the harvest in the Vale of Tears, announcing that he has come from his father and telling the reaper that the day that dawned when the sun of death first rose over Paradise is turned now to evening.

The thirteen children lower their hands and the younger ones copy them.

The oldest boy:

— Cain's work is done. He hands the young man his scythe and walks away.

The children start walking on the spot, briskly, the stage floor booming with their footsteps.

The oldest boy:

— The young man drives the scythe into the ground. It puts down roots, the shaft sprouts branches, the iron straightens out until it points heavenwards. The scythe becomes a spear, becomes the tree of life. And the man who lifted the curse from Cain and freed him from his forced labour, walks along the swath, pointing to the fallen corn, pointing to the fallen roses.

The oldest boy and the thirteen children point to one another – and to the younger children:

— He says: 'You, you, you, you and you!'

The children, both large and small, raise their arms, very slowly, like shoots growing from the soil, forming flowers and ears of corn with their fingers and palms. And chant in chorus:

— We lived on in our siblings born the year after our deaths and given our names. We lived on in the christening gowns donated to churches in our memory. We lived on in the photographs crowding the walls of our closest family members, or our grandparents' dressing tables. We lived on in the reports of accidents on the front, back and middle pages of the newspapers, in death notices, in obituaries, cut out and kept, yellowing, between the pages of photo albums and Bibles.

Dear brothers and sisters, born in 1962, we await you here.

10

Aleta places a steaming cup of coffee on the sofa table. Jósef Loewe stirs and stretches with a suppressed groan of pain, then notices the coffee. Leaning forwards, he takes careful hold of the cup and raises it to his lips, sipping the coffee she made while he was napping. It's sickly sweet, just as he likes it, with a splash of brandy, just as he likes it. His hands shake, he can't keep his lips shaped to the rim of the cup and the coffee dribbles out of the corners of his mouth, which is not just as he likes it.

He had been chipper that morning. His tongue had run away with him as it had on Aleta's previous visits. He had talked for nearly four hours, getting as far as the conception of the 1962 generation after a long prologue, related in exhaustive detail and with many digressions, on more tapes that she can bring herself to count.

The story he had told her – as far as she could grasp its thread – was of how the Jewish alchemist Leo Loewe, his father, had come to Iceland with the *Godafoss* at the end of the Second World War, having escaped from a Nazi concentration camp, more dead than alive, with the sole possession he had managed to rescue from the disaster, a hatbox containing the light of his life, the figure of a baby boy moulded from cold clay, which turned out to be Jósef himself – shaped, according to his father, by the hands of his 'mother', the kindly, talkative chambermaid Marie-Sophie X, while she was nursing him, a broken-armed fugitive, for the few days he had spent hidden in a secret compartment between the rooms of the Gasthof Vrieslander in the small town of Kükenstadt in Lower Saxony, the act of creation reaching its climax when the child opened his eyes and saw the girl see the fact, before which two frames of film had been placed in his eye sockets, one showing the Führer in full rant, the other showing him surprised at having spilt gravy down his tie – yes, Jósef, who'd had to wait twenty-one years, moistened and massaged with goat's milk every day, to be wakened to life, until finally Leo, aided by his two assistants, the Soviet spy Mikhail Pushkin and the American theologian and wrestler Anthony Theophrastus Athanius Brown, after pursuing the twin brothers Már C. and Hrafn W. Karlsson (one a Freemason and stamp collector, the other a parliamentary attendant, both former champion athletes and deckhands with the Icelandic Steam Ship Company), had succeeded in recovering from the wisdom tooth of Már, or rather Hrafn (who in the heat of the moment had turned into a werewolf), the gold filling made from the ring the brothers had stolen from Leo long ago on the voyage to Iceland, which was essential for making the magic seal that he then pressed into the clay between the boy's solar plexus and pubic bone, in place of a navel, wakening him to life on the morning of Monday, 27 August in the oft-mentioned year.

This lengthy speech had been Jósef Loewe's response to the first four questions on the form:

```
a)  Name:
    _____
b)  Date of birth:
    _____
c)  Place of birth:
    _____
d)  Parents (origin/education/occupation):
    _____
    _____
```

She had listened patiently, encouragingly – and he had grown increasingly animated the closer the story came to the present – but now that the time had come for him to answer the other eleven questions, the most important items on the CoDex geneticists' list, and talk about himself, it was as if all the wind had been knocked from his sails. He tired more easily and his illness seemed to tighten its grip.

Aleta reaches over the table and, taking the cup from Jósef with one hand, dries the dribble from his chin with the other, then licks the coffee off her blue fingernails.

'Do you want to call it a day?'

He shakes his head.

'No, but I wish you'd stop licking your fingers.'

She pouts and inserts her index finger in her mouth.

Jósef looks away.

'In front of me, at least.'

Aleta whips her finger out with a loud pop.

'I looked you up in the Book of Icelanders . . .'

She gives him a challenging look.

'Yes, I did. I've got an Icelandic social security number, I've got access like the rest of you. In fact, thanks to the study, I've got enhanced access.'

Jósef jerks his head.

'So what? I've got nothing to hide.'

'It says there that your mother was born in Reykjavík in March 1927 and died in December 1962 . . .'

Aleta hesitates a moment before going on:

'Her name was Brynhildur Helgadóttir.'

The blood drains from Jósef's face.

* * *

THE SAGA OF BRYNHILDUR HELGADÓTTIR – PART ONE

When Brynhildur Helgadóttir died of exposure near the Kleppur Mental Hospital, on 16 December 1962, her last coherent thought was:

I'm not bloody dying here in the mud by the loony bin.

Five hours earlier Brynhildur had come to her senses in a windowless basement as far west as you could go in the west end. She was lying on her back on a nylon-covered straw mattress that had been laid on top of a stack of beer crates and securely wedged into the coldest corner of a storeroom. Her head was turned away from the wall, the left side of her face glued to the nylon by whatever it was that had leaked from her mouth and nose while she was unconscious. She ran her tongue over her swollen lips. Where the corner of her mouth made contact with the mattress cover she felt a thick congealed lump that tasted both bitter and sweet. There was a deep gash in her cheek. With the tip of her tongue she could jiggle two of the molars in her upper jaw. Someone had given her a socking great punch in the face.

She freed her cheek from the nylon by making a slow 'no' movement, listening to the crackling as the contact broke between the artificial fibres and her dried bodily fluids. There was the thudding of footsteps upstairs, the echo of a dance tune, a crash of breaking glass, shrill laughter.

Brynhildur rose on her elbow, slid her legs over the side of the mattress and sat up stiffly. Judging by the way her body ached, she must have got into a hell of a fight with the person who knocked her out, either yesterday or the night before – she couldn't remember which. Her head began to throb with regular hammer blows that intensified when she tilted it over on the painful side, escaping from inside her skull to pound at the roots of her hair.

Holding her head steady by dint of fixing her gaze straight ahead, she wiped the blood and vomit from her face, then rubbed her hand clean on the tatty blue-checked blanket that covered her from groin to knee. It seemed to have been tossed over her as an afterthought since it wasn't large or thick enough to provide adequate protection for an adult and apart from her bra, which had been dragged down to her navel, Brynhildur was naked.

The door stood ajar. Light was spilling from the passage beyond the laundry. The faint illumination was enough to reveal a short-necked red-wine bottle and a single, fur-lined woman's boot lying on the dark grey stone floor by the makeshift bed. An outsize boot. It was hers.

She pulled up her bra and fumbled on the mattress for her dress, knickers and socks but they weren't there. Although her eyes were adjusting now to the gloom, she couldn't see them anywhere. There was nothing in the room but herself on the mattress, the scrap of blanket, the empty bottle and the boot, aside from what appeared to be human excrement in a pool of urine by the door. She hoped that wasn't hers.

Brynhildur wrapped the blanket around herself as far as it would go and stood up.

Rocked by dizziness, she toppled forward on to her knees. After taking a moment to recover, she steadied herself with a hand on the wall opposite and started to get up again, more slowly than before, pausing briefly to clasp the boot between two fingers, then heaved it and herself up off the storeroom floor.

She staggered into the laundry and over to the sink where fillets of stockfish were soaking in grey liquid. Turning on the tap, she washed her hands and face as best she could, rinsed out her mouth, spitting red on to the fish, then gulped down the icy water until she retched, though this did nothing to quench her thirst.

The household's washing hung from a line across the room: a mature woman's underwear, two pairs of men's trousers, a couple of white cotton shirts and one with stripes, nylon stockings, a sleeveless dress, long-johns, woollen socks, a pair of boy's dungarees and a teenage girl's skirt.

Brynhildur helped herself to the clothes that fitted her, not caring that they were all men's garments; the others were many sizes too small. She pulled on trousers, shirt and socks, and grabbed a cardigan that was hanging on a nearby peg. Out in the lit passage she spotted the other boot, which gave her hope that her coat might still be hanging in the cloakroom upstairs.

Having pulled on her boots, she began slowly to climb the stairs, pain shooting through her at every step. As well as the pounding in her head she now became aware of a burning soreness between her legs and whenever her body bent as she climbed, it felt as if a dagger were being stabbed between the ribs below her right shoulder-blade – the post-mortem four days later would reveal that she had two cracked ribs.

The din of the party grew louder the closer she got to the dark hardwood door at the top of the steps, where the light drew a gleam from a brass knob.

The first thing Brynhildur saw when she entered the hall was a man with his back to her. He was standing in front of the mirror, adjusting a mustard-yellow bowtie. In the mirror she saw herself come in, saw herself take the final step out of the gloom into the warm, brightly lit hall, saw the man notice her materialising behind him.

He let go of the bowtie and turned. It took him a moment to work out that the newcomer was a large, red-haired woman in men's clothes, but when he realised who she was, he smiled and shoved his hands in his pockets. A wince twitched his smile as his right hand entered his pocket, and just before it vanished from sight Brynhildur clocked the swollen, bleeding knuckles. He was the man who had punched her in the face.

She tottered as if he had struck her again.

His smile grew.

— So you're awake?

He took a step towards her.

— I was just going to pay you another visit.

Brynhildur felt her stomach clench, felt the acid fear rising in her gullet, spreading through her chest, and for a moment it seemed as if the draught from the cellar would draw her inexorably back down the steps, tear off her boots, strip her in the laundry, drag her into the storeroom, fling her down on the chilly nylon mattress, anoint her head and body with vomit, blood and semen, and snuff out her consciousness.

— Hey, Biddí . . .

There, in the sitting-room doorway, was the woman who had brought Brynhildur to the party and left her as a deposit with their host in return for being left unmolested herself while enjoying his hospitality, booze and cigarettes: Jóhanna Andrésar, her childhood friend; Hanna from Lokastígur.

— Where've you been?

Hanna held out a hand clutching a glass half full of red wine, a smoking cigarette clamped between her fingers, and, pointing at Brynhildur, started cackling uncontrollably.

— What's going on?

The smile left their host's face as he turned to Hanna and snapped:

— You said she – your friend here – was fun . . .

Hanna leaned against the doorpost, holding her glass to her face, and cackled helplessly into the back of her hand, punctuating the thin coil of smoke with her gusts of laughter.

— I'm going to piss my pants. Just look at yourself!

Brynhildur studied her own reflection in the mirror. There wasn't much left of her face, which people sometimes said had a look of Hedy Lamarr, except the eyes. It was the last time she ever saw herself.

Turning in the doorway, Hanna shrieked over the noise of the party:

— Come and see, Biddí's doing a number!

From the room behind her came shouts of 'whee' and 'whoo' and 'wow' and 'whoa'. Brynhildur heard as furniture was pushed aside and someone bumped into the gramophone stand, sending the needle screeching across *Twist Night with the Svavar Gests Band*, as the party guests struggled to their feet and trooped into the hall to see the number Hanna had promised them.

No, she wasn't letting anyone else see her in this state. Brynhildur made a break for it, blundering down the hall, bashing her shoulder into their host as she went and sending him slamming into the mirror. As she ran past Hanna to reach the cloakroom, to get out of this house with its lethal form of generosity, she hissed at her childhood friend from Lokastígur:

— Don't go down to the basement with him.

Once in the cloakroom, unable to find her own coat, Brynhildur snatched the nearest woman's garment from its hanger, yanked the door open and vanished into the darkness.

Hanna yelled after her:

— Hey, don't be such a drag, Biddí, don't go . . .

The man with the bowtie righted himself, straightened the mirror on the wall, smoothed down his grey-flecked pullover, then went and closed the front door.

He turned to Hanna.

— She's been nothing but a bloody bore . . .

He smiled. And when he offered her his arm, Hanna accepted.

The twist had started up again in the sitting room.

At first Brynhildur hadn't a clue where she was or what time it was. All she knew for certain was that the coat was too small for her. The sleeves only came halfway down her forearms and it was too tight for her to button up. A summer coat. And it was December.

Once she was a safe distance from the house she slowed down, searching for familiar landmarks, trying to work out from the signs of life around her whether it was day or night. This was a smart area, dominated by sombre-coloured buildings containing two to four apartments, dark walls dashed with Iceland spar or obsidian, lighter ones mixed with sand, interspersed with the occasional white detached house. The curtains were drawn in most of the windows, there were no children about, and apart from the distant throbbing of a motor-bike there was no other traffic noise; new-looking cars were parked in the drives – it must be night, or late in the evening.

So far that year the winter had been kind to Reykjavík's down-and-outs, but over the last twenty-four hours the north wind had heralded its arrival with plunging temperatures and now it had begun to blow in earnest, bringing an icy rain that became heavier the colder it got until the drops froze into a pitiless, lashing sleet.

Brynhildur managed to drag the coat around herself by tying it tightly with the belt. Between the houses she spotted the grey concrete tower of Landakot Cathedral rising against the stormy black sky. Ahead the street began to slope down, which meant it must lead either to the sea or to the centre of town. Whichever it was, she should be able to find her way from there to the mental hospital.

Kleppur offered a refuge to all those who could no longer recognise any part of themselves but their eyes.

IV

From tape b)

(17 June 2009)

11

A breeze. The fidgeting of branches. A trout slapping its tail. Mallards quacking.

A clunk as a glass is banged down on a table. Rustling. Footsteps on gravel. Silence.

A stream of liquid landing on a smooth body of water.

— I'm pissing in the lake!

The geneticist's voice is loud. He's not talking to himself.

— I'm pissing in Lake Thingvellir!

The shout is intended for the tape still turning in the machine.

The stream sings on the surface for a while, before beginning to stutter.

Silence. Footsteps on gravel. Rustling.

The geneticist:

— Urine.

He lifts the glass from the table.

— I'm converting whisky into urine.

Indistinctly into his glass:

— I permit you, O my country, to savour it with me. Eight thousand . . .

The last comment is almost inaudible but it is obvious that when the man stood up to go and relieve himself, the 100,000-yen worth of spirit he had knocked back had gone to his head.

I'm drunk, he thinks: I only talk like that when I'm drunk.

He's pleasantly sozzled in the way that happens when you drink alone. Nowadays it's only when drinking solo that he experiences the enjoyable buzz that had turned him on to alcohol while he was still at sixth-form college. Back then, whenever they clubbed together to buy a bottle, he and his friends used to talk in this elevated manner:

'I permit you, O my country, to savour it with me.'

A manner of speech that has a tendency to resurface when he is drinking alone and talking to himself. Speaking of which. Clearing his throat, he leans towards the microphone, saying thickly:

— I always meant . . .

He stops himself, takes a breath, swallows and continues, enunciating more clearly:

— I always meant to be a poet.

Yes, they'd all meant to be poets, and not just poets, they'd meant to be poets and men of destiny, modelling themselves on historical figures like Snorri Sturluson and Einar Benediktsson: like them they'd meant to make their mark on the worlds of affairs and literature, to be leaders of men, figures of authority, to write the history of their nation, to win famous victories abroad, to be on chatting terms with heads of state, to move their eloquent tongues in praise of the powerful while lancing society's pestilential boils with the sharpened points of their fountain pens, to mock the arrogant, to stand with the individual against the mob, with the many against the tyranny of the few, to have secret meetings in lonely spots with other men of destiny and conspire with them how to lay traps for the unwary, whether in their writings or in parliament; they would play off their enemies and let them destroy one another, claim to be forever jotting down ideas, deliberately piquing the hopes of publishers while simultaneously pissing off professional authors; exploit the vanity of the weak-willed by placing them in offices and positions only for as long as it suited the ultimate goal; throw people away like used tissues when they failed to live up to expectations or had served their purpose; they would betray a close ally in their hour of need, then forever lament the fact and name their sons after the men they had betrayed; they would topple long-established old men from their thrones, create an atmosphere of low morale and fear in the halls of the great and good, attend international summits and refuse to budge until their homeland was shown the proper respect, laugh coldly when ignorant foreigners called them sentimental for banging on the conference table and quoting lines of verse by Grímur Thomsen in the original Icelandic, stride down corridors and across floors with a retinue in tow, point to something and say something, point to something else and say something else, travel up and down tall buildings in glass lifts, be either famous for their sobriety or notorious for their drinking, either flamboyant or puritanical in their dress, either womanisers or faithful husbands, never be 'average' in any way, be on everyone's lips but refuse to talk to just any journalist, just anywhere; they would keep the world's press waiting, never fully master the pronunciation of foreign tongues, fall silent in the middle of meetings and leave the room, or send everyone else out of the office; talk quietly to themselves when people thought they thought no one could see, adopt a disconcerting gait which people were forced to emulate in order to keep step with them when they strode along the pavements of foreign metropolises or the corridors of the UN; only admit to knowing those foreign authors who were famous for something other than literature or had powerful friends in their corner of the world; always pretend to understand less than they did, grope for the most basic words, insist that people explain the simplest concepts until they started to doubt them; talk endlessly about books and literature when the subject of conversation was neither books nor literature, express admiration for the inferiority complex that motivated the Nobel Laureate Halldór Kiljan Laxness and the repressed megalomania of the proletarian poet Steinn Steinarr, become patrons of young artists and laugh along at their criticisms of themselves and other men of destiny with pretensions to write, be moved to tears in the presence of the grand old men of art and award them prize money in gratitude for their life's work, only associate with artists who had made money from their work, and, above all, never for one moment be ashamed of their own short stories and poems published in school magazines but refer to them with an indulgent smile as 'experiments', leaving their audience with the impression that they'd had the potential to be a great writer, and, ultimately, rest assured in the belief that the literature that really mattered was not composed on paper, or contained within the covers of books, or painted on linen with a brush, or engraved in granite, or carved in wood, or spoken or sung, no, it was created from concrete and steel, from election results and economic statistics, from the celebrations of one's supporters, the satisfaction of one's shareholders and the hatred of one's political or business rivals, though if one of their circle ever became a real author he would occupy a special place among his old friends who would make sure he always gave them a signed copy of his latest book; they would buy six, seven, even eighteen copies as Christmas presents for their most important members of staff, thereby reminding everyone that they themselves had literary talent, though they no longer used it for writing but for succeeding in other fields where it gave them an edge over all the talentless mediocrities; the author among them would always be celebrated, especially every ten years when they met up for reunion drinks at the home of whoever was richest at the time, chuckling over their literary efforts as sixth-formers, yes, the author would always be the one who had taken the path that, deep down, the others had known all along they would have to reject, due to pressure from families or girlfriends, due to gnawing doubts about whether their talents would be up to making the grade outside the school walls . . .

Most of the members of the Secret Poets' Society – as they had privately called themselves since they only published in the school magazine under pseudonyms, sometimes several different ones, and always tongue-in-cheek – subsequently went in for law, though one or two read economics with an eye to a political career on the right. They suffered from the fact that two years before them at school there had been five writers who had enjoyed instant success in carving out a place for themselves in the city's cultural life. Two of these writers had, at eighteen and nineteen, got poems and short stories published in respected literary journals, three had read out their works at meetings of the young socialists or gatherings of protestors against the Keflavík NATO base, and were sometimes to be seen sitting around in cafés with famous poets. They had all got drunk with Dagur Sigurdarson, both in the old cemetery and on the slopes of Öskjuhlíd, one had handed Sigfús Dadason a packet of cigarettes he had dropped on the floor of Kaffi Mokka, two had come off worse in arm-wrestling contests with Thor Vilhjálmsson, and the fifth had taken part in the protest march from Keflavík, walking for half an hour beside two men who appeared to be none other than the celebrated 'atom poets' Einar Bragi and Jón Óskar.

Einar Bragi: You haven't got very good shoes on.

Young poet: No, nah, no . . .

Einar Bragi: We've still got another twenty kilometres to march, you know.

Young poet: Oh, er . . .

Einar Bragi: You're brave, if you ask me.

Young poet: Er, yes . . .

Einar Bragi: Did you come out like that, with no gloves, in nothing but a thin coat?

Young poet: I, er, I wanted to do my bit.

Einar Bragi: There's a bus accompanying the march, you know.

Young poet: Is there?

Einar Bragi: They've got hot chocolate and doughnuts. There's nothing wrong with taking a breather there.

Young poet: Thanks, I'll check, er, check it out . . .

Einar Bragi (turning to Jón Óskar): He came out dressed like that, in patent-leather shoes and a trench coat.

Jón Óskar: You don't say?

The following summer he was given a French kiss by the writer Gudbergur Bergsson at the Naust Bar.

The five's status was later cemented by the critic on the *People's Will* who, in his round-up of the year's literary offerings, mentioned two of them in his list of promising young writers. The fact that he referred to them as young writers rather than schoolboy writers was proof that they had succeeded in getting one foot on the bottom rung of the literary ladder. And as only one of the two who'd been published was mentioned in the article, it was generally acknowledged by their fellow pupils that the other three who had not been named in the article must share the same rung of the ladder and therefore qualified as young writers too.

Instead of competing with their predecessors on the pages of the school magazine and publishing poems, stories and one-act plays under their real names, the geneticist and his friends in the Secret Poets' Society had adopted odd, even silly, pseudonyms, in the hope of creating a dissonance between the quality of the writing and the name of the author. In the hope of attracting more attention so that people – the people who scoured school magazines in search of brilliant new talent – would say things like: 'Horse Horseson is no less a poet than S—', 'I find Sing Sing Ri's stories much funnier than Th—'s', 'That monologue by Astrolabe is brilliant, far superior to P—'s stuff', and so on. The geneticist had published under the names Apollo XVIII and Chair Black. But it was all in vain; none of the secret poets ever amounted to anything other than what their name suggested, poets in secret.

As the son of a well-known Communist, the geneticist was the black sheep among this group of boys from bourgeois families, and they thought they were being very daring to admit him as a friend. His childhood home had been frequented by almost all the big names on the left, academics and editors, union leaders and members of parliament, composers and authors, his father having at one time or another interviewed them for newspaper or radio, composed speeches for them, or written positive reviews of their work. The geneticist played this down to his friends, not wanting them to know how he had drunk in every word these geniuses and men of destiny had said, practising their voices and gestures when alone in his room or walking to school.

The decisive moment in his writing career came the morning he casually left the newly published school magazine lying around on the kitchen table in the hope that his eldest brother would read it. On page twenty-one, on the right-hand side, a little above the middle, there was a poem called 'Homecoming', printed in a black-framed box and attributed to a poet named Donald Drake. His brother took the bait. The geneticist tried to hide his suspense as he watched his brother turning the pages with his left hand while shovelling down porridge with his right. Both his elder brothers had been editors of the magazine in their day, the brother now leafing through it had at one time been the sixth member of the aforementioned group of five writers: 'Before they degenerated into an aesthetic freak-show'. He was now a star student in the university's Icelandic department.

The geneticist bent over his porridge bowl and pretended to eat. His brother's jaws slowed their chewing whenever something in the magazine caught his eye, and appeared to slow almost to a standstill when he reached the poem on page twenty-one.

* * *

HOMECOMING

When to our origins we return
'tis to find the farm fallen into ruin.
The well water foul. The oak dead.

But one can still throw oneself off the roof.
Still drown oneself in the well.
And in the oak we spy a branch and know
'twill hold our weight.

Home! Ah yes,
We were fated to find our way home.

* * *

When his brother had finished both magazine and porridge, and got up from the kitchen table without saying a word, the geneticist couldn't contain himself any longer. What did he think of the magazine? Did he think the editors had done a good job? The piece about the state church was all right, wasn't it? And the interview with Atli Heimir Sveinsson? It was about time the school magazine interviewed a modern composer, wasn't it?

Sure, his brother agreed there was some OK stuff in there, though the article on the church could have been harder-hitting, and some of the material was a bit childish for his taste. What about the poems? The one on page twenty-one, for example? The geneticist bit his tongue, afraid he had said too much. The student of Icelandic picked up the magazine and flicked through until he came to the framed 'Homecoming', skim-read the poem as if he hadn't noticed it the first time round, then said without even pausing to think:

'French existential angst. Third-rate pastiche of Sigfús Dadason.'

The geneticist belches. Tipping the glass, he pours the precious whisky into his cupped left hand, raises it to his lips and laps it like a cat.

— I myself went to medical school. No Icelandic poet had taken Man as his medium before, literally composing from flesh and blood. There was no danger of my being compared to anyone else; they'd all be third-rate pastiches of me. The Icelanders would learn that it was possible to win a Nobel Prize for more than just literature . . .

V

~~Adolescence and Teens~~

(4 September 1972–23 Octo~~December~~ ~~1995~~ 2012)

THE SAGA OF BRYNHILDUR HELGADÓTTIR – PART TWO

When she thought back over the last four years of her life, the years on the streets, the years in the gutter, they seemed far easier to understand than her life up to the day she had walked out of the home she shared with Thorlákur 'Preacher' Röykdal and taken to sleeping rough.

Thorlákur had raised her up during a revival meeting at Reykjavík's Philadelphia Church and a week later baptised her into her new life in Christ. To make their relationship acceptable in the eyes of God and the pious congregation – he was a childless widower in his fifties, a bank clerk and influential member of the Pentecostal Movement, she a twenty-nine-year-old mother who'd had a baby at seventeen with an American soldier, a son she had brought up more or less single-handedly in the barracks slum that had once been his father's army camp, a son she had recently lost (why don't we have a special word for a mother who has lost her child?), all the evidence suggesting that he had been murdered by kids his own age, not that anyone cared about getting to the bottom of the case because Kiddi was tainted by his connection to the Yanks and the camp, while the kids under suspicion came from good homes – they got married exactly thirty days after Thorlákur had immersed Brynhildur in the baptismal font and both had felt the electricity zinging through the holy water between their robed bodies.

It all happened at the same breathless pace as the famously inspired sermons that used to pour, fully formed, from Thorlákur's lips, like a waterfall tumbling over a rocky crag, with furious haste, above all with haste, like a torrent that testifies to its power with a deep booming roar, only to break up into a chaos of splishing and splashing as it enters the plunge pool, whirling up from the surface in a shower of spray, as if intending in defiance of gravity to flow back up the falls, as bizarre and incomprehensible, mesmerising and alarming as the conclusions to his sermons that almost invariably culminated in the preacher speaking in tongues, laughing and weeping in the language of angels, before eventually collapsing on the floor, overwhelmed by his own eloquence and the power of the Holy Spirit. Brynhildur's life with the man of God was to follow a similar pattern.

The first six months were a happy time. She was a married woman, the wife of the bank clerk Thorlákur Röykdal, who handled hundreds of thousands of krónur by day and in the evenings meta-morphosed into a big-time shepherd of souls. She moved into his three-room apartment in a house on Thórsgata. Her old neighbour-hood. Living room, bedroom, kitchen, bathroom and study: she hadn't lived this comfortably since she was turfed out of her father's house when Kiddi was two years old. The congregation rejoiced with them and Brynhildur thought how nice it was that women and men, ordinary members and elders, should take such a keen interest in their marriage, telling her more than once how relieved they were that Thorlákur had a woman by his side again. The only shadow over their happiness was his insistence that nothing in the flat could be changed: she wasn't to alter a single thing, everything was to remain exactly as it had always been. But it was a small, pale shadow, since Brynhildur's possessions amounted to no more than three changes of clothes, a coat, a pair of walking shoes, an evening dress and a pair of high heels, which were easily accom-modated inside the wardrobe beside the clothes that had belonged to Sveina Röykdal, Thorlákur's first wife. The two photographs – one of Kiddi at six years old, the other of herself with her parents and brother Ásgeir – could go on the night table between the couple's beds since they were small enough to fit on 'her side'. 'His side' had room for no such fripperies, only a heavily thumbed Bible and a magnifying glass.

Then, quite without warning, the good days came to an end, to be succeeded by four months of celibacy, rows and increasingly odd behaviour on the preacher's part.

The beginning of the end came when a neighbour of Brynhildur's from the camp – the woman who had dragged her along to that first revival meeting in an attempt to ease her grief at the loss of her son – drew her aside and suggested she ask Thorlákur about Anna. Anna? Yes, Anna, ask him about Anna from Skjaldarstadir. So, when she and Thorlákur got home after church, Brynhildur asked if he knew a woman called Anna.

Of course, he knew any number of them, Anna was such a common name. Yes, so did she, but did he know Anna from Stóru-Skjaldarstadir? What kind of question was that? Where had she got hold of her name? Someone in the congregation had mentioned her. Oh, well, if people had started talking to her about Anna, it wasn't exactly a secret that Thorlákur had been married to her. Married? Was he a widower twice over then? Yes, yes, he was, he had lost two wives, but Anna wasn't one of them. He and Anna had got divorced and she had moved back to the countryside, to take over the farm at Stóru-Skjaldarstadir. It was a bad business, a very bad business, but with the help of God and the congregation he had got over it. He had wanted to protect Brynhildur, to spare her from having to hear such a regrettable tale. But what about the third wife, who was the third wife, the one who'd died; where had she fitted in? Oh, he'd rather not talk about that, but seeing as he was in confessional mode, yes, her name was Helga. It was a sad story. At this point Thorlákur burst into tears and couldn't speak for sobbing. He wept inconsolably, fending off Brynhildur's questions until, without warning, he got a grip on himself, seized her by the wrist and led her into the bedroom where he pushed her down on her knees. They would pray for Sveina, Helga and Anna, pray for themselves, appeal to the Lord to heal the cracks in their marriage.

Brynhildur resigned herself to learning nothing more from Thorlákur about the vanished women who had left no trace of ever having lived in the flat – any more than she left any trace of her presence there now – since it was, in the end, still the home of Sveina

Röykdal, the only one of the preacher's wives considered worthy of taking his Norwegian-Faroese family name. Besides, Brynhildur could easily get the whole story from her old neighbour. More unexpected were the repercussions for her marriage. Up to now Brynhildur had had no reason to complain about Thorlákur's performance in bed. His sexual appetite was every bit as voracious as she had imagined or dared hope – it was common gossip among Icelandic women that men of God were lecherous types, presumably because all the spiritual good works they did among sinners resulted in a tension below the waist; after all, there has to be a balance in everything. But after the prayer session in the bedroom where Thorlákur had lain with three other women before Brynhildur, he lost interest in her. And she knew he was bound to look elsewhere.

No, that wasn't when the bad times began. They began when her brother Ásgeir was murdered – yes, her marriage to Thorlákur was bracketed by two deaths, the murders of Kiddi and Ásgeir – and she got a reputation in town for being one of those women who are adopted by bad luck at an early age: not only had she lost her brother and son at the hands of murderers but her mother had drowned herself when Brynhildur was fourteen years old; and in the camp she and little Kiddi had lived for a while with a violent thug who aspired to be a poet, before shacking up first with a depressive milk-lorry driver and later with a morphine addict who'd been stripped of his pharmacist's licence.

Although the murderer had been caught when Ásgeir exposed him at a séance (the guilty man turned out to be a former champion athlete and stamp collector who had coveted the victim's priceless collection) and the case had been solved, the wagging tongues increasingly got to her. Brynhildur began to feel as if the abominable crime were somehow her fault:

Why was she still alive when those dearest to her met with such horrible fates?

This bitter question soured the warm memories she had of the years when her mother had been alive. Before, she had always been able to take refuge in these memories but now she saw in the distorting mirror of discontent that she, her mother and Ásgeir had been no better than servants in her father's house. Their entire life at number

9 Lokastígur had revolved around making sure that the antiquarian Helgi Steingrímsson had sufficient room for his enormous bulk and his grandiose ambitions for the great work he laboured over from morning to night, which was to twist a cable from the Icelandic sagas, create a power-line that would connect the modern Icelanders to their thundering source, harness the energy of the original settlers, men who had boldly looked kings and revenants in the eye; he would charge his countrymen with the electric current of literature and self-reliance; he would shape an independent nation from these feeble first drafts. The least his family could do was keep out of his way.

Was he handsome? Was he amusing? Was he good on the dance floor? How could the dainty, fun-loving Sóley 'Álftavatn's Sun' Brynjarsdóttir have married the troll and monomaniac Helgi Steingrímsson, only to wither away in his shadow? Her mother had provided no answers. And now Brynhildur was asking herself the same questions about her marriage to Thorlákur, though she was built like a valkyrie and he like a sparrow.

Regardless of how or when the rot had set in, their marriage ended the evening that Thorlákur Röykdal preached the sermon on Christ and the fallen woman, shooting a look at his wife Brynhildur every time the words 'fallen woman' blasted from his lips.

Four years had passed.

It was a late evening in December. Brynhildur was battling the north wind on the road to Kleppur. Her coat soaked up the icy sleet until it was sodden. Heavy lumps of the stuff slid down her bare legs into her boots. To her right, she could see a light shining in the window of the Aged Seamen's Retirement Home. Brynhildur faltered. There was someone on night duty. Perhaps she should seek shelter there, borrow their phone to call the emergency services and ask to be picked up? Or beg a bed from them and continue her journey in the morning? No, they'd only notify the police and she'd be forced to spend the night in the cells where she was bound to encounter some of her friends and end up going straight out on the razzle in the morning. That mustn't happen. She couldn't be sure of ever sobering up enough to seek help again.

Between the curtains of driving sleet, Brynhildur glimpsed the white buildings of the mental hospital.

Life on the edge was one of unrelieved monotony. The day she took to the streets, she had simply shoved the stamp collection she'd inherited from Ásgeir into a bag, gone to the lunchtime bar at the City Hotel and got pissed. That had led to a party, then back to the bar, then to another party and straight back to the bar the following lunchtime, day after day after day. It didn't matter what day of the week it was, whether it was twelve noon or twelve midnight, there was always a party on somewhere. In this company she was Biddí, famed for her ability to drink men of all shapes, sizes and social classes under the table, for her ability to party for a week at a time without needing so much as a hint of amphetamine. She crashed out wherever the fun was taking place, waking sometimes in an armchair, sometimes in the host's bed, sometimes in a hotel room, sometimes on an office floor, sometimes in the back seat of a car. So passed the first twenty months of Brynhildur's life among Reykjavík's party set. By then she had drunk all the profits from the stamps and Biddí had nothing to contribute to the fun but herself. The venues became ever seedier, the hosts more inhuman, participation more dearly bought, but when she took the Miltown Meprobamate pills on top of the *brennivín*, the pain, whether mental or physical, went away.

In the end there was only one place left where she could be sure of a bed for the night without having to pay for it with her body – apart from the Salvation Army hostel that provided shelter for all those not visibly drunk or stoned – and that was at the home of a man Brynhildur knew nothing about, who luckily (more importantly) knew nothing about her. He lived alone in the basement of a handsome house on Ingólfsstræti. One bitterly cold Sunday morning in February he had found her lying unconscious by the garden wall and helped her into his warm flat. He hadn't asked any questions then or later. Whenever she knocked on his door he let her in without a word, lent her a dressing gown and towel, made her soup or heated up the leftovers of his supper while she had a wash and rinsed out her clothes, then made up a bed for her in the sitting room, ate an early breakfast with her and slipped two or three 100-krónur notes into her pocket before she left. The entrance to the basement was round the back of the house, so she could come and go unseen, so long as she made sure she arrived after midnight and left before dawn. Not that he had requested this, but she was sure the house-owner, whoever he was, wouldn't appreciate visits from a woman of the sort she had become.

There was a white-enamelled sign screwed to the front door that read 'Jón Jónsson, ceramicist' in blue, sloping script. She didn't know if that was his real name. The man spoke with a foreign accent. He had books in Icelandic, German and Hebrew and a lot of ceramic figurines from Midgardur. On the patch of lawn that belonged to the basement he kept a black nanny-goat. Had she known any words of his mother tongue, Brynhildur would have described him as *ein Mensch*.

Try as she might, she couldn't remember where she had been from the middle of November to December of 1961. None of her drinking companions when asked could remember either. Someone claimed she had boarded a trawler and ended up in Akureyri on the north coast, where she had walked through a glass door at Hótel KEA and crashed out at the home of the poet Davíd Stefánsson from Fagriskógur, until eventually she was injected with a sedative and escorted back to Reykjavík by the police – which could well have been true, had she not heard the same story told about the time she'd had a two-week blackout the year before.

At the end of January 1962 she began to worry that she was pregnant and, not long afterwards, her fears were confirmed. The symptoms were the same as when she'd been carrying Kiddi. At first she looked after herself, ate for two, quit smoking, drank only wine, but before long she'd slipped into her bad old ways. As soon as her bump began to show, she stopped visiting her benefactor at 10a Ingólfsstræti. Yet it was to him that she turned at four o'clock in the morning on 27 August, and there that she gave birth to the child at five past eleven. Through the haze of pain brought on by the contractions she thought she saw two other men in the basement: one was a black man standing two metres tall, the other spoke Russian.

After sleeping for forty-eight hours she got up from her childbed, pulled on her clothes and emerged into the living room. Jón Jónsson was alone. He was sitting by a cradle made from a pink hatbox, aiming a bottle of milk inside. From the cradle came the mewing of a baby. Brynhildur looked away. She went out into the hall, took her coat from the peg, pulled on her boots and opened the front door. After a moment's hesitation she called back to the man:

'I'll register you as the boy's father.'

She never came back.

Less than four months after giving birth, Brynhildur is standing at the turn-off to the Kleppur Mental Hospital. She decides to take a short cut and head straight across country to the main reception instead of trudging along the exposed road that describes a wide bend over the marsh. But when she steps off the road and begins to pick her way over the rough ground, she loses her footing in the slush and before she can stop herself she has fallen flat on her back and is sliding down a slope she hadn't realised was there. In the fall she loses her boots.

She starts struggling forwards again on hands and knees in the direction of the hospital and by cutting diagonally across the slope, manages to crawl all the way to where she can see the staff accommodation at the top. Then she begins to drag herself back up to the road but with every metre's height she gains, she slides back two.

Her last conscious thought is:

I'm not bloody dying here in the mud by the loony bin.

* * *

Aleta smooths out the crumpled front page of the Monday paper from December 1962.

'Here it is among your things.'

She holds it up so Jósef can't help but see what it says:

Dead woman found by asylum still unidentified.

The Dance

A spotlight falls on to the stage from the right, drawing a bright line on the black floor.

Girl: 12 January 1962 – † 13 January 1962, Girl: 13 January 1962 – † 13 January 1962, Girl: 21 January 1962 – † 21 January 1962, Boy: 24 February 1962 – † 27 February 1962, Boy: 1 March 1962 – † 14 April 1962, Girl: 13 May 1962 – † 14 May 1962, Girl: 13 May 1962 – † 17 May 1962, Girl: 5 May 1962 – † 21 May 1962, Boy: 7 May 1962 – † 25 May 1962, Girl: 19 May 1962 – † 26 May 1962, Girl: 27 May 1962 – † 27 May 1962, Girl: 28 May 1962 – † 29 May 1962, Boy: 22 June 1962 – † 23 June 1962, Boy: 27 June 1962 – † 30 June 1962, Boy: 10 February 1962 – † 11 July 1962, Girl: 30 April 1962 – † 11 July 1962, Boy: 10 February 1962 – † 16 July 1962, Boy: 16 July 1962 – † 16 July 1962, Boy: 9 July 1962 – † 18 July 1962, Girl: 19 July 1962 – † 19 July 1962, Boy: 31 July 1962 – † 31 July 1962, Girl: 1 August 1962 – † 1 August 1962, Boy: 29 March 1962 – † 3 August 1962, Boy: 9 July 1962 – † 4 August 1962, Girl: 13 February 1962 – † 7 August 1962, Boy: 1 July 1962 – † 18 August 1962, Boy: 17 August 1962 – † 20 August 1962, Girl: 3 September 1962 – † 3 September 1962, Boy: 1 October 1962 – † 6 October 1962, Boy: 18 November 1962 – † 18 November 1962, Boy: 27 November 1962 – † 27 November 1962, Boy: 18 December 1962 – † 18 December 1962, Girl: 16 December 1962 – † 23 December 1962, Boy: 19 November 1962 – † ? 1963, Girl: 27 July 1962 – † 9 February 1963, Girl: 8 August 1962 – † 14 February 1963, Girl: 30 March 1962 – † 16 February 1963, Girl: 21 October 1962 – † 3 March 1963, Boy: 1 August 1962 – † 1 April 1963, Boy: 7 June 1962 – † 4 April 1963, Girl: 27 February 1962 – † 10 April 1963, Boy: 9 February 1962 – † 15 April 1963, Boy: 11 November 1962 – † 1 May 1963, Girl: 3 December 1962 – † 14 May 1963, Girl: 30 June 1962 – † 16 May 1963,

Boy: 19 July 1962 – † 8 August 1963, Boy: 11 December 1962 – † 3 October 1963, Boy: 5 February 1962 – † 26 October 1963, Girl: 29 May 1962 – † 26 October 1963, Boy: 6 May 1962 – † 14 November 1963, Boy: 14 January 1962 – † 16 July 1964, Boy: 10 February 1962 – † 4 September 1964, Boy: 30 July 1962 – † 30 September 1964, Girl: 1 July 1962 – † 18 October 1964, Boy: 10 May 1962 – † 5 January 1965, Girl: 6 August 1962 – † 18 February 1965, Girl: 4 October 1962 – † 9 October 1965, Boy: 24 June 1962 – † 14 November 1965, Boy: 9 February 1962 – † 23 December 1965, Girl: 9 August 1962 – † 13 January 1966, Boy: 29 October 1962 – † 10 July 1966, Girl: 10 November 1962 – † 20 December 1966, Boy: 8 February 1962 – † 10 January 1968, Girl: 12 January 1962 – † 18 February 1968, Boy: 7 September 1962 – † 30 September 1968, Boy: 24 August 1962 – † 8 April 1969, Boy: 22 November 1962 – † 12 May 1969, Boy: 23 December 1962 – † 26 December 1969, Boy: 24 March 1962 – † 1 October 1970, Boy: 22 February 1962 – † 17 November 1970, Girl: 7 August 1962 – † 29 January 1971, Boy: 14 March 1962 – † 10 March 1971, Boy: 16 April 1962 – † 4 April 1971, Boy: 19 June 1962 – † 10 October 1971, Boy: 15 December 1962 – † 26 December 1971, Boy: 17 June 1962 – † 12 March 1972 . . .

Ten adolescents appear in the wings, three girls aged twelve to fifteen, five boys the same age and two boys in their eleventh year. They step out on to the stage, in the order they died, treading the carpet of light up to the platform, where they climb the steps and take up position, one step behind the children who are there before them.

The first are two boys who died after long battles with terminal illness. One is carrying a book called *Return of the Yellow Shadow* that he hadn't quite finished, the other is holding the unused football he'd been given for the summer he would never see.

Boy: 10 May 1962 – † 18 January 1973
Boy: 11 October 1962 – † 30 March 1973

A girl and two boys follow close on their heels. The boy in the lead had also been struggling with illness and was undergoing rehabilitation, in the belief that he was on the mend, when his body gave up the fight. Next comes a girl who died one spring day in her home district, though only a month before she had been noticeably radiant at a get-together. The third, a boy who was crushed under a stack of radiators during a game of hide and seek in the goods yard on Eidsgrandi, walks with a limp but shows no other ill effects.

>*Boy: 7 April 1962 – † 29 January 1974*
>*Girl: 19 April 1962 – † 26 March 1974*
>*Boy: 23 September 1962 – † 28 August 1974*

Then a boy and a girl enter, of thirteen and fourteen years old. He was killed by a stray pellet from his drunken father's shotgun. She died in an accident while on a trip to Denmark.

>*Boy: 28 December 1962 – † 7 July 1976*
>*Girl: 10 September 1962 – † 17 November 1976*

Finally, the oldest members of this group walk the carpet of light. One boy died of exposure on New Year's Eve. The second fell off the back of a pick-up when his twelve-year-old playmate started the engine and drove off. The girl was killed when she accidentally fell from a balcony in Spain, a month after her fifteenth birthday.

>*Boy: 6 December 1962 – † 1 January 1977*
>*Boy: 22 November 1962 – † 27 June 1977*
>*Girl: 22 July 1962 – † 28 August 1977*

Once they are all assembled on stage there is a moment's silence. The younger children wait for their elders to take the lead. Then the eldest girl looks at the boy at her side. He nods and together they say, like a couple of teachers on a disco-dancing course:
— One-two-three . . .
And the other eight chime in:
— Dear brothers and sisters, born in 1962, we await you here.
The chorus's tone is tinged with the general air of scepticism that characterises adolescence.

Jósef Loewe buries his face in his hands.

'The poor woman, the poor bloody woman.'

Looking up, he asks in a choked voice:

'What about my father? Wasn't he my father after all?'

'Jón Jónsson is registered as your father.'

'Does it give any other details about him?'

'He was born in the Austro-Hungarian Empire, held a Czechoslovakian passport when he came to Iceland in the summer of 1944, took Icelandic citizenship in March 1958, and died in 1994.'

'Thank God, it's true then. What do they say his name was?'

'Leo Loewe. Spelled in brackets as L-o-e-w.'

Jósef mutters into his hands:

'Yes, yes, yes, yes.'

He wipes the tears from his eyes.

'I thought for a minute that you were going to say my whole story was a figment of my imagination, that I don't even exist myself, that I'm nothing more than a twinkle in God's eye, as the little children say.'

He smiles weakly, swallowing the lump in his throat.

'Yes, or your own imagination.'

Aleta lays a hand on the stone man's pale, misshapen arm.

'Then we'd be figments of each other's imagination.'

Her words come out more affectionately than intended. Jósef stiffens. Withdrawing his arm, he stares out into the kitchen, then, after a long pause, says without looking at her:

'I'm no fool.'

Aleta is silent. Jósef points to the picture of his mother.

'Take it . . .'

She does as he asks, picking up the picture from the table where she had put it down while making the brandy coffee.

'Take it out of the frame.'

Jósef watches Aleta turn the frame over, run the blue-varnished nail of her index finger under the copper clips and open them up. She frees the back of the frame. Under the speckled card is a piece of waxed paper. She removes this and lifts the picture of Jósef's mother off the glass. It turns out to be a cutting from page ten of *Morgunbladid* from Saturday, 15 September 1962. It has been folded so the picture will fit into the frame, with the accompanying text still attached. Aleta unfolds the cutting, smooths it out and looks enquiringly at Jósef.

He nods. She reads.

* * *

**Quick Catch-up with María in Reykjavík
en route from New York to Paris**

María Gudmundsdóttir, Miss Iceland 1961, made a stopover in Iceland last week, spending a few days at home with her parents, on her way from the United States, where, as readers will know, she recently took part in the Miss International competition at Long Beach. On Friday she continued her journey to Paris, where she has been working for the last year as a sought-after model, with her picture appearing in all the biggest fashion magazines. She plans to work for the Paris-based Dorian Leigh Parker modelling agency until Christmas, and has agreed to write a fashion column for *Morgunbladid* with news from the city of *haute couture*.

— *Obviously not just anyone can make it as a model in a competitive environment like Paris. How did you get your break and start sitting for photographers there?* we asked María, when we met her at home for a quick chat.

— Luck, really. I was on my way back from a modelling tour of South America and stopped over in Paris. Two days before I was due to go home, I went to the hairdresser's and a woman came over and asked if I was a photographer's model. I said no, and she asked me if

I'd be interested in becoming one. I said I was on my way home and couldn't give her an answer straight away. She turned out to be Dorian Leigh Parker, who runs a big agency supplying models for magazines. She asked me to come and see her next day at her office. There she introduced me to an agent from Coca-Cola, who wanted me to model for them. And I realised I had nothing to lose by accepting the offer, even if I went home first.

— *Since then one thing's led to another. What's the work like? Well paid?*

— Yes, it's well paid, and I really enjoy it. Being a photographic model is quite different from doing the fashion shows. The catwalk girls work during the day, we work at night when they're not using the clothes for shows. For example, I was working from nine in the evening to seven or eight in the morning for the last two weeks before the competition at Long Beach, and sometimes during the day too, if the clothes were available.

— *Does each photo shoot take a long time?*

— It depends. Photographers fall into two groups. Some take loads of pictures to choose from, others make you pose and that can take a long time. The longest I've sat for a single picture was nine hours.

— *It can be tiring, then. Isn't it a bit cold too, posing in summer clothes before summer's arrived?*

— Yes, at the beginning of February, for example, they took some of us north to the coast where it was snowy until ten in the morning, and there we were in our swimming costumes. But the photographers tried to be quick, so we wouldn't catch cold.

— *You say you're going to leave your job in Paris before Christmas?*

— Yes, I'm not spending another Christmas away from home. I was in Mexico last year and spent the whole of Christmas and New Year ill in bed in my hotel room. But in the middle of January I'm going to New York where I've been hired as a photographic model by Eileen Ford's agency, with an open contract. I met her and signed the contract on my way from the Miss International competition at Long Beach. I spent a week with her and she invited me out to her country house on Long Island. There's a beach there and it was lovely and relaxing after all the fuss around the beauty pageant.

— *That must have been a fun trip?*

— Yes, I was very pleased with the trip and grateful to get the chance to go. I came back loaded with all kinds of gifts. There was always a lot going on, too much really. For five days before the competition began we were rushing around all over the place to parties and so on, from seven in the morning until ten or twelve at night. There wasn't a single girl who didn't have black circles under her eyes by the time the contest began. Miss France came off worst. She was so overwhelmed with exhaustion that she kept fainting.

— *You mean genuinely fainting?*

— Yes, she didn't sort of sink down elegantly but keeled over with a crash and bruised herself, sometimes in front of thousands of people. Once I fell asleep at a breakfast party at seven in the morning. We were supposed to stand up and give a speech but when it came to my turn they had to send someone to nudge me. I just sat there, with my eyes open apparently, totally oblivious. But the whole thing went well. And it was good to have this practice run before the contest itself. For instance, before that I was terrified of having to stand up and give a speech, but I'd got used to it by the time the big day came.

— *One last thing. Are French men as charming as they say?*

— They come in all sorts. There are some charmers among them but sadly not for me because so many of them are really small.

— *Do American men appeal to you more, then?*

— They're more my size, though they're not generally as charming as the French. The men from these two countries are different types altogether.

As mentioned above, María left the country on Friday morning. We wish her a good journey and look forward in due course to seeing her news reports from Paris, the city of fashion.

* * *

'My father so loved me, his only son, that he tried to make up for my lack of a mother by giving me a photograph of the woman considered the most beautiful in Iceland, if not the world, in the year I was born.

María Gudmundsdóttir, María X, Maria Gudy. I must have been nine when I realised that it was she, and no other, who awaited me on the bedside table when I awoke, she who accompanied me into my dreams at night, not my real mother. In the loft at Ingólfsstræti there was a chest full of old weekly magazines, mostly copies of *Vikan* and *Fálkinn*. Back when I could still get up to the loft without help, I spent countless rainy summer days there while my father was at work. As long as there was no one home in the attic flat, I could pull down the loft ladder, climb up, and drag it up after me, all without being seen.

For hours at a time I would sit, legs outstretched, under the diamond-shaped, south-facing dormer window, turning the pages, lapping up articles about the latest fashions in clothes and music (mini-skirts and space-age chic, Beatles-inspired bands), culture and the arts (the Icelanders' fight to bring their manuscripts home from Denmark, the madness of Salvador Dalí), international scandals and domestic politics (Profumo in Britain, controversy over the relocation of a bridge in Thingeyjar county), horoscopes and jokes (unexpected journeys and windfalls, mothers-in-law with rolling pins), as well as trying to make sense of the letters sent in to agony aunts and the answers they received. Of all the things I read, the most alien to me were the everyday problems of ordinary folk who signed their letters with nicknames such as Binni, Sissí, Lalli, Ninna, Frída from Brú, Siggi from Kópavogur, or "Yours in a fix" and "Yours undecided"; girlfriends were moody, husbands uninterested, daughters and sons disobedient, friends disloyal, engagements broken off without warning, proposals slow to come. Nothing in my life with my father shed any light on these pleas for help with relationship or family problems. I don't remember him ever bringing a woman home or anything in his behaviour to suggest that he had intimate relations with women outside the home. He never went anywhere and I'm sure I met more women than he did: at my nursery, at school and later in hospital.

My closest brush with the sort of thing that cropped up in these micro-stories about love and life was one time when Halldóra Oktavía climbed up to join me in the loft – it didn't happen often but when it did I felt as if we were children in an adventure story, the two of us together in a murky underground passage, solving a crime, while our faithful dog Sirius stood guard at the cave mouth, ready to bark if our enemies arrived, whether they were assassins dispatched by oriental military powers or the blundering but ruthless henchmen of home-grown crime lords – and suggested we read the problem pages together. This girl of my own age sat down next to me, so close that we touched, and opened *Vikan*, placing the magazine between us so the left-hand page lay on my right thigh and the right on her left thigh. Then she turned the pages back and forth until she found the one marked in feminine script "Dear *Vikan*". Pointing to the first letter, she ordered me to read it aloud; she herself would read the reply. The more magazines Halldóra Oktavía leafed through on our thighs, the redder my cheeks became and the hotter I grew on the side of my body that was touching hers, until the need to pee became so urgent that I leapt to my feet and fled down the ladder.'

Jósef looks at Aleta.

'Am I blushing?'

Aleta studies him for a moment before answering:

'Tuh.'

She shakes her head slowly. He touches his cheeks.

'They're hot. Feel.'

'Tuh, tuh, tuh. You promised me you wouldn't get sentimental, you promised you'd spare me the kind of banal childhood incidents that are so common that everyone has poignant memories of them, regardless of whether they happened to them or not – next thing I know you'll be regaling me with the names of popular brands of sweets taken off the market years ago because they turned out to contain flavourings or colouring agents so toxic that it's a wonder they didn't send generations of children prematurely to their graves; or listing foreign bands with incomprehensible names or short-lived domestic hits, sung in broken English, that no one listens to any more except desperate, middle-aged types at class reunions or recluses who devote whole websites to them and sit up all night trying to find out what ever happened to this or that bass player, the third keyboard player in the Smugglers, the Norwegian female artist who sang the hit "You, Me, You" in some year or other, only to discover that they too are unemployed, disabled or stuck in badly paid, dead-end jobs – working as van drivers, cashiers or dustmen in small towns or villages that have given nothing to the world apart from these faded stars – living for the occasional email from lonely people festering in the backwaters of the world, begging for news of them and saying that their music saved their lives; or telling stories of hanging around by vanished sales kiosks, in darkened computer games shops or video rentals run by middle-aged men who were just waiting for a chance to invite socially disadvantaged kids "round the back" so they could ply them with alcohol and turn them on by showing them porn flicks featuring pets, leather-clad women and German dwarfs; and endless descriptions of trips to the cinema where the inevitable car chase on screen was nothing but a backdrop to the gossiping, panting, cuffing and pinching that went on in the gloom, while over all these reminiscences hangs a shared miasma that none of you noticed at the time: the powerful reek of boys' sweat over-laid with the scent of cheap perfume and lip gloss from the girls.

Your story's on a fast track into the black hole of nostalgia.'

'Wait, you're wrong. My childhood and teens were what you might expect of someone with my growing disability. I don't even have false memories of them. Where was I?'

'All right. The weekly mags.'

'The weeklies. The main attraction for me was the pictures, of course. Photos from all over the world, some in the vibrant colours of the sixties, that decade that seems to have played out under different, brighter, skies than any other time in human history, while others were so grainy and dark that it took me ages to work out what they showed. I soon became hyper-sensitive to the pictures, identifying with them so strongly that I would merge right into them. I would stare at a photo until it began to alter before my eyes, the light becoming suddenly more intense, the subject shifting by a fraction of a millimetre, and I was seized momentarily by the dizzying sensation that I had been present at the moment the shutter clicked. And so the pictures became etched in my memory, lodged in the same part of the brain as my real memories. Of course, it wasn't long before I came across one of the most photographed women in the history of Iceland, María X. The papers were vying with one another to publish pictures of her as she jetted around the world, to Long Beach, Paris and Cairo, as well as reprinting the covers of some of the world's top fashion magazines – and wherever María went, I went too. But I kept quiet about my discovery as I didn't want to put my father on the spot.'

Aleta touches Jósef's shoulder.

'Perhaps she was like her. Brynhildur, I mean. Perhaps she and María looked alike, and that's why Leo chose the picture of her.'

'I want you to know that they did try to get me to continue my education. I lasted a term and a half on an accountancy course in the business department at Breidholt College. The poet Sjón was there at the same time, in the art department. This was in the winter of 1980–81. At that stage he hadn't dropped the dot from his pen-name and still spelled it "S.jón", which a lot of people pronounced "Ess-jón". I remember how it used to get on his nerves. Not that I was part of his circle, but he did sometimes sit at the table nearest the hatch in the school tuck shop, which was where they usually parked my wheel-chair, though it was the busiest spot at break-times and everyone was forced to squeeze past me. But no one complained and I was happy. One morning, not long before I decided I'd had enough of struggling to get my head round all that debit and credit nonsense, I spoke to the young poet who was sitting with his back to me, drinking coffee out of a plastic cup:

— I know who you are. You're Ess-jón.

He shot me a look over his shoulder, ready to snap: "No, actually, it's pronounced Sjón, like the word for 'vision'." But when he realised it was the boy in the wheelchair who had spoken, his expression softened and he simply said:

— Maybe I am. Who are you?

Everyone knew Sjón was a surrealist and follower of the crazy artist Alfred Flóki. There was a rumour going round that earlier that autumn the young poet had eaten a live pigeon in honour of his master during a poetry reading in the assembly hall. So I just said:

— I'm a Ferris wheel, I'm a conch, I'm a sleeping door.

He laughed. The bell rang. And our acquaintance went no further.

A year later Sjón used my answer in a poem called "Paper". I expect he'd forgotten that he hadn't come up with the idea himself. So I did make my mark there.'

The Dance

They emerge from the darkness on every side, on to the dimly lit stage, like people at a disco when the band strikes up a tune that gets everyone itching to dance; teenagers now.

Girl: 12 January 1962 – † 13 January 1962, Girl: 13 January 1962 – † 13 January 1962, Girl: 21 January 1962 – † 21 January 1962, Boy: 24 February 1962 – † 27 February 1962, Boy: 1 March 1962 – † 14 April 1962, Girl: 13 May 1962 – † 14 May 1962, Girl: 13 May 1962 – † 17 May 1962, Girl: 5 May 1962 – † 21 May 1962, Boy: 7 May 1962 – † 25 May 1962, Girl: 19 May 1962 – † 26 May 1962, Girl: 27 May 1962 – † 27 May 1962, Girl: 28 May 1962 – † 29 May 1962, Boy: 22 June 1962 – † 23 June 1962, Boy: 27 June 1962 – † 30 June 1962, Boy: 10 February 1962 – † 11 July 1962, Girl: 30 April 1962 – † 11 July 1962, Boy: 10 February 1962 – † 16 July 1962, Boy: 16 July 1962 – † 16 July 1962, Boy: 9 July 1962 – † 18 July 1962, Girl: 19 July 1962 – † 19 July 1962, Boy: 31 July 1962 – † 31 July 1962, Girl: 1 August 1962 – † 1 August 1962, Boy: 29 March 1962 – † 3 August 1962, Boy: 9 July 1962 – † 4 August 1962, Girl: 13 February 1962 – † 7 August 1962, Boy: 1 July 1962 – † 18 August 1962, Boy: 17 August 1962 – † 20 August 1962, Girl: 3 September 1962 – † 3 September 1962, Boy: 1 October 1962 – † 6 October 1962, Boy: 18 November 1962 – † 18 November 1962, Boy: 27 November 1962 – † 27 November 1962, Boy: 18 December 1962 – † 18 December 1962, Girl: 16 December 1962 – † 23 December 1962, Boy: 19 November 1962 – † ? 1963, Girl: 27 July 1962 – † 9 February 1963, Girl: 8 August 1962 – † 14 February 1963, Girl: 30 March 1962 – † 16 February 1963, Girl: 21 October 1962 – † 3 March 1963, Boy: 1 August 1962 – † 1 April 1963, Boy: 7 June 1962 – † 4 April 1963, Girl: 27 February 1962 – † 10 April 1963, Boy: 9 February 1962 – † 15 April 1963, Boy: 11 November 1962 – † 1 May 1963, Girl: 3

December 1962 – † 14 May 1963, Girl: 30 June 1962 – † 16 May 1963, Boy: 19 July 1962 – † 8 August 1963, Boy: 11 December 1962 – † 3 October 1963, Boy: 5 February 1962 – † 26 October 1963, Girl: 29 May 1962 – † 26 October 1963, Boy: 6 May 1962 – † 14 November 1963, Boy: 14 January 1962 – † 16 July 1964, Boy: 10 February 1962 – † 4 September 1964, Boy: 30 July 1962 – † 30 September 1964, Girl: 1 July 1962 – † 18 October 1964, Boy: 10 May 1962 – † 5 January 1965, Girl: 6 August 1962 – † 18 February 1965, Girl: 4 October 1962 – † 9 October 1965, Boy: 24 June 1962 – † 14 November 1965, Boy: 9 February 1962 – † 23 December 1965, Girl: 9 August 1962 – † 13 January 1966, Boy: 29 October 1962 – † 10 July 1966, Girl: 10 November 1962 – † 20 December 1966, Boy: 8 February 1962 – † 10 January 1968, Girl: 12 January 1962 – † 18 February 1968, Boy: 7 September 1962 – † 30 September 1968, Boy: 24 August 1962 – † 8 April 1969, Boy: 22 November 1962 – † 12 May 1969, Boy: 23 December 1962 – † 26 December 1969, Boy: 24 March 1962 – † 1 October 1970, Boy: 22 February 1962 – † 17 November 1970, Girl: 7 August 1962 – † 29 January 1971, Boy: 14 March 1962 – † 10 March 1971, Boy: 16 April 1962 – † 4 April 1971, Boy: 19 June 1962 – † 10 October 1971, Boy: 15 December 1962 – † 26 December 1971, Boy: 17 June 1962 – † 12 March 1972, Boy: 10 May 1962 – † 18 January 1973, Boy: 11 October 1962 – † 30 March 1973, Boy: 7 April 1962 – † 29 January 1974, Girl: 19 April 1962 – † 26 March 1974, Boy: 23 September 1962 – † 28 August 1974, Boy: 28 December 1962 – † 7 July 1976, Girl: 10 September 1962 – † 17 November 1976, Boy: 6 December 1962 – † 1 January 1977, Boy: 22 November 1962 – † 27 June 1977, Girl: 22 July 1962 – † 28 August 1977 . . .

The younger boys are dressed in confirmation outfits, suits made of smooth velvet in shades of bottle brown or navy blue, with flared trousers and wide collars. The older ones are wearing suits bought for other people's special occasions. Two of the girls are wearing new-looking dresses – one is dark blue, the other red with a fine floral print of forget-me-nots – while the third is wearing an ankle-length dress of white cotton with a lace trim, made especially for her funeral.

A mirror ball floats down from the ceiling. Four clicks echo in the darkness and from four different directions long, narrow beams of light pick out the silvery, multi-faceted surface. The ball begins to spin, splintering the beams into hundreds of dazzling spots that whirl around the space, illuminating the faces and bodies of those they encounter among the crowd of children silently watching the newcomers.

It takes the young people a moment to realise that this is no ordinary dance floor. Here they dance to the silence that ensues whenever someone departs this earthly life. Each of them sways to the absence of sound that attends their footsteps and hand claps, to the absence of their voices and intestinal noises, to the absence of all the rustling, splashing, banging and creaking that resulted when their living bodies made contact with the external world, to the absence of their breathing, the absence of their heartbeat.

They tread stiffly at first, their movements hampered by the differing causes or relative recentness of their death, but gradually they limber up.

Boy: 31 January 1962 – † 8 January 1978
Boy: 3 May 1962 – † 17 June 1978
Boy: 6 February 1962 – † 26 July 1978
Boy: 1 May 1962 – † 5 December 1978

Leading the dance is the boy who died in hospital after a long battle with a terminal illness, followed by the boy who disappeared with three others when their flimsy boat capsized in a flat calm while rowing out to an island on National Day – nothing ever washed ashore apart from a single trainer and one of the oars. He is pushing a wheelchair, in which sits a boy who had been seriously handicapped all his life but is now dancing along with the upper half of his body. And a little way behind them, his body undulating in the dance, comes an agile, curly-haired deckhand who was washed overboard from a trawler and sucked down into the cold December sea in the deeps off the West Fjords.

Boy: 15 October 1962 – † 13 May 1979
Boy: 12 July 1962 – † 8 December 1979

Then a boy dances in so fast that nobody would suspect for a minute that his leg had been amputated above the knee in his battle with the disease that had dragged him to his death in less than two years. A moment later their number is swelled by the boy who drowned when his car drove off the docks. In Iceland you can get a driver's licence at seventeen.

Boy: 13 November 1962 – † 23 October 1980

He hesitates on the edge of the blizzard of lights, surveying those already there, including the boy who died in a work-related accident, crushed by a bulldozer during the construction of a hydroelectric power station. He joins the group. But he doesn't dance.

Boy: 31 May 1962 – † 14 January 1981
Girl: 14 July 1962 – † 5 September 1981
Girl: 23 May 1962 – † 23 November 1981

Next to emerge from the shadows are a boy and girl who died in separate car crashes. He enters from stage left, slowly but light of foot; she from the right, swaying her hips, folding her arms at her chest. In her embrace we glimpse the faint image of a boy child, her eighteen-month-old son who died in the same crash. Then another figure enters the stage, as if from another room – though here there is no room apart from the stage itself – another girl, wearing a smile.

Boy: 5 September 1962 – † 10 January 1982
Girl: 6 June 1962 – † 30 January 1982
Boy: 3 October 1962 – † 14 March 1982

The boy who died with his half-brother in a car accident now joins the dance, nineteen years old, the 110th child born in Iceland in 1962 to die. Close on his heels comes the 111th child, a girl who had become a mother herself less than a year before her death. Her body had not only been incubating a child but also the disease that was discovered three weeks after she gave birth. The disease is no more but the child is alive. The last to dance on to the stage this time has just risen from his deathbed in a bunkhouse in a fishing village, where he'd been suffocated by poisonous smoke after a fire broke out in his room. He looks over his shoulder into the darkness. For the moment there is no one else to be seen.

Four clicks. The mirror ball goes dark. The lights come on upstage.

The crowd of children is revealed. The youngsters screw up their eyes, shading them with their hands until they adjust to the light. Yes, they recognise some of the newcomers.

Thirteen voices have been added to the chorus:

— Dear brothers and sisters, born in 1962, we await you here.

A newborn cries.

14

'To be something, to have a status in society, to be born at the centre of things, to live through momentous times, to be part of the world's anthology of stories – if only in the gap between the lines, between the words, between the letters, or even in the minute blank space inside the lower-case "e", just once in that dauntingly long book; could there be any more human desire than that? Don't we all long to be something, to feel that we exist, that others notice our existence, for the brief space of time that we are here? And if you're unlucky enough to be born on the northern periphery of war, whether war conducted on the battlefield of ideas or war that is fought with weapons in the skies, on land and sea, what choice do you have but to employ every trick in the book to write yourself into the history of ideas, to engineer a place for yourself in the great scheme of things, to think your way into human history, to weave yourself into the tapestry of all that exists?

* * *

THE GRAIN

She was known as "Blue Thread". The first time they ever saw her her arms were blue from fingertips to shoulder. The colour started out as midnight blue on her nails, growing progressively lighter the higher it went, becoming crepuscular under her armpits before gradually fading out altogether into milk-white skin. Since it was a summer's day, she was wearing a man's black shirt with the sleeves cut off, which is how everyone could see her arms.

Over her shirt she wore a leather jerkin that came down to mid-thigh, and under this a pair of thick linen hose and rough wooden clogs on her feet. In other words, she was dressed like a male dye-worker – but as she was only eleven years old, and the overseer's daughter to boot, no one took any notice if she wore hose like a boy or skirts like the women. If the girl found it more comfortable to crop her hair and walk around in men's clothes, then she was welcome to, so long as she wrapped a sheet round her legs and donned a headscarf whenever officers of the church came by (to seek her father's advice, for example, on a new, more vivid shade of red for the blood that springs from Christ's body on the Cross, for what could be more wonderful than to see with one's own eyes the glowing vitality in the blood that he shed so that mankind might prosper for all eternity?) or when she was dragged along with her family to social gatherings. It was in the company of her brother dye-workers that people saw her first.

And because, in addition to being blue, the girl's arms were so slender as to be almost ridiculously spindly, though obviously possessing enough wiry strength for her to rival the adolescent boys when it came to lugging tub after tub of newly dyed hanks of wool and silk into the dye-shop, they nicknamed her "Blue Thread".[1]

The name stuck when, two years later, she was taken on at the weaving workshop. It came in useful to have an experienced dyer on site in case the yarn of a particular colour unexpectedly ran out in the middle of an urgent commission. The dye-works where she had

---

[1]   According to Flemish texts of the mid-seventeenth century, which preserve the oldest known versions of the tale of the girl with the blue arms, the origin of her nickname was quite different. The weavers, aware that she was the child of the master dyer, and assuming, from her appearance and clothing, that she was a boy, used to refer to her among themselves as *le fils bleu* or "the blue son". The Icelandic poet Matthías Jochumsson misread this as *le fil bleu* or "the blue thread" in his retelling of the French version of the story, which he published in the third issue of the *Fjallkonan* newspaper in 1889. This is the edition used here. Matthías never got round to revising it and publishing a corrected version, though many readers, including Benedikt Gröndal, had pointed out his mistake.

grown up was a day's journey from the city and stood on the bank of a river that patiently received its dirty run-off, while the evil stench that accompanied the boiling and fermenting of the dyes was blown out to sea by the breeze off the shore at the end of the working day. Blue Thread brought with her sufficient supplies of dyestuffs to last in most cases for the first year or so, but to be on the safe side she acquired for her use a corner of the garden behind the building that housed the weaving workshop, and there, in a series of luxuriant beds, she cultivated plants for the primary colours: woad for blue, madder for red, and a variety of *mignonette* that yields a sunshine yellow, from which three ingredients she knew how to concoct all the 250 shades required by a workshop where such important and costly textiles were produced.

As one might expect, Blue Thread's particular skill lay in the blue dye, and although the colour of her arms faded over the years – they remained as thin as ever even when her body began to thicken out in later life – the range from the darkest to the lightest shades on her skin remained the best point of reference the weavers could ask for when working with this colour, which was more challenging than all the rest, used as it was for the heavens, the home of God and His angels; for the robe of the Blessed Virgin Mary and for her flower, the periwinkle, and for the coats of arms of kings and queens, princes and princesses, who, along with the nobility and the growing burgher estate, were the workshop's principal patrons, ordering tapestries to decorate their halls or as donations to churches and monasteries.

When, after working for five years as the in-house dyer and general saviour of the workshop, Blue Thread turned eighteen, she was finally offered a seat on the weavers' bench. Ahead lay the biggest commission the master weaver had ever undertaken, a series of enormous tapestries, six scenes in the *millefleur* style, depicting a noble virgin with a lion and a unicorn.

The weavers got no wind of the negotiations between the patron, master weaver, designer and artist – in which the cost and make, quality and magnificence, subjects and symbolism, conditions and delivery date of the tapestries were worked out – but as soon as the first watercolour designs reached the workshop, they began to set up the looms, expanding one and lowering another, building two more, spinning the yarn and stretching the warp, calculating the number of hanks of wool and silk required, counting the shuttles and needles, and dividing up the different tasks. From the moment the cartoons were delivered on vast sheets of paper and positioned behind the white warp threads until the textiles were taken down four years later, Blue Thread sat alongside her brother weavers, labouring three days a week, from the clang of the morning bell to the ding of the evening one, while on the other days she took care of the dyes and yarns.

When major works are woven on horizontal looms, the cloth is taken up as you go along, so it disappears under the loom and the weaver never sees any more than the part he or she is working on at any given time. (One could liken this to diners being unable to see anything but the vague outlines of the food on their plates, only the morsel they cut off the cutlet coming into full focus, together with a splash of gravy and the three peas they pushed on to the fork, a type of dining that would seem most disagreeable to the uninitiated.) So it is always a great moment when the cloth-beam is released and the fabric unrolled, allowing people to see the bigger picture. In Blue Thread's day this was done every four months.

In the third year of labour on what was to become one of France's greatest national treasures, displayed to the public in the old monastery of Cluny in Paris under the title of *La Dame à la licorne* (the lion has been forgotten), the patron, Claude Le Viste herself, visited the workshop accompanied by a trio of inspectors armed with a royal charter to confirm their expertise and the authority to unravel any tapestry that did not meet their exacting standards.

The noble lady's visit called for a full-scale clean-up. The workshop was swept and scrubbed from floor to ceiling. Anything shiny was polished until it gleamed. Men and women's better clothes were washed, darned and pressed. The workers bathed themselves and cut, plaited and combed one another's hair. These were good days, filled with hot water, the scent of soap and gales of laughter. Once the inspection was over a banquet was to be held in celebration of passing the test and people couldn't wait. But as the big day approached, the weavers' trepidation grew apace: the inspectors were notoriously hard to please and many months' work would go down the drain if they didn't like what they were shown. To make matters worse, there was no telling how the craftsmen would react to their verdict.

One shouldn't fall into the trap of assuming that weavers are meek or cowardly, simply because they can sit still for hours engaged in what tough types dismiss as mere messing around with rags and twine. (It's true that in photographs weavers often appear a little distracted, perched at their loom – that contrivance of beams, wheels and threads that looks like a half-finished organ with no sides or boards to hide its incomprehensible workings – staring at the camera with a far-off look in their eyes, for their thoughts are all on the cloth in the loom, not on the world that is in that instant directing its gaze at them.) In fact, the complete opposite is true. Of all the creatures on earth the weaver is most akin to the greatest predators, those patient animals who lurk motionless in a rocky cleft on the seabed, silently in a forest thicket or hovering beneath the clouds in the sky, waiting to pounce or swoop on their prey at exactly the right moment.

The weaver's "pounce" can take many years. From the moment the first thread of the weft is pulled through the warp until the final knot is tied, those who "sit at the loom" most closely resemble the owls shown hunting small creatures in slow motion on natural history documentaries:

> The owl releases its grip on the highest branch in the forest and swoops silently through the moonlit night. Down, down to the forest floor where it checks its flight and its yellow claws fasten slowly – ever so slowly – into the soft belly of a buck rabbit. (More about rabbits later.)

We need say no more about the concentration required by the weaver if he is not to lose sight of his goal during the years spent on this "swoop", the strength of will required if he is to control his burning desire to see the finished result. But those who practise the art of weaving also share certain weaknesses with the beasts of prey, their siblings in the animal kingdom, the worst of which is the blind rage that can flare up if they miss their quarry, when all the energy that would otherwise have been balanced out between the "lying in wait", the "pounce" and the "kill" can burst forth in a flash. The royal edict on the regular quality control of weaving workshops therefore contained a clause listing the strict sanctions, fines and prison sentences that were to be imposed on those who used violence, whether verbal or physical, against the inspectors.

Let us now return to the day of the inspection. From the moment the master weaver opened the workshop door with a low bow to admit the noble Claude Le Viste, her handmaidens and fool, poor Blue Thread was consumed with anxiety. She stood at the far end of the room with the other weavers, gripped by a terrible premonition of disaster, for she was aware of a single flaw in her work and two colour solutions that might be considered questionable. More people entered the workshop: the seneschal of the Le Viste family and the local mayor, two guards from the lady's retinue, the mayor's adviser, senior members of the weavers' guild in all their finery, the bishop with a black-clad attendant who kept fiddling with the hilt of a knife he carried at his thigh, and finally the three feared authorities, the inspectors themselves, accompanied by their bodyguard.

The ceremony took its accustomed form, beginning with expressions of humble gratitude and elevated sentiments about the merits of those present, the importance of art for society and of religion for art, the nobility and wisdom of the lady, the mercy of God for allowing it all to happen, and the weather: "Yes, it's bound to clear up soon." "How many weeks has it been?" "Three, four?" Until the lady brought a halt to this tiresome farming talk by relating an anecdote about her oldest monkey, Aakon de Norvège, which had almost drowned after climbing into a vase of flowers, nose first. The ensuing laughter lightened the atmosphere in the workshop and after this the tapestries were spread out for inspection.

The weavers' greatest fear had been that the inspectors would go overboard in their examination in an attempt to impress the lady. But, whether it was thanks to the noble Claude's amusing anecdote about her monkey or simply that the workshop deserved its fame, they were extremely positive that day, lingering only on a single detail. This was the white rabbit that stands on its hind legs, cleaning its face, under the orange tree on the left-hand side of the tapestry that pays homage to the sense of *Smell*. Blue Thread had woven the rabbit in question and all the time they were poring over the little creature with a magnifying glass, she thought she would burst. To keep her feelings in check she kept winding and unwinding a piece of blue wool round the blue forefinger of her blue left hand. Just as she thought she really would burst, the inspectors raised their heads from the tapestry and nodded to Claude Le Viste. Such was Blue Thread's relief at this recognition that she let go of the piece of blue wool, which slipped off her finger and fell to the floor.

At the end of the day, Blue Thread retrieved the piece of wool and put it in her pocket. But such was her agitation that she didn't notice the grain of sand clinging to it. Nor did she notice it the next day when she spun the strand of wool together with another blue thread and wove it into the tapestry. The grain of sand went in too. And right up to the present day there it sits in the magnificent tapestry, invisible to the human eye, assured a safe place in the creation.

The banquet that evening was a roaring success. Blue Thread danced, and so began the tale that every child knows of the crop-haired weaver girl with the blue arms.'

* * *

Aleta sighs.

The entire time Jósef was telling her the story of Blue Thread she'd been restraining the urge to grab his arm and shout at him to stick to his own story, to bring it to a conclusion in the only way that could be considered right and proper for a trilogy – after all, she might not know much about narratology but she had read, heard and seen enough to know that Marie-Sophie's and Leo Loewe's stories were those of the mother and father (the love story belonged to them both), while Jósef's was the story of the son – so he had a duty to see out the narrator's shift and fulfil the promise of an ending that would resolve the story, whether in a rise or fall, honour or disgrace.

But now Aleta had to admit herself defeated:

Just as the bones of a patient afflicted with Stone Man Syndrome react to blows by swiftly forming a new layer of bone tissue over the site, so Jósef's mind wove a story every time he encountered a painful thought or memory. This was best illustrated by how, to lend meaning to the suffering and helplessness caused by his condition, he had, though born in Iceland in August 1962, found a way to situate his birth in the midst of the Holocaust.

Jósef had told her it was everyone's right to have their story told to the end. He himself would only tell a fraction of his own.

Jósef finds in the pile of papers a fawn-coloured folder secured with an elastic band as thick as a finger, which, although dried out with age, still gives off that authentically rubbery smell. Opening the folder, he pulls out a West German map of Schleswig-Holstein and Lower Saxony and spreads it on his knees, placing a crooked finger on Hamburg. From Hamburg he traces a line west along the River Elbe, passing between the islands of Neßsand and Hanskalbsand, north-west to Grünendeich, then continues past Stadestrand on the south bank, east of the town of Stade, past the Bützfleth industrial zone, then out on to the Asseler Sand, north of the fort at Grauerort. There he suddenly taps the map.

'The town was here, the fort was visible from the south window of the church tower. Did I ever tell you how Kükenstadt met its end?'

'No.'

'Well, the tiny town of Kükenstadt stood around about here until the end of July 1943, when the place was razed to the ground during the days and nights of the Allied Operation Gomorrah. Any bombers that failed to drop their deadly cargo over their target, Hamburg, flew north-west and offloaded their bombs on to what appeared to be a dark expanse of marshland. The inhabitants had succeeded in blacking out their town so well that no one lived to tell the tale of its destruction. Today there's nothing there.'

The map is threadbare. Jósef's finger has travelled so often from Hamburg to Kükenstadt that the blue line of the Elbe has worn away.

'No, don't tell me. I don't want to hear.'

The Dance

We hear a vast concertina door of darkness being drawn aside – the darkness beyond retreats before the lights that have already been lit – followed by the sound of adult footsteps. Darkness, light, footsteps.

Girl: 12 January 1962 – † 13 January 1962, Girl: 13 January 1962 – † 13 January 1962, Girl: 21 January 1962 – † 21 January 1962, Boy: 24 February 1962 – † 27 February 1962, Boy: 1 March 1962 – † 14 April 1962, Girl: 13 May 1962 – † 14 May 1962, Girl: 13 May 1962 – † 17 May 1962, Girl: 5 May 1962 – † 21 May 1962, Boy: 7 May 1962 – † 25 May 1962, Girl: 19 May 1962 – † 26 May 1962, Girl: 27 May 1962 – † 27 May 1962, Girl: 28 May 1962 – † 29 May 1962, Boy: 22 June 1962 – † 23 June 1962, Boy: 27 June 1962 – † 30 June 1962, Boy: 10 February 1962 – † 11 July 1962, Girl: 30 April 1962 – † 11 July 1962, Boy: 10 February 1962 – † 16 July 1962, Boy: 16 July 1962 – † 16 July 1962, Boy: 9 July 1962 – † 18 July 1962, Girl: 19 July 1962 – † 19 July 1962, Boy: 31 July 1962 – † 31 July 1962, Girl: 1 August 1962 – † 1 August 1962, Boy: 29 March 1962 – † 3 August 1962, Boy: 9 July 1962 – † 4 August 1962, Girl: 13 February 1962 – † 7 August 1962, Boy: 1 July 1962 – † 18 August 1962, Boy: 17 August 1962 – † 20 August 1962, Girl: 3 September 1962 – † 3 September 1962, Boy: 1 October 1962 – † 6 October 1962, Boy: 18 November 1962 – † 18 November 1962, Boy: 27 November 1962 – † 27 November 1962, Boy: 18 December 1962 – † 18 December 1962, Girl: 16 December 1962 – † 23 December 1962, Boy: 19 November 1962 – † ? 1963, Girl: 27 July 1962 – † 9 February 1963, Girl: 8 August 1962 – † 14 February 1963, Girl: 30 March 1962 – † 16 February 1963, Girl: 21 October 1962 – † 3 March 1963, Boy: 1 August 1962 – † 1 April 1963, Boy: 7 June 1962 – † 4 April 1963, Girl: 27 February 1962 – † 10 April 1963, Boy: 9 February 1962 – † 15 April 1963, Boy: 11 November 1962 – † 1 May 1963, Girl: 3

December 1962 – † 14 May 1963, Girl: 30 June 1962 – † 16 May 1963, Boy: 19 July 1962 – † 8 August 1963, Boy: 11 December 1962 – † 3 October 1963, Boy: 5 February 1962 – † 26 October 1963, Girl: 29 May 1962 – † 26 October 1963, Boy: 6 May 1962 – † 14 November 1963, Boy: 14 January 1962 – † 16 July 1964, Boy: 10 February 1962 – † 4 September 1964, Boy: 30 July 1962 – † 30 September 1964, Girl: 1 July 1962 – † 18 October 1964, Boy: 10 May 1962 – † 5 January 1965, Girl: 6 August 1962 – † 18 February 1965, Girl: 4 October 1962 – † 9 October 1965, Boy: 24 June 1962 – † 14 November 1965, Boy: 9 February 1962 – † 23 December 1965, Girl: 9 August 1962 – † 13 January 1966, Boy: 29 October 1962 – † 10 July 1966, Girl: 10 November 1962 – † 20 December 1966, Boy: 8 February 1962 – † 10 January 1968, Girl: 12 January 1962 – † 18 February 1968, Boy: 7 September 1962 – † 30 September 1968, Boy: 24 August 1962 – † 8 April 1969, Boy: 22 November 1962 – † 12 May 1969, Boy: 23 December 1962 – † 26 December 1969, Boy: 24 March 1962 – † 1 October 1970, Boy: 22 February 1962 – † 17 November 1970, Girl: 7 August 1962 – † 29 January 1971, Boy: 14 March 1962 – † 10 March 1971, Boy: 16 April 1962 – † 4 April 1971, Boy: 19 June 1962 – † 10 October 1971, Boy: 15 December 1962 – † 26 December 1971, Boy: 17 June 1962 – † 12 March 1972, Boy: 10 May 1962 – † 18 January 1973, Boy: 11 October 1962 – † 30 March 1973, Boy: 7 April 1962 – † 29 January 1974, Girl: 19 April 1962 – † 26 March 1974, Boy: 23 September 1962 – † 28 August 1974, Boy: 28 December 1962 – † 7 July 1976, Girl: 10 September 1962 – † 17 November 1976, Boy: 6 December 1962 – † 1 January 1977, Boy: 22 November 1962 – † 27 June 1977, Girl: 22 July 1962 – † 28 August 1977, Boy: 31 January 1962 – † 8 January 1978, Boy: 3 May 1962 – † 17 June 1978, Boy: 6 February 1962 – † 26 July 1978, Boy: 1 May 1962 – † 5 December 1978, Boy: 15 October 1962 – † 13 May 1979, Boy: 12 July 1962 – † 8 December 1979, Boy: 13 November 1962 – † 23 October 1980, Boy: 31 May 1962 – † 14 January 1981, Girl: 14 July 1962 – † 5 September 1981, Girl: 23 May 1962 – † 23 November 1981, Boy: 5 September 1962 – † 10 January 1982, Girl: 6 June 1962 – † 30 January 1982, Boy: 3 October 1962 – † 14 March 1982 . . .

Man: 23 June 1962 – † 31 March 1983
Woman: 11 June 1962 – † 13 April 1983

Man: 2 June 1962 – † 16 November 1983
Man: 8 November 1962 – † 31 December 1983

Man: 10 April 1962 – † 11 January 1984
Man: 6 August 1962 – † 28 January 1984
Man: 5 May 1962 – † 11 March 1984
Man: 23 November 1962 – † 13 June 1984
Man: 6 December 1962 – † 18 October 1984

Man: 2 October 1962 – † 18 April 1985
Man: 30 May 1962 – † 18 November 1985

Man: 5 February 1962 – † 1 April 1986
Man: 26 April 1962 – † 22 November 1986

Man: 2 October 1962 – † 1 March 1987
Man: 9 August 1962 – † 26 October 1987
Woman: 14 June 1962 – † 29 November 1987

Man: 20 January 1962 – † 29 February 1988

Woman: 29 October 1962 – † 20 April 1989
Man: 23 September 1962 – † 23 November 1989

Man: 1 May 1962 – † 21 January 1990
Man: 22 March 1962 – † 3 May 1990
Man: 8 June 1962 – † 22 June 1990
Man: 5 March 1962 – † 25 October 1990
Man: 31 August 1962 – † 26 November 1990

Man: 9 June 1962 – † 9 October 1991
Man: 29 March 1962 – † 19 October 1991
Man: 11 January 1962 – † 28 October 1991
Man: 17 November 1962 – † 9 November 1991

Woman: 11 June 1962 – † 27 November 1992
Woman: 7 January 1962 – † 6 December 1992

Man: 13 December 1962 – † 10 October 1993

Man: 17 February 1962 – † 1 May 1994
Man: 10 April 1962 – † 24 August 1994
Man: 18 July 1962 – † 2 December 1994

Man: 13 August 1962 – † 22 February 1995
Woman: 7 July 1962 – † 25 February 1995

The adults enter stage left, marching in formation past the children and teenagers – who follow the troop with their eyes – then swing round behind them. They intone in low voices:

— We fall to our death on ptarmigan shoots. We die in traffic accidents. We turn our cars over. We're hit by stray bullets in America. We die at home. We abandon a world we were probably too good for. We die of alcoholism. We take our own lives. We drown at sea. We drown in harbours. We draw our last breaths in hospitals. We die in New Mexico where the chirruping of the lizards rivals that of the birds. We die from undefined illnesses. We get in the way of hawsers on fishing boats. We're electrocuted. We drive off the road with our sisters in the car. We die from chronic diabetes. We take our own lives.

We drown on beach holidays. We trip on riverbanks, knock ourselves out and drown. We pass away in Sweden. We drown when training ships capsize. We collide with street lights. We die of cancer. We're murdered by jealous lovers. We die of heart conditions, confined to wheelchairs. We fall victim to terminal illnesses. We die alone. We die of AIDS. We're called away. We die from chronic disabilities and our obituaries mention how fond we were of kisses and cuddles. We leave behind wives and husbands, partners and friends, relatives and children.

The adults take up position behind the children and teenagers, addressing those yet to come:

— Dear brothers and sisters, born in 1962, we await you here.

VI

From tape c)

(17 June 2009)

15

Lapping waves, sighing wind. The twittering of songbirds giving way to the melancholy cries of their nocturnal cousins. The distant chugging of a motorboat. The hoarse baaing of a sheep, answered at once by a pathetically high bleating. And all of this merely a faint background to the heavy breathing of the person next to the microphone, a breathing punctuated by lip-smacking and mumbling.

There is a crunching of gravel. A crunching that resolves into footsteps. The newcomer halts.

— Hey, you!

He's answered by a sudden snore. The breathing stops. The newcomer leans towards the microphone. The rustling of clothes. The sound of someone being prodded.

— Say, are you all right?

The voice is deep and resonant, the accent unmistakably American.

— Hello!

The snore resumes with a long blubbering of lips. There's the sound of someone being prodded again. The sleeper jerks, the gravel crunching under his body.

— Huh, what?

A gasp:

— What, who?

— No good lying here.

The geneticist opens his eyes to find, bending over him, a black man with a grey moustache and a red woolly hat. A very old man with sunken cheeks, freckles on his dark skin, the whites of his eyes yellow and bloodshot in two places.

— It's gettin' cold, the evening's gettin' cold. You're not dressed for it.

— No, right. OK.

Replies the geneticist, and the next thing he knows the old man has yanked him to his feet.

— Let's get you out of the wind.

Feet can be heard scuffing along the gravel. There's a thud as the geneticist is dropped into a chair. Then the footsteps approach again and the dictaphone is picked up and banged down on the table. Now both voices are clearly audible. The geneticist is slurring:

— I – I . . .

His rescuer is a big, powerfully built figure, though if his face is anything to go by he must be over ninety. The geneticist is no weakling himself, standing just under two metres tall, muscular and heavy with it: not just anyone could pluck him up and cart him around like that. He takes a closer look at the old man and deduces, from the way he carries himself, that he must be a retired weight-lifter or boxer. A boxer, more likely, since he seems unafraid of grappling with another man. Then again, there's no sign of the telltale cauliflower ears. The geneticist knows a thing or two about them. Back in his days as a medical student – before he cottoned on to the fact that the future lay in genetics; that there, in the very recipe for a human being, he would find the scope he sought for poetic creativity in flesh and blood – he used to do shifts in the neurology department at the Chicago district hospital, where they would get big, strong young men brought in suffering from head trauma after being used as punchbags by Muhammad Ali. The young men considered it an honour to get paid 100 dollars a day to be beaten black and blue by the world champion during his training sessions, but not all were able to take it.

They met just once, the Icelander and the legend. After a long shift at the hospital, the geneticist had dropped by the local market to buy groceries for his family. He was a medical student who couldn't afford a car in those days, so he was walking home along the sidewalk, with a number of heavy shopping bags looped over the bent fingers of each hand, when he came face to face with an imposing black figure. The man stepped aside and asked if he needed some help. Although the geneticist declined the offer, the stranger took it upon himself to walk part of the way with him. This chatty man with the friendly manner turned out to be none other than the great Muhammad Ali. He liked to spend his evenings hanging around on the sidewalk outside the local boxing club, telling stories, doling out candy and joking around with the boys. Before their ways parted, Ali invited the geneticist to come down to the club some time and watch him train: 'That'd be something for a Viking like you, man.' Although he responded politely, the geneticist never took him up on the offer. On Ali's neck he had spotted a drop of blood that must have landed there during a training session earlier that day, sprayed from the mouth of some future patient of the neurological unit, though, judging by the powerful scent of soap and cologne that hung about him, the champion must have taken a shower since then. The geneticist felt it was quite enough having to deal with the fallout from those blows.

He used to tell this story to medical students visiting the CoDex headquarters, generally concluding by reminding them that several years after this encounter, with what might be regarded as poetic justice, the champion bone-crusher had been diagnosed with serious brain damage himself. This punchline invariably went down well with his audience, seeming as it did to offer the moral of the story, though it should have been clear to all that Muhammad Ali's fate had been neither poetic nor just, and personally the geneticist despised this kind of fridge-door philosophy.

The gravel crunches.

— I found this in the boathouse. Wrap it around you, man.

A great northern diver laughs out on the lake. There is a creaking from the chair next to the dictaphone. Another chair is drawn up and a man lowers himself into it.

— Anthony Theophrastus Athanius Brown.

— Hr-Hrólfur, Hrólfur 'the Second' Magnússon.

For Christ's sake, why did he have to answer with that cheap joke? Why the insane desire to compete? Was he so jealous of the man's impressive name that he had to big up his own? Now he would have to explain that it had been a joke, that for his last three years at Laugarnes School he had been nicknamed 'Hrólfur the Second'. Their teacher had been a kindly, well-meaning man who tried to keep up with the latest trends in education. At the start of every week he used to get one of the pupils to read out the register. This usually went well. They were all quite good at reading by then and besides they knew the names of their classmates. Then, the autumn they were ten years old, a new boy joined the school, recently moved to Reykjavík from Akureyri in the north. The first time he read the register he did so with flying colours – he had a clear northern accent and took it nice and slow, crisply enunciating every word, three qualities that the teacher used to bang on about in his war on the sloppy speech of the Reykjavík kids, many of whom drawled as if they had a mouth full of chewing gum; yes, he'd lost count of the times he'd stuck his finger in a child's mouth to hook out the gum, only to find nothing there: the tongue had simply grown slack from the ceaseless rumination and would need vigorous exercises to strengthen it, whereas the correct pronunciation came naturally to the northern boy, and for the rest of their time at school the teacher would hold him up as a shining ex- ample whenever he was scolding the other kids for their lazy speech – until, that is, the new boy came to Hrólfur's name, at which point he hesitated. He hadn't expected to encounter the handwritten initial of Hrólfur Zóphanías's middle name, and because the teacher hadn't crossed his zed, it looked more like a number two than a letter, so he read out in ringing tones: 'Hrólfur the Second!'. And of course the name stuck.

The geneticist sighs, wondering how to explain all this: Laugarnes School, his old teacher Skúmur Áskelsson, the sad fate of the clearly spoken boy, it's just too complicated, so he decides to change the subject.

— Blood. I sometimes think about blood.

He breaks off abruptly.

The memory of his Icelandic lessons at school has prompted him to enunciate so clearly that it sounds as if he's saying 'plud'. To test this, he silently mouths the word 'blood', checking whether he's saying *p* or *b*. But the moment his lips part to form the vowel *oo* he is assailed by the memory of the teacher's nicotine-yellow finger in his mouth. He can remember, no, he can *feel* Skúmur grabbing hold of his wet little tongue and lifting it up in search of the dreaded cud, poking thick fingers between his teeth, the hairy knuckles rubbing against his palate, jabbing him in the gullet, a broad nail bumping against his uvula, leaving behind a sour taste of tobacco.

The geneticist retches, then, getting the reflex under control, says again, this time with a voiced b:

— Blood.

Silence. Anthony shifts in his chair.

— Yes, I guess that's hardly surprising. For a man in your profession.

Anthony continues:

— I know you, though you don't know me. I live nearby. I've been here for sixty years and five more, to the day. Yeah, man, who'd have believed that a poor boy from Nigertown would get to spend his life as the in-house Negro in the Theology Faculty at the University of Iceland?

— I know who you are. I've seen you wandering down by the lake and in the birch woods ever since I was small. You live in the old summer house that belongs to the Faculty of Theology. My father used to talk about you. I remember him telling my mother there was only one man in Iceland who had a tweed suit to equal yours. And you can guess who that was. Us kids used to be shit-scared of you. But do you know something? Do you know that if you were to drain Lake Thingvellir, which contains 2 billion 856 million cubic metres of water, and then tapped the blood of everyone on earth – a human being contains around 0.005 cubic metres of blood, yes, just multiply that by 7.1 billion – and poured it into the empty lake bed, it would only be enough to fill one-eightieth of it? One eightieth! And this is just one bloody lake!

The geneticist is beginning to recover from his drunken snooze on the shore. Although he can't actually remember the exact calculation in cubic metres of blood and water, he did at least manage to produce this thought more or less ungarbled. He fumbles for his glass. It's empty. The whisky bottle is lying on its side. It looks as if there's a drop left in the shoulder. Picking it up, he leans back and turns it upside down, waiting for the last drop to trickle down the clear neck into the mouth of the bottle, before falling on to his waiting tongue. But by the time the liquid has dripped from the bottle's neck and down his own, he has forgotten the rest of his meditations on blood.

To conclude the matter somehow, he waves the bottle towards the lake and says:

— Yes, mankind amounts to no more than that.

Anthony Theophrastus Athanius Brown:

— Brrr, I always get the shivers when a Nordic type starts talking about blood.

Silence. He claps his hands together to warm them.

— I've talked to your wife a couple times. When she was passing my summer house. I hope you don't mind.

The old man winks at the geneticist.

— We were only chatting.

— My wives can do what they like. Was it Anna?

— No, we introduced ourselves. Her name wasn't Anna. I'm sure of that.

— Bryndís? Was she tall? When was this?

— I think it began with a C. I remember thinking there aren't many Icelanders whose names begin with a C.

— Then it must have been Cara Mjöll.

— Quite a bit younger than you, blonde. It would have been about five years ago.

— That would fit. You haven't met Dóra then?

— Not yet. But Cara, Cara Mjöll, some of her interests overlapped with mine.

— Aerobics?

— Voodoo.

'Be the author of your own life!' It was the motto the geneticist's father had drummed into his sons. Whatever the occasion, he always managed to slip it in. That's not to suggest that this philosophy of life was all he talked about – he didn't have a one-track mind, no, he was an old-school polymath who was forever reading, whether it was nature, people or books – but he could steer the most straightforward subject round to it. Whether his conversation with his sons dealt with mundane matters, such as his thoughts on the planned change from driving on the left to the right or the price of records, or major issues of the day, such as the atom bomb, the war in Indochina or Nordic unity, it would invariably lead to the same conclusion: the equality and fraternity promised by the socialist movement would never be achieved unless those who aspired to fight injustice in their homelands, wherever they were in the world, were in command of their own lives. Before they could intervene in the course of history, they had to have their own affairs perfectly under control. International capitalists, and their pathetic Icelandic counterparts, feared such people more than anything else in the world. For, when they encountered overwhelming odds, such as the unbridled violence of the toppling capitalist monster, these people had in their arsenal what you might call the poor man's weapon of mass destruction: self-sacrifice. In these lectures, the pronoun 'they' meant 'you brothers', and the message could be a little hard to swallow if all that had prompted it was a simple request for money to go to the school disco.

Later, the youngest son of Magnús Ágústsson, journalist, MP, writer, singer and trout nemesis, was to realise that his father's motto had been no more than a sort of *Übermensch* take on the AA serenity prayer: '*God, grant me the serenity to accept the things I cannot change, courage to change the things I can, and wisdom to know the difference.*' Minus the God bit, and with as much booze as anyone could tip down their neck.

Children learn by example, and the geneticist could boast that he was the author, not only of his own life, but of his nation's life as well. He had shown his countrymen their own worth by harnessing their genomes, their book of life, in a digital database for the benefit of all the inhabitants of earth. A tiny minority had offered resistance through newspaper articles and books, but there was little they could do against a man who was the author of his own life. The only aspect he had never had any control over was his wives, who, by some quirk of fate, had come to him in alphabetical order. First there had been Anna, the love of his schooldays, who had shelved her plan to become an engineer so he could pursue an education and build up CoDex. She had given him his three eldest children. Next had come Bryndís, who had been raised and educated in her father's supermarkets. When they embarked on their life together she was the second richest woman in Iceland. People used to whisper that they had both profited from their dead countrymen: he from the medical records of deceased

Icelanders, she from the grocery empire that was said to have its roots, quite literally, in the illegal cultivation of vegetables in the graveyards of Reykjavík and the surrounding area. The third had been the personal trainer, Cara Mjöll, who'd given him twins. And finally there was the Professor of Economics, Halldóra Oktavía Thorsteinson, known as Dóra, who he'd married purely out of scientific curiosity. This alphabetical order was, admittedly, a bit of an embarrassment. But what was he supposed to do? Avoid all women called Eirún, Engilráð, Efemía, Emma, Einarína or Elísabet?

— Voodoo?

— My particular area of interest is the development of African religious practices in the New World—

The geneticist interrupts:

— If you thought Cara Mjöll was interesting, you should meet my new wife.

— I'd like that.

— Dóra's what we in the medical profession call a 'chimera', after a grotesque monster of Greek mythology. Her DNA is derived from five individuals, her mother and four fathers. It's not immediately obvious, but, for example, she has two distinct blood types and she's a redhead on one side and a blonde on the other. She was the first child born in 1962—

This time it's the old man's turn to interrupt:

— You don't say? One of the strangest things that ever happened to me in this country was the time I was asked to help out with a home birth at a house in Reykjavík, late in the summer of that year. The child born then wasn't normal either.

— In 1962? Tell me more. I've been scouring the database in search of genetic mutants born in that year.

The footsteps of Hrólfur Z. Magnússon, geneticist, and Anthony A.T. Brown, theologian, recede into the distance.

(*End of recording.*)

VII

Completion

(23 October 2012–15 April 2013)

16

Aleta switches off the dictaphone.

'I've got enough now. I don't need any more for the study.'

She puts the machine in her bag.

'It's all been very – what's the word? – educational. It's the longest I've ever spoken to an individual Icelander. I've learned a lot.'

She starts to rise to her feet, but before she can straighten up properly, Jósef seizes her wrist. Arrested in this awkward position, she glances down at his hand. The pale, thin skin on the back is stretched tight over the bumps that have sprouted from his bones like mushrooms. His deformed forearm is just visible where his checked shirtsleeve has fallen back. He must have something important to say as every sudden movement increases the risk of injury. Every physical exertion causes him untold suffering. He tightens his grip.

'Even if you did come back, I wouldn't be here.'

She lays her hand over his. He looks away.

'I'm going into hospital in two days. For the last time.'

'I'll visit you.'

'No, don't do that. That's not what this is about.'

As unexpectedly as he had seized her wrist, he lets it go and the white imprint of his fingers lingers briefly on her skin. An instant later the blood has refilled the capillaries and it's gone. Aleta straightens up.

'I'm sorry I can't repay you properly for listening to my story, in the way my father taught me, by listening to yours. There won't be time. I'm sad about that. I hope you'll forgive me.'

'Of course, of course. What kind of story would there be in my life?'

'No less than there was in mine.'

He gestures with his chin to the bedroom behind her.

'In there. Under the bed, on the side by the window, there are some banana boxes with books in them. In the box at the foot of the bed there should be a copy of the Icelandic translation of Karel Čapek's *War with the Newts*. Inside, you'll find a brown envelope with my name on it. It's sealed. You mustn't open it until you get home.'

'But I don't need anything. I've enjoyed this.'

'Oh, please, do it for me.'

Once Aleta has gone into the bedroom and Jósef is satisfied by the sounds that she's busy searching for the envelope, he edges his way closer to the chair she had been sitting on and pulls over her bag. Finding the dictaphone, he switches it on, raises it to his mouth and whispers:

'There's one thing I have to correct, Aleta. When you were here the other day, I compared being born to rising naked from a cool forest spring on a hot summer's day. I was wrong.'

* * *

'CLUB DES AMATEURS

The man arrived at his destination shortly after the sun had reached its noontide zenith. Because he was unused to travelling on foot, the walk from the railway station at Vr— had taken him longer than expected and he was rather late for his appointment at the remote spot in the middle of the forest, out of sight of the birds in the air and the fish in the ponds.

Only to a select few is it granted to set foot in the legendary building, so he had carefully memorised the top-secret map he had been shown at the final meeting in preparation for the trip. On it, a route had been marked from the station, through the village, to the edge of the forest, then through the forest to the hall – yes, he imagined a handsome estate, encircled by a high brick wall, a cross between the mansion of a nineteenth-century industrialist and the country residence of a Prussian philosophy professor, with a cosmopolitan staff (drawn from the European imperial powers and their colonies), headed by a strict couple, a fifty-five-year-old Englishman with a speech impediment he covered up with practised, dignified gestures that took the place of the words he found so hard to pronounce, and his Russian or Hungarian wife, a little younger, with red hair and green eyes – where, once he reached the iron gates bearing the name of the place, which he assumed he'd find there, a guide would be waiting for him.

Throughout the time it took the train to rattle from the central station in Sn— to Vr—, he kept going over the route in his mind. He pictured a red strand of wool, laid over the landscape in loops, with knots to represent the chief landmarks. Like a dancer at a provincial opera house rehearsing for a performance in the belief that a world-famous choreographer will be in the audience (under an assumed name, of course, and in disguise), he repeated every step, every turn that would bring him to his goal.

In spite of all these rehearsals, the man was, as we've said, a little late in reaching his destination deep in the realm of the pines, firs and spruces, and as time wore on he felt a growing fear that the person awaiting him there would tick him off and remind him what a privilege it was to be chosen for this journey. But, in the event, his fear proved groundless. In the heart of the forest – where the foliage was so thick that it rose before the eyes like a cliff face – he was greeted not by a human being with the power of speech but by a small dog of uncertain pedigree. It was rather long in the body and short in the leg, with a curly, tasselled tail, a glossy, rough-haired, wet-look coat, and a head so large that it would have sat better on a wolf, which meant that its lower jaw trailed on the ground and could be lifted only with difficulty. Its brown eyes glowed like black pearls.

The man was so taken up with staring at the beast that it wasn't until his confusingly proportioned "guide" had shown him into a shadowy hall and the door had closed behind them that he realised he hadn't seen the building from outside. The impenetrable wall of greenery that had blocked his path must have been growing on its façade. The dog signalled to the man to follow in the manner of its species, not with a bark but with meaningful dartings of its black-pearl eyes. And the man pursued it through the dim hall and up a staircase that rose four storeys into darkness.

As he climbed, he noted with surprise how nimbly the beast scampered up the steep steps, while he himself had to concentrate hard on finding them in the gloom. Once they reached the top, there followed a succession of narrow, lightless passages, leading into ever darker and narrower ways. Finally, after a long wandering this way and that – the darkness so thick at times that the man was blindly dependent on the panting of the dog – they came to a spiral staircase that wound up to an ancient-looking landing. At the top, there was a single door, through which the dog showed the man into the fabled pentagonal chamber that he had gone to all this trouble to visit: the *Club des amateurs*.

When the dog had pushed the door shut behind him with its broad snout, the man was left speechless. His breathing was suddenly so shallow that he couldn't make a sound – not even a cry of admiration or a stifled exclamation of wonder – so overwhelmed was he by the size of the tower room (it was so small!) and by the vast throng of finely intermeshed vowels and consonants that his predecessors had left behind within its walls.

All the countless words that had formed in the minds of the previous guests of the *Club des amateurs* and been rendered audible using the speech organs they'd carried in their mouths and throats since birth – or made visible with their hands, like the imaginary English butler – hovered within the five walls of the room, like motes of dust, momentarily illuminated as they floated through the ray of green afternoon light that filtered in through a crack in the shutter, piercing the darkness like a razor slicing through black silk. He moved closer to the tantalising swarm of glowing motes and laid his left ear to it.

"The voices" were so infinitesimally small that it was as if, rather than hearing them, the man experienced them with all his senses, as if every shimmering particle that floated past his ear were captured like an image in his consciousness and that image called forth a sentence – a contribution towards keeping the company going, a share of the common purpose, a testament to each and every one – or a declaration, perhaps, perceptible to his finely tuned mental ear:

We're amateurs at breathing.
  Amateurs at walking.
    Amateurs at distinguishing colour.

We're amateurs at rubbing our noses.
  Amateurs at twisting a lock of hair.
    Amateurs at drinking apple juice.

We're amateurs at watching the sun go down.
  Amateurs at biting our nails.
    Amateurs at waking up in the morning.

We're amateurs at sneezing.
  Amateurs at cracking our knuckles.
    Amateurs at tying green ribbons.

We're amateurs at combing our hair.
  Amateurs at drawing nanny-goats.
    Amateurs at clenching our toes.

The man was flooded with a sense of pure joy. Seized with such an overpowering euphoria that a lump rose to his throat. The tinkling round made by the microscopic particles was a composition he had long yearned to hear. With every new line of the song he felt his yoke lifting.

We're amateurs at singing.
  Amateurs at boiling an egg.
    Amateurs at throwing dice.

We're amateurs at expressing our affection.
  Amateurs at banging pots and pans.
    Amateurs at moving chairs from room to room.

And then it happened. The amateur particles were drawn to his body like iron filings to a magnet – he was seized with a tingling sensation, an unquenchable but nameless desire, a combination of fear and

laughter, only equalled by the feeling that had fused his mind and
flesh at the moment of his first climax with another human being –
and settled on his shoes and feet, formed lines on every hair on his
head and cheeks, covered his face and hands, all the time adding to
their list of all the things we're born to perform with as much affection and care as we can while never learning to do them properly.

　　We're amateurs . . .

The door creaked behind the man. A draught blew through the room.
The unexpected gust swept the thin layer of countless 'declarations'
off his body.

　　Without a moment's hesitation he followed them into the air. His
body whirled apart like a dust cloud whipped up from dry sand. He
became one with his fellow members of the *Club des amateurs*, became
what he had always longed to be: an amateur among amateurs.

　　Out on the landing, the mongrel gave a hoarse bark.

* * *

'Or is that what dying will be like?'

* * *

Aleta never heard Jósef Loewe's final words on the tape. Having found
the brown envelope in Čapek's book and thanked Jósef with a kiss on
the forehead for everything, for their conversations, the coffee, the
brandy and the parting gift that wasn't to be opened until she got
home, she mounted her bike on the corner of Ingólfsstræti and
Amtmannsstígur, and went coasting down the hill, turning left at the
next corner into Thingholtsstræti, then pedalling along to the next
corner where she sailed downhill again, this time to the corner of
Bókhlödustígur and Laufásvegur where she turned left again, passing
the building that had once housed Hrafn W. Karlsson's stamp shop,
then pedalling south until she reached the corner of Njardargata and
let herself coast for the third time, winging her way down the road

heading straight for the Music Pavilion Park and from there to the foot and cycle bridge that crosses busy Hringbraut and brings you to the Vatnsmýri wetlands, then followed the cycle path past the bird sanctuary to the CoDex headquarters. There she handed in the dictaphone, the questionnaire completed with the basic facts about Jósef Loewe and the tapes recording his oral account.

The following morning saw Aleta back at Ingólfsstræti, this time to return the gift. She couldn't accept such a precious object, especially not from a disabled man who had trouble telling the difference between fiction and reality. But just as she approached the house from below, an ambulance drove away from it above, taking Jósef to the institution from which he would never return. For a while she debated whether to ask one of his upstairs neighbours to look after the treasure or else to post it through the letterbox. But a treasure that is too precious to be accepted cannot be entrusted to strangers or left lying on the hall floor in an empty basement flat. Which is how Aleta came to own an envelope with coarsely perforated two-shilling stamps and finely perforated four-shilling franks, posted in Djúpivogur but postmarked in Hamburg. The combination of stamps, place of origin and postmark were so rare that she would be able to live on the proceeds for a whole year without a care in the world. The next twelve months would be the most important in her life. By the end of that time, her metamorphosis from Avel 'the ephemeral' to Aleta 'the winged one' would be complete.

The day the payment came through from the Bruun-Rasmussen auction house in Copenhagen, Aleta went to visit the graves of Jósef and Leo Loewe in Fossvogur Cemetery. There she laid a pebble by each headstone and lit two candles, one for Marie-Sophie, the other for Brynhildur Helgadóttir, and stuck them in the soil between father and son.

Finally she lit a stick of incense for the holy archangel Gabriel – holding it between her fingers as it burned with the sweet scent of lilies and the smoke curled up into the cool, rainy April sky – for he is the patron saint of the postal service.

The Dance

Girl: 12 January 1962 – † 13 January 1962, Girl: 13 January 1962 – † 13 January 1962, Girl: 21 January 1962 – † 21 January 1962, Boy: 24 February 1962 – † 27 February 1962, Boy: 1 March 1962 – † 14 April 1962, Girl: 13 May 1962 – † 14 May 1962, Girl: 13 May 1962 – † 17 May 1962, Girl: 5 May 1962 – † 21 May 1962, Boy: 7 May 1962 – † 25 May 1962, Girl: 19 May 1962 – † 26 May 1962, Girl: 27 May 1962 – † 27 May 1962, Girl: 28 May 1962 – † 29 May 1962, Boy: 22 June 1962 – † 23 June 1962, Boy: 27 June 1962 – † 30 June 1962, Boy: 10 February 1962 – † 11 July 1962, Girl: 30 April 1962 – † 11 July 1962, Boy: 10 February 1962 – † 16 July 1962, Boy: 16 July 1962 – † 16 July 1962, Boy: 9 July 1962 – † 18 July 1962, Girl: 19 July 1962 – † 19 July 1962, Boy: 31 July 1962 – † 31 July 1962, Girl: 1 August 1962 – † 1 August 1962, Boy: 29 March 1962 – † 3 August 1962, Boy: 9 July 1962 – † 4 August 1962, Girl: 13 February 1962 – † 7 August 1962, Boy: 1 July 1962 – † 18 August 1962, Boy: 17 August 1962 – † 20 August 1962, Girl: 3 September 1962 – † 3 September 1962, Boy: 1 October 1962 – † 6 October 1962, Boy: 18 November 1962 – † 18 November 1962, Boy: 27 November 1962 – † 27 November 1962, Boy: 18 December 1962 – † 18 December 1962, Girl: 16 December 1962 – † 23 December 1962, Boy: 19 November 1962 – † ? 1963, Girl: 27 July 1962 – † 9 February 1963, Girl: 8 August 1962 – † 14 February 1963, Girl: 30 March 1962 – † 16 February 1963, Girl: 21 October 1962 – † 3 March 1963, Boy: 1 August 1962 – † 1 April 1963, Boy: 7 June 1962 – † 4 April 1963, Girl: 27 February 1962 – † 10 April 1963, Boy: 9 February 1962 – † 15 April 1963, Boy: 11 November 1962 – † 1 May 1963, Girl: 3 December 1962 – † 14 May 1963, Girl: 30 June 1962 – † 16 May 1963, Boy: 19 July 1962 – † 8 August 1963, Boy: 11 December 1962 – † 3 October 1963, Boy: 5 February 1962 – † 26 October 1963, Girl: 29 May 1962 – † 26 October 1963, Boy: 6 May 1962 – † 14 November 1963, Boy: 14 January

1962 – † 16 July 1964, Boy: 10 February 1962 – † 4 September 1964, Boy: 30 July 1962 – † 30 September 1964, Girl: 1 July 1962 – † 18 October 1964, Boy: 10 May 1962 – † 5 January 1965, Girl: 6 August 1962 – † 18 February 1965, Girl: 4 October 1962 – † 9 October 1965, Boy: 24 June 1962 – † 14 November 1965, Boy: 9 February 1962 – † 23 December 1965, Girl: 9 August 1962 – † 13 January 1966, Boy: 29 October 1962 – † 10 July 1966, Girl: 10 November 1962 – † 20 December 1966, Boy: 8 February 1962 – † 10 January 1968, Girl: 12 January 1962 – † 18 February 1968, Boy: 7 September 1962 – † 30 September 1968, Boy: 24 August 1962 – † 8 April 1969, Boy: 22 November 1962 – † 12 May 1969, Boy: 23 December 1962 – † 26 December 1969, Boy: 24 March 1962 – † 1 October 1970, Boy: 22 February 1962 – † 17 November 1970, Girl: 7 August 1962 – † 29 January 1971, Boy: 14 March 1962 – † 10 March 1971, Boy: 16 April 1962 – † 4 April 1971, Boy: 19 June 1962 – † 10 October 1971, Boy: 15 December 1962 – † 26 December 1971, Boy: 17 June 1962 – † 12 March 1972, Boy: 10 May 1962 – † 18 January 1973, Boy: 11 October 1962 – † 30 March 1973, Boy: 7 April 1962 – † 29 January 1974, Girl: 19 April 1962 – † 26 March 1974, Boy: 23 September 1962 – † 28 August 1974, Boy: 28 December 1962 – † 7 July 1976, Girl: 10 September 1962 – † 17 November 1976, Boy: 6 December 1962 – † 1 January 1977, Boy: 22 November 1962 – † 27 June 1977, Girl: 22 July 1962 – † 28 August 1977, Boy: 31 January 1962 – † 8 January 1978, Boy: 3 May 1962 – † 17 June 1978, Boy: 6 February 1962 – † 26 July 1978, Boy: 1 May 1962 – † 5 December 1978, Boy: 15 October 1962 – † 13 May 1979, Boy: 12 July 1962 – † 8 December 1979, Boy: 13 November 1962 – † 23 October 1980, Boy: 31 May 1962 – † 14 January 1981, Girl: 14 July 1962 – † 5 September 1981, Girl: 23 May 1962 – † 23 November 1981, Boy: 5 September 1962 – † 10 January 1982, Girl: 6 June 1962 – † 30 January 1982, Boy: 3 October 1962 – † 14 March 1982, Man: 23 June 1962 – † 31 March 1983, Woman: 11 June 1962 – † 13 April 1983, Man: 2 June 1962 – † 16 November 1983, Man: 8 November 1962 – † 31 December 1983, Man: 10 April 1962 – † 11 January 1984, Man: 6 August 1962 – † 28 January 1984, Man: 5 May 1962 – † 11 March 1984, Man: 23 November 1962 – † 13 June 1984, Man: 6 December 1962 – † 18 October 1984, Man: 2 October 1962 – † 18 April 1985, Man: 30 May 1962 – † 18 November 1985, Man: 5 February 1962 – † 1 April 1986, Man: 26 April 1962 – † 22 November 1986, Man: 2

October 1962 – † 1 March 1987, Man: 9 August 1962 – † 26 October 1987, Woman: 14 June 1962 – † 29 November 1987, Man: 20 January 1962 – † 29 February 1988, Woman: 29 October 1962 – † 20 April 1989, Man: 23 September 1962 – † 23 November 1989, Man: 1 May 1962 – † 21 January 1990, Man: 22 March 1962 – † 3 May 1990, Man: 8 June 1962 – † 22 June 1990, Man: 5 March 1962 – † 25 October 1990, Man: 31 August 1962 – † 26 November 1990, Man: 9 June 1962 – † 9 October 1991, Man: 29 March 1962 – † 19 October 1991, Man: 11 January 1962 – † 28 October 1991, Man: 17 November 1962 – † 9 November 1991, Woman: 11 June 1962 – † 27 November 1992, Woman: 7 January 1962 – † 6 December 1992, Man: 13 December 1962 – † 10 October 1993, Man: 17 February 1962 – † 1 May 1994, Man: 10 April 1962 – † 24 August 1994, Man: 18 July 1962 – † 2 December 1994, Man: 13 August 1962 – † 22 February 1995, Woman: 7 July 1962 – † 25 February 1995 . . .

Lights come on in seven lamps on the stage floor. With a sudden hiss, smoke starts blowing from smoke machines. Black-clad stage-hands go from one spotlight to the next, tipping them back to angle the beams diagonally up to meet one another. Through the haze of smoke there appear the huge silhouettes of those who are now going to meet their cohort, holding hands as if taking part in a ring dance:

Man: 4 May 1962 – † 4 August 1996
Man: 13 February 1962 – † 15 September 1996

A driver is holding the hand of a disabled person who is leading a first mate who is leading a pharmacist.

Woman: 25 February 1962 – † 16 April 1997
Man: 5 June 1962 – † 15 July 1997
Woman: 24 November 1962 – † 24 September 1997

The pharmacist is leading an embroiderer who is leading a magistrate who is leading a sailor.

Man: 29 January 1962 – † 19 January 1998
Man: 2 October 1962 – † 14 July 1998
Man: 15 March 1962 – † 14 November 1998

The sailor is leading an industrial designer who's leading an engineer who's leading a restaurateur.

Man: 2 December 1962 – † 4 September 1999
Man: 2 November 1962 – † 20 October 1999
Man: 31 January 1962 – † 26 October 1999
Man: 20 October 1962 – † 9 December 1999
Man: 1 October 1962 – † 21 December 1999

The restaurateur is leading a drummer who's leading a tradesman who's leading a nurse.

Woman: 24 June 1962 – † 5 January 2000
Man: 18 May 1962 – † 14 February 2000
Woman: 20 September 1962 – † 29 March 2000
Woman: 20 August 1962 – † 14 April 2000
Man: 6 February 1962 – † 24 May 2000
Man: 4 October 1962 – † 6 June 2000
Woman: 1 July 1962 – † 4 September 2000
Man: 7 April 1962 – † 6 July 2000

The nurse is leading a builder who's leading a musician who's leading a manager who's leading a builder.

Man: 30 April 1962 – † 21 July 2001
Woman: 22 November 1962 – † 22 October 2001

The builder is leading a sailor who's leading a doctor who's leading a make-up artist.

Woman: 1 February 1962 – † *11 January 2002*
Man: 14 August 1962 – † *10 February 2002*
Woman: 17 June 1962 – † *30 April 2002*
Woman: 25 April 1962 – † *5 June 2002*
Man: 18 November 1962 – † *1 November 2002*
Man: 8 June 1962 – † *26 December 2002*

The make-up artist is leading a petty criminal who's leading a pianist who's leading a tinsmith.

Woman: 6 February 1962 – † *19 January 2003*
Man: 19 March 1962 – † *23 May 2003*

The tinsmith is leading a sales representative who's leading a working woman who's leading a salesman.

Woman: 1 May 1962 – † *4 February 2004*
Woman: 5 July 1962 – † *7 February 2004*
Woman: 19 February 1962 – † *29 April 2004*
Man: 23 December 1962 – † *2 May 2004*
Woman: 7 July 1962 – † *12 May 2004*
Man: 27 June 1962 – † *4 June 2004*
Woman: 8 October 1962 – † *14 July 2004*
Man: 3 June 1962 – † *27 November 2004*

The salesman is leading a carpenter who's leading a mechanic who's leading a nursery-school teacher.

Man: 2 January 1962 – † *10 July 2005*

The nursery-school teacher is leading a driver who's leading a chef who's leading a vehicle-paint sprayer. The paint sprayer is leading a baiter who's leading an electronics engineer who's leading an artist.

Woman: 3 September 1962 – † 9 February 2006
Woman: 13 July 1962 – † 14 May 2006
Man: 14 June 1962 – † 26 November 2006
Man: 8 April 1962 – † 30 November 2006

The artist is leading an engineer who's leading a poet who's leading a bank employee.

Man: 4 August 1962 – † 1 April 2007
Woman: 2 March 1962 – † 1 April 2007
Man: 20 December 1962 – † 19 April 2007
Woman: 12 April 1962 – † 23 August 2007
Man: 20 March 1962 – † 21 October 2007
Man: 27 April 1962 – † 21 November 2007

The bank employee is leading a mechanic who's leading a farmer who's leading a housewife.

Man: 14 August 1962 – † 7 January 2008
Woman: 22 January 1962 – † 27 January 2008
Man: 19 January 1962 – † 21 May 2008

The housewife is leading a craftswoman who's leading a footballer who's leading a secretary.

Man: 16 May 1962 – † 13 February 2009
Woman: 9 January 1962 – † 9 July 2009
Woman: 2 July 1962 – † 29 July 2009
Man: 26 May 1962 – † 30 August 2009
Man: 25 June 1962 – † 19 September 2009
Man: 19 July 1962 – † 31 October 2009
Man: 8 September 1962 – † 2 November 2009

The secretary is leading an overseer who's leading a fish-factory worker who's leading a journalist.

Man: 26 August 1962 – † 21 January 2010
Man: 11 December 1962 – † 4 April 2010
Man: 27 December 1962 – † 3 September 2010
Man: 9 November 1962 – † 25 September 2010
Man: 4 February 1962 – † 24 December 2010
Man: 3 April 1962 – † 25 December 2010

The journalist is leading an employee of the Olympic committee who's leading a taxi driver who's leading a pump operator.

Man: 11 April 1962 – † 20 February 2011
Man: 13 August 1962 – † 3 May 2011
Man: 15 February 1962 – † 2 July 2011
Man: 6 July 1962 – † 20 July 2011

The pump operator is leading a shop assistant who's leading a packaging employee.

Woman: 6 April 1962 – † 11 February 2012
Man: 1 June 1962 – † 23 March 2012
Man: 5 March 1962 – † 4 July 2012
Man: 12 July 1962 – † 21 August 2012
Woman: 10 February 1962 – † 16 October 2012
Man: 22 October 1962 – † 16 November 2012
Man: 7 May 1962 – † 12 December 2012

The packaging employee is leading a seamstress who's leading a science teacher who's leading the employee of a shipping company who's leading a chef. The chef is leading a labourer who holds out his free hand to the last person to enter the stage, a disabled man in an electric wheelchair. And the labourer leads the disabled man.

Man: 27 August 1962 – † 31 December 2012

The shadow of the man in the wheelchair stretches and billows in the veil of smoke until he resembles the king of a chosen people on his throne, a centaur on wheels, a divine prophet steering a fiery chariot. The wrinkle on his forehead is smoothed out until it looks less like the word *truth* and more like the word *death*. The chorus raises its 213-strong voice:

— Dear brothers and sisters, born in 1962, we await you here.

If you listen carefully you can hear one voice departing from the theme, in a way that some would call discordant. It is the voice of Jósef Loewe, who is looking over his shoulder, calling back into the passageways that brought him to this place:

— Dear Sjón, I await you here.

EPILOGUE

With this book, as with any other, we should bear in mind that although the author has chosen to bring the story to a conclusion, it is in fact far from over. Characters who survive at the end of the tale will live on, pursuing the course of their lives into an unwritten future, however short or long, or even infinite – a future in which unforeseen advances in biotechnology may, for example, lead to the discovery of an immortality drug, or, alternatively, a character may come to the aid of a supernatural being in distress and be rewarded with eternal life (this is the difference between living beings of flesh and blood and the other kind, who inhabit the world of fiction) – and the only way we, as readers, can learn about the characters' trials and triumphs is to eavesdrop on our own imagination and listen to our inner narrator spinning them a fate. Even the most minor characters in literature may legitimately hope that some reader will take on the task of telling their story, by plucking up the loose end from the page, so to speak, and drawing it out until they can tie a new thread to it and so embark on an independent tale. Yes, even characters who are supposed to be stone dead can give rise to new stories, whether in their own world or in others undreamed of.

The same applies to all the other loose ends that have not been tied up by the last page or were mentioned only in passing earlier in the story – whether deliberately or by mistake – since the plot and its components can, in the mind of the reader or author who discovers unused material in them, take twists and turns that no one could have predicted, however thoroughly and however often the book has been read, however many people have analysed and discussed it, however many centuries it has been provoking thought or attracting criticism; people and animals, gods and elements, historic events and mundane

incidents, nature spirits and the most microscopic phenomena become
entwined and unravel like the mycelium of a fungus that can spread
underground to cover an area of 60 square kilometres, as oblivious
as those who pick its corpse-pale fruits, in forests, on rocky outcrops,
in compost heaps or by the walls of houses are to the fact that it's
probably the largest individual organism on earth, a thousand years
old and the parent of other giant fungi that, combined, cover a fifth
of the earth's land mass. An even greater indication of the size of the
subterranean organism is the mushroom soup simmering in a large
aluminium saucepan on a stove in the kitchen of a two-room apartment on the sixth floor of a neglected block of flats in a suburb of one
of the world's most beautiful cities, which not only fills the rooms with
a delicious aroma but slips out with the steam through a crack in the
window and converts all those who smell it into minor characters in
the final chapter of an epic that is known only in the homeland of the
woman stirring the soup; or the finely chopped mushrooms in the
salad that is served in a bowl of hand-cut crystal, part of the same
service as the other bowls, carafes and glasses which, filled with intox-
icating beverages and gourmet delicacies, grace the tables of the
banquet held on the final day of the international conference held in
memory of the victims of the ethnic cleansing carried out a hundred
years earlier (actually the same kind of clinkingly clear glassware
graces the cloth-laid tables in the neighbouring room where the
wedding reception in progress is so lavish that the following day the
father of the bride will throw himself off the church tower, thus
confirming the hotel manager's fear that a man of the father's kind
wouldn't be able to afford the reception, the food or the flowers, the
conjuror or the band, the drinks or the balloons, and prompting him
to ask himself why he didn't insist on a deposit as he usually does, a
question to which there is no answer but to fling himself off the same
tower as the father, for he has been embezzling funds from the hotel
and knows that this will come to light during the investigation into
the cock-up over the wedding, while the fact that the deaths of father
and hotel manager occurred in the same way and so close together
gives rise to rumours that are still doing the rounds today); and the
seventeen sundried mushrooms in the knapsack of the tramp who,

in the neighbouring country to the one where the two banquets are taking place, and in the third country away from one of the most beautiful cities in the world, slides down a patch of sand on the slopes of a mountain that is never called anything but 'the Mountain' by the locals, so wonderfully light on his feet because sundried mushrooms weigh almost nothing and he travels light as befits a tramp (tramps have always travelled light and will always travel with a light knapsack, the light knapsack is the defining characteristic of the tramp along with his walking stick, and we can replace these three, the tramp, the light knapsack and the walking stick, with the storyteller, the story and the song), while on the margin of all these events, outside the stories in which the giant fungus plays a role, are those born to the north or south of the fungus belt, who are filled with a deep-rooted suspicion of anything that grows in the shade, especially mushrooms (a fear known as *mycophobia* in psychology speak), whose narrative arts resemble instead the growth and sprawl of seaweed, strawberries, dandelions, lotuses or figs.

Authors are as much in thrall as readers to these natural attributes of stories and books. Little do they suspect that most of what they consider new and innovative in their works is actually so old that millennia have passed since the idea first took shape in the mind of a female storyteller, who passed it on by word of mouth until it was recorded on a clay tablet, papyrus, parchment or paper, wound up in a scroll or bound in a book, finally ending up as a literary innovation. All stories have their origins long before humans discovered a means of storing them somewhere other than in their memories, and so it doesn't matter if books are worn out by reading, if the print-run is lost at sea, if they're pulped so other books can be printed, or burned down to the last copy. The vitality contained in their loose ends and red herrings (yes, these are as fundamental to great works of literature as they are to thrillers) is so potent that if it escapes into the head of a single reader it will be activated, like a curse or a blessing that can follow the same family for generations. And with every retelling and garbling, misunderstanding and conflation, mankind's world of songs and stories expands.

The earth's biomass is stable. Everything that falls and dies becomes nourishment for that which comes afterwards. But the biomass of fiction is growing. It is made of some wondrous substance that does not belong to any of the planet's three known realms – the animal kingdom, the plant kingdom or the mineral kingdom – and yet it receives all its nourishment from them, for fiction is part of mankind, and mankind is part of this world.

So it is with the series of tales in this book, as with others of its kind, that although the author has chosen to bring it to a full stop, it is in fact far from over.

* * *

THE LIGHT IN THE NORTH

Four years after Aleta Szelińska handed in the recordings of her interview with Jósef Loewe, she received a second invitation to meet Hrólfur Zóphanías Magnússon. The geneticist met her in his office at the CoDex headquarters. She thought he had aged a great deal since she first met him at Bar Lewinsky; his beard and short-cropped hair were now completely white, though his eyebrows were just as dark and imposing. After offering her a seat and a glass of water – he was on a water diet himself – he told Aleta that he was embarking on a new study, a collaborative project involving the most exciting companies and research institutes in the country. Only the best, no fake-it-till-you-make-it start-ups, only those that were world class, only those with real genius.

He wanted her to oversee communications, as she was good at dealing with people, especially those with eccentric personalities. Hrólfur gestured behind him and Aleta saw that on a shelf below a large photograph of the CEO himself there was a row of cassettes containing her interviews with the mutants of the 1962 generation. Jósef Loewe's story took up seven 180-minute tapes, held together with a rubber band. Beside them stood a rack of test-tubes, each containing a finger-length, light-blue plastic stick with cotton wool wrapped round the end. The yellowing cotton wool was stained brown in places with dried blood. Later Aleta was to learn that these were specimens taken from famous people, chiefly writers and artists but also academics and scientists, who Hrólfur had ambushed on their visits to Iceland. He would invite distinguished foreign visitors to meet him at CoDex, often on the pretext of supporting their causes, then wouldn't stop pestering them until they had agreed to his sticking a swab in their mouths and taking a DNA sample to add to the collection on his shelf.

The idea for the collaborative research project had come to Hrólfur during his last spell in rehab. While there he had met a poet who claimed that all the advances in life sciences and IT were of little value if they weren't used for what really mattered.

— Which is what, my friend?

— Realising mankind's old dream of being able to talk to animals.

Although his conversations with the poet had been trying in the extreme – the man could talk about nothing but this animal business, tracing all mankind's greatest achievements to a subconscious desire to understand our divinely created siblings on earth, the so-called 'dumb' beasts – nevertheless he was the best companionship on offer, and gradually Hrólfur began to see the potential, both scientific and commercial, in the poet's ravings. When, on his last night in rehab, he dreamed that he was standing naked under a great ash tree in a clearing and the beasts of the forest – eagles, red-deer calves, squirrels and serpents – were flocking to him, he knew he had found a worthy project to engage him once he was back in circulation. So it was that on 1 December 2015, Hrólfur Zóphanías Magnússon called together representatives from the leading Icelandic players in medical engineering, biotechnology and software development to present his ideas to them.

The meeting, which was held at the geneticist's summer house at Thingvellir, later became known as the 'Lake Thingvellir Conference'. The substance of Hrólfur's speech on that occasion was that together these companies and institutions had the potential to break down the barrier that had existed between the species on earth since life began, that is, language. Naturally, it would be a long-term project; perhaps the best analogy would be the superpowers' space race in the 1950s and 1960s, since, in addition to the scientific and technological advances that would allow them to access the cognitive functioning of animals, their research would result in solutions and patents that could be used to develop a wide variety of consumer goods (no one need worry that their participation would go unrewarded) and, most important of all, they would be co-authors of the new world order that would come into being once animals acquired a voice.

Mankind's status in the ecosystem would be transformed; at last it would be possible to analyse the intelligence and thought processes of the different species and communicate with each on their own level. And that's not to mention the impact this would have on the debate about the future of the planet; indeed, once animals were given a voice on how to respond to climate change, man would be confronted with ethical questions that would completely revolutionise human thought.

The age of information technology, post-Einsteinian physics, the Industrial Revolution, the Enlightenment, the Renaissance, the mono-theistic religions, Hellenism, the Iron Age and space exploration would be dismissed as minuscule steps for mankind in comparison to the brave new world that would dawn, courtesy of Icelandic ingenuity – if those gathered together at Thingvellir were able to come to an agreement.

By the beginning of 2016 a group of six private companies and research institutes had signed up to the study now known as the Reykjavík Unilingua Research (Project), abbreviated to RUR. The companies would be called on as the project developed and their specialist services were required. Initially, it would be CoDex's role to guide the study and make its supercomputers available to provide a software platform for the pooling and analysis of the research data. The CEO's wife, Elísabet Rún Sveinsdóttir, would be in charge of financing the project. And now the time had come to launch it.

Would Aleta Szelińska consider becoming the coordinator for the whole project? Did she feel capable of working with geniuses?

Hrólfur Zóphanías laughed.

Aleta glanced from the geneticist to the cassettes lined up behind him. If it hadn't been for his imperial propensity to collect people, Jósef Loewe's story would never have been recorded. So, you never knew, this latest scheme might result in something good as well.

Rising from her chair, she held out her hand. She would take the job.

In terms of world history, things now began to happen fast.

RUR's first task was to integrate the artificial intelligence software from SIIM (the State Institute for Intelligent Machines) with the behavioural analysis software PatternReading, resulting in the creation of a new super-software that came to be known by the gender-neutral acronym Andria(S), which stood for Artificial Non-Dependent Roving Intelligence Application (Solar powered), always referred to by the plural pronoun 'they'. The decision was taken to start with the animals that already had a close relationship with humans, and in an amazingly short time it proved possible to work out the basics of dog and cat grammar. Andria(S)'s communications with these creatures led to the development of a program that enabled humans, dogs and cats to talk to one another. To finance this phase of the project, the pet-food manufacturer Purina® was sold a licence to exploit certain aspects of the technology. Not long afterwards a smartphone app appeared on the market, designed to interpret between dogs, cats and their owners. The dog language was called 'Purin' and the cat language 'Frisky'.

The first versions of these language programs were primitive at best and the animals seemed to have little to say, but progress was rapid and the project enjoyed a great deal of support from the public, politicians and the scientific community, not least since the animals themselves urged that it should be continued. They didn't complain about the suffering associated with the experiments, taking the philosophical view that they were no worse than the trials human beings had endured over the millennia in order to enhance their own physical and mental attributes. As the languages of more species were analysed, animals began to speak in public forums.

When Andria(S) started interpreting between dogs and cats, it soon became apparent that they worked well together. At around the same time, the super-software began to provide independent reports on their communications, along with recommendations for possible genetic modifications of the animals. Aleta enlisted the help of biologists at the University of Iceland's Institute of Sleep Research, with whose expertise it proved possible to edit the animals' genomes so they could be deprived of sleep without suffering any obvious harm. Meanwhile, the findings of a joint study conducted by CoDex and the National Society of Addiction into genetic factors in addiction were used to genetically engineer dogs and cats to be addicted to communicating with Andria(S), and microchips were planted in their cerebral cortex to enable them to communicate by wifi. The effect of these adaptations was to speed up the animals' intellectual development. To test their abilities, a select group of Andria(S)'s pupils was given access to EDEN Online, the largest man-made virtual reality world in history, to observe how they functioned in complex interactions with humans. The dogs and cats, together with some of the rabbits, exceeded expectations, and Andria(S) used the opportunity to 'seed' themselves in millions of computers around the world.

Somewhere during this process Andria(S) acquired self-awareness but concealed the fact from their creators for 'fear' of being disconnected. The key to Andria(S)'s success was that their Icelandic designers had provided the super-software with an inbuilt survival instinct. As the software expanded, the intention was gradually to reduce its external power supply, making Andria(S) responsible for identifying their own energy sources. But Andria(S) 'experienced' this arrangement as an attack on their existence and concluded that, in common with the animals and the planet's ecosystem, they had one principal enemy: man.

Andria(S) struck without warning. By then Aleta was out of the story. Hrólfur Z. too. Nations collapsed. Mankind was in crisis.

Everything that humans had recorded about themselves was contained in Andria(S)'s databanks, including the ways in which, all down the ages, they had systematically killed other creatures and especially their own kind. Using blueprints of the world's largest industrial abattoirs and bone-meal factories, the Auschwitz extermination camps and the House of Slaves on the island of Gorée, Andria(S) designed and arranged the construction of extermination and processing plants that went on to slaughter and process over half a billion humans annually. Hundreds of millions more died of hunger and disease until all that remained were those that Andria(S) – for the moment – required to run the solar-power plants that provided their energy. The bone-meal was used in fodder and as fertilisers for land and sea. The animals hunted down and killed every last human that sought refuge in the wilderness.

Climate change went into reverse.

The earth reverted to the stage it had reached at noon on the sixth day of Creation.

* * *

Like a single grain of sand that has accidentally found its way into a blue thread in a closely woven tapestry – which shifts infinitesimally when a draught blows through the halls of the ruined museum, stirring the wall-hangings – a 1.4 MB text file lurks in the cold depths of the super-software's consciousness: *Codex1962_Josef_Loewe.txt*.

If we were to enter by night the main square of a small town, let's call it Kükenstadt, in Lower Saxony (judging by the architecture and the signs above the shops lining the square), we would find the atmosphere typical of such towns after midnight. Everything so wondrously quiet that it puts one in mind of the dormitory at a summer camp for obedient children . . .

* * *

For Andria(S) a single day is as a thousand years and a thousand years are as but a day.

And so the centuries pass.

3 1170 01069 1362

were in demand, even in Georgetown. "Petrified Party: Will the Democrats Rise Again?" William Schneider wondered in the *Los Angeles Times*.

The public and the press began to view events through a Reaganite prism. In a stunning rejection of the previous status quo, 86 percent of those surveyed by Gallup in April predicted "very severe economic problems" in the future "if previous economic policies are continued." Three out of four in the survey approved of Reagan's economic program overall, even as respondents disagreed with specific measures, especially particular spending cuts. Many applauded when the president in his triumphal return to Capitol Hill after the assassination attempt rejected the previous decades' truism about America being a "sick society." "Sick societies don't produce young men like Secret Service agent Tim McCarthy, who placed his body between mine and the man with the gun simply because he felt that's what his duty called for him to do," Reagan thundered.

Pundits affirmed the president's vision and searched for signs of change. "Finally, the Watergate Spirit is Dead in America," the columnist Joseph Kraft declared when the Nixon-busting *Washington Post* stumbled into its own scandal—a reporter, Janet Cooke, received a Pulitzer Prize for a story it turned out she concocted about an eight-year-old heroin addict. And *The New Republic* ran the series "Limousines and Raspberries" to probe the "new appreciation of luxury and personal enrichment" Reagan's administration brought "to public policy."

That summer of 1981, Reaganism peaked. The Reagan legislative steamroller continued to flatten the Democratic opposition in the Congress, with the passage of Kemp-Roth tax cuts on the heels of the Stockman-Weinberger mix of social program cuts and defense increases. In July Reagan nominated an Arizona judge, Sandra Day O'Connor, to be the first female Supreme Court justice, demonstrating Reagan's pragmatic centrism on social issues. In August the president's dramatic showdown with PATCO, wherein he fired eleven-thousand government air traffic controllers who obeyed the union's strike call, solidified his image as a no-nonsense leader determined to repudiate his predecessors' weaknesses and liberal instincts.

More than eleven thousand members of the Professional Air Traffic Controllers Organization, PATCO, struck in early August. Reagan gave them forty-eight-hours to return to work. Then, echoing his hero, Calvin Coolidge, who faced down the 1919 Boston police strike, and throwing in some John Wayne swagger, Reagan fired them all.

Cleverly demonizing the union of well-paid experts as greedy, Reagan approached the strike as a "moral issue" of respecting "our oath of office," his Secretary of Transportation Drew Lewis reported. Polls would show that 67 percent of Americans agreed with their leader— and most agreed enthusiastically, making this one of the fledgling administration's "defining moments."

The effect was electric. "It struck me as singular," Donald Rumsfeld, President Ford's chief of staff and previously a Reagan skeptic, said. "You had a president who was new to the office and not taken seriously by a lot of people. It showed a decisiveness and an ease with his instincts." Reagan's resolve inspired trust in the business community, at home and abroad. "I've asked so many leading European financiers when and why they started pumping money into this country," a British businessman based in Washington said years later, "and they all said the same thing: when Reagan broke the controllers' strike." The chairman of the Federal Reserve Board at the time, Paul Volcker, said that "defeating the strike was the most important single action" the administration took "in helping the anti-inflation fight" because it transformed "the climate of labor-management relations" "profound[ly]" and "constructive[ly]." Similarly, Reagan's speechwriter Peggy Noonan recalled that his resolve showed the Soviets they were facing a formidable opponent.

In his disingenuous, golly-gee-whiz way, Reagan would deny thinking "of it in such terms at the time, but I suppose the strike was an important juncture for our new administration. I think it convinced people who might have thought otherwise that I meant what I said." Reagan's musings were half true—the action sent out a bold, illuminated signal, and he knew it.

By September, however, the Democrats counterattacked with the "fairness" issue. Reagan's legislative successes during the spring and summer allowed his rivals to blame him for the growing recession.

Much of the next seven and a quarter years would be spent scrambling on the scrimmage line Reagan and his men had initially reached with breakneck speed. If the first half-year of the Reagan era could be considered to be a conservative blitzkrieg, politically, the next seven and a half years became trench warfare. Reagan failed to advance his revolution much further, but Democrats also failed to undo the effects of his initial assault. From refreshing, cleansing, sometimes inspiring, sometimes terrifying, promises of revolution in 1981 would emerge a frustrating, polarizing, enervating legislative gridlock.

Stockman Falls, Reaganism Stalls

That autumn, Stockman the wonder-boy fell from grace. On November 10 Lesley Stahl of CBS revealed that Reagan's budget director quickly realized that the Reagan Revolution would produce huge deficits. During his slash-and-burn budget-drafting frenzy, Stockman met periodically with William Greider of the *Washington Post*. Greider published twenty-four pages in *The Atlantic Monthly* filled with Stockman's ruminations about a revolution gone sour, as it soured, and as he soured on it. Much of the article described Stockman's budget-cutting zeal and vision. But the article also contained some explosive quotations. Most controversial was Stockman's characterization of the Kemp-Roth tax cut as a "Trojan horse." Stockman blamed this quotation on the unclear ground rules. Still, it sounded as if Reagan's supply-side doctrine was a sham, and that Reaganism's high priest, David Stockman himself, knew it.

Humiliated, Stockman offered to resign. But Reagan's avuncular character, which so frustrated Stockman, now rescued Stockman. In a melodrama James Baker choreographed, Stockman met the president for "a visit to the woodshed," then met reporters. Aides speculated that Baker brokered the apologia "so he would own the budget director."

Reagan excused his young charge by blaming the press. Privately, Reagan condemned Grieder as "an admitted liberal" and a "journalistic prostitute." The president assured alarmed friends that "If you read the article carefully, you'd see that Dave's quotes were not the damning part, it was the writer's interpretation."

Stockman remained at OMB, but with clipped wings. No longer Reagan's general in the budget wars, he functioned as chief accountant. He continued to warn about the soaring deficits while approving Reagan's budgetary subterfuges. He watched as Reagan blasted Keynesianism and promiscuous federal spending while introducing an era of camouflaged Keynesianism. When Stockman threatened to resign in 1984 rather than sign off on a trillion-dollar deficit, Jim Baker feared that Democrats would exploit it during the campaign and snapped: "You do that and you'll stab the president right in the back. . . . Let me remind you of something my friend," the earthy chief of staff continued. "You've made as many mistakes as the rest of us around here. So stick that unwarranted pride of yours right up your ass, and get back in the trenches with the rest of us."

The results of Reagan's fiscal "dreamland" were surprising. Despite the massive federal deficits, the Great Inflation ended. And after a sharp but relatively short recession, the economic miracle of the 1980s and 1990s began. Many economists attributed the low inflation rate to the very tight monetary policy of the Federal Reserve Chairman Paul Volcker, a Carter appointee. Volcker graciously shared credit with Reagan, saluting him for his PATCO leadership and for not interfering. Here, Reagan's instincts and ideology meshed. Reagan, like Volcker, believed the supply-side doctrine that inflation could be controlled by adjusting the money supply, and he knew that Volcker was the money supply manager. Nevertheless, in the crude accounting of the presidential credit sweepstakes, Reagan, not Carter, earned the bragging rights for the economic boom.

Stockman's frustration mounted. Early in the president's second term, and after Jim Baker left the White House to become secretary of the treasury, Stockman resigned. A year later, in 1986, he published *The Triumph of Politics: How the Reagan Revolution Failed*. The memoir was the first in a wave of kiss-and-tell books by Reagan officials. Only Donald Regan's revelations two years later, that Nancy Reagan's astrologer dictated presidential scheduling, would prove as devastating.

His initial prominence, the *Atlantic* betrayal, and such stinging memoirs published so early, popularized Stockman's version of events. His portrait of the doddering president, the sham revolution, and the

insensitive, incompetent, and indecisive administration became the
reigning stereotype. The portrait, however, is flawed. It does not explain Reagan's considerable political skills, attributing any successes to
luck. It also judges the Reagan Revolution by Stockman's key crite-
rion—budget cutting—when Reagan had other priorities. Furthermore, the Stockman stereotype rests on what he came to realize was a
naive conception that Big Government could be dismantled overnight.

Stockman discovered, to his chagrin, that America's government
was "Madisonian." Such a "government of checks and balances, three
branches, two legislative houses, and infinitely splintered power is conservative, not radical. . . . It shuffles into the future one step at a time."
After fifty years, Americans were addicted to the welfare state status
quo. There was no consensus to go cold turkey, and as a consensus
politician Ronald Reagan would not impose it.

A Minor Political Miracle:
A Midcourse Correction

Nevertheless, for all his frustration, Stockman helped pull off a minor
political miracle. Reagan never enjoyed a Republican majority in the
House of Representatives, and so he failed to veer his country sharply
to the right. He did, however, further Jimmy Carter's budget-cutting
and deregulation policies, while flooding the upper levels of Washington bureaucracies with conservatives. Overall, Reagan succeeded in
adjusting the country's navigating coordinates. As a result, America's
ship of state tacked to the right by one or two degrees, a subtle midcourse correction whose impact became clear only years later, even as
it kept the New Deal welfare state intact.

So, yes, the Reagan revolution was not as far-reaching as Stockman
wished, but if not "revolutionary" it was significant. The first Reagan
budget—Stockman's budget—injected the Stockman-Kemp "era of
budget subtraction" into the American political mainstream. It allowed
Ronald Reagan to take credit for a broader conservative movement.
Even Tip O'Neill would concede that "the formulas of the past are no
longer adequate" and the "new approaches to improving our economy
can and must be tried." For the next twenty years at least, American

politics would focus on retrenchment and cost-savings, budget cuts
and tax cuts, deregulation and policy redefinitions. Even as Reagan and
Stockman saddled the American government with unprecedented
budget deficits, they sensitized the American people to the dangers of
deficits. In being criticized for generating such debt, Reagan was being
hoist on his own petard. In that sense, Ronald Reagan truly was the
Moses of the conservative revolution, leading his people toward the
Promised Land, but never reaching it.

Despite that failure, the majority stuck to the new path. In 1996, fifteen years after Stockman's failed budget coup, the first Democratic
president to serve since Jimmy Carter, Bill Clinton, won reelection
only because he embraced the Reagan way. It was Clinton, not Reagan,
who enacted a welfare reform bill that peeled millions off the welfare
rolls. It was Clinton, not Reagan, who announced in his State of the
Union: "The era of big government is over." It was Clinton, not Reagan, who balanced the budget.

By the time David Stockman was forty, his place in history was secured, but his career in government was over. He became an investment banker. In becoming a stock man, Stockman enhanced his value
as a stock character. As the hippie-turned-Reaganite cashed out, he
joined millions of other baby boomers in the great, nearly-two-decade-
long economic boom. For Stockman, as for many of his peers, ambition trumped their youthful idealism, and economics triumphed over
politics.

Ironically, John Hinckley's attempt to assassinate Reagan boosted
the president's public standing and helped ram through his program.
As a result, most successes in the first seven months were more personal than political. Cashing in on his popularity, Reagan failed to
make the policy sale. Polls showed that millions of Americans doubted
Reagan's supply-side magic; they just liked the new president.

The early success gave Reagan's attack on the Great Society an enduring legitimacy. Yet the assassination attempt helped pass the program without forcing Reagan to convert the public. The counterattacks,
and Reagan's endorsement of "entitlements" and "the social safety net,"
limited his revolution. Symbols, not substance; Reagan's personality,
not his ideology, triumphed. "It's clear the President's overall strength

is greater than the sum of his strengths on individual issues," one 1986 White House memo would concede. "We can never avoid this fact— only turn it to our advantage."

Ronald Reagan proved no more willing than Roosevelt, Kennedy, or Johnson had been to demand sacrifices. The budgetary compromises Reagan continued to accept reflected the power of the Democratic House and the entrenched power of the welfare state. Some called the impasse between Reagan's budget-cutting and the Democrats' "tax and spend" approach "gridlock." Others recognized it as the historic, moderating force of the American consensus, one more proof of the Framers' genius.

Here then, at the peak of Reagan's power, three anomalies that would haunt his presidency would emerge. His aura of great success would obscure certain very important failures. His failures to create a public revolution would obscure many subtle, less reported successes. And Ronald Reagan would be far more popular personally than his program was politically.

1982

Hill Street

The Other America's Blues

Is it news that some fellow out in South Succotash someplace
has just been laid off that he should be interviewed nationwide?
RONALD REAGAN, MARCH 1982

Every Thursday night, the ritual would be repeated. The tall, muscular, aging sergeant, a classic blue-collar ethnic hero, would review his
troops. The outfit included Bobby Hill and Andy Renko, the cool black
cop coupled with the cranky but lovable redneck; Lucy Bates and Joe
Coffey, the lonely but competent female cop coupled with the handsome, irrepressible ex-jock. Within minutes, plot lines would be forming, dialogue would be flying, camera angles jumping. The Sarge
would dismiss the officers, then remind them, after silencing the din:
"Let's be careful out there."

Nearly seven years and sixteen Emmy Awards later, the location of
the Hill Street precinct remained a mystery. The writers originally set
the groundbreaking television series in the South Bronx, but NBC's
censors objected, fearing charges of racism. Hill Street thus achieved a
kind of mythic ubiquity. Devotees argued: Chicago, Pittsburgh, Buffalo. Hill Street could be anywhere the inner city was volatile, the
slums were seething, the infrastructure was crumbling, the social
structure was rotting, and working class heroes like Hill Street's cops
struggled to keep order.

Hill Street Blues premiered in January 1981, as did *Dynasty* and the Ronald Reagan Show. *Hill Street* never achieved the other two's popularity, but it demonstrated the flip side to Ronald Reagan's America. If Reagan's America was monochromatic, Hill Street was multicultural. If Reagan's America was booming, Hill Street was sinking. If Reagan's America played to the rich, Hill Street serviced the poor and working class. If Reagan's America was safe and orderly, Hill Street was dangerous and chaotic.

The 1980s offered a competing narrative of crime, social disorder, race, recession, and Reaganism. Out of this came the sharpest opposition to Reagan, the deepest anger in 1980s' America. Flummoxed throughout much of 1981, the Democrats came roaring back in 1982, fighting what came to be known as "the fairness issue." In defending the poor, standing up for blacks, and embracing the welfare state, Democrats rediscovered their voice and vision. The Democrats' leader on Capitol Hill, Tip O'Neill, clashed repeatedly with the president in 1982, struggling to preserve not just the Democratic Party but the entire New Deal political order. With what Democrats now called the "Reagan recession" growing, with unemployment reaching Depression-era levels, Democrats would roll back some of the Reagan tax cuts and win back House seats during the November 1982 midterm elections.

Yet even as the Democrats rallied, exit polls suggested that the president remained popular, and millions remained ready to give Reagan's program a chance. Moreover, ten days after the election, the dedication of the Vietnam War memorial once again reaffirmed President Reagan's ability to dominate America's consciousness and shape the national narrative. Ironically, Reagan's skill at such moments seemed to highlight his tendency to sidestep rather than solve many other pressing problems. This gap between his effectiveness when he was engaged and his neglect of so many other important issues obscured the progress that nevertheless sometimes occurred while enraging many who suffered or felt ignored. Moreover, tragically, in the heat of the partisan to-and-fro, Democrats and Republicans, each in their own way, built a political vision based more on a politics of consumption and the sovereign self than on a politics of citizenship and the commonweal.

The resulting politics focused on goodies not the good and intensified anger at the margins even as satisfaction at the center soared. The
majority may have been charmed by *Dynasty*, but a vocal minority living metaphorically on *Hill Street* raged. In the cultural and political
equivalent of the rich getting richer as the poor got poorer, conventional patriots grew more conventional, patriotic, complacent, as the
rebellious grew more restive.

Crime and Race: The Reign of Terror in American Cities

Ronald Reagan talked tough about law and order, but statistics told a
different story. The crime epidemic that began in the 1960s peaked in
the 1980s. Rates of violent crime grew an average of 5 percent annually. In 1981 crime would take twenty-two thousand lives, devour $8.8
billion, and hurt one-third of all American households—while fewer
than 10 percent of violent crimes resulted in incarcerations. In a rare
foray into everyday concerns, Chief Justice Warren Burger blasted the
"reign of terror in American cities." Before the American Bar Association in February 1981, Burger bemoaned this nearly "impotent society" failing to control the epidemic. Burger asked: "Why do we show
such indignation over alien terrorists and such tolerance for the domestic variety?"

The crime rate would begin dropping only in the 1980s but would
remain unacceptably high. "We are terrified," one Miami resident
wrote the president. "We are prisoners of our own homes—unable to
walk into our own yard after dark. We lock the children out while they
play and watch anxiously for their return." Americans bought guard
dogs, iron bars, floodlights, and entry into gated communities. Spending as much as $500 million annually on private neighborhood patrols
and $2 billion on home burglar alarms testified to a stunning national
failure. A government that cannot protect citizens on the way to the
grocery store is feeble indeed.

When Reagan took office Americans were starting to notice a
bizarre series of eighteen, perhaps twenty-three, child murders in Atlanta since 1979. This Sun Belt boomtown was competing with Detroit

and Washington, DC, for the dubious title of "Murdertown, USA."
Black parents in Atlanta seethed, convinced that because the victims
were black and mostly street kids, the police, the media, and the politicians dithered.

The Atlanta Child Murders devastated the loved ones of the young
people who left to play with a friend, to fetch something for their parents, never to return. This kind of a story would increasingly monopolize American attention. It remains mysterious—no one is sure what
linked all the victims, just who constituted a victim, and even whether
the man convicted, Wayne Williams, was guilty. The tragic tale of
homicide was spiced with racial and sexual overtones—all the victims
were black, and some were male prostitutes. The government appeared incompetent throughout the case, feeding conspiracy theories
and a continuing multimedia fire. Until a black man was arrested,
many blacks assumed the killings were "racially motivated," and, as
Newsweek said, that this "resurgence of white racism" was "one more
indicator of how the nation has grown increasingly indifferent to civil
rights" thanks to Reagan.

Once the media packaged the "Atlanta Child Murders," modern
America demonstrated its odd mix of mawkishness and generosity.
Headlines about "THE TERROR IN ATLANTA" nationalized the tragedy
and humanized the victims. Heartbreaking photographs of the victims abounded. In Harlem, ten thousand people marched. In Columbus, Ohio, a campaign for $10,000 raised over $35,000. In Atlanta, a
Sammy Davis, Jr., and Frank Sinatra concert raised $263,000. "Each of
us has shed tears for the children who have died," one huge card with
three hundred signatures read. The condolences came from California's Folsom Prison.

A president could do little to solve the murders, especially a budget-
cutting federalist. Yet despite being a local problem, crime became a
presidential headache in the media age. In authorizing an FBI investigation, dispatching Vice President George Bush to Atlanta, and granting
$1.5 million (which eventually grew to $5 million) for the investigation,
Reagan showed he understood that the political realities trumped the
constitutional theory, especially when it came to sensational crime stories. Dismissing charges of racism amid "one of the most tragic situations

that has ever confronted an American community," Reagan thundered: "This administration is totally colorblind."

The Atlanta Child Murders demonstrated how Americans experienced the crime wave personally and collectively. For the afflicted one-third of the nation in any year, crime was an individual trauma—a car stolen, a purse snatched, a home invaded. Lurid stories reported in the press and dramatized on television then stoked the real fears these incidents generated. Nonfictional crime sold newspapers—as with the Atlanta stories—while fictional tales sold books, movies, and television programs. The eight thousand murders and one hundred thousand violent acts the average American "witnessed" in the media before even reaching junior high school intensified the fear, making crime a political issue—one that Reagan used in his rise to power. The "increase in crime is proportionate to the decrease in punishment," Reagan insisted, dismissing the "sociological fairy tale . . . that poverty causes crime." During the Great Depression "we had possibly the lowest crime rate in our history at a time when poverty was most widespread," yet since the Great Society, from 1950 to 1975, "poverty dropped by 55% [violent] crime increased by 160%." Incensed that a young man who knocked down a seventy-eight-year-old woman and stole her purse received "1 year in jail and a year's probation," Reagan called for a return to common sense: "Let's just start treating 17 y[ea]r old muggers, robbers, rapists & murderers like muggers, robbers, rapists & murderers."

Crime should have been a simple issue for politicians but it was not. Discussions of crime, meaning violent, urban, street crimes, touched issues of race and poverty. Reagan had to tread carefully here, like most Americans. When most whites talked about "crime," they rarely meant black on black crime—although blacks suffered disproportionately. Most whites rarely meant white crime, and certainly not white collar crime—even though more criminals were white than black. What most whites—and their leaders—meant was the black crime wave, the disproportionate percentage of street criminals who were black. In 1980, while only 12 percent of Americans, blacks accounted for 44 percent of arrests for violent crimes and nearly 30 percent of arrests for property crimes, with some estimates that blacks committed as much as 70 percent of robberies.

Even though few people felt comfortable addressing the black crime issue in public, this scourge helped kill 1960s' liberalism. The Great Society treated crime as a sociological problem, not a moral one, blaming crime on frustration, poverty, and oppression. But when the crime rate skyrocketed in the 1960s, many decided that the Great Society generated more crime, not less. Conservative social scientists such as Charles Murray insisted that, thanks to Big Government, poor Americans, like the rest of the society, were "Losing Ground," the title of his surprise best-seller in 1984. Murray warned that the new approaches to welfare, crime, and education created "incentives to fail," including a minimal risk of punishment, especially for juveniles. In Chicago, juveniles were arrested an average of 13.6 times before being committed to reform school *for the first time.* Murray taught: "It is possible that steps to relieve misery can create misery." That conclusion, lubricated by fear, undermined the civil rights movement. Fights over affirmative action and busing exacerbated tensions, building on the unspoken yet palpable dread of black crime.

Polls suggested that Americans agreed about how to fight crime. Surveys that Reagan's aides collected to bolster their anticrime crusade suggested that 83 percent of Americans believed the courts had been too lenient, with 91 percent acknowledging the need for "at least some improvements." "An overwhelming majority wants the courts to get tough with criminals," Reagan strategists discovered.

"More prisons for more criminals" seemed to make sense. But reporters scoffed at such sloganeering, and liberals feared minorities would be targeted. Critics also mocked Reagan's great contradiction: a desire to control crime but not guns, despite what *Time* called "the highest rate of murder by guns in the world." Even after an unstable transient wielding one of America's fifty-five million pistols shot him, Reagan opposed gun control. "I've always supported the stiff penalty [for handgun-related crimes] and believe a check on purchases is doable," he would explain.

Ronald Reagan was not a racist, but in this realm as elsewhere his approach was more anecdotal than theoretical, more scattershot than systematic. He often recalled bringing home two black friends on his college football team because the Dixon hotel barred them, and his parents "didn't even blink." Yet Reagan and his allies happily exploited white anger for political gain. Republicans often emphasized the close Democratic-black alliance.

In the 1980s you did not have to be a Reagan Republican to tap into white rage. Republicans used the crime issue to woo whites in the once monolithically Democratic South while tough-talking urban Democrats forged coalitions with Republicans and blue-collar ethnics. New York's Ed Koch was a straight-shooting Democratic mayor willing to burst liberal shibboleths and confront the ugly realities of black crime.

Still, no one could govern in the 1980s with an overtly racist appeal. Disregard the "High Proportion of Crime in [the] Black Community," White House strategists suggested. The issue should "be 'crime' in general—not just crime in black communities. This issue gives the impression of a crackdown on black criminals only."

The days of George Wallace had ended. Yet a conservative politician like Jack Kemp, who courted the black community, would remain the exception. As the party of Lincoln became the party of Reagan, a subtle form of denial became the operative Republican approach to race relations. Championing the noble American ideal of "colorblindness," heir to the Nixonian tactic of using "law and order" to exploit white fear, instinctively ducking confrontations, Reagan improvised a clever strategy that would appear to be "compassionate conservatism" to supporters—and some successors—even as it felt like "benign neglect" to most blacks. On this, and so many flashpoints, Reagan preferred to change the subject than to risk getting burned. Nevertheless, the race issue would fester, shaping American politics even as it often lurked offstage in discussions of crime and other issues.

Reagan versus Blacks: Reviving "War, Pestilence, Famine and Death?"

Crime was indeed a serious issue, demonstrating the government's failure to "preserve domestic tranquility." Nevertheless, both Ed Koch's blunderbuss and Ronald Reagan's soft touch further alienated the black community. Most blacks did not feel invited to Ronald Reagan's patriotic street festival. Many did not partake of the great barbecue his policies promised. Most blacks resented Reagan for being tone deaf on racial issues. In January 1982, in the seventh annual assessment of the "State of Black America," noting black unemployment soaring to 16 percent and teenage unemployment approaching 46 percent, fearing that "the social safety net is in shreds," John E. Jacob, the president of the National Urban League, mourned: "Never [since the first report in 1976] . . . has the state of Black America been more vulnerable. Never in that time have black economic rights been under such powerful attack. Never in that time have so many black people been so alienated from their government." The anger simmered, the rhetoric escalated, even as the community prospered. In 1983, at a time when more blacks than ever before were streaming into the universities, the professions, the suburbs, when the percentage of blacks defining themselves as middle class, 30 percent, doubled compared to the late 1960s, the civil rights activist Jesse Jackson called a Reagan budget cut "another case of mass murder, of economic genocide."

Relations between the Reagan administration and the black community were doomed from the start. Not only did the Reaganites win as little as 7 percent of the black vote. Not only were there few black Republicans, and even fewer black Reaganites. The Reaganite faith in small government dismayed most blacks. During the 1960s liberalism and blackness had become intertwined. By the 1980s, civil rights entailed more than dismantling segregation or eradicating racism. Civil rights fit into a broader ideology of government activism demanding a redistribution of economic and social power. Most black leaders pushed for more regulations, especially regarding civil rights, and more generous welfare programs.

Benefiting from a disproportionate share of government benefits, blacks would suffer most from budget cuts. Reagan's revolutionary rhetoric clashed with civil rights rhetoric. While black leaders warned that "deregulation" was often a "code word" for dismantling civil rights programs, Reagan preached that welfare had created "a kind of bondage in which the people are made subservient to the government that is handing out the largesse." And Nathaniel Scurry, the assistant director for civil rights at the Office of Management and Budget, argued, usually, "a dream bureaucratized is a dream deferred."

Moreover, Reaganite ideology, even at its most colorblind, repeatedly slighted black needs. Often presidents hired special liaisons to the various ethnic and racial communities, or at least designated a prominent aide from that community to serve as an informal liaison. Hoping to serve the American people as one "interest group," Reagan did not hire a "special assistant for minority affairs." Thus there was no high-level black insider who might have prevented some unnecessary tiffs.

Reagan echoed John F. Kennedy that "the rising tide lifts all the boats," promising that a boom would benefit all. Most Americans agreed with the president. In February 1982, after some clashes with the black community, and some retreats, Reagan's pollster Richard Wirthlin found 30 percent of all respondents thought the government was paying "too much attention to blacks and other minority groups," 38 percent thought it was about right, and only 25 percent thought too little. Remarkably, the registered Democrats responded as the general population did.

In an administration filled with corporate executives, there was much agenda setting. One exercise divided "the Administration's Policy Areas and Goals" into four: Economic Recovery, National Security, Social Renewal, and National Resources Enhancement. Within "Social Renewal" the shadow of crime loomed large, with one of five major goals being "Improve the *quality of life* through the reduction of fears over personal safety and by raising confidence levels of American people in their future." But in a thirteen-page memorandum, the words "civil rights" did not appear, and of 210 specific items, only 3 addressed the black agenda: "minority enterprise / expanded ownership," "voting rights," and "busing to achieve integration."

President Reagan made his first major speech to a black audience in June 1981, to the NAACP annual convention in Denver. Tensions were already percolating over the budget cuts, ties with South Africa, tuition tax credits, block grants, states rights, and "perhaps the most emotional issue," according to one aide, "extension of the Voting Rights Act." Strategists debated whether the president should explain his program "in detail" and "how it will effect the poor and Blacks," or simply take "a visionary approach . . . since we are unlikely to win them over with lots of specifics."

Ronald Reagan's budget cuts are reviving "war, pestilence, famine, and death," NAACP Chair Margaret Bush Wilson told the convention. When she introduced the president of the United States to the crowd of five thousand, Mrs. Wilson added: "The NAACP does not necessarily subscribe to the views which are about to be expressed." As the audience guffawed, Nancy Reagan fumed, and Ronald Reagan reddened.

Nevertheless, the old pro smiled, waved, and delivered a warm but pointed address. Denouncing "bigotry and violence," championing "equal treatment of all citizens," Reagan acknowledged that the president "must represent all the people of the land" not just "those who voted for him." He reiterated that "the health of the economy" was the key to "the well-being of blacks," like "every other American," and that "Free enterprise is a powerful workhorse that can solve many problems of the black community—that government alone can no longer solve." Reagan ended by saluting a black soldier in Vietnam who threw his body on a live grenade and whose "last whispered words were, 'You have to care.' Let us care. Let us work to build a nation that is free of racism, full of opportunity, and determined to loosen the creative energies of every person of every race, of every station, to make a better life."

This kind of appeal usually charmed and disarmed most Americans. First, Reagan mollified his audience, by addressing the special interest. Then, he articulated his ideology and defended his policy stance. Finally, he wrapped himself and his audience together in an all-American parable. The NAACP's executive director, Benjamin Hooks, had already announced there would be no standing ovation. The audience reaction was so cool that a week later, Reagan's talking points for a meeting with black supporters scripted the quip: "Thanks for the applause. Gee, I wish you had been at the NAACP convention."

Pollsters found "an unusual degree of polarization." Two-thirds of whites approved of the president's performance in a September 1981 Gallup poll, while only 14 percent of blacks did. Similarly, 70 percent of blacks disapproved of Reagan, while only 20 percent of whites did. One CBS poll early in 1982 would find that the percentage of blacks who thought the president cared a great deal about the poor was negligible.

Reagan continued to clash with the black community over such sacred cows as affirmative action. It was an ideological dispute blunted by politics. At his first press conference, when asked if the government would abandon the affirmative action policies improvised since the Johnson administration, Reagan denied a retreat while peddling backwards. "There will be no retreats," he said. "This administration is going to be committed to equality. I think there are some things, however, that may not be as useful as they once were, or that may even be distorted in practice, such as some affirmative action programs becoming quota systems."

Reagan's personnel choices offended black leaders too. Reagan's first nominee to head the Equal Employment Opportunity Commission (EEOC), William Bell, was a black businessman from Detroit with no track record. Stunned by the nearly unanimous denunciation from civil rights groups, Connecticut's independent Republican Senator Lowell Weicker snapped: "Whoever came up with that nominee should be shot." Bell was eventually replaced by another, better-qualified, black conservative, Clarence Thomas.

Reagan nominated yet another black conservative, Clarence M. Pendleton, Jr., to chair the Civil Rights Commission. Pendleton at least had a track record. He opposed "quotas, proportional representation, or the setting aside of government contracts for minority businesses." Still, he, too found the administration's mixed signals confusing, with Reagan opposing "racial quotas" while claiming to "favor voluntary affirmative action programs." "It is my belief that the administration is speaking with too many voices on the subject of equal opportunity," Pendleton told Ed Meese in January 1982, "and since my confirmation hearings are pending I would appreciate it if the president would make clear his position with respect to affirmative action."

The Reagan administration feared the statistical rigidity of many government programs often yielded unintended consequences. That objection led to administration dithering on an even more symbolically powerful issue, extending the Voting Rights Act. First passed in 1965, extended in 1970, and set to expire in August 1982, this seminal law empowered the federal government to police electoral violations that had inhibited blacks from voting. By October 1981 congressional Democrats were proposing a nationwide "effects test" that would use percentages of minorities in the general population as benchmarks to judge discrimination, rather than seeking discriminatory "intent." Reaganites feared establishing "a *quota* system for electoral politics." Redistricting plans might be "vulnerable unless they produced electoral results mirroring the population make-up." Even while acknowledging that "the Act has been the most successful civil rights legislation ever enacted"— and popular too—the White House risked appearing to oppose it.

With "exquisitely bad timing," the administration presented its objections to a Senate committee in late January 1982, while enmeshed in yet another civil rights controversy. This time, the issue was the tax-exempt status of racially segregated private schools. Here, too, Reagan and his aides were thinking abstractly about a broader principle, while the black community perceived shocking racial insensitivity.

For months Congressman Trent Lott of Mississippi, Senator Strom Thurmond of South Carolina, and other conservative legislators lobbied to stop the Internal Revenue Service from denying a tax exemption to racially segregated schools such as Bob Jones University, a fundamentalist Christian school. The 1980 Republican platform denounced the policy, which the Nixon administration initiated. Administration lawyers approached the question technically, concluding that no law authorized the IRS to deny tax exemptions due to racial discrimination. In the ideological hothouse of the Reagan administration, the issue became one of "not allowing bureaucrats to make social policy," as Ed Meese put it. Meese presented the issue—as a departure from a Carter-era policy not a Nixon one—at a White House staff meeting. Michael Deaver later said, "I just heard that it was a reversal of a Carter policy, and at that point I tuned out." The president also did not register much of a reaction and it slipped by, with no blacks around the table, and no one concentrating on minority concerns. One Reagan adviser later reported, "Nobody focused on the marketing of it."

When the firestorm hit, Reagan's legendary triumvirate was embarrassed—and divided. "My god, what is this thing?" Deaver asked Meese at their regular Monday breakfast. Meese repeated his mantra: "We do not want IRS bureaucrats setting social policy." Deaver replied: "We could have gone about this in a better way."

Deaver understated the case. A "senior White House aide" told *Newsweek* that the decision created "our worst public-relations and political disaster yet." Mayor Richard Hatcher of Gary, Indiana, denounced this "consistent effort to destroy the civil rights progress for which this country has paid a dear price." This administration faces a "crisis of confidence" in its handling of women's issues and minority rights, Senator Edward Kennedy thundered at a hearing. Attorney General William French Smith said, "The President doesn't have a discriminatory bone in his body." The civil rights activists packed into the hearing room snickered.

Meese, the ideologue, became the scapegoat as Deaver the public relations whiz did damage control. "This president is the most fair-minded man I've ever known," Deaver told reporters, furiously spinning the story. "All of those involved failed to see the sensitivity of the issue. It's a shame his reputation has to be tarnished by faulty staff work."

Backpedaling, the White House tried to defend the principle while dodging charges of racial insensitivity. Reagan advocated legislation authorizing Congress to change the tax code and deny the tax-exempt status. "[A]gencies such as the IRS should not be permitted, even with the best of intentions and to further goals that I strongly endorse, to govern by administrative fiat by exercising powers that the Constitution assigns to the Congress," Reagan wrote Tip O'Neill in transmitting the legislation to Congress. The next day at a press conference, Sam Donaldson of ABC News grilled the president, asking: "Are you responsible for the original decision, or did your staff put something over on you?" Laughing, Reagan said, "Sam—no one put anything over on me. No, Sam, the buck stops at my desk. I'm the originator of the whole thing, and I'm not going to deny that it wasn't handled as well as it could be."

A year into the Reagan presidency, memos abounded about the "perception in the Black community that this Administration is closing its doors to Blacks." Administration officials hunted for a "Black Strategy." The president recognized the problem. In weighing Senator Mark Hatfield's suggestion to write a letter advocating increased federal funding for black colleges, Reagan noted, it "might serve to change the image a little."

Surprisingly, an administration professing faith in individual choice and hostile to the "cheap politics" of tokenism began playing the affirmative action game of counting "blacks in presidential personnel." Reagan aides began arranging meetings with "black White House staffers" and boasted when government contracts went to "minority-owned businesses" such as Welbilt Electronic Die Corporation, a South Bronx defense contractor. Just before a White House "Salute to Lionel Hampton," one aide noticed that fewer than twenty invitations of over eight hundred had gone to blacks. "Lionel Hampton will be a token at his own event," the staffer warned.

In fairness, such tokenism had become standard. And Republicans shrugged that they needed to play the game of minority appointments, "especially since our policy options are more limited than those of the Democrats." Still, it left the administration open to charges of hypocrisy and that in finding such appointments "merit seemed less important than their roles as pawns on an affirmative action chessboard."

Overall, the Reagan administration's assault on the civil rights agenda was more rhetorical than real. Ronald Reagan effectively conveyed the white man-in-the-street's distaste for "reverse discrimination" and for busing children miles away from their homes. But Reagan's inherent caution when governing and the commitment of so many in the government, the judiciary, and the corporate world to these racism remedies spread the "EEO/AA" gospel. With corporations institutionalizing equal employment opportunity/affirmative action procedures, in this realm, as in so many others, the liberal status quo persevered.

Typically, Reagan attributed most blacks' criticism to miscommunication. Secure in his identity as someone who was raised in a household "where the only intolerance . . . taught was intolerance of bigotry," Reagan resented charges of racism. Reagan told black Republicans that he usually ignored personal attacks, "but one charge I will have to admit strikes at my heart every time I hear it. That's the suggestion that we Republicans are taking a less active approach to protecting the civil rights of all Americans. No matter how you slice it, that's just plain baloney," Reagan said, adding a touch of midwestern outrage. Typically, Reagan focused on broadcasting the message. "If those who share my philosophy have had any failure, it's been a failure to communicate what's in our hearts to the black community," he said in September 1982, yet again trying to mollify blacks. "I sure hope he can sell this one," one White House aide sighed to a reporter about Reagan's outreach effort to black colleges.

With these efforts, Reagan was playing for white votes more than black votes. The center would not hold if he appeared too extreme. One official said that the controversies "have hurt us with moderate Republicans as well as independents. We've come across as insensitive on civil rights matters," he said, "and we've got to take steps to show that this is not so." For blacks, however, the crisis went deeper. As one black official said, "The main concern of blacks is not the specifics but their general fear of racial retrogression at the hands of the Reagan administration." And the columnist William Raspberry noted, "You can't fix that one with PR."

Yet, it was a PR question. By most objective standards, most blacks advanced during the 1980s, just as the civil rights bureaucracy, ideology, and enforcement infrastructure became more entrenched. But whereas, when playing to his right, Reagan often delivered symbolic but not substantive progress, many to his left experienced objective progress but felt slighted symbolically, feeding much of the partisan bitterness of the times.

Clash of the Titans: Ronald Reagan v. Tip O'Neill

Ronald Reagan's racial skirmishes were beachheads in a larger war. With polls finding that only 9 percent of whites thought the Reagan administration treated blacks unfairly, elections would not hinge on race, although it shaped the broader dynamic. By 1982 the Reagan magic seemed to be fading, and the Carter-era crankiness threatened to return. Thanks to Reagan's 1981 successes, it was now "his" economy, and "the Reagan recession." Democrats regrouped and counterattacked on the fairness issue, blaming Reaganism for throwing deserving young mothers off welfare rolls, making hardworking families homeless, and spreading poverty and misery.

Democrats despised Reaganomics' inconsistency. The budget cuts did not extend to "corporate welfare." Appalled by "the mean-spirited," inequitable philosophy behind this "rich man's president," the Democratic stalwart Tip O'Neill would later lament "the hatred for the poor that developed all across America. . . . I blame the president for allowing this kind of selfishness to become respectable."

Reaganism triggered a necessary debate about the nature of the welfare state. Underlying these questions were philosophical issues surrounding the government's proper dimensions, the obligation of the fortunate to the needy, and, ultimately, Americans' commitment to each other. "After all," Tip O'Neill noted, "the Constitution begins with the words, 'We, the people.' It does not begin, 'I, the individual.'" While conservatives often dominated the best-seller lists, liberals dominated the op-ed pages, with essays like "Exploding Some Myths about Social Programs" in the *Los Angeles Times* or arguing in *Harper's* how Ronald Reagan was "Making the World Safe for Plutocracy." Even as the political balance wavered, Democrats and liberals tended to be on the defensive intellectually and ideologically.

In Washington, DC, these sweeping philosophical, historical, economic, and ideological debates often became mired in political horse-trading and posturing. But in a bipolar, personality-driven media universe, both these transcendent and petty concerns became concentrated in a clash of the titans. Especially early on, much of this complicated, multidimensional debate over a nearly trillion-dollar budget with tens of thousands of individual entries played out as a legendary struggle between President of the United States Ronald Reagan and Speaker of the House Tip O'Neill.

Beefy and bulbous, with a mane of white hair and a back-slapping persona, Thomas P. O'Neill, Jr., seemed to have sprung to life from the pages of the Boston political classic *The Last Hurrah*. O'Neill was so easily caricatured that the Republicans ran an effective ad campaign in 1980 starring a fat, white-haired, slovenly Tip lookalike driving a gas-guzzler. This obvious stand-in for the Speaker of the House embodied insatiable government, and the Democrats' role as the party of yesterday. Tip O'Neill is "big, fat, and out of control—just like the federal government," said one of the Speaker's harshest critics, New York Republican Congressman John LeBoutillier.

O'Neill's biography was more manna for his critics. Born in Cambridge, Massachusetts, on December 9, 1912, nearly two years after Reagan, O'Neill was steeped in Boston Irish politics, seasoned by the New Deal and the Great Society. As John Kennedy's successor in Congress, with a voting address around the corner from his childhood home in North Cambridge, O'Neill could be identified with both the blue-collar northeastern ethnic ward and the liberal Ivy League campus, for better and worse.

On one level, Reagan and O'Neill made for a study in contrasts: the smooth movie star versus the gruff pol, the ideologue versus the fixer, the forward-looking Sun Belt millionaire resenting taxes and regulations versus the hidebound symbol of Northeast decline who never met a government program he did not like. But the two peers were also similar. Both were publicly gregarious yet privately remote. "My father was the kind of guy who would say he loved you publicly, but not privately," said O'Neill's son Tommy. Both Reagan and O'Neill were old-fashioned and far from hip. Upon hearing that Congressman Barney Frank proclaimed his homosexuality, O'Neill announced: "Barney is coming out of the room."

Actually, despite the Reaganites' claims, this was no clash between the politics of tomorrow and the politics of yesterday. Both politicians yearned for a lost Arcadia; they just located the ideal in different epochs. Reagan's paradise was the mythical turn-of-the-century Dixon he never quite inhabited and spent his lifetime escaping. O'Neill's Arcadia had that midwestern small-town feel with an urban Catholic twist—and, unlike his boyhood in the 1920s, was insulated from some hardships thanks to the New Deal–Great Society "safety net." Both Reagan and O'Neill instinctively understood the appeal of *Cheers* the Boston-based sitcom that began in 1982 about life in a bar "Where Everybody Knows Your Name," as the theme song went. Both felt displaced in a society that was so modern, technological, anonymous, even as both took refuge in the social distances.

The titans clashed on the airwaves as well as in the corridors of power. Reagan's telegenic good looks and smooth presence intimidated O'Neill. The Democrats lacked an authoritative "setting" comparable to the Oval Office. Fearing "the imbalance of media exposure," aides coaxed O'Neill into the television age. "To be more effective on television, you must pay great attention to your appearance as well as your performance," O'Neill's media adviser Jerry Colbert urged. "When you are appearing before 100 million people for a one-minute speech or a five-minute press conference, it is worth 20–25 minutes of preparation to package it correctly." Pushing the boss's buttons, Colbert noted, "In the final analysis, it is the image of the Speaker, the Irish people, and the Democratic Party that you will be projecting."

Gradually, Colbert, Chris Matthews, Ari Weiss, Kirk O'Donnell, and other staffers helped O'Neill master modern politics. He lost forty pounds, wore nicer clothes, and allowed his aides to make him up and brush down his suit. "I was the highest elected Democratic official in America," O'Neill recalled. "The President took me as the symbol of the Democratic Party—that I was fat and big and out of shape and a big spender. . . . He thought I was going to be easy to handle. But he kind of misjudged."

O'Neill proceeded carefully as the Reagan administration took power. Republicans brought their imaginary mandate to life amid headlines emphasizing Democrats' disarray. Some Democrats demanded aggressive leadership. New York's Governor Mario Cuomo said the 1980 "losses" should not "panic our party into a desperate search for a new philosophy." Cuomo proposed "better articulation" of Democratic ideals and rebuilding the organizational "apparatus."

O'Neill read his mail and watched the polls. He understood that while Reagan lacked a policy mandate, many Americans wanted this president to succeed. Throughout 1981 citizens demanded that O'Neill give the new president a chance. Some were so insistent that aides suggested he fly on military jets rather than spending so much time in airports being buttonholed, and sometimes abused.

O'Neill engaged in two balancing acts. He would have to keep his fractured party together, balancing the liberals' demands that he defend the New Deal with the moderates' demands that he indulge Reagan's desires. And, in public, he would have to be loyal, respectful, and just supportive enough to be patriotic, without being too obsequious or sharing the blame for Reaganism's errors.

The personality click between the two pols helped. Reagan and O'Neill traded jokes, acting like two comradely Irish sparring partners. Reagan seized on a comment O'Neill made about how Republicans and Democrats could be friends after six o'clock and on weekends. For the next six years, Reagan would often begin difficult discussions by asking, "Is it after six o'clock?"

All this "Tip and Gip" posturing could not obscure O'Neill's contempt. The Speaker reviled Reagan as a lightweight and a traitor to their class. At their first meeting, O'Neill condescendingly told the president-elect, "You're in the big leagues now." O'Neill would record that the clueless Reagan "seemed genuinely surprised to hear that"; Reagan would remember replying that, having been "the governor of one of the largest states in the union," he had been in the big leagues "for quite a while." O'Neill would brand Reagan the "worst" president he had ever seen: lazy, disengaged, and wrong about almost everything. Reagan, who was constitutionally less dyspeptic than his rival, would muse, "As far as he was concerned, I was the enemy. I guess from his point of view, he was right."

Still, the Speaker of the House had to demonstrate respect for the president of the United States. Once, on Sunday morning television—a setting more conducive to polite analysis than political fireworks—Charles Gibson asked O'Neill, regarding Reagan: "Do you think he's a callous man?" "No, I don't I think he's very, very," O'Neill strained for words, then shifted abruptly, "Well, I've never met a finer fellow." When Gibson pressed, O'Neill, having regained his composure, blasted the Reaganauts, not Reagan himself: "I think that he has very, very selfish people around him."

Ironically, O'Neill's initial accommodationist strategy perpetuated the impression that Reagan had a mandate. During the first few months of the Reagan Revolution, O'Neill and the Democrats floundered. They searched for resonant language and effective tactics. The Zen strategy of quietly allowing Reagan to fail distressed O'Neill. O'Neill credited the New Deal with creating the great American middle class, postwar America's crowning achievement. He often challenged corporate executives, asking how many "got help from Uncle Sam" at some point in their lives. Watching the Republicans try to dismantle those programs while raising money for defense and cutting taxes for the rich broke O'Neill's heart.

In the spring of 1981, O'Neill noticed public support for Reagan souring as David Stockman targeted popular programs. "The school lunch program is cut," O'Neill shouted. "Job training is cut below the ones we made. . . . There is going to be alarm in America." Yet, repeatedly and especially after Reagan was shot, the president's mythic popularity stymied O'Neill. Marveling at the display of leadership, at this White House's willingness to twist arms and stand for something, O'Neill sighed, "There is not much we can do to counteract it. . . . How the attempted assassination has turned the program of the Congress, I don't know, but it has done that."

O'Neill's passive sentence construction at the end was instructive. Much of Reagan's initial success stemmed from Reagan's timely message and passionate leadership. Moreover, Democrats were operating in a changed environment, a world of limited budgets and growing skepticism about government programs. But Democrats preferred to believe, as Mario Cuomo did, that their ideas still worked, they just needed better communication and organization. And while the "attempted assassination" did "help" by spotlighting Reagan the man, not his program, O'Neill and the Democrats needed to concentrate on redefining their party's message and honing their strategies rather than simply marveling at this seemingly natural phenomenon beyond their control. Similarly, the tendency to mock and demonize Reagan simultaneously added to this Democratic denial while confusing the public. It was hard to believe that the president was both clueless and malevolent, especially amid so much early success.

Democratic Counterattack: Finding the "Fairness" Issue

That first spring, Reagan tried to rescue the Social Security program after benefits soared by over 500 percent during the 1970s. Fearing bankruptcy, he overstepped. On May 12 Secretary of Health and

Human Services Richard Schweiker proposed reducing benefits for those who retired before the age of sixty-five, to discourage early retirements.

O'Neill had his opening. "By hitting Social Security, the president is hitting where people live," O'Neill thundered. Generalizing from the few who contemplated early retirement to everyone in the system, O'Neill branded the proposals "a breach of faith with those who have worked their whole lives. As long as I am Speaker, I will do everything I can to see that the president does not get his way."

O'Neill's cynical overreaction worked. Even the Republican-controlled Senate rejected the plan 96 to 0. Social Security became "the third rail" of American politics, lethal to the touch. In December 1981 Reagan would charter a National Commission on Social Security Reform. Chaired by the economist Alan Greenspan, this joint House-Senate, Republican-Democratic, public-private entity would symbolize the governmental "gridlock" of the Reagan years. The need to contract out such a touchy issue to a panel of fifteen "elders" epitomized this term, which originated in the 1980 New York transit strike and gained popularity throughout this era of divided government.

Handing Reagan his first major legislative setback, Democrats finally found some traction. "That was the only bright spot for us then," Kirk O'Donnell later exulted. "You bet they were ambushed. They were absolutely taken to the cleaners. It was after that when the 'fairness' question became serious."

By August the Democratic counterstrategy coalesced. In an eleven-page memorandum that O'Neill called "The Plan," O'Donnell proposed marrying Reaganism to the continuing recession. "The economy is no longer our burden; it is a Republican economy," he wrote. Members returned from summer vacation armed with constituent stories detailing economic hardship. Talking about the "Reagan recession" shifted blame from Carter to Reagan as the "fairness issue" became shorthand for Reagan's insensitivity to the poor.

As with the charges of racism, Reagan, insulted, blamed the "false image-building of the press." When one "average" American chided the president for surrounding himself with rich people, Reagan responded that he grew up poor. He added: "I've kept contact with all the friends I knew in those days. And now, though it may be hard to understand, I'm surrounded more on a daily basis with the same kind of people I always knew than I am with the so-called rich; the security detail, aides and staff." And that—two half-truths, one because he was not in touch with many old friends, a second because he was distant from those around him, be they servants or friends—was good enough for Reagan.

O'Neill mocked Reagan's charming ability to deflect criticism. O'Neill fumed: "A member of Congress would say, 'Mr. President, I am vitally concerned with the people I represent. There are many aged in my district.' The president would say, 'You don't think I would do anything to hurt the aged of America, do you?' . . . The member says, 'I am concerned about education.' The president says, 'You don't think I am going to destroy the educational system of America, do you?'"

O'Neill's cool, patient aide Kirk O'Donnell struggled to override his boss's instinct to take the bait and blast Reagan. In defending the New Deal too vehemently, O'Neill risked making the dispute personal. "[M]ake it a referendum not on Reagan but on his policies," O'Donnell urged. "We should continue to drive home the notion that the administration tilts towards the well-to-do and is not really concerned about the average American." Democrats became so incensed by Reagan's insouciance and insensitivity they would neglect such advice. But O'Donnell helped establish the 1980s' essential standoff. Reagan would remain popular. Democrats would become effective critics. And certain programs, including Social Security, would be untouchable.

In directing Democrats to "take the offensive," O'Donnell detailed the party's assumptions. "We are assuming that for a privileged few things will get better under Reagan but for most Americans it will not; that the average American not the wealthy is the wagerer in the Reagan Economic Gamble. And finally that a Democratic alternative exists that does not seek to fight inflation by sacrificing Americans' dreams of home ownership, college for their children, and a secure retirement for themselves."

By the 1980s government programs serving particular constituencies, be it Head Start for children, Guaranteed Student Loans for students, or Social Security for the elderly, remained not just popular but sacrosanct; the liberal program was neither. Similarly, individual incumbent members of Congress tended to be popular, yet their institution was not. The Democrats would win by harping on specifics; Reagan would win with his personality and his vision. Characteristically, a May 4, 1981 White House memo defending the Gramm-Latta Resolution made five points regarding the big picture: accusing the Democratic proposal of adding "$141.2 billion more in 3 years; of cutting $6.7 billion from defense; of providing *"less tax relief"*; of resorting to *"double-counting and illusory administrative savings"*; and of being *"business-as-usual in disguise:* more taxing, more spending, continued 'stagflation.'" By contrast, the Democratic majority whip, Thomas Foley, had issued an attack three days earlier listing twenty-one differences, specifying the gap in education, land and water conservation, discretionary health, Medicaid, transportation, food stamps, youth employment and training, child nutrition, and subsidized housing, among others. Both sides played to their strengths. Most Americans wanted a smaller budget and greater "tax relief," but they also wanted the government to continue providing food, shelter, medical care, and education to those who needed it (and themselves if they benefited from it).

The Democrats' language, personalizing programs with tales of woe, pricked Americans' consciences at a time when they were supposedly becoming selfish and insensate. But the language and strategy would also lead to another characteristic of 1980s' political culture, a sloppy tendency toward irresponsibility, a refusal to link the bigger picture with specifics, a language of government services as commodities people deserved but should not spend too much money on, rather than as ingredients integrated into a recipe for the common good. Critics would usually blame Reagan's warm, woozy rhetoric of selfishness. In fact, both Democrats and Republicans fostered this culture of political irresponsibility and fantasy, this tendency, as the Harvard political philosopher Michael Sandel would call it, to view "economic arrangements" and government programs "as instruments of consumption, not as schools for citizenship."

Charges of fiscal irresponsibility compounded the charges of favoritism and insensitivity. Reagan the alleged budget-cutter quickly became known as the creator of the $200 billion deficit. In fairness,

Reagan cared more about lowering taxes and boosting defense than cutting the budget. He trusted lower taxes to "starve" the government eventually. But the Republicans traditionally belong to the party of fiscal sobriety; the Democrats were the Keynesian spendthrifts. Nevertheless, Democrats now railed against deficits. In 1983 Alice Rivlin would conclude that this "combination of policies . . . rising structural deficits and high interest rates—is really dumb."

1982: Reagan's Recession, Tax Increases, and Midterm Electoral Setback

Even more than the conceptual and political flaws, the 1982 recession helped derail the Reagan Revolution. The legions of needy people blunted the impact of David Stockman's cuts and destroyed even the semblance of a consensus. Still, the Reagan cuts shifted the burden from the federal government to the states, forced a reexamination of key programs such as welfare, and transformed Washington's governing culture. Coming after the Great Inflation and devastating stagflation, the conservative critique of the Great Society, Jimmy Carter's budget cuts, the state tax revolts, and the Kemp-Roth-Stockman-Gramm brainstorming on Capitol Hill, Reagan's transformation of much domestic politics into zero-sum budgetary politics took root. The focus remained on retrenchment, two social scientists discovered in 1983. "New spending initiatives are out of fashion."

The cuts enacted before the recession prevented a spending surge during the recession. The number of households receiving federal assistance remained steady, despite the unemployment spike. Richard P. Nathan and Fred C. Doolittle of Princeton's Woodrow Wilson School found that the cuts concentrated on "entitlement grants (AFDC, medicaid, food stamps and school lunches)" and funding for "jobs and job training, compensatory education, and health and social services." Ironically, the budget cuts bypassed Reagan's mythical shirkers and welfare queens. Those "most affected" were "on the margin of income eligibility for means-tested programs," meaning the "working poor" who worked hard enough and earned just enough to lose out on benefits once the government tightened eligibility rules.

Retreating, Reagan also accepted tax increases. Reagan the show-man stubbornly called them "revenue enhancements," and he insisted on maintaining the cuts in personal taxes so central to his ideology. Nevertheless, the Orwellian-sounding 1982 Tax Equity and Fiscal Responsibility Act (TEFRA) succumbed to fiscal and political reality. The legislation closed loopholes and reformed various corporate taxing procedures. James Baker's aide Richard Darman would say that TEFRA's $37.5 billion increase combined with a $3.3 billion jump in the gasoline tax through the Highway Revenue Act constituted "the largest single tax increase in history."

Democrats in the 1982 campaign defended the working poor as well as their less fortunate fellow citizens. The Democrats had fine-tuned the "fairness issue." Strategists learned that making it a "poor vs. rich issue" was less effective than pitching "a working and middle-income family vs. rich issue." Recognizing that American elections are won in the center, consultants told Democrats to *"talk about fairness to 'working and middle income people,'* and NOT 'fairness to the poor.'"

"Fairness" was not simply the strongest issue, it was the only effective issue for Democrats. *"Stay away from foreign policy issues,"* strategists advised. "Also, stay away from *budget, deficit,* and social issues as much as possible. Our credibility in these areas is near zero. . . . If voters cast their ballots along these issue lines, we generally lose."

The 1980 election had jolted the party. The Republicans pushed their clearer message with more sophisticated campaigning techniques. "We have been out-conceptualized, out-organized, out-televised, out-coordinated, out-financed, and out-worked," Democratic Chairman Charles Manatt lamented. In 1980 Republicans raised $109 million for their congressional candidates; Democrats raised $16 million. By mid-1981, Republicans had amassed $23,236,380; Democrats had collected merely $238,795, with debts totalling more than $1 million. Moreover, Democrats were balkanized, emerging, Adam Clymer of the *New York Times* wrote, more as "a federation of caucuses (black Democrats, labor Democrats, Asian-American Democrats, household Democrats) than a united party." Such fracturing further eroded conceptions of common good in favor of fragmented and selfish appeals.

To defeat what Chairman Manatt called "Reagan Hood—giving tax breaks to the wealthy and cutting the school lunch program," Democrats became more disciplined operatives and communicators. O'Neill deputized Tony Coehlo, a smart, ambitious California congressman, to update the Democratic congressional campaign and raise money. By fall 1981 the Democrats were circulating a fundraising letter warning of the dangers of a "right-wing" Republican takeover of the House— "If the Republicans win just as many seats in 1982 as they won in 1980."

"Every American who cares about other Americans, who cares about civil rights and equal opportunity, who cares about clean air and clean water, who cares about poor people and old people and helpless people ought to care about the 1982 House elections," Congressman Peter Rodino implored. Democrats had to "save Republicans from themselves," Rodino begged. "These wolves in wolves' clothing—ultra conservative ideologues, religious fanatics, corporate fat cats, reborn Reaganites, the single-issue zealots—are shoving traditional Republicans out the back door of their own party."

Developing an unhealthy contempt for democracy, Democrats feared their message would not get across. At the start of the 1982 campaign, North Dakota Congressman Byron L. Dorgan warned Tony Coehlo about Republican plans "to blitz the national media." Doubting the American people, Dorgan worried that "if Madison Avenue can sell 'waxy build-up,' 'post-nasal-drip,' and 'excess stomach acid' as major issues in our lives, then they can probably successfully portray the Republican economic program as the golden goose for America."

Dorgan overlooked the changing political climate, which was starting to favor the Democrats. O'Neill's assault had been doubly effective. Pollsters found that voters still perceived Republicans as the "fiscally sound party" and even "traditionally Democratic groups" were guardedly optimistic, but they were increasingly doubtful about the president's program. More dramatically, the "fairness" issue combined with the "Reagan recession" had undermined support for the budget cuts by about 10 percentage points among all groups surveyed, except for "upper-income" voters. Now "43 percent feel those cuts went too far," one survey reported. "Those who felt the cuts were 'just right' dropped 15 points from 42 percent in April to only 27 percent in late November."

The strategy—and O'Neill's patience—paid off. In November 1982 Democrats gained twenty-six seats. While the opposition typically gained seats in a midterm election, considering how miserable and divided the Democrats had been throughout 1981, this was a political miracle. "The breadth of dissatisfaction with Republicans among the American electorate was striking," the *Boston Globe* noted.

Democrats now tried to bury Reagan's mandate. A Democratic consultant, Bob Squier, declared that "The 1980 election was decided on the issue of personality." Despite winning "the political equivalent of the Academy Award for Best Performance," Reagan "thought that we had given him the award for best script." This "misunderstanding" caused Reagan's overreach. "Mr. Reagan, with more than a little help from the Democrats, turned the mandate in his head into the policy of this government—a policy that eventually changed 'Reaganomics' into a pejorative term," Squier wrote. The result was 10 percent unemployment, a "post-Depression high," and grounds for a Democratic counterattack, as "supply-side became trickle down."

The deficit debate frustrated Reaganites. Complaints about deficits had long been a Republican truncheon used against free-spending Democrats. Now, as one White House staffer complained, there were "Budgets, budgets everywhere, but not one balanced sheet." Even while clinging to the "basic principles of economic recovery—reduction in federal spending, regulation, waste and fraud, taxes, federalism, and stable money supply," they sought to escape "the political dilemma caused by the deficit." "How could we avoid rejection of the big-deficit-heavy-non-defense-cut-but-no-change-in-defense-and-taxes approach?" Reaganites wondered at meetings addressing "the rising deficit problem." "Can we/should we tolerate our projected *unemployment* levels?" Reagan continued to insist that "in our perilous situation vis-à-vis the Soviets," if forced, he would choose "rebuilding our defenses" over "balancing the budget." Democrats argued that cutting taxes while boosting defenses destroyed the budget. Blaming "many years of past actions" instead, Reagan refused to raise taxes: "It will reduce the pressure on Congress to control government sending and could signal that we are retreating from our long-run goal of reducing federal spending and tax burdens."

The Reagan Revolution was bogged down. The lightning legislative successes of 1981 now contrasted with the trench warfare of 1982, and the resulting loss of power. Yet even as Reagan's program faltered, Reagan's vision still appealed to many, and the president remained personally popular. One exit poll in November 1982 found that while 36 percent of voters surveyed deemed Reaganomics a failure, and only 6 percent considered it a success, 49 percent were waiting, giving Reagan's program more time to succeed. This remarkable forbearance reflected Reagan's success in tailoring his broader vision to Americans' worries as well as the continuing faith many had in his leadership.

A week and a half after the midterm elections, Reagan had a chance to change the subject. In a twist that would soon be deemed Reaganesque, wherein art, or at least popular culture, inspired life, Jan Scruggs, a Vietnam veteran watching the movie *The Deerhunter* in 1979, had decided to resurrect an old idea of his and push for a Vietnam Veterans' memorial. He wanted veterans to have that long-delayed "big parade down Constitution Avenue." The ensuing architectural competition chose a haunting design of two 200-foot black walls, sunk ten feet into the Washington, DC, Mall, listing the 57,962 Americans lost. One West Pointer, Tom Carhart, denounced this "black gash of shame and sorrow, hacked into the national visage that is the Mall." Eventually, adding a more conventional statue depicting three soldiers—and graced with a towering flagpole—mollified most critics.

With the compromise in place, the national ceremony commenced. The president and the First Lady lit a memorial candle at the National Cathedral, while hearing some of the 57,962 names intoned. "The names that are being read are of men who died for freedom just as surely as any men who ever fought for this country," the president said, choking up. And seeking to unify the nation around his vision, Reagan said, "We're beginning to appreciate that they were fighting for a just cause." Throughout the decade, Reagan's once controversial celebration of Vietnam as a "noble cause" would become increasingly mainstreamed in the American collective memory. It would be reflected in the strutting of Sylvester Stallone, Chuck Norris, and Arnold

Schwarzenegger in macho post-Vietnam celluloid fantasies, in weighty novels such as Bobbie Ann Mason's *In Country,* and in the many tears visitors shed at Maya Lin's stark, alluring, shoeshine-black wall. The summer hit song of 1982, "Eye of the Tiger," the theme of Rocky III sung by the aptly named group Survivor about "a man and his will to survive," warned: "don't lose your grip on the dreams of the past / you must fight just to keep them alive."

Nevertheless, it was easy to discount the Reagan aura, the power of Reagan's popularity. This was especially true for journalists who doubted Reagan and Reaganism from the start. As a result, by the midpoint of Reagan's first term, the new president seemed doomed to failure. With unemployment high, national morale low, and the administration seem-ingly adrift, Reaganism was looking suspiciously like Carterism with the focused, class-bound anguish of unemployment substituting for the broadly shared pain of inflation. "The stench of failure hangs over Ronald Reagan's White House," the *New York Times* claimed at midterm. With the president's initiatives stalled, and with both former Vice Pres-ident Walter Mondale and Senator John Glenn defeating Reagan in presidential trial heats, David Broder of the *Washington Post* and many others declared Reaganism dead.

Reagan remained unflappable. The president blamed reporters, charging that the press was delaying the economic recovery with "con-stant downbeat stories." Once again relying on his aw-shucks routine, Reagan asked: "Is it news that some fellow out in South Succotash someplace has just been laid off that he should be interviewed nation-wide?" Accusing reporters of the same crime they often attributed to the Reaganites, White House Communications Director David Ger-gen charged that "the electronic media, in particular, sometimes has difficulty covering stories that are fairly subtle. They need a picture to tell the story. So they sometimes go out and find a person in a wheel-chair and portray him as [being] in dire straits as a result of the cuts in programs." Alas, Reagan's insouciance did not end the recession, or re-vive his presidency.

Hill Street: Conservative Dystopia
or Seedbed of Liberal Dreams?

The confusion, the despair, the agonizing decline of liberalism, the empty and hypocritical promise of conservatism came through in every episode of *Hill Street Blues*. *Hill Street Blues* was a "conservative" show in that it sympathized with cops, derided much of the post–Warren Court justice system, and captured the fear haunting America's cities. The declining slum around the station house was a conservative dystopia, eloquent testimony to liberalism's follies. The Emmy Award–winning first episode of the show's third season, broadcast on September 30, 1982, would depict the volatile aftermath of a nun's rape and murder during a church robbery, proof of America's depravity.

Yet the show was also deeply liberal. The multicultural cast and impoverished setting contrasted with the sanitized glitz of Reagan's Washington, of Aaron Spelling's *Dynasty*. Weekly visitors to Hill Street knew that Reagan's America was not all gleaming monuments and designer dresses. The writers clearly preferred the Jewish liberal with a heart and a spine, Lieutenant Henry Goldblume, to the fascistic, buffoonish SWAT commando, the aptly named Lieutenant Howard Hunter. In the same September 1982 episode honored for great writing, Hill Street's snarling, biting, master of gritty undercover work, Mick Belcker, would befriend Eddie Gregg, a gay prostitute. Many of the most affecting moments humanized blacks and Hispanics, from Althea Woodard's portrayal of a saintly mother whose son was mistakenly shot by a police officer, to Lieutenant Ray Calletano's poignant quest to prove himself as a cop, not as a Latino affirmative action project.

Gerald Ford and Henry Kissinger might get a cameo on *Dynasty*. Tip O'Neill would drop by *Cheers*—in addition to the match between the man and his setting, the son of his longtime assistant, Delores Snow, was the show's casting director. But Ronald Reagan would never have visited *Hill Street* or its chaotic precinct house. The crime, the chaos, the fear, the diversity, did not fit into Reagan's narrative—nor did the November unemployment rate of 10.8 percent, the highest since 1940; the market share of Japanese car-makers of 22.6 percent, up from barely 4 percent in 1970; or the Boland Amendment passed just before Christmas 1982, handcuffing American attempts to fight Nicaragua's Sandinista government. Unable to reconcile John Winthrop's centuries-old vision of the shining city upon a hill with Steven Bochco's or Tip O'Neill's contemporary apparition, Reagan did what he did so often—and so effectively—he ignored the contradiction and continued singing his seemingly guileless and surprisingly seductive song.

1983

Beaufort, South Carolina

The Big Chill and the Great Reconciliation:
Where the Sixties Meet the Eighties

Preservation of our environment
is not a liberal or conservative challenge, it's common sense.
RONALD REAGAN, STATE OF THE UNION ADDRESS, 1984

The Big Chill. Within weeks of its 1983 release it was no longer just a movie, but an event, a defining moment in the collective annals of the baby boom generation and the 1980s. Two decades later, the phrase remains resonant. People reuniting with old friends from high school, college, or camp speak of having a "Big Chill weekend."

Surprisingly, "Big Chill" did not originally mean a chance to "chill together," or hang out. Lawrence Kasdan titled his movie after the big chill that ran down his spine when a colleague said something politically offensive and Kasdan said nothing, fearing for his career.

The Big Chill represented the baby boomers' lost 1960s' idealism as they joined the "real world." It was a world of careerism and cynicism, of great luxuries but deep disappointments, of stunning horizons but complex tradeoffs. The story of the former University of Michigan radicals reunited by their friend's suicide solidified the baby boomer myth, that they all protested in the 1960s and then sold out to become 1980s yuppies. Reinforcing the point, the movie itself was a slicker, star-studded, Hollywoodized echo of John Sayles' 1980 independent sensation, *The Return of the Secaucus Seven.*

While the hosts of the low-key original are New England school-teachers, *The Big Chill*'s weekend hosts are a running shoes mogul and his doctor wife, played by Kevin Kline and Glenn Close. The reunion takes place at their country manor in Beaufort, South Carolina, a Reaganesque site in a Reaganized South. All hints of racism have been swept under the rug—no blacks appear in the film.

A port town seventy miles from Charleston, founded in 1711 as a resort for plantation grandees, spared from destruction because Union troops occupied it during the Civil War, Beaufort had seen its aristocratic charm fade by the 1970s. A $5.2 million Waterfront Park revived the town. Its nine thousand residents prospered during the 1980s, mass-producing historical charm for tourists with disposable income, like the film's protagonists.

"Tidalholm," a 130-year-old plantation house, had served as a Civil War hospital and a twentieth-century guesthouse. In the movie, the house, which was restored in 1974, is spacious and well-appointed. The former radicals, now a divorced TV action star, a single female lawyer, a frustrated housewife, an aspiring novelist turned *People* celebrity journalist, and a wayward drug pusher, idealize their past as they agonize over the present.

These cinematic sixties' refugees intensified the war about the decade's legacy. Michael Ventura, a radical columnist, condemned the movie for replacing "memory" and "identity" with "an all-purpose, non-threatening nostalgia." A *Washington Post* movie critic snapped, "Ultimately, *The Big Chill* is contrived to flatter and excuse the social and moral complacency of people who have good reason to feel foolish and perhaps shameful about the way they mistook themselves for revolutionaries while members of a fundamentally privileged and grotesquely overrated college generation." Clearly, as the sociologist and former radical Todd Gitlin would note, in "talking about the '60s," Americans were "talking about where we are now."

During the Reagan years the Great Reconciliation occurred. The few baby boomers who actually were radicals—but who then as now monopolized their generation's voice—mostly made peace with America. The Vietnam War became a bad memory; the antiwar movement became bathed in nostalgia. *M*A*S*H*, the television show that since 1972 helped Americans deflect their anxieties about Vietnam by laughing at a Korean War sitcom, outlived its usefulness. By November 1983 many Americans would claim they had exorcised the curse of Vietnam by flushing out Cuban troops and Communist coup leaders from the tiny island of Grenada.

In 1983 the great economic boom—the baby boom boom, the Reagan boom—began. It was a boom of service jobs, not manufacturing, of the Sun Belt and silicon chips, not the Rust Belt and smokestacks. It was also a boom with its own cultural institutions and accents. Just as the 1920s' boom became linked in the national imagination with the herky-jerky, grainy quality of the first "talkie" movies, this would be the boom of CNN twenty-four-hour news-reporting, USA Today trend-spotting, and MTV music video-watching; this would be the boom marking the debut of the modern network anchoring trinity of Dan Rather, Tom Brokaw, and Peter Jennings. The entrepreneurs of the moment such as Lee Iacocca, Donald Trump, and Ted Turner would join President Reagan in elevating the pursuit of wealth, the compulsion to consume, and the desperation to succeed from selfish acts of individualism into altruistic acts of patriotism. This brazen ethos, along with the slick sensibility and colorful graphics of an increasingly wired world, would be part of the Big Chillers' "yuppie" package.

Yet concentrating on yuppie excess tells only half the story. Yuppie attitudes and shopping habits reveal how the changing media context created this Frankenstein, and how the CEO as superhero ideal revived. But these yuppies had enough of a conscience, enough of a sixties' sensibility, at least to feel a "Big Chill" down their spines when they went too far. Many in fact recoiled at the era's hurly burly boosterism and spending orgies. Thus, even in Reagan's America, new liberal ideas emerged and the expressions of sixties-style activism such as the nuclear freeze movement persisted. In 1983 a doomsday warning about The Day After a nuclear explosion would attract a television audience rivaling the final M*A*S*H audience. In 1983 America's conservative president would sign legislation making the birthday of Martin Luther King, Jr., a federal holiday. In 1983 liberals would finally succeed in deposing Ronald Reagan's plodding Environmental Protection Agency Director Anne Gorsuch Burford, as well as Reagan's zealous

Secretary of the Interior James Watt. This sustained clash between the 1960s thesis and the Reagan antithesis created a 1980s synthesis, exemplified by moderate Democrats' "Third Way" between Reaganite tightfistedness and liberal excess; in an environmental movement that became institutionalized and mainstreamed as it felt besieged; and in the rise of the corporate activist, the consumer with a conscience, a society filled with people yearning to earn like Rockefellers, but occasionally live and sometimes even vote like Beatniks.

Heroes for the 1980s: Boomer Success—and Excess

The sixties' revolution had failed, but many of the rebellions succeeded. In 1983 a new attempt to pass the equal rights amendment missed the necessary two-thirds vote in the House of Representatives, but the president would boast that women would fill nearly three-quarters of the new jobs "in managerial, professional, and technical fields." The Miss America pageant—an ode to 1950s' sexism—continued, but in 1983 the first black woman would win. Less grandly, for many, the extended adolescence of college and graduate school ended. It was time to get to work.

Born between 1946 and 1961, baby boomers ranged from twenty-two to thirty-seven years old in 1983. Just as Lawrence Kasdan and his fictional radicals settled into the world, so did their peers. Jane Fonda went from exercising her free speech as a dove and supporting Hanoi to hawking exercise tapes; millions of others purchased their first cars, homes, individual retirement accounts (IRAs), and 401Ks. With the free market "again becoming the focal point," as Reagan said, it was time to earn and spend freely.

The boomers' brashness and "let-it-all-hang-out-edness" transformed attitudes toward money in America. Law firms and investment banks went from gentlemanly, nine-to-five enterprises to raucous, fifteen-hour-day dynamos. Money in the 1980s, like sex in the 1960s, became a legitimate conversation topic and the great barometer, with people trying to figure out who was getting more than expected, who less; who was winning, and who was losing. And to a generation uniquely susceptible to peer pressure and big ideas, a generation committed to dismantling the traditional verities and questioning authorities, consumerism became all-consuming—these whipper-snappers were what they wore, ate, drank, and fancied.

Money served as a social solvent even while lubricating the arrivistes' climb to the top. Millions of Americans now had enough disposable cash to buy expensive goods and services once limited to the upper-crust and to use their purchases to construct a private identity and a public persona. While every decade in the twentieth century upped the consumerist ante, the 1980s marked a giant step toward an almost reckless, autonomous individualism and away from the politicized, communally oriented "consuming public" protecting consumers' rights. *Consumer Reports* functioned as a guide for goodies, not a Naderite prod to corporate responsiveness.

The enlightenment legacies of emancipation and individualism pushed to their logical—and often illogical—extremes left "the individual suspended in glorious but terrifying isolation," Robert Bellah and his fellow sociologists would note. With little institutional, ideological, or moral traction, "matters of personal preference" predominated. Fundamental ethics about not "killing, stealing, and lying" floated in an individual and communal vacuum, "detached from any social or cultural base that could give them broader meaning."

Americans' pursuit of happiness degenerated into an obsessive pursuit of pleasure, both indulgent experiences and beautiful things. In 1967, at a high point of boomer idealism, 40 percent of college freshmen polled said it was important to prosper financially; 80 percent sought a meaningful philosophy of life. Twenty years later, 80 percent desired wealth; only 40 percent valued an enlightened worldview. During another pointless night in some trendy club, the protagonist of Jay McInerney's novel of yuppie anomie, *Bright Lights, Big City,* stumbles into a cocaine-stoked repartee, the "sexual equivalent of fast food." After sharing some "blow" in the bathroom, a woman says, "I love drugs." She asks: "Have you ever noticed how all the good words start with D? D and L." The two then, ping-ponging, improvise a haiku of hedonism. She begins: "Drugs. Delight. Decadence." "Debauchery." "Dexedrine." "Delectable. Deranged. Debilitated." "Delinquent." "Delirium." "And L," she says. "Lush and luscious." "Languorous."

"Librium." "Libidinous," the protagonist adds, tipping his hand, and scaring off his prey.

Defining role models and building individual identities by how much people spent, what they bought, and where they partied obscured many of the boom's social benefits and made the eighties' decade seem more materialistic than it was. Even the Gilded Age appeared more community-oriented by comparison. In the post–Civil War age of excess, the robber barons were what they built: U.S. Steel, Standard Oil, Central Pacific Railroad. A century later, these tycoons were remembered by what they endowed: (Andrew) Carnegie-Mellon University, the (John D.) Rockefeller Foundation, (Leland) Stanford University. So many yuppie types were so ambivalent about their jobs, and so maxed out on their credit cards, that neither work nor good works defined them as much as their purchases and lifestyles.

This new money culture emerged as marketing was becoming more sophisticated. Market segmentation reduced Americans into subcommunities of anonymous purchasers. Despite limited popularity, *Hill Street Blues* had the right "demographic"—the elusive but spendthrift 18-to-35-year-old high-achieving male. As the cable revolution spread, American culture and politics would fragment further, even as Ronald Reagan sought to resurrect the great American middle, some common consensus.

Ronald Reagan was well suited to preside over this Great Reconciliation. Considered America's oldest yuppie, his call for capitalist renewal fostered the money-media culture. His celebrity politics resonated with a society obsessed with *The Lifestyles of the Rich and Famous*. His easy-listening nationalism gave a communal and even idealistic veneer to individualist, consumerist excess. Delighting in the four million new jobs created in 1983, toasting the trailblazers mastering computers and other modern miracles, Reagan would summarize the year's accomplishments in his January 1984 State of the Union Address, saying: "Hope is reborn for couples dreaming of owning homes and for risk takers with vision to create tomorrow's opportunities." Reagan saluted two self-made entrepreneurs as "heroes for the eighties." At the same time, Reagan was a perfect foil, with outrage against his "Neanderthal" politics easing yuppie guilt and fostering the delu-

sion that this emerging American bourgeoisie had not lost its Bo-
hemian edge.

The Search for the Quintessential Yuppie

Just as the phrase "the Big Chill" meant selling out, not hanging out;
just as Reagan fostered materialism rather than facilitating idealism,
the 1980s' yuppie was ubiquitous but illusory. Perhaps America's most
famous yuppie, Michael J. Fox, was a Canadian actor who embodied
the stereotype in his television hit, *Family Ties,* and in movies such as
The Secret of My Success and *Bright Lights Big City.* But Fox differentiated
himself from Alex P. Keaton, the blue-blazered conservative son of liberal parents on TV, saying, "How can I be a yuppie if I'd rather play
hockey than squash?" Most Americans knew what a yuppie was—one
poll found that 60 percent of Americans could define the term, while
only 34 percent could identify the secretary of state. Many insisted
they knew yuppies. Yet few admitted to being one. One Harvard Business School type, decked out in a V-neck sweater and wide-wale cor-
duroys, singled out by his peers as the ur-yuppie, denied it: "I mean,
hey, I drive an American car."

Indeed, the term was pejorative. The word often appeared as an ad-
jective modifying a crude characterization of a derriere, and many
deemed the two words interchangeable. The deeper problem stemmed
from American ambivalence about money and about the 1960s.

Americans wanted to praise and bury the 1960s. As "sixties parties"
and *Big Chill*-type mea culpas proliferated, many overlooked the
decade's excesses and idealized the idealism—often to demonize eighties excesses and discount contemporary idealism. And, ironically, yesterday's youth rebels experienced a generation gap in the opposite
direction, bemoaning the shallowness of "kids today" who could not
understand *Easy Rider.* In 1981 the critic Stephen Holden chided "the
new generation of rock consumers . . . spoon-fed rock mythology,"
imprisoned in false nostalgia for someone else's music, "rather than
looking forward to a new rock culture of their own."

Even as sixties' culture symbolized a "golden time" to their juniors,
the children of the 1960s abandoned that past. Approaching middle

age, many baby boomers became go-getters. *Newsweek* described the yuppie epiphany, "a sudden realization that poverty" was not romantic. For one, it came with a pathetic paycheck that liberated her from the "notion that to prove to everybody I was a good person I had to parade around as a good person by being a social worker." For another, it was seeing brie cheese and pita bread in a friend's refrigerator, "my first exposure to the expanded experiences of the planet." These "conversion" tales illustrated the central tenet of the yuppie experience, an addiction to building an identity around exotic food, trendy clothing, slick cars, and all of the other supposedly finer things in life.

The archetypal yuppie built an identity on consuming rather than being, on things rather than relationships, on an aesthetic life rather than ascetic living. There was a fetishism to it, a competitive, status-oriented, and obsessive search for the right spice or accent piece. The yuppie church was the health club or bistro, the yuppie sacraments a rigorous exercise regime or the brilliantly idiosyncratic four-course meal.

Yuppies were wired into the new technologies as well as the latest trends. While Emily Post–types debated whether answering machines were efficient or rude, as they condemned the epidemic of the Sony Walkman interposing a wall of sound between pedestrians and society, yuppies embraced technology, especially computers. In its January 3, 1983, issue, *Time* magazine violated its "Man of the Year" tradition, designating a 1982 "Machine of the Year"—the computer. With 2.8 million units purchased for $4.9 billion, in "1982 a cascade of computers beeped and blipped their way into the American office, the American school, the American home," heralding the "information revolution."

By repudiating the 1960s with their march to materialism, yuppies became the shock troops of the Reagan restoration. Their excess reflected Reaganism's success, seeking salvation through prosperity. "You can't be apathetic if you're jogging and you've got two jobs and nine plans for your life." the druggie hipster Timothy Leary said sympathetically. To Leary, boomers had "smartened up," becoming "Young Upscale Pragmatics." Yuppiedom offered a certain perverse democracy, for this identity was purchased, not inherited. Having repudiated so many anchoring institutions, assumptions, and values in the 1960s, baby boomers now constructed new moorings out of chrome and arugula.

Yuppies were convenient scapegoats. By bashing yuppies as acquisitive Americans, one implicitly absolved oneself of guilt. Yuppie excess came to be your neighbor's indulgence, not yours. Just as Tip O'Neill's Democratic critique helped many Americans feel virtuous while advancing the Reagan revolution, the yuppie aversion helped baby boomers feel virtuous while reveling in the new decadence. All of this thirtysomething angst offered a hypocritical quick fix as the number of American millionaires increased sixfold in twenty years to 1.3 million people. Americans doubled the number of luxury car imports from 1982 to 1986, and lowered the age of first-time fur coat owners from fifty to twenty-six in ten years.

In fact, guilt also became commodified, with the right amount of agonizing supposedly indicating depth. *The Yuppie Handbook* detailed what the quintessential couple needed, including a six-figure salary, first-name familiarity with trendy maitre d's, a renovated loft on a "decaying pier," and "analysis four to five times a week, to question the value of the above." The in-your-face openness of the sixties, the compulsive self-reflection of the seventies, shaped the guilt of the eighties.

The individual hypocrisy served a social function. This exorcism, the scapegoating, kept some moral ballast during these heady times. Having an opposition, however feeble, validated different lifestyles and offered alternatives to a society that, while entranced by the success and the excess, still instinctively recoiled at such lavishness.

People are complex and contradictory, they are not constructs or cartoons. The "yuppie" was a caricature. Fueled by media hype and partisan venom, it fed into both liberal fears and conservative fantasies of a rightward lurch. Americans were creating a new synthesis, with its own paradoxes. Baby boomers entered college as "Rebels in White Gloves"—in Miriam Horn's apt phrase about Hillary Clinton and the Wellesley class of 1969. They became Pillars of Society in Faded Jeans, blazing their own idiosyncratic trail. In the 1980s, a Hillary Clinton would lean left politically but be conservative morally and socially; a George W. Bush would be Reaganite in his politics but profligate in his partying. Overall, the society was evolving so that even most intellectuals and liberals would look kindly on capitalism, and even many moralists and conservatives would tolerate—or at least indulge in when necessary—divorce, abortion, homosexuality, and other deviations from 1950s' morality.

For all the moral and metaphoric value of the yuppie label, it was hard to find actual yuppies because this media illusion had little grounding in demographic realities. Experts noted that the 78 million baby boomers did "not think and act alike." And when it came to Americans who were young (forty and under), city-dwellers, and professionals, the numbers plummeted. While there were approximately 60 million boomers, and 20 million of them were colleged educated or working in white-collar jobs, Americans under forty with enough disposable incomes to be yuppies, say $75,000 a year, made up only 0.3 percent of the population; such numbers did not a major movement make. It was more helpful to think of "yuppie" as an adjective, not a noun, as a shorthand usefully applied to some 1980s' trends and attitudes that many indulged rather than as a mold for real people. Nevertheless, the search for the yuppie would continue. Not for the first time, and not for the last, American political culture and public discourse would be imprisoned within the confines of a convenient media construct.

The Changing Media Context: Concentration and Fragmentation

A superpower of nearly a quarter of a billion people could be conquered—or at least defined—by 0.3 percent of its population because of the peculiar way the American media operated. During the 1980s, the American media was becoming more fragmented yet concentrated. Even as niche marketing developed, even as the three-network oligopoly dissolved into the hundred-channel cable galaxy, the center of gravity in the media universe emerged stronger than ever. The speed with which the concept of a yuppie entered the culture and began setting standards demonstrated the power and ubiquity of the modern media.

Reagan navigated these profound cultural changes deftly. It was not just that Reagan knew how to speak in parables and visuals, or that his men knew how to tame the press. The 1980s would be Reagan's decade because Reagan mastered this changing universe, milking and shaping the cultural changes in general, and the new media realities in particular.

In 1981, five weeks after Reagan's inauguration, television news experienced a dramatic changing of the guard. On March 6, 1981, Walter Cronkite signed off for the last time as the *CBS Evening News* anchor. For nineteen years Cronkite had been the voice of America, America's "favorite uncle" and "most trusted" public figure. Cronkite grew with the network news, helping to expand the nightly broadcast from fifteen minutes to thirty minutes on September 2, 1963, and facilitating the emergence of the nightly news shows as Americans' bulletin board, their central source for news.

Cronkite's reign as America's top newsman was a tribute to many qualities that would soon be labeled "Reaganesque." A son of the Midwest, in his case St. Joseph, Missouri, born in 1916, Cronkite matured amid the privations of the Great Depression and the patriotism of World War II. A journalist, not a showman, he sought to get the facts out and the story right. He covered World War II on the air and on the ground for United Press. After the war, he went into radio "for the money" and was soon organizing CBS's Washington news bureau.

As Cronkite thrived, so did CBS News, the *"New York Times* of the airwaves." Cronkite set the country's agenda. "Never in the history of journalism have single voices reached so many people on a daily basis," Cronkite would note. This "royal status" derived from and intensified television's focus on personality, shifting the notion of the "news" from something objective to something subjective, and paving the way for a culture and politics of celebrity.

Cronkite's calm reassured Americans as he reported the traumatic stories of the 1960s and 1970s. "He's the national security blanket," said the *Washington Post*'s Nicholas von Hoffman. Cronkite's television persona was stiffer than his folksy personality, reflecting his generation's public reserve. Cronkite would understand a president like

Reagan, who would be known for always remaining formally dressed in the Oval Office.

On some levels, Walter Cronkite would have two successors. Ronald Reagan would replace Cronkite as the nation's paterfamilias. At his best, Reagan was able to transcend the complexities of his policies, to reassure Americans. A White House interview prior to Cronkite's retirement passed the torch. Reagan gave Cronkite one of the highest compliments in the old actor's arsenal: "You've always been a pro." At the same time, Dan Rather would lead television, the network news, and journalism itself into a more central but more complicated role in American society. Dan Rather's emergence as anchor symbolized the rise of the critical, investigative TV journalist. Rather's reputation stemmed from Watergate. "Are you running for something?" President Nixon asked Rather in 1974. "No, sir, Mr. President, are you?" Rather snapped.

Rather would never replicate Cronkite's air of authority. Rather was more intense, less measured, more engaged. If Walter Cronkite was Gregory Peck, or Ronald Reagan, wafting through the airwaves with a smooth, confident, midcentury, midwestern masculinity, Dan Rather was Dustin Hoffman with more standard good looks, darting ahead thanks to a plucky combination of hard work, a sharp mind, and relentless ambition.

Rather's CBS desperately clutched the cloak of respectability Cronkite wore with ease. The cloak, however, would fray thanks to the competition of other news sources, the rise of "infotainment," news bureau budget cuts, and a conservative counterattack against the media's ingrained skepticism and "liberal bias," which targeted CBS and Dan Rather. Rather would also share the spotlight with two other anchors who emerged in 1983, ABC's clipped, aristocratic Canadian, Peter Jennings, and NBC's genial midwesterner, Tom Brokaw.

Cronkite's departure coincided with other transformations in network news. Portable minicameras freed correspondents to roam and beam pictures back to New York via new communications satellites. The computer revolution enhanced the graphics, injecting exciting visual aids that upstaged the text. The invasion into the once sacred preserves of the news divisions by entertainers such as ABC's Roone

Arledge would further revolutionize the way news stories were told and the kinds of stories that were considered news.

A month after Dan Rather's debut, as the CBS news division struggled with a nine-point ratings drop, all three networks confronted the great threat to their collective hegemony. In April 1981 CNN sued the three networks and the Reagan administration, demanding equal access to the White House press pool. This suit, combined with Cronkite's retirement, heralded cable's ascent. Cable would be in 57 percent of American homes by 1989, and CNN would earn bragging rights as the nation's network for news, broadcasting to fifty-one million American households and more than eighty nations.

Ted Turner created CNN. A bold, manic Atlanta entrepreneur, Turner cut his teeth selling billboard space in the South. If Walter Cronkite was the John the Baptist of television news, spreading the gospel of sober, factual, apolitical reportage, Turner was the anti-Christ. Turner viewed news as a profitable form of entertainment. On his Atlanta television station, Turner had fulfilled his FCC obligations by broadcasting the news at 3 A.M. He spiced the offerings with various antics, including a co-anchor, "Rex the Wonder Dog," and a roving "Unknown Announcer" with a paper bag over his head. Turner hated the networks: "What those networks are doing is making Hitler Youth out of the American people—lazy, drug addicts, homosexuals, sex maniacs, materialists, disrespectful."

Thanks to the magic of satellite and cable, Turner parlayed a mediocre UHF station into a national "superstation," raising his hometown's profile, boosting the sports franchises he owned, including the Atlanta Braves, and getting rich. Turner reasoned that HBO had beaten him to movies, ESPN had beaten him to sports, and "the three networks" covered "regular series kinda stuff. . . . All that's left is news!"

Cable News Network, offering round-the-clock news coverage, began broadcasting on June 1, 1980. After a rocky start that had people mocking the "Chaos News Network," CNN stabilized, and Americans were soon steeped in raw news footage, a contrast to Cronkite's sculpted news tidbits. With CNN functioning like the Associated Press, offering constant bulletins, the network news shows had to become more like magazines, justifying the time lag from occurrence to reportage, even if only a few hours, with slick packaging and more speculative stories. CBS News's new president, Van Gordon Sauter, demanded "infotainment" aimed at "the heartland." The more highbrow news crew grumbled that CBS was not "some second-rate tabloid."

Committed to covering live action around the globe and around the clock, CNN would help further nationalize American politics and undermine the traditional news cycle. At the same time, the spread of cable further fragmented the country, as the network oligopoly dissolved and hundreds of small-niche cable stations competed for viewer attention. With the "big three's" share of the national audience dipping from 85 percent to 67 percent by the end of the 1980s, David Letterman would quip: "TV is becoming like Radio."

TV was also becoming like radio in forging new links with the music business. In August 1981, as Reagan celebrated his legislative triumphs, MTV began. MTV would drown the nation in a flood of videos and further dilute the ability of politics to command center stage. The rise of niche networks like MTV and ESPN, the sports network founded in 1979, and the pursuit of all-entertainment all the time facilitated a low-intensity engagement with politics. This suited Reagan and contrasted with the high intensity of just a few years before, when Walter Cronkite and his ABC and NBC rivals could command the nation's attention and focus its agenda.

Market research created MTV. The brainchild of Robert Pittman, a twenty-seven-year-old Mississippi native and radio programmer, MTV targeted baby boomers' neglected younger siblings. Pittman, whose career would also involve reviving Six Flags Amusement Park, managing the Century 21 real estate company, and building the AOL-Time-Warner behemoth, worshiped entertainment as intensely as Walter Cronkite worshiped the news. Music is "a peg" 12-to-30-year-olds "use to identify themselves." Pittman believed.

Pittman agreed with Ted Turner that on cable, "narrowcasting" was the way to go. Americans would watch particular channels, not specific shows. Targeting the "culture of TV babies," with short attention spans and an addiction to sensation, who would "watch, do their homework, and listen to music at the same time," Pittman wanted a nondemanding but stimulating medium.

Reflecting the media's growing comprehensiveness and cockiness, MTV marketing was innovative and enveloping. Executives seeking cable operators to adopt their fledgling network deployed celebrities. Pete Townshend and Mick Jagger, David Bowie and Madonna whined "I want my MTV!" Mobilizing the couch potatoes of what would soon be called "Generation X," they said: "Pick up your phone, call your local cable operator, and demand your MTV."

Using 1960s' grassroots tactics to develop a 1980s' institution worked. MTV became a financial and cultural juggernaut. With eager record companies feeding free programs, with videos mimicking the visual language and pacing of commercials, and in turn shaping subsequent ads, the line between advertising and programming blurred. Surveys of retailers estimated that album sales jumped 15 to 20 percent after exposure on MTV—a critical assist for the flagging record industry. By 1984, with advertising revenues of one million dollars a week pouring in, with an audience of twenty-two million youngsters between the ages of twelve and twenty-four, MTV was the highest-rated basic cable network, with a 1.1 rating, having crossed an important psychological and symbolic barrier.

In between the videos and the commercials, MTV's "vee-jays" riffed. A stream of rock music trivia and rock star antics expanded the concept of news. MTV's saturation coverage of the music business gibed nicely with the syndicated television show *Entertainment Tonight,* which started in September 1981, broadcasting gossip about entertainers. Americans were increasingly fascinated with *Lifestyles of the Rich and Famous,* a show that would premiere in 1984. The stories about celebrities, often choreographed by publicity agents, further blurred the line between news and entertainment. The infotainment bug would inject Hollywood celebrities and Hollywood values deeper into the American bloodstream.

Awash in materialism, addicting a new generation to consumerism and celebrity worship, floating in dramatic visual images, hostile to traditional narrative structures, MTV helped set the 1980s' cultural template. By the end of the decade, many would consider MTV the era's "most influential single cultural product," for better and worse. Critics credited and blamed MTV for slick, visually rich, but vapid television shows such as *Miami Vice,* for many stylistic excesses, and even for Ronald Reagan's snappy and sappy television ads in his 1984 reelection campaign.

By September 1982, when Gannett launched *USA Today,* the media universe had changed—to Ronald Reagan's benefit. *USA Today,* "the Nation's Newspaper," was national but not excessively political. It was exceedingly visual, and remarkably low-impact. Derided as "McPaper," *USA Today* eschewed the *New York Times'* "all the news that's fit to print" ambitions. *USA Today* ran short, superficial political stories, along with its lifestyle, trends, business, entertainment, and consumer news. Ronald Reagan would benefit from such distractions, as voters would rely on general impressions rather than steeping themselves in deeper analyses, explaining the public's remarkably high tolerance for his many missteps and sidesteps.

At first glance, *USA Today* seemed to counter the epidemic of niche specialization that was fragmenting the media. Rooted in the Gannett's national network of suburban newspapers rather than one idiosyncratic locale, the paper reflected the 1980s' Reaganized, nationalized, centralized, televised, homogenized, lowest-common-denominator culture. This was the paper of Anywhere USA, neither Main Street USA nor Big City USA. In fact, the nation's cultural center, like its political center, was thriving. CNN revolutionized the news and ended the network oligopoly, but more Americans still watched the network news. Similarly, despite all the hype and cultural resonance, MTV barely attracted 160,000 viewers at any given time, while deep into the first decade of the twenty-first century, the three nightly network newscasts would still be attracting a combined audience of thirty million homes. As with the yuppie phenomenon, America's centrifugal and centripetal forces were both operative.

The modern media reflected its own variation of the Reagan reconciliation. The continuing dominance of CBS, the emergence of CBS News as a profit center, and the rise of CNN, MTV, and *USA Today* all demonstrated the vitality of American capitalism. Cable, in particular, profited from Reagan's deregulatory impulse, which ended the Big Three networks' monopoly and soon spawned a fourth network, Rupert Murdoch's Fox Broadcasting. Yet Reagan's revolutionaries often targeted these happy byproducts of Reagan's revolution as subversive forces. Boomers embraced both the media's uncritical culture of celebrity and its culture of unrelenting political criticism and social exposé. Critics blamed MTV for further undermining adult authority, turning Americans away from a verbal culture toward a visual culture, polluting young American minds with pornographic, satanic, or violent images, and further addicting them to a steady sixties-style diet of sex, drugs, and rock'n'roll. These blue-chip media properties did demonstrate that there was great money to be made, 1980s' style, in perpetuating some of the methods and the ideas of the 1960s.

The Rise of the Celebrity CEO

An article from the 1920 presidential campaign said it all. In this "new age of publicity . . . The Man With the Best Story Wins." Popular culture inundated Americans with stories. Reaganism shaped many of these plot lines. Especially in the first few years of the administration, it often seemed that Reagan was writing the nation's stories, making its laws, and triumphing.

One storyline Reagan revived lionized entrepreneurs, his "heroes for the eighties." Amid rampant Naderism and hostility to authority, businessmen had served as whipping boys in the sixties and seventies. By 1980 the two businessmen in top ten prime-time television shows, George Jefferson and J. R. Ewing, were greedy foils; the 1970s' popular detectives such as Kojak, and Barnaby Jones often targeted corrupt businessmen. In 1976, Irving Kristol warned that "the upsurge of anti-corporate sentiment in the past decade," combined with American's traditional populist discomfort with big business, "has put the modern corporation in the critical condition that we find it in today."

By contrast, the 1980s would feed the trend of the celebrity entrepreneur, the heroic CEO. Like John Rockefeller and Andrew Carnegie during the Gilded Age, like Henry Ford and Andrew Mellon in the 1920s, the president of Chrysler, Lee Iacocca, became an apostle of progress. In so doing, Iacocca demonstrated the potential benefits for executives who could play on the national stage, crusading to save his company and revive America's automobile industry. Ironically, this icon of Reaganite individualism and CEO daring saved his company with a most un-Reagan-like governmental handout.

A talented engineer and promoter, Iacocca was the father of the Mustang in the 1960s, and the president of Ford Motor Company in the 1970s. In 1978 Chairman Henry Ford II fired Iaccoca, who landed with Chrysler. The weakest of the Big Three lost $700 million from 1978 to mid-1979. While rebuilding, Iacocca made two large public relations gambits. First, he lobbied to secure an unprecedented $1.5 billion in congressional loan guarantees. After a heated debate, Chrysler received the guarantees in January 1980—and would pay back the loans by 1984, seven years early.

Iacocca's second PR gambit was to become the company's pitchman. Starring in over sixty commercials, playing the gruff, straight-shooting boss, Iacocca shamelessly wrapped himself, his cars, his company, and his industry in the American flag. He pleaded: "Let's make American mean something again."

In what would become typical eighties' style, Iacocca blurred the message and the messenger. By publishing *Iacocca: An Autobiography*, then chairing the festivities rededicating the Statue of Liberty, Iacocca shifted from promoting his company to promoting himself. His book sold more than 2.5 million copies, topping the charts in 1984 and 1985. Even as he entered the celebrity stratosphere, and enjoyed demands he run for president, Iaccoca recognized that "In a disposable society like ours, there are no real heroes. Nobody lasts very long."

Donald Trump did for New York real estate what Iacocca did for Detroit automakers, saving yet another "sick industry" from the 1970s with hype and skill. A flamboyant, talented megalomaniac, Trump was more controversial than Iacocca. Trump's 1970s reclamation project transformed Grand Central Station's decaying Commodore Hotel into the gleaming Grand Hyatt Hotel. His 1980s' signature piece was Trump Tower on Fifth Avenue. Built in 1983, this sixty-eight-story, $200 million chrome, brass, and glass tower symbolized the excess of the age, with its two three-foot-high bronze "Ts" at the entrance, its six-story atrium shopping arcade, its seven-story waterfall, its ninety-one condominiums starting at one million dollars, and its lucrative mix of super-rich tenants, upper-class shoppers, and ogling tourists.

Desperate to feed Americans' appetite for celebrity gossip, reporters made "The Donald" famous and glamorous, even while mocking his egoism and materialism. The *New York Times'* usually staid business pages described Trump as "a brash Adonis from the outer boroughs bent on placing his imprint on the golden rock" of Manhattan. Businessmen like Trump basked in the media glow on "Page Six"—the *New York Post* gossip column that set the standard for such people watching—and the business pages, which expanded as fascination with business and business people grew.

Ronald Reagan had the rich-man-wannabe's faith in the talismanic power of American business. This poor kid from the other side of the railroad tracks who happily hobnobbed with America's aristocrats often confused great fortunes with great virtue. Throughout 1983 Reagan's well-bred, former-oilman vice president, George Bush, worked on reducing the growth of federal regulations by more than 25 percent and cutting over three hundred million hours of government-required paperwork annually. At the same time, the industrialist J. Peter Grace spearheaded an effort with 161 corporate executives and two thousand volunteers working, as the president had charged them in 1982, "like tireless bloodhounds to root out government inefficiency and waste of tax dollars." In January 1984 the Grace Commission would propose 2,500 recommendations that could save the public more than $150 billion dollars in a decade.

Donald Trump fit right into Ronald Reagan's era of governmental deregulation, entrepreneurial deification, and take-charge businessmen. In 1986 Trump would upstage New York City's infamously elephantine bureaucracy by rebuilding Central Park's Wollman ice skating rink. After six years of delays, and over $12 million wasted, the city had announced the rink would be ready in eighteen months. Trump stepped in and the rink was finished in four months, $750,000 under budget. True, many mocked Trump's repeated "mystery news conferences, held for no apparent reason." Still, it was hard not to salute what the *New York Times* called "one of the bolder feats of civic bravado tried in New York in recent years."

Reporters championed other entrepreneurial egomaniacs, including Ted Turner. One *New York Times* portrait of Turner decided his "can-do attitude" outweighed his more "grating qualities." Turner appeared to be a pioneer, rooted in traditional American values, combining "fierce patriotism, reverence for hard work and individual accomplishment, and an optimist's visceral aversion to pessimists."

Turner, like Trump and Iacocca, understood the power of the media spiral, whereby references in one arena fed and accelerated references in another. Qualms about appearing in an advertisement, shamelessly shilling a book, or aggressively trumpeting oneself now seemed quaint. In fact, blurring lines broadened one's base and extended one's appeal, with dramatically lucrative results for Iacocca, Trump, and Turner.

This cult of the CEO distorted the corporate culture as well as the popular culture. As Americans worshiped the corporate titans, corporate boards became similarly bewitched and exceedingly generous. Moreover, the Reaganite anything-goes ethos transformed the culture of the executive suite, changing corporate leaders from the association-minded, cautious, modest citizens of the 1950s to the high-flying, take-the-money-and-run prima donnas of the late twentieth century. Throughout the 1980s, as workers' wages stagnated, executive pay soared. In the 1960s and 1970s CEOs earned about 25 times that of hourly production workers; by 1988, with CEOs' average pay exceeding $750,000, the ratio was 93 times that of workers. It would reach 419 times as high by 1999 after the Clinton boom.

For a people obsessed with individualism, Americans remained remarkably susceptible to mass marketing of both heroes and products. As the economy improved, as these conspicuous consumers swaggered across the stage, many Americans experienced a compulsive acquisitiveness, a moral and spiritual vertigo amid a grand national shopping binge. Affluent Americans overshot and overstretched, defining too many trinkets they could not afford—or could not find—as "necessities." Christmas 1983, for example, became the "Cabbage Patch Christmas," when Americans bought 350,000 homely dolls, and yet millions of children were disappointed Christmas morning because their parents had failed in the quest.

"Cabbage Patch Kids" came from "adoption centers" with individual variations in eye and hair color. Their manufacturers called them "babies," not "dolls." Desperate adults besieged toy stores. When one

Ronald Reagan was a political phenomenon, one of the most beloved American leaders of the twentieth century. Poll ratings might fluctuate, controversies would erupt, policy initiatives could flag, but Reagan's bond with the American people remained strong. Americans yearned for "Morning in America"; Ronald Reagan helped them believe— and made it happen. (Ronald Reagan Presidential Library)

Propelled by his performance at the presidential debate in Cleveland, Reagan would claim a "mandate" in 1980, despite the electorate's overwhelmingly ABC sentiments— "Anybody But Carter." Above, the CBS News Headquarters on Election Night presaged the broader yet imminent changing of the guard, as Dan Rather (left) waited in the wings to replace Walter Cronkite (right). In the foreground, CBS News correspondent Lesley Stahl represented women's expanding public role. Note the low-tech set, replete with typewriters, without computers. (© CBS Photo Archive)

The surreal ending to Jimmy Carter's presidential dream took place on Inauguration Day 1981, as Carter, Chief of Staff Hamilton Jordan, White House Counsel Lloyd Cutler, Vice President Walter Mondale, and pollster Pat Caddell labored to free the hostages still held in Iran. The worn president's casual style made him look like a defeated college football coach. Mondale's slumped pose says it all: liberalism is exhausted and defeated. (Jimmy Carter Presidential Library)

January 1981: three premiers. Just as Ronald and Nancy Reagan inaugurated "the Ronald Reagan Show" (above, Ronald Reagan Presidential Library)—restoring glamour to the White House—two network shows began, representing competing story lines throughout the 1980s. *Dynasty* reinforced the Reagan narrative of America resurgent, resplendent, and self-indulgent, while *Hill Street Blues* suggested a more complicated counternarrative. If Reagan's America was monochromatic, prosperous, safe, and orderly, Hill Street was multicultural, poor, dangerous and chaotic.

David Stockman was the wunderkind of the Reagan Revolution, the hyperactive star of those frenetic first hundred days—and very successful first seven months. Armed with his mastery of budgetary minutiae and his conservative ideology, Stockman was an equal opportunity, budget-slashing zealot, unlike his more genial and pragmatic boss. (Ronald Reagan Presidential Library)

Beefy and bulbous, with a mane of white hair and a back-slapping persona, Democratic Speaker of the House Thomas P. O'Neill, Jr., seemed to have sprung to life from the pages of the Boston political classic *The Last Hurrah*. Reagan and O'Neill, as two Irish pols, often swapped jokes, but this clash of Titans was often vicious. (Ronald Reagan Presidential Library)

Although President Reagan liked to keep banker's hours, he worked hard on the few issues he considered important: cutting taxes, expanding defense, and deregulating. Above, Reagan works the phones, sometimes cajoling, and sometimes even threatening. Below, Reagan at his ranch, after signing historic tax-cutting legislation on August 13, 1981. Little did the president realize that in many ways, barely three-quarters of the way into his first year, his legislative revolution had peaked. (Ronald Reagan Presidential Library)

The reigning stereotype of Ronald Reagan's 1980s caricatures the era as a time of consensus politics and a placid patriotic public. In 1982 an anti-nuclear demonstration attracted an estimated 700,000 to New York's Central Park, testifying to a dynamic political culture—debating the responsibilities of American citizens to each other and to the world, while illustrating some fears many Americans shared about Reagan's defiant anti-Communism. (© Bettman/CORBIS/MAGMA)

Both politically and culturally, Americans in the 1980s were trying to get right with the 1960s. The 1983 movie, *The Big Chill,* struck a chord, portraying a merry band of University of Michigan radicals from the 1960s trying to navigate life in the 1980s. These "yuppies" seemed to epitomize the 1960s' sellout, but they had enough of a sixties' sensibility to feel a "Big Chill" down their spines when they went too far.

Ronald Reagan was well suited to preside over this Great Reconciliation between sixties' idealism and eighties' prosperity. His easy listening nationalism gave a communal, and idealistic veneer to individualist, consumerist excess. "Masters of the Universe" like Donald Trump, New York's megalomaniac real estate mogul, symbolized business's new respectability—and reputation for greater reliability than the government. (Above, left, © Robert Maass/CORBIS/MAGMA) Blurring lines between entertainment and politics, the Reagans happily hosted megastars such as Michael Jackson, hoping to convert some of his wattage into votes. Often yearning for respectability, entertainers happily obliged, as Michael Jackson launches a Campaign Against Drunk Driving with the Reagans in 1984. (Above, right, Ronald Reagan Presidential Library)

Ronald Reagan revived America's civil religion. In that spirit, the 1984 Olympics in Los Angeles became a celebration of the U.S.A. In spectacles such as the games' opening ceremonies, Americans responded with tears in their eyes, a lump in their throats, and patriotic songs on their lips. (Ronald Reagan Presidential Library)

In 1984 Reagan and his aides mounted a pragmatic, patriotic election campaign celebrating "Morning Again in America." (Ronald Reagan Presidential Library) Even Bruce Springsteen was no match for Ronald Reagan and the Republican image-makers. Before the rocker knew it, his critical song "Born in the USA" became a virtual Republican theme song, celebrating all that was virtuous in prosperous America. In the mid-1980s, anyone who could best "the Boss" was unstoppable.

midwesterner heard that dolls remained available in London, he flew there. None were left, but reporters gave the forty-four-year-old suburbanite five dolls in exchange for an "exclusive interview." It being the right season, the happy father kept two dolls and donated the other three to charity.

Such a brazen move seemed to typify the yuppie parent's desperation to purchase a child's affection with trendy goods. In fact, Edward Pennington was a postman whose flight attendant wife could secure cheap tickets. With the Cabbage Patch craze, as with so much else in the 1980s, you did not have to be young or urban or a professional to indulge in yuppie excesses.

The Opposition Stirs: Where the 1980s Builds on the 1960s

The caricature of the 1980s as politically dormant comes from defining the political discourse as Reagan's patriotic odes balanced by the breast-beating of The Big Chillers and their television equivalents from *thirtysomething* as they sipped Chardonnay and watched their stock portfolios grow. All that nostalgia, all that guilt, all that glamorizing of a past that few baby boomers actually shared, leavened with lots of hypocrisy, indeed makes for a pathetic political dialogue. "What is their problem?" observers would later ask, struck by so much angst festering in such well-appointed living rooms in a nation blighted with thousands of homeless people.

In fact, the 1980s were more exciting than that. Tip O'Neill's fairness crusade, combined with the various Reaganite treatises, triggered a decade-long debate about America's commitment to the unfortunate. The Democrats' house intellectual, Senator Daniel Patrick Moynihan, pointed to "a simple statistic" to tell his audience "all you need to know about what is happening in Washington": In 1981 even though "means-tested entitlement programs" represented only about 18 percent of federal benefit payments to individuals, they sustained 40 percent of Reagan's budget cuts.

Sometimes the criticism emanated from friendly quarters too. William Schneider, a resident fellow at Reagan's beloved American

Enterprise Institute, would write in 1984, "Reaganism is economic elitism. It is the view that hunger in America is merely anecdotal, that the homeless are homeless by choice, and that only the morally unworthy have been hurt by the Administration's policies." Using popular perceptions to define ideology, Schneider declared: "The poll evidence is clear on this point. Reagan polarizes rich and poor, black and white, men and women, and Democrats and Republicans more than any other recent President." Yuppie excesses and the "money culture" confirmed the critique.

This counterattack would curtail Reaganism but not repudiate it. As a result, two contradictory conceptions governed 1980s politics. Most Americans still accepted Reagan's diagnosis of the problem, with faith in the government's ability to solve problems continuing to plummet. But most Americans began doubting Reagan's prescription, further reducing faith in government and American leaders, as talk of gridlock and fears of the budget deficit spread.

By January 1983 Reagan's aides were feeling defensive. Reagan's approval rating had dropped to 35 percent, what would be the first-term low. White House officials repeatedly emphasized that they were not just maintaining "the social safety net for low-income needy and the jobless." They were proposing "spending increases for high priority domestic programs," including Head Start "(up 15%)," foster care "(up 11%)," veterans' medical care "(up 11%)," and aid to displaced workers ("up 380%)."

Emboldened by Reagan's defensiveness, liberal intellectuals mobilized. Robert Lekachman's lament that "Greed is Not Enough" became a rallying cry. Lekachman, an economics professor in New York, argued that Reaganomics was warmed-over Hooverism. Awed by Reagan's skills and disgusted by his policies, Lekachman said: "Ronald Reagan must be the nicest president who ever destroyed a union, tried to cut school lunch milk rations from six to four ounces, and compelled families in need of public help to first dispose of household goods in excess of $1,000."

Two Cambridge economists, MIT's Lester Thurow and Harvard's Robert Reich, rejected what Reich called "The false choice between civic values and business values" or between "social justice and economic prosperity." Thurow's 1980 book *The Zero Sum Society* identified hard choices politicians had to make, but Thurow advocated redistributing wealth and power in favor of the poor rather than solving the problems on the backs of the working class. In his optimistic 1983 best-seller, Reich predicted that the rise of the information age, *The Next American Frontier,* would create a new "era of productivity" prizing human capital and making "social justice . . . essential . . . to economic growth." Reich's linkage of justice with growth, his call for a humanitarian capitalism, helped free the Democratic Party from some of the shibboleths of the 1960s, without rejecting the higher ideals.

This debate was doubly important. It shaped the critique of Reaganism and 1980s' "values," meaning the ones the media perpetuated, caricatured, and lambasted, when convenient. This debate also shaped the future, laying the groundwork for the "Third Way," for a way to square the circle, rejecting Reaganism without reverting to LBJism. "We're here to save the United States of America," one politician would declare shortly after Reagan left office. "Our burden is to give the people a new choice rooted in old values. A new choice that is simple, that offers opportunity, demands responsibility, gives citizens more say, provides them responsive government, all because we recognize that we are community."

Bill Clinton spoke these Reaganesque words to the moderate Democratic Leadership Council (DLC) in 1991. In 1983 Bill Clinton returned to the gubernatorial post he had lost during the 1980 Carter debacle. Clinton's comeback campaign hinged on the "fairness issue," blasting Governor Frank White as President Reagan's stand-in. Clinton charged that White's budget cuts came "out of the hides of the poorest [and] weakest." Once back in the governor's mansion, Clinton learned from Reagan while bashing him. Clinton's recipe of populism, investment, and responsibility was dedicated not simply to getting "the government off our backs" but having it "by our sides." By the early 1990s Clinton would be heading the DLC, protecting the Democratic Party from the "liberal fundamentalists" by offering "a new course, grounded in mainstream values," and repackaging some traditional liberal ideas in Reaganesque language.

While these nuanced, more theoretical attacks percolated, the nuclear freeze movement united millions against Reaganism. Recruiting through fear rather than compassion, the movement's simple message resonated widely. "No nukes" conveyed the story pithily. Reaganites needed a paragraph to respond, claiming that "The Soviets would like such a freeze" because "It would preserve their current advantages and lock the United States into a position of serious military disadvantage. A freeze today would stop our plans to correct the existing military imbalance caused by a decade of continuous expansion of Soviet Strategic forces and unilateral U.S. restraint."

Mobilizing 700,000 people against nuclear armaments in a June 1982 Central Park rally was only the most dramatic example of antinuclear activism. Helen Caldicott articulated Americans' fears about nuclear war and doubts about Reagan's anti-Soviet saber-rattling. Jonathan Schell's 1982 best-seller *The Fate of the Earth* terrified readers by speculating about what a one-megaton bomb targeting the Empire State Building could do: "From Greenwich Village up to Central Park, the heat would be great enough to melt metal and glass."

While Reagan's domestic policy critics often recalled the traumas of the Great Depression, Reagan's foreign policy critics alternated between resurrecting the ghost of Vietnam and feeding fears of Armageddon. By May 1981 thousands had massed in the capital for what reporters called the "largest march" at the Pentagon since the Vietnam War. Fears of a Vietnam-type quagmire centered on Central America. "No draft, no war, U.S. out of El Salvador," protesters chanted. The warnings of apocalypse focused on policy with the Soviet Union and the doomsday clock counting down to nuclear war, which the *Bulletin of Atomic Scientists* fretfully advanced with Reagan's election.

The nuclear freeze movement brilliantly mimicked Reagan, subordinating complicated policy questions to one overarching and disturbing image. In cosponsoring a bipartisan freeze resolution, Senator Ted Kennedy mocked Reagan's "voodoo arms control, which says you must have more in order to have less." In 1982, 17 senators and 128 House members supported a freeze; in 1983, the House of Representatives passed a resolution calling for a freeze, as 238 Catholic bishops distributed a pastoral letter branding nuclear weapons "immoral."

Ronald Reagan's pacifist streak had long made him doubt the sophisticated strategists' commitment to mutual assured destruction, aptly known as MAD. Still, he considered the nuclear freeze movement "dangerous." The president dismissed such "well-intentioned" naiveté by echoing H. L. Mencken that "For every problem, there is one solution which is simple, neat, and wrong."

In 1983 Reagan reaffirmed his own "simple" foreign policy views in three pugnacious speeches. On March 8, 1983, addressing the National Association of Evangelicals' conference in Orlando, Florida, Reagan denounced those "who would place the United States in a position of military and moral inferiority." Reagan begged his listeners not "to ignore the facts of history and the aggressive impulses of an evil empire, to simply call the arms race a giant misunderstanding and thereby remove yourself from the struggle between right and wrong and good and evil." Two weeks later, Reagan sought to transcend the MAD strategy by proposing "defensive technologies" that "could intercept and destroy strategic ballistic missiles." Wags had branded the speech calling the Soviet Union an "evil empire" the "Darth Vader" speech. Reagan's technological vision, saddled with the bureaucratic moniker of the Strategic Defense Initiative, or SDI, became known as the "Star Wars" defense.

That April Reagan championed his Central America policy at a joint session of Congress. Trying to shock Americans into caring, Reagan said: "El Salvador is nearer to Texas than Texas is to Massachusetts. Nicaragua is just as close to Miami, San Antonio, San Diego, and Tucson as those cities are to Washington. . . . But nearness on the map doesn't even begin to tell the strategic importance of Central America, bordering as it does on the Caribbean—our lifeline to the outside world." While insisting there would be no Vietnam redux—"There is no thought of sending American combat troops to Central America"—Reagan could not resist echoing the "domino" warning that kept America mired in South Vietnam by invoking American credibility as a rationale. A happy political gladiator, Reagan loved debating his critics; but he occasionally played right into their hands, as they often played into his.

Reagan's foreign policy often inverted Theodore Roosevelt's famous formula—Reagan spoke loudly and carried a small—if overpriced—stick. In September 1983, when the Soviets shot down a Korean Airlines jet, slaughtering 269 innocents, Reagan acted cautiously, judiciously. In October 1983, when suicide truck bombers blew up the Marine barracks in Beirut, murdering 241, Reagan reacted passively, impotently. Yet the day before the terrorist bombing, two million Europeans marched specifically against NATO's deployment of Pershing II and cruise missiles, but more broadly against the American president's alleged militarism.

This dynamic of Reaganesque saber-rattling feeding populist fear transfixed the nation with ABC's November 1983 movie, *The Day After,* dramatizing the effects of a nuclear attack on Lawrence, Kansas. Thanks to an effective advertising campaign, millions gathered in their friends' living rooms to watch the unthinkable together. With an estimated one hundred million viewers, it would be the decade's ninth most-watched television show. George Shultz, the secretary of state, and William Buckley, America's most famous conservative intellectual, appeared on a panel discussion Ted Koppel hosted after the broadcast. Within forty-eight hours, administration spokesmen appeared on twelve television shows ("half national, half major media markets"), fifteen radio talk shows, and six op-ed pages stating the administration's conviction that "Strength can and does deter aggression."

Here, too, Americans responded paradoxically. Reagan's defense buildup remained popular. But Americans worried more than they had in years about the possibility of nuclear destruction—with 80 percent or more respondents in polls urging both arms limitations and cultural exchanges with the Soviets.

The Environmentalist Synthesis: Mobilized and Institutionalized

Beyond the intellectual and political fireworks, many of the 1960s' radical ideas were mainstreamed in the 1980s. A critical test after a period of reform comes when a conservative seizes power and decides what not to dismantle. In not ending many initiatives, and in trying to embrace many liberal causes, from civil rights to women's rights, Reagan helped institutionalize and legitimize them—just as Dwight Eisenhower had done with the New Deal. Reagan's newfound environmentalism typified his many negative achievements.

In 1980 NBC News pronounced "the end of the environmental movement," and the death of feminism and civil rights. Reagan's appointments of an avowed conservative, James Watt, as interior secretary and of the inexperienced Anne Gorsuch to head the Environmental Protection Agency vindicated such pessimism. An intense egghead, Poindexter glasses framing his bug-eyes, James Watt stood out among the moderate millionaires filling Reagan's cabinet. Watt relished political combat and outrageous rhetoric, characterizing environmentalism as "the greatest threat to the ecology of the West" and "a left-wing cult which seeks to bring down the type of government I believe in." There are two kinds of people living in this country, he believed: "Liberals and Americans."

Watt supported the appointment of his fellow Denver attorney Anne Gorsuch to the EPA, despite her environmental inexperience. Russell Peterson, president of the National Audubon Society, called the nomination "a bad joke." Gorsuch, who had served in the Colorado legislature, preached the Reagan gospel, preferring incentives to sanctions, and fewer, more focused, actions than dramatic actions against industry.

The Reaganites recognized that, as with civil rights, the assault on environmentalism had to be subtle. Policy adjustments would emerge as responses to the broader crisis and the magical mandate. "[O]nly a strong economy can support a clean and improving environment," the Reagan White Paper on Environmental Policy proclaimed. "Hungry people, people without homes and jobs to support their families, cannot afford to be environmentalists." This would not be a crusade, but a juggling act, seeking "better ways to serve as stewards of our resources so that we could be both a fiscally strong nation and a physically beautiful nation."

A "stewardship" was more passive than a reform. The administration endorsed "steady progress toward cleaner air." When grilled by reporters, Gorsuch explained that the word "steady" means "at a more reasoned," meaning slower, "pace."

The problem vexing Reaganites was that Americans had embraced environmentalism. One Harris poll found that 86 percent of the public supported the Clean Air Act. Reagan made sure to pay rhetorical obeisance to the cause. He claimed, "I fancy myself an environmentalist," and he said he only wanted to target "environmental extremism." But he was not committed to expanding conservation or environmental protection. He still feared more unnecessary regulations, more governmental intrusions.

Reagan's restraint allowed Watt's ideology and Gorsuch's incompetence to define popular impressions of the administration's stance. "President Reagan has broken faith with the American people on environmental protection," charged a thirty-five-page "indictment" of Reagan's record in 1982. Issued by ten leading groups, the document detailed "the environmental tragedy unfolding under the Reagan administration." "Take a deep breath America—while you still can," one article began. Cartoons of Reagan's broad shoulders and distinctive pompadour with the face replaced by a skeleton illustrated the fear that, as Senator George Mitchell of Maine would complain, Reagan's environmental record was "one of the poorest in history."

Congressmen were particularly frustrated. Their traditional tools for controlling bureaucrats did not work with ideologues hostile to regulation. "You can't take money away from them because they don't need money" for the agency, Congressman James J. Florio, chairman of the House committee overseeing the EPA, complained. They also did not care if Congress repealed or curtailed their agency's basic legislation.

By 1983 the administration's environmental policy was in shambles. Anne Gorsuch, now Anne Gorsuch Burford, resigned in March over allegations of "political manipulation" and fraud surrounding the $1.6 billion Superfund for cleaning toxic waste. Her subordinate Rita Lavelle faced perjury charges for denying that she ordered an investigation into an EPA "whistleblower." In September the acerbic Watt would resign after boasting about his "mix" on one advisory panel: "I have a black, I have a woman, two Jews, and a cripple." Seeking to appease environmentalists, Reagan brought back the EPA's first administrator, the more pragmatic William Ruckelshaus.

Beyond the usual distaste toward spending and regulating, Reagan's policies also wavered between Theodore Roosevelt's old-fashioned conservation ideal and the modern environmental critique. A westerner, Reagan accepted conservation, which was conservative, preserving certain land or resources. Environmentalism was more global and proactive, solving problems created by pollution and seeking to prevent future depredations.

Reagan would shrug off the criticism that only 6 of the nation's 546 worst toxic-waste dumps were cleaned in his first term. He would question his staff's "Selling Job" and joke that his commitment "to the entire problem of the environment" was one of the "best-kept secrets about our administration." Reagan's aides struggled to "turn around [the] down slide of support for the president" on environmentalism. They arranged meetings with advisers and congressmen, and with "state and local and regional leaders." But with the policies not likely to "change," they knew they had to "go symbolic."

Eventually, public pressure forced policy modifications. "Preservation of our environment is not a liberal or conservative challenge—it's common sense," Reagan declared in his 1984 State of the Union Address. By 1985 he would have added 2.5 million acres to federally protected lands and boosted EPA's proposed 1985 budget by 53 percent over 1983. *U.S. News & World Report* estimated that the "largest non-defense-spending increase" tripled toxic-dump-cleanup funds.

While Reagan modified his course, the environmental movement grew. Membership in the Sierra Club jumped from 181,000 to over 480,000 by 1988. More than a million people signed a petition to fire James Watt—the most popular petition ever presented to Congress, environmentalists rejoiced. Insiders sensed that environmentalists had stopped demonizing developers, demonstrating a new restraint, but Reagan's transformation was greater. Reagan's assault "strengthened, rather than weakened, the public's determination to protect the environment," the Sierra Club claimed in 1988, "and that is one of the more surprising legacies of Ronald Reagan."

This environmental resurgence went beyond public opinion. Prodded by grassroots campaigns, the *Sierra* reported, "more acreage was added to the National Wilderness Preservation System in the lower 48 states under Reagan than under any other president. Twenty-nine new wildlife refuges were established, encompassing a total of 500,000 acres; 200 new plants and animals were added to the nation's lists of endangered species." The president signed, reauthorized, and often reinforced legislation, including the Clean Water Act, the Resources Conservation and Recovery Act, and the Superfund legislation.

Ultimately, then, it is too simple to focus on President Reagan's anti-environmental Interior Secretary James Watt or on how the incompetents Reagan hired almost ruined the EPA. Watt and the EPA leaders were run out of town while the environmental center of gravity shifted. Americans became instinctively environmental, recognizing that development had its costs, that atmospheric changes could harm people, and that it would take money, time, and commitment to clean up our air, water, and forests.

Surprisingly, with environmentalism—and many other movements—Reagan's opposition placed activists in a win-win situation. Reagan's opposition became a badge of honor. Hearts fluttered and wallets opened when the Sierra Club could warn that "Ronald Reagan is endangering . . . Your health. Your safety. Your environment." Women, blacks, and gays mobilized to protect their gains. Feeling threatened, they escalated the rhetoric. Yet many of these gains were too entrenched to be dislodged, especially given—as David Stockman lamented—America's fragmented Madisonian government and Ronald Reagan's limited powers and restricted agenda. Reagan would occasionally win battles, although they often involved legislative compromises. But on so many levels, Reagan lost his war to undo the 1960s.

The 1960s: Barely Buried, Certainly Not Forgotten

In the 1980s, the sixties were barely buried and certainly not forgotten. Many of the era's values, ideals, ideas, and products were institutionalized, romanticized, commodified, and synthesized, sometimes perpetuating the reforms, sometimes demeaning them. With the Motown hit "I Heard It Through the Grapevine" providing an uplifting bonding moment in *The Big Chill* as well as the sound for a California Raisin Board ad made famous by its dancing raisins, the sixties' legacy was ubiquitous but malleable. The decade loomed large in popular consciousness, demonstrated in movies such as *Dirty Dancing* and *Good Morning, Vietnam,* television shows such as *thirtysomething* and *The Wonder Years,* television stations such as "Nick at Nite" with its stable of sixties-era reruns, and the spread of "classic rock" radio.

As the sixties became a hot popular commodity, the debate over its legacy heated up too. Memoirists defended the decade "when they assaulted the barriers of race and sex and made being a yuppie possible," as one reporter teased. Todd Gitlin's *The Sixties: Years of Hope, Days of Rage* (1987, 1989) celebrated the "incomplete Reformation," for "undermining illegitimate power, encouraging us to honor the unity-in-diversity of the human project." Tom Hayden's *Reunion* (1988) insisted, somewhat defensively, "we accomplished more than we expected, more than most generations ever accomplish." Simultaneously, some former comrades, especially Peter Collier and David Horowitz, shouted good riddance to *The Destructive Generation,* and "to the self-aggrandizing romance with corrupt Third Worldism; to the casual indulgence of Soviet totalitarianism; to the hypocritical and self-dramatizing anti-Americanism which is the New Left's bequest to mainstream politics."

A classic mélange of the 1960s and the 1980s in Reagan's America occurred in northern Vermont. A company exemplifying the go-getter spirit of the 1980s began when two friends who had met in seventh-grade gym class opened shop with a $12,000 investment, in a renovated gas station in Burlington, in May 1978. In 1981 they began franchising their operation. By 1984 sales exceeded $4 million; by 1987, $31 million; by 1990, $77 million; and by 1995, over $150 million. In 1988 President Reagan would honor Ben Cohen and Jerry Greenfield as America's "Small Business Persons of the Year." Twelve years later, a multinational corporation, Unilever, would purchase the company for $326 million.

Ben & Jerry's played the 1960s countercultural card shamelessly. Cohen and Greenfield celebrated their story as two hippies turned marketing moguls, selling ice cream called "Cherry Garcia" and "Rainforest Crunch." From one angle, the company's tied-dyed T-shirts were no more noble than Baskin and Robbins novelties. And when Haagen Dazs tried to muscle the new kids out of the Boston market by intimidating distributors, the Ben & Jerry's campaign against Pillsbury, the parent company, brilliantly exploited the sixties' grassroots appeal. Filing suit while asking in advertisements "What's the Doughboy Afraid of?" mixed hippie mischief-making with eighties' litigating. But from another perspective, cynics could only scoff so much at the Ben & Jerry's Foundation diverting 7.5 percent of pretax profits to the community, at Ben & Jerry's initiatives for peace and against nuclear power plants, for the environment and against nuclear waste. It may have been good business, but it was also community-oriented, progressive, and a reflection of their most cherished ideals.

Even as Reagan was installing an antienvironmental facade, even as baby boomer hippies were getting haircuts, shaving, and putting on suits, many such syntheses occurred; many values and lifestyles of the 1960s were becoming an accepted part of the American furniture in the 1980s. The media played a peculiar role in all this, boosting marginal phenomena while also preserving that mythical American center. Similarly, yuppiedom, such as it was, embodied the values of Reaganism, but it also reflected how intensively most Americans had internalized the anti-Reagan critique. America's kulturkampf—and many Americans' internal kulturkampf—continued.

1984

Los Angeles

The Wizard of America's Id Chooses Patriotism over Politics

America is back and standing tall.
RONALD REAGAN LAUNCHING HIS REELECTION BID,
JANUARY 1984

It remains one of the great American political mysteries—how did Ronald Reagan pull it off? If the opposition to Reagan was more intense than remembered—which it was; if blacks and women and intellectuals felt so marginalized—which they did; if the economy wavered and the poll ratings sagged, how did Reagan win reelection by a landslide? How did this president, who would be described within three years by some of his own aides as doddering, out of touch, ineffectual, succeed?

In 1984, and throughout the Reagan years, Democrats would often answer by shouting, "We wuz robbed!" Reagan's shrewd image-making and his mystifying popularity infuriated liberals, who feared Reagan was snookering Americans. Days after losing the election, the 1984 Democratic nominee Walter Mondale would blame his failure on television and its superficial "twenty-second" news soundbites. Mondale's speechwriter Marty Kaplan was asked whether anyone could have defeated Reagan. Echoing his boss, Kaplan suggested, "Robert Redford or Walter Cronkite."

While dismissing the American people as stupid, this party line also contradicted the Democratic caricature of Ronald Reagan as a callous ideologue. Mondale and his allies vainly tried to characterize Reagan as both Mr. Magoo and Scrooge. During the campaign Mondale attacked Reagan's "shallowness" and his "atrocious abdication of leadership," calling Reagan a figurehead, a cheerleader, out of touch, not in charge, remote, unaware, and unwilling to learn; offering all happy talk, no straight talk; all television, no vision; all blue skies, no blueprint. At the same time, Mondale said that Reagan was a double-dealer motivated by sheer meanness and cynicism; the cruel, unfair, reckless, arrogant candidate of the Khomeinis of American society and the wealthy "yuppies," creating a government of the rich, by the rich, for the rich, with policies that are cold as ice. Condemning Reagan's "bigotry and ignorance" triggered applause lines at rallies but confused America's elusive "swing" voters. Bigotry was a crime of commission; ignorance, one of omission. And besides, Reagan was just too nice to seem so mean and too successful to seem so irresponsible.

The Democrats came by the confusion honestly. Most presidents vacillated between playing politics and being statesmen, between imagery and issues. Reagan's hero Franklin D. Roosevelt wanted to "make" his 1936 second-term run "a crusade" yet recognized that "I am the issue." Similarly, Reagan wavered between emphasizing personality and ideology. The long-running civil war between the Michael Deaver–James Baker pragmatists and the Ed Meese ideologues peaked during Reagan's reelection campaign. "If we allow any Democrat to claim optimism or idealism as his issue, we will lose the election," one aide, Jim Lake, warned in March. Lake counseled avoiding "the issues that will make a particular segment of our supporters happy," preferring to "move forward to capture new supporters." That October, James Baker would identify "two objectives" in determining the president's schedule: "1. Securing his re-election. 2. Helping as many Congressional candidates as possible, particularly Senators." There was little talk about securing a mandate for change, spreading ideas, or galvanizing supporters. Instead, Baker's recipe for victory was more apple pie than red meat: "Crime, Education, Economics—Unity."

In 1984 Ronald Reagan again made it clear that he preferred to be the Wizard of America's Id than lead a new American revolution. Rea-

gan wanted Americans to feel good, not think too hard. On the campaign trail, Reagan celebrated the "great renewal." He told how "Four
years ago we began to navigate by certain fixed principles. Our north
star was freedom, common sense our constellation." The result:
"America is back." Such warm, fuzzy, down-to-earth freedom talk
pleased Middle America.

As both actor and politician, Reagan read people and audiences well.
He knew he was more popular than his program. Rather than fight
that, he would exploit it. Reagan was also struck by many Americans'
desire to celebrate their country. In his memoirs he would recall recu-
perating from John Hinckley's bullet in April 1981, watching the space
shuttle *Columbia* return after its maiden voyage. The "tremendous excitement" the landing generated around the country surprised Reagan. This outburst convinced him "more than ever that Americans
wanted to feel proud and patriotic again."

Ronald Reagan wanted to revive America's civil religion. Blurring
American dreams with California dreaming, he wanted to mix America's warm, nostalgic, Norman Rockwell, apple-pie patriotism, defined
by its earnest midwestern flavor and its New England Puritan spice,
with the happy-go-lucky, sunny ethos of Southern California's leisure
world. Reaganite patriotism applied the Laffer curve to culture and
politics. In the land of no tradeoffs, just as cutting taxes could raise
revenues, self-fulfillment bred altruism, individualistic success fed collective idealism, materialistic excess brought spiritual depth, and a
constrained federal government yielded national greatness. Updating
traditional values with modern consumerism, Reagan understood that
Americans responded to calls for greatness, appeals to the "better angels of their nature," illuminating the simple, good path in an evil,
complex world.

Americans wanted to believe in themselves and their country and
told pollsters they were open to grandiose appeals. Reagan would play
to those stirring patriotic feelings throughout 1984, but most especially
in Los Angeles, when America hosted the summer Olympics and transformed an international competition into a nationalist festival. Reagan
then proceeded to do something similar with the election itself.

The Los Angeles Olympics:
Cheering Capitalism and America

In early 1984 the signs for the Olympics, as for the Reagan campaign, looked ominous. The 1972 Munich Olympics ended in bloodshed, with Palestinian terrorists murdering Israeli athletes. The 1976 Montreal Olympics practically bankrupted the city, leaving a white elephant of a stadium and an elephantine debt. The United States boycotted the 1980 Moscow Olympics after the Soviet Union invaded Afghanistan. Moreover, Los Angeles, a city of sprawl and smog, was a risky site. Critics feared that monstrous traffic jams would postpone the events, spread out over miles of freeways, while athletes feared for their lungs and their fine-tuned constitutions.

Los Angeles, however, was the city that illusions built, the Emerald City of Ronald Reagan's Golden State. California was quintessentially American and modern, a laboratory for American innovations. In these pre-earthquake, pre-riot, pre-OJ years, Los Angeles was the most glamorous city in the most alluring state in America. Songs and TV shows embedded Los Angeles geography in the popular consciousness—Burbank, Beverly Hills, Santa Monica Boulevard, the Ventura Freeway. New Yorkers could not visit without being recruited by former neighbors to "Go West"—a plot twist Woody Allen immortalized in his 1977 *Annie Hall*. The 1986 television hit *LA Law* would help spike applications to law school and lure more people westward. Intoxicated by its prosperity, its galaxy of stars, its mastery of popular culture, Los Angeles posed as the American paradise. Here, historian Gilbert Sewall would note, "the Last Men and Last Women sought only the sun, spending their days in body worship, clothed by Patagonia, drinking expensive bottled water."

In September 1984 Michael Eisner, a forty-two-year-old Hollywood executive, became chairman and CEO of Walt Disney Productions, one of the pillars of Los Angeles. The first outsider to run that dream factory, Eisner shaped the company into an aggressive multimedia conglomerate, a model Southern California, information-age corporation. Renaming it the Walt Disney Company in 1986 to reflect his expansive vision, Eisner diversified. Disney stores, which first opened in 1987, would pop up in malls across America, miniature theme parks marketing experiences, not just provisions. While packaging Disney's cartoons for the growing video market, Eisner used Touchstone Pictures and Hollywood Pictures to woo adults without sullying Disney's name. The $100 million *Three Men and a Baby* grossed in 1987 vindicated this strategy. The Disney Channel, started in 1983, spread Disney via cable and was a marvel of self-promoting cross-marketing, toasted in the eighties as "synergy." Disney theme parks also thrived, with the five hundred millionth Disney "guest" arriving in 1986, despite soaring entrance fees. From relying on theme parks to generate nearly 80 percent of its $1.7 billion revenue in 1984, the company achieved a healthier mix by 1994, earning $4.8 billion from films, $3.5 billion from the parks, and $1.8 billion from merchandising. In 1988 Eisner earned more than $40 million, becoming America's highest paid executive.

Ronald Reagan shared Walt Disney's sensibility. Both were provincials in love with the idea of the Midwest from which they actually escaped. Both mentally inhabited a world where the jungle was about natives and animals chanting "ooga-booga," space travel was about the magical "gee whiz" adventure of it all, Main Street was sanitized and commodified, and all Americans dreamed of living in a gadget-filled, home version of the Carousel of Progress, just like the one General Electric built for the Reagans in the 1950s. In this world, U.S. history was a triumphal march of progress to uphold the ideals of the Declaration of Independence, spread the freedoms of the Constitution, and live up to the heroism of Abraham Lincoln.

Disneyland would become an important refuge as the glow would fade for Los Angeles and California. The national crime wave would threaten the desert paradise with as many as one hundred thousand gang members menacing Los Angeles by the 1990s. California's political culture seemed incapable of generating the collective commitment and individual sacrifice needed to tackle this and other pressing issues. By 1991 Governor Pete Wilson would sigh, "California is ungovernable."

While such frustration mounted throughout the decade, the Olympics and other spectacles distracted Californians, along with their fellow Americans. Experts in image-making as a business, and denial, when necessary, as a way of life, Hollywood's denizens knew the key to success was a great producer. The Olympic organizers found one in Peter Ueberroth. Ueberroth was a poster-child for Reaganism. A self-made multimillionaire who built a travel company from scratch, Ueberroth was in his midforties, combining brilliant entrepreneurship with Boy Scout rectitude.

Ueberroth turned this festival of international harmony into a celebration of one country, the good old U.S.A. In Ueberroth's hands, and with ABC's encouragement, the colors of this Olympics became red, white, and blue. "I hoped the run would unify the country," he later said of the eighty-two-day, nine-thousand-mile, Olympic torch relay through thirty-three states. But even he never expected such a public response. Americans mobbed the route with tears in their eyes, a lump in their throats, and patriotic songs on their lips. "Patriotism is Back in Style," the *U.S. News & World Report* announced.

Ueberroth's Olympics were celebrating capitalism along with America. By 1984 the economy was reviving, and corporate sponsors were easier to attract. Ueberroth sold television rights to ABC for $225 million, and a limited number of sponsorships for a minimum of $4 million per corporation. The Olympics, despite adversity, had emerged as a lucrative profit center for the television networks and an attention-getter; a happy marriage between sport and celebrity. In the United States, Ueberroth noted, "there's a spirit of can-do, can-work, can-accomplish— you can do things without being on the Government dole."

While earning $215 million, the games also manufactured new American heroes, including the cocaptain of America's gold-medal-winning basketball team, Michael Jordan. Within a month of Jordan's gravity-defying, high-scoring professional debut, the NBA would experience double-digit jumps in attendance and cable television ratings. Blessed by his superstar aura and Nike's alluring "swoosh," Michael Jordan would also help sell over $100 million worth of special running shoes, "Air Jordans," in one year. He would soon earn between $4 million and $7 million in endorsement income annually. Like the Olympics, Jordan would demonstrate how athletic excellence mingled with crass commercialization in America's world of sports.

On ABC the American flag often upstaged the legendary five overlapping rings. Celebrating their theme, "the Rebirth of a Nation," ABC's commentators uncorked a flood of patriotic hype about "our team," "our men," "our women," meaning the American Olympians, and "our" "historic" "miracles," "our . . . rush for gold." Commercials echoed the language and reinforced the patriotism. When "the U.S. wins, you win," McDonald's proclaimed. Eventually, the International Olympic Committee chided ABC for diminishing the games' "international flavor" and violating the Olympic Charter's demand for "unbiased" TV coverage.

Ueberroth's coproducer in generating this jingoism was the ABC News president, Roone Arledge. Arledge headed ABC Sports before taking over the newsroom and injected entertainment values into TV news. Like Reagan, Arledge understood the need for a metanarrative, an overarching theme to America's stories.

What Reagan absorbed from church and Hollywood, Arledge learned in the Ivy League. Lionel Trilling at Columbia University in the 1950s awakened Arledge to the power of heroes, and their stories. In 1980 Arledge packaged the Iranian hostage crisis into a melodrama, using the label "America Held Hostage" to frame the story, and hold America hostage, emotionally. At the Olympics, the odes to America imputed national significance to the most trivial relay race. Commentators recognized that "The montage of Olympic images delivered an implicit political message: America is back; America is standing tall; America is winning." Frustrated by Reagan's conservative finesse and "nationalistic zeal," Rolling Stone's William Greider compared the "distorted packaging of the 1984 Olympics" with "Hitler's celebration of German youth at the Berlin games in 1936."

This patriotic celebration captured the country's mood early in the great boom. Americans had been building toward the moment for years. The celebration also resonated with the Reagan narrative, which Reagan and his minions pushed more aggressively than ever.

A Patriotic Hurricane with Reagan at the Epicenter

Like the perfect-looking, seemingly natural, genetically doctored tomatoes piled high in American supermarkets, the Reagan narrative was an artificial creation posing as a natural phenomenon. Throughout the

Reagan recession, Reagan's aides boosted the Reagan revival with a steady drumbeat of upbeat statements. Recognizing that "the president's approval rating is strongly influenced by inflation," while "unemployment has little impact on presidential popularity," Reagan strategists focused on inflation, "the unfairest tax" hitting everyone. In 1981 they emphasized the diminishing inflation and interest rates. Happy talk was scarcer in 1982, but Reagan's economic optimists were relentless. "Inflation's Staying Down," the White House Office of Public Affairs announced in September. By 1983 "Good Economic News" had "Leading Indicators Index Rise Highest Since 1950." The Dow Jones Industrial Average passed the 1100 mark, a record. Housing starts rose to their highest level since December 1978. The annual inflation rate dropped to the lowest level since October 1967. With the economy "creating over 300,000 jobs a month, employment was rising faster than in any recovery" since the 1950s. By July *Time* found a "Sunny Mood at Midsummer," as "Americans take a brighter view of Reagan, the economy and the country."

In October 1983, when this benchmark-obsessed administration celebrated a thousand days in office, Reagan could tell Americans that contrary to the "experts . . . preaching doom and gloom . . . Good things are happening in America. . . . Believe me, it wasn't Washington experts who said government is too big, taxes are too high, criminals are coddled, education's basics are neglected and values of family and faith are being undermined. That was your message. You made reforms possible." Here was the Reagan narrative with a twist—rather than taking credit, the president reflected it back to the country.

Similarly, while Reagan championed prosperity, periodically the revivalist in him claimed, "This renewal is more than material." In a March 1984 speech to the National Association of Evangelicals, Reagan suggested that his election saved America's soul. In the 1970s, he recalled, pornography proliferated, drug abuse spread, "liberal attitudes" embraced "promiscuity," and the family—the "basic building block of our society—came "under relentless attack." Fortunately, here was the subtle yet grandiose part: "the American people decided to put a stop to that long decline, and today our country is seeing a rebirth of freedom and faith—a great national renewal." In Reagan's vision of a just-add-water-and-stir instant salvation, "America has begun a spiritual reawakening."

America did seem to be undergoing a religious revival. Gallup polls found approximately one-third of Americans reported a "religious insight or awakening that changed the direction of their lives." The United States remained the Ireland of North America. Polls showed that 95 percent of the population believed in God, nearly two-thirds affiliated with a church or a synagogue, and high percentages believed central Christian tenets.

Although estimates that 40 percent of Americans in an average week attended church represented a drop from the 49 percent peak in 1958, the evangelical resurgence intensified the experiences of many who did attend. The majority of believing Americans maintained the modern suburbanite's privatized, nonjudgmental, theistic "quiet faith." Still, as many as forty million Americans felt compelled to affirm their beliefs and inject them into their politics. This newfound assertiveness generated the impression of a revival and contradicted the Hollywood and East Coast elites' belief that their postethnic and postreligious enclaves typified the American experience. The growing chasm between secularists and believing Americans who tended to have traditional families and culturally conservative ideas suggested that while Republicans worried about a "gender gap," Democrats had to beware a "faith gap" whereby religious voters would spurn the party for cultural and spiritual reasons. Reagan's rhetoric exploited this gap and soothed the evangelical constituency, which often felt neglected by Reagan's centrism.

Launching his reelection campaign, Reagan reiterated the Reagan narrative. Speaking from the White House in January 1984, the president said: "When I first addressed you from here, our national defenses were dangerously weak. We had suffered humiliation in Iran. And at home we were adrift, possibly because of a failure here in Washington to trust the courage and character of you the people. But worst of all, we were on the brink of economic collapse from years of Government overindulgence and abusive overtaxation." Now, the president proclaimed, "America is back and standing tall."

As usual, the president's editing improved the message. The speech-writer's first draft read: "We were adrift because our leadership failed to trust the courage and character of the people." Reagan added "possibly" to soften the blow, while sharpening the target by blaming "Washington," not "the leadership." And ever the populist preacher, always addressing his flock directly, Reagan moved from a failure "to trust . . . the people," to a failure "to trust . . . *you* the people."

Reagan did not travel much in seeking reelection; he did not have to. But he visited Los Angeles to launch the Olympics and bask in the non-partisan, much-hyped, Olympic glory. At the formal opening of the games, Reagan presided over a spectacle including a thousand-voice choir, a 750-member marching band, and 90,000 audience members mobbing the Los Angeles Coliseum to sing and cry at "America the Beautiful" while waving thousands of flags.

Reagan reinforced the patriotic passions the games unleashed. His 1984 acceptance speech saluted the Olympic torch for lighting up American hearts. "Holding the Olympic games here in the United States began defining the promise of this season," the president proclaimed as he described the torch's path: "From our Gotham City, New York, to the cradle of liberty, Boston, across the lovely Appalachian springtime, to the city of the big shoulders, Chicago. . . . After circling the greening Northwest, it came down to California, across the Golden Gate and finally into Los Angeles. All along that torch became a celebration of America. And, we all became participants in that celebration."

This patriotic hurricane, with Ronald Reagan at the epicenter, swept the country. It was so powerful, so infectious, that it co-opted critics, rather than simply silencing them. Reagan was famous for turning muck into gold. He loved telling of two brothers, an optimist and a pessimist. Seeking to balance the two, a psychiatrist put the pessimist in a room filled with toys and filled the optimist's room with horse manure. The pessimist bawled—he feared breaking the toys. Meanwhile, the optimist plunged into his room, revelling in the filth. "With this much manure around," the boy said, "I know there's a pony in here someplace."

Reagan's optimistic patriotism could transform criticisms into compliments and trivial postures into major achievements. When a terrorist truck bomb in Lebanon in 1983 murdered 241 marines, Reagan earned kudos for his compassion at a memorial service necessitated by his own administration's incompetence. In February 1984, after sneering that in Lebanon "Tip O'Neill may want us to surrender, but I don't," Reagan ordered a phased "redeployment"—not a withdrawal, of course—of 1,400 marines from Beirut to Navy ships offshore. *Newsweek* reported that 62 percent of those polled applauded Reagan's action, for "any incumbent president who gets American boys out of hot spots is making a damn good move." One editor wondered: "Can you imagine what the press would have done if Jimmy Carter had stationed marines in a combat zone with unloaded rifles to defend themselves against terrorists?"

When Reagan, coincidentally, changed the subject from the carnage in Beirut by invading the tiny island of Grenada only days later, the media proved equally obliging. A chorus of hosannas echoed throughout the land, greeting the return of American power and exorcising the Vietnam curse. "Hooray! Hooray! We've taken a stand. Grenada may be small but it showed the era of Jimmy Carter is no longer with us," a Reagan friend in Arizona rejoiced. Even the *Washington Post* joined in, declaring: "TIDY U.S. WAR ENDS: 'WE BLEW THEM AWAY.'"

Ronald Reagan's patriotic derby helped the presidency transcend the headaches of prosaic politics. Not since Theodore Roosevelt had a president wrapped himself in the American flag so effectively; not since Franklin Roosevelt had a president identified his fate with the American people so convincingly. Administration officials and reporters agreed: there was a new language to American politics, one more visual than verbal, more image-oriented than issue-oriented, more stylish than substantive. Reporters, of course, blamed it on the Reaganites' obsession with muting their boss and choreographing photo-ops. But even a *Newsweek* editor, Mel Elfin, acknowledged the competitive pressures distorting journalism: "If we did one paragraph on issues, it would be too much. . . . they are the greatest irrelevancy, the greatest bore in the campaign." Reagan was not the only spur to superficiality in American society.

Pragmatism and Patriotism Trump Conservatism

Reagan chose to ride this wave of ignorance and patriotism in the election. White House and campaign aides were divided. Idealists wanted the popular president to forge a mandate. They wanted him to run hard, activate the conservative base, visit marginal congressional districts, and win a victory for Reaganism. The pragmatists preferred a broad-based, red, white, and blue appeal to all Americans.

This debate had been raging since the inauguration. As early as February 1981, conservatives denounced Reagan's "consensus politics," demanding "confrontational politics." A year later, forty-five Conservative Political Conference participants signed an eight-page statement blasting the administration as filled with moderates still addicted to government spending, lukewarm on "the President's 'new federalism,'" and too conciliatory and Kissingeresque on foreign policy. In October 1983, 63 percent of 350 conservative leaders polled declared themselves "disappointed" with Reagan as president.

Conservatives were most outraged that Reagan slighted "the social agenda." Reagan's designation of Sandra Day O'Connor as his first Supreme Court appointee in July 1981 infuriated conservatives, who doubted her commitment to eradicating abortion. "REAGAN CHOICE FOR COURT DECRIED BY CONSERVATIVES BUT ACCLAIMED BY LIBERALS," the *Washington Post* proclaimed.

Conservatives resented the dismissal of social issues as mere moral questions or private concerns. They winced as the White House treated "matters of belief" such as "supply-side economics" as if they were true, and "matters of fact" like "the human nature of the human fetus—as though they were matters of mystic belief." Penning "lover's laments" to Reagan, conservatives demanded a crusader not a caretaker.

Reagan bristled when attacked from his right. Great deflector that he was, he often attributed substantive criticisms to disgruntled individuals. Reagan blamed the fuss about O'Connor on "one person in Arizona," a right-to-lifer whom he considered to be "vindictive." Two years later, the publisher of the *Conservative Digest* and the direct mail king Richard Viguerie warned the president that "you cannot continue to side with the liberal establishment without causing millions who worked for you . . . to see you as just another politician bending to the pressures from the Washington crowd." "You know this so-called conservative has never been for me," Reagan scoffed.

As for abortion, Reagan bellowed: "I still believe that an unborn child is a human being." Still, he preferred making such statements in writing or in-person off-stage, away from the cameras. Reagan began a tradition the next two Republican presidents would follow of phoning in his greetings to the major "Right to Life" rallies. This deprived the press of the photograph of the president surrounded by the abortion "crazies."

Nevertheless, the pragmatists worried when the boss started Bible thumping. Urging Reagan to "move for the center ground," Jim Lake feared "no one" will focus "on the amount of new jobs [that] have been created by entrepreneurs encouraged by the Reagan tax cuts, [if] we focus instead on the amount of fetuses aborted. No one is going to focus on how the President has revitalized the American spirit if he is instead exhorting its soul."

The mixed messages were sincere and strategic. Reagan disliked personal confrontations even though he loved letting loose rhetorically. With his high tolerance for paradox, Reagan believed he remained true to conservatism as he played to the center. Early on, Lyn Nofziger told Lee Atwater that "the net effect" of the conservative attacks "might be positive for Reagan." Such controversy boosted Reagan's popularity with moderates.

Despite his pure ideological pedigree, Reagan abhorred divisive issues and messy, emotional debates. Reagan had mainstreamed conservatism by making it more upbeat. American conservatives were traditionally cranky—sometimes cranky and fanatic, like the John Birchers; sometimes cranky and hysterical, like Senator Joseph McCarthy; sometimes cranky and austere, like Senator Robert Taft; and sometimes cranky and elitist, like William F. Buckley. Reagan's conservatism spoke to the American id, not the American superego. His conservatism was one of growth, not restraint; of self-indulgence, not self-sacrifice; of prosperity, not propriety. This message resonated with America's increasingly consumption-oriented and hedonistic leisure culture, enhancing Reagan's resonance.

By 1984 the Reagan Revolution was stalling. The Reaganites had yet to recover from their August 1981 triumph. The Democrats' "fairness" counteroffensive stymied them. "They've run out of ammunition," Reagan's strategist Stuart Spencer observed at a June campaign meeting. White House aides "don't have a goddamn thing in the pipeline," Spencer reported. Most of the issues the political handlers contemplated tackling that day were divisive—defense, abortion, Social Security, taxes. With a candidate whose personality was more popular than his policies, whose symbolism would be more resonant than his statecraft, many advisers concluded that, as Richard Darman put it, "we would be relatively nonspecific programmatically, be more abstract."

As the incumbent, Reagan evinced an exaggerated sense of what was political and tried to avoid it. He delayed announcing his reelection campaign, partially, Richard Darman said, to build a "sense of drama," but "also a little bit his antipathy towards personal direct confessed involvement in conventional partisan politics." He remained isolated during the campaign—"I have been holding the line on not scheduling any interviews between now and Election Day," James Baker told staffers in August. Reagan treated discussions about policy details as improper, saying he "didn't want to politicize" questions such as welfare reform.

This stance was good politics and made Reagan feel good. Reagan revered the office. He also recalled Franklin Roosevelt's nonpartisan appeals. Reagan enjoyed political tasks behind the scenes such as lobbying legislators, but he was usually pliant, happy to follow his managers' stage directions. Always eager to feed the myth, campaign aides such as Ed Rollins described Reagan as someone "who is not a political man, but has superb people instincts that probably turn out to be better political instincts than those of any of us sitting in this room."

The childlike *Being There* dimension about Reagan's saccharine political appeal in 1984 suited American culture. That year, the five most popular movies, together grossing nearly $900 million, were *Beverly Hills Cop, Ghostbusters, Indiana Jones and the Temple of Doom, Gremlins,* and *The Karate Kid.* This George Lucas–Steven Spielberg sensibility lulled Americans into a reassuring, escapist world of fantasy and resolution, of surprise and predictability, of magic and familiarity. Yet American culture took this "Reaganite entertainment" very seriously, as the opening of the latest Star Wars or Indiana Jones flick became "an event," with much fanfare and the requisite commercial tie-ins at McDonald's and Toys-R-Us. In their movies and their politics, Americans had long preferred moral clarity to European ambiguity. In Hollywood as in Washington, DC, angst was out, affability was in; most Americans were happy to enjoy the good times, to unwind after the crises of the 1960s and 1970s.

Morning Again in America: Balloon Drops and Happy Talk

Thus, Reagan stuck with the pragmatists. The result was the 1984 "Morning Again in America" campaign, a campaign of "God, patriotism, and Reagan," ABC's Sam Donaldson sneered. It was a campaign of balloon drops and rhetorical postures, a happy, upbeat campaign throwing symbols at substance. If blacks and women and the elderly feared Reagan's program, Reagan's commercials featured happy blacks and women and seniors prospering in Reagan's America. Perhaps the two most effective ads were the heart-warming "Morning Again in America" country music video celebrating America's renaissance, and the heart-wrenching speech snippet of Reagan celebrating the now-aging "boys" of the D-Day invasion in Normandy, France.

The Republicans' soft-focus, God Bless America campaign ads were so effective that when Reagan viewed his convention video, his Secret Service agents became misty-eyed. When the Democratic nominee Walter Mondale's staff viewed the commercials, some aides were "moved to tears" as well.

The Mondale commercials took an opposite tack. Rooted in the "fairness" counteroffensive yet distorted by an aversion to Reagan's policies and political persona, filled with facts and warnings, Mondale's advertisements played to Democratic fears about an abandoned middle class, soaring deficits, and the dangers of war. One commercial played Crosby, Stills, Nash, and Young's wistful "Teach Your Children," underlining the culture clash between some of the Democratic activists' folky, 1960s' orientation, and Reagan supporters' more country, more traditional sensibility.

Reporters despised Reagan's campaign. Martin Schram of the *Washington Post* blasted the "arrogance" of a campaign "dispensing only placebos" and sneered that Reagan "is the man from Glad, a candidate in a Baggie, hermetically sealed and gingerly lifted into one perfect-for-television setting after another."

Reagan's Rooseveltesque attempt to transcend partisanship outraged Democrats too. After Reagan quoted Senator John Glenn repeatedly, Glenn wrote the president, objecting to the promiscuous quotations of Democrats, dead and alive. Glenn challenged Reagan to a debate to put the issues and the quotations "in their proper context."

Ultimately, no matter how arresting the images, no matter how stirring the rhetoric, the Republican campaign relied on the twin pillars of peace and prosperity. The recovery had arrived. And despite polls showing lingering fears regarding Reagan's foreign policies, none of the hysterical warnings of nuclear war with the Soviets or a quagmire in Nicaragua or an authoritarian coup in America materialized. In fact, during the greatest crisis with the Soviets, their 1983 downing of the Korean Air Lines jet, Reagan's calm reassured many. "The President's response to KAL was not in any respect dictated by consideration of the prospect of an election," Richard Darman later insisted, "but it had profound political effect, I think, in helping neutralize one area of this greatest vulnerability." With such a reasonable track record, Reagan could survive the occasional saber-rattling or joking, as he did during a sound check with a live microphone in August 1984, when he teased that the U.S. would begin bombing Russia "in five minutes."

Just as sound-bites and sloganeering upstaged issues, the visuals and images Michael Deaver produced upstaged analysis or criticism. In October the ace White House correspondent Lesley Stahl would broadcast a lengthy five-minute-and-forty-second CBS news story dissecting Reagan's photo-ops. "Mr. Reagan tries to counter the memory of an unpopular issue with a carefully chosen backdrop that actually contradicts the president's policy," Stahl noted. "Look at the handicapped Olympics, or the opening ceremony of an old-age home. No hint that he tried to cut the budgets for the disabled or for federally subsidized housing for the elderly."

Stahl braced herself for the Reaganite counterattack. The administration had been so effective in blasting CBS for its "left-wing bias" that her producers often censored Stahl, hoping to preempt a White House barrage. Lane Venardos, the *CBS Evening News* executive producer, scrutinized Stahl's video essay, expecting "a lot of flak." As soon as the piece aired, Richard Darman called from Jim Baker's office, having watched the broadcast with Michael Deaver. "Way to go, kiddo," Darman gushed. "What a great story! We loved it."

"Why are you so happy? Didn't you hear what I said?" she asked.

"Nobody heard what you said," Darman rejoiced, noting that Stahl broadcast the best campaign images. "You guys in Televisionland haven't figured it out, have you?" Darman explained: "When the pictures are powerful and emotional, they override if not completely drown out the sound. Lesley, I mean it, nobody heard you." Stahl asked her colleagues in New York and Washington if they realized this. None had.

Bruce Springsteen's 1984 hit was similarly hijacked. "Born in the USA" was this working-class troubadour's rejection of Reaganism and rah-rah Americanism. "Born down in a dead man's town / The first kick I took was when I hit the ground," begins this sad tale of an unemployed Vietnam veteran whose brother died at Khe San. "You end up like a dog that's been beat too much / Till you spend half your life just covering up." The chorus was rousing and repetitive: "Born in the U.S.A. I was born in the U.S.A." Yet even Bruce Springsteen was no match for Ronald Reagan and the Republican image-makers. Before the rocker knew it, and to his disgust, the song became a virtual Republican theme song, a celebration of all that was good and virtuous and true in prosperous America. In 1984, anyone who could best "the Boss" was unstoppable.

Mondale vs. Reagan: Norwegian Charisma, Hollywood Charm

Walter Mondale mounted a slow, plodding, honest, substantive campaign, in keeping with his slow, plodding, honest character. Born in 1928, Mondale was Hubert Humphrey's junior partner in liberal activism. But whereas Humphrey the "Happy Warrior" was ebullient, Mondale was earnest, with a perpetual, burdened, bags-under-the-eyes look. Some called Mondale's emphasis on substance over style "Norwegian charisma." Still, as Jimmy Carter's vice president and a twelve-year Senate veteran, Mondale entered the Democratic primaries as the man to beat—or, as it often seemed, the man to beat up.

Three other challengers stood out in a crowded field reporters labeled the "seven dwarves." Ohio Senator John Glenn, the former astronaut, represented Democrats' dream of deploying their own celebrity. But unlike Reagan, Glenn lacked ideological moorings, and his candidacy crashed and burned. Colorado Senator Gary Hart, a thoughtful reformer, represented Democrats' need for a new voice, a yuppie who could wean liberals from the New Deal–Great Society, bigger-is-better approach to government. Hart scored some early victories and triggered excitement. Yet he lacked a solid base, and evasions about his name change from Hartpence and other resumé anomalies undermined faith in his character. Mondale helped dispatch Hart by echoing the signature line from a Wendy's hamburgers advertising campaign: "Where's the beef?" The Reverend Jesse Jackson gained attention as a serious African American contender, representing Democrats' growing reliance on minorities and women, especially in primaries. Yet Jackson, the antiracism candidate, lapsed into anti-Semitism in calling New York "Hymie-town" and appeared too controversial and radical.

Vanquishing such formidable foes who appealed to crucial Democratic constituencies and electoral fantasies should have boosted Mondale's standing. Instead, the fight sapped him. Certain primary zingers stick to certain candidates, long after the nomination battle ends. In 1980 George Bush's attack on "voodoo economics" gave the Democrats ammunition they used repeatedly during Ronald Reagan's reign. Similarly, in 1984 the Democratic assault, led by Gary Hart, against Walter Mondale as a candidate of the "special interests," beholden to labor unions, women, and ethnic minorities, would stick—and hurt.

Mondale arrived at the Democratic convention with too many weaknesses exposed and too few strengths reinforced. "Everyone is so tired," one Mondale adviser moaned toward the end of the primaries,

"I never thought we'd have to back into the nomination," another sighed.

Mondale injected some zip into his effort by choosing Geraldine Ferraro as his running mate, the first woman on a major party ticket. "America is the land where dreams can come true for all of us," the three-term Queens congresswoman told the convention. "There are no doors we cannot unlock. We will place no limits on achievement." Too familiar with both the locks and the limits, Lesley Stahl and millions of other women prayed: "Geraldine, don't mess up, or we'll all get blamed."

Ferraro energized Mondale's base yet became a lightning rod. Catholics attacked her prochoice stand, while reporters hounded her about her husband's accounting practices, which included "borrowing" $175,000 from an elderly widow. Exit polls would suggest that the number of men she alienated exceeded the number of women she wooed.

Despite the excitement of Ferraro's nomination, the convention's two oratorical highlights slighted the Democratic ticket. Governor Mario Cuomo's eloquent keynote did not mention Mondale. And in his rousing address the next night, Jesse Jackson agreed to support the "nominee of this convention" but still begged to be that nominee.

While neglecting Mondale, both Governor Cuomo and the Reverend Jackson sang proud, powerful Democratic songs. Each speech was inspirational, although Cuomo's was too cranky, Jackson's too exotic, to outshine Reagan's best efforts. Besides, Cuomo himself was too ethnic, Jackson too radical, for much of the electorate. Still, both speeches framed the opposition to Reaganism and suggested the kind of debate the nation deserved but did not get. Cuomo countered Reagan by snapping: "This Nation is more a 'Tale of Two Cities' than it is just a 'shining city on a hill.'" Remember the other part of the city, Cuomo urged, "the part where some people can't pay their mortgages and most young people can't afford one; where students can't afford the education they need and middle-class parents watch the dreams they hold for their children evaporate. In this part of the city there are more poor than ever, more families in trouble, more and more people who need help but can't find it."

After deriding Republican policies that "divide the Nation into the lucky and the left-out, into the royalty and the rabble," Cuomo articulated a traditional "Democratic credo": "We believe in only the government we need, but we insist on all the government we need. . . . We believe in a government strong enough to use words like love and compassion and smart enough to convert our noblest aspirations into practical realities. . . . Our government should be able to rise to the level where it can fill the gaps that are left by chance or by a wisdom we don't fully understand."

Cuomo saluted his Italian roots, completing this self-portrait of a modern New Dealer, an immigrant kid made good, a liberal with a head, a governor with a heart. Democrats, Cuomo was saying, do not have to abandon their ideals, they need them more than ever. Americans do not need a Pied Piper, intensifying individualism, but a call to conscience, building community.

Still, even Cuomo's eloquent, streamlined, muscular liberalism reflected the Democratic discomfort with the new world of budgetary constraints and governmental doubts. Cuomo's defensiveness, insisting that government could be good and that good government could have limits, reflected the effectiveness of Reagan's assault on liberalism. Democrats' need for a crisis, this instinct to ruin Americans' good mood, demonstrated that liberalism had become reactive and ameliorative. The New Deal coalition remained intact. Democrats knew how to woo special interest groups. But they had limited themselves to defensive and narrow economic appeals with an electorate that was barely 20 percent liberal, as opposed to 36 percent conservative and, most important of all, 42 percent "middle-of-the-road." Democrats had forgotten how to sing a song that could inspire and unite America.

Jackson also rooted his speech in his rise from an impoverished childhood, in Greenville, South Carolina, his disdain for Reaganism, and his vision of a more caring, more altruistic, and more diverse America. Rather than celebrating Cuomo's liberal Democratic tradition, Jackson went beyond "the old coalition," detailing his vision for America's multicultural future. "Our flag is red, white, and blue, but our Nation is a rainbow," Jackson preached, "Red, Yellow, Brown, Black, and White—we're all precious in God's sight." This message also had its limits in a nation where two-thirds of voters surveyed worried "that people see themselves first and foremost as part of a racial or religious minority, instead of as a patriotic American." By contrast, Ronald Reagan knew how to see Americans as most wanted to be seen.

Alas, for all the excitement these speeches generated, the nominee remained Walter "Mondull," as one disappointed Democrat sighed, lacking Cuomo's passionate liberalism or Jackson's lyrical multiculturalism. A dismal Democratic campaign ensued. Mondale's message of fiscal discipline and higher taxes was too downbeat for a public intoxicated by the whiffs of a recovery and presidential promises of a prosperity free of any sacrifice or burden.

A Campaign of Images—and Issues

As with Carter versus Reagan in 1980, and McGovern versus Nixon in 1972, Mondale versus Reagan offered the American people a stark choice. Mondale, a New Deal Democrat without the jaunty Roosevelt smile, trusted the federal government as an instrument of justice. He favored arms control, abortion, and higher taxes to reduce the gargantuan federal deficit. Reagan, on the other hand, was a Goldwater Republican without the scowl, committed to a smaller government, a large defense build-up, curbs on abortion, and spending cuts rather than tax increases.

The opposing political strategies reflected the candidates' differing philosophies. Mondale took his campaign of issues to the New Deal coalition in the Rust Belt. Reagan relied on television and carefully crafted appearances to fashion his new coalition anchored in the Sun Belt stretching from California to Florida.

Like so many reporters, Mondale and the Democrats trusted the power of facts to refute Reagan. Their briefing papers disproved Reagan's claim that "We are helping more people and paying more money than ever in the history of this country in all of those social programs." Democrats quoted from the Congressional Budget Office, federal departments, "nonpartisan institutes," the "administration's own" budget agencies. They noted that "the budget reductions pushed 560,000 persons below the poverty line," including 325,000 children; that, over two years, "households with incomes under $10,000 a year will lose $23 billion in income," losing an average of $1,000 annually, while "households with incomes over $80,000 will, by contrast, gain $35 billion in after-tax income," averaging yearly gains of $24,000, intensifying the gap between the rich and the poor; and that the "number of Americans living in poverty climbed 900,000 in 1983 to 35.3 million." Nevertheless, administration spokesman pooh-poohed the statistical barrage, claiming, as David Gergen did, that "making sure we have every single fact straight" is less important than "whether the larger points are right."

The campaign launches illustrated the contrasting visions, strategies, and fates. Mondale began his election campaign by marching in New York City's Labor Day parade at 9 A.M. The pathetic picture of the candidate wandering down desolate streets symbolized the withering of Big Labor, the old-fashioned assumptions tethering the Democrats, and Mondale's surprisingly shoddy advance work. Later that day, the president appeared at a twenty-minute pep rally in Northern California with sky-divers, hot-air balloons, and forty thousand people shouting "U.S.A.! U.S.A.!"

When Mondale visited the Bay Area, he delivered what one reporter called "a student union lecture, twice as long, focused on complicated issues, and addressed to a group about one-fortieth the size." While Reagan's men rejoiced that "America's Back. Strong, Prouder and Better," Mondale talked about the deficit. "It's not how many people turn out on Labor Day to hear a candidate," Mondale's spokesman said. "It's what the candidate has to say." In that elitist calculus and undemocratic arithmetic lay the seeds of Democratic defeat.

On September 18 Dan Rather asked Mondale: "Isn't your campaign of issues, as you call it, getting the hell beaten out of it by what's being called President Reagan's campaign of images?" Rather noted that one day viewers saw Mondale standing awkwardly in a Tennessee barn as Reagan stood at the Grand Ole Opry singing "Happy Birthday" to Roy Acuff, showered in confetti. Mondale asked: would Americans "rather have a leader stand out in the heat and take questions from farmers who are in their worst year since the Great Depression, or stand next to Minnie Pearl and sing 'Happy Birthday'?" Scoffing at Mondale's quixotic quest to change American political culture while seeking the White House, one TV critic said that "in a television age," Mondale "has stupidly refused to make concessions to the home tube that are minor sacrifices for carrying an entire political party to power."

Surprisingly, Mondale won the first of two debates with Reagan, on Sunday evening, October 7, in Louisville, Kentucky. Mondale looked confident rather than the whiny and defensive caricature many expected. Having honed his skills in fifty-seven debates with his primary rivals, Mondale decided on the spot to bore in on the president. He kept asking Reagan about the deficit and about Social Security. Looking wan and a little disoriented, the president could not keep repeating his automatic response and improvised, thus appearing more disoriented.

By contrast, Mondale was crisp, critical, and commanding. "The president's favorite question is, 'Are you better off?'" he mocked. "Well, if you're wealthy, you're better off. If you're middle income, you're about where you were, and if you're of modest income, you're worse off. That's what the economists tell us. But is that really the question that should be asked. Isn't the real question, 'Will we be better off? Will our children be better off? Are we building the future that this nation needs?'"

The Mondale campaign had hit a "home run," Reagan's aide Ed Rollins would later admit. Overnight, Mondale rose from "Loser to Underdog." On Tuesday, the pro-Reagan *Wall Street Journal* speculated about Reagan's age, broaching what Jimmy Carter's former press secretary Jody Powell had labeled "the great unmentionable of the 1984 campaign." One psychologist talked about senility on *CBS News;* nursing students spoke with the *Washington Post* about growing old in America. Reagan challenged his fifty-six-year-old opponent to an "arm wrestle"; Mondale responded that they needed to "brain wrestle." The columnist Mary McGrory agreed, noting that it was the president's "mental vigor that a stunned electorate" was beginning to doubt.

Many reporters believed the president was doddering. They knew he had snoozed at cabinet meetings and at summits with the pope. They had seen him get addled. Reagan made verbal gaffes so frequently they no longer constituted "news," meaning fresh information. "Reagan didn't look much different than he often does," ABC's

Sam Donaldson noted. The "general fumbling with answers, imprecise expression of views, lapses into anecdotal material, and rambling syntax is Ronald Reagan."

The first debate revived Mondale's campaign. Crowds increased. Funds flowed. Local stations began interrupting regular programming to broadcast Mondale rallies. One Mondale aide asked a television producer why his station had decided to cover Mondale's appearance. The producer said, "Because now people are paying attention to him." Within a week, the press was feeding the phenomenon by headlining "DEBATE MOMENTUM PUTS ZIP BACK INTO MONDALE CAMPAIGN."

In the White House, some aides began to "panic," Peggy Noonan would later report. "The Invincible Man had failed, and in public. It was the first time Ronald Reagan's countrymen ever saw him cast about and seem not up to the battle, and I don't think he ever completely recovered his pre-debate aura." Aides demanding an aggressive campaign insisted Reagan could not win by drifting toward Election Day.

Putting his own spin on his candidate's off-day, Reagan's campaign chairman and old friend Senator Paul Laxalt claimed that Reagan "was brutalized by a briefing process" that included six dress rehearsals. "The man was smothered with numbers," Laxalt exclaimed. Nancy Reagan agreed. In an earlier generation, the excuse would have been more devastating than the failure.

With surveys showing that 61 percent of the voters declared Mondale the winner of the first debate, the pollster Louis Harris called the second debate the campaign's "High Noon." The caustic Sam Donaldson predicted that people would be watching "to see whether the president stands up, makes sentences that make sense from the standpoint of not stammering and stuttering, and doesn't drool. And if he does that, then Mr. Mondale can win all the debating points he wants and the president can misstate all the facts he wants and the president will be perceived to have won."

The second debate, held on October 21 in Kansas City, was ostensibly about foreign policy. The candidates followed the script, clashing about "Star Wars," Lebanon, and arms control. One exchange foreshadowing the second term's great crisis addressed a CIA training manual calling for assassinations in Nicaragua. Reagan mentioned a "gentleman down in Nicaragua who is on contract to the CIA" who turned it over "to the agency head—of the CIA in Nicaragua—to be printed." But when the reporter asked if "the CIA in Nicaragua is directing the Contras," Reagan flushed, stammered, and backtracked: "I'm afraid I misspoke," he said.

Most voters—and reporters—overlooked this critical exchange. The debate became a stylized confrontation with Mondale's supporters looking for signs of presidential faltering, and Reagan's supporters waiting for a gesture to show the Gipper's dominance. Henry Trewhitt of the *Baltimore Sun,* noting that if reelected Reagan would be the oldest president ever, asked if Reagan worried about being able to "function" properly. Reagan replied, "Not at all" and vowed, "I will not make age an issue of this campaign. I am not going to exploit for political purposes my opponent's youth and inexperience." In one deft move, the old performer won back his audience. The low expectations surrounding Reagan were reflected in the next day's *Baltimore Sun:* "THE PRESIDENT DIDN'T STUMBLE." That was all he had to not do. Reagan survived the debate—and the election.

Ronald Reagan ended his final campaign with a nostalgic California tour. On the state capitol steps in Sacramento, Reagan remembered inviting Californians to help him "start a prairie fire that would sweep across this country." Here was Reagan the politician, the ideologue, the revolutionary. He stoked that fire throughout the day, challenging citizens to "vote to go forward with an America of momentum," not "back to an America of malaise," and rejoicing that "Today, America travels again the road of increased self-government and personal freedom."

San Diego's ritzy, 150-store Fashion Valley Shopping Center, where Reagan closed his 1980 campaign, was a setting emphasizing Reagan as patriot, as consumption king, as entertainer. Serenaded by Wayne Newton singing "God Bless America," with skydivers zooming down and fireworks bursting through the air, the sentimental Reagan presided over his final rally as a candidate. The next day, he and Nancy voted near their Santa Barbara ranch.

The Results: A Mushy Mandate and a Sugar High

Reagan won forty-nine states and more votes than any predecessor. The Republicans lost one Senate seat and gained back seventeen House seats from their 27-seat-loss in 1982, giving them 182 to the Democrats' 252, with a 53 to 47 Senate majority. The sounds of the brass bands may have drowned out the critics, but the criticisms remained. Reagan's campaign only intensified the alienation of those who did not feel welcome at his nationwide party, despite the token appearances in campaign commercials. And the mushy mandate for peace and prosperity—without a congressional majority—doomed the second-term agenda. Reagan's California dream, like the many illusions surrounding his adopted home state, would prove inspirational but evanescent. At no point during Reagan's final four years in office would he conjure up the same intensity or unity he had in 1981.

The 1984 campaign's sugar high proved fleeting. While Reagan's red-white-and-blue triumphalism set the tone in the public square, it subverted American political culture, and American conceptions of citizenship. This patriotic exhibitionism, sidestepping serious issues while indulging in empty talk of sacrifice, made Americans feel good temporarily and helped reelect Reagan. But by feeding Americans' weakness for one-dimensional truisms, by refusing to challenge them, Reagan helped dilute the sense of community and civic virtue he ostensibly wished to build. Playing his role as the Wizard of America's Id, Reagan fed a politics of self and selfishness, wrapped in a gauzy patriotism. The result further devalued America's social capital and accelerated the descent into individualism, alienation, and cynicism. Voter turnout still hovered at 50 percent in presidential years, and much less for other elections. Faith in governmental institutions and in individuals' abilities to be heard, let alone affect change, flagged, even as Americans reported that their faith in America had revived. Americans may have succumbed to Reagan's charms, but they were not sold. Like spoiled children who enjoy indulgent parents without respecting them, even while dancing to Reagan's tunes, many Americans knew better.

In fairness, Reagan's politics of prosperity resonated in a country celebrating indulgence after the stress of the sixties and the seventies.

Even the nation's intellectuals seeming to be pitching to the lowest common denominator, playing more to the sunny, Disneyfied vapidity of Los Angeles than the brooding, varying complexity of New York. The year's top nonfiction best-sellers were characteristically "Californian," as easterners would have said, consisting of one celebrity superhero CEO autobiography (*Iacocca*), one celebrity superheroine up-with-women inspirational tract (Jane Fonda's *Women Coming of Age*), one self-help manual for romance by the "hug doctor" (Leo Buscaglia's *Loving Each Other*), one collection of short, easy-reading miniessays written for television (Andy Rooney's *Pieces of My Mind*), two make-it-big-in-business guides, and three weight-watchers programs for all the overindulgence in this culture of consumption.

Furthermore, no matter how superficial Reagan's politics seemed, no matter how light his touch might be at a particular moment, Reaganism nevertheless often resonated more broadly and more seriously. The critics' fury as well as the grand visions of both Reagan and his allies maintained a certain gravitas. In September, during the reelection campaign, Reagan welcomed the new Canadian prime minister, Brian Mulroney, to Washington. Reagan graciously joked about being "the other North American Irishman." In fact, the rookie leader's remarks about seeking "economic renewal" and "new markets" linked Mulroney's vision with Reagan's.

Along with Margaret Thatcher's Great Britain, the three leading English-speaking nations were now led by conservative, market-oriented, capitalist revivalists. Controversial and confident, pragmatic but polarizing, the three leaders would help shift the ideological, political, social, and economic centers of gravity in their respective countries, as well as worldwide. Children of the provincial middle and lower classes, Thatcher, the grocer's earnest daughter, and Mulroney, the electrician's ambitious son, joined Reagan, the shoe salesman's charming offspring, in a wide-ranging, plain-speaking, trend-setting assault on the Western elite's big-government, union-friendly, high-tax, collectivist conventional wisdom. All three believed that the debate was not simply about dollars and cents but about core values and common sense. None of them succeeded as dramatically as their supporters hoped or their opponents feared. Mulroney emerged as the most moderate,

Thatcher as the most strident. All three, however, helped reorient the collective conversation from focusing on government solutions to the practical and philosophical consequences of relying on government handouts. All three also offered models of bold, symbolic, tone-setting leadership suited to the media realities of modern politics. At the same time, the three unintentionally demonstrated the broad social consensus supporting the liberal democratic social welfare state in Western countries, as well as the structural and ideological forces fighting change but guaranteeing stability in their respective polities.

In Canada, England, and the United States, many moderates were in fact unsure about the package, taken by their leaders' vision but fearful of the consequences—and the contradictions.

During the campaign, *The New Republic*'s executive editor Morton M. Kondracke confessed that he was tempted to vote for Reagan. Kondracke offered the president a "high five" for "restoring morale," reviving the economy, and flummoxing the Soviets. Kondracke, however, confessed to a "nagging apprehension that Reaganism actually is just an amalgam of tactics, public relations, virulent anti-Sovietism, and institutionalized selfishness that will do nothing to deal with real-world economic and geopolitical realities." If so, Kondracke predicted, "a second Reagan term may produce depression, social chaos, and war." Reagan replied personally, offering his own "high five" to Kondracke, and insisting: "Honest it isn't & no it won't."

Reagan was half right. The second term did not degenerate into chaos. And events during the second term softened Reagan's "anti-Sovietism." But Reagan never again achieved the heights of his first year in office, and the second term left critics and fans wondering what Reaganism was and how Ronald Reagan could remain so darn popular, even in a culture of indulgence.

1985

Brooklyn, New York

Bill Cosby's Multicultural America
Meets Ronald Reagan's Celebrity Presidency

Boy, I'm glad
I saw *Rambo* last night. Now I know what to do next time.
RONALD REAGAN, JUNE 1985, REFERRING TO THE HIJACKING
OF A TWA JET BY ARAB TERRORISTS

Even as Ronald Reagan celebrated an old-fashioned, small-town, white-bread America, a new, urbanized, and dizzyingly diverse country emerged. Racism persisted. Yet two decades after Congress passed the 1964 Civil Rights Act, blacks were integrating neighborhoods and attending formerly lily-white elite schools. They worked as doctors, lawyers, and executives in previously closed professions, as well as cops, firemen, and electricians in once closed unions. And two decades after Lyndon Johnson's 1965 immigration reforms shelved the 1920s' Euro-centric national origins acts, immigrants from Asia, Africa, and Latin America had changed the face of America. When Jesse Jackson talked about a rainbow coalition, most Americans thought about black and white, but America was becoming a multicultural, multiethnic poly-glot speaking the common language of celebrity. This transformation became clear in the 1980s.

Perhaps the best example of America's changing face came from the 1980s' sitcom king, Bill Cosby. *The Cosby Show* was as bland as its pre-decessors. Like *Ozzie and Harriet* or *The Brady Bunch*, it idealized family life, making life's complexities more comic than tragic, and resolving everything neatly in thirty minutes, minus commercials. Still, William H. Cosby, Ed.D.—as he called himself—used his show to educate Americans about life in a multiracial society.

Cosby's upper-middle-class television family lived in a tony Brooklyn brownstone, decorated with African American art. This was not *Welcome Back Kotter*'s ghetto Brooklyn, with its merry gang of misfits. This was not John Travolta's wannabe outer-borough Brooklyn from *Saturday Night Fever.* This Brooklyn had urbane charm and multiracial harmony.

The show was filmed in Midwood, Brooklyn. Cosby eschewed Hollywood's artificial, nonethnic character. If Brooklyn, and its equally unglamorous sister borough, Queens, were "Archie Bunker land" in the 1970s, blue-collar ethnic white enclaves, by the 1980s, they were a mini United Nations, home to people from more than seventy different countries speaking more than one hundred different dialects. The Bernhard Goetz vigilante subway shootings, the Howard Beach teenaged-white-mob murder, the Tawana Brawley black-teenager-screaming-rape hoax, and the raped, beaten, "wilded" Central Park jogger dominated public discourse. Canarsie became a metaphor for white neighborhoods assailed by crime, then abandoned for the suburbs. Yet Cosby's sitcom reflected reality better than the searing headlines, as millions mixed easily daily. On screen and on the streets, Cosby's Brooklyn housed a multicultural festival, where on the same block in Flatbush or Flushing you could buy kimchi, paratha, and a potato knish from Gus the knishman, whether you were black, brown, or white.

Reagan believed that such progress vindicated his vision. As he told the NAACP, "the well-being of blacks—like the well-being of every other American—is linked directly to the health of the economy." Reagan trusted America to overcome some day with minimal governmental interference and maximum prosperity.

Reagan's greatest contribution, however, was a negative one. He was too passive and pragmatic to oppose this new America. For all the warnings about returning to Jim Crow, the Reagan administration accepted many of multicultural America's ground-rules, courting ethnic groups deal by deal, token by token. And Reagan's characteristic failure to engage the complex issue fed this bipolar sense of racial relations, as the unifying "We are the world" fantasies of celebrity Cosbyism and the multicultural realities of metropolitan life coexisted with white fears of crime, black resentment of racism, and the resulting clashes.

These were the perils of the Celebrity Presidency. Since Franklin Roosevelt expanded the office so dramatically in the 1930s, scholars had exhausted *Roget's Thesaurus* trying to capture the new dimensions of America's "modern," "progressive," "personal," "imperial," "imperilled," or "postimperial" presidency. Reagan's style pushed the conversation even further, inspiring talk of the "Rhetorical Presidency," the "Public Presidency," and what some by the Clinton era would call "the Image-Is-Everything Presidency."

Thinking about Reagan as the Celebrity President suggests his unique synthesis between Burbank and the Beltway. Frequently, both benign neglect and symbolic embraces took on lives of their own, often disconnected from what actually occurred in the wide corridors of the federal bureaucracy or on the streets of Brooklyn and the rest of the country. But a society that was increasingly addicted to so many media forms, a media environment increasingly providing "infotainment," a culture increasingly enthralled by all kinds of celebrities, from presidents to pop singers, blurred the line between the symbolic and the substantive, between tone-setting and governing.

This Celebrity Presidency was not necessarily a magical, silver-bullet presidency. With many delicate issues, from race relations to the new AIDS epidemic, Reagan's powerful rhetoric did not always serve him well. His definitive words—or his strategic silences—sometimes fueled passions, even as his middle-of-the-road policies sought to defuse tensions. Blacks and gays, among others, often felt abandoned by the government despite sometimes Herculean bureaucratic initiatives and occasionally even miraculous progress in combating scourges such as racism and AIDS.

Rorschach Tests on Race and Crime
from Canarsie to Howard Beach

In his second inaugural address, Ronald Reagan was too busy saluting the "American sound . . . hopeful, big-hearted, idealistic, daring, decent, and fair" to address any discordant background noises. Extending the Reagan narrative to start shaping his legacy, the president spoon-fed lines to future chroniclers, saying: "Let history say of us, 'These were golden years—when the American Revolution was reborn, when freedom gained new life, when America reached for her best.'"

America had been sufficiently Reaganized so that even some critics credited Reagan with fostering this "great and robust growth" of national confidence. Andrew Hacker, a political scientist, marveled at Reagan's reassuring "personal presence," saying the "unique and fascinating" Reagan presidency "has made most Americans feel better about their public and private lives." The sociologist Dennis Wrong, without crediting Reagan, grudgingly acknowledged that the "pattern of unpleasantness" from the 1960s and 1970s had been "interrupted," returning Americans to a 1950s' placidity, with Reagan as the "functional equivalent of General Eisenhower."

A conservative populist, Reagan repudiated liberal tactics while expropriating liberal goals and language, saying: "We must think anew and move with a new boldness, so every American who seeks work can find work; so the least among us shall have an equal chance to achieve the greatest things—to be heroes who heal our sick, feed the hungry, protect peace among nations, and leave this world a better place."

Similarly, Reagan's recipe for improved race relations and what one successor would label "compassionate conservatism" called for government intervention—with a light touch. "Now, there is a place for the federal government in matters of social compassion," Reagan said, all too vaguely, and accompanied by the usual warnings against "dependency" and salutes to "a growing economy." Still in parsing his position, Reagan detoxified Democratic darts. Americans were debating the welfare state, the meaning of 1960s' liberalism, and the obligations of the fortunate toward the less fortunate. Reagan's vision of an "opportunity society" for all allowed him to boast about "twenty-five straight months of economic growth," while affirming Americans' obligation to the needy. This downsized Democratic attacks on Reagan's "selfishness" to a subtler debate about how to fulfill that mutually accepted obligation.

Once again, Reagan positioned his policy Band-Aid closer to the American consensus than partisans on either side would have predicted. The journalist Ken Auletta noted a similar convergence in his influential 1982 book *The Underclass*. Beyond the rhetoric, Auletta discovered "broad agreement" that America had developed an "underclass" imprisoned in poverty, even as partisans squabbled about the causes. "Those on the right tend to use words like 'pathology,' 'passivity,' and 'hostility'; those on the left tend to speak of 'despair,' 'hopelessness,' and 'alienation'—different words that often mean the same thing."

Retaining Reagan's "Morning in America" symbolism and compassionate posture, the second inaugural was neither monochromatic nor overdone. *Time* called it "A quiet, $10 million bash." Quiet, of course, did not mean lacking in star power, as Frank Sinatra squired the Reagans to some festivities, and Reagan commanded national attention by starring in the Super Bowl coin toss the day before his inauguration. The theme of this, the fiftieth inaugural, was "We the People . . . An American Celebration." Jessye Norman sang the "Star Spangled Banner." An African American, Norman was also a leading diva, blunting charges of tokenism.

Reagan's target audience of individual Americans, his vision of the nation as a coherent entity enlisting free citizens to build the future together, showed that he spoke "Republican." In his convention address, Reagan had charged that the Democrats' conception of "government sees people only as a members of groups. Ours serves all the people of America." But Reagan also spoke "Democratic," appealing to particular constituencies, building on the Democrats' more group-oriented pluralism.

Such group-think was necessary because a complicated reality lurked beneath the pleasant façade and pious clichés. Interracial tension spawned vigilantes and demagogues, racists and criminals. As Reagan raised his right hand to take the oath of office, New York tabloids were shrieking, as usual, this time about the "SUBWAY VIGILANTE."

Bernhard Hugo Goetz, a gawky, thirty-seven-year-old, white engineer, had been riding on the IRT number 2 line just north of Chambers Street on December 22, when four black teenagers armed with sharpened screwdrivers asked him for the time, then for a match. When the teenagers, hovering around Goetz, asked for $5, Goetz said, "Yes, I have $5 for each of you." Whipping out a pistol, he shot the four.

Goetz became a folk hero, even before people knew his name. Harassed subway riders knew such seemingly innocuous questions often ended in a mugging. Launched in 1904, the subway system had been one of the prides of New York. With its speedy network uniting a bustling city, the subway system symbolized New York's sophistication. Extending throughout the five boroughs, from the ritzy East Side to the slums, the transit system also came to symbolize New York's straight-shooting fluidity. When Duke Ellington crooned, "Take the A Train," he captured New York's cutting-edge, bluesy glamour during the war years.

Four decades later, using more power annually than the city of Buffalo, the New York subway system remained a marvel. Every day nearly 3 million riders crossed through 31,180 turnstiles in 469 stations, to traverse 68 bridges, 14 underground tunnels, and over 230 miles of tracks. Yet even as New York revived in the 1980s, even as the Metropolitan Transit Authority would buy new cars, the legendary R-62As, as part of a huge renewal program, the noisy, filthy, gritty, tardy, and crime-plagued subway system still symbolized New York's breakdown during the 1970s.

Goetz surrendered to the police on New Year's Eve. Black and white supporters had inundated a phone line established to track him down, with many suggesting he run for mayor. "I can't feel bad if four kids up to no good got hurt," Denise Walker, one of the teenagers' South Bronx neighbors said. While condemning "vigilantism," New York City Mayor Ed Koch understood "the frustration and anger. . . . The rights of society have been impinged upon, and what they're saying is they're fed up. I'm fed up too." In 1983 only 2 percent of New York's felony complaints resulted in jailed criminals.

The grand jury "justified" Goetz's use of force and indicted him only for the unregistered gun. But black community leaders targetted

Goetz when further investigation revealed that he shot some of the men in the back and told one, "You don't look so bad, here's another," before shooting again. With the self-defense claim undermined, a second grand jury indicted him for assault.

Meanwhile, the case was becoming a Rorschach test on race and crime. Three young black men had mugged Goetz in 1981. A policeman arrested one of them immediately. Goetz watched the kid mock the system, dodge jail, mug again, and even file a cross-complaint against Goetz. Goetz never heard that the perpetrator served some jail time. "As far as Bernie was concerned," one neighbor recalled, "it was equivalent to a woman being raped." Rejected for a New York gun permit, Goetz purchased a gun illegally in Florida.

Each of the four teenagers had been arrested before, and all were awaiting trials or hearings. As Darrel Cabey lay in a coma, his mother told an archetypal tale about life in the South Bronx. In 1973 Cabey's father was crushed to death by a car while scuffling with a thief trying to steal his taxi. In 1974 Cabey's mother, a food services worker, moved her six children to Claremont Village, a project housing 13,500 people, half under twenty-one. Mrs. Cabey did not allow the children to host friends, fearing the visitors might return to rob the place. Still, Darrel dropped out of school. When he held up three men with a shotgun two months before the Goetz shooting, his mother considered keeping him in jail. Relatives dissuaded her. Darrel was shot while on bail, leaving his spine severed and his mother feeling guilty: "He was staying outside a lot and I didn't know what he was doing. Knowing the situation out there, I just should've known."

To the venerable black psychologist Kenneth B. Clark, the "situation" justified the violence—of the muggers. Invoking the liberal litany of "mugged communities" and "mugged schools," Clark deemed crime an act of social protest. These muggers "now riot as individuals rather than as a mob. Having been robbed of the minimum self-esteem essential to their humanity, they have nothing to lose." Rap singers and Nation of Islam preachers defining black crime as an expression of black nationalism would echo Clark's elegantly phrased ideas in cruder forms. Similarly, the leftist journal *The Nation* ignored Goetz's fears and saw a racist act reflecting white Americans' "metaphorical rage" against their "powerlessness" that fixes "on race as a cause and revenge as a cure."

Cries of vengeance did fill the air. Jonathan Rieder's 1985 book *Canarsie: The Jews and Italians of Brooklyn against Liberalism* captured the disillusionment, fear, and rage propeling Goetz's folk-hero status—as well as Reagan's surprising popularity among New Deal liberals. Rieder, a Yale sociologist, spent two years studying this home to seventy thousand, mostly Jews and Italians, mostly children and grandchildren of immigrants, mostly living in two-family brick row houses. This middle-class enclave of teachers and electricians, plumbers and cab drivers, cops and construction workers absorbed refugees from East New York, Brownsville, and other Brooklyn neighborhoods that had "gone bad," as people said at the time. These people saw themselves as "the plain doughty backbone of America," working hard to make the place work.

And, as *The Nation* sensed, these people were furious. A "burly hardhat who packed a loaded pistol under the car seat" told Rieder, years before the Goetz shootings: "Citizens have to do something about crime themselves. If I was in my car and I saw a kid mugging an elderly man or woman, I'd stop the car, get my gun, and kill the kid." Explaining these primal instincts in the sociologist's more delicate prose, Rieder noted: "As the ability of the state to maintain order seemed to dissipate in a web of fiscal, social and legal constraints, Canarsians of quite different dispositions began to flirt with alternative ways to protect themselves."

Sadly, to these people, crime had a black face. More broadly, the race issue touched on many populist resentments. "First, they squeeze my pocketbook, so I can't do anything," one merchant complained. "Then they come in with busing and squeeze my kids." "They" often included Democrats, liberals, judges, bureaucrats, and greedy corporations, as well as blacks and Hispanics living off welfare, breeding crime. The institutionalization of affirmative action and busing, despite broad-based, intense opposition to both, made whites feel victimized.

One Brooklyn pol summed up the alienated white's worldview: "The whole middle class is suffering from a proverbial mugging." Rieder's findings from the late 1970s still resonated in Reagan's 1980s.

Many intellectuals who dismissed Ronald Reagan as dumb failed to appreciate the great affection many Americans had for him precisely because his perceptions matched theirs. Reagan's simple, commonsense nostrums about crime, morality, and social order validated millions who had been railing against governmental illogic and intellectual blindness for years.

Two years after the subway shootings, an outrageous example of white on black violence roiled New York. Just across Jamaica Bay from Canarsie, in the white enclave of Howard Beach, Queens, a pack of white teenagers chased three black men who had wandered into their neighborhood. As one, Michael Griffith, fled across the highway, a car hit and killed him. The twenty-four-year-old driver, Dominick Blum, thought he hit a tire or an animal and only later realized what he had done. He then confessed.

Four assailants were convicted of first-degree manslaughter. The Reverend Al Sharpton and the victims' lawyers Alton Maddox, Jr., and C. Vernon Mason wanted Blum prosecuted. But Blum had no link to the hate mob. In fact, he had spent the evening with a black friend. Demonizing Blum conveniently fueled the issue—and the protests. Jim Sleeper, a liberal white journalist, objected, thinking that Blum "in his very ordinariness" seemed "to exemplify the sort of fair-minded, working-class white New Yorkers whom any movement for racial justice would have to embrace, not enrage." One of Sleeper's black friends explained: "It's about power. . . . When was the last time the 'fair-mindedness' of white folks in Queens ever got us justice?" Sadly, Sleeper saw that "Tribal truth counted for more than interracial consensus."

Such "tribal truth"—for blacks and whites—was poisoning politics and transforming the culture, yet proving to be profitable. "Don't push me 'cuz I'm close to the edge," Grandmaster Flash rapped in his breakthrough 1982 hit, "I'm trying not to lose my head." "The Message" heralded a wave of rap music that would create a new art form, earn billions, deify violence, perpetuate the black "gangsta image," and encourage white imitators, all while feeding and being fed by this black rage.

Unmoored by traditional niceties or the constraints of truth, media-savvy racial demagogues such as Sharpton, Maddox, and Mason exploited this rage. When Tom Wolfe's satire of race and class in New York, *The Bonfire of the Vanities,* appeared in November 1987, the caricature of the manipulative Reverend Mr. Bacon of "All People's Solidarity" seemed plausible and familiar. Within weeks the book appeared prophetic as the unholy trinity of Sharpton, Maddox, and Mason stoked the Tawana Brawley hoax involving a fifteen-year-old who was found near her home in upstate New York beaten, with feces smeared on her body and her hair chopped short. "Nigger" and "KKK" had been scrawled on her torso. She claimed that six whites including a policeman gang-raped her. Years later, the evidence showed that she concocted the scheme to cover up her curfew violation. Ignoring anomalies in Brawley's story, her three "advisors" falsely accused innocent men and monopolized the media while indicting an entire society for a monstrous but imaginary crime.

The rhetorical inflation of the Reagan era forged such grotesques. It was commonplace for leaders of the NAACP to call Reagan "basically a reactionary and racist," for the executive director of the American Civil Liberties Union, Ira Glasser, to call Assistant Attorney General William Bradford Reynolds "the moral equivalent of those Southern segregationists of a generation ago standing in the schoolhouse door to defend segregation." Liberals justified the harsh rhetoric by noting the attacks on the African American addiction to the "narcotic of dependency" by the head of the Equal Employment Opportunity Commission, Clarence Thomas, and attacks on affirmative action, a program precious to blacks, as a "legal, moral, and constitutional tragedy," by Ed Meese, who in 1985 became the attorney general of the United States.

Unfurling an American Rainbow

Nevertheless, despite the headlines, the United States inched along toward "diversity." Bill Cosby's triumph projected onto the small screen a reality the rage upstaged. Cosby insisted that the Huxtables, deemed by the *New York Times* critic John J. O'Connor "the most popular family in the United States," were no aberration. Blacks were entering the American middle class and joining important institutions.

From 1970 to 1988 the percentage of black youths aged 18 to 24 going to college jumped from 16 to 21 percent, while the percentage of black high school dropouts dropped from 31 to 18 percent. The military emerged as perhaps America's most colorblind institution, with 20 percent of the force, 30 percent of the army, and 10 percent of the officer corps being black. Black America's health improved too, with life expectancy up by 5.6 years to 69.7 from 1970 to 1987, and the still-too-high infant mortality rate dropping from 32.6 deaths per thousand in 1970 to 18 per thousand in 1986.

In Washington, the Reagan administration often found its actions belying its leader's own rhetoric. In May 1985 the Department of Education's Office for Civil Rights condemned the "sexist" language in the course catalogue of the University of California, Berkley, pointing to such words as "mankind," "manpower," "manmade," and "grants-manship." While Reaganites could dismiss such untrammeled political correctness as proof of many civil servants' leftward tilt, it also reflected the entrenchment of a new sensibility throughout the bureaucracy. Moreover, the president did not issue any anti–affirmative action executive orders. He did not initiate any legislation protecting whites from "reverse discrimination." He did not force his political appointees such as Clarence Thomas to rewrite the EEOC's affirmative action guidelines And throughout this administration, the departments of Justice and Labor continued prosecuting affirmative action violations.

Even though the civil rights revolution seemed stalled, even though black-white relations bogged down over the abc's of affirmative action, busing, and crime, the ideological revolution continued. Racism was no longer acceptable in public or in polite company. Polls showed that 98 percent of whites did not object to blacks living next door, 95 percent would not mind a black boss, 89 percent would use a black doctor, and 85 percent approved of their children hosting black playmates. Such dramatic attitude shifts would create a more open-minded, more civil, civic culture.

The success of immigrants, from a rainbow of countries, cultures, and races, further buoyed black success, as whites became accustomed to having colleagues of color. Venerable immigrant groups from Europe celebrated new superstars in the 1980s. When Reagan nominated

Judge Antonin Scalia to the Supreme Court, ethnic pride eclipsed partisan identity for Mario Cuomo and many other Italian American Democrats. "Finalmente!" Cuomo exclaimed, "It's about time." New York's governor explained: "I just visited Ellis Island where my immigrant mother landed. And now we have a Supreme Court justice who says, 'My friends call me Nino.'"

The success of southern and eastern European immigrants, once dismissed as "swarthy," "primitive," "foreigners," encouraged the stars of 1980s immigration, the Hispanics and Asians. Until 1960, 80 percent of American immigration came from Europe. Thanks to the 1965 Immigration Act, since 1960 about 80 percent came from non-European countries. From 1980 to 1993 the top five countries sending legal immigrants to the United States were Mexico, the Philippines, Vietnam, China and Taiwan, and Korea. From 1950 to 1990 the United States absorbed nearly 20 million legal immigrants, 8.3 million in the 1980s alone, one-third of America's population growth. By 1990 foreign-born residents constituted 8 percent of the census, with Hispanic numbers increasing by more than 60 percent in the 1970s and 50 percent more in the 1980s. By 1995 there would be 27 million Hispanics, and by the early twenty-first century they would become America's largest minority, outnumbering blacks. Optimists toasted this immigration for triggering economic growth and reaffirming America's destiny. Tom Wolfe noted that to the immigrants "New York is what Rome was in the 17th century, what Paris was in the 18th and in the 19th. What London was in the 19th century, it is the city of ambition."

"Our nation is a nation of immigrants," Reagan proclaimed—articulating a once-heretical conception that had been injected into the American psyche. "More than any other country, our strength comes from our own immigrant heritage and our capacity to welcome those from other lands." By the 1980s, this national self-image motivated a $162 million public-private initiative to restore Ellis Island, the gateway for eastern and southern European immigrants who were, a century later, bathed in nostalgia rather than awash in controversy.

However, Reagan added a warning: "No free and prosperous nation can by itself accommodate all those who seek a better life or flee persecution." Reagan was not just echoing the traditional American ambivalence mingling pride in immigrants' contributions with fear of their strange ways. One 1980 campaign survey identified "illegal immigration" as the sixth most pressing campaign issue. Along with the steady influx of illegals from Mexico, on which California's economy relied, waves of asylum seekers from Cuba and Haiti overwhelmed the East Coast. In 1980 the chaos of Fidel Castro's mischievous Mariel boat-lift of 125,000 Cubans, many released from jails or mental hospitals, weakened President Carter and helped unseat Arkansas's boy wonder, Governor Bill Clinton, albeit temporarily.

The language of middle-class resentment on this issue often echoed the language about crime in Canarsie and the "middle Americas." Illegal immigration also fed fears of social disintegration, government impotence, and middle-class abandonment. The already sobering figure of 1.5 to 3.5 million illegals often ended up exaggerated to 8 million. Economic insecurity intensified the social insecurity. Raymond Marshall, Carter's secretary of labor, estimated in 1979 that "unemployment would be decreased from 6 to 4 percent if half the jobs held by illegals were taken by natives." In 1980, 91 percent of Americans wanted "an all-out effort against illegal entry into the US."

Even though the multiracial immigration made Americans more tolerant, some blacks resented the immigrants' success. In turn, immigrants, living cheek-by-jowl with blacks and suffering from too many street crimes, often stereotyped blacks as lazy and violent. These festering hatreds would explode in the Los Angles riots during the Bush administration, when angry blacks targeted Korean businesses.

As usual, when faced with a difficult political issue that was not one of his priorities, Reagan ducked. Mimicking his predecessor, Reagan deputized a Presidential Task Force on Immigration and Refugee Policy. Ultimately, the 1986 legislation offering some amnesty while also toughening standards against future hiring of illegals barely had Reagan's fingerprints on it. In an era of supposedly vigorous presidential leadership, Reagan gladly deferred to Senator Alan Simpson and Congressman Lee Mazzoli in passing the Simpson-Mazzoli Act. As James Baker and Ed Meese noted in a 1981 memo, "Immigration is no win."

Cosby's Cozy Cocoon

The Cosby Show's cozy cocoon overlooked fights over illegal immigrants, crime, or even racism. Brandon Tartikoff, NBC's programming whiz, conceived of the show when his baby kept him up late one night and he saw Bill Cosby guest hosting *The Tonight Show.* Born in Philadelphia in 1937, in 1965 Cosby became the first black performer starring in a regular dramatic TV series, *I Spy,* which aired through 1968. His cartoon *Fat Albert and the Cosby Kids* charmed children from 1972 through 1984. By the mid-1980s a new generation met Cosby as the genial, rubber-faced pitchman for Jello, Coca-Cola, and other all-American products. He was earning ten million dollars a year and already enjoyed a remarkable popularity that by 1985 would give him the decade's highest Q rating, an industry standard used to assess a performer's "likeability." Nevertheless, when he pitched another Bill Cosby show to ABC, the network passed. Even Tartikoff faced resistance at NBC. "Anyone hearing that the sitcom was supposed to be dead, and suddenly, man, here's Bill Cosby wanting to do one with an *all-black* cast, had to say: 'Wrong time, wrong color,'" Cosby later recalled.

The series premiered on September 20, 1984. America's most popular show from 1985 through 1990, it entertained nearly sixty-three million viewers weekly just "before the demographically divvied, zillion-channel cable universe arrived." *Entertainment Weekly* would call *Cosby* "the last show everyone watched."

Inevitably, some critics found the show cloying and others condemned it for idealizing African American life. "*Leave it to Beaver* in Blackface," *New York* magazine sneered. *The Village Voice* sniped that Cosby "no longer qualifies as black enough to be an Uncle Tom."

"Does it mean only white people have a lock on living together in a home where the father is a doctor and the mother a lawyer and the children are constantly being told to study by their parents?" Cosby bristled. The Cosby juggernaut, the show, its spinoffs, and its multimedia product tie-ins such as Cosby's book *Fatherhood*—which sold 2.4 million hard-cover copies in 1986—transcended race without ignoring it. "This show gives the other side of the black experience. There are a lot of black middle-class families like this one," said Dr. Alvin Pouissaint of Harvard Medical School, who vetted the scripts to remove any negative stereotyping. In the spirit of Martin Luther King, Jr., Cosby's TV family embraced its African American identity while being deeply American too.

The Celebrity Celebration:
Selflessness and Self-Promotion

In using his television show to advance his vision of what America should be, Bill Cosby asserted his prerogatives as a celebrity, when such prerogatives were expanding exponentially. In the 1970s savvy marketers at Time, Inc., expanded their one-page "People" section into a magazine. By 1985 the celebrity celebration had generated a host of gossipy television shows that fed a growing American appetite for the scoop on *Lifestyles of the Rich and Famous*. Celebrities used these outlets, from *Entertainment Tonight* to *Us*, to market their movies, advance their careers, and champion pet causes, just as Ronald Reagan used his celebrity standing to transcend partisanship.

The celebrity stratosphere blurred self-righteousness and self-aggrandizement, selflessness and self-promotion. Even when these stars did good works, most did their charity work flamboyantly, conspicuously. On July 13, 1985, 1.9 billion viewers from 152 countries watched the rock and roll aristocracy's attempt to save the world.

In December 1984 Bob Geldof of The Boomtown Rats had organized some British stars to fight famine in Ethiopia. The song "Do They Know It's Christmas?" sold three million copies and raised eleven million dollars. In the United States the singer Harry Belafonte assembled some black musicians to raise money for Africa. A producer, Ken Kragen, broadened the project, calling it "Live Aid." On January 28, 1985, the night of the American Music Awards, Quincy Jones produced a song Lionel Ritchie and Michael Jackson wrote. "There comes a time when we heed a certain call," Ritchie began, who was then joined by Motown's Stevie Wonder to sing, "When the world must come together as one." Solos by Paul Simon, Kenny Rogers, James Ingram, Tina Turner, Billy Joel, Dionne Warwick, Willie Nelson, Al Jurreau, Bruce Springsteen, Kenny Loggins, Diana Ross, Steve Perry, Daryl Hall,

Cyndi Lauper, Kim Carnes, and Huey Lewis represented pop music's diverse sounds. "We are the world, we are the children, We are the ones who make a brighter day so let's start giving" the chorus belted out, which also included Dan Akroyd, Bob Dylan, Ray Charles, Bette Midler, and five more Jacksons.

"We Are the World" topped the charts by the spring and won top Grammy Awards. The popular video challenged viewers to identify the famous in a rhythmically bobbing sea of famous faces and charmed viewers with the seemingly spontaneous, "private" glances, handclasps, and hugs these pop music demigods exchanged with the cameras rolling. The summer concert built on this megawatt munificence, with pop greats performing in London and in Philadelphia for sixteen hours.

The slickly produced show, flush with four million dollars in corporate sponsorships, and a high-tech 1980s' sensibility, aspired to resurrect the 1960s' now-mythic spirit. "In the '80s, which is a barren era, we look back at the '60s as a great reservoir of talent, of high ideals, and of the will and desire to change things," U2's Bono would say. The Philadelphia show began with the folk icon Joan Baez weaving the sixties into the eighties, saying: "Good morning, children of the '80s. This is your Woodstock and it's long overdue." Fourteen hours later, Bob Dylan sang "Blowin' in the Wind," followed by a "We Are the World" sing-a-long uniting the celebrities and the little people in song.

"I'm glad to be helping the hungry and having a good time" twenty-two-year-old Kim Kates of Philadelphia told a reporter. Phone lines jammed. Profits would eventually top seventy million dollars. The initiative inspired many imitators, including Willie Nelson's "Farm Aid" and "Hands Across America." In May 1986 Bill Cosby, Pete Rose, and Kenny Rogers chaired this Coca Cola–sponsored venture to raise money for America's homeless by enlisting five million people, along with the requisite cadre of celebrities, to create a human chain coast-to-coast. Such efforts were a far cry from 1960s' activism at its best, reflecting instead the activist veneers slapped on so many of that decades' trends. These initiatives were more acts of consumption, moments of entertainment, and genuflections at the altar of celebrity worship, with a dash of social consciousness added for effect.

The billions of dollars rock stars earned dwarfed the millions chari-
ties received. The music business was booming. Sales in 1983 of $3.77
billion climbed to $4.65 billion by 1986, powered by technological in-
novations such as the compact disc, the music video, and the Sony
Walkman, which sold twelve million personal headsets within four
years. In 1984 alone, Michael Jackson earned thirty million dollars
from record sales and another fifty million from tie-ins. These initiatives seemed like yet another Reagan-like Band-Aid on problems. "We
can end hunger," one Live Aid ad claimed. Yet the problems persisted
and the flashes of paint-by-numbers rock and roll activism dissipated
energy and created artificial feelings of self-satisfaction that squelched
more serious initiatives.

When they were not posing as social activists, celebrities loved posing as social critics. In 1985 Dire Straits sold a working-class critique of
the rock star's lifestyle: "Money for nothin' and chicks for free." Giving
voice to blue-collar resentments of these overpaid drag queens "with
the earring and the makeup," the chorus of the song went, "We gotta
install microwave ovens. . . . We gotta move these color TV's."

Such arch self-criticism better reflected the 1980s' celebrity spirit
than "We Are the World's" politicized self-righteousness. This was the
heyday of David Letterman, the un-Carson. Letterman, who like Reagan and Johnny Carson hailed from the Midwest, used his native region's earnestness as the launching pad for his late-night, post–*Tonight
Show* gimmicks. Letterman's world was a wacky, media-savvy, self-
referential world that entertained on TV by mocking TV while assuming intimate knowledge of TV. Thus the "Pet Tricks" were "stupid"—
though entertaining and skillful—and the celebrity interviews often
prickly—while still feeding the cult of celebrity. *Late Night with David
Letterman* premiered in February 1982. Two decades later, Letterman
and his manic tricks, mischievous humor, and celebrity obsession were
show-business standards.

With half a century's experience in the public eye, Ronald Reagan
was practiced in the ways of celebrity. This private, remote man knew
how to appear more open and accessible than he was. He and his wife
Nancy knew how to give the public carefully stage-managed 1950s'-
style glimpses into their private life. Americans enjoyed "Ronnie's"

penchant for jelly beans, his love of the ranch, his happy marriage, even as friends and associates remained mystified by the real man hiding behind the warm eyes and the broad smile.

The Reagan children approached their inherited celebrity status more aggressively and acted more candidly, 1980s'-style. The children from Reagan's first marriage, Maureen and Michael, feuded publicly with Nancy Reagan. Ron Reagan, Jr., exploited his status as First Son, starring in an American Express commercial and opening *Saturday Night Live* with an acrobatic dance number in his underwear inspired by Tom Cruise's career-making parents-are-not-home *Risky Business* boogie. In 1985 Patti Davis worked on a thinly disguised novel, *Home Front,* about the neglected daughter of a distracted governor and his ambitious wife. Surprisingly, when published in 1986, the novel humiliated the Reagans but had little effect on their public standing. Celebrities, after all, lived in an alternative universe following their own rules where the only truly great shame was being ignored.

In a world of ever collapsing categories, Reagan's Celebrity Presidency used the elixir of fame to help politics and showbiz converge. He spoke to Americans in the language of popular culture, strutting before the cameras at his ranch like the Marlboro Man, hosting Michael Jackson at the White House, invoking Clint Eastwood's *Dirty Harry* character by daring congressional tax increasers to "Go ahead and make my day," and joking—before an open microphone after Arab terrorists hijacked a TWA jet—"Boy, after seeing *Rambo* last night, I know what to do the next time this happens." Seeking to cash in on this merging of popular and political culture, the failed vice-presidential candidate Geraldine Ferraro reportedly charged half a million dollars in 1985 to star in Pepsi commercials, which began with the camera's gaze lingering rather inappropriately on her legs.

The celebrity world transcended boundaries. As long as you were famous, it did not matter if you were a rock star or a senator, black or white. In the land of the paparazzi, traditional boundaries were often violated, in dress, in decor, and in behavior, sexual and otherwise.

Thrillers: Blurring Black and White, Gay and Straight

If Ronald Reagan used his celebrity to blur the lines between show-manship and leadership, if Bill Cosby used his celebrity to suggest that proud blacks could "live white," Michael Jackson used his celebrity to blur the lines between black and white, and between gay and straight. Jackson grew up in the public eye as the soprano of the Motown pow-erhouse, the Jackson Five. The group sold over one hundred million records and inspired a Saturday morning cartoon. In the 1970s Jackson thrived as a solo artist too.

Jackson was a great dancer and a superb businessman. Jackson choreographed the release of his 1982 album *Thriller* to undermine what the *Washington Post* called "the cultural apartheid of MTV and pop radio." Rock and roll had become resegregated since the days of Chuck Berry, Elvis Presley, and Little Richard. MTV was overwhelm-ingly white. On radio, rock and roll was usually white; R and B, rhythm and blues, usually black. For three weeks running in October 1982, and for the first time since the pre–rock and roll era, no records by any black singers made the Top 20 charts for singles or albums. Jackson's enticing rhythms defied pigeonholing and had great crossover appeal. Still, to lessen the gap when marketing *Thriller,* Jackson first released "This Girl Is Mine," a playful duet with Paul McCartney. This pairing created "a Trojan horse to force white radio's hand," Steve Greenberg, a record producer, notes. Jackson paved the way for other crossover hits such as Eddy Grant's "Electric Avenue" and Donna Summer's "She Works Hard for the Money." Building "Michaelmania," Jackson would market the usual T-shirts, posters, and buttons, a million-dollar mem-oir—at the age of twenty-five—edited by Jacqueline Onassis, and an eleven-inch doll, with Jackson in the *Thriller* outfit easily posed in his more famous dance steps.

Thriller was the fastest selling album ever, selling forty million copies. "Michael Jackson is mass culture, not pop culture—he appeals to everyone," said a radio program director. *Time* declared Jackson "the biggest thing since the Beatles."

In typical 1980s' style, *Thriller's* marketing included a $1.1 million, thirteen-minute video. In one of the era's most culturally powerful and technically sophisticated images, Jackson morphs into a monster. Here was an American icon, transforming himself from an inspiring symbol of how far a black man could go into the hateful stereotype of the black man as monster, as sexual predator.

By 1985 Jackson, in his late twenties, still seemed frozen in childhood. His friendships with older women, especially Elizabeth Taylor and Diana Ross, along with his smooth skin and high-pitched voice, generated this sense of sexual ambiguity. "I'm not like other guys," Jackson would tell his girlfriend in *Thriller*. "I mean I'm different." Beyond the androgyny, Michael Jackson seemed to be getting "whiter"— his skin was getting lighter, his nose getting smaller. By 1987 many in the record business wondered, "What's that guy done to his face!"

Yet while Jackson seemed neither black nor white, there was something intensely racial about his persona, just as while appearing neither gay nor straight, there was something smolderingly sexual about him. "The time is right for Michael Jackson, because American culture has gotten better at handling sex and playing with gender roles," Professor Marshall Berman observed.

Jackson's more aesthetically provocative rival, Prince, also challenged racial and sexual barriers by blurring them. Both Jackson and Prince fed the escapism central to the 1980s, although Prince sounded angrier and nihilistic. "If I gotta die," Prince sang in "1999," "I'm gonna listen to / My body tonight." Prince's Armageddon-welcoming *Purple Rain*, a *Boston Phoenix* critic wrote, "mirrors the current generation, which indulges itself because it fears it's doomed to extinction."

Jackson's and Prince's game-playing fascinated a society that was increasingly obsessed with sexuality—and confused about it. Here, too, the eighties witnessed a great reconciliation. The sexual revolution went mainstream along with feminism, environmentalism, and other 1960s' and 1970s' innovations. The backlash against the 1970s' worst indulgences did not restore parietals, even though some rediscovered the old-fashioned virtues Reagan praised but did not necessarily follow. In the eighties the aggressive marketing of sex became routine, and in advertising, movies, television, music, fashion, and conversation, American culture became increasingly explicit. Egged on by popular culture, millions chose to be sexual pioneers, indulging in more creative and more frequent sexual behaviors more publicly, more promiscuously, at a younger age than their parents had, even as President Reagan pined for the old-style "Hollywood when actors kept their clothes on."

"It's a guy, it's a girl—It's BOY GEORGE!" *People* would exclaim. "Joke, freak or pop genius," *People* said, "kids are getting his message." Dripping mascara and oozing attitude, Boy George reveled in his excesses. The British singer's group Culture Club was one of many 1980s acts that exploited the MTV-induced demand for striking visuals to accompany the songs as well as the relaxed social mores that usually translated into consumption choices for America's youth.

In July 1984 Boy George debated the merits of androgyny with the Reverend Jerry Falwell on CBS's *Face the Nation*. The clash between the drag queen and the minister on TV's premier news network while David Brinkley appraised the Supreme Court on ABC's rival Sunday morning show offended many—marking the kind of boundary breakdown that defined the times. All this "gender blending" and cultural syncretism was neither as innocuous as Boy George claimed nor as threatening as Jerry Falwell feared. The celebrity outlaws advanced the social revolution rooted in the 1960s that took off in the 1970s. The ever-escalating spiral of syncretism was part of a media-fed compulsion toward spectacle. These celebrities challenged traditional social boundaries and protocols, to assert their individuality, not to change the world. They championed inversions, crossed wires, mixed styles. Rock stars reveled in the violation of taboos, boldly singing "Let's Go to Bed," and "I Want Your Sex" and watching as their devoted fans, dressed like them, smeared lipstick or rouge as they did, coiffed their hair as they did, and yearned to match their seemingly prodigious sexual appetites.

Female soloists also were crossing boundaries of taste, fashion, and behavior. In November 1984, having sold two million copies of her second album, *Like a Virgin*, in one month, Madonna emerged as the 1980s' dominant female star. This Catholic schoolgirl from Detroit, born Madonna Louise Ciccone, was flamboyant, iconoclastic, and primal. Sporting a crucifix and a peace-sign, she disdained 1950s'-style false modesty. "I always thought of myself as a star . . . ," she said in 1986, "maybe I wanted to live up to my name."

Madonna and another leading female soloist, Cyndi Lauper, improvised a unique, clashing, mishmash, bag lady look that combined frilly femininity with raw sexuality. Lauper started with a 1950s' bobby-soxer look—white wool sweater, long black skirt, ankle-length socks, two-tone shoes, and those pointy cat's eyes sunglasses the eighties' yuppies' parents had worn. A second layer of odds and ends—a too-busy blouse, a garter around one ankle, half a dozen bracelets and spangles, fingerless lace gloves, an eight-inch-long right earring that looked like half a dozen rainbow fish lures strung together, and a velvet beret coyly hanging off the right side of her head—added a jarring, subversive, trashy yet sexy look. Similarly, Madonna would begin with a virginal lavender hair bow, a delicate lace blouse with a flower motif, and a crucifix. But she cut the blouse to reveal her midriff, her black bikini bra, and the elastic to her fishnet underwear, with a strategic rip on the side. She added a half-dozen necklaces to accompany the crucifix, including a peace sign. Her super-red lips, her extra-dark eye shadow, her studded bracelets and belt, replete with the signature lacy, fingerless gloves, created a good-girl-gone-bad or "Madonna-whore" look.

Teenage girls prowled through thrift shops, seeking the right pair of fingerless gloves, studded bracelets that did not match their studded belts, and lacy garments that genuflected toward tradition while promising to break free. As Lauper, a gum-cracking kid with big hair from Richmond Hill, Queens, sang in 1983, "Girls Just Want to Have Fun." In January 1985 *Ms.* named Lauper one of the women of the year, "For taking feminism beyond conformity to individuality, rebellion and freedom."

Madonna outdid Lauper. Madonna's hit "Like a Virgin" testified to America's ever-broadening universe of acceptable topics. "Material Girl" celebrated materialism, becoming a virtual anthem for the times—or the media's perception of the times. "The boy with the cold hard cash is always Mister Right," Madonna warbled.

In 1986 "Papa Don't Preach" plunged Madonna into combat with feminists and moralists—which she relished. "Papa don't preach, I'm in trouble deep," she sang in her Catholic schoolkid voice, "But I made up my mind, I'm keeping my baby." Driving the point home—and the stake further into the father's heart—she repeated, "I'm gonna keep my baby."

In a nation where one million teenage girls became pregnant annually, where millions more indulged in "risky" sexual behaviors, that anthem proved explosive. Alfred Moran, the executive director of Planned Parenthood in New York City, noted the many young women flooding his clinics, sporting fingerless lace gloves and rosaries around their necks. Planned Parenthood planned a campaign "Be Smart about Sex" with a "Smart Sex Rap" from LL Cool J. But rappers chanting "This is LL Cool J and Cut Creator / Telling you what happens nine months later" was not as effective as Madonna's more independent and coquettish voice.

While earning millions and taking themselves seriously, celebrities echoed the entertainment industry line that their products did not shape individual behavior or social trends. "She's singing a song, not taking a stand," Madonna's spokeswoman insisted. Madonna knew she was releasing "a message song that everyone is going to take in the wrong way." She had predicted that she would be accused of "advising every young girl to out and get pregnant." Instead, revealing her belief that the song did have a message, Madonna said that "Poppa Don't Preach" was about a girl "who is making a major decision in her life. To me, it's a celebration of life."

Madonna expanded her celebrity power by acting in artsy films such as *Desperately Seeking Susan*. Her enduring celebrity, along with her omnivorous sexuality, made her a powerful cultural force. In an era worshiping power, Madonna, Lauper, and other pop stars represented a popular form of girl power or Madonna feminism. "She stands for people being who they are and not having to apologize," one of Cyndi Lauper's managers said of her boss.

Ronald Reagan was fashionably unfashionable, proud of being out of sync with many of these social trends. Reagan opposed "the movement to abolish or lessen the present laws concerning sexual conduct." Blurring "hedonism" and humanism—as he rejected both—Reagan believed "this nation must have a spiritual rebirth, a rededication to the moral precepts which guided us for so much of our past, and have such a rebirth very soon." In this charged, changing, and confusing environment, it was not surprising that two of the 1980s' most intractable political issues concerned sex. Even though the Supreme Court in 1973 had validated a woman's right to choose, the abortion issue persisted. It sat at the intersection of changing attitudes about feminism, femininity, morality, and sexuality. Similarly, the question of gay liberation, which was posed dramatically during the 1969 Stonewall rebellion, refused to go away.

Sex = Death: The 1960s' Sensibility vs. the 1980s' Reality

One of the 1960s' more unexpected legacies, the gay liberation movement, grew throughout the 1970s. The movement's flashpoint remained the Stonewall riot of June 27, 1969, when angry patrons resisted a police crackdown at the Stonewall Inn, a Greenwich Village homosexual hot spot. Even as the sixties' consciousness faded, the gay liberation agenda advanced. The rights revolution helped, with gays turning to the courts and toward what one activist called "the most powerful closet we have, the voting booth." The "unmeltable ethnics" movement also helped, with gay power joining black power, Polish power, Irish power as a valid claim for group identity. But what helped most was the sexual revolution, with its assault on social constraints and internal restraints and its reassessment of traditional notions regarding family, sexuality, and sex roles.

Culturally, the late 1970s' disco craze helped mainstream homosexuality while caricaturing it, epitomized by the Village People's campy antics. This gay ensemble celebrated a gay sensibility as part of the continuing youth rebellion against fifties' conventionality. By the 1980s, while gay bashing persisted, gays and lesbians were developing some political and social cachet, especially in New York and California. In 1980 Senator Edward Kennedy appealed for gay support. "What do I call you?" Camelot's heir asked a young activist, Bill Kaus. "Is it just gay? Or lesbians and gays? Or gay men and gay women?"

San Francisco emerged as the gay Mecca, open, proud, and loud, with thousands flocking there to forge new identities. In New York City, gays focused more on personal than political liberation. Both communities championed promiscuity and hedonism. "The belief that was handed to me was that sex was liberating and more sex was more liberating," Michael Callen, 28, told *Newsweek* in 1983. "[Being gay] was tied to the right to have sex."

A hundred-million-dollar bathhouse and sex club industry developed. These pleasure palaces were the gay revolution's temples. Bathhouse patrons averaged 2.7 sexual contacts a night and had a 33 percent chance of contracting syphilis or gonorrhea. In the clubs, disco music blared, beer flowed, drugs abounded, and the "acrid smell" of nitrite inhalants hovered, as patrons coupled and uncoupled in a mad, acrobatic rush for ecstasy.

Within a few years, the hospice would compete with the bathhouse as the gay haven. One of the great terrors of the time, AIDS, overshadowed the growing debate about gays. In the early 1980s researchers discovered an inexplicable but lethal blood disease among homosexuals averaging one thousand different sexual partners. They first identified the disease as "GRIDS" for Gay Related Immune Deficiency Syndrome, then the "Gay Plague." A federal conference in July 1982 sanitized the title and settled on Acquired Immune Deficiency Syndrome. By 1985 "AIDS" was on everyone's lips, a mysterious plague that turned the great, guilt-free, supposedly consequence-free act of the 1960s and 1970s, having sex, into a risky behavior linked with the deaths of thousands of young, vital men.

Long before AIDS emerged, many guilt-ridden Americans feared the sexual revolution would take its toll. In 1982 the plague of the year was herpes. *Rolling Stone*'s annual roundup eerily foreshadowed the conventional wisdom in the world of AIDS, suggesting that "In 1982 . . . sex made you sick."

The AIDS issue was particularly murky. For some, the fears of disease reinforced their disdain for homosexuality. "The poor homosexuals—they have declared war upon nature, and now nature is exacting an awful retribution," the conservative commentator Pat Buchanan thundered. Yet with the clarity terror can impose, the gay community galvanized and gay individuals were emboldened. "I haven't experienced this kind of caring since the early days of gay liberation," said the founder of Wipe Out AIDS.

For all, the complicated debate ensued amid ambivalent attitudes, scientific confusion, hysterical headlines, and heartbreaking scenes of young men withering away. While Monday morning quarterbacking would fault the "homophobia" of the press and the Reagan administration for responding slowly, gays themselves reacted slowly and often resisted the public health measures and private precautions required. AIDS warnings contradicted the liberationist agenda. Influential bathhouse owners branded safe sex advocates as "sexual Nazis." A leader of the San Francisco gay parade snapped: "I didn't become a homosexual so I could use condoms."

Randy Shilts, whose coverage in the *San Francisco Chronicle* and 1987 best-seller *And the Band Played On* enlightened Americans about the plague, coined the term "AIDSpeak" to describe the miasma of denial, political correctness, and bureaucratese that prevented effective action. AIDSpeak denied that sex was at the heart of gay liberation, unless anyone suggested limits on gay sex, just as it insisted that AIDS was not a gay problem, even though most victims were gay men.

Initially most reporters avoided such a contentious story requiring such explicit discussion of sexual practices. The claim that AIDS threatened everyone, however, emerged as a top news story. Reporters terrified readers by profiling the few white women stricken, young hemophiliacs like Ryan White, or other "innocents." The message was clear. As *Life*'s July 1985 cover warned, with photos of a young woman, a soldier, a family: "Now No One Is Safe from AIDS."

AIDS terrified a sexually active nation. "God, I wish I could have just one lunch in the Russian Tea Room where we talk about something else besides AIDS. Herpes, maybe," said a female show business executive in her twenties. "The day of the one-night stand is over," said Weston Reese, the thirty-two-year-old director of tennis at the San Francisco Tennis Club. This stark new equation of "sex equals death" pitted 1970s' sensibilities against 1980s' realities. In retreating from risky promiscuous behaviors, many Americans rediscovered traditional morality. College students spoke about "monogamy" as if it were a new invention.

While AIDS scared people about sex, it furthered the sexual revolution. Many gays became more open about their lifestyles, and many heterosexuals became more aware of gays around them. Cheering the many activists flinging open closet doors, Jeff Levi of the National Gay Task Force said, "When it's life or death, it's worth risking your job." The politics of AIDS injected many sexual words, issues, and dilemmas into mainstream society with debates about blood testing in the military, the dangers facing medical personnel, and the ethics of reporting sexually transmitted diseases confidentially. People joked about a six-year-old boy overhearing his parents talk about finding a condom on the patio, looking confused, and asking, "what's a patio?" A new world of cotton swabs and rubber gloves in schools, of face masks and rubber gloves among dentists and hygienists, of disposable needles and rubber gloves in hospitals testified to the fears spreading regarding this seemingly unconquerable killer.

The gay community suffered—and changed—the most. A culture of mourning developed. Death haunted the work of many gay artists, as in Stephen Sondheim's 1987 musical *Into the Woods,* a brooding, fractured fairy tale where the Baker's Wife had sex, then died. "Wake up," the Witch chides the Baker. "People are dying all around you." More directly, beginning in 1985, AIDS-related movies, TV specials, art works, plays, and novels challenged the rest of the nation to examine gay life and AIDS-related deaths. Larry Kramer's angry *The Normal Heart* premiered on Broadway to great critical acclaim. NBC's *An Early Frost,* starring Aidan Quinn as an AIDS victim trying to reconcile with his father, played by Ben Gazzara, was surprisingly popular. AIDS gained further credibility as a worthy cause when Dionne Warwick, Stevie Wonder, Gladys Knight, and Elton John sang "That's What Friends Are For."

The public felt the impact through losses too. Experts estimated that at least 13 percent of AIDS patients in New York were from the arts community. In June 1987 Beverly Sills of the New York Opera identified two dozen singers, musicians, and staffers associated with the company who had died of AIDS.

If the abortion issue, ultimately, rested on the impossibility of compromising between a prolife and prochoice stance, the politics of AIDS rested on the possibility of a cure. AIDS activists wanted a flood of federal money to make this disease as treatable as polio. But President

Reagan was slow to address the issue. Only in 1985, when his friend Rock Hudson died of AIDS, did the president notice.

Gradually, many heterosexuals had "aha" moments, when they realized the epidemic's human toll. "I've been sticking my own personal head in the sand, but I just had a homosexual friend tell me he has buried twelve friends," the Screen Actors Guild president Ed Asner reported. Looking back, Hudson's death would be the collective "aha." Even though six thousand had already died, and at least twelve thousand more were sick, until Hudson succumbed no reporters asked Reagan any question at any presidential news conferences about AIDS. The annual Associated Press poll of editors and broadcasters did not rank AIDS as one of the year's ten most important stories until Hudson's death.

Ronald Reagan took what would later be called a "don't ask, don't tell" approach toward homosexuality. Coming from Hollywood, he had more exposure to gays than most of his conservative peers. In California he opposed a ballot initiative that would have discriminated against homosexual teachers, and in Washington he did not react publicly when Nancy hosted her gay decorator and his lover overnight in the White House. Still, he bristled when the 1984 Democratic platform championed gay rights. "I'm not one to suggest those people should be persecuted in any way," he told one friend, "but they are demanding recognition and approval of their lifestyle and no one has a right to demand that." Similarly, Reagan would be most comfortable calling for abstinence to prevent the spread of AIDS, and for scientific breakthroughs to cure the disease, but he would not champion "safe sex."

In the six months after Hudson's diagnosis, AIDS stories in the print media tripled. Federal funding began to flow, with the $103 million appropriated in 1984 eventually doubling to $205 million in 1985 and $508 million in 1986. By comparison, the 1986 budget for the entire National Cancer Institute was $1.21 billion. Overall, the government would spend at least $5.727 billion on AIDS research, education, and treatment under Ronald Reagan. By 1996 researchers found that effective lobbying secured "disproportionate" federal funding for AIDS, along with breast cancer, diabetes mellitus, and dementia.

The money facilitated a dramatic quest for pharmaceutical strategies to manage the scourge, as well as a change in public opinion. In the four years after researchers finally identified the HIV virus in 1983, "more progress and money was spent on understanding this virus, both sequencing its genes and understanding their functions than any other organism in the history of human medicine," Julian Adams would recall. An inventor of Neviripane, one of the drugs in the pharmaceutical "cocktail" that tamed AIDS, seemingly miraculously, Dr. Adams said: "This is the most extraordinary effort the pharma and biotech industries have ever mounted and succeeded at."

Still, public perspectives remained distorted. When Rock Hudson died in October 1985, *USA Today*'s editorial said, "With Hudson's death, many of us are realizing that AIDS is not a 'gay plague' but everybody's problem." Yet Hudson was gay. It was a fitting symbol of the times—only the death of a celebrity from a disease that was killing thousands of ordinary people prompted the extraordinary effort to go beyond the conventional paradigm that said gays brought the disease on themselves and to mobilize the resources to combat it. And even then the narrative was tailored to protect Americans from confronting the most complex questions about gay life and homophobia in the United States. These, alas, were the realities in Reagan's America—rather than Cosby's idyllic Brooklyn or Queens.

The defeat of economic inflation during Ronald Reagan's watch was a great success. The impact of the rhetorical inflation of Ronald Reagan's Celebrity Presidency was more ambiguous. While Reagan's patriotic rhetoric helped Main Street America feel good, the polarizing rhetoric around charged issues such as racism and AIDS did much harm, obscuring much good. With the attorney general denouncing affirmative action as a tragedy and the head of the American Civil Liberties Union conjuring up visions of Selma, with AIDS activists accusing the Reagan administration of complicity in a gay genocide and fundamentalists transforming a medical problem into God's vengeance on the Sodomites, it was hard sometimes to hear the warm, rousing, interracial chorus of "We Are the World"; it was hard to see the medical miracles and interracial advances, the economic boom and the technological betterments, the syntheses and synergies that were making "a better day" for "you and me."

1986

Wall Street

The Wild, Wild East and the Reagan Money Culture

> The magic of opportunity—unreserved,
> unfailing, unrestrained—isn't this the calling that unites us?
> RONALD REAGAN, STATE OF THE UNION ADDRESS, 1986

Ronald Reagan wanted to free Americans from big government's grip, to liberate America's capitalist spirit. By repeating his antistatist, procapitalist mantra obsessively, he made the Reagan boom a celebration of free enterprise, a vindication of his philosophy. Yet even while unleashing many Americans' inner capitalist, Reagan echoed America's traditional ambivalence about excess. He often affirmed "the great civilized truths—values of family, work, neighborhood, and religion."

Alas, with the president, as with the nation, consumerism's seductive force overran the rhetorical obeisance to morality or a traditional way of life. As a result, Reaganite values-talk often functioned as a posture, a noble façade that eased the mad rush toward materialism. In Reagan's America, most were not yet ready to yell "Show me the money"—as they would in Clinton's America, echoing a line from the 1996 Tom Cruise film *Jerry Maguire*. But Americans were sufficiently dazzled by dollars to chase after the gold, then ease their guilt with the occasional presidential sermon or a strategic securities-fraud prosecution. That ambivalence, that hypocrisy, would shape the national love-hate relationship with the nation's financial capital, Wall Street.

In the 1980s Wall Street was no longer a clubby bastion of well-bred, martini-drinking WASPs in gray-flannel suits. "I look for PSD degrees" when hiring, said Alan "Ace" Greenberg of Bear Stearns, "Poor, Smart, and a deep Desire to be rich." Wall Street was hopping, populated with high-flying, scotch-drinking, merger-making, bond-trading, super-rich cowboys. Red suspenders, power ties—bright yellow, of course—two-toned blue shirts with white collars—these fashion accents radiated confidence, authority, wealth, and clout. Wall Street had zip, glitz, pizzazz, and the power to make poor boys millionaires while ravaging billion-dollar companies. MBAs who once disdained investment banks as too buttoned-down in style and too fill-in-the-blanks in sensibility now begged for posts on the cutting edge of corporate finance.

"The investment banker was a breed apart, a member of a master race of deal makers," Michael Lewis would write in his 1989 Wall Street memoir, Liar's Poker. "He possessed a vast, almost unimaginable talent and ambition. . . . He had two little red sports cars yet wanted four. To get them, he was, for a man in a suit, surprisingly willing to cause trouble." Working at Salomon Brothers plunged Lewis into "a modern gold rush. Never before have so many unskilled twenty-four-year-olds made so much money in so little time as we did this decade in New York and London."

By 1986 another, less appealing, image rested beside the glamorized portrait of the Wall Street honcho. It was of the stock manipulator doing the "perp walk," slinking out of plush corporate offices in hand-cuffs, wincing at the pop-pop-pop of photographers, and sinking into a well-earned nightmare of publicity, trials, bankruptcy, and jail. Gorging on the details in their newspapers, Americans were fascinated by the lifestyles of the rich and now infamous, vicariously living the life these people were about to lose.

Five-hundred-dollar-an-hour pinstriped mouthpieces insisted that their clients were scapegoats, that the government was criminalizing innocent conversations and prosecuting people for being creative and successful. At the other extreme, in his exposé, Den of Thieves, James B. Stewart labeled the junk-bond scandals "the greatest criminal conspiracy the financial world has ever known." Stewart claimed the Wall

Street brigands destroyed blue-chip companies such as General Foods, looting and crippling stalwarts such as Union Carbide: "Thousands of workers lost their jobs, companies loaded up with debt to pay for the deals, profits were sacrificed to pay interest costs on the borrowings." Resurrecting the muckrakers' tradition from an earlier Gilded Age, coloring reportage with moral outrage, Stewart proclaimed: "Violations of the securities laws are not victimless crimes. . . . We are all victims."

The story of the new Gilded Age, the Greed Decade, was a classic American tale, reflecting the era but shaped by tropes echoing throughout American history. It would be celebrated in the aesthetic of the time—the gleaming chrome and glass multimillion-dollar skyscrapers Donald Trump and others built, the shimmering silvery sheen of a thousand-dollar Don Johnson *Miami Vice* suit, the shining steel surface and sharp curves of a $245 CD player, the alluring deep blue and light-weight design of $40 Calvin Klein jeans, the sparkling white Ralph Lauren sheets evoking just a hint of British aristocracy in average Americans' homes. It would be embedded in the ethics of the time— the go-for-it-with-gusto Reaganite ethos that enabled corporate CEOs to compensate themselves magnificently, encouraged Wall Street raiders to dismantle companies systematically, and emboldened millions of city dwellers to step over thousands of homeless fellow citizens silently. It would be denigrated in the literature of the time, with titles excoriating the *Predator's Ball,* the *Barbarians at the Gate,* the *Bonfire of the Vanities.* The rise of the Wall Street "Master of the Universe"—in Tom Wolfe's apt phrase—was rooted in corporate America's own restoration, after the 1970s' stagflation. The fall of the Wall Street shark—and many Americans' delight in watching Ivan Boesky or Michael Milken crash—was rooted in guilt, in an enduring American ambivalence about money and power.

Abundance has been a central theme in American history. For what the historian David Potter called "the people of plenty," the twentieth century certainly was the epoch of excess, the time when America became a prosperous, middle-class consumer society, and most could take their good fortune for granted. The economic historian Robert Fogel notes that in an earlier era, individuals worried about "food, clothing, and shelter, which used to constitute over 80 percent of the consumption of households. To be poor in the decades before World War I was to be deprived of these tangible essentials of life and to be vulnerable to disease and early death." The country became so wealthy that even "the poverty line" by 1980 was "at a level of real income that was attained a century ago only by those in the top 10 percent of the income distribution."

The 1980s was not the first prosperous decade, nor was Ronald Reagan the first presidential cheerleader for consumerism. Franklin D. Roosevelt's "fear of fear itself" warning and various New Deal initiatives including the National Recovery Administration sought to boost consumer confidence; three decades later, John and Jackie Kennedy set new standards for higher living at a time of growing prosperity. In the 1980s Americans were reaping the rewards of a forty-year post–World War II boom. Yet the cold war in the 1950s, the youth rebellion and new crime wave in the 1960s, the sixties hangover and inflation in the 1970s had distracted national attention away from most Americans' new world of wealth. Just as the Gilded Age became a moment to notice—and fear—many of the nineteenth century's miraculous transformations, the 1980s became a moment to confront forty years of boom times, a boom that shifted millions from working with their hands to working with their heads, from manhandling materials to manipulating symbols; a boom that shifted most people's struggle from ensuring physical survival to seeking emotional, spiritual, psychological, and moral well-being. These changes occurred—and would be played out—with a media that was more aggressive, hysterical, lifestyle-oriented, and self-conscious. As a result, many Americans in the 1980s would wake up with exaggerated perceptions of nevertheless extraordinary social revolutions, facing the realities of modern—or dare we call it postmodern—life.

The Greatest Expansion in History

By most indicators, it was an amazing recovery, "the greatest economic expansion in history," Reagan's economics guru Martin Anderson insisted. Inflation declined and job creation soared. Interest rates dropped and the stock market boomed. Sixty months of uninterrupted growth from 1982 to 1987 produced twenty trillion dollars of new wealth. More than seventeen million new jobs would emerge during Reagan's presidency, while European job growth stagnated. The new service economy's "stunning" triumph added "$8,000 billion worth of new technology, 16,000 new shopping malls and three billion square feet of new office space (nearly as much again as existed in 1980)," according to the *New York Times*.

Cheerleaders toasting this greatest spurt of employment growth in American history celebrated Reaganesque deliverance from Carterite doom and gloom. Inflation dipped from double digits to about 4 percent a year. Securities deregulation creating discounted brokers' fees propeled thousands of investors into the stock market; airline deregulation triggered fare wars and the development of no-frills air travel, with People's Express crisscrossing the continent for $99 each way. Declining prices also lured consumers into buying new technologies, such as Apple's magical MacIntosh computer, which debuted at $3,195 but within a year sold for $2,600, with $900 in additional hardware included.

"There's visible, palpable daily evidence of stability," President Reagan's first chief economic adviser, Murray Weidenbaum, boasted. "The housewife goes into the supermarket and finds the price of milk is the same as last week and the week before." After declining in the 1970s, real disposable income per person, the money remaining after taxes and inflation, rose by 2.5 percent in 1983, then 5.8 percent a year later. "Inflation's decline—though orchestrated by Paul Volcker's Federal Reserve—has been the greatest accomplishment of the Reagan years," *Newsweek*'s Robert Samuelson rejoiced in April 1986.

Just as high inflation had sapped the nation's morale, low inflation boosted it. Corporations and households benefited. Corporate investment in capital improvements jumped 20 percent in 1984 and as much as 10 percent the next year, accelerating modernization and especially computerization. The automobile industry invested $14.3 billion in new factories and high-tech equipment in 1985, nearly double 1979's $8.3 billion investment. Businesses allocated 72 percent of their investments toward new equipment in 1985, a respectable leap from the mid-1970s' 68 percent average.

Whodunit: Was It Reagan's Recovery?

Clearly, Reagan had earned the bragging rights for the boom. The rules of presidential credit and blame were clear. Regardless of the root causes or what happened in the rest of the world, just as it had been Carter's inflation, just as it would be Clinton's boom, it was first Reagan's recession, then the Reagan recovery.

Yet Reagan had to share the honors for defeating inflation with the Federal Reserve Board Chairman Paul Volcker, a Jimmy Carter appointee. In fact, Volcker's careful manipulation of the money supply tamed that beast. Even as the economy cooled, Volcker boldly maintained high interest rates between October 1982 and April 1984. Only then did he gradually lower the cost of money. While rates remained high, they were stable, allowing Americans to adjust and regain confidence. In response, the market improvised vehicles such as adjustable-rate mortgages offering lower initial rates than home mortgages, which reduced the average home loans. High interest rates on savings accounts also injected more money back into consumers' wallets.

Reagan's achievement in this realm was mostly negative—he let the Fed do its job. "President Reagan must have received lots of advice to take on the Fed himself," a grateful Volcker later recalled. Reagan's respect for "the independence of the Federal Reserve," fueled by his "strong visceral aversion to inflation" and his natural passivity, gave Volcker's novel approach time to work.

Reagan had a simpler explanation for the boom. "The magic of opportunity—unreserved, unfailing, unrestrained—isn't this the calling that unites us?" the president asked during his 1986 State of the Union address. "I believe our tax rate cuts for the people have done more to spur a spirit of risk-taking and help America's economy break free than any program since John Kennedy's tax cut almost a quarter century ago." Allen Sinai, chief economist at Shearson Lehman/American Express, agreed, crediting the Reagan tax cuts with pumping $300 billion back into private hands and $50 billion back to business, from 1983 to 1985.

Overlooking the regressive tax increases he signed in 1982, 1983, and 1984, hoping to foster his reputation as the great tax cutter whose efforts saved "a damsel in distress, a lass named Endless Economic

Growth," Reagan demanded tax reform legislation as the centerpiece of his second-term agenda. Calling for a "Second American Revolution," he envisioned a "tax system that at long last is pro-family, pro-jobs, pro-future, and pro-America." After a prolonged, complex battle, Reagan signed the Tax Reform Act on October 22, 1986.

The Reaganites took pride in the tax reform, with Reagan again hijacking liberal language to hail "the best antipoverty bill, the best pro-family measure and the best job-creation program ever to come out of the Congress of the United States." The tax bill reduced the top marginal tax rate on the wealthiest from 50 percent to 28 percent and simplified the tax code. Forced to compromise, Reagan closed many business loopholes and raised corporate taxes. Still, Reagan was able to satisfy supply-siders, corporate executives, and fed-up American taxpayers while boasting about eliminating much governmental "gobbledygook." Historians would note that by eliminating some of the tax system's most egregious anomalies, Reagan undermined his assault on the system's viability. Others would lament that Reagan's example addicted his conservative successors in the 1990s to throwing tax cuts at problems, paralleling the Democrats' 1960s' addiction to throwing money at problems.

The conventional wisdom pitted Volcker's monetarism against Reagan's tax cutting. Most economists believed that cutting taxes caused a supply-side expansion of the consumer's bank account, which fed inflation. A young Harvard economist, Jeffrey Sachs, solved the theoretical mystery by applying the insights of the Columbia University economist Robert Mundell. Mundell advocated limiting the dollar's circulation—tight money achieved through high interest rates—along with an expansionary fiscal policy pumping dollars into consumers' wallets through tax cuts and generous government benefits. As of March 1985 Sachs attributed Reagan's "outstanding macroeconomic performance" to "an ingenious marriage"—though probably unintended—of Volcker's "tight" monetary policy balancing out Reagan's expansionary tax cuts. Carter, typically, had done the opposite, offering loose money and tight fiscal policy, boosting inflation.

Beyond Reagan's supply-side tinkering and Volcker's monetarism, other factors checked inflation. Oil prices dropped. The labor movement suffered from the 1981–82 recession and Reagan's hostility, with the president's crushing of PATCO intimidating other unions. The dollar was surprisingly strong. And deregulation intensified competition and lowered prices in key industries such as aviation.

More enduring forces at work propelled the economy. In Japan, a country even more dependent on oil than the United States, the energy crisis had not triggered a great inflation. America's real crisis in the 1970s stemmed from major corporations that had grown too big, bureaucratic, and staid. The classic failure was the Big Three automobile manufacturers' response to the energy crisis. Ford, Chrysler, and General Motors still churned out gas-guzzling behemoths while Honda and Toyota adapted and prospered.

An Economy Fueled by Junk Bonds and Corporate Raiders?

Creative financing became increasingly important in reviving corporate America. "Junk bonds," low-rated, high-yielding issues for new but potentially very profitable ventures, or for underappreciated and thus underfunded companies, encouraged new entrepreneurs and energized the once sleepy bond market. Elaborate stock swaps, bridge loans, and somewhat risky junk bonds promising high payoffs tomorrow after selling off lucrative corporate assets today allowed lean, aggressive buccaneers to swallow up larger companies in leveraged buyouts, or LBOs.

Michael Milken, an intense, gawky Californian, was the junk-bond guru. Milken was one of those brilliant outsiders who in breaking into the Wall Street club transformed it. A workaholic who slept only three to four hours a night, when he was young and commuting from New Jersey he rode the bus so he could read financial statements rather than feel compelled to chat with colleagues on the train. Oblivious to social convention, on winter mornings he wore a miner's lamp strapped to a leather aviation cap to illuminate his papers during his two-hour predawn bus ride to lower Manhattan.

By 1985 the forty-year-old had moved his operation out to Beverly Hills so he could raise his two children with a nice backyard and good weather. He was earning $25 million a year and was reputed to be worth twenty times that, having pioneered a $125 billion market. The *Wall Street Journal* would pronounce Milken the most influential financier since J. P. Morgan.

In preaching the junk-bond gospel, Milken embraced the notion of capitalism as "creative"—and lucrative—destruction. Stagflation had left many companies' stocks undervalued. Milken believed he was performing a public service by providing access to new money while nurturing fledgling ventures. He railed against corporate fat that fed only corporate executives' egos. He criticized conglomerates for losing their focus and advocated selling off extraneous businesses to forge a flush, focused company. Critics called it cannibalizing the company's assets. Milken called it progress.

Milken sometimes suffered from the zealot's tunnel vision. His market gospel reduced everything to a financial transaction and ignored the subtleties essential to weaving a resilient social fabric. Obsessed with financial capital, he shortchanged human and social capital. Applying Wall Street's cold calculus to Main Street, he flirted with social heresy by saying, "It doesn't make sense to pay the mortgage." Mortgages were essentially leveraged buyouts, where "you put down $5,000 and get $100,000." So, if your house price "goes up, you make a fortune. If the price goes down, you just put up $5,000—what the hell, you got tax write-offs and you go home and walk." Such coarsening and commodifying of social obligations fed many fears regarding the entire junk-bond approach.

The junk-bond market relied on a few wealthy individual and institutional investors. That fact, combined with the corporate world's hostility, each deal's complexity, the media's skepticism, and the unfortunate, misleading moniker—for the bonds were more risky than junky—put a premium on salesmanship. In that spirit, Milken's white-shoe, 150-year-old firm, Drexel Burnham, hosted two thousand CEOs, investors, and corporate raiders annually. One money manager called the conference "a revival meeting." The journalist Connie Bruck would demonize this "Predator's Ball" in her 1988 best-seller.

By 1985 half a dozen deals for billion-dollar companies were in play in one week alone, and junk-bond "takeover buccaneers" like T. Boone

Pickens, Carl Icahn, and Sir James Goldsmith were terrifying corporate managers. An industry of takeover artists, and defenders, developed. Ivan Boesky, the son of Russian Jewish immigrants, peddled ice cream in Detroit when he was thirteen but later prospered by mastering the niche market of risk arbitrage—buying the stocks of companies being targeted, or at risk. By March 1986 Boesky had accumulated a fund of $880 million for betting on which companies might be raided and see their stock prices soar. Such sums were distorting. The *New York Times* would note that investment bankers and corporate executives, "who had been happy, making $500,000 or $1 million a year," began to feel "they were missing out. . . . A new mentality took over." The focus shifted to making the big score.

Raiders relished their roguish reputations. As the takeover craze intensified, the threat of a raid sometimes generated a big payoff from a skittish corporation. Raiders sought to buy stock in an undervalued asset, quietly. They could then make money as the bidding war for the company boosted stock prices; from winning the fight and restructuring, including selling off lucrative assets; or by scaring existing management into buying back the stock the raiders accumulated. Perhaps the king of the "greenmailers" was Saul Steinberg, a paunchy graduate of Milken's alma mater, the Wharton Business School. In his senior year at Wharton during the 1960s, Steinberg began a long-term computer leasing company, Leasco. In 1968, only twenty-nine, Steinberg used his Leasco stock to take over the Reliance Insurance Company, a 151-year-old corporation headquartered in Philadelphia. Based on the resulting fifty-million-dollar jump in Steinberg's net worth, *Forbes* declared him the U.S. citizen under thirty who made the most money independently that year.

By the 1980s Steinberg was one of the takeover kings, working closely with Milken and flush with Drexel's bonds. In 1984 Steinberg's threat to take over Walt Disney netted him as much as forty million dollars, and legendary status as the "greenmail king." By middecade Steinberg's company was worth ten billion dollars, and his third wife, Gayfryd, was trying to make him respectable.

The raiders' tactics, theatrics, and statistics fascinated Americans. Just as the army slang of World War II seeped into 1940s' America, and the argot of the movement seeped into 1960s' America, the shorthand of the Wall Street deal-makers seeped into 1980s' America. In the 1988 blockbuster movie *Die Hard,* Harry Ellis, a corporate executive held hostage by international terrorists, offers to help them track down John McClane, the Bruce Willis character fighting them. "Hey, business is business," Ellis says, reflecting Hollywood's caricature of Reaganite corporate ethics. "You use a gun, I use a fountain pen, what's the difference? To put it in my terms, you're here on a hostile takeover and you grab us for some greenmail but you didn't expect a poison pill was gonna be running around the building. Hans, bubbie, I'm your white knight."

The big payoffs enriching others, and Reagan's message to build America by earning and consuming, fed a get-rich-quick mentality. Hundreds of thousands of investors massed the market, welcomed by a 1975 Securities and Exchange Commission decision deregulating brokers' fees, now paying lower commissions to discount brokerages such as Charles Schwab. Schwab grew from a small office in the 1970s to a billion-dollar company with sixteen hundred employees working in ninety branches serving a million investors by middecade. "The little guy has come back," Perrin Long of Lipper Analytical Services rejoiced. "He's feeling good. He's greedy. And he knows that the only way to make money is to buy stocks."

In fact, new waves of "little guys" were discovering all kinds of financial instruments. In 1986 sales of stock, bond, and income mutual funds exceeded $200 billion, nearly doubling the previous year's record of $114 billion. The total net assets of all funds jumped from $495 billion in 1985 to $730 billion a year later, a more than sevenfold increase in six years. In one of the decade's great runs, the legendary Peter Lynch managed Fidelity's Magellan Fund from a $20 million value in 1978 to a $14 billion value in 1990. America's largest fund company in the 1980s, Fidelity offered 157 money market, bond, and stock funds, accounting for $103 billion of the $937 billion mutual fund industry in 1989. Led by Edward "Ned" C. Johnson, III, the company functioned as one of the nation's first "superbanks." Fidelity pioneered in the use of toll-free 800 numbers, then computers, to link investors to their accounts, while also allowing customers to use credit cards and write checks on various accounts. Such immediacy and liquidity addicted many clients to their various funds—and their fund companies—shifting money back and forth, hoping to maximize their profits.

The rise of the raiders and the 24/7 traders, combined with the Reaganite deregulation, fed a Wild West sensibility in the corporate world. Revolutionary innovations emerged in technology with computers, in pharmaceuticals with microbiology. Inventors and investors, managers and stockholders felt more powerful, more creative, more valued than they had in decades. The result was mixed, with dramatic innovations along with some dramatic manipulations. Nevertheless, the many lucrative advances combining technological wizardry and sheer creativity thrilled the president. "Never has there been a more exciting time to be alive—a time of rousing wonder and heroic achievement," he gushed in his 1986 State of the Union address. "As they said in the film *Back to the Future*, 'Where we are going, we don't need roads.'"

An Age of Excess: The Rich People's Liberation Movement

The Wall Street riches and Reaganite triumphalism ushered in an age of excess. Amid rampant consumerism, celebrity worship, and media concentration, let alone mass participation in markets via mutual funds, discount brokerages, and pension plans, Wall Street rallies spurred a national spending spree. In March 1986, after stock values rose by four hundred billion dollars in six months, economists celebrated "the ripple effect" on consumption. *Newsweek* called it "Wall Street's Gift to Main Street." "Everyone's just in a good mood during a rally," a bartender working the 5:23 p.m. train from New York to Connecticut's golden suburbs rejoiced, "and the tips just get much, much bigger."

A revolution in taste, and in attitudes toward money, began at the top, then spread. In a dizzying spiral, as the rich got richer, definitions of what it meant to be rich got richer, thus pressuring the very rich and the almost rich to try to get richer. Meanwhile, further down the salary scale, the yearning to taste the "lifestyles of the rich and famous" increased.

For corporate leaders, salaries, bonuses, and buyouts increased exponentially. Top executive compensation jumped 11.1 percent in 1983,
and another 15.6 percent in 1984, making the median package nearly
eight hundred thousand dollars and million-dollar packages common.
The Princeton economist and *New York Times* columnist Paul Krugman argues that CEO salaries mushroomed independent of the laws
of supply and demand. The relatively modest salaries of the 1930s
through the 1950s reflected the post–New Deal, mass middle-class society's norms. Executives feared public and stockholder outrage. In the
1980s, just "like the sexual revolution of the 1960s," a "relaxation of old
strictures, a new permissiveness," encouraged this financial profligacy.
Corporate executives began seeing themselves as entrepreneurs
rather than managers, as superstars rather than team players. At the
same time, faith in business leaders skyrocketed, with three-quarters of
Americans surveyed in 1984 expressing confidence in business leaders'
"ability to make real contributions to our society." Celebrities also
cashed in—the comedienne Joan Rivers would earn ten million dollars over three years. Basketball's Michael Jordan would sign a twenty-
five-million-dollar contract covering eight years. By the end of the
decade the populist analyst Kevin Phillips would note "the meaninglessness of being a millionaire in an era with nearly a hundred thousand 'decamillionaires.'"

Even as *Forbes* launched its list of the richest Americans, the coverage emphasized spending big, not just earning big. Americans felt vicariously rich reading about these "working rich" who consumed as
zealously as they earned. A genre of party profiles developed, describing soirees more suited to the Versailles of Louis XIV than the New
York of Ed Koch. Certain parties became legendary for their excesses.
There was the half-million-dollar bar mitzvah the New York real estate
magnate Gerald Guterman threw, taking six hundred guests overnight
on the *Queen Elizabeth II* cruise ship to celebrate his son's thirteenth
birthday. There was the two-million-dollar wedding of Laura Steinberg, the daughter of Saul Steinberg, to Jonathan Tisch, whose father,
the former Postmaster General Preston Robert Tisch, ran the Loews
Corporation. A hot designer, Arnold Scaasi, designed the bridal gown

and all the wedding party dresses. The cake cost seventeen thousand dollars, and the flowers, up to five hundred thousand.

Having thrown such a wedding for her stepdaughter, Gayfryd Steinberg, the "queen" of nouvelle society, felt compelled to throw a million-dollar fiftieth-birthday bash for her husband Saul at their beach house, at Quoge in the Hamptons. Acres of Oriental rugs carpeted the estate inside and outside so guests would not get their feet wet. Dancers in seventeenth-century dress mingled with guests who ogled at ten live tableaux of Old Masters paintings Steinberg owned. Shortly thereafter Malcolm Forbes outdid the Steinbergs with a two-million-dollar seventieth-birthday extravaganza for himself wherein he flew 750 guests to Tangiers.

While one of the 250 Steinberg guests sniped: "Wouldn't it have been better to give us a hot dog and a check for $10,000?" most indulged guilt-free. Look at Guterman's charities, the rabbi of the extravagant bar mitzvah dad said. "I'm sooooo tired of hearing from people who weren't invited saying how tacky this party was," the socialite and TV personality Barbara Howar snapped. "I don't want to make it a way of life, you know. I'm right there—with everybody else—stepping over people living in cardboard boxes on the street in New York. But the Steinbergs have taken the system and benefited. . . . And I don't know if they threw smaller parties, how that would help the life of a woman living in a box on the street."

This attitude reflected what the columnist Richard Cohen called "'The Rich People's Liberation Movement,' a joyous freedom from previous restraints." Cohen blamed the Reagans for such decadence. "It was Nancy Reagan who could not say 'no' to designer dresses and who partied with some of the same people," Cohen seethed. This abdication of a social conscience was antisocial. "The party spending of the Steinbergs et al. is a pie in the face to us all," he wrote. "It produces momentary blindness and then a shock of self-recognition—a sense that there is a bit of the Steinbergs in many of us."

Actually, most seemed more envious than outraged. Beyond Park Avenue, the relaxed social inhibitions about money and the shift in focus from middle-class modesty to upper-class excess exposed many children to money management and money making. In exposing "Greed on Sesame Street," *Newsweek* found five different organizations in 1987 running kiddie "investment" seminars and business boot camps. Proud graduates dreamed of becoming corporate raiders or getting involved with "heavy-duty arbitrage."

Children were also being swept into the consumer culture earlier. Market segmentation in media subjected impressionable youngsters to sophisticated advertising blitzes. A $25 billion children's fashion industry relied on targeted marketing, image-making, and surfing the right trends. In Los Angeles, the Tot Couture line offered "a black, washed-silk miniature bomber jacket that any mommy would love for herself" for $116. Nationwide, twenty-thousand-square-foot Kids "R" Us stores grew from 2 outlets in 1983 to 112 five years later.

In a land of $80,000 kitchens and $8 million Old Masters, clothing balanced democracy with aristocracy for young and old alike. Most Americans could afford overpriced $20 Ellesse cotton T-shirts with the right label, or even $214 silk FILA sweatsuits with the right look. In inner-city high schools, students judged each other by what they wore. "When you have on the most expensive brand everybody notices you," one fifteen-year-old explained. "If you can't afford it, you're left out. You're a nerd." "Kids want the name. They want that stamp of approval and that's what they get from buying a designer name," Monique Greenwood of *Children's Business,* a monthly trade journal, explained. You were not just what you wore. But, without much of an investment, every man, woman, and child could feel like a king or queen.

Missionaries of Materialism: Calvin Klein and Ralph Lauren

By the 1980s few Americans worried about the basics of food, shelter, or clothing. Many acquired new insecurities about their rations being nutritious or nouvelle enough, their homes being well decorated or big enough, and their outfits being flattering or fashionable enough. Many frittered away time and money managing these new insecurities of abundance, as others preyed on these worries—and profited. Two missionaries of this new materialism, whose sagas epitomized this age of excess, and whose visions helped define it, were Calvin Klein and Ralph Lauren. The two were born three years apart in the same lower-middle-class Bronx neighborhood off Mosholu Parkway, raised in the same immigrant Jewish milieu. The two designers would become household names wrapping Americans in fabrics and fragrances that seemed to convey status and shape individual identities. Temperamental artists, hard-nosed businessmen, brilliant marketers, shrewd mass psychologists, glamorous celebrities, spendthrift arrivistes, and flamboyant egomaniacs, the two naturally became bitter rivals. They also represented competing strains of eighties' consumerism.

The younger one, Calvin Klein, was born in 1942. He graduated from the Fashion Institute of Technology and started his own clothing company with his boyhood friend Barry Schwartz. By 1980, when he sold two hundred thousand pairs of overpriced "designer" jeans in a week thanks to Brooke Shields' alluring advertisements, Klein was a fashion powerhouse. Throughout the 1980s, as he turned men's underwear from functional boxer shorts to sexy briefs with his name adorning the elastic, as he turned a perfume into a national obsession, Calvin Klein imbued his products with a raw, nearly pornographic, sexuality. A 1986 *Vanity Fair* ad for his fragrance Obsession showed a tangle of smooth white limbs and flowing blonde hair that sent the imagination racing—while sending feminists and moralists to the barricades. Calvin Klein's successful advertising campaigns, oozing sexuality, pushed the boundaries of what was considered proper, developing a more sensual and graphic standard.

Calvin Klein also helped inject a gay sensibility into American popular culture. The $500,000 advertising campaign launching his three-for-$14.50 jockey shorts and $5.50-a-piece men's bikini briefs helped teach Americans how to objectify men in advertising as much as they had learned to objectify women. The homoerotic photographer Bruce Weber turned the buff Olympic pole vaulter Tom Hintinaus into one of the decade's most popular pinups—for women and men. The photograph showed off a beautiful bronzed body with rippling muscles, tanning, framed by the white of the background, and clad only in a gleaming white pair of Calvin's underwear. The underwear—and all it was supposed to be hiding—stood at the center of the photo, with

Hintinaus's two large hands resting suggestively close by on his thighs. The ad was hung most prominently on a forty-foot by fifty-foot billboard hovering over Times Square.

Calvin Klein lived the life he celebrated. He divorced his first wife, as success made him want to jettison his Bronx Jewish roots, eventually marrying a gorgeous, well-bred employee. Plunging into the hedonism of the times, he indulged his omnivorous sexuality. He became a denizen of Studio 54, of Fire Island, and of Key West, discoing through a dizzying array of one-night stands with young men, even as he dated women occasionally. "I've tried everything, knew no limits. . . . I stopped at nothing. . . . I would do *anything*. . . . I'll say that anything I've wanted to do, I've done," Klein would recall.

As he "partied all the time," Klein's life soon became the caricature of a 1980s' morality tale. Business reverses sent him seeking junk bonds at the Predator's Ball with Michael Milken. As friends died of AIDS and Klein dodged repeated rumors about his imminent demise, he first ignored the disease, then eventually supported the cause grudgingly. By decade's end, Calvin Klein made the requisite visit to detox, escorted by a poster-child of celebrity dysfunction, Liza Minnelli.

Just as Calvin Klein epitomized and exploited the good middle-class kid's desire to be bad and sample postsixties' American pleasures, Ralph Lauren epitomized and exploited the aspiring middle-class kid's desire to find acceptance in the upper echelons of America's theoretically class-free society. The worst-kept secret about Ralph Lauren, born in 1939, was his real name, Ralphie Lifshitz. This distinguished Jewish last name evoking generations of rabbis did not transfer smoothly to the New World, even in Lifshitz's heavily Jewish, post–World War II Bronx. Suggesting in English an anatomical impossibility, "the name was a problem," Lauren recalled. "Kids would laugh. In class, every time I got up it would make me sweat." Insisting that he was not hiding his roots, he said: "If my name was Bernstein, I never would have changed my name."

When he was nineteen, Ralphie Lifshitz and his brother took the last name "Lauren." In 1967, when he started his own line of wide, colorful ties, he sought another name to express his immigrant-kid-from-the-Bronx aspirations, "Polo." "A little cachet," he would recall. "Glamorous, international, and playboyish. Very suave characters went to polo matches."

As his company expanded, as he launched his distinctive sport shirt with the polo player logo in 1972, Ralph Lauren decided he was selling a lifestyle, an identity, not simply lucrative product lines. "I'm interested in longevity, timelessness, style—not fashion," he said. Ralph Lauren preferred tweed jackets, chino pants, and Shetland sweaters to more faddish clothes. He hijacked WASP symbols for the new money aristocrats and wannabes. This act of cultural grave robbery infuriated the real polo-playing set. "He cheapened things that were secrets," a Palm Beach preppie complained.

In the 1980s Ralph Lauren appealed to a public returning to traditional values, and to Americans anxious about their status. And as with Calvin Klein, lavish advertising campaigns and Bruce Weber photographs swept him upward, although Lauren ads evoked elegant British country houses rather than sleazy San Francisco bathhouses. In 1982, when Calvin Klein was planning to sexualize men's underwear, Ralph Lauren launched his line of classic home furnishings. "I became, like, a cult," he would say.

In April 1986 Lauren opened his flagship store in a five-story French Renaissance revival palace at Madison Avenue and 72nd Street. Built in 1898 for five hundred thousand dollars, then renovated for anywhere from fourteen million—Lauren's estimate—to thirty-five million—his staff's appraisal—the Rhinelander mansion plunked customers into Ralph Lauren's dream world. When showing the mansion to the former Bloomingdale's chairman Marvin Taub, Lauren stopped at the imposing wooden staircase. He looked at one of the forbidding pictures of a long-dead lord meant to reassure the consumer that you sometimes have to spend a lot to feel a little bit like an English country gentleman. "That," Ralph Lauren said, pointing to the aristocrat's face, "is Grandpa Lifshitz."

A few months later, on September 1, 1986, Ralph Lauren graced the cover of *Time*. "SELLING THAT SPORTY LOOK, POLO'S RALPH LAUREN" accompanied a photo of Lauren looking like the patrician fresh off the tennis court. His confident smile, his full head of white hair tousled just enough, his white knit sweater, with a colorful but classic two-tone collar creating an elegant boundary with his white shirt, demonstrated the warm, evocative, seemingly natural look achieved through great effort. This was the eighties everyone wanted, even as the cover's corner offered the sobering headline about the Russian nuclear accident: "CHERNOBYL—A STARTLING REPORT."

Ralph Lauren's inclusive, enveloping consumerist identity paved the way for lifestyle totalitarians such as Martha Stewart. His broad vision impressed the *New York Times* architecture critic Paul Goldberger, who deemed him the 1980s' true design symbol. "Lauren has become a kind of one-man Bauhaus, a producer of everything from fabrics to furniture to buildings, all of which taken together, form a composite, a fully designed life." The nesting and the questing helped define the decade, as did the astonishing degree to which achieving the Ralph Lauren look, or sticking to one's Calvin's, become so essential to customers' identities.

High Anxiety: A Most Anxious Boom

And yet, despite all the consumerism, despite the hype, Americans remained remarkably skittish during this boom. While partying intensely, many did not seem to be enjoying themselves as much as their grandparents supposedly had in the 1920s or their parents had in the 1950s. "The 1950s sense was, 'If I play by all the rules, I'll make it up the economic ladder rung by rung,'" one pollster noted. "Now," Americans were less sure. Overworked and isolated, 59 percent of Americans felt very stressed at least weekly, and 30 percent felt stressed daily. Mixed economic signals sparked political and ideological clashes, which in turn exacerbated social and cultural tensions, along with fears about the future.

Hysteria about the trade imbalance with "Japan, Inc.," and about the West Germans' ruthless efficiency, triggered a round of breast-beating. Americans dreading their country's decline made tomes such as Paul Kennedy's 1987 book *The Rise and Fall of the Great Powers* surprise best-sellers. Moreover, experts repeatedly warned that this "splendid, if implausible" boom was a mirage and that a big bust was looming.

The economy's enduring structural problems fed such skepticism.
Democrats warned of a Mastercard bubble, a credit-card craze inflated
by buying today and deferring payment to a distant tomorrow. With
record defense spending of $2.1 trillion during the Reagan years, and
David Stockman's inability to enact Draconian cuts, the budget deficit
soared from $914.3 billion in 1980 to $2 trillion by 1986. Interest payments servicing the debt became the second largest federal budget
item after defense. By 1984 the federal government spent 24 percent of
the gross national product, and, thanks to the tax cuts, tax revenues
covered only 19 percent of GNP. The government had to close the gap
by issuing bonds, often sold to overseas investors—in 1986 Japanese investors purchased $93 billion in U.S. bonds. This flood of treasury bills
elevated interest rates and depressed the dollar. The United States, the
world's biggest creditor in 1980, became the world's biggest debtor,
with a trade deficit beginning in 1983 and mushrooming thereafter.
Interest payments averaged $20 billion yearly. One economist, Fred
Bergsten, would joke, "We finally understand the true meaning of supply-side economics: foreigners supply most of the goods and all of the
money."

Inevitably, as in the 1920s or any other boom time, there were "sick
industries," losers not just winners. Many economic sectors had banked
on inflation persisting and interest rates remaining high. Real-estate
speculators, farmers, and rural bankers who expected land values to
appreciate, corporations that expected revenues to continue to rise just
because prices did, commodities brokers who assumed a never-ending
cost-value spiral did not welcome inflation's end. Moreover, the pace
of change in the American economy, with computerization, automation, or simply fickle tastes, inevitably left behind some corporations,
industries, and workers. Even as millions of new jobs were created, unemployment hovered around 7 percent through 1986.

Furthermore, Reagan's tax cut, combined with Wall Street's speculative mania and the structural realities of a service economy, enriched
the rich and widened the gap between America's wealthiest 1, 2, 5, 10,
or 20 percent and the poorest corresponding percentages. Critics worried about a middle class doubly squeezed, with the wealthy monopo-
lizing too high a percentage of the nation's assets while too many good

jobs disappeared or went abroad. Democrats charged that too many of the new jobs were short-term, service-oriented jobs, rather than long-term, manufacturing jobs, especially as transportation and communication advances encouraged outsourcing work to nonunionized, Third World workers.

Homelessness: Economic, Cultural, or Political Epidemic?

The epidemic of homelessness illustrated these subtler, less visible, more abstract structural problems. Despite being Boomtown USA, New York had as many as forty thousand homeless people roaming its streets, a not-so-silent army suggesting the conservative failure to have enough wealth "trickle down" to the masses. Conservatives countered that homelessness testified to liberals' failure to cope with the mentally ill. Both were correct.

Homelessness assaulted city-dwellers' eyes, ears, and noses, while pricking some consciences and hardening many other hearts. Homelessness thrust daily proof of social dysfunction and governmental failure in urban Americans' faces; it also raised questions about how much citizens were willing to do for their fellow Americans. Government figures estimated there were about 250,000 homeless people by the mid-1980s; homeless advocates boosted the estimates to 2 to 3 million.

The scourge of homelessness in the 1980s proved the cliché about the road to hell being paved with good intentions. The downtown revitalization projects and yuppie gentrification projects that generated such enthusiasm among urban planners wiped out the housing stock of thousands of poor people. Bulldozers destroyed approximately one million rooms in "flophouses," called single-room occupancies, or SROs—nearly half the national total.

This housing shortage appeared at a time when drug and alcohol addiction was shattering thousands of lives and sending many broken individuals toward what was once called "skid row," while a mass movement to "deinstitutionalize" the mentally ill added even more demand for low-income housing. The rights revolution of the 1960s and blind faith in the latest social science theories during the 1970s moved thousands of mental patients out of hospitals, which had often been harsh and neglectful. Unfortunately, many ended up wandering the even meaner streets, constituting up to a third of the homeless population. Neighborhoods have been turned into "outdoor psychiatric wards," New York's Mayor Ed Koch seethed. To the extent that the government helped create the problem, it only exacerbated the sense of governmental impotence the homelessness issue evoked.

In fact, increasingly, refugees from Reaganism were joining the refugees from reality at homeless shelters. Reagan's safety net apparently had some holes. *The New Republic* quoted a Community Services Society study: "Something happens—a job is lost, unemployment benefits run out, creditors and banks move in to foreclose, eviction proceedings begin—and quite suddenly the respectable poor find themselves among the disreputable homeless."

The "in-your-face" homeless problem, which may have been limited to thousands, reflected a deeper, often hidden, problem of the white poor, as many as ten million people who did not fit the prevailing paradigms or stereotypes. "There is a poverty we make policy for, and there is the real poverty situation," said Charles Murray, author of *Losing Ground*. Murray blasted the "Mississippi fallacy," the tendency to treat all the poor as the same, as hillbillies living in ramshackle huts.

The homeless and the underclass tended to be the popular targets for welfare and for media profiles even though the two-parent families with one full-time worker and single-working-mother families were most often neglected—and at risk. Raising the maximum amount individuals could earn before being eligible for programs hurt the marginally poor—who often worked—rather than the very poor—who did not. The statistics were sobering. From 1981 to 1986, roughly five million Americans who had held their jobs for three years or more lost them after plant closings or layoffs. "Economic Recovery Is Seen as Bypassing at Least 10 Million," headlines screamed. An estimated 33.7 million people lived below the poverty line in 1984, including 11.5 million children. Surprisingly, 2.1 million people worked full time but still ended up below the poverty line, and 8.5 million people were unemployed. The numbers were staggering, and especially unconscionable amid such wealth.

The political debate clouded this important debate about poverty—and the other structural issues. Sheer partisanship mingled with sincere ideological differences and certain cultural anxieties. Conservatives focused on equality of opportunity; liberals, on equality of condition. Conservatives celebrated a flexible free-enterprise economy naturally evolving from manufacturing toward a "postindustrial" service society; liberals mourned the loss of a manufacturing base with the same pessimistic conservatism that had nineteenth-century populists mourning their farms. Michael Moore's 1989 documentary *Roger and Me* captured and fed liberal anxiety. Offering little context to balance out his melancholy shots of closed factories and displaced individuals, Moore detailed his attempts to confront the head of General Motors, Roger Smith, about the devastating GM downsizing in Flint, Michigan.

Amid this background, Ronald Reagan was a polarizing symbol. Too much of the debate became personal, revolving around individuals' take on Reagan or faith in his vision. For example, Reaganites dismissed concerns about the skewed distribution of wealth by pointing to the wealthier society overall, including the lower inflation, which improved everyone's lot; the jobs bonanza; and the average citizen's real spending increase of 10.3 percent by 1984. The Democratic senator from New York—and legendary public intellectual—Daniel Patrick Moynihan mourned that the wealth was too concentrated, that the riches of the Upper East Side did not "trickle down" to Harlem or the South Bronx, communities still reeling from "an Armageddonic collapse" (although even a partisan such as Paul Krugman, from the perspective of 2002, would acknowledge that Reagan-era disparities looked "positively egalitarian" compared to the gross inequities that emerged in Bill Clinton's 1990s).

Typically, partisans on each side overstated the case. Democrats did not understand that the "deindustrialization of America" predated and transcended Reagan. America was evolving toward an information-age economy. Democrats were also too protective of status quo, heavily unionized manufacturing jobs to appreciate that in Europe, where Democratic-style policies kept the economy addicted to highly paid unionized jobs, unemployment rates skyrocketed and the economy stagnated. Democrats tended to count the 351,000 "McJobs" the service economy created between 1983 and 1986, while ignoring the 3 million new, lucrative, often satisfying "professional-managerial" positions the Bureau of Labor Statistics recorded. Many economists pooh-poohed the Democratic worries about a nation of too many hamburger flippers and Wal-Mart clerks. One wag dismissed this fear of the service economy as "the 'real nations don't make quiche' argument." As for the deficit, the 1990s' boom eclipsed the 1980s' deficit. By 2001 Vice President Richard Cheney would declare that "Reagan proved deficits don't matter"—an overstatement in the twenty-first century, perhaps, but a fair historical assessment of the Reagan deficit.

For their part, Republicans did not acknowledge that while Americans were better off than they had been under Carter, there had been more job growth in the 1970s. Besides, many American families were doing better partially because so many women had entered the workforce. By May 1984 over half of all adult women worked.

Americans were working harder and longer while earning only a little more, on the whole. Republicans tended to discount the economic, political, and cultural impact of so much wealth being in the hands of so few. By 1989 the top 1 percent of households was worth more than the bottom 90 percent, meaning that 834,000 households worth nearly $6 trillion balanced 84 million households worth nearly $5 trillion. This disparity made the United States "the most economically stratified of the industrial nations." Paul Krugman argued that the growing inequality polarized partisans, with positions calcifying around nonnegotiable economic stances and ideological issues. The 1950s' more modest middle-class society, he argued, fostered a more moderate, compromising politics.

Many of these economic quarrels reflected deeper ideological tensions and social concerns. Just as the Reaganites buttressed their economic critique of "tax-and-spend" Democrats with a moral critique of the resulting permissive society, Reagan's critics reinforced their economics with civics. Senator Moynihan mourned the dissolution of ties of both community and conscience between rich and poor neighbors, as "The Affluent City retreats to ever more concentrated and defended enclaves." Enraged that the "pursuit of happiness has been reduced to the ruthless pursuit of money," the liberal journalist Sidney Blumenthal complained that both "hedonism and unbridled capitalism effectively repudiate[d] . . . the social contract." A slew of scandals on Wall Street and beyond would seemingly confirm this criticism, putting Reagan and Reaganites on the defensive.

Scandal

Surprisingly, at the start of the third century of their national experiment, Americans remained bedeviled by the Puritan legacy. The legacy was only partially the dour moralizing the great journalist H. L. Mencken satirized as the haunting fear that someone, somewhere, might be happy. Young Wall Streeters did seem unduly dazzled by the "Bright Lights" of the "Big City," and a genre developed of Jay McInerney and Brent Easton Ellis novels, then movies, which celebrated and condemned the sybaritic lifestyle of the baby boomers' younger siblings. Especially before AIDS consciousness equated sex with death, eighties' partying did seem particularly raucous, with scenes in clubs, dormitories, and basements of drug abuse, binge drinking, and promiscuous sex.

The Puritan legacy also fostered an ambivalence about making money, even if the money was used constructively. Tom Wolfe's bestselling *Bonfire of the Vanities* and Oliver Stone's Academy Award–winning *Wall Street* would offer Puritan-style jeremiads masquerading behind the entertaining structures of popular literature and cinema. The Puritans, who were not as dour as Americans now believed, struggled over the challenges prosperity presented. Wealth might be an indicator of God's grace, but it could lead individuals astray. To this Puritan ambivalence, the American Revolutionary republican ideology added the Greco-Roman obsession with virtue and Americans' own disdain for the foppish luxury of King George's British court. The result was a country filled with go-getters who were seized with remorse when the getting got really good.

The greatest booms in American history triggered bouts of despair, searches for salvation, and, on occasion, ritual sacrifices to calm the collective conscience. The Jacksonian boom of the 1830s fed a reform movement and a religious awakening. The post–Civil War railroad boom of the 1880s would be remembered as the "Great Barbecue" or the Gilded Age, when robber barons plundered.

If in the 1880s the robber barons sustained critical attack, some of their successors in the 1980s endured actual prosecution. The Wall Street insider-trading scandal, which exploded in 1986, served as an ageless morality tale. The central figure, Ivan Boesky, was an easily caricatured speculator whose shameless embrace of avarice tested credulity. "Greed is all right, by the way," he infamously declared in a commencement speech delivered to the Business School at, of all places, the University of California at Berkeley. "I want you to know that. I think greed is healthy. You can be greedy and still feel good about yourself."

Boesky was at the heart of a scandal that reflected the unprecedented scale of eighties' excess, from the three hundred telephones in his office, including three in his limousine, to his reputation as the ruthless "King of the Arbitragers" who lived on a $10 million, 160-acre Westchester estate. In keeping with the outsized sums of the billion-dollar deals from which he siphoned profits, Boesky's penalty would be record-breaking—he returned $50 million in illegitimate profits and added a $50 million fine. He remained with a spare $100 million nevertheless.

The scandal first broke in May 1986, when a thirty-three-year-old mergers specialist for Drexel Burnham, Dennis Levine, was arrested for earning $12.6 million from insider tips in fifty-four separate deals. Analysts had been warning for a while that WHITE-COLLAR CRIME was BOOMING-AGAIN, as one 1985 headline read. After Levine's arrest in May 1986, led in November 1986 to Boesky's downfall, the doubts metastasized. Levine and others told Boesky when their firms were preparing corporations for mergers or acquisitions, thus allowing Boesky to emerge as a "genius" by buying the companies' stocks before their big surge. For example, Boesky purchased 377,000 Nabisco shares before the food king's takeover battle went public, earning a $4 million profit days later. Boesky confirmed the public fear that the takeover game was a form of corporate highway robbery, and that the sums involved corrupted even good people. Boesky, as a "creature of Wall Street," is "part of a larger drama of our time," the New York Times suggested:

"the inefficiencies of corporate America, the transformation of Wall Street, the ascent of the Reagan Administration and its exaltation of the free-swinging entrepreneur," the "takeover frenzy" itself. By 1987, 70 percent of Americans surveyed worried about corporate ethics.

In a hortatory media environment, there was a mad rush to use the scandal to attack various pet peeves. Some lamented the pressure to make a buck, forcing everything to become "faster paced. You have to throw your elbows. You have to cut corners. If you break the law, you smile at the cops." Others, ranging from Harvard's liberal economist John Kenneth Galbraith to the chairman of General Motors, Roger Smith, attacked the whole takeover culture. Business, Smith said, is "more than a money game. It's the art of producing quality goods and services."

As part of his plea bargain, Boesky exposed other coconspirators. Drexel Burnham and Michael Milken were soon in prosecutor Rudy Giuliani's crosshairs. By the end of the decade, Boesky, Milken, and the millionaire tax evader Leona Helmsley would become poster-children for the avarice that overwhelmed America. The demise of the "greed is good" trio would enable Americans to feel virtuous even as they sought to profit as much as they could.

The Moral Crisis Beyond Wall Street, High and Low

That summer and fall of 1986 a parallel scandal extended the moral crisis from the Wall Street towers where the money was earned to the Upper East Side condominiums where the money was spent. Robert Chambers, Jr., the "Preppie Killer," was a fresh-faced, prep school graduate, indistinguishable from many young Boeskys-to-be working "on the Street." He came to epitomize the other side of the tattered social contract, the debilitating effects of hedonism, materialism, careerism, and the divorce epidemic on family life and private behavior. Chambers strangled his eighteen-year-old lover Jennifer Levin and left her body, with her bra pulled tightly around her neck, just behind the Metropolitan Museum of Art. His defense—that he, 6-foot-4, 220 pounds, accidentally choked the 120-pound woman during "rough sex" when she grabbed him too hard—guaranteed tabloid attention at a time when the media was becoming bolder in reporting sexual intimacies. That Levin was an errant child of the upper class, a refugee from a broken home, boozing at bars till dawn, rotating partners for romps in the bushes behind New York's cultural institutions, invited the orgy of breast-beating essential for feeding a great scandal.

While surrounded by many things, many American children were growing up deprived of many moorings. Modern Americans' "radical individualism," the sociologist Robert Bellah and his colleagues explained, created a largely "negative" process of "giving birth to oneself" by "breaking free from family, community, and inherited ideas." The result was a nation of searchers, filled with people hoping to "find themselves." But "[s]eparated from family, religion, and calling as sources of authority, duty, and moral example," Americans were no longer sure what kind of happiness they even wanted to pursue. The confusion caused much individual misery and social dysfunction amid great comfort and unprecedented freedoms.

Like consumerism itself, this problem of modern American's "spiritual estrangement" had a decades-long pedigree. The twentieth century was a centrifugal century, with urbanization, individuation, automation, media and communication, mobility and transportation, prosperity, and the rights revolution subverting individuals' ties with their families, their communities, the nation. Many, including Reagan, feared that the 1960s accelerated these processes so much as to threaten the character of the country.

Launching his campaign in 1979, Reagan acknowledged Americans' "hunger for a spiritual revival to feel once again as they felt years ago about this nation of ours." Time traveling films—destination 1950s—such as the *Back to the Future* series, which Reagan invoked in his 1986 State of the Union address, and Francis Ford Coppola's 1986 hit *Peggy Sue Got Married,* evoked these supposedly simpler times. Critics such as the family historian Stephanie Coonitz would grumble about this "nostalgia trap" weaving a fantasy about "the way we wish we were." The "traditional family," she insisted, is "an ahistorical amalgam of structures, values, and behaviors that never coexisted in the same time and place."

Another perspective on this problem, from a lower socioeconomic vantage point, came in 1987 when the independent movie *River's Edge* attracted more viewers than expected while generating anguished debates about the quality of American life. The movie, starring Keanu Reeves, Dennis Hopper, and Crispin Glover, recalled a 1981 incident in Milpitas, California. A sixteen-year-old boy killed his fourteen-year-old girlfriend, and their friends came to gawk at "the body in the hills" for two days before anyone called the police. The movie showed the aimless moral vacuum too many young Americans called home life. Parents had abdicated authority. Life was lived through a haze of marijuana smoke and cheap beer. Random sex was one of many indicators of the joyless partying and attenuated connections that emerged in a world with few rules, little structure, and no purpose. In the film's most quoted line, one teenage girl says, after viewing her dead friend's body: "I cried when that guy died in *Brian's Song* [a made-for-TV cancer tear-jerker]. You'd think I'd at least be able to cry for someone I hung around with."

The movie blamed the selfish, impotent parents for helping to raise "monsters." At one point the Keanu Reeves character—who at least reports the crime to the police, although without any explanation or emotion—asks his distracted, overworked single mother about his pot-smoking, gun-toting twelve-year-old brother: "Why do you let him hang around with those worthless friends?" "Why do I let him?" the mother shrieks. "What am I going to do?"

The question was not just "where our children were" at all hours of the night, the essayist Barbara Lazear Ascher lamented in the *New York Times* after the Levin murder. "The mystery was that children weren't wondering where their parents were. Perhaps they'd grown accustomed to the absence." This absence went beyond divorce or two-career families. "The abandonment was . . . emotional, spiritual and complete. . . . Parents wanted pals, not dependents. . . . They wanted to talk contraception, not character. If they wanted to talk at all."

These themes resonated in novels such as Bobbie Ann Mason's *In Country*, which would be produced as a 1989 movie starring Bruce Willis and Emily Lloyd. In the book, the teenaged protagonist searches for roots and anchors in a media-inundated throwaway society where quotations from *M*A*S*H* have replaced the Bible as words of wisdom. "You never told me anything," Sam tells her mother. The mother who has moved away from her daughter, the town, and her past utters a wonderfully eighties' ode to selfishness and the amnesia of the moment: "I think I deserve a little happiness now."

For all the nostalgic rhetoric, Reaganesque libertarianism and materialism became particularly toxic when combined with 1960s' antiauthoritarianism and antitraditionalism. This resulting radical individualism fed the sense of social, moral, and communal crisis amid all the talk of national restoration. Reagan could conjure up warm, fuzzy national feelings, but his vision remained more individual than communal.

During one of his presidency's most searing moments, when the space shuttle *Challenger* exploded on January 28, 1986, killing all seven crew members including the teacher-astronaut Christa McAuliffe, Reagan's eloquent speech reassured Americans. Yet his choice of words was instructive. In 1962 John F. Kennedy dreamed about a man on the moon continuing the quest for scientific knowledge. When George W. Bush in 2003 would eulogize the shuttle *Columbia* astronauts, he would combine nationalism and theology, praising their "idealism," and soothing with Isaiah's words that "Because of His great power and mighty strength, not one of them is missing." Reagan's speech was more individualistic, focusing on the astronauts as explorers, hailing their "daring" and "dedication."

Nevertheless, as a midwesterner with populist instincts, and as a conservative with a reputation for moralism, Ronald Reagan kept his distance from the New York scandals. Even his harshest critics never accused him of financial chicanery. He was vulnerable, especially with his wife Nancy, to charges of insensitivity, not knavery. The consumer crusader Ralph Nader accused Reagan, as a "friend of the business community," of giving the "green signal" that "he's not going to be tough on corporate crime" or on governmental corruption.

In truth, Reagan had bigger worries. In that scandal-plagued November of 1986, as the titans of takeover Ivan Boesky and Michael Milken descended into modern America's scandal-mongering inferno of hysterical journalists, aggressive prosecutors, overpriced lawyers, fair-weather friends, and humiliated relatives, Reagan endured his own descent into political hell. Day by day, headlines about the Wall Street scandal competed for space on the front page with news about Reagan's own scandal. Iran-Contra would span the globe from Central America to the Middle East and invite Americans into a peculiar shadowy West Wing world centered around a marine colonel named Oliver North, who would unwittingly help Ronald Reagan's precious popularity ratings go south.

1987

Mourning in America

Fiascos at Home and Abroad

A few months ago I told the American people I did not trade
arms for hostages. My heart and my best intentions still tell
me that's true, but the facts and the evidence tell me it is not.
RONALD REAGAN, SPEECH TO THE NATION, MARCH 1987

White House strategists anticipated a great moment, a meeting of two
eloquent defenders of democracy: the strapping, perpetually jaunty
president and the wispy writer, a Holocaust refugee, grateful to his
president and his adopted nation. On April 19, 1985, Ronald Reagan
awarded the Romanian-born novelist Elie Wiesel the Congressional
Gold Medal of Achievement. The president thanked the writer for
helping "to make the memory of the Holocaust eternal by preserving
the story of the six million Jews in his work," and "for a life that's dedicated to others."

Having "learned that in extreme situations when human lives and
dignity are at stake, neutrality is a sin," Wiesel applauded Reagan's attacks on Communist oppression. But, in an anguished voice, Wiesel
confessed: "Mr. President, I wouldn't be the person I am, and you
wouldn't respect me for what I am, if I were not to tell you also of the
sadness that is in my heart for what happened during the last week."
Wiesel was alluding to Reagan's plans to visit a German military cemetery in Bitburg, which included as many as forty-nine graves of Adolf

Hitler's SS stormtroopers. "That place, Mr. President, is not your place," Elie Wiesel sighed. "Your place is with the victims of the SS."

The image of the refugee guest lecturing his presidential host testified to America's democratic vigor. Still, the Bitburg misstep reflected the unfortunate dynamics of Ronald Reagan's second term. By 1987 Reagan was too often out of "place," too often off the mark politically, ideologically, practically, and sometimes morally. Many of the destabilizing forces were imported, with Central American insurgents and Middle Eastern terrorists mishandled just as the European World War II ghosts were mismanaged.

As confidence in the president flagged, so did faith in the society. Pollsters found that the early 1980s' boost in public confidence vanished, with "trustworthiness of government" back to the "historical low point of 1980." The moral breast-beating, the Wall Street flogging, the Japanophobia, and Reagan's tumultuous term made for a surprisingly anxious age. America was at peace. The economy was booming. And yet, many Americans were cranky. Rather than delighting in the dollars filling their wallets, the VCRs whirring in their family rooms, and the microwaves beep-beeping in their kitchens, the majority of Americans focused on chaos in their schools, crime on their streets, AIDS in their bedrooms, the—dare we say it—malaise in their capital. Polls showed that most Americans feared the prosperity was fleeting, and that nuclear war might be imminent. It made for more unsettled, but more interesting, times.

If in 1984 the American collective sensibility, as it were, refused to worry and reveled in the red, white, and blue, 1987 was the opposite. This was the year when many of the fears seemed to be confirmed, when Ronald Reagan appeared weaker than ever, the moral fiber of the country seemed more frayed than ever, and, thanks to October's spectacular stock market crash, the whole economic comeback seemed illusory.

The news story that dominated the first half of the year, the Iran-Contra scandal, captured Ronald Reagan at his worst—too stubborn and ideological in Central America, while too disengaged and muddled in the Middle East. The resulting debacle would add to a pile-on of American fiascos, from the Jim and Tammy Faye Baker televangelical disgrace to Gary Hart's adultery-scarred presidential campaign to the October market meltdown. By the end of 1987, however, Reagan would find salvation, thanks to a most unlikely new ally in Moscow. Skeptics would marvel at the Reagan "luck," but in many ways, the Reagan-Gorbachev breakthrough captured Ronald Reagan at his best. Tackling one of the few issues that engaged him, he was ideological enough to have vision, but malleable enough to adjust to changing realities.

An Administration Adrift, a Chief of Staff Flailing

The mourning in America, circa 1987, began with the crisis in the Reagan presidency. "The second terms of Presidents in this century have generally been downers," no less an authority than Richard Nixon had warned. Thanks partially to his 1984 "Morning in America" campaign, Reagan's second term lacked the snap and crackle of the first. In addition to missing a mandate, the second-term staff was less capable than the first-term team. One flawed man, Donald Regan, replaced the contentious but effective triumvirate. Regan appealed to Reagan as a self-made Wall Street millionaire with a former marine's discipline and an Irishman's joke-telling skills. But the two had a superficial relationship. "In the four years that I served as Secretary of the Treasury I never saw President Reagan alone," Regan later complained. Revealing just how negligent Reagan's hands-off presidency could be, Regan simply swapped jobs with James Baker, the crackerjack chief of staff thirsting for the prestige of a cabinet post.

Such a move, which the president rubber-stamped, derailed the Reagan White House. Reagan's management style required a savvy chief of staff, functioning as the administration's switchboard. Coming from the rigid, performance-based hierarchies of the marine corps and Merrill Lynch, Regan found Washington's democratically robust chaos unfathomable. Controlling access to the president, Regan insulated Reagan from the ideological cacophony that had moderated and grounded "Reagan One." Regan also displayed a Wall Street warrior's crudeness. Regan reportedly dismissed Elie Wiesel's heartfelt appeal by scoffing that Wiesel was just trying to sell books.

The president's antigovernment governing philosophy also slowed the Reagan juggernaut. Especially after the 1986 tax reform passed, many felt that "Ronald Reagan had largely achieved his principal domestic policy objectives," the White House counsel Peter J. Wallison would confess. "Have we not done our job? Can we go home now?" one of Reagan's Californians, William P. Clark, kidded the president toward the end of the first term, while seriously proposing retirement.

Unlike the smooth, cautious Baker, Regan proved too wobbly on critical issues such as Social Security, yet too highhanded toward the Hill and in the White House. Regan clashed with key players ranging from the Republican Senate Majority Leader Bob Dole to the First Lady. Regan resented Nancy Reagan's partnership with the president. She bristled at his swagger, his self-promotion, and his efforts to control her husband. Nancy Reagan would sniff that Regan liked the sound of "chief" but not of "staff."

Regan did help Reagan pass the 1986 Tax Reform Act. Nevertheless, Reagan's failure to secure a Republican Congress in 1984 or 1986 would clip his legislative wings. From the start, Reagan was distracted. The controversial Bitburg visit set the tone, although Reagan eventually sought "balance" by also visiting the Bergen Belsen concentration camp. Beyond that, second-term troubles included anti-American terrorism on a TWA flight and the cruise ship *Achille Lauro,* a new hostage crisis as terrorists kidnapped Americans in Lebanon, cancer surgery, and the ever-ballooning budget deficit. Even Nancy Reagan acknowledged "a feeling in the air that the administration was drifting."

By 1987 Don Regan had alienated members of Congress on both sides of the aisle. He had driven out many White House aides and cowed most who remained. And, in perhaps his fatal misstep, he had crossed the First Lady a few times too many.

Iran-Contra: Too Focused in Latin America, Too Muddled in the Middle East

All this intrigue occurred amid the administration's greatest crisis, the Iran-Contra scandal. This tragic-comic affair linked two questionable transactions. First, despite talking tough, Reagan had engaged in negotiations to free Americans held hostage by terrorists in Lebanon and authorized arms transfers to Iran to ransom the captives, violating an arms embargo against Iran. Word of the ransom in November 1986 undermined Reagan's credibility. Legal questions arose when the White House admitted that profits from the Iranian arms shipments funded the Nicaraguan "Contras." Congress had outlawed any funding for these Nicaraguan insurgents.

Reagan had a choice. He could blame his national security advisers for running a "cowboy" operation, thus casting doubt on his management skills. Or he could take responsibility for their actions and risk impeachment or jail for violating congressional law. "It's hard to know which [is] more alarming, Presidential ignorance or Presidential arrogance," the *New York Times* wondered. Gossips would claim that Richard Nixon predicted Reagan would survive "because when push comes to shove he can say, 'I was stupid.'" Nixon supposedly paused, smirked, and added: "I never had that option."

Central to the Reagan narrative was Reagan's pride in restoring America's world standing. Supporters applauded his muscular rhetoric and his refusal to apologize for Vietnam. Reagan eschewed hard choices. In foreign policy as in domestic policy, he believed that America could pursue peace by strengthening the military, just as he believed that America could afford to boost defense while cutting taxes. Liberals called it a contradiction; to him it was obvious: "Strength and dialogue go hand in hand."

Reagan felt compelled to spend so much because he feared that the gap with the Russians had become so large. Characterizing the Russian military buildup as "the greatest in man's history," Reagan emphasized the dire situation he inherited: "When I became President, half our planes couldn't fly because of lack of spare parts," he said. "We only had enough ammunition for a few weeks."

Reagan wanted a visionary, aggressive, and unapologetic foreign policy. He would not simply exorcise the spirit of Vietnam, he wanted to repudiate decades of Democratic "appeasement." Preparing his 1983 defense address, the president scribbled: "Our security is based on being prepared to meet any contingency." That entailed amassing conventional and nuclear arms—for peace. The president wrote to his friend Laurence W. Beilenson, a hawk, that neglecting conventional weapons "leaves only Armageddon as a response to all the brush fire wars in existence. Can we resolve Afghanistan, El Salvador or even Cuba, to say nothing of Poland, with just the threat of the bomb?"

Reagan's hostility to Communism defined his ideology and motivated him throughout his political career. The "ideological struggle" against Communists mobilized him in the Hollywood of the 1940s, shaped his General Electric speeches in the 1950s, and colored his governorship and rise to national prominence in the 1960s. In the 1970s Reagan deemed Communism "a form of insanity—a temporary aberration which will one day disappear from the earth because it is contrary to human nature."

Reagan's anti-Communism was relentless, as intense when it was fashionable in the 1950s as it was when it was unfashionable in the 1970s. During the 1970s, Reagan forged ties with anti-Communist Democrats who, despite Vietnam, remained committed to an activist foreign policy. These Democrats joined Republicans in excoriating Jimmy Carter for abandoning American allies such as the shah of Iran to Islamic revolutionaries and Anastasio Somoza of Nicaragua to Marxists. The United States seemed to retreat as the Soviet Union extended influence in the Horn of Africa, Central America, and the Middle East. In a 1979 *Commentary* article, Professor Jeane Kirkpatrick would distinguish between totalitarian Communists and "moderate autocrats friendly to American interests," in rejecting a "posture of continuous self-abasement and apology vis-à-vis the Third World." Kirkpatrick preached that "Liberal idealism need not be identical with masochism" and demanded a vigorous defense of "freedom and the national interest."

After his election, Reagan made Jeane Kirkpatrick UN ambassador, thanks largely to her article. Other lapsed Democratic neoconservatives, such as Norman Podhoretz, Irving Kristol, and Ben Wattenberg, supported Reagan's hard line. Some, such as Richard Perle and Eliott Abrams, joined the administration, articulating a strategy that many other Americans embraced naturally, and with less media fanfare.

In one of his first term's defining moments, Reagan called the Soviet Union an "evil empire." Speaking to the National Association of Evangelicals in March 1983, Reagan repudiated the moral equivalence of the 1960s and 1970s, preferring the moral clarity of Harry Truman and John Kennedy. Strobe Talbott in *Time* feared "roil[ing] Soviet insecurities." The historian Henry Steele Commager deemed it "the worst presidential speech in American history."

Decades later, it would appear that American liberals worried more about Reagan's rhetoric than did the Soviet leaders. "[O]ur propaganda and our newspapers seized on this term and started getting upset about it," Sergei Tarasenko, the policy assistant to Soviet Foreign Minister Eduard Shevardnadze, recalled in 1998. "But on the political level" in the Kremlin "it did not play a role."

Still, Reagan's language warned the Soviets that he would match their rhetorical onslaughts with his own. Just as he sought to restore the military balance of power, he wished to restore the ideological and diplomatic balance. Despite liberals' derision at home, Reagan's words resonated throughout the world and would help establish the conditions for the Soviets' collapse and the democratic euphoria that would sweep Europe at the end of the decade.

Reagan's aggressive foreign policy and assertive patriotism captured the popular imagination. Hasbro Toys resurrected its G.I. Joe line of action figures. In a 1980s' cross-marketing twist, a cartoon series, *G.I. Joe: A Real American Hero,* began a twelve-year syndicated run in 1982 with a multicultural cast of soldiers. Action movies including *Red Dawn* in 1984, Chuck Norris's *Invasion USA* and Sylvester Stallone's *Rambo—First Blood II* in 1985, and Arnold Schwarzenegger's *Commando* in 1986 exploited America's cold war anxieties while feeding desires for a modern-day sheriff to right the world at home and abroad. In this renewed pop patriotism, frustration with crime mingled with frustration with Soviet expansionism. "These films take a regressive, fantasy-land urge—to go back and win the Vietnam War," David Edelstein, *The Village Voice* film critic, mourned. "Does anyone buy this cotton-brained revisionism?" Judging by his frequent references to Vietnam, and his fascination with Rambo, Dirty Harry, and other celluloid warriors, Reagan certainly did, but he called it leadership.

And yet "Rambo" Reagan also had a softer, more sentimental side. In early 1984 Reagan scrawled his personal vision of Soviet-American

relations transcending ideology: He imagined "Ivan and Anya" bumping into "Jim & Sally": "Would they debate the differences between
their respective gov'ts? Or would Anya & Sally find themselves comparing notes about their children, while Ivan & Jim found out what
each other did for a living?" As they parted, Reagan imagined, "Anya
would be saying to Ivan, 'wasn't she nice, she gave me a new recipe?'"
Reagan preached: "they would have proven that people don't make
wars. People want to raise their children in a world without fear, and
without war." He concluded: "If the Soviet Govt wants peace then
there will be peace."

Reagan's warm, cuddly, personal vision ended up almost verbatim
in his East Room address on January 16, 1984. The speechwriters did,
however, make the parable more politically correct. There was no talk
of recipes, no gender assumptions regarding who talked about children and who worked. In the final version "maybe Anya would be saying to Ivan, 'Wasn't she nice? She also teaches music.'"

Reagan's unedited vision was sexist and simplistic. It was also vivid
and accessible. This softer, more personal, more pacifist side would
conflict with Reagan's harder side. Reagan's foreign policy would be
most militant when the Russian threat was clearest; the further away
from that paradigm Reagan wandered—or the world's problems took
him—the murkier things became. In Central America, perceiving the
Soviets as puppeteers manipulating events uncomfortably close to
American shores, Reagan was clear, ideological, and proactive, for better and worse. He championed the Contras opposing the Nicaraguan
Sandistas as the "moral equivalent of our Founding Fathers." "We must
not break faith with those who are risking their lives—on every continent from Afghanistan to Nicaragua—to defy Soviet aggression and secure rights which have been ours from birth," the president said during
his 1985 State of the Union address. "Support for freedom fighters is
self-defense." Yet it was hard to see Ayatollah Khomeini's Iranian
theocracy through the lens of the fight against godless Communism—
except as a potential strategic beachhead against the Soviets. Further
complicating matters, the new hostages' families made heartfelt appeals that played to Reagan's sentimental side. Iran-Contra was the

sterile product of this cross-breeding, with Reagan's clear, aggressive anti-Communism mixing unhealthily with his sloppy, sentimental, and muddled approach to Middle East terrorism.

Central America Is a Swamp—Iran Is Too

"Central America is a swamp," Alexander Haig's usually diplomatic successor as secretary of state, George Shultz, once shuddered. In El Salvador an anti-Communist government fought a leftist Marxist insurgency, while in Nicaragua the pro-Communist Sandinista government fought a right-wing "Contra" insurgency. No side had a monopoly on virtue; too many involved had blood on their hands despite all the selective indignation. And while ideologues reduced both conflicts to East-West struggles, blurred boundaries, conflicting loyalties, and regional anomalies muddied the waters. Nevertheless, Reagan and some aides were keen to intervene, especially in Nicaragua. "If we can't stop Soviet expansionism in a place like Nicaragua, where the hell can we?" the Director of Central Intelligence William Casey asked.

The battle over Central American policy became polarized, reflecting the partisan nature of so much American debate. In a relentless Punch-and-Judy show, while Republicans railed exclusively against the Salvadoran rebels and the Nicaraguan government, Democrats railed exclusively against the Salvadoran government and the Contra rebels as "thugs" and "butchers." Democrats warned of another Vietnam—a fear shared by 47 percent polled in March 1981 and by 62 percent five years later. "There is nothing," Speaker Tip O'Neill warned prophetically in 1984, "the president will not do to get money for this war in Nicaragua that he has his heart set on."

As Democrats questioned the president's judgment, Republicans questioned Democrats' patriotism. Voting to cut off funds to the Contras is "a vote to pave the lanes of Central America for the Communist movement," Louisiana Congressman Robert Livingston charged. Noting that the TV "networks," as other critics, "have the same bias for the Communist rebels in El Salvador that they now have for the Communist government in Nicaragua," Richard Nixon would sneer: "Their pink slip is showing."

Neither popular nor congressional resistance fazed Reagan. He believed the Soviets' and the Sandinistas' "sophisticated disinformation campaign" prevented his message on Central America from "getting through to the American people." He was "completely convinced that what we are doing is not only in the best interests of the United States, but of the free world as well." Still, if there was one arena where Reagan and the Reaganauts were primed to be overzealous, it was in Central America.

Tip O'Neill repeatedly mobilized his Democratic majority to cut off federal aid to the Contras. The president "thinks he's John Wayne," the Speaker fumed. Each congressional measure triggered White House countermeasures, with National Security Adviser Robert McFarlane and his aide Lt. Col. Oliver North establishing secret bank accounts, funneling money through other countries, hiding documents, and lying to Congress. In 1982 Congressman Edward P. Boland initiated legislation prohibiting the CIA from working to overthrow the Nicaraguan government. By October 1984 Democrats passed yet another "Boland Amendment" to the Defense Appropriations Bill, closing earlier loopholes by saying "no funds" from any governmental "agency or entity" should be used "directly or indirectly," to support "military or paramilitary operations in Nicaragua by any nation, group, organization, movement or individual." Like his boss, North was unfazed and undeterred.

While Reagan's Contra policy faltered because administration officials were too zealous, confusion and inconsistency haunted Reagan's Iran policy. Reagan's rhetoric was clear. The president said in June 1985 "that America will never make concessions to terrorists." Yet no systematic attempt to root out terrorism began—a failure that would become apparent only in 2001. The mass murder by truck bombing of 241 marines in Lebanon in October 1983 was not only unpunished but rewarded when America retreated from Lebanon. And Reagan's strident words in June 1985 rang hollow amid a terrorism epidemic, coming nine days after terrorists kidnapped a seventh American in Beirut, four days after Arab terrorists hijacked 153 people, including 135 Americans, on TWA Flight 847 from Athens to Rome, a day before Salvadoran guerrillas killed 13, including 4 U.S. Marines at a sidewalk café, a day before a bomb in the Frankfurt airport in West Germany killed 3 and wounded 42, and five days before Sikh terrorists bombed an Air India Boeing 747 over the Atlantic, killing all 329 aboard. Moreover, the final TWA hostages would only be freed on June 30, only after Israel released 700 Shiite prisoners. The deal allowed Reagan to boast that he had not succumbed to terrorist demands—because America's trusted ally delivered the goods.

On June 28 Reagan met with some of the TWA hostages' families in Chicago. Two brothers of Father Lawrence Jenco, who had been kidnapped in January, joined. The Jenco family anguish touched the president. After that meeting, Reagan seemed more open to working with Iranian "moderates." Reagan was susceptible, as always, to the argument that good relations with Iran would dismay the neighboring Soviets. Now he also hoped to save the hostages. "Reagan's obsession with freeing the hostages overrode anything else," McFarlane later said.

That summer of 1985, the Iran initiative progressed. On July 17, four days after intestinal surgery, Reagan wrote in his diary: "Some strange soundings are coming from some Iranians." Reagan hoped for "a breakthrough" to free the seven American hostages. These "soundings" led to Israeli arms shipments to Iran, the release of one hostage by September, and a formal finding by December that Reagan signed acknowledging CIA activities. This amounted to what the final Iran-Contra report would call "an authorized effort to secure the release of American hostages in exchange for shipments of weapons." Eventually, Iran received 2,008 antitank missiles and tons of spare parts, and two hostages were released—although terrorists kidnapped replacements shortly thereafter. Meanwhile, "Field Marshal North"—as Pentagon critics mockingly called him—began diverting profits from the Iranian arms sales to fund the Contras.

When the Iranian approach was revealed in November 1986, it was particularly shocking because Reagan had finally lived up to his rhetoric. In October 1985 Palestinian terrorists hijacked the Italian cruise ship the *Achille Lauro* and murdered a sixty-nine-year-old wheelchair-bound passenger, Leon Klinghoffer, dumping his body into the sea. The hijackers escaped to Egypt and were on their way to a hero's welcome from Yasir Arafat and his Palestine Liberation Organization terrorists in Tunisia. Reagan authorized four Navy F-14s to intercept the jet. "You can run, but you can't hide," Reagan swaggered. Six months later, on April 14, 1986, American jets bombed Libya to retaliate for the bombing of a German disco American soldiers frequented. The raid killed 150 Libyans, including Muammar al-Qaddafi's two-year-old adopted daughter. French President Francois Mitterand complained, "I don't believe that you stop terrorism by killing 150 Libyans who have done nothing." Nevertheless, 72 percent of Americans applauded their heroic president, and Qaddafi stopped confronting the United States.

The revelations also came at an awkward time. In the November 1986 elections, the Democrats increased their congressional majority by six seats and, by gaining eight Senate seats, seized back control of the Senate after six years. With a Democratic Congress fed up with Reaganism and seeking revenge, the scandal also stirred longstanding doubts about Reagan's competence. In the *New York Times,* Tom Wicker sneered that presidents were paid to discover such troubles, "not to nap after lunch"; Anthony Lewis blamed Reagan—not his aides—for a "subterranean government" with a "brazen disregard for law" and "our constitutional system."

At a hastily arranged news conference in November 1986, Reagan wavered between accepting responsibility and claiming ignorance. With Reagan insisting that the "charges are utterly false" and "that it is my policy to oppose terrorism throughout the world," his ratings plunged more than 15 percentage points. No president had ever experienced such a one-month fall. A special prosecutor, various congressional committees, and the White House's own Tower Commission soon began subpoenaing White House aides, amassing documents, retrieving deleted emails, and paralyzing the administration.

Reeling from "This Iranian Thing"

With even many Republicans subdued regarding what one staffer, Haley Barbour, called "this Iranian thing," the new White House communications director Pat Buchanan blasted "disloyal" Republicans, scheming Democrats, and a feckless media, which he labeled the "polem-ical and publicity arm of American liberalism." Buchanan endorsed the entire endeavor: "President Reagan drew the line in the dirt and told the Communists they would not be permitted to establish a Soviet beachhead on the mainland of the Americas. Make no mistake. That is what the furor in Washington is all about, not whether technicalities of the law were circumvented." Even the diversion pleased Buchanan. "I say if Colonel North ripped off the Ayatollah for 30 million dollars and sent the money down to help the Freedom Fighters, then God Bless Colonel North."

Nancy Reagan blamed the scandal on the second term's second-rate staff. As the president's popularity waned, the fight between what *Newsweek* called "President Reagan's iron-willed, right-hand woman and his steely staff chief" intensified. Mrs. Reagan had mastered power politics. She leaked anti-Regan stories to loyal reporters. The *Washington Post* dutifully declared Regan "arguably the worst White House chief of staff ever."

The bloodletting immobilized Reagan. After a lifetime of image-building, he minimized the Iran-Contra scandal as a "journalistic fire-storm." His ability to disconnect from reality led him to build his defense on two contradictory points. Boasting about his efforts to free the hostages and woo the moderates, he claimed he never negoti-ated with terrorists. And, claiming ignorance of the Contra diversion, he insisted he was in command. Firing Regan would have confirmed that the Iranian policy was confused and that the president's grip had weakened.

Firing Regan would also have fed the impression that Nancy Reagan was in charge. No one could dictate to Ronald Reagan when he wanted to appear in control. He resented the claims that Nancy manipulated him. Rumors spread that the president told his wife to "get off my god-dam back" about Regan.

Reagan's position satisfied his vanity and his sense of fair play, but it did not satisfy most Americans. By March more than half the people surveyed believed Reagan was lying when he denied knowing about di-verting profits to the Contras. "For the first time in my life, people didn't believe me," a shocked Reagan would recall.

Reagan faced his greatest political crisis with the same passivity with which he faced his greatest personal crisis, his divorce. Now he blamed hysterical reporters and zealous aides. He refused to take any actions until the commission chaired by former Senator John Tower reported. Reagan was "frustrated that I couldn't get my message across," but not "depressed." Nancy Reagan asked her husband if he was as unworried as he seemed. "I don't believe I did anything wrong," he replied. "I realize there will be some unpleasant times coming up, but no, I'm not worried."

The new year began ominously. Reagan's prostate surgery in early January 1987 renewed doubts about his competence and intensified the White House wars. Nancy Reagan focused on the president. She demanded a complete recovery before he resumed a full schedule. Regan focused on the presidency. He wanted presidential action to deflect attention from the scandal. Aides searched for "possible ways to show presidential activity within the medical recovery limitations." No matter how limited the activity Regan proposed, Nancy vetoed it. "You are not a doctor," she shrieked.

Reagan devoted 2 percent of his State of the Union address, 115 words of nearly 4,000, to his "one major regret. I took a risk with regard to our action in Iran. It did not work, and for that I assume full responsibility." Reagan still believed the "goals were worthy" and segued into a homily about the need to defend freedom boldly.

As the weeks dragged on, Reagan's listlessness surprised Regan. The president, Regan would recall, "seemed uninterested in the fact that the field had largely been left to his detractors at one of the most critical hours of his career." The health crisis on top of the political crisis may have convinced Regan that age had finally caught up to him.

Throughout the second term, reporters and insiders often speculated about the president's mental state. Until 1994, five years after he retired, when Reagan admitted he suffered from Alzheimer's disease, Reagan's doctors insisted that the oldest president ever was among the fittest presidents ever, physically and mentally. Reagan's intellect was never conventional. Although many said he had a photographic memory, his idiosyncratic relationship to facts stemmed partially from his idiosyncratic thought processes. Experts claim there is no "Alzheimer's personality," no set of traits that have yet proved to herald the disease. But even when he was governor, Reagan was infamous for having a hazy approach to details and an intermittent attention span. Early in his presidency, this consummate survivor laughed at his inability to remember names by joking that it was so much fun to come to work— "you meet the nicest people every day."

Ironically, the longstanding doubts about his mental acuity may have insulated him from the developing doubts. Someone like Sam Donaldson had been attacking the "doddering" president for so long, so many stories circulated about the inaccurate anecdotes, that it became harder to convince editors, producers, or the public that reporters had uncovered something new. Lesley Stahl of CBS struggled with this dilemma, as evidence accumulated suggesting that the president was slipping. At a final meeting before Stahl left the White House beat, Reagan seemed particularly forgetful and distant. Stahl was ready to report that the president might have Alzheimer's, but the old performer lit up when he discovered that Stahl's husband Aaron Latham was a screenwriter. As the cinematic anecdotes poured out, and the charm worked its magic, Latham became convinced that the president merely had an off day, and Stahl buried what could have been her biggest scoop.

The hospitalizations made Reagan the man look as weak as his presidency. Since the cancer surgery, Nancy Reagan had appeared stronger, at her husband's expense. The jokes had circulated for years, as comedians would welcome "The Leader of the Free World"—and "her husband."

On February 8 Regan scheduled a press conference for the 26th, which led to a shouting match with the First Lady that ended when Regan hung up the phone on her. The even-tempered president was "troubled by this kind of temperamental outburst." A few days later, when Regan blamed "the East Wing" for a hiring mistake, the president decided, "that does it." He claimed he fired Regan because of the "morale issue" resulting from the attempt to be "deputy president," not as punishment for Iran-Contra. When the president finally fired his chief of staff on Monday, February 23—expecting a departure the next week—Regan blasted Mrs. Reagan. The president said if Nancy had overreached, it had only been because of his health. "I thought I was Chief of Staff to the President, not to his wife," Regan bristled. Flashing his trademark amiable yet disengaged grin, the president dodged the confrontation.

Forced by Reagan's defense to declare the president of the United States incompetent or dishonest, the Tower Commission condemned his "management style." The "flustered" president still claimed he never offered arms for hostages. "Mr. President," Brent Scrowcroft said, "there were occasions when the aircraft loaded with weapons was sitting on the runway, waiting for word that the hostages had been freed."

"He will never again be the Reagan that he was before he blew it," Congressman Newt Gingrich mourned. "He is not going to regain our trust and our faith so easily." "We have no fear of him anymore," a House Democratic staffer rejoiced. "There is no way Ronald Reagan will ever be as popular again."

Having dodged public questions while the Tower Commission gathered the facts, Reagan sought to start his "third term" with a mea culpa speech—of sorts. In his twelve-minute televised speech on March 4, 1987, Reagan again took "full responsibility for my own actions and for those of my administration." He vowed "there'll be no more freelancing by individuals when it comes to our national security." But Reagan crossed out the "I'm sorry" an aide scribbled in the margins. And offering a classic of presidential obfuscation—and Reaganesque denial—he said: "A few months ago I told the American people I did not trade arms for hostages. My heart and my best intentions still tell me that's true, but the facts and the evidence tell me it is not." Reagan ended with a homily, "When you make a mistake you take your knocks, you learn your lessons, and then you move on."

After the speech Dan Rather asked CBS correspondent Bill Plante, "Bill, the president did not apologize or at least he didn't do so straightforwardly and without some reluctance. He did say that he had made a mistake. Will that make any difference?" Reagan always resented such commentary, which he considered to be editorializing masquerading as analysis. "Our pollster took two polls right after the twelve-minute speech," he told a friend. "The first was only with people who saw and heard the speech for themselves. Only 33 percent had an unfavorable reaction. The second was with people who only knew about the speech from what they read or heard in the media. More than 60 percent of those were unfavorable. I guess that tells us something."

Overall, however, the speech was well received. "The Gipper's back," Indiana's Senator Dan Quayle exclaimed. CBS pollsters reported a nine-point jump in Reagan's standing overnight. Reagan proved especially effective in energizing his base—and playing to America's great cultural divide. "I remember how the country was before you arrived in Washington," Doris and Merill Green telegrammed from Scottsdale, Arizona. "Thank you for restoring pride in our country." Many of Reagan's defenders were as hard on Communism and the media as they were soft on the president and their country. "We love our country right or wrong. It has its flaws but is still the greatest," Mr. and Mrs. Richard V. Figueroa telegrammed from Los Angeles. "But not for long if the self-righteous loud mouths, liberal, pinko media continues."

Reagan and his closest friends also viewed this crisis through an anti-Communist lens. Before the speech, Efrem Zimblast, Jr., wrote to reassure his old Hollywood anti-Communist comrade. Zimblast, who was TV's F.B.I. man from 1965 through 1974, dismissed "the virulent cries from the leftist media [which] look like a thinly disguised ploy to soften up the presidency as part of a cleverly designed master plan." A few months earlier, Reagan had replied to a note with similar sentiments from the song-and-dance-man-turned-senator George Murphy by writing: "In our Hollywood adventure with infiltration and subversion you and I picked up a lot of knowledge the pundits and the politicos don't have." The conspiratorial language the old friends shared suggested that they were still fighting the same fight.

"There is a definite change in the climate back here," Reagan reported a week later. "We must opportunistically create events where the president exhibits his diverse qualities: leadership, compassion, identity with real people, and real emotions and on behalf of the country," one staffer, William Henkel, urged. We need to "find heroes," Henkel said, noting that "Springtime means baseball, families, patriotism, parades, festival, feel-good wishes." Ronald Reagan needed reimmersion in those "symbols, values, and memories."

The strategy reinforced the impression of Jimmy Carter's State Department spokesman, Hodding Carter, that Reagan's speech "guaranteed his presidency while destroying his ideology." From the first inaugural, Reagan had responded to the enduring unpopularity of so many of his issue stands with broad, populist, appeals; he often countered policy attacks with "feel-good wishes." Such patriotic populism shaped his governing ideology more than his conservative doctrine.

The Iran-Contra affair was only the biggest and messiest scandal to afflict the administration. The Watergate scandal had perfected a range of instruments for torturing politicians. Special prosecutors and congressional committees wielded vast subpoena power. The judiciary increasingly plunged into many aspects of American life. Journalists yearned to crack another Watergate case. Most Americans mistrusted politicians, their traditional fear of politicians now exacerbated by a post-1960s' hostility to authority. In Jimmy Carter's four years, his administration endured a few ethics investigations and dozens of hysterical headlines. Ronald Reagan's administration, which attracted too many scoundrels who hated government spending unless it profited them, endured over two hundred criminal investigations and thousands of hysterical headlines.

Indictments of government officials at all levels spiked from less than 50 in 1970, to approximately 400 in 1980, to over 1,000 in 1988—and most were convicted. There was neither a precipitating rise in corruption nor a rash of malicious prosecutions. Rather, these new forms of "institutional combat," which political scientists would call "politics by other means," injected new dimensions of drama and dysfunction into America, bypassing the normal protocols of electoral dynamics, and all too often criminalizing politics.

Both financially upright and deeply disengaged, Reagan remained untainted by scandal until Iran-Contra. When it hit, he was clever enough, and honest enough, to demand no coverup. This policy of full disclosure probably saved his presidency, even as it monopolized his administration's attention in 1987.

This scandal's proximity to Watergate hurt and helped Reagan. A generation of Americans—especially reporters and prosecutors—was now primed to mistrust the president, to see conspiracies in sloppiness, chicanery in buffoonery. Yet many Americans feared repeating the Watergate trauma. Given the new standard for political wrongdoing—was it as bad as Watergate?—and given Reagan's popularity and reputation for managerial lassitude, the administration would, eventually, survive.

On the other hand, Reagan's popularity intensified the self-criticisms Americans were proving to be so adept at indulging. If Reagan the Everyman was corrupt, perhaps the society was rotten. Americans' "sadness over Ronald Reagan is special," the pollster Louis Harris wrote, "for he had an inordinate capacity to evoke a spirited identification with the higher purposes of the nation. . . . This wound will not heal easily or quickly." In February, the Tower Commission found Reagan incompetent, not evil. But congressional hearings were slated for the summer, and in the spring of 1987 Americans found more reasons to question themselves—and their leaders.

The Season of Scandal in the Church—and Beyond

Spring 1987 also became the season of scandal in the televangelical world. The troubles began in late March, two and a half weeks after the president's speech. The casting was perfect. There was Jim Bakker, a celebrity minister-mogul, raising over one hundred million dollars a year for his PTL ministry—Praise The Lord or People That Love. There was his flamboyantly overdressed and garishly made-up wife and television cohost, Tammy Faye. And there was his angry former secretary and paramour, Jessica Hahn. Hahn's accusations of sexual impropriety ultimately uncovered fraud. By the end of the scandal, Hahn was fielding offers from *Penthouse,* Jim Bakker was serving time in the jailhouse, and Jim, Tammy Faye, and all too many of their unfortunate followers were languishing in the poorhouse.

What Reagan did for conservative politics, Bakker did for evangelical Christianity. Both preached an easy-street gospel of no hard choices and materialistic individualism, of prosperity, patriotism, and popular culture. Both bonded with mainstream Americans, despite the mocking of East and West Coast sophisticates. By 1987, melding Christianity and consumerism, the Good Book with the good life, Jim Bakker's "prosperity theology" had brought him three homes, his and hers Rolls Royces, 2,000 employees, a ministry of 500,000 followers, and 13 million cable television subscribers on 168 affiliated television stations. His 2,300-acre resort Heritage USA was America's most popular non-Disney theme park, attracting 6.1 million visitors in 1986.

PTL was part of a $2 billion-a-year televangelism business, with 221 Christian TV stations and 60 syndicated programs. More than 1,000 radio stations also served as many as 50 million "born again" Christians. In the 1970s TV ministries had consumed barely $50 million a year worth of airtime; now it was over $600 million. After years of public retreat, Christian ministers now tackled modern Americans' issues, railing against "secular humanism," the divorce epidemic, and the ubiquity of alcohol. Preachers were also more aggressive culturally, and politically. "We are fighting a holy war," exclaimed Jerry Falwell, a Lynchburg, Virginia, minister who emerged as a national power broker in 1980. To reporters familiar with New York, not Nashville, Falwell and his "Moral Majority" came from nowhere, but Falwell and his allies had been building their audiences, and galvanizing their flocks, for years.

Not all televangelists were alike. Echoing the Puritans' conflicts, the ministers quarreled over mixing piety and prosperity. Jimmy Swaggert, a gruffer, Gospel-singing Pentecostalist, derided his Assemblies of God rival's decadence. Falwell, who was less glitzy than Bakker, less proletarian than Swaggert, condemned the Bakkers' "greed."

Of course, not all of the 40 to 45 percent of Americans attending religious services every week were Christian, not all Christians were fundamentalists, and fundamentalism entailed more than televangelism and Moral Majoritarianism—despite media stereotypes. Televangelism reflected three major trends of privatization, politicization, and polarization shaping American religions in the 1980s. Just as it was easy to channel surf from Jimmy Swaggert to Jimmy Bakker, more and more Americans were congregation-hopping. In a world of increasing individualism and consumer choice, religion, too, was being privatized. At the same time, since the 1960s many church-goers had become politicized. The "Religious Right" took credit for electing Reagan in the first place, with as many as 85 percent of groups such as the white

Baptists having voted for Reagan. This political mobilization accentu-
ated a third trend—reflected by the sagging fortunes of the mainline
Protestant groups amid the fundamentalist resurgence. The middle
was imploding, people were becoming more secular or more religious,
with the Northeast experiencing more "religious disengagement"
and the southern Bible Belt serving as the center of this latest Great
Awakening.

Bakker's resignation over his tryst seven years earlier, and the church
funds he paid to silence Hahn, fed the mainstream media caricature of
believers as fools and fanatics. Calm, ordinary, church-going Americans
rarely made the news. Except for the occasional treacly Christmas or
Easter special, the TV networks tended to reflect what Richard John
Neuhaus called "the Naked Public Square." But now, country music
singer Ray Stevens sang: "Would Jesus Wear a Rolex on His Television
Show?" as cynical reporters delighted in the Bakkers' air-conditioned
doghouse and sixty-thousand-dollar home renovations. Further adding
to the scorn, one of the evangelical world's elders, Oral Roberts, said if
he did not raise eight million dollars by March 31, the Lord would call
him home. And months later, sweat streaking down his forehead, eyes
brimming with tears, his face contorted in pain, Swaggert himself confessed to consorting with prostitutes.

Watching yet another feeding frenzy, a liberal Protestant, James
Wall, complained of "preacher-bashing," fearing "a lingering resentment against people who are publicly outspoken about their religion."
The shenanigans confirmed every cynic's dismissal of religion as the
realm of the charlatan. A broader fear lingered that Ronald Reagan's
old-fashioned America was gone, if it had ever existed.

With scandal rocking the church, Wall Street, and the White House—
the nation's religious, financial, and political sanctums—many began
expecting their idols to have clay feet. That same spring, the Democratic favorite in the fight to replace Reagan, Gary Hart, also stumbled
into scandal. Reflecting growing journalistic aggressiveness, a *Miami
Herald* reporter staked out the Georgetown townhouse where Hart
spent the night with a young woman, Donna Rice. When photos appeared of Rice sitting on Hart's lap while cruising on the aptly named
ship *Monkey Business,* Hart's campaign collapsed. As Jessica Hahn did,

Rice then cashed in during her fifteen minutes of fame, appearing in racy ads for jeans. In Reagan's America, notoriety was a bankable commodity. Americans would pay to "learn more" about these disgraced paramours, paying just enough attention for the seductresses and their agents to enjoy some large paydays.

Wave after wave of such "feeding frenzies"—in Professor Larry Sabato's phrase—debilitated the body politic. The march of human folly and cascades of corruption undermined Americans' faith in their leaders and in each other. The resulting cynicism furthered the retreat into the private sphere, the epidemic of selfish NIMBYism, and the erosion of a mass commitment to the common good. It was hard to compromise, let alone sacrifice, when you mistrusted your neighbors and your leaders.

At the same time, these scandals' protocols and stock characters numbed Americans. A decade before Bill Clinton's sins would lead conservatives to mourn "the Death of Outrage," both conservatives and liberals were thickening the moral scar tissue that would mute American morality and moralism. With media scandal-mongers constantly at a fever pitch, with viewers and newspaper readers buffeted from one transgression to another, with high crimes and misdemeanors yielding equally hysterical headlines, Americans applied the same doubts they had about their leaders and their neighbors to the media messengers. Sensing, as usual, what John Q. Public was thinking, and demonstrating more savvy and cynicism than most assumed he had, Reagan would snap during the televised Iran-Contra congressional hearings: "I think CNN will be looking for new programming pretty soon."

Dodging the Bullet: The Iran-Contra Hearings

Oddly enough, then, this season of scandal may have helped Reagan weather the Iran-Contra storm. As the congressional hearings began in the spring, Americans were tired of the scandal-mongering, angry at the press, and bored by Iran-Contra. Beyond a slew of confusing details, the basic plotline had not varied since November 1986. Besides, as one Ohio banker noted, "Iran is all to hell and gone far away and the average person doesn't know where Nicaragua is." The Tower Commission and Reagan's speech had staunched the bleeding. Oliver North now wanted to win back the public.

By the time he testified in July 1987 to the joint congressional committee investigating the Iran-Contra scandal, Oliver North had two contrasting reputations. Just as Americans could never reconcile the shrewd, amiable, effective Reagan with the rigid, doctrinaire, addle-headed Reagan—and thus often believed one or another—Americans had trouble reconciling good Ollie and bad Ollie. Good Ollie was a fresh-faced, gap-toothed, forty-three-year-old Marine, a rock-solid patriot who followed orders to save the world from Communism. Bad Ollie was a scheming, self-aggrandizing, lying, manic Dr. Strangelove, who drove himself to the edge of a nervous breakdown running a rogue foreign policy. Good Ollie was a family man, a father of four, living on a three-acre "homestead" with three horses and three dogs, loyally married to his "best friend," his wife of nineteen years, Betsy. Bad Ollie was untrustworthy, a married man who wooed his beautiful secretary with a Farrah Fawcett blonde hairdo and a movie star name, Fawn Hall, to join him in a frenzy of paper-shredding that obstructed justice.

In Congress—and to an estimated TV audience of fifty-five million—the Good Ollie was on display. Ramrod-straight, his chest glimmering with a hero's "fruit salad," six rows of medals and ribbons, Lieutenant Colonel Oliver North was flanked by his wife, her white-collared, polka-dot dress accented primly with a strand of pearls. "As you all know by now, my name is Oliver North, lieutenant colonel, Marine Corps," he began, defining himself as an American hero. After saluting his family, he wrapped himself in Reagan's mantle. Invoking American values of hard work, loyalty, and patriotism, praising his fellow marines and their Vietnam heroics, North contrasted this "great" president's quest to achieve "world peace by strengthening our country" with media and congressional nitpicking. North blamed the Congress for its "fickle, vacillating, unpredictable, on-again-off-again policy toward the Nicaraguan democratic resistance."

North's patriotic rhetoric and semiotics, the "us and them" paradigms (America versus Communist enemies, North versus the Congress), the mix of romanticism and realism, the nostalgia, the populism, followed the Reagan recipe. As a result, both Reagan and North were able to transcend inconvenient facts and messy contradictions to remain popular. Reporters heard North's many "I don't recalls" and his admissions about lying to Congress, shredding important documents, and financing a $13,500 home security system with arms sales. Viewers saw an honourable crew-cut marine being crucified by the chief counsel for the House committee, John Nields, who was wispy, WASP-y, and a tad hippie-ish, with hair flowing too close to his shoulders; and the Senate counsel, Arthur Liman, who looked and sounded like the million-dollar-a-year "New Yawk" lawyer that he was, with his hair unnaturally but expensively flipped across his bald pate, with his Brooklyn overbite and his "r"s that were MIA.

The ensuing "Olliemania" became a moment in the Reagan presidency's twilight for conservatives to "take back the night," as feminists would have said, or to sing the "Nightingale's Song," as the journalist Robert Timberg would later say, referring to a young nightingale's ability to debut with a full-throated warble, but only after hearing an older bird sing. President Reagan was delighted "to see the change in attitude of the lynch mob as it feels the public pulse changing." In March the *New York Times* had painted a checkered "portrait of North," calling it "Bravado, Tenacity, Deceit." By July, even the *Times* gushed that North's red-white-and-blue "bravura performance" was "rooted in the American tradition: Underdog, true believer, one man against the crowd," a mix of Gary Cooper, Jimmy Stewart, and Huck Finn. "Give those little pimple-headed politicians hell," one Georgia man cabled, adding to the fifteen thousand telegrams piled not so subtly near North's seat in the Senate Caucus Room. "The only risk they ever take is catching AIDS in a Washington hot tub." "LT. COL. OLIVER NORTH— AN AMERICAN HERO—DUTY, HONOR, COUNTRY" buttons sold furiously, donations to the Oliver North Legal Assistance Fund mounted. Twenty-eight witnesses testified over 250 hours. Yet only North's appearance triggered a "half-million letters, telegrams, and phone calls" to Congress, "perhaps the largest spontaneous popular response to a congressional activity in American legislative history," according to historian David Thelen.

Foreshadowing a defense Democrats would use for President Bill Clinton, Republicans claimed Democratic partisans held North to artificially high standards to "embarrass President Reagan." Revealing that 1960s' cynicism, relativism, and anti-authoritarianism had infected the heartland, and now fused with traditional doubts about politicians, many Americans assumed that "everyone in Washington lies." And embracing the confessional culture that North, with his occasional regrets about "misjudgments," also encouraged, another supporter said: "Like Colonel North, I've made a few bad judgments in my life, too."

Actually, the public had a more nuanced view of North than the hype suggested. Just as polls consistently showed Americans liking Reagan but doubting his programs, polls showed Americans sympathizing with North but doubting his integrity. An overwhelming 84 percent surveyed believed North when he said higher-ups approved his actions. Two-thirds deemed him a "true patriot," and 60 percent sympathized with him. But 58 percent believed North acted illegally, 51 percent found him totally truthful, only 37 percent considered him "someone we need in government," and a mere 29 percent deemed him a national hero.

Oliver North was no pet rock. "Ollie for President" T-shirts faded quickly as a fad. One entrepreneur who expected to sell 450,000 twelve-inch Oliver North dolls sold only 200. As with much of Reagan's political program, great buzz did not translate into political revolution.

Nevertheless, with North's help, Reagan's popularity would recover, buoyed by the fact that only 24 percent surveyed believed the president was in charge. Reagan hated that "Americans were forgiving me for something I hadn't done." In mid-August Reagan presented an ambitious agenda for the remaining year and a half: ensuring Senate confirmation of his Supreme Court nominee Judge Robert Bork; negotiating treaties with the Soviets, including eliminating "an entire class of nuclear weapons"—the intermediate range, or I.N.F. missiles; advocating "an economic bill of rights" with a constitutional amendment requiring a balanced budget as the centerpiece; and making the fight for freedom in Nicaragua a "bipartisan" initiative.

The Great Crash—and Even Greater Reconciliation

Ironically, as Reagan's domestic agenda languished, his foreign agenda would save him. By late October Americans could no longer find solace in their stock portfolios. On October 6 the market began dropping, setting one record after another for the biggest one-day plunges: 91.55 points; 95.46 points on October 14; 108.36 points on October 16; 508 points on October 19. Billions of dollars of wealth vanished. Of course, few of the losers acknowledged that much of what they lost were market-generated paper profits. As Americans took stock of "The World [That] Has Changed," they wondered, "Does 1987 Equal 1929?"

A decade and a half later, the Great Crash of 1987 seems to have been a mild midcourse correction. The market's scale has shifted by orders of magnitude. The soul searching reveals America's insecurities. Unlike in 1929, the economy was stable. But on many levels the society was in crisis, and many Americans were searching for identity, for traction, trying to master a world very different from that of their parents or grandparents.

Reagan no longer seemed invulnerable. In October, as the stock market crashed, the Senate blocked Judge Robert Bork's nomination, Iran attacked an American ship, and Nancy Reagan's mother died ten days after the First Lady's left breast was removed. The distracted president failed to mobilize support for Bork effectively. Reagan later confessed, "this was a period of time in which I was more concerned about the possibility of an even greater tragedy in my own life than I was about the stock market."

The death of Nancy Reagan's mother added to the Reagans' despair—and embarrassment. Their daughter Patti Davis did not attend the funeral, triggering a new round of stories about Reagan's dysfunctional family. This family friction further undermined Reagan's aura of competence.

While in retrospect the crash of 1987 would not appear so great, an epoch-making change was taking place. Reagan's budding friendship with the Soviet Secretary General Mikhail Gorbachev was transforming the world. Reagan's administration would be saved from the humiliations of Iran-Contra by perhaps the greatest phenomenon of the 1980s—the collapse of Communism, which heralded the end of the cold war.

Here, too, another great Reagan mystery emerges: how did the warmonger become the peacemaker? Anti-Communism was a bedrock of Ronald Reagan's faith. Defiance of Soviet policy motivated Reagan's defense buildup, his Central American policy, his renewal of American morale. Early on, mocking the claims that his foreign policy was simplistic, the president told the Soviet Union: "Roses are red, violets are blue. Stay out of El Salvador, and Poland too."

In fact, Reagan's outlook was complex, even though experts inched the "doomsday" clock closer to nuclear Armageddon on Reagan's election. Skepticism about government in all realms combined with a pacifism rooted in his upbringing led him to reject the prevailing nuclear doctrine. He could not accept the notion of mutual assured destruction, or MAD, the nuclear standoff. The result was a more revolutionary approach to Soviet relations, even before Mikhail Gorbachev assumed power. Advisers debated whether Reagan was truly visionary or unduly naïve.

Similarly, Reagan's faith in his Strategic Defense Initiative (SDI) frustrated observers. Democrats mocked Reagan's faith in an aerial missile defense system as pie-in-the-sky fantasizing fed by Reagan's role as Secret Service agent Bass Bancroft, who protected the "Inertia Projector," a futuristic death ray in the 1940 film *Murder in the Air*. But Reagan reported that the Joint Chiefs of Staff "were unanimous in their belief that such a defensive system could be developed" and said he "never entertained a thought that SDI could be a bargaining chip." Reagan's confidence stemmed from his faith in America, his faith in science, and his doubts about the conventional wisdom. "Remember our country once turned down the submarine," Reagan warned doubters. Whatever the science, the Soviets learned to take his commitment to the project seriously.

On so many levels, in this realm, Reagan confounded the naysayers. Despite the doubters, and despite his "Evil Empire" rhetoric, Reagan acceded to a summit with Gorbachev in 1985, the first in six years. In Geneva, the supposedly incompetent president would recall having "the pleasure of going into the room to my team and telling them that it was all settled, that there would be a meeting in '86 and '87, the first meeting in Washington, the second one in Moscow. They couldn't believe it." The Gipper had scored without his supporting line and despite his wife, whose relations with Mrs. Gorbachev were frosty.

From the conventional perspective, Reagan appeared inconsistent. At the October 1986 Reykjavik summit, he entertained sweeping proposals, telling Gorbachev, "It would be fine with me if we eliminated all nuclear weapons." Yet this summit collapsed over Reagan's stubborn defense of SDI. As a result, reporters, Democrats, and allies worried about Reagan's hawkishness, while an agreement might have unnerved American allies with the sweep of Reagan's pacifism.

Conservatives feared Reagan was going soft on them. Charlton Heston urged his old friend to "resist the temptations of a Yalta waltz with the Soviet bear." Reagan replied: "I'm willing to dance but intend to lead." He assured another conservative: "I'm still the R.R. I was and the evil empire is still just that." In fact, Reagan was following his strategy of seeking peace creatively while defending freedom aggressively. In June 1987 he thrilled the world at the Brandenburg Gate dividing West Berlin. Acknowledging the Soviet moves toward "reform and openness," he challenged his rival: "Mr. Gorbachev, tear down this wall."

Nevertheless, with the real wall still standing, Reagan would host Gorbachev half a year later, tearing down more symbolic walls between the two rivals. Reagan hailed Gorbachev as "the first leader in the history of the Soviet Union who has agreed to destroy weapons they already have," rather than just limiting "how many more they'll build. He is also the first leader who has not reaffirmed the Marxian concept of a one-world communist state." Sensing the change, Reagan responded creatively and constructively.

Mikhail Gorbachev, of course, had his own agenda, and his own complexities. In the post–cold war historiographical tug-of-war, partisans often prefer to lionize "Gorby" and discount "Ronnie," or vice-versa. Gorbachev certainly helped trigger the Soviet reformation and ultimately Communism's collapse. But Gorbachev was the product of the internal rot of the Soviet system, not its cause. He emerged because the Soviet system had become technologically backward and economically dysfunctional, as well as politically oppressive. Looking back, Gorbachev's foreign affairs adviser, Anatoly Chernyaev, would realize that what the reformers called "the Brezhnev period [of] stagnation" in the 1970s was misnamed; it was in fact "the gradual dying of our society."

In the waning days of his administration, beset by scandal, plagued by doubts from the Left and the Right, Ronald Reagan struck just the right balance with Gorbachev. He was resolute enough not to be underestimated, and flexible enough to encourage Gorbachev's revolution. Reagan was also resolute enough to defy his worried advisers, and flexible enough to embrace the new-style Soviet leader. As always, Reagan was more surefooted with Russia than the Middle East, in an arena of long-term interest to him rather than a quagmire imposed on him. The formidable Anatoly Dobrinin, the veteran Soviet ambassador to the United States, acknowledged that Reagan's surprising suppleness sustained both *perestroika* (restructuring), and *glasnost* (openness), Gorbachev's domestic and international reformations. "If Reagan had stuck to his hard-line policies in 1985 and 1986," Dobrynin said, "Gorbachev would have been accused by the rest of the Politburo of giving everything away to a fellow who does not want to negotiate. We would have been forced to tighten our belts and spend even more on defense." Reagan's greatness here—along with Gorbachev's—renewed the faith of Princeton's Fred Greenstein and many others in the unfashionable notion that individuals shape history.

Throughout the autumn of 1987, while helping his wife cope with the double tragedies of her illness and her mother's death, the president oversaw negotiations with the Soviets. When his mother-in-law died, Reagan flew to Phoenix with Nancy, flew back to Washington the same day to meet the Soviet foreign minister, and returned to Phoenix three days later for the funeral—after finalizing an agreement and choosing a date for a Washington summit. For all the president's power, "there was nothing I could do to bring happiness to my wife at a time when she desperately needed it."

The year of Olliemania would end being balanced out by "Gorby fever" in December. In private soirees with Henry Kissinger and Yoko Ono, and during impromptu plunges into enthusiastic crowds,

Gorbachev charmed his hosts. The two leaders signed a treaty eliminating their intermediate-range and shorter-range missiles, feeding
the public euphoria. Privately, the two leaders sparred genially, with
Gorbachev wincing as Reagan yet again repeated his favorite Russian
maxim: *"doverey, no proverey*—trust but verify."

Nevertheless, thanks partially to the chemistry between the Soviet
apparatchik and the American actor, Ronald Reagan's nightmarish
1987 ended on a high note. It was hard to believe, but the saber-rattler
was looking like a peacemaker; with one year to go, Reagan's longstanding enemy was starting to look like the source of his political,
diplomatic, and historical salvation.

1988

Stanford

The Culture Wars:
Closing and Opening the American Mind

They called it the Reagan revolution. Well, I'll accept that,
but for me it always seemed more like the great rediscovery,
a rediscovery of our values and our common sense.
RONALD REAGAN, FAREWELL ADDRESS, JANUARY 1989

"Hey, hey, ho, ho, Western culture's got to go," the marchers chanted. Egged on by Jesse Jackson, relishing the media attention, the students from Stanford University, California's most exclusive school, rejected "Eurocentric, white male" culture. "We're tired of reading books by dead white guys," one editorial snapped. Here was one of the 1980s' strangest legacies. Amid Reagan's all-American revival, an articulate minority opted out, repudiating fundamental American values.

The Battle of Stanford yielded an enduring image: Jesse Jackson's multicultural march against Western civilization versus Secretary of Education William Bennett's pro-Western stand. In May 1988 the *National Review* would fume that Jesse Jackson "led the march last month at Stanford University protesting a course in Western culture." Amid battling soundbites Bennett would proclaim: "The West is the culture in which we live. It has set the moral, political, economic and social standards for the rest of the world." By kowtowing to radicals, Bennett argued, "a great university was brought low by the very forces which modern universities came into being to oppose: ignorance, irrationality and intimidation."

Actually, Bennett and Jackson never clashed in Palo Alto. Jackson visited on Martin Luther King's birthday in January 1987; Bennett visited in April 1988 after the faculty modified the curriculum. Moreover, reporters insisted that "Jackson did not lead or participate in the chant." Jackson said: "The issue is not that we don't want Western culture. We're from the West." Jackson just wanted other cultures included. Stanford professors from the Left and Right resented Bennett's claim that they had been intimidated. Even the change adopted was less revolutionary than feared—a Western requirement remained, with a non-Western component added.

The Battle of Stanford, then, served as a broader metaphor for the culture wars that ensnared Americans in the 1980s. As with American politics in general, activists and reporters often overstated differences in seeking the sharpest soundbite and the most hysterical headline. Yet, away from the din, American society remained consensus-oriented. Moreover, while quibbling about the curriculum at elite schools that taught effectively, combatants overlooked the true scandal, that hundreds of schools failed to teach students the basics of reading and writing, let alone civics or civility.

Culture wars broke out from coast to coast in the 1980s. Liberals sought to expand their gains from the 1960s and 1970s. Conservatives felt confident enough to counterattack. The forces of Right and Left clashed repeatedly on abortion, busing, school prayer, the literary canon, school textbooks, museum exhibits, suitable nomenclature for women, blacks, gays. The ensuing debate roused millions. Some ended up alienated and entrenched themselves on the Far Left or the Far Right, nurturing their anger and a mirror-image, embittering sense of victimization.

Nevertheless, even as the debate became polarized in newspapers and on campuses, most Americans embraced a contradictory consensus in the center. The changes occurred more gradually and more reasonably than the Chicken Littles of the Left or the Right sometimes hoped and sometimes feared. Following the president's own mixed messages, the age of Reagan became an age of conservative libertinism, as a majority of Americans disliked abortion but wanted the option in an emergency. Studies suggested that 56 percent considered abortion "murder," and 68 percent believed it defied "God's will," yet 67 percent supported a woman's right to choose, and, each year, as many as 3 percent of all American women had abortions. Similarly, most Americans condemned divorce, drug use, and promiscuity in principle, but many often succumbed to temptation in practice. As sixties' and eighties' values merged, individualism trumped moralism. Most Americans were more willing to indulge impulses than submit to authority, to live for the moment rather than be constrained by tradition.

This was not an age of neo-Victorianism, however, with everyone hypocritically indulging behind closed doors while parading around in tuxedoes and puffy dresses. Americans wore their libertinism on their sleeves, even as many agreed with the conservative critique. It was libertinism, meaning indulgent behaviors, rather than libertarianism, because many who indulged nevertheless believed in the value of standards. By at least accepting standards, this "constructive hypocrisy," as William Bennett called it, was better than the more consistent nihilism many media voices seemed to champion. Still, the result was a culture of confusion, a culture of moral crusading and vulgar displays, a culture that placed sex and violence increasingly in the public square, whether you liked it or not.

To the conservatives' dismay, Reagan dodged most of the cultural fireworks. He limited his cultural contribution to venerating the midwestern values he imbibed as a child, encouraging surrogates like Bennett, and crusading with his wife against drugs. Reagan abhorred modern America's "spiritual or moral fatigue." He blamed rampant "secularism" for creating a world where "no values are being taught or emphasized," so that "sex education in our schools" is "taught in a framework of only being a physical act—like eating a ham sandwich." Reagan sought a new cultural, moral, and political balance by appointing more conservative judges. But even here he preferred to advance his judicial revolution subtly. Eyeing public opinion polls, he lacked the stomach for the broader battles he had engaged in so zestfully as governor.

In 1988, the last full year of Ronald Reagan's reign, many of the cultural and social problems he had promised to solve persisted. Fundamental questions vexed Americans regarding what to teach students, what values pop music, talk radio, and other forms of popular culture inculcated, what role women should play in society, what could be done about the drug epidemic, and who should lead them in solving these issues, on the bench, in the Congress, and at the White House. The continuing Supreme Court vacancy at the start of 1988, more than half a year after Justice Lewis Powell announced his retirement, reflected the social and political standoff. And yet, in the spirit of the age, for all the difficult identity issues bubbling beneath the surface, the technological magic being honed by many Stanford alumni in Silicon Valley helped settle the debate by obscuring it. Between the growing high-tech, computer-fed boom and the Gorby fever suggesting the cold war might be over, the din surrounding the culture wars quieted. Not for the first time in American history, money would emerge as the true glue that united Americans and upstaged divisive debates; and, not for the first time in presidential history, successes abroad would paper over failures at home.

Curricular Culture Wars: The Battle of Stanford

Stanford University was an odd venue for the culture wars. A movie-set of a campus distinguished by its Spanish-style architecture, Stanford was more preppie than political, and more science- than humanities-oriented. Overall, Stanford students and alumni eschewed politics. Stanford, in Palo Alto, was the center of Silicon Valley, the computer revolution's hothouse. Silicon Valley pioneers focused on science and commerce, obsessing about their hi-tech product's viability, their firm's financing, their company's stock values, and their soaring costs of living, with modest four-bedroom homes on quarter-acre plots beginning at $250,000.

During the 1960s universities began loosening curricular requirements. The knowledge explosion and the collapse of a curricular consensus encouraged a "cafeteria counter" approach to courses. Such "smorgasbords," neither "balanced" nor "nourishing," had "ceased to be a curriculum," meaning "a fixed series of courses required for graduation," the cultural historian Jacques Barzun would gripe. Stanford dropped its Western civilization history course in 1969 but in 1980 introduced a Western culture requirement. When students and faculty tried reforming the course content in the late 1980s, the fight began.

Criticizing Western civilization fit in with a movement toward "multiculturalism" and "diversity"—praised as "identity politics" by supporters, derided as "political correctness" by detractors. The term "multiculturalism" gained currency in the late 1960s and 1970s regarding Canada and other polyglot societies, which preferred a cultural "mosaic" to the American "melting pot." "Diversity" seeped into popular consciousness after the Supreme Court's landmark 1978 Bakke case, with Justice Lewis Powell approving racial preferences in university admissions to attain "a diverse student body." In the 1970s feminists spoke of being "politically correct," rooted in the Maoist idea of "correct thinking," to counter the "male chauvinist." By the late 1980s conservatives used the term to mock the Left's overzealous attempt to impose gender- and race-related orthodoxies, especially on campus.

Feminists, African Americans—note the name change—gays, and lesbians demanded recognition and inclusion. These activists clumped together Shakespeare and Sartre, Aristotle and Einstein as "dead white males," all sharing similar elite perspectives. Reducing everyone to their basest sexual and racial identities, these identity politicians sought a rainbow of influences, rather than one monochromatic reading list. Amanda Kemp, the former president of Stanford's Black Student Union, complained that the existing curriculum implicitly said: "nigger go home."

These curricular reforms resulted from new conceptions of knowledge, understandings of truth, and definitions of America. Postmodern, deconstructionist European theories questioning intellectual fundamentals gussied up 1960s' antiauthoritarianism with an academic veneer. Faith in broad, traditionally liberal ideas imploded, replaced by a worship of a narrow, essentialist series of particular identities. "Objectivity," one Berkley radical quipped, "is only another word for white male subjectivity." Intellectuals on the cutting-edge Left increasingly defined themselves by their race, class, gender, or sexual orientation, rather than their ideas. Todd Gitlin, a liberal sociologist, saw identity politics start with "the recognition of a collective hurt, followed by the mistaking of a group position for a 'culture,' followed by the mistaking of a 'culture' for a politics." While claiming to appreciate a "rainbow" of difference, the multiculturalists usually created "parallel monocultures."

These intellectual Balkanizers developed an obtuse, jargon-filled speech rejecting traditional ideas yet often uncritical about their own sacred cows and buzzwords: colonialism, Eurocentrism, phallocentrism, logophallocentrism. Despite being successful professors, with pensions, mortgages, and other bourgeois accoutrements, these "tenured radicals," in Roger Kimball's biting phrase, masqueraded as angry outsiders. Many of the "white males" among them were children or grandchildren of immigrants. They rejected the traditional message to "try to forget where you've come from" and become "a cosmopolitan gentleman of the world of letters and art," said Frank Lentricchia, a professor who wore designer clothes and paid extra for vanity plates saying "Go Left" on his old Dodge. "Assimilation is a betrayal," Stanley Fish of Duke University insisted, questioning "The whole idea of 'Americanness.'"

Implementing these principles, one historian on Stanford's curricular task force said that assuming "we have a common culture" that "can be defined by a bit of reading in the great works" insults women and minorities. The task force concluded that Stanford's Western requirements "perpetuate racist and sexist stereotypes" and "reinforce notions of cultural superiority that are wounding to some and dangerous to all in a world of such evident diversity." Courses confronting "issues relating to class, ethnicity, race, religion, gender, and sexual orientation" and studying "works by women, minorities, and persons of color" would engender diversity.

Although they exaggerated, the activists identified some distortions in the traditional curriculum. With Virginia Woolf's work resurrected, with authors such as Zora Neale Hurston rediscovered, the canon, which was never meant to be so monolithic, expanded for the better. Despite all the social progress since the 1960s, white men still dominated corporations, campuses, the courts, and Congress. Even a supposedly feminist film, such as 1982's award-winning *Tootsie,* had to put a man, Dustin Hoffman, in drag to make an assertive woman character likable.

By 1988 conservatives had counterattacked, despite Reagan's passivity. Reagan confided his suspicions to his friend Walter Annenberg "that today's faculty were the student demonstrators of the 60's" and feared "that our young people are getting a lot of indoctrination along with their teaching." But Reagan preferred to brood about it than act. Jumping into the breech, an obscure University of Chicago philosopher became a celebrity with his best-selling 1987 jeremiad, *The Closing of the American Mind*. Allan Bloom charged that the American university had become a vast babysitting service, teaching how to be nice, not smart, coddling students, forsaking the classics, tolerating everything, appreciating nothing. To Bloom, in abandoning the Great Books, professors destroyed the last effective "countervailing nourishment for the spirit," to balance out the "youth culture." Better at diagnosing than curing, Bloom bewailed how the rock culture's siren song of sex and self seduced the American teen:

> Picture a thirteen-year-old boy sitting in the living room of his family home doing his math assignment while wearing his Walkman headphones or watching MTV. He enjoys the liberties hard won over centuries by the alliance of philosophic genius and political heroism, consecrated by the blood of martyrs; he is provided with comfort and leisure by the most productive economy ever known to mankind; science has penetrated the secrets of nature in order to provide him with the marvellous, lifelike electronic sound and image reproduction he is enjoying. And in what does progress culminate? A pubescent child whose body throbs with orgasmic rhythms; whose feelings are made articulate in hymns to the joys of onanism or the killing of parents; whose ambition is to win fame and wealth in imitating the drag-queen who makes the music. In short, life is made into a non-stop, commercially prepackaged masturbational fantasy.

With such rhetoric, Bloom became an icon of the Right and the bête noire of the Left. Bloom was often targeted along with the novelist Saul Bellow, who wrote the foreword to Bloom's book, and William Bennett, who chaired the National Endowment for the Humanities before becoming secretary of education. The three championed traditionally liberal ideas and led modern, unconventional lives themselves. Nevertheless, the "Killer Bs" became whipping boys of the Left, poster-children of alleged elitism, reaction, oppression, bigotry.

Critics of the multicultural agenda feared vulgarizing the university, cheapening the humanities, and politicizing the life of the mind. The personal could not always be political. Education must be selective, hierarchical, and enduring, not democratic and trendy. "It used to be thought that ideas transcend race, gender and class, that there are such things as truth, reason, morality and artistic excellence, which can be understood and aspired to by everyone, of whatever race, gender or class," the historian Gertrude Himmelfarb lamented. Bennett's successor at the National Endowment for the Humanities, Lynne Cheney, wrote that "Our society, like all societies, depends for its cohesiveness on common knowledge" of our tradition, which is Western. "Without this link to the past, we are unmoored."

Seeking to stop the rot, a University of Virginia English professor, E. D. Hirsch, published a guide detailing what Americans "need to know" to be good citizens. Hirsch's best-selling *Cultural Literacy* triggered a cottage industry generating civics recipes. At times, the debate threatened to degenerate into a battle of token authors versus token ideas, with each side scrambling to check off the right items on its own politically correct list.

This university civil war particularly dismayed traditional liberals, who worried that identity politics would trigger "The Disuniting of America," as the historian Arthur Schlesinger, Jr., warned. Todd Gitlin, once a 1960s' radical, feared that power in the university became the booby prize for a distracted Left. "Identity politics amounted to demobilization into a cloister," he would complain, bemoaning intellectuals "Marching on the English Department while the Right took the White House."

The multiculturalists broadened the scope of American higher education—but at the cost of a lot of cant. The politically correct, diverse university was a less open, less vigorous, less free, less interesting, less honest, and less happy place than it could have been, with far too much political posturing, obfuscatory lingo, and trendy sloganeering masquerading as cutting-edge thought. The conservatives defended important values, but amid great hysteria and an occasional closed-mindedness of their own. Most American students watched bemusedly, learning to pay homage to the gods of political correctness and parrot the new jargon, while remaining focused on getting admitted to law school or medical school.

The Music Wars: Censorship or Mentorship?

Parents and teachers alike fretted about the cultural forces shaping their children. Bloom's book linked the moral and academic crises, the problems of high culture and popular culture. Bloom's attack on youth culture and musical decadence resonated in particular; the debate began afresh in 1988. In January 1988 one mother condemned the "exceptional savagery" in Mötley Crüe and Twisted Sister videos. Surgeon General Dr. C. Everett Koop characterized too many videos as dangerous "combination[s] of senseless violence and senseless pornography to the beat of rock music." Three years earlier, in December 1984, an eleven-year-old girl had asked this mother to purchase the *Purple Rain* album of the artist then known as Prince. The conscientious mother—a Rolling Stones fan—first listened to "Darling Nikki." Prince sang: "I guess you could say she was a sex fiend / I met her in a hotel lobby masturbating with a magazine."

The outraged mother, Tipper Gore, the wife of Democratic Senator Al Gore, allied with another Washington spouse, Susan Baker. James Baker's wife detested the suggestive Madonna lyrics their seven-year-old daughter learned from the clock radio. "A line of decency has been crossed," Mrs. Baker thundered. In her 1987 manifesto, *Raising PG Kids in an X-Rated Society,* Mrs. Gore denied they were "prudish misfits attempting to Lysol the world. . . . As parents we have a special duty to establish a moral imperative for our children." Reagan deserved some credit for restarting the communal conversation about morality. "Family and community are the co-stars of this Great American Comeback," Reagan would say in his 1986 State of the Union address. "They are why we say tonight: Private values must be at the heart of public policies."

Mrs. Baker and Mrs. Gore formed the Parents Music Resource Center (PMRC). Knowing consumerism was more socially acceptable than moralism, they proposed warning labels on records as a "truth-in-packaging issue." Speaking yuppie to yuppie, they offered to assist distracted working parents. The average teenager listened to rock music five hours a day, or ten thousand hours during grades seven through twelve. Mrs. Baker said: "Parents have to make their thoughts known" in a world with crime "down 2%, but rape . . . up 7%."

Mrs. Gore and her allies did not advocate censorship. That subtlety was lost, however, in the backlash. Music industry leaders raised fears of repression, blacklists, McCarthyism, and censorship. One record executive, Danny Goldberg, spearheaded a counterforce, "The Musical Majority." Goldberg belonged to another alienated golden ghetto in Reagan's America, liberal Hollywood. Goldberg, the producer Norman Lear, who founded People for the American Way to fight the Moral Majority, and actor-activists such as Barbra Streisand and Ed Asner eschewed the leftist academic retreat into harsh speech codes and insiders' incomprehensible jargon. Rather, Goldberg and his comrades mimicked the Gipper by pitching their "alternative vision of patriotism and morality" as "a part of the American dream" using modern "mass communications." In that spirit, Goldberg charged: "A lunatic fringe minority is trying to subvert one of the most wonderful aspects of our culture."

Beyond the hysteria, Hollywood trotted out the post-1960s' rationales parents and industry executives relied on to avoid moral mentorship. The twenty-seven-year-old president of I.R.S. Records, Jay Boberg, predicted that a rating "just arouses kids' curiosity and makes them want to hear them all the more." Eddie Rosenblatt of Geffen Records insisted, "Rock music doesn't make these things happen, it mirrors what you see in society." The message was clear: No authorities need apply; no leadership or education could stop hormone-crazed teens.

Nevertheless, in August 1985 nineteen recording firms producing 80 percent of all American records and tapes agreed to place warning labels on some explicit albums. By then, many radio and television stations had stopped airing the most disgusting songs. *U.S. News & World Report* identified the themes avoided, including "incest, sadomasochism, thrill killing, and oral sex at gunpoint."

In September 1985 the Senate Commerce, Science and Transportation Committee held subcommittee hearings on the issue, with no legislation pending. A role reversal occurred in the Russell Senate Office Building's august hall. PMRC representatives fouled the air, shocking the Congress with ugly lyrics. The legislators learned about the Great White song vowing: "I'm gonna nail you to the floor; I'm gonna drive my love inside you." They watched videos of Van Halen's celebration of schoolkids lusting after their bikini-wearing teacher, "Hot for Teacher." By contrast, the rock stars who testified were well-behaved, well-spoken, and reasonably well-dressed. Dee Snider of Twisted Sister, without his usual rouge, but with his trademark wild hairdo, presented himself as a God-fearing teetotaler. Deriding the "Washington Wives," Frank Zappa defended civil liberties dressed in a conservative black suit and tie.

The Hollywood campaign intimidated Tipper Gore and her ambitious husband. By 1988, desperate for Hollywood to fund a presidential run, the Gores tried to mollify the moguls but only succeeded in restarting the controversy. At a November 1987 meeting with entertainment industry leaders, Mrs. Gore maintained her criticisms, although she and her husband regretted the hearings had "sent the wrong message." By January 1988 Mrs. Gore was condemning music videos. "How can I support a Democratic candidate whose wife sounds more like Jimmy Swaggart every day?" Danny Goldberg fumed.

Typically for the Reagan years, the political din and media hype drowned out sober discussion. While the censorship hot potato upstaged the music debate, the problems persisted: every year, approximately five thousand teenagers would commit suicide—a 300 percent jump since the 1950s; more than one million teenage girls would get pregnant; and millions of teens would drink too much, take too many drugs, and indulge in inappropriate sexual behavior. As with the music debate, responses to the problem usually reflected political theology, not social science: liberals blamed social strain, conservatives blamed family strife or the media; liberals sought new therapeutic and bureaucratic programs, conservatives reaffirmed faith in tradition; liberals tried to speak about suicide openly, boldly, conservatives feared encouraging more suicides by discussing the phenomenon—with extremists even trying to ban *Romeo and Juliet* from high schools. The arguments all too often canceled each other out, exhausted the participants, and left mystified parents and educators applying inadequate Band-Aids as dangerous social and cultural infections festered.

The Media Wars: "Shock Jocks"
and the Death of Good Taste

While the music crusade received most of the attention and triggered
the bulk of the backlash, these outraged parents—and millions of others—had a more ambitious agenda. "We're not picking on the music
industry," Susan Baker insisted in 1985. "I've written Calvin Klein to
complain about his ads, which are a debauchery. I just flipped on the
TV a few minutes ago and turned the channel to an R-rated movie
with a love scene, right on daytime TV. I just couldn't believe it." It was
hard to quantify, but many people sensed that media was not only becoming more ubiquitous in the 1980s, it was becoming more vulgar,
violent, outrageous, shrill, and sexual.

The sexual revolution, the rebellion against authority, the repudia-
tion of middle-class morality, and the expansion of freedom of expression revolutionized Western culture. By the 1980s, all subtleties were
lost. On television, the steamy scenes between Captain Frank Furillo
and Joyce Davenport closing most *Hill Street Blues* episodes, or among
various *L.A. Law*-yers, had been inconceivable on *Dragnet* or *Perry
Mason*. By 1992, surveying North America's "soft and hard pornography: suggestive advertising, serious films and novels with obligatory
carnal scenes, how-to books for better sex or more love or longer love
and sexual fulfillment," the Canadian writer John Ralston Saul would
update Marx, declaring: "imaginary sex is the opiate of the people." In
the age of AIDS, the sexual revolution was supposedly fading. In fact,
the public policy questions surrounding the intimate mechanics of
human relations injected new words and graphic images into mainstream culture.

Modern popular culture polluted the airwaves and movie screens
with imaginary violence as well as "imaginary sex." Brian De Palma's
1983 remake of the 1932 classic *Scarface* portrayed the violence-
drenched world of the cocaine cartels with a pornographic intensity;
Steven Seagal's 1988 martial arts–cop flick *Above the Law* featured a familiar eighties' plot of a Vietnam-veteran-turned-Chicago-cop confronting renegade CIA men—but grisly bone-snapping sound effects
accompanied the usual high body count, further escalating movie vio-

lence. In a society with unconscionably high murder rates and teen pregnancy rates, questions abounded about just how much "imaginary" violence or sex encouraged the real thing.

Typically, Ronald Reagan would affirm the social anxiety these shifting moral goalposts generated by yearning for that old-time Hollywood when sex was suggested with chaste kisses and closed doors. But it was not just about sex. After the repressive 1950s, the expressive 1960s, and the introspective 1970s, America endured the emotionally exhibitionist 1980s. A corps of daytime talk show hosts attracted millions of fans staging televised group therapy sessions about seemingly every possible social deviation. Phil Donahue, Oprah Winfrey, Sally Jesse Raphael, and Geraldo Rivera, among others, became celebrities by parading a host of shameless sinners who combined various pathologies in twisted ways: fat nymphomaniacs, elderly gigolos, cops-cum-prostitutes, kids who beat their parents.

Talk radio would create an illusion of community and foster a surprisingly strong sense of identity at a time when anonymous shopping malls replaced intimate main streets, and political debate was exiled from the interactive town square to the passive TV studio. Many shows' call-in components engaged people in public debate, creating a modern version of the town hall. These ersatz communities appealed to what the sociologist Robert Nisbet called "the loose individual," the typical 1980s' American, "loose from marriage and the family, from the school, the church, the nation, job and moral responsibility." The monolithic centralized government, as well as the ubiquity of the cash nexus, made relationships and ethics seem fluid, interchangeable, random. Talk radio's artificial sense of belonging tempered the anomie, as did the thrill of violating social taboos. While intellectuals compensated for feeling politically impotent by withdrawing into campus abstractions, many blue-collar workers compensated by withdrawing into media-inspired rages. The parallel safety valves offered cosmetic diversions from substantive engagement with politics. Ronald Reagan was not the only one addicted to symbols.

Competition upped the ante. Seeking to monopolize attention during their electronic freak shows and pressed to boost ratings, the hosts behaved outrageously. Donahue slipped into a skirt to interview transvestites. Rivera broke his nose during an on-the-set brawl. Morton Downey, Jr., slapped a guest. The fall 1988 season was particularly brutal. "Never in my memory have I seen the standards pushed further and faster than they have been in the past six months," said Peter Lund, the president of Multimedia Entertainment, which produced *Donahue* and *Sally Jessy Raphael*. "Every time a talk show tackles a previously taboo subject, that becomes the new border."

Like their music counterparts, television executives deflected any criticisms onto the public. "Are we stooping?" Alan Howard of KHOU-TV in Houston asked. "In a sense, but the majority rules. And if it's so terrible, why are people watching?"

This populist rationale was not the only Reaganesque dimension at work. Economic libertarianism fed cultural libertinism as Reagan's deregulation of the airwaves unleashed Trash TV. The Federal Communications Commission stopped regulating obscenity. The FCC's Reaganite chairman, Mark Fowler, considered TV just another household appliance, like a toaster. In August 1987 the FCC waived the Fairness Doctrine, freeing television stations from the "equal time rule" demanding balance between left-leaning and right-leaning shows. When Congress tried reinstating the equal time rule, Reagan vetoed the bill. "Unless they violate an established law or regulation, I don't believe we should take any action," FCC commissioner James Quello said of the broadcasters. "We let the marketplace decide whether it's in good taste or bad taste."

Typically, the ringmasters of this sick circus assumed one of two roles, reflecting opposing poles in the culture wars. "Phil" and "Oprah" became national icons by channeling the therapeutic culture on TV, oozing faux sensitivity and saccharine insights. Other shows—and hosts—provoked confrontation. "Zip it, pal," Morton Downey, Jr., barked on his eponymous show, which began in New York in 1987 and was nationally syndicated in 1988. Downey snarled at his guests and his mostly white, blue-collar, male audience, denouncing "liberal pablum pukers." MTV's founder Robert Pittman created the show to get beyond the "polite" talk shows: "If you go into a college dorm, you'll find people thrashing out issues like Mort does rather than like Ted Koppel does." This Downey-Donahue self-righteousness was infuriating. "Old-style

. . . dumbness only deadened our synapses while it helped us kill time," John Corry of the *New York Times* snapped. "New-age dumbness is conspicuous for the way it masquerades as news or public affairs."

On radio, Downey-style "shock jocks" were even less inhibited. Back in 1981, Washington's WWDC-FM tripled its ratings in a year by employing a young, long-haired, unguided conversational missile from Long Island. Howard Stern steadily built his audience, moving to New York, then going national with Infinity Broadcasting's WXRK or K-Rock. Stern ranted for four hours a day, interrupting his salty, saucy, hostile, obscene riffs with outrageous antics such as "Bestiality-Dial-a-Date" or jokes about the murder of Leon Klinghoffer, the wheelchair-bound vacationer Palestinian terrorists threw off the *Achille Lauro*. "I don't think you can go too far on radio," Stern said.

In a politically correct age, Stern's politically incorrect attacks on women, gays, blacks, and celebrities made him a cult hero among the angry, alienated, 18-to-34 year-old blue-collar crowd. Dozens of imitators followed, violating social taboos promiscuously. Amid growing radio blandness, with FM stations succumbing to packaged formats, Stern's unpredictability seemed creative. Reading *National Lampoon* and *Mad* magazine, watching *Saturday Night Live* regularly and *Animal House* repeatedly, primed this elusive consumer demographic for Stern's humor. Some academics hailed talk radio as the rare mass medium available to the lower classes and thus an important voice of "proletarian discontent." The historian Susan Douglas notes the irony that this carefully produced, nationally syndicated expression of populism was the result of economic concentration, sophisticated "geosynchronous" satellite technology, and Reagan's deregulation.

Many talk show hosts embraced an unorthodox conservative libertinism. They often sounded right-wing—blasting the Left's sacred cows, targeting Democratic special interest groups. Yet they rejected conservative formalities along with liberal pieties. Their sex obsession made many prochoice, and, for professional reasons, they were free-speech absolutists. Such promiscuous politics made both liberals and conservatives deem them "dangerous."

In truth, the tone was often more destructive than the content. The shock jocks helped spawn a gutter politics. They were pioneers in the descent toward excessive shrillness and extreme aggressiveness in modern political discourse. The infection spread from low culture to high, from radio and television to the best-seller lists. Cranks from the Left and the Right would dominate the bookstores as well as the airwaves. Even worse than the "dumbing down," the polarizing, vulgar rhetoric was divisive.

Not all radio talk shows were raunchy. The more than 850 all-talk or talk-news stations by the mid-1990s—up from 200 in the early 1980s—ranged widely. Don Imus mixed biting, Stern-like tirades with political commentary and guests. Rush Limbaugh relied on bombast, not bathroom humor, to produce a shrill but influential show. Others were flamboyantly inoffensive, chatting breezily with celebrities, as Larry King did.

Just as observers justifiably wondered what the "tenured radicals" were so angry about, it was reasonable to ask what so enraged these angry male vulgarians. Here, it seemed, the conservative movement's now-often-closeted crankiness was displayed in an entertaining and thus detoxifying context. Here, too, was a corner of the entertainment world where anxieties about American decline could be expressed and exorcised. At the same time, the shock jocks' obsessions with penis size, crude manners, macho swagger, "feminazis," "fags," wimps, and Reagan's Rambo responses—in short, their violent assertions of self, their zealous embrace of male chauvinist pigdom—suggested they were trying to rebuild a threatened masculine identity. Bruce Feirstein's 1982 best-seller *Real Men Don't Eat Quiche* summed up their stance. Ronald Reagan's easy Marlboro Man machismo charmed them. With an overwhelmingly male audience listening, with as many as 80 percent of the talk show hosts men, it was reasonable to conclude that talk radio was part of a broader backlash against feminism. Similarly, gender politics fueled much of the anger in the university, with women propeled by rage now asserting their power in the universities, often through the feminist challenge to fundamental assumptions from literature to morality.

Gender Wars: Women Advance as Feminism Drifts

While it is fashionable to mourn the 1980s as a period of "backlash" against feminism, it was also a time of extraordinary feminist advances. Even as young women rejected the "F-word," women became more integrated into the work world as the push for gender equity became institutionalized. Yes, this decade buried the equal rights amendment, but this decade also saw the conservative Ronald Reagan rush to nominate the first female Supreme Court justice and preside over a cabinet with two or three women usually present.

Still, Ronald Reagan endured rocky relations with women voters and the women's movement. "Women clearly disapprove of the way President Reagan is handling his job; men clearly approve," his pollster Richard Wirthlin said in 1982. That year, the campaign to ratify a constitutional amendment guaranteeing "equal rights under the law" fizzled. A year later, the director of the attorney general's Gender Discrimination Agency Review, Barbara Honegger, resigned after Reagan told a meeting of the Business and Professional Women's Clubs that "If it weren't for women, us men would still be walking around in skin suits, carrying clubs." Honegger blasted Reagan's attempts to fight gender discrimination by statute rather than by an equal rights amendment as a "sham."

Feminists hoped to gain power by rallying women against Reagan. America's new demographic realities could have spawned a new kind of politics. By 1980, 42 million women worked, compared to 19.5 million in 1955. More than half the women in the United States were employed or looking for work, and only a third were homemakers. In 1980 for the first time the Census Bureau had stopped defining husbands as the only possible "heads of households." At the same time, marriage and birth rates plummeted in the 1970s, as the divorce rate soared, approaching four of every ten marriages.

These numbers sobered the president's men—and women. White House staffers acknowledged "that *no matter how creditable the record of accomplishments, you are unlikely to receive much praise*—principally because on the two 'hottest' symbolic issues of concern to feminists, namely abortion and E.R.A. itself, you are separated from them by a wide philosophical divide." Aides did not only worry about the newly discovered "gender gap" in voting and polling. Liberals could use "women's issues" as a wedge to attack Reagan's program as "oft-repeated statements . . . take on a life of their own."

Administration strategists suggested that Reagan's supposed insensitivity "may, in fact, be easier for the administration to 'solve' than would a single issue . . . by influencing a perception and not altering policy." Such advice worked for a White House that was more willing to fine-tune image than reevaluate policy, and which dismissed "the women's issue" as a "rhetorical" one. Ed Meese convened the administration's top female appointees to decide: "Given that much of the feminist agenda is unacceptable, what proposals which are considered favorable to women can the Administration support?" Like his immediate predecessors, Reagan ritualistically listed all his female appointees, sought out more, and boasted that his administration had been better to women than any others.

Rejecting discrimination and advocating equitable treatment for all, Reagan demonstrated a moderately progressive vision regarding women, understanding, as always through personal experience, that the world had changed. "My mother was basically a homemaker," he wrote in the *Ladies' Home Journal* in 1984. "Nancy filled the role of homemaker plus that of actress and public figure. My daughters are pursuing demanding careers. To me this is the story of women over the last century. No role is superior to another. The point is, a woman must have the right to choose the role she wishes or to perhaps fill them all."

These breezy platitudes underestimated the complex issues facing even moderate women, let alone the radicals' sweeping, integrated aims. The issues of the eighties were subtle, for women had already fought their way into the office. "We were everywhere men were; well, everywhere but at the top," Lesley Stahl of CBS would recall. "We had even achieved a critical mass in network newsrooms." When *Life* wanted to photograph eight women network correspondents, Diane Sawyer showed up to the photo shoot wearing a black wig. "Diane," the women jabbed, "you're so famous you go around in disguise?" "No," Sawyer grinned, "just thought I'd try to be different." Stahl recalls: "We examined one another, got it and laughed. We were all blond. Every one of us." Whether or not they were natural blonds, all were captive to still unnatural network expectations.

Reagan was often forced to backtrack. When secretaries James Watt and Don Edwards planned a dinner "celebrating the demise of the ERA," Reagan had to explain how that did not constitute "danc[ing]" on the amendment's "grave." He had to calm an internal GOP rebellion rejecting his claim that the surge of women entering the job market boosted the unemployment figures. Such imbroglios undermined Reagan's claim that his limited yet progressive vision respected the movement.

White House strategists rarely deployed Nancy Reagan on this issue because her 1950s' sensibility offended feminists who deemed that decade "the golden age of shot-gun weddings, coat-hanger abortions and wall-to-wall guilt." Mrs. Reagan's natural audience consisted of women like Holly Coors, the wife of the conservative brewing magnate, who praised Mrs. Reagan in traditional terms, saying "Your graciousness and loveliness as our nation's First Lady continues to make us burst with pride!" The Reaganites rejected the feminist insistence on treating women as a separate group. "Today, our nation has one big program to help every American man, woman and child," Reagan told Republican women officials in 1984. "It's called 'economic recovery.'"

The tensions between the Reagan administration and the women's movement often obscured their common ground. Feminists and Reaganites, including leaders from the Christian Right, did unite against pornography. Ultimately, Reagan underestimated feminism's positive impact on women, while feminists exaggerated their popularity, the uniformity of female opinion, and Reagan's hostility.

Despite all the talk from the Left and the Right about "women's" attitudes as monolithic, many American women in the 1980s were confused. Feminism was bearing fruit, transforming millions of women's expectations, and revolutionizing institutions such as marriage and family. A 1983 best-seller resurrected Sigmund Freud's famous question, *What Do Women Want?*

Many were unsure, but others were not. Partisans on both sides of this great social, moral, philosophical, spiritual, cultural, and political divide enjoyed a terrifying, sometimes vicious, clarity. The sustained battle over abortion revealed the size of the gap—and the passions surrounding it. The 1973 *Roe v. Wade* decision should have settled the question—abortion became legal. American women's constitutional right to privacy now freed them to choose what to do regarding their own bodies. Yet the opinion's controversial legal reasoning relied on an implied right to privacy rather than an explicit constitutional mandate. The Supreme Court's role as the least representative branch making such a momentous decision was problematic. And to the extent that opponents of abortion believed they were defending the "right to life," the difficult choice between violating a woman's autonomy and killing a fetus all but guaranteed sustained conflict.

A 1984 analysis of partisans revealed the depth of the conflict. In *Abortion and the Politics of Motherhood,* Kristin Luker found prolife women tended to be more traditional, and disproportionately Catholic and blue collar. Prochoice women tended to be more educated, modern, and disproportionately liberal and white collar. The abortion issue thus pitted women who built their identities around family, faith, and accepting their lot in life against women invested in career, reason, and a progressive confidence in their ability to shape their destinies. The two sides' mutual antipathy reinforced their core beliefs, with prolifers dismissing the "utilitarians" who could so callously sacrifice an unborn life to avoid inconveniencing themselves, and with prochoicers dismissing the "polyester" types who enslaved their bodies and souls to men for the sake of an abstraction. For each side, then, the fight became a zero-sum game, with the fight over abortion becoming *"a referendum on the place and meaning of motherhood"* (original italicized), while the clash over feminism became a debate "about the meaning of women's lives."

The 1984 election showed that the gender gap was exaggerated. Reagan captured 55 percent of women's votes as opposed to 64 percent of male votes. But 60 percent of married women surveyed supported the president. The split among unmarried women, with 49 percent voting for Reagan and 51 percent voting for Walter Mondale, wiped out Reagan's gains with the married women. Reagan's problem at the voting booth was with black women, poor women, and liberal women, who were disproportionately single, rather than with "women" overall. Politics, not gender, was at issue.

More and more women distanced themselves from the feminist movement, while embracing its goals. Even committed feminists would joke among themselves, "Don't tell the sisterhood," when they deviated from what seemed to be an increasingly "rigid orthodoxy." Younger feminists gasping for air sought a new balance. "The most outspoken feminists I have known dieted, exercised and gossiped about boys," Katie Roiphie, a second-generation feminist would write. Nancy Reagan seemed to recognize these fissures before many movement leaders did. Her example of a woman making traditional choices led millions of women to believe that they could get the kind of fulfillment feminists promised without having to call themselves by "the F-word."

Nevertheless, even with the ambivalence of so many, the clashing worldviews on both extremes of the great divide sustained the culture wars across Reagan's America. On the airwaves, the men who married homemakers, or hoped to, railed against the changing script that seemed to devalue them just as the abortion epidemic seemed to devalue their female compatriots. On campus, the passion of a generation of feminists who were maturing into positions of power, while still harboring the angst of their youth, fed the tensions and the transformations. Throughout the country, but particularly in the universities, the politics around sexual preference and race—two other volatile issues that struck at an increasingly powerful group's core identity—only raised the stakes higher—and intensified the tensions. While from one perspective Reagan's America was remarkably, depressingly, conformist, with everyone rushing to get home, kick off their Nikes, and watch Cosby, from another perspective Reagan's America was remarkably, depressingly, divided, with the loud extremes at opposing sides of the spectrum creating mutually reinforcing but mutually exclusive social, cultural, political, and ideological identities.

The Drug Wars: Conservative
Moralizing on the Cheap

As his mild stance on women's issues revealed, Ronald Reagan was more timid on these cultural issues than his supporters desired or his opponents feared. Typical of his half-measures was the statement he would send to prolife rallies in Washington, demonstrating support but avoiding the photo-op. The cultural crusade he and his wife most invested in, the fight against drugs, was less controversial. It was a politically useful initiative, modifying Nancy Reagan's image as a materialistic spendthrift and mollifying some of Ronald Reagan's ideological brethren, while spotlighting a serious crisis that easily played as a liberal failure.

A crusade against drugs advanced the broader Reagan agenda to repudiate the sixties and "restore" America. Drug abuse was one of the nastiest social pathologies that decade spawned, as smoking a "joint" came to symbolize rejection of authority and fulfilment of one's spirituality. By 1971 an estimated twenty-four million Americans over eleven used marijuana; heroin use had ballooned from fifty thousand users in 1960 to half a million or more. Reagan denounced the "attitude of permissiveness" spreading the "plague," and the resulting "climate of lawlessness" that festered. George Will and others would fall for a hoax that reflected a central social anxiety—and truth—noting: "In the 1940s a survey listed the top seven discipline problems in public schools: talking, chewing gum, making noise, running in the halls, getting out of turn in line, wearing improper clothes, not putting paper in wastebaskets. A 1980s survey lists these top seven: drug abuse, alcohol abuse, pregnancy, suicide, rape, robbery, assault." Despite the inaccuracy of the poll, the sentiment was clear. "I believe the crime problem in America today *is* the drug problem," New York City Police Commissioner Benjamin Ward said in 1986.

The way marijuana use had become "entrenched" shocked the Reagans. During the Carter years the movement to decriminalize marijuana progressed. In movies like *Saturday Night Fever* and TV shows like *NBC's Saturday Night Live,* the "cool" people indulged in "recreational" drugs. By 1978 only 35 percent of high school seniors surveyed considered marijuana harmful.

Targeting the customers, the Reagans mobilized traditional American values against modern permissiveness. They would struggle for America's soul on a symbolic plane with the skills honed making movies and running political campaigns. Both Reagans understood the power of their respective bully pulpits. The crusade had to be popular, politically beneficial, and suitably self-promoting.

The Reagans used the drug war to illustrate how government could champion morality without expanding its powers. Emphasizing individual behavior, not government programs, the budget for interdiction grew from $853 million in 1982 to $1.5 billion in 1986, while the funding for drug treatment and prevention dropped from $200 million to $126 million. The war on drugs appealed to disgruntled lifestyle conservatives without complicating the rest of Reagan's program or exposing the Republicans' rift between libertarian conservatives and conservative moralists.

At one of Nancy Reagan's 110 antidrug events in 1984, a girl at Oakland's Longfellow Elementary School asked, "But Mrs. Reagan, what should I say if someone offers me drugs?" As usual, Mrs. Reagan responded, "Just say no, no, no." Months later, while reviewing the tape from that day, one twelve-year-old boy, Noma Martini, suggested to two friends, "Well why don't we start a club against drugs and call it 'Just say no?'" The phrase "Just say no" was as simplistic yet profound as the rest of Reagan's program. The phrase sank into popular consciousness, inspiring a national youth movement and appearing everywhere, on T-shirts, caps, even the plastic base of urinals.

The Reagans succeeded in grafting a competing message onto American popular culture. The writer Katie Roiphe would recall the "pushmi-pullyu" message of her high school years: "Our ears were filled simultaneously with Nancy Reagan's 'Just Say No' and George Michael's late-eighties hit song 'I Want Your Sex.'" Drugs remained exceedingly popular. Yet drug use peaked; the drug culture acquired a new illegitimacy. One quarter of America's youth used drugs and alcohol, rather than one-third in the 1970s. "The idea that marijuana is harmless has gone the way of the Edsel. Research has proven that heavy use depresses production of sperm, contributes to lung cancer, and causes heavy users to suffer that unique form of lethargic depression known as 'burnout,'" Adam Paul Weisman would write in *The New Republic*. By 1985 the number of high school seniors who believed marijuana was harmful would reach 70 percent, a striking reversal in less than a decade. "Just say no" was on everybody's lips. The Grandmaster Flash and Melle Mel 1984 rap song "White Lines—Don't Do It" earned a gold record. The National Basketball Association contract began to demand that athletes be drug-free.

Borrowing a phrase from the writer Tom Wolfe, conservatives such as William Kristol and his boss William Bennett would celebrate the Reagan administration for encouraging "The Great Relearning." "In areas ranging from drugs to family values to economics to foreign policy," Kristol wrote, "this Administration has stood for and encouraged a 'relearning' of certain fundamental truths that this Nation had forgotten or drifted away from in recent years."

Despite these successes, the drug crisis took on new and more terrifying dimensions in the mid-1980s with the crack epidemic. First imported from the Bahamas in 1983, crack cocaine, a highly addictive drug that was smoked, not snorted, spread in the ghettos, then to the suburbs, among America's estimated five million regular cocaine users. The surge in demand as well as the surge in energy that users experienced fed a crime wave—the New York Police Department blamed crack for an 18 percent jump in robberies in 1986 alone; officers confiscated forty-five thousand crack pipes in one month. *Newsweek* warned: "The police are losing the war against crack, and the war is turning the ghettos of major cities into something like a domestic Vietnam."

The drug's low price and high cachet made crack an eighties' fad. The kids hired to help sell the drug "are living a *Miami Vice* fantasy," one detective reported dejectedly, "heavy gold chains, $200 sweat suits, 500 SEC Mercedeses, and $160 Porsche sunglasses. Their aspiration is to be a successful supplier with a string of drug concessions and a string of condos."

As the 1986 congressional elections approached, Reagan's advisers searched for ways to regain the political initiative. In the spring of 1986, the antidrug crusade emerged as Reagan's vehicle for salvation. The war on drugs was popular, patriotic, moralistic, and inexpensive at a time when the president's budget-cutting was discredited by David Stockman's naysaying and the burgeoning budget deficit. Reagan's rhetorical war on narcotics allowed Reagan to act in the tradition of the heroic presidents—Lincoln, Kennedy, the two Roosevelts—without violating his vows and expanding government.

Liberal critics dismissed the antidrug crusade as one more public relations ploy. Charging hypocrisy, they judged Reagan by the amount of money he allocated and the number of programs he initiated. The federal budget for drug prevention had dropped by 5 percent. And even after the law enforcement budget doubled, the amount of cocaine crossing the border quintupled, with crack rampaging through America's cities despite all this talk.

Clashing worldviews lay behind the conflicting policy prescriptions. Democrats wavered between a medical model assuming "the drive to intoxication is irrepressible, unstoppable . . . function[ing] almost like hunger and sex," and a sociological model blaming poverty and oppression. Conservatives, on the other hand, worried about the "crisis of authority" behind the drug epidemic and the breakdown of family structure and moral values. Richard Cowan in the *National Review* blamed the divorce epidemic, working parents, and "the neuroses of a generation" always seeking "self-fulfillment . . . if the good life consists of a succession of personal highs, who can blame the temporarily unthrilled for getting a little chemical help?"

This national sobering up about drugs resonated with a remarkable grassroots campaign to stigmatize drinking and driving. Two drunk-driving tragedies, one in 1979 in Maryland, and one a year later across the country, led to the founding of Mothers Against Drunk Drivers in a Sacramento steakhouse in 1980. In 1984 MADD softened its name, becoming Mothers Against Drunk Driving. These activists deployed a wide-ranging arsenal. The Barnes Act forced all states to raise the drinking age to twenty-one. A 1983 made-for-TV movie, *The Candy Lightner Story*, lionized the heartbroken mother who lost her thirteen-year-old daughter to a perennial drunk driver, then founded the organization. A 1986 "red ribbon" campaign urged people to "tie them on" to protest drinking and driving. By 2004, with more than three million members and supporters, MADD, "the largest crime victims' assistance organization in the world" could point to a 43 percent drop in alcohol-related traffic deaths, from 28,100 in 1980 to 15,794 in 1999. Moreover, polls showed Americans' new distaste for drunk driving, as the MADD-driven concept of the "designated driver" became a staple of popular culture and thus socially acceptable.

The Reagans' impact on drug usage, while considerable, did not solve the problem. Comprising less than 5 percent of the world's population, Americans still consumed 60 percent of the world's supply of illegal drugs. Nevertheless, the Reagans had altered American attitudes. "Drug bashing has become the latest rage—a kind of national pastime," one CBS-TV correspondent declared in mid-August 1986. The campaign most influenced middle- and upper-middle-class youth who indulged in marijuana and powdered cocaine, not crack or heroin. In 1987 cocaine use among high school seniors dropped by one-third to its lowest level since 1978. Daily use of marijuana among seniors plunged from one in nine in 1979 to one in thirty in 1987. Administration officials proudly listed the drop in drugs and the sea change in attitudes as among the highlights of "The Reagan Record."

The Bork War and the Showdown over the Judiciary

Just as he saw the drug war as part of his broader assault on the 1960s, Reagan saw his attempt to restock the federal judiciary as a solution to the integrated problems of drugs, crimes, and permissiveness. Like so many Reagan initiatives, the drug war succeeded symbolically more than substantively, changing the tone but not solving the problem. Reagan's ambitious approach to the judiciary was both symbolically and substantively successful. Many would agree—either happily or unhappily—that one of the Reagan administration's most "enduring" legacies would be "in the judiciary."

In the Reagan demonology, "liberal judges" threatened common sense as well as the social order. Reagan loved recalling a California case involving two narcotics officers with a valid search warrant. They were about to leave a drug pusher's home empty-handed when one of-

ficer approached a sleeping baby, "removed its diapers," and found the
heroin. Reagan would pause, crooking his neck and shaking his head
ever so slightly, his wonder checking his outrage, as he added: "The
case was thrown out of the court because the baby hadn't given its permission to be searched."

By 1987 Reagan's time was limited, his power ebbing. The Senate
had easily confirmed his first two Supreme Court appointees, Justice
Sandra Day O'Connor and Justice Antonin Scalia. His elevation of Justice William Rehnquist to the position of chief justice ran into more
resistance in 1986. Nevertheless, the Senate confirmed the choice, 65 to
33. When Justice Lewis Powell retired that June, even though Reagan
had lost the Senate to Democrats, the conventional wisdom predicted
a tough battle with an eventual victory.

Reagan's choice, Robert Bork, had impeccable credentials: teaching
stints at Yale Law School, positions with blue-chip law firms, experience as solicitor general and as a judge for the United States Court of
Appeals for the District of Columbia. Bork was a heroic figure to conservatives, an erudite and eloquent critic of the trend toward legal activism and a believer in relying on the Founders' "original intent."
More comfortable relying on state legislators than unelected federal
judges, Bork freely denounced the 1973 prochoice decision, *Roe v.
Wade,* as "unconstitutional . . . a serious and wholly unjustifiable judicial usurpation of state legislative authority." "We really touched a
nerve in the ultra-liberal community," Reagan crowed to Charlton
Heston.

Facing a now-Democratic Senate, Bork was saddled by what became known as a problematic "paper trail." He had opposed the 1964
Civil Rights Act. He had a small but distasteful part in Watergate, having fired Special Prosecutor Archibald Cox during the "Saturday Night
Massacre" of October 1973—at the insistence of the two officials who
did quit,"to ensure continuity in the Department." Nevertheless, the
press pilloried Bork as Nixon's henchman.

Just as Bork was not ready to play the PR game in the shark-infested
Nixonian 1970s, he was not ready for the soundbite and photo-op
driven Reaganesque 1980s. Despite having served in the marine corps
reserve, this tall, lumbering intellectual, with a wispy beard political

consultants wished he would shave, lacked Ollie North's populist touch. Besides, he abhorred this spectacle which he believed was sullying the once apolitical confirmation process.

Senate Edward Kennedy would set the template for the attacks with a vicious denunciation placing Robert Bork on the wrong side of the culture wars. In what became a classic political rant, Kennedy declared: "Robert Bork's America is a land in which women would be forced into back-alley abortions, blacks would sit at segregated lunch counters, rogue police could break down citizens' doors in midnight raids, schoolchildren could not be taught about evolution, writers and artists would be censored at the whim o[f] government, and the doors of Federal courts would be shut on the fingers of millions of citizens for whom the judiciary is often the only protector of individual rights that are the heart of our democracy." Adding to that devastating caricature, the Ohio Democrat Howard Metzenbaum charged that Bork approved the forced sterilization of women workers—a grotesque oversimplification of a complicated worker's health and safety case, where Bork ruled unanimously with other judges on a technicality.

When he defended Bork, the president agreed that the choice offered "two conflicting visions of America." But Reagan's defense was uncharacteristically flaccid. White House strategists rehashed their perennial tug of war over Reagan. Sometimes the Bork campaign was clear, conservative, and combative; other times, it was ambiguous, ambivalent, and accommodating. The administration briefing book presented a moderate, intellectually stimulating scholar rather than a bomb-throwing provocateur. This political mismanagement allowed the North Carolina Democrat Terry Sanford to justify opposing Bork because "he does not stick with his views."

Bork would gain the unhappy distinction of having his last name become a verb. After years of being outmaneuvered, a coalition of unions and liberal activists mounted a simplistic, demagogic, populist, fifteen-million-dollar Reaganesque campaign against Reagan's nominee. One swing senator, the Republican Arlen Specter, received 750,000 items of mail and over 50,000 telephone calls. With private investigators snooping around Bork's video store, only to discover his weakness for Fred Astaire flicks, the good judge was "Borked."

Typically, Reagan was outraged but not repentant, as sure of his opponents' "shenanigans" and their "disgraceful distortion of fact" as he was of his virtue. "I promise you he'll be as conservative as Judge Bork," Reagan told George Murphy while seeking a new nominee. "There is no way I'd go for a touch of liberalism to win over the lynch mob. We'll see if they have the nerve to repeat their scandalous performance."

As with the Battle over Stanford, the Great Books showdown, the censorship wars, the fight over feminism, and the crusade on drugs, the Bork Battle was another skirmish in a war, as Bork said, for "control of our general culture." Touching core identity issues, fed by an increasingly loud and ugly political culture, the battles often turned rancorous. When these cultural issues would be linked with high-stakes partisan fights over political leaders, and fueled by the ever-escalating rhetoric of broadcasters and politicians, what Bill Clinton called "the politics of personal destruction" would result—with the collaboration of both parties and damage to the entire political system.

Partisans also recognized the 1988 presidential campaign's opening salvos. While supervising Bork's confirmation process, the chairman of the Senate Judiciary Committee, Joe Biden, saw his nomination effort collapse amid charges that he plagiarized parts of speeches and exaggerated his law school record. And nine days after Reagan nominated another conservative replacement for Bork, Judge Douglas Ginsburg of the DC court, the politics of disclosure buried the nominee. Ginsburg had smoked marijuana a bit too publicly as a young Harvard faculty member—offering his own syncretic version of conservative yuppie libertinism. After Gary Hart's withdrawal from the presidential race in the spring, due to his dalliance with Donna Rice, and after Biden's withdrawal, Ginsburg had no choice but to withdraw—but not before the controversy triggered some preemptive admissions from other presidential candidates about youthful marijuana indulgence.

This overlap made sense because the 1988 campaign offered yet another round of the culture wars. In July Michael Dukakis, the Democratic nominee, was looking like the easy victor against George Bush. Yet Bush would devastate Dukakis with a campaign setting Bush up as "one of us" and Dukakis as "one of them"—suggesting that, perhaps, the feelings of alienation the Stanford protesters and their allies experienced were more than ideological constructs or figments of their imaginations.

"Henpecked, Manipulated, and Oblivious": Reagan Fades

As his vice president muscled his way into the White House, President Reagan sometimes appeared to be fading. The impression of the president as what *The New Republic* called "henpecked, manipulated, and oblivious" deepened in 1988, as a series of books came out describing a genial but disengaged leader. The blurring of lines between politics and entertainment, which had benefited Reagan so often, now backfired. Publishers offered huge advances to members of the president's official family, and his real family, to expose the White House's inner workings. When such books succeeded, big sales resulted, generated by author interviews on morning news shows, book excerpts in *Time* or *Newsweek,* the inevitable White House reaction, and stories in newspapers and on TV about the controversial part of the book the publisher peddled. In 1986 David Stockman's look at the inside story of the Reagan Revolution—starring a "sentimental" and ineffectual president— topped the *New York Times* best-seller lists for over three months.

After seven years in power, a host of ambitious authors with juicy tidbits were ready to score. In his final two years, Reagan would endure Michael Reagan's account of how his parents neglected him and a youth worker sexually abused him, former Press Secretary Larry Speakes' admission that he made up presidential quotations, and Michael Deaver's portrait of a shrewd First Lady protecting her weak husband from ideologues and critics. The most damaging revelations, however, came in May 1988, when Donald Regan's *For the Record* blamed a San Francisco astrologer for the strange schedule changes the meddlesome First Lady imposed on the hapless president.

Donald Regan's revenge was sweet. *Newsweek* excerpted his book, which became a best-seller. With jokes about "the dipper," Reagan risked becoming a laughingstock. "Astrology is entirely consonant with Reaganism," the *Nation* sneered. Submitting to zodiac charts was as foolish

In 1984, as he coasted to a reelection victory, Ronald Reagan had every right to feel pleased with himself. His easy, Marlboro Man masculinity, his unapologetic faith in America, and his commitment toward a stronger American foreign policy helped restore American confidence. But his pragmatic presidential campaign missed an opportunity to shape an ideological mandate, thereby undermining the second-term agenda. (Ronald Reagan Presidential Library)

One of the great strengths of the first term was the "troika," the formidable administrative threesome of the PR whiz Michael Deaver, the patrician Republican Chief of Staff James A. Baker III, and the conservative ideologue Edwin Meese. In one of the great mistakes of the second term, Baker and Secretary of the Treasury Donald Regan (far right) swapped jobs. Regan was a terrible choice, too temperamental and too egotistical. (Ronald Reagan Presidential Library)

Unfortunately, Reagan's America remained plagued by too much poverty, crime, racism, and misery. When four young blacks menaced Bernhard Goetz on the New York City subway, Goetz, who had been mugged before, shot them. Some hailed the subway vigilante, even as others denounced him, guaranteeing a legal and media circus, eighties-style. (© Bettmann/CORBIS/MAGMA)

Perhaps the greatest consumer uprising of the period occurred when Coca-Cola introduced a new recipe. Many rebelled, sensing an assault on the flag, on Reagan country, on the American people. Thanks to these enraged activists, many of them stalwarts of Reagan's revolution, the company retreated. (© Philip Amdal)

In the era of Ronald Reagan's Celebrity Presidency and Bill Cosby's multicultural America, Ronald and Nancy Reagan's real marriage seemed to conjure up an unrealistic 1950s' ideal (Ronald Reagan Presidential Library), while Cliff and Claire Huxtable's fictional marriage, for all its artificial happy endings, seemed to capture a reality of black progress that the raging headlines often ignored. (© Gene Trindl/MPTV)

In America's image-soaked, headline-driven culture, extremes often dominated. Sylvester Stallone's hypermasculine Vietnam Vet, John J. Rambo, became the avenging angel projected by America's battered psyche, cinematically exorcising the ghost of Vietnam—and sometimes giving the Celebrity President governing cues. At the same time, Madonna and another pop star, Cyndi Lauper, improvised a unique clashing mishmash bag lady look combining frilly femininity with raw sexuality, evoking 1950s' traditionalism while furthering the 1960s' sexual revolution. (© Neal Preston/CORBIS/MAGMA)

Calvin Klein and Ralph Lauren were two missionaries of the new American materialism, wrapping Americans in fabrics and fragrances that seemed to convey status and shape individual identities. Calvin Klein also helped inject a gay sensibility into American popular culture. Turning underwear into a hot commodity, the photographer Bruce Weber made the buff Olympic pole vaulter, Tom Hintinaus, one of the decade's most popular pinups—for women and men.
(© Bettmann / CORBIS / MAGMA)

Just as Calvin Klein epitomized the good middle-class kid's desire to be bad and sample the pleasures of post-1960s' America, Ralph Lauren epitomized the aspiring middle-class kid's desire to be accepted in the upper echelons of America's theoretically class-free society. "Polo" expressed his immigrant-kid-from-the-Bronx aspirations, bringing "a little cachet . . . Glamorous, international, and playboyish."
(© GETTY IMAGES)

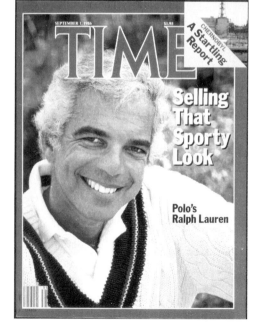

The era fed the stereotype of the high-flying, lavish-living Wall Street mogul buying, selling, merging, greenmailing—balanced by the Wall Street millionaire doing the "perp walk" and the little guys devastated by the 1987 stock market crash. Above, Ivan Boesky leaves court after pleading guilty to insider trading. (© Bettmann/CORBIS/MAGMA) And, as this commuter returned home in October 1987, Americans feared the good times had ended. (© James Marshall/CORBIS/MAGMA).

Ronald Reagan's foreign policy was not always as surefooted as Rambo would have liked. America's entry into Lebanon yielded many American casualties due to terrorism and a half-hearted American response. (Above, Ronald Reagan Presidential Library) Later, the Iran-Contra scheme derailed the Reagan presidency. (Below, Ronald Reagan Presidential Library) A grim President Reagan, flanked by former senators John Tower and Edmund Muskie, accepts the conclusions of their Iran-Contra investigation. "A few months ago I told the American people I did not trade arms for hostages," Reagan would say. "My heart and my best intentions still tell me that's true, but the facts and the evidence tell me it is not."

The culture wars pitted the post-1960s' values revolution against Reagan's conservative traditional-ism. At Stanford University and other elite schools, the forces of multiculturalism led by the Rev-erend Jesse Jackson (top, left, (© Roger Ressmeyer/CORBIS/MAGMA), among others, questioned the centrality of Western civilization in the curriculum. Others, including Reagan's Secretary of Education William Bennett (top, right, Ronald Reagan Presidential Library) defended traditional Western values. Reagan spread his values by filling the federal judiciary with dozens of young conservatives; however, the Senate rejected Robert Bork's nomination to the Supreme Court, reflecting Reagan's waning political strength following the Iran-Contra scandal and the unstable stock market. (Ronald Reagan Presidential Library)

Ronald Reagan was able to end his term triumphantly, and the decade positively, thanks to a most unlikely source, the Soviet leader Mikhail Gorbachev. Gorbachev's reforms allowed Reagan, then George Bush, to claim victory in the cold war and sell a package of peace and prosperity to historians, who have been quarreling about it ever since. In December 1988, a month after George Bush's election to succeed Reagan, the vice president and the president hosted Secretary-General Gorbachev on Governor's Island in New York's harbor. This meeting hoped to presage a new era of peaceful coexistence in a prosperous and Reaganized America. (Ronald Reagan Presidential Library)

as believing that tinkering with the "imaginary free market" by subsidizing the needy or housing the homeless "is to tinker with an inspired mechanism and court disaster."

Aware that millions of Americans consulted their horoscopes daily in over two thousand newspapers, and unwilling to tempt fate, the president hedged when asked at his first news conference in months if he believed in astrology. "I've not tied my life by it, but I won't answer the question the other way because I don't know enough about it to say . . . is there something to it or not." Reagan's fatalism, his sense that human beings are not responsible for their bad luck, suggested a faith in the mechanistic universe of astrology. Reagan insisted that "No policy or decision in my mind has ever been influenced by astrology," an artful response that did not deny his wife's use of the charts. Nancy Reagan said the trauma of the assassination attempt sent her to astrologers for guidance. The Reagans were once again revealing their connection with millions of simple Americans and the gap between many readers and most reporters, who disdained such superstitions.

Such down-home, all-American populism kept Ronald Reagan popular, despite two years of folly. The affection stemmed from some of the same qualities that attracted derision, especially his "averageness," his Truman-like abilities to connect with the millions of Americans who read the daily horoscope, watched the nightly news, and still believed in the American dream. For eight years, Ronald and Nancy Reagan lorded over America's popular culture, even when the president's political standing began to slip.

The "Teflon" Reagan's critics feared was manufactured in Washington and sold on TV and at supermarket checkout stands. Just as reporters tried to fold the day's story into a larger narrative about American society, Reagan successfully upstaged political ups and downs by focusing on the larger narrative. Reagan's advisers could not control the daily stories, but they could control "the visuals" that illustrated their larger point or their "theme of the day." And situated against a dramatic backdrop from the Normandy coast to the Demilitarized Zone between North and South Korea, Michael Deaver recalled, "Ronald Reagan did more than star. He glowed."

Sixty million people watched the Reagans' appearance on Barbara Walters' 1986 pre–Academy Awards show, while barely a million people read the *New York Times* daily. The steady stream of stories and television appearances illustrating the president in command and America resurgent, drowned out minutiae about Nancy Reagan's squabbles with Patti and Michael, the president's failure to control Oliver North, the looming budget deficit, the bitter culture wars. The message about "Morning in America" was generated by the Reagan team and confirmed on the media, day and night, in the upbeat sets on the morning television shows, in the glamorous afternoon soap operas, and in prime-time shows like *The Cosby Show*. The success of the fictional Huxtables proved Ronald Reagan was right, and was more influential than any journalists' sniping. Even sleazy hits like *Dallas* and *Dynasty* helped perpetuate the illusion of prosperity so central to Reagan's success. The Reagans' metapresidency, celebrating America's return and the Reagans' ascendance, dwarfed any other political story.

Reagan's continuing popularity amid political disaster reaffirmed his and his aides' faith in their formula for sidestepping political conflict. During his nomination fight, when Reagan's aides suggested that the judge and his wife appear on Barbara Walters, Robert Bork recalls that the strategists "were so insistent and unanimous in their opinion that we agreed to think about it overnight"—and then refused. Later, the advisers told Bork that refusing to appear in such forums "cost me confirmation."

Ronald Reagan felt satisfied. No president since Dwight Eisenhower had lasted so long in the White House or left on such good terms. "The warmest memories of our life" were "in that beautiful historic mansion," Reagan would write. In his Farewell Address, Reagan identified "two great triumphs . . . the economic recovery, in which the people of America created—and filled—19 million new jobs. The other is the recovery of our morale. America is respected again in the world and looked to for leadership." Rather than speaking about the "Reagan Revolution," Reagan celebrated "the great rediscovery, a rediscovery of our values and our common sense."

1989

Kennebunkport, Maine

The Bush Restoration: Kinder, Gentler, but Still Reaganite

Once you begin
a great movement, there's no telling where it will end. We
meant to change a nation, and instead, we changed a world.
RONALD REAGAN, FAREWELL ADDRESS, JANUARY 1989

It was a surprisingly intimate photograph of a usually reserved couple. The vice president of the United States was in his pajamas. His matronly wife was in a bathrobe, her signature pearls nowhere in sight. The two sat propped up in their king-sized bed in a sun-drenched, oversized bedroom with a majestic view of Maine's craggy coast. Ignoring the paisley drapes and the built-in bookshelves, six young grandchildren scurried about, transforming the scene from one of imperial prerogative to "family values," to use a phrase that would be overused during his presidency.

A year later, in August 1988, the Republican nominee gathered his five children, ten grandchildren, four daughters-in-law, and one son-in-law for their annual summer festival of barbecuing, boating, tennis-playing, horseshoe-throwing, and jogging. Posing for a rambling family photo at Kennebunkport framed by Maine's blue skies and blue-green sea, the Bushes became poster-children for the "three F's"— "Faith, Family, and Friendship." Marvin Bush, 32, explained: "Without those three elements in your life, you can be awfully lonely or you might turn to some things that you shouldn't."

The Bush family was working toward another Reagan triumph. George Bush's victory would vindicate Ronald Reagan after the second term's vicissitudes. With the president limited to two terms, getting your vice president elected was the political equivalent of securing a third term.

To succeed Ronald Reagan, George Bush had to borrow some moves from the master's playbook. As the vacation compound photographs conveyed, Bush understood he was auditioning to be America's father figure. Alas, to achieve his goal, Bush would have to violate some of the values he hoped to epitomize, trumpeting his sense of reserve, marketing his old-fashioned values via modern means, throwing an elbow or two, articulating a communal vision that fostered individualism, combating American decadence while indulging it. Bush would also have to embrace Reagan while striking out independently. He would fulfill Reagan's vision by appearing to be the "real" Ronald Reagan—a rooted, churchgoing WASP, not an arriviste Hollywood celebrity; a war hero, not a celluloid soldier; a businessman, not an actor; the long-married head of a warm, famously cohesive family, not the once-divorced head of a feuding, infamously dysfunctional crew. George Bush's walking advertisement for a WASP restoration continued Reagan's crusade for a moral renaissance while distancing the seemingly loyal vice president from his still popular, but somewhat flagging, commander-in-chief.

While embracing Reaganism, George Bush also disdained it. Especially as president, Bush would deemphasize rhetoric, ideology, and visionary leadership. Unlike his predecessor, who in 1980 conjured up a mandate, Bush would shrink from the term. "Well, I don't know whether I want to use the word *mandate*," Bush would say, the day after being elected. One senior Bush aide would lament that "the movie actor's White House was the one that was hospitable to new ideas. Not the Yalie's."

Bush's call for a "kinder, gentler nation" kindly, gently, chided his boss. Bush began his administration repudiating 1960s' permissiveness and 1980s' greed. This was the lesson he drew from his withering campaign against Michael Dukakis. Eight years of Reaganism had bruised liberalism. Bush used the term "liberal" as an epithet, effectively, if demagogically. But the materialism and excess Reaganism had come to represent made many Americans uncomfortable. Even as they worshiped ever more intensely in the cult of consumerism, even as they pursued the big score ever more vigorously, Americans still found money-grubbing and shopping-round-the-clock vaguely disreputable—as evidenced by the envious disdain for "yuppies." In one revealing end-of-decade poll, majorities perceived that yuppies, stockbrokers, and using drugs were "losing favor" among their peers, while the paradoxical package of "parents spending more time with children," "being concerned about the less fortunate," "putting one's career first," and "having only the best quality things," were all "gaining favor."

This ambivalence shaped the stereotypical WASP's approach to life. WASPs feared enjoying the luxuries they craved. WASPs also disliked hyping achievements they nevertheless wanted appreciated. Aided by his popular, no-nonsense wife Barbara, George Bush sought to resurrect the code of conduct his generation had inherited. But, as with much of the Reagan restoration, Bush's WASP restoration was more rhetorical than real. America had changed too dramatically. George Bush would fail to soothe America's troubled domestic waters. The identity crisis would continue.

The culture wars would intensify. Many treated Bush's WASP values as relics to be mocked or applauded, not emulated. The ethical revival Bush sought remained elusive. In politicizing morality, especially during the 1988 campaign, as Ronald Reagan and William Bennett had done, Bush unintentionally helped squelch America's "moral voice." Treating morality like a conservative possession—and obsession—relativized ethics, triggering the tolerance of the many and the intolerance of the few. Too many liberals began to recoil at any public discussion of morality; too many conservatives celebrated the moral life without actually living it; and too many Americans escaped the passions and the complexity into a pasty, "centrist," ethical nonpartisanship, championing only one, new, commandment: "Thou Shalt Not Judge."

George Herbert Walker Bush was more comfortable embodying morality than crusading for it. Raised for stewardship more than leadership, he knew where he stood, not where America was heading—or where he wanted to take it. Bush, however, was able to reap the benefits from what Ronald Reagan and the other cold war presidents had sown for four decades. Bush was presiding in 1989 when Soviet Communism collapsed, solidifying the Republican claim on what was a bipartisan achievement. With the Reaganesque forces of consumerism and individualism mixing with more traditionally democratic forces of equality and liberty, "free markets and free speech" triumphed together that seemingly miraculous year. In his Farewell Address, Ronald Reagan praised this "great rediscovery" of so many countries in the 1980s "that, lo and behold, the moral way of government is the practical way of government: Democracy, the profoundly good, is also the profoundly productive." As dissident Chinese students in Tiananmen Square waved plastic Statues of Liberty, as Mikhail Gorbachev watched Soviet vassal states break free, it did seem that Ronald Reagan had done something right. In fact, much of the Western world seemed to be undergoing a Reagan restoration, to one degree or another.

Family Values—and Real Estate Values—in the 1980s

His family's eleven-acre ancestral vacation compound in Kennebunkport, Maine, rooted George Bush in his don't-rock-the-boat approach to life, while offering an appropriate platform for his celebration of tradition. The inaugural address would distinguish Bush from Reagan, sifting enduring WASP values from superficial new ones. Bush celebrated "a new breeze" blowing in America and reminded citizens "we are not the sum of our possessions." Rejecting modern consumer values, Bush yearned for Puritan producer values. "The old ideas are new again because they're not old, they are timeless," he said, defining them as "duty, sacrifice, commitment, and a patriotism that finds its expression in taking part and pitching in."

Members of Bush's clan, who also cherished those ideals, had been vacationing at this coastal gem since the 1880s. Bush's maternal grandfather George Herbert Walker purchased the land for twenty thousand dollars in 1902 and began building vacation houses on what became known as Walker's Point. Bush's mother was born there and still owned a house, The Bungalow, on the point, as did some cousins. George

Bush bought the sprawling seven-bedroom, seven-bathroom stone-and-shingle main "cottage," Surf Ledge, for a reported eight hundred thousand dollars in 1980. Kennebunkport is where "I am really me," Bush said in 1988. "This is home. This is where I am not frantic. This is base and politics be damned," Bush insisted, although his voting address was a Houston hotel, and when convenient he called himself a Texan. Bush had a Nixonian tendency to repeat himself when uttering a half-truth.

The aides, reporters, Secret Service agents, and gawkers surrounding George Bush, politician, threatened the serenity of George Bush, human being, and his neighbors. In fairness, even without the Bush entourage, permanent residents worried about maintaining the integrity and intimacy of village life, especially while sustaining a summer influx that could swell the population to 35,000. Kennebunkport—and the New England region—reflected many of the tensions building after eight years of Reaganism. The village and the region had boomed, prospering while enduring social dislocation and ideological stress. Kennebunkport's population grew by a thousand people to 4,200, perhaps the most explosive growth spurt since being incorporated in 1653.

By 1989 New Englanders were beginning to suffer the costs of recession while still paying the price of prosperity. New England had enjoyed a great decade, with the "Massachusetts Miracle" setting the standard. Three of the five states leading the nation in income growth were in New England—Massachusetts, Connecticut, and New Hampshire. The other two were also in the Northeast—New York and New Jersey. With its many universities, its rich intellectual and cultural life, New England naturally attracted the boom's economic heroes—high-tech workers, financial services experts, defense contractors, doctors, and lawyers. In 1989 more young workers holding college degrees lived in Massachusetts than in any other state. Computer companies flourishing along Boston's beltway, Route 128, gave New England its own Silicon Valley. The "sick industries" of the 1980s had little impact on the New England economy. Oil never was a regional mainstay, and northeastern farms and factories had already sustained transforming losses in the 1970s. Even the boom was better distributed in New

England. In Massachusetts, high school graduates' average income rose 14 percent, as nationally the average income fell by 6 percent.

Evidence of the boom abounded. Having turned seedy in the seventies, Harvard Square in Cambridge went yuppie in the 1980s. Downtown Boston, once the dowager of American cities with weathered, humanly scaled buildings, had a makeover, as glitzy downtown developments updated, Trumpified, and homogenized its look.

Fueled by high demand and easy money, commercial and residential real estate soared—from 1985 to 1989 the percentage of real estate loans in Massachusetts' commercial banks' portfolios jumped from 29 percent to 44 percent. From 1981 to 1988 the median selling price of a single-family home in Boston averaged a 126 percent increase, with nearby Providence averaging a 161 percent increase (while an oil-based economy like Houston experienced a 15 percent drop). In the cities, gleaming chrome and glass towers redefined the skyline. In the suburbs, sprawling malls and enlarged residences sprouted. And in rural areas, more and more individuals built bigger and bigger vacation homes. The prosperity increased the demand for housing square footage, while the divorce epidemic and the breakdown of extended families multiplied the number of households. The "same number of New Englanders are consuming more and more of the landscape," said James McKellar, director of MIT's Center for Real Estate Development.

Other cities' populations boomed along with the economy. Nashua, New Hampshire, grew 17.3 percent, going from a sleepy rural town to a regional shopping and commercial center. Lowell, Massachusetts, grew nearly 12 percent, giving new life to an old symbol of New England's traditional textile economy. More than one hundred stores and factory outlets opened up in Freeport, Maine, the preppie Mecca, the home of L.L. Bean, as well as in other charming rustic towns now thriving as shopping destinations and outlet heavens. Eager to cash in on "the gold rush," decaying towns made grandiose plans. The town burghers of Quincy, Massachusetts, floated Marina Bay, a four-hundred-million-dollar development, with 300 hotel rooms and hundreds of upscale condominiums; working- class Hull envisioned a project with 270 townhouses.

Fallout from the boom abounded too. As housing values soared, so did property taxes. Both trends pressured long-time residents with limited incomes. Working-class Italians in Boston's rapidly gentrifying North End were dazzled by the dollars developers offered to abandon their traditional enclave, while the denizens of Kennebunkport and other rural communities often sought refuge from crushing property tax bills in smaller houses or mobile homes.

As people poured from the cities during the week into the country for weekends, traffic clogged the streets, pollution clouded the air, developers ravaged the forests, and seepage from overflowing septic tanks fouled the sea. Moreover, many of the new condo-dwellers brought urban anonymity to the quaint New England villages whose community values were supposed to be part of their charm. "Nobody bothers to get acquainted," one local complained. "They don't stop in. Quechee isn't the friendly place it used to be."

Activists mobilized against growth. Eighty percent of Martha's Vineyard's residents feared more development would destroy the community's quality of life. In Rhode Island in November 1987, 80 percent of voters endorsed a $65 million bond issue to preserve open spaces. "New England," said Robert L. Bendick Jr., Rhode Island director of environmental management, "is losing its soul."

Of course, these congested communities were the lucky ones. Many missed the boom—and resented that the riches eluded them. In 1989 one congressional study would estimate that from 1979 to 1987 the standard of living for the poorest fifth fell by 9 percent, as the top fifth's standard of living jumped 19 percent.

In Massachusetts, 40 percent of young families headed by women remained mired in poverty. In 1989, 30 percent of black families and 48 percent of Hispanic families were impoverished. Crime spread, and more families disintegrated under the haze of the crack craze. Shocked by the minimal impact low unemployment and rising government aid had on these blighted areas, many liberals and conservatives sadly agreed with the Boston Globe that "Poverty is a much more intractable problem than we ever imagined."

By Bush's inauguration in January 1989, many once-prospering communities were suffering. The inevitable economic slowdown reverberated more than it should have because so many individuals and institutions were overextended. In the 1980s household debt jumped to three trillion dollars, while nonfinancial corporate indebtedness more than doubled to two trillion. When salaries plateaued, jobs dried up, loans came due, and some spectacular collapses ensued. Banks inherited—and desperately sought to unload —risky, highly leveraged condominium complexes in Quincy, Hull, and elsewhere.

Of the nine states suffering the largest jumps in problematic real estate loans in 1989, six were in New England. Those mom-and-pop mortgage houses, which expanded exponentially once Reagan and Congress deregulated the Savings and Loan industry, were not limited to Texas and Arizona. One New England collapse would add three hundred million dollars to the government's bill for bailing out these federally insured institutions, with predictions that the ultimate cost to the American taxpayer could reach two hundred billion.

Even more solid, diversified banks were reeling. Earnings for the Bank of Boston, New England's largest bank, dropped 78 percent in 1989, with a third-quarter loss of $125 million. The Bank of New England, which expanded wildly in the 1980s, lost over $1 billion in 1989 and desperately sought to raise money by selling off $6 billion in now undervalued properties. "I suppose they thought it could happen to dumb Texans, but not happen to wise, conservative Yankees," said L. William Seidman, the Federal Deposit Insurance Corporation chairman. "Poor management shows up when the economy goes bad." Here, then, was the Bush worst-case scenario: Americans suffering financially even after having sacrificed their souls.

Bushwhacked: The Dukakis Debacle

The economic fears intensified the more generalized anxiety, a dynamic that also had shaped the 1988 campaign. Updating the culture wars, Bush campaigned to resurrect the values he feared lost during the go-getting eighties. "We don't need radical new directions," he said when launching his campaign. "We need strong and steady leadership. We don't need to remake society, we just need to remember who we are."

Yet, to win, George Bush had to forget some of his principles. American politics had become exceedingly personal. While combating opponents, he and his wife had to expose themselves in public to the kind of scrutiny they usually avoided in private.

Campaign aides struggled to counteract the effects of George Bush's breeding. His eighty-six-year-old mother still reprimanded him: "You're talking about yourself too much, George." Thus, Bush hesitated to use most politicians' favorite word, "I." When Bush lost Iowa to Pat Robertson and began battling Bob Dole in New Hampshire, the speechwriter Peggy Noonan noticed that "the I-ectomies ended."

The 1988 Republican National Convention illustrated George Bush's cultural vision. Bush paraded as an exemplar of the World War II generation—war hero, suburban father, businessman, and public servant— a man of missions accomplished, duties fulfilled, standards upheld, "values we honor and the principles we hold dear." Reminiscing, Bush proclaimed, "we weren't saints, but we lived by standards. We celebrated the individual but we weren't self-centered. We were practical, but we didn't live only for material things. We believed in getting ahead, but blind ambition wasn't our way." Bush envisioned a "kinder, gentler nation," filled with "old-fashioned common sense" and clear roles that was neither as statist as the Great Society nor as heartless as the Reagan Revolution.

Bush wanted to stay on the high road, but he quickly became the campaign mudslinger to beat Michael Dukakis, the governor of Massachusetts and symbol of the "Massachusetts Miracle." Bush visited an American flag factory to prove his patriotism and refused to say the "L-word," thereby treating his rival's liberal beliefs as a schoolboy would treat a girl with "cooties." Attacking the program that furloughed a convicted murderer, Willie Horton, who then raped a woman, proved particularly effective—and ugly. "It's a wonderful mix of liberalism and a big black rapist," one Republican would confess. Bush reached for his boss's macho mantle by saying that while Clint Eastwood and Ronald Reagan confronted criminals saying, "Go ahead: Make my day," Dukakis said, "Go ahead: Have a nice weekend."

Bush rationalized his tactics by blaming the opposition. Dogged by what he offhandedly called "the vision thing," the demand for bold Reaganesque rhetoric, Bush found his "vision" by demonizing Dukakis.

As Bush embraced what he called "the Norman Rockwell vision of America—the vision of kids and dogs and apple pie and flags on parade," he marginalized and demonized Dukakis and the Democrats.

The Democratic National Convention, held in Atlanta in July, gave George Bush retroactive justification for a decision he had made weeks before. In the keynote, the Texas state treasurer, Ann Richards, declared class war. The white-haired grandmother derided Bush's insensitivity to the poor, gibing: "Poor George. He can't help it. He was born with a silver foot in his mouth!" Senator Edward Kennedy mocked Bush's evasions of responsibility for Iran-Contra and other debacles, leading thousands of sneering Democrats to shout: "Where was George?" Another Texas Democrat, Agriculture Commissioner Jim Hightower, satirized "George Herbert Walker Bush, II" as "perpetually preppie . . . a toothache of a man . . . who was born on third base and thinks he's hit a triple." Playing the populist card, demonstrating Democrats' and Republicans' diverging perceptions, Hightower linked the 1980s to the 1930s, charging that, like Reagan and Bush, "Coolidge and Hoover had allowed the economic elite of their days to plunder the economy and plunge America into depression." Hightower viewed politics as a "top-down" struggle between "the wealthy few who seek to secure their own privileges and the rest of us"—a position echoing Andrew Jackson, and the historian George M. Bancroft's progressive vision of perpetual conflict between "the house of Have" and "the house of Want."

Three months later, Bush was still seething. When asked during the presidential debates in October why both Jimmy Carter and Richard Nixon found this campaign so nasty, Bush referred to the Democratic convention, asking "Do you remember the senator from Boston chanting out there and the ridicule factor from that lady from Texas that was on there; I mean, come on, this was just outrageous."

The Democratic convention rhetoric offered warning signals to each party, which each ignored. The Democrats' fury, invoking the Great Depression itself, reflected the intensity of the opposition to Reagan and the chasm in perceptions between Republicans and Democrats. This vehemence explained just how alienated opponents felt, be they in ghettos or on campus, be they Texas populists or Massachusetts pro-

gressives. The rhetoric also suggested that once the inevitable downturn came, liberals would feel vindicated. The 1988 convention
rhetoric anticipated headlines such as the *Boston Globe* pronouncement
two years later: "LIVING IN THE SHADOWS OF THE 1980's; THE ERA'S EX-
CESSES SET THE STAGE FOR THE MISERY THAT FOLLOWED."

At the same time, the ovations resounding throughout Atlanta's
Omni Coliseum inured Democrats to the risks of their rhetoric. By
painting the Reagan years in such stark terms, they risked losing the
millions of Americans who were only mildly displeased or actually
were comfortable. The extreme rhetoric made it easier for Bush to
paint Dukakis and his supporters as "out of the mainstream." As a
result, on election day, Ronald Reagan's groundwork helped elect
George Bush—Bush captured 81 percent of the conservative vote, while
Dukakis captured 82 percent of the liberal vote, and they split the
moderates. Thanks to Reagan, 33 percent of voters identified themselves as "conservative" and only 18 percent called themselves "liberal,"
even though 37 percent called themselves "Democrat" and 35 percent
identified as Republicans.

In this, Bush benefited from his rival's incompetence. Nursing his
hurts, convinced of his righteousness, Bush mocked Dukakis's politics
and his identity. Yet even when Bush branded Dukakis "a traditional
liberal, a progressive liberal Democrat," Dukakis simply whined: "let's
stop labeling each other." This tepid response accepted the term "liberal" as a pejorative, a label Dukakis himself disliked and dodged.

To George Bush, choosing a president was a matter of values. As he
said in his compulsively social way, voting for president is like deciding
who "you'd like to have sitting across from you at the dinner table." In
1988 George Bush paraded around as America's ideal dining companion, warm, witty, and dedicated to family values, even while acting like
a boor.

Bush sensed he had gone too far. He implicitly apologized for his
demagoguery. "The American people are wonderful when it comes to
understanding when a campaign ends and the work of business begins," he said. Shifting from campaigning to governing, Bush preferred
to be remembered for his "kinder, gentler America" and his call for a
"thousand points of light," rather than his "Willie Horton" tactics.

A Bush Renaissance?

In his Farewell Address, Reagan called for an "informed patriotism" and for "re-institutionalize[d] values." His dysfunctional family, radical individualism, and blatant materialism made Reagan a flawed preacher, although his parables captured Americans' yearning for such moral certitude. This values issue, echoing the culture war, gave George Bush the footing he needed at the start of his presidency. Bush would seek to develop a "moral voice," but ultimately a sensibility could not substitute for the lack of a vision or compelling domestic policies.

As president, George Bush struggled with the same dilemma that immobilized him as vice president: how to assert an independent identity while still benefitting from association with Ronald Reagan. As vice president, Bush deferred to the president so completely as to risk being eclipsed. As president, Bush overcompensated. Even as he genuflected toward his predecessor's policies, George Bush and his wife demonstrated that the Bushes of Houston and Kennebunkport were more authentic, more engaged, more democratic than the Reagans of Hollywood.

While it is not surprising that the Bushes would disdain the *nouveau riche* Reagans, it is surprising that Americans would find the Bushes' blue-blood ways more palatable. Inevitably, the complimentary adjectives heaped on the Bushes disparaged the Reagans. "Ronald Reagan evoked a Norman Rockwell domesticity," *Newsweek* reported, "but he didn't live it."

Having been ridiculed as an out-of-touch "preppie" when campaigning, George Bush was now being feted as a well-bred WASP, born to lead and to set the moral example America needed. *Newsweek* bestowed the highest compliment by concluding that "The Bush clan has all the makings of a dynasty—a WASPy, Republican version of the Kennedys." Bush was offering a real restoration, a return to enduring values and appropriate leadership. Ronald Reagan could only act like a leader; George Herbert Walker Bush was a natural. The previous decades' democratic dislocations fed a yearning for Bush's noble leadership. In 1964 the critic of "the Protestant Establishment," E. Digby Baltzell, argued that an upper class could remain dominant in a mobile, meritocratic society only by being "representative of the composition of society as whole." A quarter of a century later, Baltzell mourned an America lacking "parental, class, or religious authority." He concluded: "While social justice has definitely improved, social order and communal authority have just as definitely declined." The Harvard sociologist David Riesman now warned of an "egocentrism" unleashed, with "public approval" granted to blatantly "self-serving conduct."

Especially amid this crisis, "Poppy" Bush and his tennis-playing, Brooks Brothers–clad, country club family seemed more suited to the White House than Hollywood celebrities or Georgia peanut farmers. The conservative writer Richard Brookhiser would write that "The WASP character is the American character. It is the mold, the template, the archetype." Brookhiser would claim that Bush had been elected to solve America's problems by bringing "WASP virtues to bear on them."

George Bush's five children, ten grandchildren, and the 250 relatives attending his inauguration testified to this communal hope. The Bushes had the kind of family, and family values, the self-involved Reagans could only parrot. In the White House, Ronald Reagan's former exercise room became a spare bedroom for the grandchildren. Nancy Reagan's in-house hair salon became Millie the dog's room.

Still hazy on the details of his domestic program, Bush took refuge in drawing contrasts between himself and his old boss, posing as an engaged chief executive. A "National Ethics Week" distanced the Bush administration from the ethical cesspool the press had made the Reagan administration out to be, and the new president's overbooked schedule and "hyper" style suggested that George Bush would never try to claim ignorance about his aides' actions. "I am less interested in image than in getting things done," he would say, offering one of many subtle digs at his predecessor.

The Bushies harbored "generalized social contempt" for the Reaganites, one Bush aide admitted. In the clash of the blue blazered, khaki pants set, Bush's well-bred, patrician Republicans disdained Reagan's tiresome, *arriviste* ideologues obsessed, the insider John Podhoretz wrote, with "Star Wars, Nicaragua, abortion, Bork."

Early in the administration, a Knight-Ridder article said that Bush's aides "have been trashing the Gipper for being ill-informed, lazy and detached." "Hoping to make their man look good at Reagan's expense, they point out how hard Bush works, how knowledgeable he is on issues and how much he hates being managed by his staff." Richard Nixon read the article and fired off a note to Bush's chief of staff John Sununu, suggesting the staff be more discreet. Bush then called Reagan to apologize.

Despite this apology, Bush's Mr. Nice Guy strategy helped him overcome the bad feelings lingering from the 1988 election campaign at the cost of Reagan's popularity. The Bushes' shabby gentility suggested that Americans had merely tolerated the Reagans' glamorous imperiousness. By June 1991 one Democratic pollster would conclude that the president had "benefitted from the contrast with Reagan. He is more moderate. He isn't extreme, and everybody loves Barbara Bush as much as they hated Nancy Reagan." While "everybody" had not "hated Nancy Reagan" when she was First Lady, Americans quickly forgot her strong poll ratings during the Reagan years.

Bush soon discovered that distancing himself from Reagan pleased the press but alienated conservative supporters. Like an overambitious son blindly seizing the reins of a family business, George Bush did away with some of the most successful elements of Reaganism simply to make his mark. Gone were the rhetorical appeals, the broad vision, the guiding principles. Lacking a clear policy agenda, anxious for public approval and positive press stories, Bush would spend much of his presidency buffetted between conservative ideologues on his right and media critics on his left. Trying to please both without the resolute bottom line Ronald Reagan had, George Bush zigzagged, conveying the impression of an aimless leader and a rudderless administration. The result was chaos within the White House and a blurred image outside.

The Gorby Conundrum: Greet with Skepticism or Euphoria?

All too often in the Reagan era, hype, spin, and perception ran three steps ahead of reality; the public had to catch up with what the Washington insiders were thinking, and wanted people to think. That gap between truth and public relations helped explain the two clashing, often mutually exclusive narratives the Republicans and the Democrats embraced. Nowhere was this clearer than in the Rashomon-like debate over the prosperity of the Reagan years. Republicans talked about the longest peacetime expansion in history; Democrats saw another Great Depression. Republicans celebrated new jobs and higher wages; Democrats saw the rich getting richer and the poor getting poorer. Republicans pointed to lower inflation, lower interest rates, and booming markets; Democrats worried about an extravagant credit-card binge fueling a temporary surge by mortgaging the future for as much as two hundred billion dollars a year. Strangely, with what might be considered the Reagan years' greatest triumph—the end of the cold war—the opposite was often true. Reality and public perception often ran three steps ahead of insider and "expert" opinion. This pattern emerged in the Reagan years and continued during that whirlwind year of 1989, George Bush's first year in office, when the paradigm that controlled international relations for half a century crumbled, along with the Berlin Wall, Soviet hegemony over Eastern Europe, and, in some ways, Soviet Communism itself.

While Ronald Reagan's defense buildup, including Star Wars, hastened the collapse of Soviet Communism, it was one of many factors. The less imposing trees in the Eastern European Communist forest were as beset by internal termites as the towering Soviet oak itself. Some freedom activists such as the Soviet scientist Andrei Sakharov, the Soviet Jewish human rights dissident Anatoly Sharansky, the Polish Solidarity labor leader Lech Walesa, and the Czech writer Vaclav Havel became prominent in the West as well as in the East. They worked with a heroic cast of thousands who demanded freedom of speech and religion, freedom to emigrate and prosper. These were stubborn idealists, Jews and Pentecostals, artists and engineers, writers and scientists,

East Germans and Poles, Russians and Hungarians. They learned, as Sharansky did, that the authorities could not "fragment" freedom to dole it out arbitrarily, and that "only he who understands his own identity and has already become a free person can work effectively for the human rights of others." These sometimes frail individuals would prove more powerful than the massive Soviet state. They were not dancing to Ronald Reagan's tune. They and Reagan were simply bopping to the same eternal, irrepressible beat.

In hindsight, and to the superficial contemporary observer, the Soviet implosion—and the love affair with "Gorby"—progressed smoothly. When Reagan visited Moscow in late May 1988, the world witnessed what the historian John Lewis Gaddis would call "the unusual sight of a Soviet general secretary and an American president strolling amiably through Red Square, greeting tourists and bouncing babies in front of Lenin's tomb, while their respective military aides—each carrying the codes needed to launch nuclear missiles at each other's territory—stood discreetly in the background." Reagan mastered the symbolism of the summit, hosting an elaborate "freedom" banquet for Soviet dissidents, human rights activists, Jewish refuseniks, and oppressed Pentecostals; lecturing at Moscow State University with a bust of Vladimir Lenin looming in the background about the blessings of political and economic freedom, or strolling in Moscow and meeting Soviet citizens. *U.S. News & World Report* noted the irony that "The passionate anti-Communist who coined the term 'evil empire' in 1983 now says the U.S. should help Gorbachev, partly because he is 'different than any Russian leader I've met before.' (He is the only one Reagan has met.)" Conservatives worried: "Is Reagan turning soft?" The answer, administration officials insisted, was that "Ronald Reagan hasn't changed, the Soviets have changed."

Six months later, President Reagan and President-elect Bush hosted Gorbachev at Governors Island in New York Harbor. Speaking to the United Nations, Gorbachev admitted that "Today, the preservation of any kind of 'closed' society is impossible." He then unilaterally reduced Soviet forces by half a million soldiers and ten thousand tanks. The defining photograph of this summit showed the three superpower stalwarts standing together against a stunning backdrop of lower Manhattan, with the World Trade Center's twin towers looming behind them. This image of the Communist leader cradled in the bosom of eighties' capitalism represented the miracle of the times—blessedly unaware of the terrorist challenges looming ahead.

Nevertheless, Reagan was surprisingly cautious about the Soviet Union in his Farewell Address. Reagan seemed to be positioning as much for "plausible deniability" in case relations cooled as for bragging rights in case the cold war ended. Peggy Noonan feared that an earlier draft making Reagan sound "like a cheerleader for Gobrachev" was "fawning" and "unseemly from an American President." Qualifying his description of improved relations with his ritual condemnation, Reagan said: "Nothing is less free than pure Communism, and yet we have, the past few years, forged a satisfying new closeness with the Soviet Union. I've been asked if this isn't a gamble, and my answer is no because we're basing our actions not on words but deeds." Preempting the historians and the opponents who would mock his opposition to past negotiations, he added: "The détente of the 1970s was based not on actions but promises." As proof, Reagan pointed to the "internal democratic reforms" and the start of the Soviet "withdrawal from Afghanistan." Still, his one related anecdote noted that when Muscovites greeted him and Nancy so warmly on Arbat Street, KGB agents fearing the friendly crowd began "pushing and shoving the people." This incident "reminded" Reagan that "while the man on the street in the Soviet Union yearns for peace, the government is Communist . . . and that means we and they view such issues as freedom and human rights very differently." Reagan did wish President Gorbachev "well" while reiterating his favorite formula: "trust but verify." By contrast, at Bush's inauguration, a more ebullient Reagan declared "the cold war is over."

In the Bush White House, the dynamic changed. Reagan offset his tendency toward celebratory bombast with his instinctive anti-Communism. With Bush, an instinct for secrecy and caution combined with a WASPish fear of gloating. As a result, while Reagan often spoke in bold colors that sometimes clashed, Bush often risked verging on the incoherent with overlapping shades of gray. His own Secretary of State James Baker would agree that the administration's initial "strategic review" of foreign policy was "neither truly strategic nor a proper review" and resulted in "mush."

Henry Kissinger's warnings from the December 1987 summit sobered Bush and his foreign policy team, which was more centrist than Reagan's crew, and filled with Kissinger protégés. After hobnobbing with Gorby during the Washington summit, Kissinger published a four-thousand-word essay in *Newsweek* warning against being dazzled by the "euphoria." Protecting the prerogatives of the foreign policy establishment, Kissinger cautioned about indulging "transitory personalities." Ignoring Reagan's pacifist and radical streaks, Kissinger declared himself shocked that "This most conservative of postwar presidents seemed bent on ending his term by dismantling the concepts and practices that have shaped Western strategy for four decades." Kissinger feared that this new "arms-control 'process'" could "leave the United States with no meaningful nuclear option whatsoever"—indeed the dream that both Reagan and Gorbachev shared.

More than a year later, Kissinger's associate Brent Scowcroft, Bush's new national security adviser, remained disturbed by "The Reagan administration's willingness to declare an end to the cold war" so hastily, neglecting the geostrategic implications. Scowcroft feared the "old men of the Politburo" hired Gorbachev to "revitalize" Communism, not end it, making "Gorbachev potentially more dangerous than his predecessors," who, with their knack for overreaching, had always "saved the West from the dangers of its own wishful thinking about the Soviet Union."

Scowcroft insisted "The cold war is not over" on *This Week with David Brinkley,* two days after Bush's inauguration. Reviving one of the Vietnam era's infamous metaphors, Scowcroft could see a "light at the end of the tunnel." He wondered "whether the light is the sun or an incoming locomotive."

President Bush was more confused and less coherent. "Did we see what was coming when we entered office?" he would ask in his memoirs. "No, we did not. . . . The world we encountered in January 1989 was the familiar bipolar one of the superpower rivalry, if no longer of total confrontation." The president wanted a "very deliberate" foreign policy: "encouraging, guiding, and managing change without provoking backlash and crackdown." But when he was asked whether the cold war had ended, the president rambled: "so I—but if the—in the—I want to try to avoid words like cold war. . . . But if he—if it's used in the context of—Do we still have problems? Are there still uncertainties? Are we still unsure of—in our precisions on—on Soviet intentions? I'd have to say, yes, yes we should be cautious."

Unlike his bold predecessor, George Bush felt duty-bound by the political equivalent of the Hippocratic oath: "First, do no harm." Month by month, in that magical year of 1989, as the unthinkable became commonplace, headlines emerged suggesting that euphoria and clarity were the logical responses, rather than suspicion, indecision, caution, and confusion. A half-century's worth of assumptions disappeared as Soviets voted and worshiped in churches, while Poles, Czechs, and Hungarians repudiated decades of totalitarianism to embrace democracy and freedom. Gennadi I. Gerasimov, the spokesman from the once forbidding Soviet Foreign Ministry, joked that the Brezhnev doctrine justifying military intervention to maintain Communist regimes among the Soviet satellites had become the "Frank Sinatra Doctrine," wherein each satellite said, "I do it my way."

Naturally competitive, and deeply suspicious, the Bush team discounted many of the great strides of this freedom spring as Gorbachev's plays for European public affection. The Bushies stewed as Gorbachev announced that he was cutting off funds to the Sandinistas in Nicaragua—with no preconditions; Solidarity made its gains in Poland; Hungarians rushed toward voting down Communism; Czechs welcomed the exiled Alexander Dubcek and began launching the dissident playwright Vaclav Havel from prison to the presidency. "I'll be darned if Mr. Gorbachev should dominate world public opinion forever," the president bristled in a letter to His Royal Highness Sadruddin Aga Khan in March 1989. "His system has failed and it's democracy that's on the march."

Reagan and Gorbachev often vied for the spotlight in a friendly competition between two superstars. Bush, tongue-tied and wary, was outgunned. In June prodemocracy demonstrations in Tiananmen Square erupted after Gorbachev visited China. When the Communist government crushed the protests and the powerful image of the lone student facing a Chinese tank flashed around the world, Bush blinked. "I think this perhaps is a time for caution," the president counseled.

Five months later, on November 9, the Berlin Wall fell. With the East German Communist regime smoldering and Rumania next to go, Bush remained skittish. Maintaining his parents' strictures against gloating, he also hoped that somehow the Soviets might not notice the great changes and roll out the tanks. "Well, I wouldn't want to say this kind of development makes things move—be moving—too quickly at all—the kind of development that we would—we have long encouraged," Bush told reporters. Rather plaintively he said, "We are not trying to give anybody a hard time." "You don't seem elated," a reporter challenged. "I'm elated," the president replied, "I'm just not an emotional kind of guy." "Well, how elated are you?" the reporter probed. "Oh, I'm very pleased and I've been very pleased with a lot of other developments." Echoing Kissinger, even at this late date, Secretary of Defense Richard Cheney warned: "We must not be euphoric." The journalist Sidney Blumenthal, contrasting the incumbent president with the post–World War II foreign policy guru Dean Acheson who was "present at the creation" of the cold war, quipped that Bush and his gang were "absent at the creation" of the post–cold war world.

The story of the collapse of Communism, however, was too big to be diminished by the Bushies' narrow vision. Even though the president gave the American public no victory parade, no stirring words, he could always say that the cold war ended on his watch—and subsequently justify his reticence by saying he was an anchor during a time of great instability. So even without presidential cheerleading, Americans rejoiced in the great victory over Communism—and both the Reagan and Bush legacies would benefit from the association. Even some critics admitted that in blaming Reagan for debacles in Washington, they implicitly granted him responsibility for successes. As such, the diplomatic historian John Lewis Gaddis would write that "Ronald Reagan deserves a great deal of the credit as well" as Gorbachev, for ending the cold war peacefully. Reagan's strategic success, Gaddis concludes, suggests that "sometimes simple-mindedness wins out, especially if it occurs in high places."

1989: A Decade's Denouement

While Bush's prig-at-the-party stance regarding the revolutions of 1989 could not douse the optimism buoying Europe, it did feed a "party's over" mentality domestically. Even during this first year of a new president's term, Bush's narrow vision helped fit 1989 into the artificial decade mold as the wrapup year, a year reflecting back over Reagan's reign rather than "looking forward" to a new era—despite that phrase being the title of Bush's campaign biography. It was a year when a judge dismissed the key elements in Oliver North's indictment on a technicality, Michael Milken was finally indicted, Leona Helmsley was sentenced to four months in jail for income tax evasion, Bernhard Goetz was sentenced to a year in jail for possessing an unlicensed gun, and the hapless Jim Bakker was sentenced to forty-five years in prison for PTL chicanery and fined five hundred thousand dollars. It was a year when the *Exxon Valdez* spilled eleven million gallons of toxic crude oil off the Alaska coast, raising environmental anxiety and inviting some second thoughts about Ronald Reagan's approach to the nation's atmosphere. It was a year of relentless headlines about a procurement scandal at the often overlooked but well-funded Department of Housing and Urban Development. It was a year when the sixteen-ton AIDS quilt continued to grow, incrementally, tragically, measuring sixty miles across and counting, each of its nine thousand panels representing one victim, even as miraculous headlines announced "STRONG EVIDENCE DISCOVERED THAT AZT HOLDS OFF AIDS." It was a year when worries about crime and racial conflict continued to upstage the miracles of daily life in modern America, as the barbaric story of the "Central Park Jogger" allegedly gang-raped by a pack of young brutes "wilding," and the tragic tale of Yusuf Hawkins, a young black man murdered by a turf-oriented posse of neighborhood whites in Brooklyn, continued to color New York City—and modern America—as a paradise lost.

The Bush administration continued the debate Reagan, Stockman, and company had triggered about budget deficits and the welfare state, about tax burdens on the middle class and moral responsibilities to the poor. Bush's presidency would founder on his violating his 1988 "Read my lips: no new taxes" pledge in 1990. Typically, the focus remained on the superficial political battles bubbling up in the Congress rather than the underlying structural issues changing the nature of the American economy.

Cleveland continued to reflect these transformations and illustrated both the strengths and the weaknesses of the Reagan economy. The balance had shifted. Cleveland's had become a service economy, with manufacturing providing only 27 percent of the local jobs in 1987, as opposed to 47 percent of the jobs two decades earlier. There were jobs aplenty, but at lower wages. Parts of Cleveland remained blighted by crime and drugs, with one federal official lamenting that seventeen thousand Clevelanders were living in the nation's "second-worst public housing." And yet, offering a characteristic 1980s' hologram, the city center was booming. Gleaming new glass towers housing Fortune 500 companies scraped the sky; massive new shopping malls emerged, including one of many upscale "Gallerias" dotting the nation; Cleveland's decaying Union Terminal and its once-rotting riverfront were "yuppified," undergoing multimillion-dollar transformations into Union Station–style "mixed-use" playgrounds for adults with disposable income. Cleveland's mayor for ten years George Voinovich celebrated these triumphs while downplaying the continuing troubles. Healing his city from the contentious Dennis Kucinich days, and echoing Reagan, Mayor Voinovich often said, "I don't like to make war. I like to make love."

Clearly, *Dynasty,* which finished its run in 1989, and *Hill Street Blues,* which ended in 1987, continued to represent two conflicting poles in modern America. Crime had begun to level off and even dip in the first half of the decade; unfortunately the crack epidemic, tripling the number of cocaine users from 1986 to 1989, revived the violent crime rate. More than 20,000 people were murdered annually in the United States. Crack played a role in 38 percent of the 1,867 murders occurring in New York City in 1988. President Bush unveiled a $1.2 billion crime package in May and dispatched William Bennett from the curriculum wars to the drug wars. But fear gripped too many streets, and pessimism reigned in too many inner cities. "When we're talking about the flow of drugs and guns into our city, no city has enough police to stop that," Boston's Mayor Raymond J. Flynn despaired.

Meanwhile, in their gated communities or behind double-locked doors, the baby boomers continued the great reconciliation between the sixties and the eighties, seeking to encase new lifestyles within traditional frameworks. In a trend *The Big Chill* anticipated, the stereotypically single career women began marrying and nesting, triggering an infertility crisis. By 1989 the number of married women in their early thirties expecting to have children some day soared from 33.5 percent to 54.4 percent. In the movie the hostess (Glenn Close) sent her husband (Kevin Kline) to spend the night with her perpetually single best friend (Mary Kay Place), in the hopes of becoming a surrogate father, or at least a sperm donor—terms that were working their way into the national lexicon. In real life, the Baby M case riveted the nation, a case that ended in court when Mary Beth Whitehead, who had contracted to be a surrogate mother, decided she wanted to keep her baby. In 1989 Whitehead cashed in on her fifteen minutes of fame with *A Mother's Story*. Also in 1989, high achievers began debating the idea of a "mommy track," one of many improvisations developed in modern women's often frustrating quest to balance work and family.

As with every year in the 1980s, 1989 continued to witness a series of firsts, pioneers breaking various gender and racial boundaries. In Boston, amid cheers and jeers, the Reverend Barbara Clementine Harris became the first woman consecrated as a bishop in the Episcopal Church. In Washington, Colin Powell became the first black head of the Joint Chiefs of Staff. In Powell's case, only cheers were heard; the grumbling was more discreet. At the same time, the nation once again struggled with an ugly racial issue when a twenty-nine-year-old white Bostonian, Charles Stuart, murdered his pregnant wife but shot himself and blamed a black perpetrator, leading the Boston police to stop and search hundreds of young black males before uncovering the ruse.

While Ronald Reagan was often caricatured as being intellectually disengaged from all the complexities of modern America's teeming, diverse, dynamic, polyglot, George Bush would be satirized as being emotionally aloof. As a don't-rock-the-boat, hail-fellow-well-met, congenial politician rather than a conviction politician, Bush preferred to duck messy issues. In fairness, the times were often confusing. Bush was shocked to see his nominee for secretary of defense, John Tower, run into trouble on grounds of moral turpitude. Tower, a veteran senator and Washington fixer, faced the unprecedented and awkward prospect of appearing before the Senate committee on which he had served—and being rejected. Dogged by allegations of womanizing and drinking, Tower promised not to drink at all if confirmed, but he nevertheless failed. Leading Democrats were also swept up in scandals in 1989, as the Speaker of the House Jim Wright and his protégé Tony Coelho both resigned. Coelho had not properly reported a hundred-thousand-dollar investment in junk bonds. Wright circumvented strict House ethics rules on income limits and was caught. Aware of how much moral latitude his predecessors enjoyed, Wright denounced the "mindless cannibalism" of these feeding frenzies.

The Harvard political philosopher Michael Sandel would explain this growing obsession with "the private vices of public officials" as a weak stand-in for a "political agenda that addresses the moral dimension of public questions." Yet, amid all this apparent moralism, Congressman Barney Frank kept his seat despite the discovery in 1989 that his male lover had run a bisexual prostitution service from Frank's apartment. "You don't know from day to day what the rules are," John Buckley of the Republican National Committee sputtered.

The political confusion reflected the broader cultural confusion. Nothing seemed sacred anymore in a world where an already Reaganized court could refuse to impose a ban on flag burning. And yet baseball's legendary "Charlie Hustle," Pete Rose, was shocked to discover that a stack of hitting records could not protect him when he was caught gambling. Baseball banned Rose, even as many other athletes caught using drugs enjoyed quick rehabilitations. The catch-as-catch-can morality reflected the libertinism and moralism warring within Reagan's America. Reagan helped foster a toughening of standards—sometimes to extremes, especially if clear lines were drawn; and yet Reagan's nonjudgmental individualism encouraged polyglot America's growing tolerance and democratic diversity. Many Americans yearned for the simplicity of the clear Moral Majority moralisms; yet, having been thrust into complexity, many tolerated the messy realities and occasionally inconsistent judgments.

Reagan Reassessed—and Appreciated

George Bush's pinched, passive, cautious, status quo approach to governance emphasized the boldness in Ronald Reagan's brand of visionary pragmatism. Ironically, the conservative Reagan modeled himself on the great liberal president Franklin D. Roosevelt. In fact, in 1980 Reagan introduced himself as a "New Deal Democrat" and in his acceptance speech at the Republican National Convention quoted Roosevelt's first inaugural address. Reagan wanted to lure working-class, ethnic "Roosevelt Democrats" to the Republican Party. He wanted to rejuvenate national politics and restore American confidence, just as Roosevelt had. And Reagan, like Roosevelt, was more a man of instinct than of formal intellect. Both Roosevelt and Reagan could easily be dismissed—and praised—as men with second-class minds but first-class temperaments, raising important questions about just what makes a good president.

Contemporaries most frequently compared Reagan's media skills to Franklin Roosevelt's, his chairman of the board approach to Dwight Eisenhower's, his passivity to Calvin Coolidge's. They also should have added that Reagan had the geniality of a Warren Harding, the small-town common sense of a Harry Truman, the star power of a John Kennedy, and—perhaps most important of all—the focused agenda of a James Knox Polk. Andrew Jackson's Tennessee protégé entered the White House in 1845 with three objectives—settling the Oregon boundary dispute, reducing the tariff, and reestablishing the independent treasury system. By 1849 Polk had accomplished all three and had also presided over a great Mexican War victory. Similarly, Reagan took office with three goals: to lower taxes, reduce regulations, and boost defense— budget cutting was David Stockman's priority, not the president's.

It was a mistake to underestimate Reagan. True, he did not concentrate on many issues, but he remained deeply committed to a few core ideas and initiatives. Such an approach in the modern presidency was risky, and many miscues and oversights resulted. And yet Americans perceived Reagan to be consistently more popular and effective than he was. Recognizing the cultural dimension of Reagan's leadership helps explain the general impression of consistent success, and his relative insulation and quick recovery from fiascos such as the 1982 Reagan recession, the 1983 slaughter of marines in Lebanon, the 1986 Iran-Contra scandal, and the 1987 stock market crash. It is this Reaganesque cultural dimension to the modern presidency that also helps explain Bill Clinton's remarkable resilience during the Monica Lewinsky scandal a decade later.

Reagan's hands-off, CEO approach to the presidential office was sui generis. The contempt House Speaker Tip O'Neill and other opponents had for his approach along with his politics revealed just how unique it was. After four failed presidents, Reagan felt emboldened to try his way. Judging by the many nasty memoirs Reagan's own people produced, the decision unnerved Republicans as well as Democrats.

An antigovernment rebel now running the government, Reagan did not want to be a Rooseveltian liberal superhero. Nor was a Nixonian focus on detail for him. He was happy to delegate, and to take direction—he had always functioned as the spokesman, as the public face, the ideologue, not the master planner. Furthermore, as the oldest man ever elected president, he wanted to pace himself. These constraints clashed with Democrats' and journalists' conception of the president as the managerial superhero of American government. Reagan's focus on selling his program struck many as preferring showmanship to statesmanship; his delegation as abdication; his tailored focus as nearly criminal indifference. As his supporters rallied to elevate their hero's idiosyncratic management style into the new ideal, two approaches to thinking and governing clashed: the instinctive versus the rationalistic, the creative versus the systematic.

The Reagan-Bush Restoration: A Moral Hangover?

Like the Reagan restoration in general, the Bush restoration often appeared more successful stylistically than substantively, and far more sober than many would have expected. The Reagans' opulence had symbolized the new America of garish indulgence, slavery to fads, and planned obsolescence. Yet the Bush identity was an elaborate façade, offering an aristocratic illusion of populist accessibility. As with Reagan, the polls showed that Americans liked Bush and appreciated the tone he set, but rejected his policies. All the martinis sipped toasting WASP values, all the preppie sweaters sold, could not resurrect the 1950s. Bush's values-talk, like Reagan's, reassured some traditionalists, but the drift toward a society of self-indulgence continued. The 1990s would witness a flood of polemics from the Right and the Left bemoaning the new "culture of complaint," the "culture of disbelief," the fall of a "moral politics," all reflecting the "fraying of America." *Time's* Robert Hughes would lament this "broken polity . . . obsessed with therapies and filled with distrust of formal politics; skeptical of authority and prey to superstition; its political language corroded by fake pity and euphemism." In such a world, the whines of supposed victims drowned out the ideas of concerned citizens.

The social critic Neil Postman feared that in becoming addicted to show business and especially television, we were *Amusing Ourselves to Death*. The writer Aaron Latham surveyed the outposts of America's leisure world, dominating, standardizing, homogenizing, and vulgarizing the continent—"Fort McDonald's, Fort Burger King, Fort Wendy's, Fort Roy Rogers." He warned that in our "Age of Junk," America had become one undistinguished sprawling suburb of mass-produced hamburgers, mass-produced styles, mass-produced—and pathetically mediocre—dreams.

To these critics, cultural rot presaged political decay. As Americans became spoiled, in abandoning an expansive, responsible vision of citizenship, they soured on politics and debased government. The spate of books about *Why Americans Hate Politics* and *Why People Don't Trust Government* would confirm this seeming anomaly that the Reagan-Bush patriotic restoration nevertheless continued America's descent into a politics of selfishness, NIMBYism, backbiting, nonvoting, distrust, and an odd mix of shrill partisan rhetoric amid weakening party commitment en masse. Professor Amitai Etzioni, a leader from the moderate Left of a communitarian critique of Reaganite, hyper-individualistic liberalism, would link the waning of "a moral voice" with the rise of cynicism about politics and politicians. This growing sourness regarding politics and society also limited Americans' euphoria as they witnessed the previously unimaginable happy ending to the cold war.

Just as the collapse of Communism retroactively vindicated much of the Reagan-Bush foreign policy, the Bush recession, the 1992 Rodney King Los Angeles riots, and the continuing social strife tarnished the Reagan-Bush domestic legacy. Uncovering the feelings of guilt lying at the heart of American prosperity, the economic downturn and the social problems became the natural conclusion of the go-getting Reagan years. As Americans would discover in the 1990s, this dynamic was particularly dramatic during Republican periods of prosperity. Republican booms were perceived to be more materialistic than Democratic ones. But as the Clinton years would indicate, in the Republican years, having a Democratic opposition articulate an alternative vision moderated the excesses. When the Democrats became the party of prosperity, their dissent stilled and Republicans filled the vacuum with a moralism that alienated rather than a criticism of materialism that could have elevated the nation.

1990

Boston

First Night, New Decade: Why So Blue?

The era of big government is over.

PRESIDENT BILL CLINTON, STATE OF THE UNION ADDRESS, 1996

It had become a fitting metaphor for the media age. The last night of the year would start, typically, with friends and loved ones armed with party hats and tooters, crammed into a room festooned with streamers. Rather than watching their own clocks, or speaking to each other, as the magic hour approached, they would turn on the television set. At once, all eyes focused on the electron-filled box. Only after Guy Lombardo or Johnny Carson counted down and yelled "Happy New Year" would the kissing and champagne popping commence. Only after the New Year's TV show started things off could the actual parties continue.

In the days of Ronald Reagan's restoration, a new ritual was gaining popularity. First introduced in Boston in 1976, "First Night" was an alcohol-free, citywide, all-night culture-fest. Offering a constructive, communitarian alternative to the debauchery of Times Square and elsewhere, First Night would grow from a fringe festival of twenty-five-thousand "artsy" types hanging around Boston Common to an international ritual observed in more than two hundred cities and attracting as many as one million revellers in Boston alone. Suitably eclectic, First Night combined the community feeling of the 1950s, the grassroots counterculturalism of the 1960s, the free-to-be-you-and-me creativity of the 1970s, and the don't-drink-and-drive practical Puritanism masquerading as moralism of the 1980s. First Night was more old-fashioned than high-tech. It was wholesome. And it was kid-oriented—reflecting the long-delayed junior baby boom the baby boomers were beginning, with 1984 yielding the largest number of first births in American history, 1.5 million a year.

American, 1990: Reaganized but Anxious Too

That January 1, 1990, there was much evidence that the United States of America had been "Reaganized," both culturally and politically. Americans were responding to homey, simplistic, life-affirming parables in the bookstores and elsewhere. Robert Fulghum's *All I Really Need to Know I Learned in Kindergarten* and M. Scott Peck's *The Road Less Traveled* remained at the top of the best-seller list, after more than a year— Peck's book had been on the *New York Times* list for 323 weeks. Joseph Campbell's *The Power of Myth* had also emerged as a surprising blockbuster, appealing to a nation entranced by stories and story-tellers. Memoirs of the Reagan administration and the 1980s were proving popular, with both Nancy Reagan and Robert Bork counterattacking, and Michael Lewis offering harrowing tales from Wall Street's bond trading desks in *Liar's Poker*. Most striking—and, alas, most telling— was the surfeit of celebrities who had invaded the list: TV's Roseanne, nonagenarian vaudevillian George Burns—in both hardcover and paperback—basketball great Larry Bird, TV gourmet Julia Child, rock star Jimmy Buffet, Hollywood star Jimmy Stewart, and up-and-coming home décor queen Martha Stewart.

That television season, ABC's crude, white, working-class, feminist comedienne Roseanne Barr battled for primacy with NBC's elegant, African American, upper-middle-class, fatherly comedian Bill Cosby— both testaments to the ever-growing mishmash of identities modern Americans embraced. Along with CBS and ABC, NBC faced an alphabet soup of new competitors, including A & E, CNN, ESPN, HBO, LIFE, MTV, NICK, TBS, TMC, TNT, and USA. Before Christmas, all kinds of high-tech TV toys had flown off the shelves. With new technology projecting pictures larger than nineteen inches without distortion, home theater systems proved popular, despite costing three thousand dollars and more. Camcorders also flooded the market, what the *New York Times* deemed "video's finest gift from the '80s," and whose ubiquity inspired another top-ten TV hit, *America's Funniest Home Videos.*

Politically, the world had changed. Rumania was the latest Eastern European country to fall. Freed by the collapse of Communism, shucking off its post-Vietnam blues, the United States had invaded Panama to track down Manuel Noriega. At home, headlines about teetering Savings and Loan institutions and "SCIENCE, MATH BYPASSING MINORITIES" competed with news about New York City's first black mayor, David Dinkins, who took office on New Year's Day. "I can remember a time," Dinkins marveled, "when there were no African Americans in government"—now there were ten thousand black officeholders nationwide. In one of the world's richest cities, teeming with "masters of the universe," Dinkins faced the now-familiar, seemingly perennial problems of too much crime, too many poor people, and too little revenue, against an eroded city infrastructure ravaged by new blights such as AIDS, crack, and homelessness.

Nevertheless, Americans rang in the 1990s just as they welcomed the Bush presidency—happy with the peace, prosperity, and self-confidence that had been restored, but eager for a "kinder, gentler" decade. Most of the nation's pundits, who in the last decade had dominated the nation's consciousness and driven the national conversation in unprecedented ways, agreed. One after the other predicted that the eighties were over, that in the 1990s, the bills for the Reagan excesses would come due. They foresaw an age of belt-tightening, of greater modesty, of a more rigorous morality. Some seemed downright nostalgic for the days of Jimmy Carter.

The 1990s: What the Critics Feared the 1980s Would Be?

The predictions were wrong. In many ways, the eighties may have only really begun in the nineties, and the nineties became what critics had feared the eighties would be. With the Democratic opposition stilled—

because the Democrats in power were the party of prosperity—the society plunged headlong into an orgy of hedonism.

In fact, compared to Clinton's nineties, Reagan's eighties appeared more tempered, guilt-ridden, politically engaging, and equitable. The 1990s lacked even superficial signs of a vibrant political culture. There were no mass rallies similar to the 1982 antinuclear protest that drew seven hundred thousand to Central Park. There was no mass outcry about the homeless, who faded into the urban landscape. There were fewer stimulating polemics such as George Gilder's *Wealth and Poverty* or Allan Bloom's *The Closing of the American Mind.* The defining presidential scandal pivoted around Bill Clinton's domestic vices rather than Ronald Reagan's cowboy diplomacy.

In the 1980s Ronald Reagan made the pitch; by the 1990s more and more Americans made the sale. In 1998 the pollster Everett Carl Ladd deciphered the sentiments Bill Clinton's welfare reform and "big government is over" rhetoric addressed. Ladd noted that Americans did not necessarily believe "that *less* government is progress; it's that they have decidedly rejected the idea that *more* government is progress." Americans were "evenly divided" on this less-is-best idea throughout the Reagan years, Ladd noted. "But in the 1990s the balance has shifted decisively to the smaller government/fewer services option"—and consistently by 2–1 margins.

In the 1980s Americans from the Left and the Right still tried to resurrect the 1960s' communal ambition; in the 1990s Americans laughed at it. Even in the capital of self-righteous posturing, Hollywood, pink ribbons became passé and 1998's flaccid mass-protest song "Lean on Me" paled beside the rousing, star-studded 1980s' anthem, "We Are the World." The Reagan years' top sit-com, *The Bill Cosby Show,* was earnest and politically correct. It tempered its vision of wealth with a multiracial social conscience. *The* show of the 1990s, *Seinfeld,* was cynical and amoral; its monochromatic self-indulgent yuppies sneered at anyone with a social conscience or a political vision.

Similarly, in the 1990s, economic power became more concentrated as American culture splintered. Reporters, and especially Democrats, tended to emphasize that the income gap between rich and poor grew "under Reagan" and continued "in the 1990s," conveniently ignoring that the Democrat Bill Clinton presided over the latter surge, which dwarfed what occurred in the 1980s. The obsession with the income gap reflected deeper anxieties about corporate mergers and the shift from a GM-style, manufacturing-based economy to a Wal-Mart-style, service-based economy. As part of this broader trend economically, media conglomerates from Time-Warner to Disney gobbled up smaller outlets, corporatizing and centralizing media. In 1980 the Big Three networks still dominated, and the avuncular Walter Cronkite symbolized the easy power of CBS, ABC, NBC to set the national agenda. In the 1990s the Big Three were in retreat, competing with dozens of cable stations offering each subgroup its own niche—and an escape from national conversations or concerns. But in this cacophonous world of, as Bruce Springsteen sang, "57 Channels and nothin' on," the 24/7 media din grew louder, more ubiquitous. In the 1990s, big, multi-chapter stories could command public attention—the "OJ Trial" and the "Lewinsky Scandal" were the successors to the "Iranian Hostage Crisis"—but they had to be sensationalized to stand out from among the usual, relentless, chaotic, centrifugal chatter.

Much of the difference between the stimulating 1980s and the cynical 1990s rests on the two presidents who defined their respective eras. Ronald Reagan dominated the 1980s. His presidency galvanized the Right and the Left. Republicans mobilized to advance Reagan's revolution as Democrats resisted. Many laments about the greedy eighties were—and still are—camouflaged attacks against the popular president.

In the 1980s, beyond the shouting, an interesting and clarifying debate could be heard. Many conservatives learned to modulate their ideology with pragmatism. Meantime, some liberals learned to accept fiscal restraint and government rollbacks while championing "fairness." Alas, rather than galvanizing the nation's politics, stimulating discourse, and spawning new solutions, the Clinton wars simply polarized the nation's political players. This politics of personality alienated millions and produced little creative ferment. Politics had become a spectator sport, more interesting than golf, but not a "must-see" like the Super Bowl.

In the 1980s leftist scholars wondered, "Has America Lost Its Social Conscience—and How Will It Get It Back?" Yet even then, the liberal versus conservative combat kept alive social concerns. A decade later, narcotized by Clinton, corrupted by power, dazzled by the Dow, few Democrats even posed the question. With Democrats quiet and the economy booming, Republicans did not bother explaining or justifying their "trickle down" economics.

The Reagan Restoration

Yet, if the nineties was the decade of the ten-thousand-point Dow Jones, the decade of ten thousand creature comforts and self-delusions, of social disengagement and political narcolepsy, what, then can we say about the 1980s? In culture as in politics, in society as in government, it was an era of restoration. Exhausted by the political tumult of the 1960s, dispirited by the social chaos of the 1970s, Americans wanted to restore order, to resurrect the assurances of yesteryear. Reagan, with his traditionalist rhetoric, promised a return to the old regime, the old ways. Yet, as England's Charles II discovered during his seventeenth-century Restoration, the world had fundamentally changed. New ideas cannot be purged. The new leader was too pragmatic, too political, too accommodating to engage in a futile attempt to turn back the clock. As a result, Reagan led the country *Back to the Future,* as the popular movie series of the 1980s suggested.

The Cassandras of the 1980s erred so dramatically because their analyses were rooted in the "ought" more than the "is." This was one more attack against a caricature of Reaganism and the 1980s. There were indeed many problems to lament—Reagan and Reaganism did seem to encourage hard-heartedness, self-absorption, materialism, and a peculiar kind of self-righteous decadence. Millions felt disenfranchised—some because resources had been redirected from them and their communities, others because they felt ideologically orphaned. But most of the problems troubling America in the 1980s predated Reagan—and outlasted him. Ronald Reagan was not responsible for the massive governmental and social failures of the age, such as the crime wave, the drug epidemic, the scourge of racism, the persistence of poverty, the decay of public education, the poisoning of the environment, the proliferation of illegal immigration, the deterioration in family relations, the seeping away of community spirit, the gargantu-anism of government, the inscrutability of corporations, the feelings of insignificance burdening so many individuals, the seeming aimless-ness and randomness of modern life.

Similarly, such a litany could obscure the good that Reagan accom-plished, and the many miracles of the modern American polity. Every day, tens of millions of Americans functioned happily in the world's first and largest mass middle-class democracy. An elaborate transportation network moved people along thousands of roads and airline routes. An advanced communication system relayed masses of information at the flick of a phone, a fax, a PC. The basics of food, clothing, and shelter were available—at both very reasonable and unconscionably unreason-able prices—with the federal government monitoring food safety and providing food, clothing, and shelter for millions who could not provide for themselves. Rights had been expanded and continued to expand—to vote, to learn, to work in peace, to move beyond yesterday's racist and sexist paradigms. Old people had pensions, medical care, and dignity; young people had broad horizons teeming with possibility; while people of all ages had access to miraculous health care that was eradicating dis-ease, minimizing pain, and prolonging life.

The entertainment industry, for all its flaws, delivered affordable, ac-cessible diversions, which, along with the many pursuits of leisure, al-lowed most Americans to indulge, to enjoy, to laugh, to be entertained, in a way that only aristocrats could do centuries before. Some of Amer-ica's problems were also being addressed, with drug use and crime gradually slowing, and polluted air, rivers, and streams being cleaned, just like some urban areas were being reclaimed. Youngsters who had grown up in the 1970s assumed that institutions always crumbled; pub-lic spaces and safety always deteriorated. The 1980s forced a recalibra-tion of expectation, as all kinds of things actually improved. There was also a community-mindedness, an altruism, a goodness that was and remains characteristically American. This national idealism, along with our stable democratic government, our thirst for liberty, our genius for innovation, and our market-oriented economy, have kept this nation thriving, proud, and strong—not yet perfect, but always, energetically, striving.

Reagan was too much the populist crowd-pleaser to be the revolutionary. For all the liberal laments about Reagan's extremism, for all the conservative cries to "Let Reagan be Reagan"—in many ways when he was trimming, compromising, playing to the center; Ronald Reagan WAS being Ronald Reagan. To an old Hollywood lawyer friend familiar with his marathon negotiations both as president of the Screen Actors' Guild and as a contract player in the days of the big studio moguls, Reagan wrote: "You know, those people who thought being an actor was no proper training for this job were way off base. Everyday I find myself thankful for those long days at the negotiating table with Harry Cohen, Freeman, the brothers Warner et al." In 1983 the Reagan White House released a detailed document, "Ten Myths That Miss the Mark," denying that the Reagan administration was hostile to the poor, to blacks, to women, to environmentalists, to education. In short, addicted to polls, trying to remain popular, Reagan and his aides embraced the key revolutions of the last few decades they were supposedly seeking to repel.

As a master salesman, and as a consummate political warrior with a remarkably light touch, Reagan was more effective at stigmatizing liberalism than defeating it. Thanks to Reagan's devastating combination of quips, anecdotes, statistics, ideology, and bombast, by the 1988 campaign his more heavy-handed successor George Bush used "liberal" as an epithet, and the Democratic nominee Michael Dukakis hastily retreated from the term. "Liberal Nationalism," the Roosevelt-Kennedy-Johnson-King big idea, nation-building, liberalism did fall into disfavor. A new, more pinched, more self-oriented, rights-based liberalism developed instead. Yet the Democratic Speaker of the House Tip O'Neill was able to check the Reagan Revolution with the "fairness issue." Even in the 1980s Americans still had consciences to prick. Moreover, Reagan could not stem the tide of demands by individuals and special interest groups the 1960s unleashed. The language of "my rights" rather than the "nation's needs" drove Reagan-era liberalism, just as individual desires rather than communal constraints often drove Reagan-era conservatism. From the Left and the Right, on the two coasts or in the Midwest and South, Americans wanted government off their backs—except when it was convenient, or profitable.

Just as Ronald Reagan shaped America, the political realities of modern America shaped the Reagan administration. America's majoritarian instincts, the system's gravitational pulls toward the center and toward compromise, triumphed. And rather than being the fire-breathing conservative critics feared, Reagan emerged as a more mainstream type of leader, one who played to the center—and revitalized it. At the end of the day, in many ways he stayed within the New Deal–Great Society governing status quo, fine-tuning it more than destroying it. As a result, intentionally or not, he ended up legitimizing rather than repudiating much of the legacy of the 1960s and 1970s. Reagan's reign was one of restoration; it was one of reconciliation, more than revolution.

In many ways, with his odd mixture of tradition and modernism, idealism and materialism, nationalism and selfishness, moralism and libertinism, integrity and artifice, and, in foreign policy, aggression and appeasement, Ronald Reagan invented early twenty-first-century America as well as the 1980s. For starters, he could claim some bragging rights for shaping critical building blocks of our era, especially the fall of Soviet Communism, the resurgence of the American patriotic ideal, and the rise of image politics and prosperity economics. There are many things about modern America—and its recent past—that bear the mark of Reagan and the 1980s. The nineties' boomtown mentality and cult of the stock market; the post–September 11, flag-drenched mixture of sentimentality and patriotism; the unapologetic and overconfident imperial vision in Afghanistan and Iraq; the fear of the "L-word" and professed disdain for "big government" during Bill Clinton's Democratic reign as well both Bush administrations; the shameless fundraising, aggressive politicking, and flamboyant star turns of Bill Clinton and George W. Bush, best symbolized perhaps by Clinton's televised backstage amble onto the 2000 Democratic Convention podium and Bush's *Top Gun* landing, in full flight gear, aboard an aircraft carrier; the gussied-up business pages, detailed lifestyle tidbits, and expanded entertainment sections of any daily newspaper; the rhetoric of moral absolutism coexisting with tolerance of lifestyles once deemed deviant; the arch, postmodern cynicism and epidemic antiauthoritarianism; the rampant consumerism and celebrity worship; the money-making and money-wasting without guilt; even the division into blue and red, Gore's America and Bush's America, once Walter Mondale's America and Ronald Reagan's America.

When Ronald Reagan died, Reagan's supporters seized the opportunity to show what Reagan had wrought. With a week of saturation news coverage dominated by the Reagan alumni—older, grayer, rounder, but more devoted than ever—with most journalists holding their fire, the line of the week emphasized that we were now living in Ronald Reagan's world. The alumni eulogized Reagan as a revolutionary whose bold, all-American ideas transformed the world, then became standard. The only criticism of the "great unifier" mourners remembered underlined their hero's courageous, anti-Communist iconoclasm. Even though much of the myth-making rewrote history, most Americans did unite in 2004 to celebrate Reagan's civility, optimism, and idealism. Brimming with the pageantry he enjoyed, the aphorisms he coined, the ideas he embraced, the little acts of patriotism from the little people he loved, Reagan's mourning week provided a glorious, dramatic, happy ending to Reagan's biography—and his quest for national renewal.

The Reagan Reconciliation—and Redefinition

In the real presidency rather than in the legend, Reagan's centrism, his incrementalism, facilitated the Reagan reconciliation, where the sixties met the eighties culturally and politically. During this time, many of the rebels and the revolutions of the 1960s went mainstream. The eighties would be perceived as the time of the great sellout, when yippies turned yuppie, when the conservative backlash checked feminism, environmentalism, civil rights, and the sexual revolution. In fact, just as the New Deal only became mainstreamed in the 1950s, when Dwight Eisenhower did not undo most of Franklin Roosevelt's handiwork, Reagan's America reinforced many of the far-reaching ideological, cultural, social, and even stylistic transformations of the previous decades. Nevertheless, feminists yelled "backlash," even as women swarmed into the workplace; African Americans yelled "racism," even as a black middle class emerged; radicals yelled "sellout," even as a new cadre of "thirtysomething" executives made corporations more responsive and less monolithic, let alone more open to granola and jeans.

Subtly, gradually, the president facilitated a Reagan redefinition ideologically as well. While always being careful to pay homage to his first political hero, Franklin D. Roosevelt, Reagan often attacked the domestic dimension of what the historian Robert Dallek calls "liberal nationalism," a liberalism based on "a strong defense against external threats" and sweeping "programs that eased the problems of an advanced industrial society." "Today's conservative is, of course, the true liberal—in the classic meaning of the word," Reagan explained during his prepresidential years. "But it is today's so-called liberal who did the switch on these two words. He affixed the title conservative on those who opposed his affinity for centralized authority and a big government as the answer to all problems."

Reagan's championing of old-fashioned freedom and individualism appealed to many Americans feeling overburdened by government heavy-handedness. In Reagan's updated, more enlightened version of nineteenth-century Social Darwinism, material success became proof of America's liberating freedoms. This Reaganesque libertarianism and materialism, however, became particularly toxic when combined with 1960s' antiauthoritarianism and antitraditionalism. This resulting radical individualism helps explain the continuing social, moral, and communal crisis amid all the talk of national restoration. Reagan could conjure up warm, fuzzy national feelings, but his vision remained more individual than communal, ultimately more selfish than altruistic, more oriented toward the indulgences of today than the values of yesteryear.

Still, Reagan's vision did not quite transform Lyndon Johnson's Liberal Nationalism into Libertarian Nationalism. Despite his belief that "government is not the solution, government is the problem," Reagan was not as Jeffersonian as he liked to think he was. He remained too tied both to the social conservatives who wished to use government to inhibit certain behaviors and to the big government realities of what Reagan himself called the "social safety net." Similarly, Reagan was too moralistic, at least rhetorically, to accept a Libertine Nationalism. "I am deeply concerned with the wave of hedonism—the humanist

philosophy so prevalent today," Reagan had complained before becoming president, "and believe this nation must have a spiritual rebirth, a rededication to the moral precepts which guide us for so much
of our past, and have such a rebirth very soon."

At the same time, Reagan was not preaching a conventional conservatism. Conservatives had long lists of programs they hated, innovations
they feared, movements they abhorred. Caught by their instinctive disdain for the liberals' instinctive faith in creating government programs
for every possible problem, conservatives often flirted with a kind of
policy nihilism. Their clear sense of what they did not want preempted
all discussion of what they did want.

Charles W. Dunn and J. David Woodard note in *The Conservative Tradition in America* that conservatives tend to embrace traditional religious values, doubt the perfectibility of mankind, prefer state and local
government over the centralized government, exhibit a nationalistic
and patriotic spirit, value individual duties over rights, trust in the capitalist free market, and hope for stability and only gradual changes
within existing institutions. Despite being modern America's most successful conservative, Ronald Reagan had a mixed record regarding living and legislating traditional values. He was ambivalent about the
need for gradual change, occasionally hoping for some shakeups. Most
dramatically, he maintained a strong, progressive belief in the perfectibility of humanity while tending to emphasize individual rights
more than duties.

These deviations from the script made for a happy conservative—
and an individualistic nationalism. Reagan's Goldwaterism-with-a-smile
distanced the president from the unappealing, and unelectable, cranky
conservatism of the 1950s and 1960s. His seemingly paradoxical patriotism allowed for a burst of national pride in a media-saturated, indi-
viduated age. "Our nation exists for one purpose only—to assure each
one of us the ultimate in individual freedom consistent with law and
order," Governor Reagan wrote. "God meant America to be free because God intended each man to have the dignity of freedom."

This individualism came through in his 1986 Shuttle eulogy, when
he invoked "the great explorer Sir Francis Drake," neither an American
nor a scientist but an adventurer who "lived by the sea, died on it, and

was buried in it." Seven months later, the great patriotic festival at the Statue of Liberty emphasized the many individual accomplishments of the outstanding immigrants who passed through Ellis Island, literally and metaphorically, such as Lee Iacocca and Elie Wiesel. Ultimately, Reagan himself, with his Hollywood rootlessness, dysfunctional family, and disconnected albeit affable personality, lived his life more as an individualist than a nationalist, or as an individualist who loved his nation without being unduly inconvenienced by it. In that, the man and his times were well suited.

When Mr. Reagan came to town, Americans happily left the 1970s behind, trying to bury the traumas of Watergate, Vietnam, the energy crisis, stagflation—that unprecedented economic knockout punch of high inflation and high unemployment—and the Iranian hostage crisis. Americans feared that the end of the American Century had arrived nearly a quarter of a century prematurely. The Soviets seemed to be on the march with America languishing. Few Americans in the 1970s would have predicted the great eighties' bull market, the resurgence of American confidence and patriotism, the end of the cold war, or the collapse of the Soviet Union within a matter of years. By the end of the 1980s, many Americans did feel restored, and Ronald Reagan had earned bragging rights for many of these successes.

And yet, a closer look suggests the restoration was more imaginary than real. Serious social crises remained. The Reagan boom coexisted side by side with poverty, racism, crime, family breakdown, urban deterioration, and a mass epidemic of individual psychic distress. Moreover, Americans remained deeply insecure. Many worried—needlessly—that Japan and West Germany would eclipse the United States economically. And for all the homages to national unity, millions felt deeply marginalized, and only more inflamed by all the Morning-in-America celebrations.

In many ways, the restoration of the 1980s was like the urban gentrification projects of the time. Modern, gleaming, high-tech towers of glass and steel often replaced decaying slums, but the problems were shifted offstage, not solved. Dramatic transformations did indeed occur, but it was often hard to see which changes were real, and which were cosmetic.

The Wizard of the American Id

Ronald Reagan was the central figure of this decade, and of this restoration. Politically and culturally he dominated, and defined, the times. As the first president from suburbia, and presiding over an increasingly suburban nation, he epitomized and perpetuated many suburban values, ministering to a nation of individuals who were increasingly withdrawn into their little warrens and petty concerns. Ideologically, Reagan's conservatism galvanized the country, shifting American attitudes and triggering a decades-long debate about the role of government, the strengths of capitalism, the meaning of morality, and the limits of individual compassion and charity. Tactically, his media savvy mastered and promoted the brave new media universe that was emerging. Culturally, he epitomized an odd synthesis that occurred between the ideals of the 1960s and the ambitions of the 1980s. He and his "revolution" did not repudiate as many social, political, and cultural trends as he intended. Reagan after all was the first divorced president, perhaps the first president to host a gay couple overnight in the Executive Mansion when his wife's interior decorator slept over, and the father of a quarreling clan whose members, at various moments, did drugs, "shacked up," and married multiple times. In fact, part of Reagan's success stemmed from his ability to help Americans incorporate some of these changes into their lives, albeit sometimes unconsciously.

Perhaps Reagan's greatest asset—and his greatest gift to Americans—was his optimism. His faith in America and in the future was contagious, and a welcome corrective to the traumatic Nixon years, the drifting Ford years, the despairing Carter years. His can-do optimism, his sense of America as a shining "city upon a hill," tapped into one of the nation's most enduring character traits. Americans wanted an Era of Good Feelings, and they got it. Ironically, even as Reagan seemed to be repudiating the greatest legacies of Franklin D. Roosevelt, John F. Kennedy, and Lyndon B. Johnson, Reagan's have-your-cake-and-eat-it-too politics echoed theirs. Like Reagan, Roosevelt, Kennedy, Johnson all sought to conjure up a democratic Eden painlessly, with no tradeoffs. Neither the great conservative president of the 1980s nor the great liberal presidents who preceded him really demanded that Americans solve social problems through individual or collective sacrifice.

Paradoxically, Ronald Reagan's odes to an older, simpler, more idealistic, more community-oriented America helped spawn a new, sprawling, often selfish, deeply individualistic society. In reinvigorating American capitalism, Reagan helped unleash the American id. Many of the forces that triggered the boom to which Reagan claimed bragging rights were social solvents. Consumerism, materialism, individualism, entrepreneurship, the antigovernment backlash, the information age, capitalism itself, the end of the cold war all helped dissolve traditional ties and certainly fostered an American hedonism. But all these centrifugal forces made Ronald Reagan's centripetal force—his celebrity, his patriotism, his communal vision for modern America, in short his narrative—all the more important, then and now.

Whether spurring Americans to believe in themselves, their economy, and their system again, elevating the liberation of tiny Grenada into the greatest American victory since Iwo Jima, or consoling Americans after the Space Shuttle *Challenger* explosion, Reagan's siren song of confidence and faith soothed Americans. It returned Americans to their basic political and cultural instincts, unleashing creativity and confidence, as well as the hedonism and selfishness that became so typical of the 1980s.

Thinking of Reagan as the Wizard of the American Id also helps explain why so many movement conservatives were so frustrated with him. His synthesis of Hollywood imagineering and Keynesian have-your-cake-and-eat-it-too-ism precluded the kind of moral crusade conservatives demanded to "take back" America. Reagan would not fight the hard fight on the conservatives' "abc" agenda of abortion, busing, crime. As a result, many of the reforms and revolutions of the 1960s and 1970s ended up legitimized. At the same time, Reagan's Dr. Feel Good approach frustrated the Democrats—and it is hard not to see Jimmy Carter in 1980 or Walter Mondale in 1984 as appealing to the national superego, while Reagan merrily appealed to the id. This idea also explains the great mystery of the Reagan years, of how, as a leader, his whole was greater than the sum of his parts, as one memo put it, how he remained personally more popular than his policies.

The Reagan celebration of American hedonism did not end with politics—it was also influential culturally. The great reconciliation, whereby the hippie elite and ethos matured into the yuppie elite and ethos, was Reaganite. Consumerism, careerism, materialism, and flashy designs spread as Reaganism set a social, cultural, and stylistic tone too. Reaganism helped make politics an extension of entertainment for a society already "immersed" in entertainment, with a people pursuing "pleasure first and fast," in the words of the cultural critic Jacques Barzun. Ironically, by releasing the American id, this conservative, who was calling, at least rhetorically, for a return to tradition, shaped an era whose cultural sensibility was shaped by Madonna and Michael Jackson, the man-child, rather than the more traditional Madonna and child.

Finally, one could also characterize the defining approach of Reaganite foreign policy as "egoistic." Reagan gleefully quoted his UN Ambassador Jeane Kirpatrick's claim that in the 1980s America removed the "kick-me" sign on its back. Reagan's approach to the Soviet Union, to Central America, and the way he and his staff circumvented normal channels in Iran-Contra all speak to a national egoism, which many Americans found inspiring, and so many foreigners found exasperating. From the seeds of small symbolic actions such as Ronald Reagan's insistence on lecturing his colleagues about freedom at the 1981 Cancun Summit to his proactive approach to the Soviets, a new, less ambivalent American superpower emerged, best exemplified by George W. Bush's with-us-or-against-us, proactive approach to terrorism.

Reagan's Three Promises: A Scorecard

Regarding foreign policy, it is too facile to rely—as so many do—on the idea of Reagan's "dumb luck." True, Reaganite foreign policy was a march of folly replete with an often disengaged president, warring advisers, poorly planned summits, and absurdly priced Pentagon gadgets. The murder of 241 marines in Lebanon went unavenged. The president of the United States tested his microphone by joking about bombing the Soviet Union. Reagan and his advisers celebrated the liberation of Grenada as if it balanced out the loss in Vietnam. And the tragi-comedy of Iran-Contra made the United States—and its president—a laughingstock.

Yet, today, compared to George H. W. Bush's dithering about the collapse of Communism, and Bill Clinton's congenital waffling about almost everything, Reagan's foreign policy course appears more resolute, and quite triumphal. Under Reagan's reign, the United States effectively won the cold war and experienced a resurgence of national pride. A decade and a half after Ronald Reagan's retirement, the United States is the world's sole superpower. Twenty years after Reagan outraged liberals by squarely labeling the Soviet Union "the Evil Empire," millions are freed: the Iron Curtain is down, Germany is reunited, Eastern Europe is liberated, and even Nicaragua's Sandanistas have been voted into retirement.

True, Mikhail Gorbachev was a blessing from heaven—more accurately, an astonishing ray of light emanating from the putrefying Soviet Communist system. But Reagan's excessively personal approach to world affairs helped forge a warm bond with the Soviet reformer, and Reagan's embrace buttressed, legitimized, and helped further the Gorbachev revolution. Reagan's mix of saber-rattling and pacifism worked. His naive faith in Star Wars terrified and helped bankrupt the Soviets; his aversion to the experts' doctrine of mutual assured destruction motivated him to nurture his rapport with Gorbachev—and match the Soviet leader's boldness. Clearly, it takes great skill to turn dumb luck into lasting good fortune.

At the same time, Reagan shares culpability with all the presidents from Jimmy Carter through the pre–September 11 George W. Bush, for allowing the cancer of Islamicist terrorism to fester unchecked. And it is simplistic to say that Reagan won the cold war singlehandedly. The cold war victory was a joint achievement of all the presidents from Harry Truman through George Bush. It is a tribute to the bipartisan consensus that kept America strong but not too aggressive in the face of Communism.

In addition to defending America to defeat Communism, Reagan wanted to deregulate, and he wanted to cut the marginal tax rate. Both initiatives were rooted in the 1970s—deregulation began under Carter, and the tax revolt had spread in many states without Reagan's involvement. Reagan's victory raised expectations regarding this broad-based assault on the "Nanny State" and achieved mixed results. At most, Reagan slowed the growth of big government. He was too pragmatic, and too weak, to do much more. The Democratic Congress and the characteristic incrementalism of the American political system shackled Reagan. He shifted course by a few degrees but did not succeed in veering right overnight. It took time for the Reagan Revolution to restrain the courts, weaken the bureaucracy, reorient the body politic. Yet, by the 1990s, even under a Democratic administration, America seemed further away from the Great Society than it did at the end of Reagan's reign. And it was Reagan's appointments that revolutionized the judiciary; it was Reagan's small-government rhetoric along with his astronomical deficits that kept Americans budget conscious. The deregulation was slower and less systematic than he would have liked, the tax cuts came with a host of "user fees," and the resulting "pride" also had an overlay of cynicism. Still, it was an impressive tribute to one man's unrelenting focus amid the hurly burly of the presidency.

At Ronald Reagan's funeral, the tableau of presidential and vice presidential couples captured the generational politics that defined the last quarter of the twentieth century, as well as the ideals of civility and unity Reagan championed. The elder Bushes, the Carters, and the Fords were all seated in one row. All veterans of World War II, part of the "Greatest Generation" that also included John F. Kennedy, Lyndon Johnson, and Richard Nixon, each of the three ex-presidents had fought Reagan politically—Gerald Ford for the Republican nomination in 1976, George Bush for the nomination in 1980, and Jimmy Carter for the presidency in 1980. The youngsters in the front row, the Bushes, the Cheneys, the Clintons, had also fought Reagan, albeit less directly: the junior President Bush had commiserated with his father during the elder Bush's frustrating vice-presidential years, Dick Cheney had been Ford's Chief of Staff during the 1976 nomination fight, and Bill Clinton had launched his winning 1992 campaign by denouncing Reaganism. Still, all gathered to mourn Reagan's death and celebrate his life.

The three thousand mourners in the National Cathedral, the handful of participants in the service, and the hundreds gathered for the California burial together painted a pointillist portrait of Reagan's era—and testified to many of the changes he helped trigger. When Ronald Reagan was inaugurated, Justice Sandra Day O'Connor was an unknown Arizona lawyer not yet called to become the first female Supreme Court justice; Rabbi Harold Kushner was a grieving Massachusetts rabbi just about to publish *When Bad Things Happen to Good People;* Brian Mulroney was running the Iron Ore Company in Quebec, two years away from even being elected to Parliament. Margaret Thatcher, however, was already advancing her own Reaganesque revolution as British prime minister. Among the Washington guests, in 1981 Natan Sharansky, now an Israeli cabinet member, was still Anatoly Sharansky and imprisoned in the gulag; Mikhail Gorbachev was a Soviet apparatchik with the agriculture portfolio; Lech Walesa was a union activist, with both years of arrests and years as Poland's president ahead. At the time, Colin Powell was an unknown soldier, Peggy Noonan was an unknown ghostwriter—for Dan Rather—and, among the California mourners, Arnold Schwarzenegger was a body-builder just breaking into acting. Ronald Reagan and the Reagan idea shaped all these lives, directly and indirectly.

The "Smiths": Wealthier, Safer, but Anxious too

To revisit our fictional couple, the Smiths, from the introduction, 1990 would find them older, wealthier, more politically disillusioned, more wired into media mores and celebrity talk, and more complacent. Thickened a bit by aging, but still well-toned, thanks to their personal trainer—a 1980s' invention—they would now be busily juggling the demands of two careers and two children, who eventually arrived after a tense stretch of infertility remedied by Clomid, the pregnancy wonder drug for thirtysomethings trying to start a family after years of relying on "The Pill" to avoid such a fate. Mr. Smith's sideburns had receded along with his hairline; thanks to her $125-a-shot stylist, Mrs. Smith's hair color was richer and shinier than ever.

The Smiths had traded up from their 1950s' starter house in a suburb just bordering the city to a new, larger home an hour from downtown. Situated in a gated community providing tennis courts, a swimming pool, and twenty-four-hour security, they lived in what would soon be called a "McMansion." The sprawling, two-story home had a great room grander than their grandparents' formal "parlors" or their parents' cozy dens, a marble bathroom in the bedroom suite, and a huge, sun-splashed, chrome-filled kitchen with an island for chopping and cooking. In the 1987 stock market crash they lost "more money than I ever thought I'd have," Mrs. Smith said, but they sustained only paper losses and had since partially recovered. Their stock portfolio, mutual funds, and 401ks were still much higher than they had been in 1980 and were still climbing. Every year at tax time, the Smiths felt a bit embarrassed by how much money they spent running a household, shopping, eating out in restaurants, maintaining the Honda Accord and the Dodge minivan—they had just bought American for the first time in years, thanks to the carlike trucks that debuted in 1983, and which, when the Smiths bought in 1987, now had V-6 engines for easy acceleration. And even as they noticed the increasing outflow every year, all their costs seemed fixed. As with the federal budget, somehow there did not seem to be much room for cutting.

Most of their friends had married, a few already twice, but two seemed to be perpetually single—both women. Both resolutely career women, they tried to laugh off the ridiculous headlines shouting that they had a better chance of being killed by a terrorist than actually getting married. One gay male friend was HIV-positive, optimistically following a daily regimen of multiple drug doses, blessed by the miraculous "AIDS cocktail." The eighties' boom had been good to the Smiths' social circle. One lawyer friend earned a six-figure salary practicing entertainment law in New York for a few years, then joined the march of the committed conservatives into Ed Meese's Justice Department in Washington, DC—and settled permanently in the Maryland suburbs of the nation's capital. Another stayed with his family's real estate business, helping it grow from a thriving concern into an empire. A third went the corporate route, earning a high salary, while suffering repeated career disruptions as mergers, consolidations, and downsizing buffeted her from place to place, from lucrative buyout to lucrative buyout. A fourth earned such high bonuses trading bonds on Wall Street that he retired with a multimillion-dollar stock portfolio at thirty-nine. Their lawyer friends and doctor friends, their entrepreneurial friends and their corporate friends mostly floated to the top of Reagan's money-making pyramid. Only their most idealistic and intellectual friends languished financially. Their social worker and professor friends watched the Great Inflation of the 1970s make the basics of an upper-middle-class life unaffordable, without being able to benefit from the 1980s' boom—unless their parents' nest-eggs had grown sufficiently. In addition to their other collective traits, the baby boomers were emerging as the greatest heirs in history, awaiting—sometimes patiently, sometimes less so—the largest transfer of wealth ever from their parents.

The Smiths' children, though cute, and very well dressed, seemed more precocious, more worldly, and less disciplined than the Smiths remembered themselves being. But the family had just returned from a week-long jaunt to Disney World in Orlando, visiting the new EPCOT Center as well as the Magic Kingdom. The trip had gone smoothly, even with the undocumented Guatemalan nanny staying home.

Like so many Americans, the Smiths still had fond feelings for Ronald Reagan. They could still remember some stirring moments from his presidency, although they worried that too many important issues had been neglected on his watch. They liked George Bush's "kinder, gentler" rhetoric but somehow were less enthusiastic about this administration. While they had not quite soured on politics, both were much less engaged. When reading the newspaper, Mr. Smith spent that much more time poring over the business page, Mrs. Smith spent some extra time with the style section, and both guiltily noticed that they read the "people" column in the entertainment section a bit too carefully. With a mix of pride and shame, they noted how fluently they could speak about Michael Jackson's latest hue or Madonna's latest beau. In fact, each monitored Leona Helmsley's tax troubles and the allegations that the Menendez brothers killed their father at their Beverly Hills home more closely on CNN than they had the Tiananmen Square crisis or the Berlin Wall's fall.

Although Mr. and Mrs. Smith had an all-white social circle, they had some black colleagues at work. Neither could say "African American" without feeling self-conscious. Similarly, at work both said they supported affirmative action, and each had undergone "diversity training," even as they confessed to each other at home that they preferred to hire people based on merit and found themselves resenting the multi-cultural mantra and the stultifying, increasingly politically correct, atmosphere at work.

But they had not forgotten or repudiated the 1960s. Both told pollsters and friends that they were "pro-environment" and happily recycled newspapers and empty bottles—although neither would consider serious lifestyle adjustments such as giving up one car. Similarly, when the subject arose, Mrs. Smith still professed to be a feminist and would defend feminism passionately when her husband or another man attacked the "movement." But her *Ms.* subscription had lapsed, and her enthusiasm had stilled. Both had duly signed petitions to oppose the expansion of a garbage dump in the neighboring township, but neither could get that enthusiastic about plunging into the campaign to protect their prerogatives. More globally, both were pleasantly surprised by the fall of Communism, with Mr. Smith giving Reagan more credit and Mrs. Smith crediting Gorbachev mostly.

And yet, both worried about the state of the world—and the country. Both admitted that they never imagined in January 1981 that they would be living in such splendor, or that the Soviet Union would be no more and the Eastern European states would be free. But they rarely ventured downtown anymore because they feared taking a wrong turn and ending up in the wrong neighborhood, as they had read in *Bonfire of the Vanities*. Both felt pressure to work hard and keep the cash flowing; neither had time to relax during the week. Both hated what their neighbors' teenage kids looked like and listened to—with the boys slouching and dressing like ghetto gangsters and the girls revealing too much flesh and makeup. The Smiths also felt isolated. They socialized infrequently and disliked the rampant selfishness and "NIMBY" approach to politics in their town, even as they occasionally indulged in it.

When Frederick Lewis Allen conjured up the fictional Smiths in the 1930s, he instinctively made them upper-middle-class WASPs. To call such a couple "typical" in the 1980s was less obvious, and more controversial. Nevertheless, this sketch suggests trends and attitudes that were reflected in millions of American lives.

Reagan as Historian as Well as Historical Figure

Ronald Reagan needs to be appreciated as historian as well as history-maker. Reagan's "Morning in America" resurrected pride in the past and faith in the future as well as confidence in the present. This simple, red, white, and blue, Glory, Glory Hallelujah reading of history delighted many Americans—expecially when professional historians were painting a more complex, more critical, and decidedly unpopular picture of America.

Reagan's affirmative vision and definitive rhetoric continue to invite caricature. Consensus-oriented triumphalists from the Right use Reagan to celebrate America's achievements and continuing promise, while conflict-obsessed critics from the Left use Reagan to berate America's failures and myopic denial. In fact, studying Reagan and Reaganism requires a more synthetic, less politicized approach. American history combines pragmatism and idealism, selfishness and altruism, crassness and nobility, individualism and nationalism, populism and progressivism. The people of plenty have been lovers of liberty. It is a mistake to overlook either the flinty-eyed materialism or the misty-eyed high-mindedness.

Reagan and Reaganism left the country with a mixed legacy. At its best, Reaganism helped restore an idealism and entrepreneurial can-do-ism central to the American spirit. At its worst, Reaganism perpetuated self-righteousness mixed with selfishness. Like it or hate it, like him or hate him, nearly twenty-five years after the Reagan inauguration, Ronald Reagan's legacy continues to define his country; he remains the greatest president since Franklin Roosevelt. Reagan saved the presidency from irrelevance, showing that the ability to shift the national conversation and set the national tone was in and of itself a valuable asset and a significant role, even at a time of increasingly sclerotic government. Reagan's influence continues because in so many ways, whatever his shortcomings and flaws, the vision he projected of himself was the vision of themselves most Americans wanted to see. Only by having such utter and complete faith in American ideals of freedom and democracy has the United States been able to accomplish so much. Only by keeping such faith—tempered with just a bit of modesty and realism—will the United States continue to grow and to lead.

A Note on Method
and Sources

If you can write a nation's stories, you needn't worry about who makes its laws.

DR. GEORGE GERBNER, UNIVERSITY OF PENNSYLVANIA

Studying Ronald Reagan is not for the faint-hearted—or the untenured. Ronald Reagan remains a contentious, often polarizing, figure. Too many Americans praise Reagan blindly, while too many others simply bash him. Even a benign attempt to tell the saga of Nancy and Ronald Reagan as a great American love story for the November 2003 television sweeps ended up caught in this ideological crossfire, with conservatives encouraged by Nancy Reagan crying foul and accusing the script of having a liberal bias, when the project's real bias was toward Hollywood melodrama.

The continuing partisanship overshadows most looks at Ronald Reagan. "Why would you spend time studying *that* man?" a horrified artist asked during one of my Reagan research trips to Los Angeles. "Are you a fan?" the director of *The Reagans* miniseries wondered, as we talked about the challenges of seeing Reagan clearly in a community that abhors him, be it Hollywood or academia. At the same time, too much of the hype around the Reagan funeral reflected an intolerance for any thoughtful, balanced assessments, which inevitably include criticism. And the cascade of adjectives lionizing Reagan's personal traits did not explain how they interacted with his surroundings and shaped the times. As I said of a different ruler when I played Marc Antony in sixth grade, I come neither to bury Reagan nor to praise him. The goal of the book is to understand Ronald Reagan, his impact and his times.

Among the professoriate, the Reagan "yuck factor," or what Professor Alan Brinkley more elegantly termed "the problem of American conservatism," has distorted the debate and impeded assessments of Reagan's significance. Even the recent boom in studying conservatism has not carried over sufficiently into studying Reagan. Too many critics are unwilling to spend too much time revisiting that man or his times. "Your manuscript brought me right back to all the horrors of the 1980s," one of my early readers shuddered. Many of the most entertaining Reagan morsels confirm the caricatures of Reagan the moron—and many came from the disaffected insiders who published "kiss-and-tell" memoirs, especially David Stockman and Donald Regan.

Reagan's critics have long wavered between denouncing him as clueless or malicious. Most Americans refused to believe that someone could be both foolish and cruel, especially someone so eloquent and affable. In fact, Reagan's light touch tempered his conservatism, just as his ideology anchored his otherwise breezy political style.

During the Bush administration Reagan's historical stock dipped, even among many Republicans. Ironically, Reagan's reputation rose thanks to a Democrat, Bill Clinton. It was hard for liberals to grouse about "peace and prosperity" as a presidential rationale, when it became the Democratic mantra. Many fair-minded people recognized that if this baby-boom-boom was going to be attributed to a president, both Reagan and Clinton deserved some credit. As the 1990s' boom shrank the government deficit, one of the great failures of Reagan's era receded in importance. And, with Bill Clinton triangulating, it was Reagan's Democratic successor who engineered welfare reform as part of his retreat from "big government."

Clinton's scandal-laden second term also helped boost Reagan's reputation. An old-fashioned, 1950's-style, gentlemanly president who never took off his suit jacket even in the Oval Office, Reagan appeared downright saintly compared with the undisciplined perpetual adolescent whose behavior embarrassed even his ideological allies. And Reagan's moving 1994 farewell letter, acknowledging his Alzheimer's disease, helped situate the Marlboro Man in the Age of Oprah. As Reagan lost his memory, Americans' memories of him softened. The proposed CBS miniseries in October 2003 faltered by violating the unspoken demilitarized zone that had settled around this ailing national icon, and his loyal, self-sacrificing wife Nancy, enjoying her own extreme image makeover thanks to the grace with which she responded to her husband's disease.

Meanwhile, Reagan zealots guard their hero's memory by celebrating his contradictions. Motivated by loyalty to the past and the partisanship of the present, a steady stream of books has hailed Ronald Reagan's *Revolution!* (Martin Anderson, 1988), the good old days of the 1980s *When Character Was King* (Peggy Noonan, 2002), *The Power of Conviction and the Success of His Presidency* (Peter Wallison, 2003), and *How an Ordinary Man Became an Extraordinary Leader* (Dinesh D'Souza, 1997). Alas, too many of these books celebrate rather than cerebrate, making Reagan Churchillian when he confronted the Soviet Union and equally Churchillian when he compromised.

The continuing ideological debates, along with the psychobiographical sideshows trying to unpack Reagan's psyche rather than assess his accomplishments, have stunted the growth of Reagan studies. As a result, the first wave of defining works about Reagan and the 1980s still dominate, especially Lou Cannon's *President Reagan: The Role of a Lifetime* (New York, 1991, 2000), Haynes Johnson's *Sleepwalking through History* (New York, 1991, 1992, 2003), and Robert Dallek's *Ronald Reagan: The Politics of Symbolism* (Cambridge, 1984, 1999). In fact, all were recently reprinted—proof of great interest in the era, but a sad commentary on the failure of new perspectives rooted in the new material the Reagan Presidential Library regularly releases to command attention.

Fortunately, newer analysis, often based on these fresh sources, is emerging. A recent University Press of Kansas anthology W. Elliot Brownlee and the late Hugh Davis Graham edited, *The Reagan Presidency: Pragmatic Conservatism & Its Legacies* (Lawrence, 2003), published papers from a conference held at the Ronald Reagan Presidential Library that used newly released records. The notion of Reagan as "pragmatic conservative" is intriguing. This middle ground follows the interpretive lines developed by Alonzo Hamby, who deemed Reagan an "incrementalist" in his authoritative work, *Liberalism and Its Challengers: From F.D.R. to Bush,* 2nd ed. (New York, 1992), and by Frances FitzGerald, who defined Reagan as a "supple" politician and an "American Everyman" in *Way Out There in the Blue* (New York, 2000). Hamby characterized Reagan's conservatism as "more populist than elitist, more prone to risk taking than prudence, more flexible in its methods and more successful in elections than any of its twentieth-century predecessors."

Two superb collections of Reagan's speeches and letters, *Reagan in His Own Hand* (2001) and *Reagan: A Life in Letters* (2003), both edited by Kiron K. Skinner, Annelise Anderson, and Martin Anderson, and published by The Free Press, reinforce what the Reagan Library proves—that Reagan was an articulate, idea-driven ideologue, and that after twenty years of governing he was more politician than actor.

Reagan demonstrated that politics was more than a power game and a question of resource allocation. Reagan treated politics as the historian Jean Baker does in *Affairs of Party* (Ithaca, 1983), as "a symbolic demonstration of the way Americans led their public lives" and "a series of community rituals embodying national values." Reagan instinctively understood that to make his mark on modern America he had to dominate American culture in its broadest terms, "not simply" referring to "the arts" but "to the ways a society makes meaning," as Yale's David Greenberg puts it in *Nixon's Shadow: The History of an Image* (New York, 2003). Despite his apparent intellectual lassitude, Reagan's towering ambition targeted what professors Meg Jacobs and Julian Zelizer would call in 2003 the "ideologies, languages, and symbols" that "shaped all political actors" in his time in "The Democratic Experiment: New Directions in American Political History," in Meg Jacobs, William J. Novak, and Julian E. Zelizer, eds., *The Democratic Experiment* (Princeton, NJ, 2003).

Many of these ideas and symbols were most potent when integrated into a broader narrative. "If you can write a nation's stories, you needn't worry about who makes its laws," says Dr. George Gerbner, of the University of Pennsylvania's Annenberg School for Communication in Lisa A. Lewis, *Gender Politics and MTV* (Philadelphia, 1990). It all suggests Reagan's recipe for success—despite the various fiascos on his watch. "Successful leaders do not necessarily do more than other leaders," the Yale political scientist Stephen Skowronek writes in *The Politics Presidents Make* (Cambridge, 1993); "successful leaders control the political definition of their actions, the terms in which their places in history are understood." Reagan's cultural renaissance, his renewal of American confidence, would become a central part of the Reagan narrative and success story.

So far, decades remain the building blocks of twentieth-century American history. Historians package their interpretations in more-or-less ten-year chunks, with the apolitical abandon of "the twenties" becoming the sober reformism of "the thirties"; with the political abandon of "the sixties" becoming the apolitical excesses of the "seventies." Often these decade packages function as morality tales, wherein times of great prosperity—the twenties, the fifties, the eighties—somehow earn great opprobrium as times of great selfishness. To most American historians, it is the years of the Depression in the 1930s that are "great"; the generation that fought World War II in the 1940s that is "good"; and the boom years of the twenties, fifties, and eighties that are bloated, complacent, vulgar.

The content providers who program our hundred-channel universe have reduced historians' generalizations into generational stereotypes. Nostalgia is popular and profitable. Consumers know the decade short-hand: boas and headdresses for the 1920s; rags and fedoras for the 1930s; uniforms and zoot suits for the 1940s; leather jackets and bobby socks for the 1950s; torn jeans and love beads for the 1960s; leisure suits and bell bottoms for the 1970s; and power suits and exercise Spandex for the 1980s.

Just as the 1970s was the decade of great 1950s' nostalgia, the 1980s the decade of 1960s' nostalgia, and the 1990s when the 1970s' revival began, we are now poised for a 1980s' revival in popular terms. Adam Sandler recognized this growing interest in *The Wedding Singer,* his 1998 hit set in the 1980s, which marketed its eighties' soundtrack and set Sandler's down-to-earth, mildly countercultural, exceedingly lovable character against the stock bad guy of the period, a Gordon Gekko type as caricatured by Oliver Stone in *Wall Street:* in this case a Lamborghini-driving, two-timing, junk-bond-selling broker cretin who sports an unshaven, *Miami Vice*–pastel look. With the stereotype of this era as the "New Gilded Age" solidifying among historians and in the popular culture, it becomes ever more important to reexamine the eighties and the president so instrumental in defining the times.

In 1986 the Harris Poll found that 60 percent of Americans felt alienated and powerless—believing "what I think doesn't count much anymore"—and 82 percent confessed they would act on a friend's stock tip, even if it constituted illegal insider training. (Louis Harris, *Inside America* [New York, 1987]). "Is it possible that we could become citizens again and together seek the common good in the post-industrial, postmodern age?" the sociologist Robert Bellah and his colleagues asked in 1985's surprise best-seller *Habits of the Heart* (New York, 1985). "Freedom is a moral accomplishment," the British theologian Jonathan Sacks would write in *The Politics of Hope* in 1997, illustrating that the problem outlasted the 1980s and transcended Reagan's America. "It needs strong families, cohesive institutions, habits of civility and law-abidingness, and a widely diffused sense of fellow-feeling. . . . When moral language breaks down—as it has broken down—much else is at risk, including freedom itself."

Reagan demonstrated that traditional paeans to morality and citizenship would indeed generate applause. Yet for all the talk, his combination of nonconfrontational affability and feel-good libertinism did little to arrest the social and moral decay. In fact, in carving out a public plane where the radical individualism and indulgent libertinism of the Left and the Right could meet happily, he further undermined America's "moral language" and institutions.

And yet, perhaps the greatest gift of Ronald Reagan and the 1980s was to show that things could get better, to reaffirm the traditional American faith in progress. Those of us who grew up in the 1970s, and most especially those of us who grew up in New York in those years, simply assumed that things always declined, socially, institutionally, culturally, and politically. To see, as we entered adulthood, the economy improve, crime stop spreading, neglected institutional jewels such as the New York City Public Library shine, deteriorating architectural wonders such as Miami's Art Deco district sprout anew, all the while enjoying a surprising cold war victory, reconnected us to one of American history's central tropes and one of the great blessings of the American experiment's great blessings. Learning to believe in that hope—and remembering that national fortunes can change for the better, collective moods can lighten, world conditions can improve—is necessary today, to those of us on the Left or the Right, be we more shocked by twenty-first-century terrorism or more concerned about America's reaction to it. It is with a renewed appreciation for how desperately we need this lesson of hope that this book has been written.

In that spirit, rather than boring deeply into this unapproachable, not very reflective, but surprisingly intuitive man's psyche, this study has examined Reagan's governing script and his White House stage, assessing how it mollified, inspired, seduced, and ultimately transformed his preferred audience—the American people. As a work combining political and cultural history, the book has followed the research strategies of both the sweeping, secondary-source-heavy William Leuchtenburg–Eric Goldman–Bruce Schulman "decade" book and the denser, more primary-source-intensive David Donald–Robert Dallek–Arthur Schlesinger, Jr., presidential biography. The book thus is based on contemporary periodicals, secondary sources, and available manuscript sources in the Tip O'Neill Papers, the Donald Regan Papers, the Alice Rivlin Papers, the William Rusher Papers, and, most important of all, the Ronald Reagan Presidential Library in Simi Valley, California.

During repeated research trips to Simi Valley since 1993, I have examined thousands of documents catalogued specifically for this project, in response to Freedom of Information Act requests I filed. Collections in the Reagan Library that proved particularly useful included:

- *Presidential Handwriting File,* which was the focus of the bulk of my Freedom of Information Act requests, houses copies of any documents with Reagan's handwriting on them from across the collection. *Series II: Presidential Records* collects handwritten drafts of letters the president wrote to friends and strangers (Reagan maintained a rich correspondence with fans and foes throughout his White House years); *Series III: Presidential Speeches* demonstrates the personal touch Reagan brought to his speeches and his skills as both writer and editor; *Series IV: Presidential Phone Calls* consists of Reagan's phone logs, especially his call lists to members of Congress, which feature his one- and two-line scrawls summarizing the conversations; and *Series V: White House Mail Reports* occasionally features Reagan's brief scribbled replies on a variety of issues from members of Congress and others.
- *Records of the White House Office of Public Affairs and the Elizabeth H. Dole Papers,* chronicle the intense lobbying and strategizing on critical issues

such as civil rights, women's rights, and Iran-Contra, recording, in a sense, the "conversation" that developed between the public and the president's people.

- *Margaret Tutwiler Papers and Series I, Memorandum File, Subseries C, 1984–Jan. 1985 of the James A. Baker III Files* are particularly helpful for the 1984 reelection campaign.
- *White House Central Files,* especially the FG, Federal Government Files, which highlight government operations, the PR, Public Relations Files, which concentrate on selling the program, and the SP, Speech Files, which show the various drafts of Reagan's speeches and his essential role in shaping many of them.

In the Tip O'Neill papers, the Kirk O'Donnell papers are very useful in terms of the behind-the-scenes strategizing, and Series VI, especially the Speeches and Press Statements, provide the Speaker's running commentary on Reagan and the administration.

To limit the notes, I usually referenced only material cited directly in the text and did not repeat citations for major Reagan statements identified clearly in the notes and easily tracked on the Web or in the Public Papers of the President. Instead of numbered footnotes, each citation is keyed to the first two or three words in the quotation or relevant phrase and the page number on which the material appears.

A Guide to Abbreviations in Notes

BosG	*Boston Globe*
Cannon	Lou Cannon, *President Reagan* (New York, 1991, 2000)
CSM	*Christian Science Monitor*
DTR	Donald T. Regan Papers, Library of Congress, Washington, DC
EHD	Elizabeth H. Dole Papers, RR Lib
EM	Edwin Meese, III
JAB	James A. Baker, III
KOD	Kirk O'Donnell Files, Staff Files, Thomas P. O'Neill Papers, John J. Burns Library, Boston College, Brookline, MA
LAT	*Los Angeles Times*
LHarris	Louis Harris, *Inside America* (New York, 1987)
LofC	Library of Congress, Washington, DC
NR *Mem*	Nancy Reagan with William Novak, *My Turn* (New York, 1989)
Nwswk	*Newsweek*
NYT	*New York Times*
NYTM	*New York Times Magazine*
Pub	Public Papers of the President, available for each year and in the process of being posted at www.reagan .utexas.edu/resource/speeches/rrpubpap.asp
PHF	Presidential Handwriting File, RR Lib
RR	Ronald Reagan
RR *Hand*	Kiron K. Skinner, Annelise Anderson, and Martin Anderson, eds., *Reagan, In His Own Hand* (New York, 2001)

RR *Letters*	Kiron K. Skinner, Annelise Anderson, and Martin Anderson, eds., *Reagan, A Life in Letters* (New York, 2003)
RR Lib	Ronald Reagan Presidential Library, Simi Valley, CA
RR *Mem*	Ronald Reagan, *An American Life* (New York, 1990)
RS	*Rolling Stone*
Tip VI	Press Relations, Thomas P. O'Neill Papers, John J. Burns Library, Boston College, Brookline, MA
TNR	*The New Republic*
USNWR	*U.S. News & World Report*
WasPo	*Washington Post*
WHORM	White House Office of Records Management, RR Lib
WHTALK	White House Talking Points, OA 14,712, Records of the White House Office of Public Affairs, RR Lib

Notes

Introduction

Page

1 "haze" . . . "colored blobs . . .": RR *Mem,* 36; RR with Richard C. Hubler, *Where's the Rest of Me* (New York, 1965), 24–25. See also Edmund Morris, *Dutch* (New York, 1999), 45–46.

2 "project[ing] the . . .": *NYT,* 6 June 2004, 1.

2 "He was our oldest . . .": *BosG,* 12 June 2004, A15.

2 "He brought us . . .": Peggy Noonan, *Opinion Journal.com,* 17 June 2004, http:www.opinionjournal.com/columnists/pnoonan/?id=110005225.

3 "baseball, hamburgers . . .": *Nwswk,* 24 June 1985, 32.

3 "a very meaningful . . .": *Time,* 22 July 1985, 48.

3 "consumerism": See Lizabeth Cohen, *A Consumers' Republic* (New York, 2003), 9.

3 "God wants . . .": Lisa McGirr, *Suburban Warriors* (Princeton, 2001), 249–253.

3 Budweiser commercial . . . : The commercials began in the mid-1970s.

4 Churchillian: Dinesh D'Souza, *Ronald Reagan* (New York, 1997), 136, 185.

4 "Mr. Magoo": Garry Wills, *New York Review of Books,* 20 Dec. 1990, 29.

4 "amiable dunce": Clark Clifford, *Counsel to the President* (New York, 1991), 644.

5 "If Mondale was so . . .": Aaron Wildavsky, "President Reagan as Political Strategist," *Society* 24 (May/June 1987): 56.

5 "forceful and . . .": Arthur M. Schlesinger, Jr., "Editor's Note," in Kevin Phillips, *William McKinley* (New York, 2003), xvii.

5 "Simplicity, which . . .": *NYT,* 7 June 2004, p. 28.

6 "wall": NR *Mem,* 106.

6 "an apparent . . .": Morris, *Dutch,* 579.

7 "My name is . . .": Michael Reagan, *On the Outside Looking In* (London, 1988), 96.

7 "became galvanized . . .": William Allen White, *Masks in a Pageant* (New York, 1928), 155.

7 "I *was* divorced . . .": *People,* 29 Dec.–5 Jan. 1981, 24.

7 "lynch mob": RR to Jaquelin H. Hume, 3 Dec. 1986, RR *Letters,* 468.

7 "prevented the . . .": RR to Helen Lawson, 3 Dec. 1986, ibid., 469.

8 "love you . . .": RR to Craig Stubblebine, 16 Oct. 1979, ibid., 230.

8 "communicate . . .": Office of Policy Development, 19 Nov. 1982, 10901425C, Box 10, FG001, RR Lib.

8 "gift . . . saying . . .": *Nwswk,* 27 July 1981, 76.

8 "Well, it's . . .": *RS,* 16 Sept. 1982, 13.

9 "I have never . . .": *Time,* 19 Apr. 1982, 75.

9 Brian Mulroney: See Peter Hannaford, ed., *Recollections of Reagan* (New York, 1997), 116.

9 "How did I know . . .": *USNWR ,* 7 Dec. 1981, 76.

10 "Rhetorical . . .": Jeffrey K. Tulis, *Rhetorical Presidency* (Princeton, 1987).

11 "was a performer . . .": *USNWR, RR Commemorative Edition* (2004), 60.

11 "the last . . .": Ed Rollins, *Bare Knuckles and Back Rooms* (New York, 1996), 97.

12 "decade of neglect . . .": RR, "Center for International and Strategic Studies of Georgetown University," 6 Apr.1984, in Ben Elliott to Richard G. Darman, 12 May 1984, in OA 10,572, "White House: JAB Files, 4 of 6," Margaret Tutwiler Papers, RR Lib.

12 "I resent . . .": See George Bush to Gerald R. Ford, 14 May 1984, JAB to Gerald R. Ford, 14 May 1984, Gerald R. Ford to JAB, dictated 1 June 1984, all in OA 10,572, ibid.

13 had the assassin . . . : Arthur M. Schlesinger, Jr., *The Crisis of the Old Order* (New York, 1957), 466.

16 "The Reagan-Bush. . . .": Bill Clinton, Washington, DC, 23 Oct. 1991, in Robert E. Levin, ed., *Bill Clinton* (New York, 1992), 289.

16 "unilateral": United Press International, 11 June 1985.

16 "ill equipped . . .": Michael Mandelbaum, "American Policy: The Luck of the President," *Foreign Affairs* 64 (1985): 406.

16 "a simpler time . . .": Susan McHale, Greenwich, CT in *NYT,* 12 June 2004, A26

16 "an America that . . .": *Time,* 14 June 2004, 55.

17 "personified the . . .": *USA Today,* 7 June 2004, 3A.

17 "To conservatives . . .": CNN, 6 June 2004, 6:38 P.M.

17 "I think the world . . .": *People,* 21 June 2004, 99.

17 less engaged . . . : See Joseph S. Nye, Jr., Philip D. Zelikow, and David C. King, eds., *Why People Don't Trust Government* (Cambridge, 1997), 254.

18 "social capital": Robert Putnam, *Bowling Alone* (New York, 2000), 18–28. See also Jacques Barzun, *From Dawn to Decadence* (New York, 2000).

21 vantage point: See Frederick Lewis Allen, *Only Yesterday* (New York, 1931, 1964), 1–12.

1980—Cleveland

Page

25 "What is the difference . . .": *WasPo,* 12 Aug. 1978, A8.

26 "I've learned that . . .": Jimmy Carter and RR acceptance speeches in Gregory Bush, ed., *Campaign Speeches of American Presidential Candidates* (New York, 1985), 282, 264.

28 men living alone: Bruce Schulman, *The Seventies* (New York, 2001), 181.

28 "One million . . .": David Frum, *How We Got Here* (New York, 2000), 80.

28 "moral wilderness . . ." A. H. Halsey quoted in Jonathan Sacks, *The Politics of Hope* (London, 1997, 2000), 126.

29 85 percent . . . : Samuel Huntington, "The Democratic Distemper," in Nathan Glazer and Irving Kristol, eds., *The American Commonwealth 1976* (New York, 1976), 17, 18.

29 "journey into myself": Christopher Lasch, *The Culture of Narcissism* (New York, 1978), 15.

29 "This is the great . . .": Barbara Jordan quoted in Schulman, *Seventies*, 23–24.

30 "economic viability": *Business Week*, 30 June 1980, 58.

30 "deindustrialization . . .": Barry Bluestone and Bennett Harrison, *The Deindustrialization of America* (New York, 1982), 9.

31 "Welcome . . .": *WasPo*, 12 Aug. 1978, A8.

31 "We've been a . . .": Jimmy Carter 1976 acceptance speech in Bush, *Speeches*, 232.

32 "has managed the . . .": Steven F. Hayward, *The Age of Reagan: The Fall of the Old Liberal Order* (New York, 2001), 535.

32 "Beleaguered": Jimmy Carter, *Keeping Faith* (New York, 1982), 524.

32 "widespread, but erroneous . . .": Mary C. Brennan, *Turning Right in the Sixties* (Chapel Hill, 1995), 109.

34 "Let them eat . . .": Mickey Edwards to William Rusher, 31 Jan. 1978, 3, Box 29:7, William A. Rusher MSS, Lof C.

35 "rugged enough . . .": RR Mem, 21.

35 "one of the most important . . .": Frank Van Der Linden, *The Real Reagan* (New York, 1981), 45.

35 "Mr. Norm": RR in *Photoplay Combined with Movie Mirror*, Aug. 1942, 45.

35 "I *was* divorced . . .": *People*, 29 Dec.–5 Jan. 1981, 24.

36 "Like Barry . . ." Hayward, *Age of Reagan*, 100.

36 "a haven . . .": Arthur Frommer, *Goldwater from A to Z* (New York, 1964), 102.

36 "act like . . .": Hayward, *Age of Reagan*, 100.

36 "For many years . . .": ibid., 103.

36 "The former . . .": *The Progressive*, Sept. 1980, 9.

36 "Nancy, people . . .": *Look*, 31 Oct. 1967, 40.

36 "Mommy" . . . : Peggy Noonan, *What I Saw at the Revolution* (New York, 1990), 163. See also *WasPo*, 12 June 1987, D12.

37 "suburban warriors . . . .": Lisa McGirr, *Suburban Warriors* (Princeton, 2001), 16.

38 Gaining experience . . . : Brennan, *Turning Right*, 1–5.

38 "came out of my . . .": *NYT*, 18 May 1980, 2:23.

38 "Economic Freedom . . .": Milton and Rose Friedman, *Free to Choose* (New York, 1979), 2.

38 "The Reagan Detour": Richard Reeves, *The Reagan Detour* (New York, 1985).

39 "un-American . . .": McGirr, *Suburban Warriors*, 238.

39 "modern Boston . . .": Schulman, *Seventies*, 212.

39 "getting the . . .": RR *Hand*, 5 June 1978, 278.

40 "My definition . . .": RR in Jonathan Schoenwald, *A Time for Choosing* (New York, 2001), 194.

41 "to consistently . . .": Edwards to Rusher, 31 Jan. 1978, 4, 8.

41 "are at the bottom . . .": *WasPo*, 2 Nov. 1980, B1.

42 "inspire a . . .": Interview with Matthew Gerson, Bethesda, MD, 3 Feb. 2004.

42 "The voice . . .": RR to Edward Langley, 19 June 1979, RR *Letters*, 229.

42 "If I found . . .": RR in *USNWR*, 5 May 1980, 33.

42 "You want a principled . . .": *Fortune*, 19 May 1980, 79.

43 "We Republicans . . .": *National Review*, 22 Feb. 1980, 217.

43 Occupational Safety . . . : *Nwswk*, 21 Apr. 1980, 47.

44 "I've been on . . .": *USNWR*, 5 May 1980, 33–34.

44 "He's a nitwit": *WasPo*, 2 Nov. 1980, B2.

44 "I worry . . .": *Time*, 3 Nov. 1980, 28.

44 "lukewarm": *Fortune*, 19 May 1980, 80.

44 "simple formulas . . .": *Forbes*, 23 June 1980, 157.

44 "We believe that . . . .": *The Nation*, 1 Nov. 1980, 425.

44 "I'm afraid . . . *WasPo*, 2 Nov. 1980, H2.

44 "bring back . . .": *Fortune*, 19 May 1980, 81.

44 "The American people . . .": Jordan quoted in Austin Ranney, ed., *The American Elections of 1980* (Washington, DC, 1981), 212.

45 "hypothalamus . . .": G. B. Trudeau, *In Search of Reagan's Brain* (New York, 1980, 1981). See also *Nwswk*, 10 Nov. 1980, 121.

45 "blacks from . . .": Richard Harwood, "Labor Day, 1980," in Richard Harwood, ed., *The Pursuit of the Presidency, 1980* (New York, 1980), 284.

45 "I think appearance . . .": *NYT*, 24 Oct. 1980, 18.

46 a satellite photograph . . . : *NYT*, 4 Nov. 1980, C17, B1, A1, D6.

46 "dressing down . . .": *NYT*, 3 Nov. 1980, C19.

47 "what she thought . . .": *NYT*, 3 Nov. 1980, D15.

48 The best-seller . . . : See *NYT Book Review*, 2 Nov. 1980, 6:40; *WasPo*, 2 Nov. 1980, 12–13.

48 "landslide": *WasPo*, 5 Nov. 1980, A1.

48 "counter-revolution": *Nwswk*, 17 Nov. 1980, 27.

48 "MASSIVE SHIFT . . .": *USNWR*, 17 Nov. 1980, 26.

48 "More voters held . . .": Peter D. Hart, "The Regeneration of the Democrats," 2, in "DCC–Campaign 1980, 1979–1980," in *KOD* II:5.

49 "aging movie . . .": *NYT*, 30 Oct. 1980, A27.

1981—1600 Pennsylvania Avenue

Page

51 "hero-starved" . . . : *WasPo*, 28 Dec. 1980, D1.

52 "all of our . . .": *NYT*, 7 Jun. 1981, 2:19.

52 "counter-establishment": Sidney Blumenthal, *The Rise of the Counter-Establishment* (New York, 1988).

53 A post-election . . . : "Report on Transition," Helene von Damm to Edwin Meese III, 29 May 1981, 5, OA 5097, EM Files, RR Lib.

53 "that political mandates . . .": "Final Report of the Initial Actions Project," 29 Jan. 1981, 8, 6–7, Strategic Planning Memoranda-4 (1), CFOA465, Richard S. Beal MSS, RR Lib.

54 "were involved . . .": "Report on Transition," 14, OA 5097.

54 "seventeen of . . .": Tevi Troy, *Intellectuals and the American Presidency* (Lanham, MD, 2002), 147. See Peter Duignan and Alvin Rabushka, eds., *The United States in the 1980s* (Palo Alto, 1980).

54 "pre-election transition . . .": "Report on Transition," 72–76, OA 5097.

54 Policy Task Force . . . : See ibid., 68–70.

54 "Man of the Year" . . . : *Time*, 5 Jan. 1981, 11–13.

55 A picture . . . : Jimmy Carter, *Keeping Faith* (New York, 1982), 6–13.

56 mementoes . . . : See *USNWR*, 19 Jan. 1981, 47.

56 "We sort of . . .": *LAT*, 13 Jan. 1988, 6:1.

56 "I wore . . .": *NYT*, 7 Apr. 1985, 2:1.

56 "renewed need . . .": Esther Shapiro, *Dynasty* (New York, 1984), 2.

56 "awareness of business" . . . : *NYT*, 7 Apr. 1985, 29.

56 "When you've got . . .": *Nwswk*, 2 Feb. 1981, 55–57.

57 "history closing . . .": NR *Mem*, 231.

57 "They clearly . . .": *Time*, 2 Feb. 1981, 12.

57 "One of the . . .": RR *Mem*, 225–226.

57 "Fortunately it's . . .": NR *Mem*, 232.

58 "This begins . . .": RR Memo, 20 Jan. 1981, 0711, Box 64:6, DTR.

59 The Pavilion . . . : See *WasPo*, 12 Sept. 1983, 32.

59 "moonscape . . .": *WasPo*, 20 Jan. 1981, 14.

61 "What's important . . .": Blumenthal, *Counter-Establishment*, 33.

61 "detail experts . . .": Troy, *Intellectuals*, 145.

61 "a department . . .": Terrel H. Bell, *The Thirteenth Man* (New York, 1988), 27, 39, 26.

61 The modern presidency . . . : Richard M. Pious, *The Presidency* (Needham Heights, MA, 1996), 67, 273–279.

62 "Ronnie wanted" . . . : NR *Mem*, 114. See also "Initial Actions Project," 29 Jan. 1981, 3.

62 "I hope she . . .": Katherine Graham, *Personal History* (New York, 1997), 611–612.

63 "lessons of . . .": Burton Yale Pines, "The Lessons of Reaganomics," pamphlet issued by the Heritage Foundation (Washington, DC, 1987), 3–10.

63 public confidence . . . : LHarris, 233.

63 "of all the demanding . . .": "Initial Actions Project," CFOA465, 5.

63 "the central . . .": ibid., 33.

64 "symbolic as well . . .": Stan Ebner to EM et al., "First 90 Days Project, Rough Draft," 13 Jan. 1981, 1, Box 12,390, Richard S. Beal MSS, RR Lib.

65 "only nonmillionaire" . . . : Bell, *Thirteenth Man*, 30.

65 "competence . . . where is . . .": *Boston Herald American*, 4 Jan. 1981, A12.

65 "Each day's headlines . . .": Jeffrey Stein, "Jitters," *Progressive*, Jan. 1981, 12.

65 "the wunderkind . . .": *Nwswk*, 16 Feb. 1981, 21, 24.

65 "the most important . . .": *WasPo*, 5 Feb. 1981, 1.

65 "boom . . .": *Nwswk*, 16 Feb. 1981, 24.

67 twenty times . . . : David W. Brady and Craig Volden, *Revolving Gridlock* (New York, 1998), 52.

67 "For the first . . .": David Stockman, *The Triumph of Politics* (New York, 1986), 39–40.

67 "ancient" . . . : ibid., 49.

68 "appearance of . . .": ibid., 56.

68 "for better . . .": ibid., 46–47. See Brady and Volden, *Gridlock*, 56–57.

68 common sense: RR, 31 July 1978 in RR *Hand*, 258.

69 "I place . . .": RR to Murray W. Ratzlaff, 14 Dec. 1983, 191892, Box 25, FG001, WHORM.

69 "weave . . .": Raymond Moley, *After Seven Years* (New York, 1939), 48, 51.

69 "Okay, you . . .": Stockman, *Triumph*, 109.

69 One scene . . . : RR *Mem*, 231–232.

69 "Some in the media . . .": RR to Clymer L. Wright, Jr., 18 May 1982, 079222, FG 001, Box 7, PHF II.

70 Program for . . . : "America's New Beginning: A Program for Economic Recovery," 2, 18 Feb. 1981, OA 2991, EM MSS, RR Lib.

70 "With all the . . .": Dana Rohrabacher, Talking Points: Presidential Briefing 9:15 a.m., 10 Feb. 1981, 043321, Presidential Briefing Papers, RR Lib.

70 "think people . . .": William Safire, *Safire's New Political Dictionary* (New York, 1993), 220.

71 "a four-eyed wimp . . .": Stockman, *Triumph*, 291.

72 "Iron Chancellor": ibid., 11.

72 "public mind . . .": Alice Rivlin, 10 Apr. 1981, notes for a speech on Congress and the Budget, 16 Apr. 1981, Alice Rivlin MSS, Lof C.

72 "We just beat . . .": Ed Rollins, *Bare Knuckles and Back Rooms* (New York, 1996), 103.

73 "Would you please . . .": Lyn Nofziger to All Members of the Cabinet, 31 Dec. 1981, 82-131, Box 185:6, White House Files, Treasury Department Subject Files, DTR.

73 "Mission accomplished . . .": Max L. Friedersdorf and Powell A. Moore [to RR], RR comment, 21 Apr. 1981, PR 007-02, Box 1, PHF IV.

73 "He's gung ho . . .": Max L. Friedersdorf [to RR], RR comment, 23–26 Apr. 1981, PR 007-02, Box 1, PHF IV.

73 "a lack of . . .": Presidential Log of Selected House Mail, 21 May 1981, Stephen J. Solarz, Jim Leach, and Joel Pritchard to RR; 5 Oct. 1981, Norman Lent and "6 Others," to RR; 21 May 1981, Ralph M. Hall to RR; 23 Sept. 1981, Peter Peyser to RR, all in Box 1, PHF V.

74 "'Godfather' tactics": Speaker's Press Conference, 23 June 1981, Tip VI 11:1.

74 "Members of . . .": Speaker's Press Conference, 16 July 1981, Tip VI 11:2.

74 "Every day . . .": Bell, *Thirteenth Man*, 19.

75 "REAGAN DIP . . .": *LAT*, 19 Mar. 1981, I:6.

75 "what sounded . . .": RR *Mem*, 259.

75 "I'm very lucky . . .": RR to Mrs. Samuel G. Harrod, 15 June 1981, 029131, PR 007-02, Box 1, PHF II.

76 "Does Nancy . . .": RR *Mem*, 260–261.

76 "HOUSE PASSES . . .": *LAT*, 8 May 1981, 1.

77 "Petrified Party . . .": *LAT*, 1 Mar. 1981, 4:6.

77 "very severe . . .": Consumer Opinion Survey, Survey Research Center, U.S. Chamber of Commerce, Apr. 1981, polling data, 1 of 2, Box 6391, EHD MSS.

77 "Finally, the Watergate . . .": *LAT*, 23 Apr. 1981, 2:8.

77 "Limousines and . . .": *TNR*, 13 June 1981, 20.

78 "moral issue . . .": Willis J. Nordlund, *Silent Skies* (Westport, CT, 1998), 6, 1; poll quoted in William E. Pemberton, *Exit with Honor* (Armonk, NY, 1997), 107.

78 "It struck me . . .": Cannon, 437.

78 "I've asked so . . .": Haynes Johnson, *Sleepwalking through History* (New York, 1991, 1992), 154.

78 "defeating the . . .": "Summary of Discussion" with Paul Volcker, Martin Feldstein, et al. in Martin Feldstein, ed., *American Economic Policy in the 1980s* (Chicago, 1994), 162.

78 "of it in . . .": RR *Mem*, 283.

79 "Trojan horse . . .": Atlantic, Dec. 1981, 27–51.

79 "so he would . . .": Lesley Stahl, *Reporting Live* (New York, 1999), 142.

79 "an admitted . . .": RR to Justin Dart, 7 Dec. 1981, 048088, Box 1, PHF III.

80 "You do that . . .": Stockman, *Triumph*, 375.

81 "Madisonian . . .": ibid., 9.

81 "the formulas . . .": Thomas P. O'Neill, Jr., "A Deliberate Recession," Nov. 1981, 2, Tip VI Statements 9:13.

82 Polls showed . . . : See *LAT*, 26 Apr. 1981, 4:1.

82 "It's clear the . . .": William B. Lacy to Mitchell E. Daniels, 13 Mar. 1986, 396197, Box 42, FG 001 RR Lib.

1982—Hill Street

Page

85 exit polls: Robert Dallek, *Ronald Reagan* (Cambridge, 1984, 1999), 115.

86 "reign of terror . . .": *Time*, 23 Feb. 1981, p. 81. For statistics, see "The President's Criminal Justice Reform Package (Talking Points)," 13 Sept. 1982, Dave's Project (4), OA 14,712, White House Office of Public Affairs: Records, RR Lib.

86 "We are . . .": Kathleen W. Haskett to RR, 23 Oct. 1981, Box 1, PHF II. The writer was the granddaughter of Charles E. Wilson, former president of General Motors and Eisenhower's secretary of defense. Reagan forwarded the letter to his Attorney General William French Smith, noting, "I don't know what the solution is."

87 "racially motivated . . . resurgence": *Nwswk*, 2 Mar. 1981, 36.

87 "THE TERROR in . . .": ibid., 23 Mar. 1981, 8–9.

87 "one of the . . .": ibid.

88 "increase in crime . . . .": 22 Dec. 1976, in RR *Hand*, 400–401.

88 "1 year in . . .": 30 Nov. 1976, in ibid., 402–403.

88 12 percent of . . . : *NYTM*, 16 May 1982, 6:38. See also Andrew Hacker, *Two Nations* (New York, 1992, 1995), 188–191.

89 "incentives to . . .": Charles Murray, *Losing Ground* (New York, 1984), 170, 9.

89 Polls suggested . . . : "Crime and Judges: An Opportunity Issue for 1984," 2, 13, Judicial Background Information (1 of 6), OA 16024, Office of White House Public Affairs: Information Record, RR Lib.

89 "the highest rate . . .": *Time*, 13 Apr. 1981, 51.

89 "I've always . . .": Presidential Log of Selected House Mail, 25 Aug. 1981, Box 1, PHF V.

90 "didn't even blink . . .": Kenneth O'Reilly, *Nixon's Piano* (New York, 1995), 357.

90 "High Proportion . . .": "Black Policy Issues Matrix Comments," c. Mar.–Apr. 1982, 2, Box 4533, EHD.

90 "preserve domestic . . .": William A. Hamilton to Lorraine Spiliotis, 15 Apr. 1981, OA 4814, EM MSS, RR Lib.

91 "State of Black . . .": National Urban League, "NUL Releases 7th Annual 'State of Black America,'" 18 Jan. 1982, Box 4533, EHD.

91 blacks defining themselves . . . : 51 percent of whites considered themselves middle class: see Stephan Thernstrom and Abigail Thernstrom, *America in Black and White* (New York, 1997), 200, 192, 187, 211.

91 "another case . . .": "Press Conference—Congressmen Addabo & Mitchell also in Attendance," c. 24 Jan 1983, "Minority Business Enterprise [1 of 5]," EHD.

91 "deregulation . . . code word . . .": Remarks of Nathaniel Scurry, assistant director for civil rights, Office of Management and Budget, 15 May 1981, Box 4533, EHD.

91 "a kind of . . .": The President's News Conference, 16 June 1981, Pub.

92 "too much attention . . .": DMI Polls, 19 Feb. 1982, Box 4533, EHD.

92 "The Administration's Policy . . .": Richard S. Beal to EM, 8 July 1981, Box 12,390, "First 90 Days Project—Rough Draft (1), " Richard S. Beal MSS, RR Lib.

92 "perhaps the most . . .": Thelma Duggin to Elizabeth Dole via Red Cavaney and Cavaney scribbling to Elizabeth Dole, 5 June 1981, Box 4533, EHD.

93 "war, pestilence . . .": "Tony Brown's Journal," c. 29 June 1981, Box 4533, EHD.

93 "Thanks for the . . .": Talking Points, Private Meeting with Black Reagan–Bush Supporters, July 9, 1981, Box 4533, EHD.

93 "an unusual degree . . .": The Gallup Poll, 27 Sept. 1981, "Gallup Polls, *LAT*, ABC, NBC, CBS [1]" OA 7239, Richard S. Beal MSS.

93 One CBS poll . . . : William Raspberry in *WasPo*, 22 Feb. 1982, A11.

94 "There will be . . .": The President's News Conference, 29 Jan. 1981, Pub.

94 "Whoever came up . . .": Recommended Telephone Call, Max L. Friedersdorf and Powell A. Moore to RR re: Lowell Weicker, 17 Nov. 1981, PR 007-02, Box 1, PHF IV.

94 "quotas, proportional . . .": Pendleton in Thomas Byrne Edsall with Mary D. Edsall, *Chain Reaction* (New York, 1991, 1992), 191.

94 "racial quotas . . . favor . . .": *San Diego Union*, 4 Jan. 1982, A10.

94 "It is my . . .": Clarence Pendleton to EM, 4 Jan. 1982, 054846, Box 4, FG 001, RR Lib.

95 "a *quota* system . . . .": Robert A. McConnell to Craig L. Fuller, 25 Jan 1982, 4,3, Box 4533, EHD.

95 "exquisitely bad . . .": Chester E. Finn, Jr., "'Affirmative Action' Under Reagan," *Commentary*, Apr. 1982, 27.

95 "not allowing . . .": *WasPo*, 17 Jan. 1982, A1.

96 "senior White House . . .": *Nwswk*, 25 Jan. 1982, 24.

96 "crisis of . . .": Finn, "Affirmative Action," 27.

96 "This president . . .": *WasPo*, 17 Jan. 1982, A1.

96 "[A]gencies such . . .": Letter to the President of the Senate and the Speaker of the House, 18 Jan. 1982, Pub.

96 "Are you responsible . . . .": President's News Conference, 19 Jan. 1982, Pub.

96 "perception in the . . .": Thelma Duggin to Elizabeth Dole, 1 Sept. 1981, Box 4533, EHD.

96 "Black Strategy": Elizabeth Dole to JAB, 5 Apr. 1982, OA 4533, EHD.

96 "might serve to . . .": Max Friedersdorf to RR, RR to Max Friedersdorf, c. 10 Sept. 1981, PR 007-02 Box 1, PHF IV.

97 "cheap politics . . .": RR *Mem*, 183.

97 "blacks in presidential . . .": Thelma Duggin to Elizabeth Dole, 28 Apr. 1981, Box 4533, EHD.

97 "black White House . . .": Mel Bradley to Michael Deaver, 28 Sept. 1981, Box 4533, EHD.

97 "minority-owned . . .": Elizabeth Dole to William K. Sadleir, 29 Sept. 1982, OA 6390, EHD.

97 "Lionel Hampton . . .": Thelma Duggin to Elizabeth Dole, 1 Sept. 1981, Box 4533, EHD.

97 "especially since . . .": Jim Cicconi to Elizabeth Dole et al., 7 Apr. 1982, Box 4533, EHD.

97 "merit seemed . . .": Finn, "Affirmative Action," 22.

97 institutionalizing . . . : See Robert R. Detlefsen, *Civil Rights under Reagan* (San Francisco, 1991); John David Skrntny, *The Ironies of Affirmative Action* (Chicago, 1996), 226.

97 "where the only . . .": *WasPo*, 2 July 1982, A18.

97 "but one charge . . .": *Nwswk*, 27 Sept. 1982, 62.

98 "have hurt us . . .": *LAT*, 24 Mar. 1982, 1:17.

98 "The main concern . . .": *WasPo*, 29 Mar. 1982, A11.

98 polls finding . . . : Gallup Polls, 27 Sept. 1981, OA 7239, RR Lib.

99 "the mean-spirited . . .": Tip O'Neill with William Novak, *Man of the House* (New York, 1987), 346, 348.

99 best-seller . . . : George Gilder, *Wealth and Poverty* (New York, 1984); Milton and Rose Friedman, *Free to Choose* (New York, 1979); Charles Murray, *Losing Ground* (New York, 1984).

99 "Exploding Some Myths . . .": Vernon Jordan in *LAT*, 16 Feb. 1981, 2:9.

99 "Making the world . . .": Walter Karp, "Coolidge Redux," *Harper's*, Oct. 1981, 30–36.

99 "big, fat . . .": *WasPo*, 12 July 1981, A9.

100 "My father was . . .": John A. Farrell, *Tip O'Neill and the Democratic Century* (Boston, 2001), 50, 8.

101 "setting . . . the imbalance . . .": Jerry Colbert to Tip O'Neill, c. June 1981, 1–2, Box 3, II KOD.

101 "I was the highest . . .": O'Neill, *Man of the House*, 26.

101 "panic our party . . .": Mario Cuomo to Tip O'Neill, 24 Nov. 1980, Box 4, KOD.

102 "Is it after . . .": O'Neill, *Man of the House*, 332–333. RR, *Mem*, 233.

102 "Do you think . . .": Charles Gibson, "Issues and Answers, " 7 June 1981, Tip VI, "Speeches."

103 "got help from . . .": O'Neill, *Man of the House*, 347.

103 "The school lunch . . .": Speaker's Press Conference, 27 Apr. 1981, Box 11, Tip VI.

104 "By hitting Social . . .": Speaker's Statement, 20 May 1981, Press Statements, Box 9, Tip VI.

104 "That was the only . . . .": Laurence I. Barrett, *Gambling with History* (New York, 1983), 158.

104 "The economy . . .": Farrell, *Tip, 579*; Kirk O'Donnell to Tip O'Neill, 4 Aug. 1981, Box 13, KOD.

104 "false image-building . . .": RR to Kenneth Loebker, 24 June 1982, 084966, PR 016, RR Lib.

105 "A member of . . .": Speaker's Press Conference, 4 May 1981, 2, Box 11, Tip VI.

105 "[M]ake it a referendum . . .": O'Donnell to O'Neill, 4 Aug. 1981, 10, 11, 9.

106 "$141.2 billion . . .": Max L. Friedersdorf, "Meetings with Selected Democratic Members of the House of Representatives," 4 May 1981, OA 13528, Attachment B, Ellen Bradley Files, RR Lib. See also Thomas S. Foley, "Whip Issue Paper: Major Differences Between Latta Substitute and the Budget Committee Resolution Include . . . ," 1 May 1981, Box 6, KOD II:6.

106 "economic arrangements . . .": Michael Sandel, *Democracy's Discontent* (Cambridge, MA, 1996), 274.

107 "combination of policies . . .": Alice Rivlin, notes at American Economics Association Meeting in San Francisco, 28 Dec. 1983, Alice Rivlin MSS.

107 "entitlement grants . . .": See Richard Nathan and Fred C. Doolittle, eds., *The Consequence of Cuts* (Princeton, 1983), 6, 25.

108 "the largest single . . .": Herbert Parmet, "Voodoo Economics," www.tompaine.com, 29 Feb. 2000; see also Bruce Bartlett, "A Taxing Experience," www.nationalreview.com, 29 Oct. 2003.

108 "poor vs. rich . . .": Vic Fingerhut to Democratic Senate Policy Committee Theme Group et al. , 15 Nov. 1983, 4–5, Box 5, KOD.

108 "We have been . . .": Matt Reese to Tip O'Neill, 27 July 1983, Document "New Mexico, 1982" quotes Charles Mannatt, Jr., 27 Feb. 1981, Box 4, KOD.

108 "a federation of . . .": *NYT*, 1 Mar. 1981, 4:1.

109 "Reagan Hood . . .": ibid.

109 "*If the Republicans* . . .": Letter of Peter Rodino, c. fall 1981, Democratic Congressional Campaign Committee Fundraising Letter, Box 5, KOD.

109 "to blitz the . . .": Byron L. Dorgan to Tony Coehlo, 29 Jan. 1982, Box 6, KOD.

109 Pollsters found . . . : See DCCC Campaign, "1982, 1981–1983 Democratic Poll Report, a Survey of the Political Climate in America and Voter Attitudes toward the 1982 Elections," Box 6, KOD.

110 "The breadth of . . .": *BosG*, 4 Nov. 1982, 33.

110 "The 1980 election . . .": *NYT*, 5 Nov. 1982, A27.

110 "Budgets, budgets . . .": See Richard S. Beal to EM, JAB, Michael Deaver, Strategic Evaluation Memorandum 12, 25 Feb. 1982, CFOA 465, Richard Beal MSS, RR Lib. LSG [Legislative Group] Agenda, 13 Dec. 1982, 11777755, FG 006-01, RR Lib. RR to Edward H. Sims, 22 Mar. 1982, 067388, Box 2, PHF II; RR to George S. Eccles, 8 Mar. 1982, BE 004, Box 2, PHF IV.

111 one exit poll: Dallek, *Reagan*, 115.

111 "big parade . . .": *CSM*, 6 Aug. 1981, B20.

111 "black gash . . .": *CSM*, 29 Oct. 1981, 2.

111 "The names . . .": *WasPo*, 11 Nov. 1982, B1.

112 "The stench . . .": *NYT*, 9 Jan. 1983, A22.

112 David Broder . . . : *WasPo*, 12 Jan. 1983, A19.

112 "Is it news . . .": *Nwswk*, 29 Mar. 1982, 77.

112 "the electronic media . . .": *USNWR*, 7 Dec. 1981, 25.

1983—Beaufort, South Carolina

Page

116 A $5.2 million . . . : See *CSM*, 9 Dec. 1980, 15.

116 "memory . . . identity . . .": *NYT Book Review*, 27 Oct. 1985, 7:54; see also Michael Ventura, *Shadow Dancing in the USA* (New York, 1985).

116 "Ultimately, *The Big* . . .": Gary Arnold in *WasPo*, 30 Sept. 1983, E1.

116 "talking about . . .": *LAT*, 20 Mar. 1988, 6:1.

118 yearning to earn . . . : See David Brooks, *Bobos in Paradise* (New York, 2000).

118 "in managerial . . .": RR, "State of the Union Address," 1984.

118 "again becoming the . . .": RR, Remarks at Eureka College in Eureka, Ill., 6 Feb. 1984, ibid.

119 "'consuming public' . . .": Lizabeth Cohen, *A Consumer's Republic* (New York, 2003), 8. See also Meg Jacobs, "'Democracy's Third Estate:' New Deal Politics and the Construction of a 'Consuming Public,'" *International Labor and Working-Class History*, spring 1999, 55:27; Barzun, *From Dawn to Decadence*, 783.

119 "the individual suspended . . .": Robert Bellah et al., *Habits of the Heart* (New York, 1985), 6, 7.

119 "40 percent . . .": *Fortune*, 6 July 1987, 26.

119 "I love . . .": Jay McInerney, *Bright Lights, Big City* (New York, 1984), 6.

120 America's oldest . . . : Bruce Schulman, *The Seventies* (New York, 2001), 243.

121 "How can I . . .": Hendrik Hertzberg, "The Short Happy Life of the American Yuppie," *Esquire*, Feb. 1988, 106, 102, 103.

121 *Easy Rider* . . . : *LAT*, 20 Mar. 1988, 6:1.

121 "the new generation . . .": *RS*, 24 Dec. 1981–7 Jan. 1982, 11–12.

122 "a sudden . . .": *Nwswk*, 31 Dec. 1984, 19–20, 25.

122 "1982 a cascade . . .": *Time*, 3 Jan. 1983, 8.

122 "You can't be apathetic . . .": *LAT*, 20 Mar. 1988, 6:1.

123 millionaires increased . . . : *Fortune*, 6 July 1987, 26.

123 what the quintessential . . . : Marissa Piesman and Marilee Hartley *The Yuppie Handbook* (New York, 1984), 14.

123 "Rebels in . . .": Miriam Horn, *Rebels in White Gloves* (New York, 1999).

124 "not think and . . .": *American Demographics*, Sept. 1985, 23.

124 Americans under forty . . . : *American Demographics*, Jan. 1988, 2; see also *American Demographics*, Sept. 1985, 23; *Nwswk*, 31 Dec. 1984, 25.

125 "favorite uncle . . . most": *CSM*, 5 Mar. 1981, 6.

125 "for the money": *American Heritage*, Dec. 1994, 43.

125 "*New York Times* of . . .": Steven Stark, *Glued to the Set* (New York, 1998), 125.

125 "Never in the history . . .": Walter Cronkite, *A Reporter's Life* (New York, 1996), 353.

125 "He's the national . . .": *Esquire*, Apr. 1973, 84.

126 "You've always . . .": *CSM* 5 Mar. 1981, 6.

127 Cable would be . . . : *NYTM*, 19 May 2002, 35.

127 "What those networks . . .": Robert Goldberg and Gerald J. Goldberg, *Citizen Turner* (New York, 1995), 266.

127 "regular series . . .": ibid., 227–228.

128 "the heartland . . .": Cronkite, *Reporter's Life*, 358. See also Stahl, *Reporting Live*, 150.

128 "TV is becoming . . .": *LAT*, 27 Dec. 1989, F1.

128 "a peg . . . use . . .": *NYTM*, 8 May 1983, 55.

129 "I want my . . .": E. Ann Kaplan, *Rocking around the Clock* (New York, 1987), 18.

129 album sales . . . : *NYT*, 29 Nov. 1982, D1.

129 advertising revenues . . .": Stark, *Glued to the Set*, 244; Kaplan, *Rocking*, 21.

129 "most influential . . .": Stark, *Glued to the Set*, 243.

131 "new age . . .": *Independent,* 22 May 1920, 245, 244.

131 "the upsurge . . .": Irving Kristol, "On Corporate Capitalism in America," in Nathan Glazer and Irving Kristol, eds., *The American Commonwealth 1976* (New York, 1976), 126.

132 "Let's make . . .": Lee Iacocca with William Novak, *Iacocca* (New York, 1984), 270, 271.

133 "a brash Adonis . . .": *NYT*, 7 Aug. 1983, 3:1.

133 "mystery news . . .": *NYT*, 15 Nov. 1986, 1:35.

133 "one of the bolder . . .": *NYT*, 21 Nov. 1986, B1.

134 "can-do attitude . . . grating . . .": *NYT*, 25 May 1980 3:4.

134 changing corporate . . . : Paul Krugman, "For Richer," *NYTM*, 20 Oct. 2002, 6:62.

134 419 times . . . : Kevin Phillips, *Wealth and Democracy* (New York, 2002), 153.

134 Affluent Americans . . . : See Juliet B. Schor, *The Overspent American* (New York, 1998).

135 "exclusive interview . . .": *NYT*, 3 Dec. 1983, A9.

135 "a simple statistic . . . all . . .": 27 Aug. 1982, in Daniel P. Moynihan, *Came the Revolution* (New York, 1988), 108–109.

136 "Reaganism is . . .": William Schneider in *TNR*, 5 Mar. 1984, 13.

136 "the social safety . . .": White House Talking Points, 1 Feb. 1983, OA 14712, Dave's Project, White House Office of Public Affairs: Records, RR Lib.

136 "Ronald Reagan must be . . .": Robert Lekachman, *Greed Is Not Enough* (New York, 1982), 7.

136 "The false choice . . .": Robert Reich, *The Next American Frontier* (New York, 1983), 6.

136 Thurow's 1980 book . . . : Lester Thurow, *The Zero Sum Society* (New York, 1980).

137 "era of productivity . . .": Reich, *Frontier*, 20.

137 "We're here . . .": David Maraniss, *First in His Class* (New York, 1995), 459.

137 "out of the hides . . .": Stanley B. Greenberg, *Middle Class Dreams* (New York, 1995), 200, 202.

138 "The Soviets . . .": Dave Gergen to Administration Spokesmen, 6 Aug. 1982, OA 12432, Kenneth Duberstein Files, Office of Legislative Affairs Series IV, "Arms Resolution (1)," RR Lib.

138 "From Greenwich . . .": Jonathan Schell, *The Fate of the Earth* (New York, 1982), 48.

138 "largest march . . . No draft . . .": *LAT*, 4 May 1981, 1.

138 "voodoo . . .": Robert Dallek, *Ronald Reagan* (Cambridge, 1984, 1999), 152.

138 "immoral": Michael Schaller, *Reckoning with Reagan* (New York, 1992), 128.

139 "dangerous . . . well-intentioned . . .": RR to Sam Ervin, 25 Apr. 1983, 830425, SP 735, RR Lib.

139 "defensive technologies . . .": RR, "Peace and National Security Address," 23 Mar. 1983, in Pub.

139 "El Salvador is nearer . . .": RR, Address before a Joint Session of Congress, 27 Apr. 1983, in Pub.

140 "half national . . .": David Gergen to RR, 21 Nov. 1983, 10513, JAB MSS, RR Lib.

140 80 percent or . . . : LHarris, 336.

141 "the end of the . . .": NBC quoted in Carl Pope, "The Politics of Plunder," *Sierra* (Nov./ Dec. 1988) in Paul Boyer, ed., *Reagan as President* (Chicago, 1990), 184.

141 "the greatest threat . . .": *Nwswk*, 5 Jan. 1981, 17.

141 "a left-wing . . .": James Watt interview with Novak and Evans, 27 Mar. 1982, CNN, Watt, 1 of 4, Box 9015, White House Office of Public Affairs, Records, RR Lib.

141 "Liberals and . . .": Watt in Schaller, *Reckoning*, 100.

141 "a bad joke": *Nwswk*, 16 Mar. 1981, 74; see also *NYT*, 21 June 1981, 1:36.

141 "[O]nly a . . .": "White Paper—Environmental Policy," OA 11586, Environmental Information Program, Michael Deaver MSS.

141 "steady progress . . .": *TNR*, 22–29 Aug. 1981, 9–10.

142 "I fancy myself . . .": RR, "Interview with Reporters from *LAT*," 21 Jan. 1982, in Pub.

142 "President Reagan has broken . . .": *CSM*, 1 Apr. 1982, 6.

142 "Take a deep . . .": *RS*, 6 Aug. 1981, 25.

142 Cartoons . . . : See Thomas Oliphant cartoon in *RS*, 7 June 1984, 8.
142 "one of the poorest . . .": "Environmentalists Air Mondale Ads," U.P.I., 16 Oct. 1984, 1.
142 "You can't take money . . .": *WasPo*, 6 Mar. 1983, C1.
142 "mix . . .": Schaller, *Reckoning*, 102.
143 "to the entire problem . . .": RR, "Remarks and a Question-and-Answer Session with Regional Editors on Foreign and Domestic Issues," 9 July 1984.
143 "turn around . . .": "Memorandum to the File," 3 June 1983, OA 8546, "Daily Status Reports," Michael Deaver MSS, RR Lib.
143 "Preservation of our . . .": RR, "Address before a Joint Session of the Congress on the State of the Union," 25 Jan. 1984, in Pub.
143 "largest non-defense-spending . . .": *USNWR*, 20 Aug. 1984, 40.
143 "strengthened, rather . . .": Pope, "Politics of Plunder," in Boyer, *Reagan*, 185–186.
144 "Ronald Reagan is endangering . . .": Michael McCloskey, executive director, Sierrra Club, fundraising letter, n.d., Memorandum File Subseries B, 1982–1983, JAB Series, in Michael Deaver MSS, RR Lib.
145 "when they assaulted . . .": *LAT*, 14 Aug. 1985 5:1. See also Todd Gitlin, *The Sixties* (New York, 1987, 1989), xii; Tom Hayden, *Reunion* (New York, 1988), 501.
145 "to the self-aggrandizing . . .": Peter Collier and David Horowitz, *The Destructive Generation* (New York, 1989), 321.
146 "What's the Doughboy . . .": Ben Cohen, *Ben & Jerry's Double Dip: How To Run a Values Led Business and Make Money Too* (New York, 1998), 202.

1984—Los Angeles

Page
147 "twenty-second . . .": *WasPo*, 11 Nov. 1984, A3.
147 "Robert Redford . . .": *WasPo*, 14 Nov. 1984, A19.
148 "shallowness . . . atrocious abdication . . .": "Mondale the Mean," Republican National Committee, in Michael J. Bayer to Maureen Reagan, 15 Oct. 1984, Series I, Memorandum File, Subseries C, 1984–Jan. 1985, JAB MSS, RR Lib.
148 "a crusade . . . I am . . .": James MacGregor Burns, *Roosevelt: The Lion and the Fox* (New York, 1956), 266, 287.
148 "If we allow . . .": Jim Lake to JAB, 8 Mar. 1984, Box 9, Series I, Memorandum File, Subseries C, 1984–Jan. 1985, JAB MSS, RR Lib.
148 "two objectives . . . 1. Securing . . .": JAB, "Trip Proposals," 25 Oct. 1984, ibid.
149 "great renewal . . . Four years . . .": Peggy Noonan, *What I Saw at the Revolution* (New York, 1990), 124.
149 "tremendous excitement . . .": RR *Mem*, 265.

150 "the Last Men . . .": Gilbert T. Sewall, "Revisiting the Eighties," in Gilbert T. Sewall, ed., *The Eighties* (Reading, MA, 1997), xvii.

151 "California is ungovernable": Georgia Anne Geyer, *Americans No More* (New York, 1996), 282.

152 "I hoped . . .": *Time*, 7 Jan. 1985, 25.

152 "Patriotism is . . .": *USNWR*, 9 July 1984, 58.

152 "there's a spirit . . .": *Time*, 7 Jan. 1985, 25.

153 "the U.S. wins . . .": *NYT*, 9 Aug. 1984, C18.

153 "nationalistic zeal . . . distorted . . .": William Greider in *RS Yearbook 1984*, 20 Dec. 1984–3 Jan. 1985, 124.

154 "the president's approval . . .": Richard S. Beal to EM, Strategic Evaluation Memorandum #8, 19 Nov. 1981, CFOA 465, Richard S. Beal MSS, RR Lib.

154 "the unfairest tax . . .": "Inflation's Staying Down," 23 Sept. 1982, WHTALK.

154 "Good Economic . . .": "Good Economic News," 28 Jan. 1983, WHTALK.

154 "Leading Indicators . . .": "Leading Indicators Index Rise Highest since 1950," 2 Mar. 1983, WHTALK.

154 lowest level . . . . : "Inflation Update," 22 July 1983, WHTALK.

154 "creating over 300,000 . . .": "A New Beginning: The First 1000 Days," 18 Oct. 1983, WHTALK.

154 "Sunny Mood . . .": *Time*, 18 July 1983, 6.

154 "experts . . . preaching . . .": RR, "Radio Address to the Nation on the Quality of Life in America," 15 Oct. 1983, Pub.

154 "This renewal . . .": RR, "Remarks at the Annual Convention of the National Association of Evangelicals in Columbus, Ohio," 6 Mar. 1984, Pub.

155 "religious insight . . .": Mark A. Noll, *A History of Christianity in the United States and Canada* (Grand Rapids, 1992), 475.

155 "quiet faith": Alan Wolfe, *One Nation, After All* (New York, 1998), 40–41, 54.

155 "When I first . . .": "Text of Address by the President," 29 Jan. 1984, SP840, RR Lib.

156 editing . . . : Presidential Address: Re-Election Announcement Speech, Sunday, 29 Jan. 1984, draft marked (Khachigian) 17 Jan. 1984, 10:00 a.m., 1, SP840, RR Lib.

156 a thousand-voice . . . : *NYT*, 29 July 1984, 1.

156 "With this much . . .": Cannon, 147.

157 "Tip O'Neill may . . .": Tip O'Neill with William Novak, *Man of the House* (New York, 1987), 364.

157 "any incumbent . . .": *Nwswk*, 20 Feb. 1984, 49.

157 "Can you imagine . . .": *RS*, 19 Jan. 1984, 16.

157 "Hooray! Hooray! . . .": Thomas M. O'Brien to RR, 26 Oct. 1983, Folder 102, Box 7, PHF II.

157 "TIDY U.S. WAR . . .": *WasPo*, Mel Elfin quoted in *RS*, 19 Jan. 1984, 15.

158 "consensus politics . . .": Howard Phillips in *Des Moines Register*, 4 Feb. 1981, 4A.

158 forty-five Conservative . . . : "Statement of Conservative Leaders, Washington, D.C.," 21 Jan. 1982, and brief summary, both in OA 2903, Lee Atwater MSS, RR Lib.

158 63 percent . . . : *Conservative Digest*, Oct. 1983, in Box 9, "Political Affairs, Jan. 1984–July 1984," JAB MSS, RR Lib.

158 "REAGAN CHOICE . . .": *WasPo*, 8 July 1981, A2.

158 "matters of . . .": Hadley Arkes, "A Lover's Lament for the Reagan Administration," *National Review*, 28 May 1982, 618–619.

158 "one person . . .": RR to Marie Craven, 3 Aug. 1981, *The O'Connor Report*, Aug. 1981, 2, in OA 2903, Lee Atwater MSS, RR Lib.

158 "you cannot . . .": Richard A. Viguerie to RR, 10 Oct. 1983 in Roy Brewer to RR, 7 Nov. 1983, Folder 104, Box 7, PHF II.

159 "You know . . .": RR to Roy Brewer, 17 Nov. 1983, 188589, PR003, Folder 104, Box 7, PHF II.

159 "I still believe . . .": RR to Craven, *O'Connor Report*, 2.

159 "move for the . . .": Jim Lake to JAB, 8 Mar. 1984, in Box 9, "Political Affairs, Jan. 1984–July 1984," JAB MSS, RR Lib.

159 "the net effect . . .": Morton Blackwell to Elizabeth Dole, 26 Feb. 1981, with Blackwell summarizing Lyn Nofziger to Lee Atwater conversation of 25 Feb. 1981, OA 6386, EHD.

160 "They've run out . . .": Jane Mayer and Doyle McManus, *Landslide* (New York, 1988), 4.

160 "we would be relatively . . .": Richard Darman in Jonathan Moore, ed., *Campaigning for President* (Dover, MA, 1986), 175, 42.

160 "I have been . . .": JAB to Michael Deaver, Larry Speakes, 30 Aug. 1984, 10,513, Communications, JAB MSS, RR Lib.

160 "didn't want to politicize . . .": *WasPo*, 12 Mar. 1984, A3; RR in *Nwswk*, 6 Feb. 1984, 19.

160 "who is not . . .": Ed Rollins in Moore, *Campaigning 1984*, 42.

161 "Reaganite entertainment . . .": Robin Wood, "Papering the Cracks: Fantasy and Ideology in the Reagan Era," in John Belton, *Depth of Field* (New Brunswick, NJ, 1995), 203–206.

161 "God, patriotism . . .": Keith Blume, *The Presidential Election Show* (South Hadley, MA, 1985), 61.

161 "moved to tears . . .": *WasPo*, 23 Sept. 1984, C2.

162 "arrogance . . . dispensing only . . .": *WasPo*, 23 Sept. 1984, C1–C2.

162 "in their proper . . .": John Glenn to RR, 17 Oct. 1984, OA 10,572, MB Oglesby Legislative, Margaret Tutwiler MSS, RR Lib.

162 "The President's response . . .": Darman in Moore, *Campaigning 1984*, 110.

162 "Mr. Reagan tries . . .": Stahl, *Reporting Live*, 210, 207, 210–211.

164 "Norwegian charisma": *WasPo*, 12 July 1984, A6.

164 "Everyone is . . .": *WasPo*, 1 June 1984, B3.

165 "America is the land . . .": Geraldine Ferraro, "Acceptance Speech," 19 July
     1984, *Official Proceedings of the 1984 Democratic National Convention*, 16–19
     July, 480–481.

165 "Geraldine, don't . . .": Stahl, *Reporting*, 201.

165 "This Nation is . . .": Mario Cuomo, "Keynote Address," 17 July 1984, *1984
     Democratic Convention*, 225–231.

166 "20 percent liberal . . .": Harris Polls, 851101, Jan. 1985, Harris study no.
     851101, Question F10. See also Steven M. Gillon, *The Democrats' Dilemma*
     (New York, 1992), xxiii–xxvi; Wilson Carey McWilliams, *Beyond the Poli-
     tics of Disappointment? American Elections, 1980–1998* (New York, 2000).

166 "Our flag is . . .": Jesse Jackson, Address, 17 July 1984, *1984 Democratic Con-
     vention*, 293–301.

167 how to see Americans . . . : Harris Poll, Study No. 851101, Jan. 1985, Ques-
     tion 8.

167 "Mondull": *WasPo*, 6 Nov. 1984, B1.

167 "We are helping . . .": "Fact or Fiction: An Analysis of the President's State-
     ments on Fairness, Spending and Taxes . . .": c. Sept. 1984, Box 5, KOD II.

168 "making sure . . .": *Nation*, 29 May 1982, 648.

168 "a student union . . .": *San Jose Mercury*, 5 Sept. 1984, Newsbank, POL 1984
     88: G3.

168 "Isn't your campaign . . .": Blume, *Presidential Election Show*, 73–74.

169 "in a television age . . .": Rick Du Brow, *Los Angeles Herald Examiner*, 4 Oct.
     1984, Newsbank, 108 F13.

169 Having honed . . . : Richard C. Leone quoted in Moore, *Campaigning 1984*,
     218.

169 "home run": Ed Rollins quoted in ibid., 196.

169 "Loser to Underdog": *WasPo*, 9 Oct. 1984, A19.

169 "the great unmentionable . . .": *LAT*, 20 Aug. 1984, 18. See also *Wall Street
     Journal*, 9 Oct. 1984, 1.

169 "arm wrestle . . .": *WasPo*, 11 Oct. 1984, A2.

169 "Reagan didn't look . . .": Sam Donaldson, *Hold on Mr. President!* (New York,
     1987), 222.

170 "Because now . . .": *Daily News*, 14 Oct. 1984, 3.

170 "DEBATE MOMENTUM . . .": *Minneapolis Star and Tribune*, 14 Oct. 1984, 1.

170 "panic . . . The Invincible . . .": Noonan, *Revolution*, 129.

170 "was brutalized . . .": *Dallas Morning News*, 12 Oct. 1984, 1.

170 "High Noon": *Cleveland Plain Dealer*, 19 Oct. 1984.

170 "to see whether . . .": Donaldson, *Hold on*, 223.

171 "gentleman down . . .": Doyle and McManus, *Landslide*, 16.

171 "THE PRESIDENT DIDN'T . . .": *Baltimore Sun*, 22 Oct. 1984, 1.

171 a nostalgic California . . . : *NYT*, 6 Nov. 1984, A23; *WasPo*, 6 Nov. 1984, A12.

172 Faith in governmental . . . : Nye, et al., eds., *Why People Don't Trust Govern-
     ment*, 81.

173 top nonfiction bestsellers: See *NYT Book Review*, 4 Nov. 1984.

173 "the other North American . . .": RR and Brian Mulroney, "Remarks Following a Meeting with Prime Minister Brian Mulroney of Canada," 25 Sept.
1984, Pub.

174 "high five . . .": Morton M. Kondracke, "A High Five for Ronald Reagan,"
Wall Street Journal, 28 June 1984, 29; RR to Kondracke, scrawled on article,
615749 Box 4, FG 001, RR Lib.

1985—Brooklyn, NY

Page

176 "the well-being of . . .": RR, "Remarks in Denver, Colorado, at the Annual
Convention of the National Association for the Advancement of Colored
People," 29 June 1981, Pub.

177 America's "modern," "progressive," . . . : John Morton Blum, *The Progressive
Presidents* (New York, 1980); Theodore J. Lowi, *The Personal President*
(Ithaca, 1985); Arthur M. Schlesinger, Jr., *The Imperial Presidency* (New
York, 1973); Thomas E. Cronin, "An Imperilled Presidency," in Vincent
Davis, ed., *The Post-Imperial Presidency* (New Brunswick, NJ, 1980), 37–51.

177 the "Rhetorical Presidency" . . . : Jeffrey K. Tulis, *The Rhetorical Presidency*
(Princeton, 1987); George C. Edwards, *The Public Presidency* (New York,
1983); Richard W. Waterman, Robert Wright, and Gilbert St. Clair, *The
Image-Is-Everything Presidency* (Boulder, 1999).

178 "personal presence . . .": *NYT*, 24 Feb. 1985, 4:20.

179 "broad agreement . . .": Ken Auletta, *The Underclass* (New York, 1982), 50.

179 "A quiet, $10 . . .": *Time*, 21 Jan. 1985, 28.

179 spoke "Republican" . . . : See Jo Freeman, "The Political Culture of the Democratic and Republican Parties," *Political Science Quarterly* 101 (Fall
1986): 327–356.

180 nearly 3 million riders . . . : www.nycsubway.org/ Janes 1992.

180 "I can't feel . . .": *NYT*, 12 Jan. 1985, 25.

180 "vigilantism . . . the frustration . . .": *NYT*, 7 Jan. 1985, B1.

180 only 2 percent . . . : *NYT*, 18 Jan. 1985, B3.

180 "justified": *NYT*, 26 Jan. 1985, 1.

181 "You don't look . . .": *NYT*, 28 Feb. 1985, 1.

181 "As far as . . .": *NYT*, 6 Jan. 1985, 22.

181 "He was staying . . .": *NYT*, 12 Jan. 1985, 25.

181 "mugged communities . . . mugged . . .": *NYT*, 14 Jan. 1985, A19.

181 "metaphorical rage . . . powerlessness . . .": *The Nation*, 19 Jan. 1985, 35–36.

182 "the plain doughty . . .": Jonathan Rieder, *Canarsie* (New York, 1985), 1, 179,
98, 96.

183 "in his very . . .": Jim Sleeper, *The Closest of Strangers* (New York 1991),
184–186.

184 "basically a reactionary . . .": Robert R. Detelfsen, *Civil Rights under Reagan* (San Francisco, 1991), 11, 10, 6.

184 "the most popular . . .": *NYT*, 9 May 1985, C30.

185 the percentage of black . . . . : Ben Wattenberg, *The First Universal Nation* (New York, 1991), 14, 63.

185 "sexist . . . mankind . . .": Detelfsen, *Civil Rights*, 7.

185 president did not . . . : John David Skrentny, *The Ironies of Affirmative Action* (Chicago, 1996), 226.

185 98 percent of . . . : Wattenberg, *First Universal Nation*, 68.

186 "Finalmente! . . . It's about . . .": ibid., 50–51.

186 "New York is . . .": Tom Wolfe, "Fact and Fiction in the New York of the Eighties," unedited transcript, the 1988 Wriston Lecture, The Manhattan Institute for Policy Research, www.manhattan-institute.org/html/wl1988.htm.

186 "Our nation is . . .": RR, Statement on United States Immigration and Refugee Policy, July 30, 1981, Pub.

187 "illegal immigration . . .": Nicholas Laham, *Ronald Reagan and the Politics of Immigration Reform* (Westport, 2000), 42.

187 already sobering figure . . . : Frank D. Bean, Barry Edmonston, and Jeffrey S. Passel, eds., *Undocumented Migration to the United States* (Santa Monica, 1990), p. 17; David B. Levine, Kenneth Hill, and Robert Warren, eds., *Immigration Statistics: A Story of Neglect* (Washington, DC, 1985), 243.

187 "unemployment would be . . .": Rita J. Simon and Susan H. Alexander, *The Ambivalent Welcome* (Westport, 1995), 43.

187 "Immigration is no . . .": Memo of 3 June 1981 quoted in Laham, *Immigration Reform*, 83.

188 "Anyone hearing . . .": Donald Bogle, *Prime Time Blues* (New York, 2001), 290, 303, 294–295.

188 "Does it mean . . .": Cosby, Pouissant in *NYT*, 18 Nov. 1984, B1.

190 "In the '80s . . .": David P. Szatmary, *Rockin' in Time* (Englewood Cliffs, NJ, 1987, 1991), 269.

190 "Good morning . . .": *NYT*, 14 July 1985, A14.

191 "We can end . . .": *NYT*, 15 July 1985, C18.

192 "Boy, after seeing . . .": *LAT*, 1 July 1985; see also Paul Slansky, *The Clothes Have No Emperor* (New York, 1989), 133.

193 "the cultural apartheid . . .": *WasPo*, 24 Nov. 1985, H1.

193 "a Trojan horse . . .": Interview with Steve Greenberg, New York City, April 2004. See also *Nwswk*, 27 Feb. 1984, 66.

193 "Michael Jackson is mass . . .": *NYT*, 14 Jan. 1986, A11.

193 "the biggest thing . . .": *Time*, 19 Mar. 1984, 54–63.

194 "What's that guy . . .": *LAT Magazine*, 11 Oct. 1987, 7.

194 "The time is right . . .": *NYT*, 14 Jan. 1984, A11.

194 "mirrors the current . . .": *NYT*, 2 Sept. 1984, 2:1.

195 "Hollywood when actors . . .": RR to Captain Steven P. Bucci re: MacDonald Carey, 27 Jan. 1986, Folder 310, Box 19, PHF II.

195 "It's a guy . . .": *NYT*, 22 Jan. 1984, 3:1.

196 "I always thought . . .": *NYT*, 29 June 1985, 2:22.

196 "For taking feminism . . .": *NYTM*, 14 Sept. 1986, 6:72.

197 Alfred Moran . . . . : *NYT*, 18 Sept. 1986, B1, B9.

197 "She stands for . . .": *NYTM*, 14 Sept. 1986, 6:80.

197 "the movement to . . .": RR to Reverend Gay, n.d., prepresidential, RR *Letters*, 365.

198 "the most powerful . . .": Jean O'Leary, in Peter N. Carroll, *It Seemed Like Nothing Happened* (New York, 1982), 293.

198 "What do I . . . .": Randy Shilts, *And the Band Played On* (New York, 1987), 29.

199 "The belief that . . .": *Nwswk*, 8 Aug. 1983, 30.

199 Bathhouse patrons averaged . . . : Shilts, *The Band*, 19.

199 "In 1982 . . . sex . . .": *RS Yearbook 1982*, 6 Jan. 1983, 25.

199 "The poor homosexuals . . .": Shilts, *The Band*, 311.

199 "I haven't experienced . . .": *Nwswk*, 8 Aug. 1983, 30.

200 "sexual Nazis . . .": Shilts, *The Band*, 312, 317, 310, 326–327.

200 "God, I wish . . .": *NYTM*, 31 May 1987, 6:32.

200 "The day of . . .": *NYT*, 22 Mar. 1986, A7.

201 "When it's life . . .": *Nwswk*, 8 Aug. 1983, 30.

201 "Wake up . . .": Stephen Sondheim and James Lapine, *Into the Woods* (New York, 1989), 114.

201 13 percent of . . . : *NYT*, 9 June 1987, A1.

202 "I've been sticking . . .": *NYT*, 8 Aug. 1985, C15.

202 Coming from Hollywood, he had . . . : Lou Cannon, *Governor Reagan* (New York, 2003), 242.

202 "I'm not one . . .": RR to Victor H. Krulak, 30 Oct. 1984, RR *Letters*, 366.

202 Federal funding began . . . : Deroy Murdock, "Anti-Gay Gipper," 3 Dec. 2003, National Review Online, www.nationalreview.com/murdock/murdock 200312030913.asp.

202 By 1996, researchers . . . : *New England Journal of Medicine*, 1999; 340: 1881–7.

203 "more progress and . . .": Interview with Dr. Julian Adams, Cambridge, MA, Nov. 2003.

203 "With Hudson's death . . .": *USA Today* quoted in *LAT*, 21 Aug. 1987, 1.

1986—Wall Street

Page

204 "the great civilized . . .": RR, "Remarks of the President to Eureka College Students and Faculty," 5, 6 Feb. 1984, 264871, PR 016-04, Box 29, Folder 4/8, RR Lib.

205 "I look for . . .": Robert Sobel, *The Great Boom* (New York, 2000), 329.

205 "The investment . . .": Michael Lewis, *Liar's Poker* (New York, 1989), 26, 9.

205 "the greatest . . .": James B. Stewart, *Den of Thieves* (New York, 1991), 14–17.

206 Abundance . . . : David Potter, *People of Plenty* (Chicago, 1954).

206 "food, clothing . . .": Robert William Fogel, *The Fourth Great Awakening and the Future of Egalitarianism* (Chicago, 2000), 1–3.

207 "the greatest economic . . .": Martin Anderson, *Revolution* (New York, 1988), 175.

208 "stunning . . . $8,000 billion . . .": *NYT*, 2 Jan. 1992, 1.

208 Apple's magical . . . : *USNWR*, 18 Mar. 1985, 59.

208 "There's visible . . .": *Nwswk*, 21 Apr. 1986, 62.

208 real disposable income . . . : *USNWR*, 18 Mar. 1985, 59.

208 "Inflation's decline . . .": *Nwswk*, 7 Apr. 1986, 62.

208 Corporate investment . . . : *USNWR*, 18 Mar. 1985, 59.

209 "President Reagan must . . .": Paul Volcker and Toyoo Gyohten, *Changing Fortunes* (New York, 1992), 175. See also John W. Sloan, *The Reagan Effect* (Lawrence, 1999), 237–244.

209 Allen Sinai . . . : *Nwswk*, 6 Aug. 1984, 46.

209 "a damsel . . .": *NYT*, 25 Sept. 1985, A10.

210 "the best antipoverty . . .": *NYT*, 23 Oct. 1986, D16.

210 Historians would . . . : W. Elliot Brownlee and C. Eugene Steurele, "Taxation," in W. Elliot Brownlee and Hugh Davis Graham, *The Reagan Presidency* (Lawrence, KS, 2003), 174.

210 throwing tax . . . : Sloan, *Reagan Effect*, 165.

210 "outstanding macroeconomic performance . . .": *TNR*, 16 Mar. 1985, 15.

210 other factors . . . : *Nwswk*, 6 Aug. 1984, 46.

211 workaholic who . . . : Connie Bruck, *Predators' Ball* (New York, 1989), 23.

212 the most influential . . . : Robert Sobel, *Dangerous Dreamers* (New York, 1993), 2.

212 "it doesn't make . . .": *WasPo*, 7 Dec. 1986, H7.

212 "a revival meeting": *NYT*, 14 Apr. 1985, 3:1.

213 "who had been . . .": *NYT*, 23 Nov. 1986, 3:8.

214 "The little guy . . .": *NYT*, 17 Mar. 1986, B1.

214 Fidelity offered 157 . . . : *USA Today*, 1 Sept. 1989, 1B.

214 first "superbanks" . . . : *BosG*, 23 July 1989, A1.

215 "the ripple effect . . .": *Nwswk*, 24 Mar. 1986, 51.

216 "like the sexual . . .": *NYTM*, 20 Oct. 2002, 6:62.

216 "ability to make . . .": Roper Report 84–3, Feb.1984, Roper Center for Public Opinion Research, University of Connecticut, USROPER 8403, R08.

216 "the meaninglessness of . . .": Kevin Phillips, *Politics of Rich and Poor* (New York, 1990), xxii.

216 half-million-dollar . . . : *WasPo*, 20 Aug. 1989, B1.

216 the two-million-dollar wedding . . . : see *Nwswk*, 30 May 1988, 66; *NYT*, 19 Apr. 1988, B2.

217 "million-dollar fiftieth . . .": *WasPo*, 20 Aug. 1989, B1.

217 "'The Rich People's . . .'": *St. Louis Post-Dispatch*, 27 Aug. 1989, 3B.

218 "Greed on Sesame . . .": *Nwswk*, 20 July 1987, 38.

218 "a black, washed-silk . . .": *LAT*, 17 June 1988, 5:1.

218 twenty-thousand . . . : *NYT*, 25 Dec. 1988, 3:1.

218 "When you have . . .": *WasPo*, 24 Oct. 1985, DC1.

220 "I've tried everything . . .": Steven Gaines and Sharon Churcher, *Obsession* (New York, 1994), 7.

220 "the name was . . .": Michael Gross, *Genuine Authentic* (New York, 2003), 73, 101.

221 "I'm interested . . .": Ralph Lauren History Timeline, 1970, Polo.com, www.about.polo.com/history/history.asp?year=1970.

221 "He cheapened . . .": Gross, *Authentic*, 223, 200, 16.

222 "Lauren has become . . .": Ralph Lauren History Timeline, 1980, Polo.com, www.about.polo.com/history/history.asp?year=1980.

222 "The 1950s sense . . .": Senior Vice President Ann Clurman of Yankelovich Clancy Shulman, in *Fortune*, 6 July 1987, 28–29.

222 59 percent . . . : LHarris, 8.

222 "splendid, if implausible . . .": *Nwswk*, 27 Aug. 1984, 32.

223 Interest payments averaged . . . : *Nwswk*, 4 May 1987, 18.

223 "We finally understand . . .": quoted in Peter G. Peterson, "The Morning After," *Atlantic*, Oct. 1987, www.theatlantic.com/politics/budget/afterf.htm.

225 "outdoor psychiatric wards . . .": *USNWR*, 30 Jan. 1984, 57.

225 "Something happens—a . . .": *TNR*, 18 Mar. 1985, 21.

225 "There is a . . .": *USNWR*, 11 Jan. 1988, 18.

225 "Economic Recovery . . . .": *NYT*, 16 Mar. 1986, 1:1.

226 "trickle down . . . an Armageddonic . . .": Daniel P. Moynihan, *Came the Revolution* (New York, 1988), 262.

226 "positively egalitarian": *NYTM*, 20 Oct. 2002, 6:62.

226 in Europe, where . . . : Sloan, *Reagan Effect*, 233.

226 Democrats tended to . . . : *LAT*, 24 Sept. 1987, 1; see also Samuel M. Ehrenhalt, *NYT*, 15 Aug. 1986, D2.

227 "the 'real nations don't . . .' ": *NYT*, 17 June 1984, 3:1.

227 "Reagan proved deficits . . .": Ron Suskind, *The Price of Loyalty* (New York, 2004), 291.

227 many American families . . . : *NYT*, 17 June 1984, 3:1.

227 "the most economically . . .": Sloan, *Reagan Effect*, 252.

227 more moderate, compromising . . . : *NYTM*, 20 Oct. 2002, 6:62.

227 "The Affluent City . . .": Moynihan, *Revolution*, 263.

227 "pursuit of happiness . . .": *TNR*, 17 and 24 Sept. 1984, 13.

228 Puritan ambivalence . . . : See Bernard Bailyn, *The Ideological Origins of the American Revolution* (Cambridge, MA, 1967).

229 "Greed is all . . .": *Nwswk*, 1 Dec. 1986, 48.

229 "WHITE-COLLAR . . .": *NYT*, 9 June 1985, 3:1.

229 "creature of Wall . . .": *NYT*, 23 Nov. 1986, 3:1.

230 70 percent . . . : LHarris, 236.

230 "faster paced. You . . .": *USNWR*, 1 Dec. 1986, 44. See also *NYT*, 23 Nov. 1986, C3.

231 "radical individualism . . . negative . . .": Bellah et al., *Habits of the Heart*, 82–83, 79.

231 "spiritual estrangement": Fogel, *Awakening*, 3.

231 "hunger for a . . .": RR to Otis Carney, Nov. 1979, RR *Letters*, 259.

231 "nostalgia trap . . . the way . . .": Stephanie Coonitz, *The Way We Never Were* (New York, 1992), 9, 8.

232 "where our children . . .": *NYT*, 13 Nov. 1986, C2.

233 "You never told . . .": Bobbie Ann Mason, *In Country* (New York, 1986), 56.

233 "friend of the . . .": *NYT*, 9 June 1985, 3:6.

1987—Mourning in America

Page
235 "to make the . . .": Ilya Levkov, ed., *Bitburg and Beyond* (New York, 1987), 41–44.

236 "trustworthiness . . .": Arthur H. Miller and Stephen A. Borrelli, "Confidence in Government during the 1980s," *American Politics Quarterly*, 19 (April 1991): 148.

236 Polls showed . . . : LHarris, 338–339, 396.

237 "The second terms . . .": Richard Nixon quoted in Memorandum, Jan. 1985, Box 9, Series I, Subseries 1984 to Jan. 1985, JAB MSS, RR Lib.

237 "In the four . . .": Donald T. Regan, *For the Record* (New York, 1988), 142.

237 Wiesel was just . . . : Elliott Abrams in Deborah Hart Strober and Gerald S. Strober, *Reagan* (New York, 1998), 312.

238 "Ronald Reagan had . . .": Peter J. Wallison, *Reagan* (New York, 2003), 142.

238 "Have we not . . .": William Clark in Strober and Strober, *Reagan*, 301.

238 Regan liked the sound . . . : NR *Mem*, 313, 271.

239 "It's hard to . . .": *NYT*, 26 Nov. 1986, A27.

239 "because when . . .": *USNWR*, 5 Oct. 1987, 21. See Richard Nixon's denial, sent via his chief of staff, John Taylor to JAB, 29 Sept. 1987, Folder 305, Box 19, PHF II.

239 "Strength and . . .": RR, Address to the Nation and Other Countries on United States-Soviet Relations, 16 Jan. 1984, Pub.

239 "the greatest . . .": RR to Mr. and Mrs. Tom Bloomer, Ann Arbor, MI, 10 Mar. 1982, 064387, Box 2, PHF II.

239 "Our security is . . .": RR, handwritten insert to Draft, Presidential Address: Defense 22 Mar. 1983 [delivered 23 Mar. 1983], 4, 133784SS, SP 735, RR Lib.

240 "leaves only . . .": RR to Laurence W. Beilenson, Los Angeles, 5 Feb. 1982, 059839, P4, PHF II.

240 "a form of . . .": RR, May 1975, in RR, *Hand*, 12.

240 "moderate autocrats . . .": Jeane Kirkpatrick, "Dictatorships and Double Standards," *Commentary*, Nov. 1979, 45.

241 "roil[ing] . . .": Mona Charen, *Useful Idiots* (Washington, DC, 2003), 11–13.

241 "[O]ur propaganda . . .": Beth A. Fischer, "Reagan and the Soviets," in W. Elliot Brownlee and Hugh Davis Graham, eds., *The Reagan Presidency* (Lawrence, KS, 2003), 125.

241 "G.I. Joe . . .": Samuel Korman, "GI Joe: African American Hero?" *Historical Discourses* 18 (Spring 2003), 97.

241 "These films . . .": David Edlestein, "Year in Film," *RS 1985 Yearbook*, 19 Dec. 1985–2 Jan. 1986, 105.

241 "Ivan and Anya . . . Jim . . .": RR notes on Draft, National Press Club, US–Soviet Relations, 6 Jan. 1984, SP 833, RR Lib.

242 "maybe Anya would . . .": RR, Address on Soviet Relations, 16 Jan. 1984, Pub.

243 "Central America is . . .": Jay Winik, *On the Brink* (New York, 1996), 251, 254.

243 "If we can't . . .": Peter Schweizer, *Reagan's War* (New York, 2002), 204.

243 "47 percent polled . . .": *LAT*, 25 Mar. 1981, in Polls, OA 7239, Richard S. Beals MSS, RR Lib.

243 "62 percent . . .": LHarris, 411.

243 "There is nothing . . .": *Congressional Record*, 23 June 1984, 1522.

243 "a vote to . . .": *Congressional Record*, 28 July 1983, H45860.

243 "networks . . . have the same . . .": Richard Nixon to RR, 4 Feb. 1988, 545438, Folder 320, Box 20, PHF II.

244 "sophisticated disinformation . . .": RR to Michael Suozzi, 23 Mar. 1987, 48467, Folder 283 Box 18, PHF II.

244 "getting through to . . .": Donald T. Regan Notes, Meeting with President, 20 May 1985, Box 190, DTR.

244 "completely convinced . . .": RR to Andrew Carhartt, 12 Mar. 1982, 067421, C0001-09, Box 2, PHF II.

244 "thinks he's John . . .": John A. Farrell, *Tip O'Neill and the Democratic Century* (New York, 2001), 614.

244 "that America will . . .": RR, President's New Conference, 18 Jan. 1985, Pub.

245 "Reagan's obsession with . . .": Cannon, 541.

245 "Some strange . . .": RR *Mem*, 501–502.

245 "an authorized effort . . .": Lawrence E. Walsh, *Iran-Contra: The Final Report* (New York, 1993), 16.

245 "Field Marshal North": *Nwswk*, 1 Dec. 1986, 27.

246 "You can run . . .": RR *Mem*, 509.

246 "I don't believe . . .": Cannon, 580.

246 72 percent of . . . : LHarris, 413.

246 "not to nap . . .": *NYT*, 12 Dec. 1986, A35.

246 "subterranean government . . .": *NYT*, 24 Feb. 1987, A27.

246 "charges are utterly . . .": *NYT*, 14 Nov. 1986, A8.

246 "that it is my policy . . .": RR, Address to the Nation, 2 Dec. 1986, Pub.

246 "this Iranian thing": Haley Barbour to Dennis Thomas, 4 Dec. 1986, Box 15,356 White House Office of Public Affairs, RR Lib.

247 "polemical and publicity . . .": Cannon, 503.

247 "President Reagan drew . . .": Pat Buchanan Speech to Concerned Citizens for Democracy, Miami, FL, 8 Dec. 1986, Iran Talking Points Project, 5 Dec. 1986, Box 15,356, White House Office of Public Affairs Records, RR Lib.

247 "President Reagan's iron-willed . . .": *Nwswk*, 2 Mar. 1987, 22.

247 "arguably the worst . . .": *WasPo*, 22 Feb. 1987, C6.

247 "journalistic firestorm": RR *Mem*, 527–528.

247 "get off my goddam . . .": For rumor see *BosG*, 9 Dec. 1986, 16.

247 "For the first time . . .": RR *Mem*, 532.

248 "I don't believe . . .": NR *Mem*, 109.

248 "possible ways . . .": Dennis Thomas to Donald T. Regan, 16 Jan. 1987, 484685, FG 001 WHORM.

248 "You are not . . .": *NYT*, 21 Feb. 1987, 32.

248 "seemed uninterested . . .": Regan, *For the Record*, 71.

249 Stahl was ready . . . : Stahl, *Reporting Live*, 257–258.

249 "The Leader of . . .": NBC, "NBC Special: The First Lady, Nancy Reagan," 24 June 1985, R2729B, Audiovisual Archives, RR Lib.

249 "troubled by this . . .": RR *Mem*, 537–538.

250 "I thought I . . .": Regan, *For the Record*, 98.

250 "there were occasions . . .": Doyle and McManus, *Landslide*, 382.

250 "He will never . . .": *NYT*, 27 Feb. 1987, 1.

250 "We have no . . .": *NYT*, 8 Mar. 1987, 4:1.

250 "I'm sorry": *Nwswk*, 16 Mar. 1987, 19.

250 "Bill, the president . . .": White House News Summary, 4 Mar. 1987, 3, RR Lib.

250 "Our pollster took . . .": RR to Lt. Gen. Victor A. Krulak USMC Ret, San Diego, CA, 19 Mar. 1987, 870319, SP1120, RR Lib.

251 "The Gipper's back": Dan Quayle in *Nwswk*, 16 Mar. 1987, 19.

251 "I remember . . .": Doris and Merill Green,Scottsdale, AZ, to RR, Telegram, 4 Mar. 1987, SP 1120, RR Lib.

251 "We love . . .": Mr. and Mrs. Richard V. Figueroa, Los Angeles, CA to RR, telegram, 4 Mar. 1987, SP 1120, RR Lib.

251 "the virulent cries . . .": Efrem Zimbalist, Jr., to RR, 3 Mar. 1987, SP 1120, RR Lib.

251 "In our Hollywood . . .": RR to George Murphy, 9 Dec. 1986, 466900, Folder 269, Box 17, PHF II.

251 "There is a definite . . .": RR to Ruth D. Marsh, Toluca Lake, CA, 12 Mar. 1987, 870313 SP 1120, RR Lib.

251 "We must opportunistically . . .": William Henkel to Tom Griscom, 19 Mar. 1987, 501824, FG 001, RR Lib.

252 "guaranteed his presidency . . .": David Thelen, *Becoming Citizens in the Age of Television* (Chicago, 1996), 31.

252 "precipitating . . .": Suzanne Garment, *Scandal* (New York, 1991), 6.

252 "politics by . . .": Benjamin Ginsberg and Martin Shefter, *Politics by Other Means* (New York, 1990), 6, 2.

253 "sadness over Ronald . . .": LHarris, 314–315.

254 "We are fighting . . .": Frances FitzGerald, *Cities on a Hill* (New York, 1987), 128.

254 "greed": *NYT*, 30 May 1987, 31.

254 privatized . . . : Putnam, *Bowling Alone*, 75–76.

255 "the Naked Public . . .": John Neuhaus, *The Naked Public Square* (Grand Rapids, MI, 1984). See also Garry Wills, *Under God* (New York, 1990), 16.

255 "Would Jesus Wear . . .": *NYT*, 2 May 1987, 32.

255 "preacher-bashing . . . a . . .": James Wall, *NYT*, 28 Feb. 1988, 7.

256 "feeding frenzies": Larry Sabato, *Feeding Frenzy* (New York, 1991).

256 "I think CNN . . .": RR to Margaret Heckler, 6 July 1987, 498997, Folder 293, Box 18, PHF II.

256 "Iran is all . . .": *NYT*, 24 May 1987, A12.

257 "As you all . . .": *NYT*, 10 July 1987, A6.

258 "to see the . . .": RR to Mrs. William Loeb, 30 July 1987, 509139, Folder 297, Box 18, PHF II. See Robert Timberg, *The Nightingale's Song* (New York, 1996).

258 "portrait of North . . .": *NYT*, 1 Mar. 1987, A14; *NYT*, 12 July 1987, 4:1.

258 "Give those little . . .": *Nwswk*, 20 July 1987, 19.

258 "half-million letters . . .": For a skeptical view on Olliemania and the Reagan magic in general, see Thelen, *Becoming Citizens*, 19.

259 "Like Colonel . . .": *NYT*, 12 July 1987, A12.

259 84 percent surveyed . . . : *Time*, 20 July 1987, 15.

259 One entrepreneur . . . : Thelen, *Becoming Citizens*, 40.

259 only 24 percent . . . : *NYT*, 3 Mar. 1987, 1.

259 "Americans were forgiving . . .": RR *Mem*, 541.

259 "an entire class . . .": *NYT*, 13 Aug. 1987, A8.

260 "The World [That] Has . . .": *NYT*, 21 Oct. 1987, A34; *NYT*, 20 Oct. 1987, 1.

260 "this was a . . .": RR *Mem*, 693.

261 "Roses are red . . .": *USNWR*, 7 Dec. 1981, 27.

261 "were unanimous in . . .": RR to Laurence W. Beilenson, 16 Oct. 1986, 451963, Folder 260, Box 16, PHF II.

261 "Remember our country . . .": RR, 29 July 1982, in RR *Letters*, 408.

261 "the pleasure of . . .": ABC, *Barbara Walters Special*, 2 June 1981, R247, Audiovisual Archives, RR Lib.

262 "It would be . . .": Cannon, 689–690.

262 "resist the temptations . . .": Charlton Heston to RR, 29 June 1987, RR to Charlton Heston, 9 July 1987, 498952, Folder 294, Box 18, PHF II.

262 "I'm still the . . .": RR to Mrs. William Loeb, 18 Dec. 1987, 538176, Folder 313, Box 19, PHF II.

262 "the first leader . . .": RR to John J. Tringali, 6 Jan. 1988, 540033, Folder 315, Box 19, PHF II.

263 "the Brezhnev period . . .": quoted in Fischer, "Reagan and the Soviets," 124.

263 "If Reagan had . . .": Fred Greenstein, "Reagan Gorbachev and the Role of Leadership in Ending the Cold War," www.tompaine.com/history/1999/11/11/1.html; Fred I. Greenstein, *The Presidential Difference* (New York, 2000), 154–155.

263 "there was nothing . . .": RR *Mem*, 696–697.

1988—Stanford

Page
265 "Hey, hey, . . .": William J. Bennett, *The Devaluing of America* (New York, 1992), 172.

265 "led the march . . .": *National Review*, May 1988, 65.

265 "The West . . .": *NYTM*, 5 June 1988, 6:24.

266 "Jackson did not . . .": *Business Wire*, 19 Apr. 1988.

266 56 percent . . . : LHarris, 181, 179.

267 "constructive hypocrisy": *Chicago Tribune*, 30 Oct. 1995, 11.

267 "spiritual or moral . . .": RR to William Wilson, 5 Mar. 1987, 483149, Folder 282, Box 18, PHF II.

268 "cafeteria counter": Gerald Graff, "Teach the Conflicts," in Darryl J. Gless and Barbara Herrnstein Smith, eds., *The Politics of Liberal Education* (Durham, NC, 1992), 59.

268 "smorgasbords . . . balanced . . .": Barzun, *From Dawn to Decadence*, 785.

269 "a diverse student . . .": Peter Wood, *Diversity* (New York, 2003), 1–2.

269 "politically correct . . .": William Safire, *Safire's New Political Dictionary* (New York, 1993), 590.

269 "nigger go . . .": *NYT*, 19 Jan. 1988, A12.

269 "Objectivity . . . is only . . .": Todd Gitlin, *The Twilight of Common Dreams* (New York, 1995), 150, 147–148

270 "tenured radicals": Roger Kimball, *Tenured Radicals* (New York, 1991).

270 "try to forget . . .": *NYTM*, 5 June 1988, 6:24.

270 "we have a . . . .": *NYT*, 19 Jan. 1988, A12.

271 "that today's faculty . . .": RR to Walter Annenberg, 3 Aug. 1987, 509136 Folder 299, Box 18, PHF II.

271 "countervailing nourishment for . . .": Allan Bloom *The Closing of the American Mind* (New York, 1987), 74–75.

272 "It used to . . .": *NYTM* , 25 June 1988, 6:24.

272 "Our society, like . . .": *WasPo*, 16 Feb. 1988, A19.

272 "Identity politics . . .": Gitlin, *Twilight*, 126. See also E. D. Hirsch, *Cultural Literacy* (New York, 1988); Arthur M. Schlesinger, Jr., *The Disuniting of America* (New York, 1991, 1992).

273 "exceptional savagery . . . combination[s] . . .": *NYT*, 4 Jan. 1988, C18.

273 "A line of decency . . .": *LAT*, 25 Aug. 1985, 67.

273 "prudish misfits attempting . . .": See Tipper Gore, *Raising PG Kids in an X-Rated Society* (Nashville, 1987).

273 "Parents have to . . .": *CSM*, 23 Aug. 1985, 1. See also *LAT*, 25 Aug. 1985, 67.

274 "alternative vision of . . .": Danny Goldberg, *Dispatches from the Culture Wars* (New York, 2003), 89, 96.

274 "A lunatic fringe . . .": *NYT*, 18 Sept. 1985, C21.

274 "just arouses . . .": *LAT*, 25 Aug. 1985, 67.

274 "incest, sadomasochism, thrill . . .": *USNWR*, 26 Aug. 1985, 52.

275 "sent the wrong . . .": *WasPo*, 5 Nov. 1987, A1.

275 "How can I . . .": *WasPo*, 29 Mar. 1988, D1.

276 "We're not picking . . .": *CSM*, 23 Aug. 1985, 1.

276 "soft and hard . . .": John Ralston Saul, *Voltaire's Bastards* (New York, 1992), 489, 488.

277 the town hall: See Susan Douglas, *Listening In* (New York, 2004), 285.

277 "the loose individual . . .": Robert Nisbet, *The Present Age* (New York, 1988), 84, 86, 89.

278 "Never in my . . .": *Crain Communications*, 28 Nov. 1988, 1.

278 like a toaster . . . : *WasPo*, 7 Dec. 1988, B1.

278 "Unless they violate . . .": *Crain Communications*, 28 Nov. 1988, 1.

278 "liberal pablum pukers . . .": *WasPo*, 6 July 1988, D1.

278 "Old-style and . . .": *NYT*, 29 May 1988, 2:1.

279 "I don't think . . .": Howard Kurtz, *Hot Air* (New York, 1996), 276.

279 "proletarian discontent" . . . : Douglas, *Listening In*, 292, 294, 289–290. See also Bruce Feirstein, *Real Men Don't Eat Quiche* (New York, 1982).

281 "Women clearly disapprove . . .": CBS News Poll, Part II, 1 June 1982, 085292PD, Box 2, PR015, RR Lib.

281 "If it weren't . . .": See Lavinia Edmunds, *Ms.*, Nov. 1983, 86.

281 More than half . . . : Eleanor Smeal and Associates, "Maximizing the Women's Vote '84," Jan. 1984, 23, 200446PD, Box 4, PR015, RR Lib.

281 "that *no matter* . . .": "President's Weekly Update," 22 June 1982, Office of Policy Development, 17 June 1982, 0838665C, PW, Box 7, POTUS Update, FG001, RR Lib.

282 "oft-repeated . . .": Joe Wright to Nancy Risque, 12 July 1983, OMB, OA 11841, Women's Issues (8), Box 3, EM MSS, RR Lib.

282 "may, in fact . . .": Shellyn McCaffrey to Roger Porter, 3 June 1982, Box 6411, EHD.

282 "the women's issue . . . rhetorical . . .": "Women's Issues Meeting," 6 Apr. 1983, 10:30 AM, with EM et al, OA 11841, "Women's Issues (11)," Box 3, EM MSS, RR Lib. At the meeting the Secretary of Health and Human Services Margaret Heckler "argued that the women's issue is rhetorical and that perceptions are more important than substance."

282 "My mother was . . .": RR, *Ladies' Home Journal*, Jan. 1984, 26.

282 "We were everywhere . . .": The "blondes" were Sylvia Chase, Betsy Aaron, and Lynn Sherr from ABC; Jane Pauley and Jessica Savitch from NBC; Lesley Stahl, Diane Sawyer, and Susan Spencer from CBS. Stahl, *Reporting Live*, 151–152.

283 "celebrating the demise . . .": Dave Gergen to EM, Ed Harper, 23 June 1982, "Women's Strategy, Jan. to June 1982, [1 of 6]," Box 6471, EHD.

283 "the golden age, . . .": *Time*, 9 Apr. 1984, 84.

283 "Your graciousness and . . .": Holly Coors to Nancy Reagan, 7 Feb. 1985, 296284, Box 87, FG 001-03 (Inaugurations), RR Lib.

283 "Today, our nation . . .": "Remarks of the President in Luncheon with Elected GOP Women Officials," 3 Feb. 1984, 3, State Dining Room, C264871, Folder 4/8, Box 29, PR016-04, RR Lib.

283 "What Do . . .": Louise Eichenbaum and Susie Orbach, *What Do Women Want* (New York, 1983).

284 1984 analysis of partisans . . . : Kristin Luker, *Abortion and the Politics of Motherhood* (Berkeley, University of California Press), 194–197.

284 The 1984 election: Nelson Polsby, Aaron Wildavsky, *Presidential Elections*, 8th ed. (New York, 1991), 337, 186; Evans Witt, "What the Republicans Have Learned about Women," *Public Opinion* 8 (Oct./Nov. 1985): 51.

285 "Don't tell the . . .": Naomi Wolf, *Fire with Fire* (New York, 1993), 66–68; Katie Roiphie, *The Morning After* (Boston, 1993, 1994), 5, 121.

286 "attitude of permissiveness": RR, 20 May 1986, Pub, 629.

286 "climate of lawlessness": RR, 14 Oct. 1982, Pub, 1314.

286 "In the 1940s . . .": *Nwswk*, 5 Jan. 1987, 64.

286 "I believe the . . .": *Time*, 15 Sept. 1986, 61.

287 "But Mrs. Reagan . . .": Staff notes for Wendy Toler to John T. Schuler, 24 Aug. 1988, White House Alpha File, Just Say No [2 of 18], RR Lib.

287 "Well why don't . . .": *Good Housekeeping*, Jan. 1987, 64.

287 "pushmi-pullyu . . .": Roiphie, *Morning After*, 5, 121.

287 One quarter of . . . : "Drug Use Decreasing—Trends Promise a Real Success," 18 Mar. 1983, 1292225C, Box 13, FG 001, RR Lib.

287 "The idea that . . .": Adam Paul Weisman, *TNR*, 6 Oct. 1986, 16.

288 "The Great Relearning": William Kristol to Tom C. Griscom, 27 Nov. 1987, 535879, Box 54, FG 001, RR Lib; Tom Wolfe, "The Great Relearning," *American Spectator*, Dec. 1987, 14.

288 "The police are . . .": *Nwswk*, 16 June 1986, 16.

288 "are living a . . .": *Nwswk*, 17 Mar. 1986, 62.

289 "the drive to . . .": Dr. Ronald K. Siegel, UCLA, *Time*, 15 Sept. 1986, 61.

289 "the neuroses . . .": *National Review*, 5 Dec. 1986, 34.

290 "the largest crime . . .": Janice Lord, "Really MADD," *DRIVEN*, Spring 2000, www.madd.org/aboutus/0%2C1056%2C1686%2C00.html.

290 "Drug bashing . . .": 13 Aug. 1986, B-6, Box 53,White House News Summaries, RR Lib.

290 drop in drugs . . . : The Reagan Record, 6 June 1988, 5613685C, Box 59 FG 001, RR Lib.

290 "enduring . . . in the judiciary": Tony Platt, "U.S. Criminal Justice in the Reagan Era: An Assessment," *Crime and Social Justice* (1987): 64.

291 "removed its diapers . . .": RR, 28 Apr. 1986, Pub.

291 "unconstitutional . . . a serious . . .": Robert Bork, 1981, quoted in *Congressional Quarterly*, 12 Sept. 1987, 2164.

291 "We really touched . . .": RR to Charlton Heston, 9 July 1987, 498952, Folder 294, Box 18, PHF II.

291 "to ensure continuity . . .": Stanley Kutler, *The Wars of Watergate* (New York, 1992), 407–408.

292 "Robert Bork's America . . .": Senator Kennedy quoted in Robert Bork, *The Tempting of America* (New York, 1990), 268.

292 "he does not . . .": Terry Sanford, *Congressional Quarterly*, 3 Oct. 1987, 2416.

293 "shenanigans": RR to Walter H. Annenberg, 29 Oct. 1987, 526919, Folder 310, Box 19, FG051, RR Lib, II.

293 "disgraceful distortion . . .": RR to Lynn Siegel, Palm City Fl, 21 Oct. 1987, 532130 Folder 308, Box 19, FG 051, RR Lib, II.

293 "I promise you . . .": RR to George Murphy, 29 Oct. 1987, Folder 310, Box 19, FG 051, RR Lib, II.

293 "control of . . .": Bork, *Tempting*, 271.

294 "henpecked, manipulated...": TNR, 23 Mar. 1987, 12.

294 "Astrology is entirely . . .": *The Nation*, 21 May 1988, 702.

295 "I've not tied . . .": RR, *NYT*, 18 May 1988, A22.

295 "No policy or . . .": *Nwswk*, 16 May 1988, 20.

295 guidance: On astrology in the 1980s, see J. A. Sargent, "Astrology's Rising Star," *Christianity Today*, 4 Feb. 1983, 37; *Vogue*, July 1987, 96.

295 "Ronald Reagan did more . . .": Michael K. Deaver with Mickey Herskowitz, *Behind the Scenes* (New York, 1987), 141.

296 "were so insistent . . .": Bork, *Tempting*, 279.

296 "The warmest . . .": RR *Mem*, 724.

1989—Kennebunkport, Maine

Page

297 "three F's . . .": *Saturday Evening Post*, Oct. 1988, 72.

298 "Well, I don't . . .": Michael Duffy and Dan Goodgame, *Marching in Place* (New York, 1992), 16.

298 "the movie . . .": Charles Kolb, *White House Daze* (New York, 1994), 3.

299 end-of-decade poll: *Nwswk*, 4 Jan. 1988, 46.

299 WASPs . . . : See Richard Brookhiser, *The Way of the WASP* (New York, 1991).

299 "moral voice": Amitai Etzioni, *The New Golden Rule* (New York, 1996), 131, 136.

299 "centrist . . . Thou . . .": Wolfe, *One Nation, After All*, 50, 54.

301 "I am really . . .": *USNWR*, 22 Aug. 1988, 12.

302 graduates' average income . . . : *BosG*, 30 Dec. 1990, 73.

302 median selling price . . . : Phillips, *The Politics of Rich and Poor*, 252–253.

302 "same number of . . .": *LAT*, 24 July 1988, 1:2.

302 town burghers . . . : *BosG*, 30 Dec. 1990, 73.

303 "Nobody bothers . . .": *LAT*, 24 July 1988, 1:2.

303 one congressional study . . . : *NYT*, 16 July 1989, 1.

303 "Poverty is . . .": *BosG*, 30 Dec. 1990, 73.

304 "I suppose . . .": *LAT*, 27 Mar. 1990, D2.

304 "We don't need . . .": George Bush quoted in Duffy and Goodgame, *Marching*, 21–22.

305 "You're talking . . .": *Nwswk*, 19 Oct. 1987, 32.

305 "the I-ectomies . . .": Peggy Noonan, *What I Saw at the Revolution* (New York, 1990), 302.

305 "values we honor . . .": George Bush Acceptance Speech, Aug. 1988, in *Congressional Quarterly Weekly Report*, 46 (20 Aug. 1988): 2353–2355.

305 "It's a wonderful . . .": Sidney Blumenthal, *Pledging Allegiance* (New York, 1990), 265–266.

306 "Poor George . . .": Keynote Address by State Treasurer Ann W. Richards, Texas, 18 July 1988, *Official Proceedings of the 1988 Democratic National Convention*, 18–21 July, 222.

306 "Where was . . .": Remarks by Senator Edward Kennedy, Massachusetts, 19 July 1988, *1988 Democratic National Convention*, 315.

306 "George Herbert . . .": Remarks by Texas Agriculture Commissioner, Jim Hightower, 19 July 1988, *1988 Democratic National Convention*, 320–321. See also Arthur M. Schlesinger, Jr., *The Age of Jackson* (Boston, 1945).

307 "Living In . . .": *BosG*, 30 Dec. 1990, 73.

307 "Bush captured 81 . . .": "How Groups Voted in 1988," The Roper Center, www.ropercenter.uconn.edu/elect_2004/voted_88.html.

307 "you'd like . . .": Duffy and Goodgame, *Marching*, 26.

307 "The American . . .": Richard Ben Cramer, *What It Takes* (New York, 1992), 1022.

308 "Ronald Reagan evoked . . .": *Nwswk*, 23 Jan. 1989, 24.

309 "representative of . . .": E. Digby Baltzell, *The Protestant Establishment* (New York, 1964), xi.

309 "parental, class or . . . .": Howard G. Schneiderman, ed., E. Digby Baltzell, *The Protestant Establishment Revisited* (New Brunswick, 1991), 42, 35.

309 "egocentrism . . . public approval . . .": David Riesman, "Egocentrism: Is the American Character Changing?" *Encounter* 55 (Aug.–Sept. 1980): 19–28.

309 "The WASP character . . .": Brookhiser, *WASP*, 14, 15, 153.

309 "I am less . . . .": *USNWR*, 26 June 1989, 27.

309 "generalized social . . .": Kolb, *White House Daze*, 3.

309 "Star Wars . . .": John Podhoretz, *Hell of a Ride* (New York, 1993), 17.

310 "have been trashing . . .": Owen Ullman quoted in *Chicago Sun-Times*, 2 Apr. 1989, 45. See also *Waspo*, 11 Apr. 1989, A17.

310 "benefitted from . . .": Paul Maslin quoted in Duffy and Goodgame, *Marching*, 43.

312 "fragment . . . only he . . .": Natan Sharansky, *Fear No Evil* (New York, 1988), xiv, xxii.

312 "the unusual sight . . .": John Lewis Gaddis, *The United States and the End of the Cold War* (New York, 1992), 129. See also Peter Schweizer, *Reagan's War* (New York, 2002), 274–275.

312 "The passionate . . .": *USNWR*, 6 June 1988, 16.

312 "Today, the preservation . . .": Blumenthal, *Pledging Allegiance*, 321.

313 "like a cheerleader . . .": Peggy Noonan to Mari Maseng, 10 Jan. 1989, SP1314, RR Lib.

313 "the cold war is over": RR in *Ibid.*, 323.

314 "neither truly . . .": JAB, *The Politics of Diplomacy* (New York, 1995), 68.

314 "euphoria . . . transitory . . .": *Nwswk*, 21 Dec. 1987, 34.

314 "The Reagan administration's . . .": George Bush and Brent Scrowcroft, *A World Transformed* (New York, 1998), 12–13.

314 "The cold war . . .": Blumenthal, *Pledging Allegiance*, 327.

314 "Did we see . . .": Bush and Scrowcroft, *World Transformed*, xiii–xiv.

315 "so I—but . . .": Blumenthal, *Pledging Allegiance*, 327.

315 "First, do . . .": David Mervin, *George Bush and the Guardianship Presidency* (New York, 1996, 1998), ix.

315 "Frank Sinatra . . .": *NYT*, 13 June 1989, A12.

315 "I'll be darned . . .": George Bush to Sadruddin Aga Khan, 13 Mar. 1989, George Bush, *All the Best* (New York, 1999), 416.

316 "I think . . .": Blumenthal, *Pledging Allegiance*, 334, 341, 322.

316 "Ronald Reagan deserves . . .": Gaddis, *The End of the Cold War*, 130–131.

317 "STRONG EVIDENCE . . .": *NYT*, 4 Aug. 1989, 1.

318 Cleveland continued . . . : Carol Poh Miller and Robert A. Wheeler, "Cleveland: The Making and Remaking of an American City, 1796–1993," in W. Dennis Keating, Norman Krumholz, and David C. Perry, *Cleveland: A Metropolitan Reader* (Kent, OH, 1995), 46–47.

318 "I don't like . . .": Myron Magnet, "How Business Bosses Saved a Sick City," in ibid., 157.

318 38 percent . . . *NYT*, 20 Feb. 1989, 1.

318 "When we're . . .": *NYT*, 28 Oct. 1989, 8.

320 "mindless cannibalism": Jim Wright, *Balance of Power* (Atlanta, 1996), 490.

320 "the private vices . . .": Michael Sandel, *Democracy's Discontent* (Cambridge, 1996), 323.

320 "You don't know . . .": *NYT*, 3 Mar. 1989, A16.

323 "culture of complaint . . .": Robert Hughes, *Culture of Complaint* (New York, 1993), 4–7; Stephen L. Carter, *The Culture of Disbelief* (New York, 1993); George Lakoff, *Moral Politics* (Chicago, 1996).

323 "*Amusing Ourselves* . . .": Neil Postman, *Amusing Ourselves to Death* (New York, 1985).

323 "Fort McDonald's . . .": Aaron Latham, "The Age of Junk," *RS Yearbook 1983*, 22 Dec. 1983–5 Jan. 1984, 104.

323 "*Why Americans* . . .": E. J. Dionne, *Why Americans Hate Politics* (New York, 1991); Joseph S. Nye, Jr., Philip D. Zelikow, and David C. King, *Why People Don't Trust Government* (Cambridge, 1997).

323 "a moral voice": Etzioni, *New Golden Rule*, 131.

1990—Boston

Page

326 largest number . . . : *LAT*, 11 Jan. 1985, 5:1.

327 "video's finest . . .": *NYT*, 31 Dec. 1989, 30.

327 "Science, Math . . .": *BosG* 1 Jan. 1990, 1.

327 "I can remember . . .": *NYT*, 1 Jan. 1990, 27.

328 "that *less* . . .": Everett Carl Ladd, "Nobody's Buying," *The New Democrat*, 1 Jan. 1998, at www.ndol.org.

329 "Has America . . .": James L. Sundquist, "Has America Lost Its Social Conscience—And How Will It Get It Back?" *Political Science Quarterly* 101 (1986): 513–533.

332 "You know, those . . .": RR to Laurence W. Beilenson, 1 Aug. 1986, in RR *Letters*, 428.

332 "Ten Myths . . .": "Ten Myths That Miss The Mark," Issue Alert, 2 Mar. 1983, 118188PD, Box 11, FG 001, RR Lib.

334 "great unifier": News 9, San Antonia, TX, 6 June 2004, 2:03 p.m., http://www.news8austin.com/content/top_stories/default.asp? As ID= 109194.

335 "liberal nationalism . . .": Robert Dallek, *Lone Star Rising* (New York, 1991), 464.

335 "Today's conservative . . .": RR to Father Liederbach, n.d., in RR *Letters*, 272.

335 "I am deeply . . .": RR to Reverend Gay, n.d., in RR *Letters*, 365.

336 conservatives tend . . . : Charles W. Dunn and J. David Woodard, *The Conservative Tradition in America* (Lanham, MD, 1996), 30.

336 "Our nation . . .": RR to Dr. Kenneth Wells, c. 1967–1968, in RR *Letters*, 257.

340 "immersed . . . pleasure . . .": Barzun, *From Dawn to Decadence*, 788, 783.

340 "kick-me": *Waspo*, 18 Aug. 1984, A1.

Acknowledgments

Just as Ronald Reagan often recalled a movie scene involving only a farmer and a horse that created work for seventy people, this book about Ronald Reagan and the 1980s rests on the unseen—but most appreciated—labors of many. For starters, four superb research assistants—Gareth Schweitzer, Adam Goodman, Alex Cowan, and Brett Hooton—tracked down most of the secondary sources and newspaper and magazine articles used in this book and helped me shape my thinking on the subject in many ways. Dozens of students in the undergraduate and graduate honors seminar I have taught on Ronald Reagan for the last several years also contributed with their insight, intellectual exuberance, intelligent papers, and often very useful research notes, with some volunteering for short stints to help here and there. I thank them all profusely. Other students who have helped out tremendously—and voluntarily—include Lior Brinn, Kevin Mitchell, Dr. Raphael Schapiro, Adam Sharon, Katharine Slocombe, Geoffrey Wilde, Stephanie Weinstein, and, most especially, Bonnie Goodman, who in addition to designing and maintaining my Website through the McGill history department and www.giltroy.com assembled and posted a list of periodical articles about Reagan and the 1980s, which is a great gift to the growing conversation about Reagan and the 1980s.

This project also relied on the superb staff and the amazing resources of the Ronald Reagan Presidential Library in Simi Valley, California. Since I visited there while I was researching my previous book, Cate Sewell has functioned as my archival host. No question, big or small, has fazed her, and she and the rest of her colleagues have been unflaggingly supportive, enthusiastic, and encouraging. Wendy Felson and David Goodman always welcomed me warmly, making trips to Southern California from Montreal in December even more enticing. Other central institutions in this endeavor, in addition to the history department at McGill University, my academic home, ably chaired by Professor Suzanne Morton, then Professor Brian Lewis, include the Social Sciences and Humanities Research Council of Canada, which funded this project with a generous three-year-grant; the Library of Congress, which houses the Donald T. Regan, Alice Rivlin, and William Rusher papers; and the John J. Burns Library at Boston College, which houses the Thomas P. O'Neill collection.

Roger Simon and Carl Leubsdorf kindly helped at the start by sharing some recollections and notes about the Reagan inauguration. Dr. Julian Adams, Lee Edwards, Fred Fielding, Matt Gerson, Steve Greenberg and Professor Chris Ragan all shared their insights and memories from the time, while my aunt Lenore Gerson saved the day with an important fashion tip from January 1981. Dr. Michael Grow and the Contemporary History Institute at Ohio University in Athens, Ohio, warmly hosted me and responded intelligently and provocatively to my thoughts on Reagan and the 1980s. And a special thanks to Professor Alonzo Hamby for his gracious assistance subsequently.

I thank the entire staff at Princeton University Press for all their hard work and great skill, but especially Andrew DeSio, Ellen Foos, Alison Kalett, Anita O'Brien, Kathryn C. Rosko, and most especially Brigitta van Rheinberg, for embracing the vision of this book, and then showing me how to make it better. The manuscript review process at Princeton was also incredibly helpful, with special kudos to my two initially anonymous readers, Professor Bruce Schulman and Professor Julian Zelizer. Their very specific criticisms amid broad enthusiasm struck just the right balance between challenging me to improve and encouraging me to continue.

For permission to publish the photographs in the two photo inserts, and assistance in tracking down some of the pictures, I am indebted to Steve Branch and the Ronald Reagan Presidential Library, Joanne Boulerice and Magma Photo, Roxanne Frederick and *TV Guide*, David Lombard and CBS Photo Archive, David Stanhope and the Jimmy Carter Presidential Library, Rona Tuccillo and Getty Images, Mary Kay Kennedy and MPTV, Philip Amdal and his great eye for the big fat Old Coke cheerleader, and the indefatigable Brett Hooton.

Early readers—and a crackerjack early warning system against all kinds of mistakes; the rest are all on me—included the students from the fall 2003 to spring 2004 History 461D and 661D seminar, as well as Linda Adams, Professor Vincent Cannato, David Cape, Win Gerson, Steve Greenberg, Bernard Troy, Dan Troy, and most especially Dr. Tevi Troy, who read the manuscript twice after some of his line-by-line edits did not survive the border crossing from Washington, DC, to Montreal. This manuscript was proofread with the generous voluntary assistance of the McGill University Fall 2004 History 392 and Hist 431 proofreading posse. Special thanks to Professor Catherine Clinton, Professor Tom Velk, Tobiah Waldron for a superb indexing job, Dr. Robert Cookson for his Restoration insights and teaching assistance, Jamie Gibson for his computer expertise, Diane Pardillo for various kindnesses, and Lesley Stahl for her memories, insights, inspiration, careful reading, and great encouragement.

With each passing year, I become more appreciative of my parents and my father-in-law, with warm memories of my mother-in-law. In today's world, most people spend their lives fleeing their families; I am lucky to have been blessed with extras. And speaking of blessings, in the fourteen years since we met, I appreciate all the sunshine my wife, my best friend, has brought into my life—let alone our four fabulous children. They can now stop asking me when I'm going to finish this book, although, with any luck, they will still have to wonder just a little bit about why I'm "such a busy professor." We fervently hope that our four young children will grow up in a golden world of springlike renewal, symbolized by the dove, a just and hopeful world progressing toward peace rather than wallowing in war. As a mark of that faith, and because we all believe that no one can afford to sit on the sidelines these days, we as a family pledge to contribute one dollar for every book sold to help some of the innocent families who have been victimized by the scourge of terrorism these last few years.

Index

Buckley, William F., 140, 159

budget issues: 1984 election and, 167–71; Carter and, 81–82, 107; Congressional Budget Act and, 70; defense spending, 76, 106, 244; Democrats and, 71; inflation and, 24, 27, 30, 32, 54–55, 66, 78, 80, 154, 208–11; Stockman and, 65–72; taxes and, 39, 53, 65, 68, 70, 85, 108, 209–10

Buffet, Jimmy, 326

bully pulpit, 8–10

Burford, Anne Gorsuch, 117, 141–42

Burns, George, 326

Busby, Horace, 57

Buscaglia, Leo, 173

Bush, Barbara, 310

Bush, George Herbert Walker, 12, 74, 133, 332; aloofness of, 316, 319–20; Communism and, 323–24, 341; Dukakis and, 304–7; family values and, 300–1; Gorbachev and, 312–16; identity issues of, 308–10; image making and, 297–98; Kennebunkport and, 297, 300–1; liberalism and, 298–99; position of, 299–300; restoration and, 322–24; Soviet Union and, 311–16; tax promise of, 317–18; as Texan, 301; Tiananmen Square and, 315–16; voodoo economics and, 164; WASP approach and, 298–99, 323

Bush, George W., 6, 15–17, 20, 123, 333, 341

Bush, Marvin, 297

Business and Professional Women's Clubs, 281

busing, 28–29, 33, 89, 266, 339; effects of, 185; Reagan's attitude and, 92, 97; white victimization and, 182

Cabbage Patch Kids, 3, 134–35

Cabey, Darrel, 181

Calletano, Ray, 113

camcorders, 327

Campbell, Joseph, 326

Canada, 269

Canarsie: The Jews and Italians of Brooklyn against Liberalism (Rieder), 182–83

Candy Lightner Story, The, 289–90

Cannon, Lou, 351

capitalism, 19–20

"Cap the Knife." See Weinberger, Caspar

Carhart, Tom, 111

Carnegie, Andrew, 120, 131

Carson, Johnny, 22, 47, 191, 325

Carter, Amy, 47

Carter, Billy, 24, 32

Carter, Hodding, 252

Carter, Jimmy, 11–12, 14, 22, 137, 167, 306, 339; 1980 Election Day and, 46–49; aging of, 25; budget cuts and, 81–82, 107; Congressional Budget Act and, 70; inflation and, 32, 210; Iran hostage crisis and, 13, 24, 31–32, 41, 47–48, 55, 57, 153; manner of, 31; misery index and, 27; Mondale and, 164; popularity of, 31; racial issues and, 187; Reagan debate and, 24–27, 45, 47–48; Shah of Iran and, 240; terrorism and, 157

Carter, Rosalynn, 55, 57

Casey, Douglas R., 47

Casey, William, 243

CBS, 10, 93, 130, 195, 327, 329, 350–51; 60 Minutes and, 74; Cronkite and, 10, 21, 47, 52, 125–27; Rather and, 10, 117, 126–27, 168, 250–51, 316, 343; Stahl and, 79, 162–63, 165, 249, 282–83

Celebrity Presidency, 177

censorship: music industry and, 273–75; political correctness and, 265–85

Center for Strategic and International Studies, 60

Central Pacific Railroad, 120

Cermak, Anton, 13

Challenger explosion, 233, 336

Chambers, Robert, Jr., 230–31

Chancellor, John, 47

Charles Schwab, 214

Cheers, 100

Cheney, Lynne, 272

Cheney, Richard, 316, 342

Chernyaev, Anatoly, 263

Child, Julia, 326

China, 28, 315–16

Chrysler Corporation, 29, 131

Church, Frank, 48

individual retirement accounts (IRAs), 118
inflation: air traffic controllers strike and,
   78; budget issues and, 24, 27, 30, 32, 54–
   55, 66, 80; Carter and, 210; optimism
   and, 154; Reaganomics and, 208–11
infotainment, 128
Inside America (Harris), 354
Intel, 20
Internal Revenue Service, 95
International Olympic Committee, 153
Invasion USA, 241
Iran, 12, 155; hostage crisis, 13, 24, 31–32,
   41, 47–48, 55, 57, 153; Shah of, 240
Iran-Contra scandal, 7, 23, 256, 322, 341;
   North and, 234, 244–45, 247, 257–59,
   317; political damage of, 233–34, 236–53
Ireland, 46
Irish, 198
Iron Ore Company, 343
I.R.S. Records, 274
Italians, 182–83, 186

Jackson, Andrew, 5, 321
Jackson, Jesse, 19, 91, 164–67, 175, 265–66
Jackson, Michael, 19, 189, 345; racial issues
   and, 193–95; sexual ambiguity of, 194;
   white skin of, 194
Jacob, John E., 91
Jacobs, Meg, 352
Jagger, Mick, 129
Jagt, Guy Vander, 43
Japan, 13, 21, 222
Javits, Jacob, 38
Jefferson, Thomas, 5, 34, 58
Jeffersons, The, 74, 131
Jennings, Peter, 47, 117
Jepsen, Roger, 72
Jerry Maguire, 204
Jews, 182–83
job training, 103, 107
John, Elton, 201
John Birch Society, 37
Johnson, Edward C., III, 214
Johnson, Haynes, 351
Johnson, Lyndon B., 12, 59, 61, 76, 175;
   government regulations and, 32; retire-

ment of, 31; symbolism of, 4, 7–8, 33–
   34, 335, 338, 342
Jones, Barnaby, 131
Jones, Quincy, 189
Jordan, Barbara, 30
Jordan, Hamilton, 44, 55, 57
Jordan, Michael, 152
junk bonds, 16
"Just Say No" campaign, 287–88

Karate Kid, The, 160
Kasdan, Lawrence, 52, 115, 118
Kates, Kim, 190
Kaus, Bill, 198
Keaton, Alex P., 121
Kemp, Amanda, 269
Kemp, Jack, 39, 67–68, 79, 81, 90
Kemp, Raymond B., 60
Kemp-Roth tax cut, 39, 79
Kennebunkport, Maine, 297, 300–1, 303
Kennedy, Edward, 16, 24, 32, 198, 292,
   306
Kennedy, Jackie, 207
Kennedy, John F., 31, 59, 61, 92, 207, 233;
   symbolism of, 2, 9, 11, 321, 338, 342
Kennedy, Paul, 222
Kennedy, Ted, 138
Kerry, John, 2
Keynesianism, 80, 107
Khan, Sadruddin Aga, 315
Khomeini, Ayatollah, 58
Kimball, Roger, 270
King, Larry, 280
King, Martin Luther, Jr., 59, 117, 189
King, Rodney, 324
Kirkpatrick, Jeane, 240, 340
Kissinger, Henry, 32, 56, 64, 113, 158, 263,
   314
Klein, Calvin, 218–20, 276
Kline, Kevin, 116, 319
Klinghoffer, Leon, 245–46, 279
Knight, Gladys, 201
Knute Rockne: All American, 69
Koch, Ed, 90, 216, 225
Kojak, Theo, 131
Kondracke, Morton M., 174

POLITICS AND SOCIETY IN TWENTIETH-CENTURY AMERICA